COMPARISONS

A SHORT STORY ANTHOLOGY

by

Nicolaus Mills

McGRAW-HILL BOOK COMPANY
New York St. Louis San Francisco Düsseldorf
Johannesburg Kuala Lumpur London Mexico Montreal
New Delhi Panama Rio de Janeiro Singapore Sydney Toronto

This book was set in Baskerville by Creative Book Services, division of McGregor & Werner, Incorporated, and printed and bound by R. R. Donnelley & Sons, Company. The designer was Creative Book Services, division of McGregor & Werner, Incorporated. The editor was Robert Fry. Alice Cohen supervised production.

•

COMPARISONS: A SHORT STORY ANTHOLOGY

Library of Congress Catalog Card Number 70-170867
07-042370-9

1 2 3 4 5 6 7 8 9 0 D O D O 7 9 8 7 6 5 4 3 2

ACKNOWLEDGMENTS

James Baldwin, "The Outing," from *Going to Meet the Man* by James Baldwin. Copyright ©1965 by James Baldwin. Used by permission of the publisher, The Dial Press.

Heinrich Böll, "Action Will Be Taken," from *18 Stories* by Heinrich Böll. Copyright © 1966 by Heinrich Böll. Translated by Leila Vennewitz. Used with permission of McGraw-Hill Book Company.

Jorge Luis Borges, "The South," translated from the Spanish. Copyright © 1956 by Emece Editores, S. A., Buenos Aires. Copyright © 1962 by Grove Press, Inc. Reprinted by permission of Grove Press, Inc.

Anton Chekov, "A Day in the Country," translated from the Russian by Constance Garnett. Reprinted with permission of The Macmillan Company from *The Cook's Wedding and Other Stories.* Copyright 1922 by The Macmillan Company, renewed 1950 by David Garnett.

Julio Cortázar, "Blow-Up," from *The End of the Game and Other Stories*, by Julio Cortázar, translated by Paul Blackburn. Copyright © 1957, 1963 by Random House, Inc. Reprinted by permission of Pantheon Books, a Division of Random House, Inc.

Guy de Maupassant, "The Model," from *Boule de Suif and Other Stories* by Guy de Maupassant, translated by H. N. P. Sloman. Reprinted with the permission of Penguin Books Ltd.

FOR

Fred, Alice-Ann, Jamie, Andrew,
and Nicolaus

CONTENTS

PREFACE

I became convinced of the need for a book like this by my students at the University of Michigan, who insisted on being bored—and proud of it—when asked to read stories that had been collected for no special reason. Whatever merit my choice of stories has is due to those who helped me to see fiction as an act of faith: Franklyn Reardon and Paul and Eleanor Roundy at the start; George Friend and Craig Stark at a time when I doubted language altogether. For the book itself, I owe a special debt to my editor, Rob Fry. It was his encouragement that started it and his trust that made me feel free to experiment and doubt.

N.M.

COMPARISONS

•

A SHORT STORY
ANTHOLOGY

INTRODUCTION

We have no doubt that, like most anthologies, this one too will fall out of use as soon as its selection of stories no longer seems novel to teachers and students. All well and good. There is no reason why a short story anthology should be used after it begins to wear.

We hope, however, that something more than the choice of stories in this anthology will draw readers to it in the first place.

We think it significant that this anthology has been designed to be read comparatively and that the relationship between the stories in it is as important as the stories themselves. Robert Frost's dictum about reading poetry comparatively,is, we believe, just as relevant to fiction: "A poem is best read in light of all the other poems ever written. We read A the better to read B (we have to start somewhere; we may get very little out of A). We read B the better to read C, C the better to read D, D the better to go back and get something more out of A. Progress is not the aim, but circulation." In this case what we have done is to make possible a much more purposeful kind of comparative reading.

In the organization of this anthology we have accepted the premise that in general literary questions, such as matters of style, point of view, and tone, become important only when a story raises problems we care about and think can be illuminated by paying particular attention to the text. For most of us close reading without such a concern is simply puzzle solving, pleasant enough at times, but certainly not compelling.

The stories in this anthology have been arranged in a pattern that has as its basis the stages in human growth that Erik Erikson describes in his *Childhood and Society*. Neither the order nor the number of stages Erikson lists (see the chart at the end of this introduction) have been strictly followed. But what has been adopted is Erikson's notion that human development is best understood in terms of a series of crises that begin with the individual's relationship to his family and eventually include his relationship to all of society.

The stories in this anthology can, of course, be approached in terms of traditional literary concerns. (The first four sections have also been arranged so that in each section a single literary element—style, perspective, setting, or tone—is sufficiently prominent that it lends itself to special analysis.) What makes these stories truly comparative, however, is that in each section a specific set of problems arises as a result of the stage of growth under consideration. These problems do not, moreover, dissolve with the close of each section. The questions of trust that are so important for the children in Section I do not, for example, cease being issues for the old people in Section V. They merely acquire new forms, ones that in broader terms challenge the comparative imagination.

The final consequence of such an approach to the short story is, we believe, not only a more intense way of reading but a more humane way, one that fulfills Arthur Mizener's observation: "What is needed [in the study of literature] is that the subject be handled in a direct and even simple way so as to bring out its humanity—if I dare say so, its moral relevance to the lives of all human beings—without cheapening its values, without reduction to an ideology, without preachment."

II

In choosing the twenty-five short stories for this anthology, we have been concerned that comparability not come at the price of uniformity. The stories in each section are thus always taken from different countries, and no author appears more than once in the anthology. In addition a deliberate effort has been made to include fiction, like Yukio Mishima's "Patriotism" and Jorge Luis Borges' "The South," which does not have the usual American or European setting. A number of the stories included here take place in the present, and some, like Julio Cortázar's "Blow-Up" and Ivan Turgenev's "First Love," have recently been made into movies. But we have strongly resisted the notion that "currentness" and readability are the same. At the center of this collection lie its nineteenth-century tales—stories by Gogol, Melville, de Maupassant, Flaubert, Tolstoy.

Nicolaus Mills
New York, N. Y.

VIII MATURITY								EGO INTEGRITY VS. DESPAIR
VII ADULTHOOD							GENERA-TIVITY VS. STAGNATION	
VI YOUNG ADULTHOOD						INTIMACY VS. ISOLATION		
V PUBERTY AND ADOLESCENCE					IDENTITY VS. ROLE CONFUSION			
IV LATENCY				INDUSTRY VS. INFERIORITY				
III LOCOMOTOR-GENITAL			INITIATIVE VS. GUILT					
II MUSCULAR-ANAL		AUTONOMY VS. SHAME, DOUBT						
I ORAL SENSORY	BASIC TRUST VS. MISTRUST							
	1	2	3	4	5	6	7	8

1

CHILDHOOD
Trust versus Mistrust

For Erik Erikson the question of trust versus mistrust arises in infancy and has its earliest manifestation in the way in which a baby eats and sleeps and begins to explore the world around him. The trust itself depends on the kind of care the infant is given and whether or not he finds that his adventures arouse feelings of familiarity and inner goodness. The infant's first social achievement, according to Erikson, is his willingness to let his mother out of sight without undue anxiety, to regard her as an inner certainty as well as an outer predictability. Later on, as the child grows, the faith he does or doesn't have in his parents becomes even more internalized, and he begins to develop a sense of his own capacity for satisfying his needs and dealing with his environment.

In this first section the question of trust versus mistrust is explored in children who have gone beyond infancy and must confront a world in which parents are often absent or unequal to the task of inspiring trust. How can children survive under such pressures? Is blame for mistrust always to be traced back to parents? Does trust make sense in a precarious society and more precarious world? These are the questions that get asked in the following stories, and sometimes answered, sometimes left unresolved.

The first story, "Father and I" by Sweden's Nobel Prize-winning (1951) novelist Pär Lagerkvist, poses all of these questions through a narrative that seems childishly simple. Nothing could be more innocent than the opening lines of Lagerkvist's story:

> *When I was getting on toward ten, I remember Father took me by the hand one Sunday afternoon as we were to go out into the woods and listen to the birds singing. Waving good-bye to Mother, who had to stay at home and get the evening meal, we set off briskly in the warm sunshine. We didn't make any great to-do about this going to listen to the birds, as though it were something extra special or wonderful; we were sound sensible people, Father and I, brought up with nature and used to it.*

The closeness of Father and son, the pleasantness of their Sunday afternoon in the woods, cannot, however, withstand the fear created by a mysterious and unscheduled "black train" which passes them "at frantic speed." The concluding paragraph of "Father and I" is the reverse of the opening one:

> *But my whole body was shaking. It was for me, for my sake. I sensed what it meant: it was the anguish that was to come, the unknown, all that Father knew nothing about, that he wouldn't be able to protect me against. That was how this world, this life would be for me, not like Father's, where everything was secure and certain.*

What remains in doubt is whether or not we can know more about the boy's fears than he does. Is the train that violates the country peace the mechanical intruder from a harsher, more complex society? Or is there something demonic about the train and its engineer, who stood in "the light of the fire, pale, motionless, his features as though turned to stone." Earlier in the story, the narrator's father had tried to calm his fear of the dark by telling him "We know there is a God," but by the end no such reassurance will work. Indeed, it almost seems as if the trust in life the narrator's father has worked to give him is the real source of his terror.

The doubts Lagerkvist raises about the world children must grow up in are pursued much more deliberately by Alain Robbe-Grillet in "The Shore." Known in this country for *The Voyeur* and *The Erasers*, and the screenplay for Alain Resnais' *Last Year at Marienbad*, Robbe-Grillet tells his story with a simplicity that is exactly the opposite of Lagerkvist's narrator. The directness of Robbe-Grillet's prose is not that of a child who naively recounts his feelings and events but that of an adult who has made sure his language is stripped of all artificiality, who, above all else, will not give meaning or comfort where none exists. The beginning of "The Shore" is in stark contrast to the beginning of "Father and I":

> *Three children are walking along a beach. They walk side by side, holding each other by the hand. They are about the same height, and probably the same age: about twelve. The one in the center, nevertheless, is slightly shorter than the other two.*

The children in Robbe-Grillet's story are silent actors for the most part, and the judgments we do or don't make about their lives occur because Robbe-Grillet's narrative voice refuses to invest purpose or compensation in what the sea is doing to their footprints and those of the birds they can never quite catch up to:

> *The birds, as the children are about to overtake them, flap their wings and fly upward, first one, then two, then ten. . . .*
>
> *Then the whole flock is again back upon the sand, moving along the shore, about a hundred yards ahead of the children.*
>
> *The sea continually wipes out the starry tracks left by their feet. The children, on the other hand, who are walking closer to the cliff, side by side, holding each other by the hand, leave behind them deep prints, in a triple line which stretches out parallel to the seashore, down the long beach.*

Will the children's footprints finally not be obliterated like those of the birds? Is there anything or anyone they can in these circumstances trust?

The next two stories suggest that the uncertainties children face may not be nearly so burdensome as the kinds of trust adults wish them to develop. In James Baldwin's "The Outing" the three boys who are the center of his story are at an age where their bodies are "troublesome" and "their voices not to be trusted." Yet, their greatest problems occur because they "tended to consider themselves sophisticates, no longer like the old folks, at the mercy of the love or the wrath of God." Baldwin, who was raised in Harlem, where his father was a minister, is particularly adept at capturing how oppressive it is for the boys to be continually reminded:

> *"We're living in the last days, children. Don't think because you're young you got plenty of time. God takes the young as well as the old. You got to hold yourself in readiness all the time, lest when He comes He catch you unprepared."*

What makes these apocalyptic warnings so terrible for the boys is not, however, the threat of annihilation they pose, but the restrictions they inflict on the boys' relationships with themselves and others. The oldest of the boys finds a girl he is courting won't see him unless he gets serious about "salvation"; and the youngest of the boys, Johnnie Grimes, finds the church service intrudes on the love he has for his friend David:

> *Yet, in the copper sunlight Johnnie felt suddenly, not the presence of the Lord, but the presence of David; which seemed to reach out to him, hand reaching out to hand in the fury of flood-time, to drag him to the bottom of the water or carry him safe to the shore. From the corner of his eye, he watched his friend, who held him with such power; and felt, for the moment, such a depth of love, such nameless and terrible joy and pain, that he might have fallen, in the face of that company, weeping at David's feet.*

At the end of "The Outing" it is still possible to ask if the boys will ever be free enough to trust their own instincts. We know that for David Grimes "where there had been peace there was only panic, and where there had been safety, danger, like a flower, opened." What is harder to tell is whether or not David's problems are uniquely his or those of the others as well.

In Graham Greene's "The Basement Room" the burden of adult trust has even more serious consequences. There is no one Philip Lane would rather trust than Baines, the family butler, and when Philip's family goes off on a holiday, it is Baines Philip turns to for comfort. Yet, much to his discomfort, Philip finds that as he trusts in Baines, Baines trusts in him. It is impossible for their relationship not to carry with it adult burdens. Philip is finally not only privy to the fact that Baines has a secret love life, but (without Baines' knowing it), he sees Baines murder his wife. In the end it is Philip, wearied that "Baines had involved him in secrets, in fears he didn't understand," who betrays Baines to the police:

> *He wasn't going to keep any more secrets: he was going to finish once and for all with everything, with Baines and Mrs. Baines and the grown-up life beyond him; it wasn't his business and never, never again, he decided, would he share their confidences and companionship. "It was all Emmy's fault," he protested with a quaver which reminded Baines that after all he was only a child . . . he didn't understand what it all meant; he couldn't read this shorthand of terror; he'd had a long day and he was tired out. . . . You couldn't blame him.*

Should Philip have done anything else? The logical answer is, of course, no. Murder shouldn't be allowed. Yet, what is upsetting about Philip's betrayal of Baines to the police is that it follows a pattern in which he has never done anything to help Baines. Is Greene suggesting that the trust between a child and an adult finally requires the child to accept adult responsibilities? It is in this regard interesting to turn to an earlier passage in "The Basement Room":

> *Let grown-up people keep to their world and he would keep to his, safe in the small garden between the plane-trees. "In the lost childhood of Judas Christ was betrayed"; you could almost see the small unformed face hardening into the deep dilettante selfishness of age.*

It is clear that the real suspense in "The Basement Room" is not that of Graham Greene the mystery writer, but that of Graham Greene the author of *The Power and the Glory* and *The Heart of the Matter*.

It is not until one comes to the final story in this section, Chekhov's "A Day in the Country," that the trust between a child and an adult seems likely to endure for an indefinite period of time. The adult in Chekhov's story is Terenty, the wise old cobbler of a small Russian village:

> *. . . there is no secret in nature which baffles him. He knows everything. Thus, for example, he knows the names of all the wild flowers, animals, and stones. He knows what herbs cure diseases, he has no difficulty in telling the age of a horse or cow. Looking at the sunset, at the moon, or the birds he can tell what sort of weather it will be the next day.*

What is crucial to ask is why Terenty should have so powerful an effect on the orphan Danilka, who trusts in him. Is Terenty any more reassuring than the father of "Father and I"? Is his religious faith so different from the fundamentalism of the "saints" in "The Outing"? Are his weaknesses so much less than those of Baines in "The Basement Room"? The answer—if there is one—would seem to have little to do with the profundity of Terenty's knowledge. At the end of "A Day in the Country" Danilka is still disturbed by all he has seen:

> *He gazes into the darkness, and it seems to him that he is seeing all that he has seen in the day: the storm clouds, the bright sunshine, the birds, the fish, lanky Terenty. The number of his impressions, together with exhaustion and hunger, are too much for him; he is as hot as though he were on fire, and tosses from side to side.*

What allows Danilka to fall asleep is his belief that he can "tell Terenty to-morrow" all that disturbs him. There is no indication that Terenty will have anything new to say or that Danilka's world will be any different when he wakes. There is only the indication that Terenty's love is enough to make Danilka feel the worth of unburdening himself.

Is such a conclusion pessimistic? Is Chekhov, whose own childhood was terribly unhappy, pointing as much to the limits as the value of the kind of trust children develop? As in the other four stories, the answers to these questions cannot be separated from how one judges the adult world in which children are expected to find a place.

PÄR LAGERKVIST

FATHER and I

When I was getting on toward ten, I remember, Father took me by the hand one Sunday afternoon, as we were to go out into the woods and listen to the birds singing. Waving good-bye to Mother, who had to stay at home and get the evening meal, we set off briskly in the warm sunshine. We didn't make any great to-do about this going to listen to the birds, as though it were something extra special or wonderful; we were sound, sensible people, Father and I, brought up with nature and used to it. There was nothing to make a fuss about. It was just that it was Sunday afternoon and Father was free. We walked along the railway line, where people were not allowed to go as a rule, but Father worked on the railway and so he had a right to. By doing this we could get straight into the woods, too, without going a round-about way.

Soon the bird song began and all the rest. There was a twittering of finches and willow warblers, thrushes and sparrows in the bushes, the hum that goes on all around you as soon as you enter a wood. The ground was white with wood anemones, the birches had just come out into leaf, and the spruces had fresh shoots; there were scents on all sides, and underfoot the mossy earth lay steaming in the sun. There was noise and movement everywhere; bumblebees came out of their holes, midges swarmed wherever it was marshy, and birds darted out of the bushes to catch them and back again as quickly.

All at once a train came rushing along and we had to go down on to the embankment. Father hailed the engine driver with two fingers to his Sunday hat and the driver saluted and extended his hand. It all happened quickly; then on we went, taking big strides so as to tread on the sleepers and not in the gravel, which was heavy going and rough on the shoes. The sleepers sweated tar in the heat, everything smelled, grease and meadowsweet, tar and heather by turns. The rails glinted in the sun. On either side of the line were telegraph poles, which sang as you passed them. Yes, it was a lovely day. The sky was quite clear, not a cloud to be seen, and there couldn't be any, either, on a day like this, from what Father said.

After a while we came to a field of oats to the right of the line, where a crofter we knew had a clearing. The oats had come up close and even. Father scanned them with an expert eye and I could see he was satisfied. I knew very little about such things, having been born in a town. Then we came to the bridge over a stream, which most of the time had no water to speak of but which now was in full spate. We held hands so as not to fall down between the sleepers. After that it is not long before you come to the platelayer's cottage lying embedded in greenery, apple trees and gooseberry bushes. We called in to see them and were offered milk, and saw their pig and hens and fruit trees in blossom; then we went on. We wanted to get to the river, for it was more beautiful there than anywhere else; there was something special about it, as farther upstream it flowed past where Father had lived as a child. We usually liked to come as far as this before we turned back, and today, too, we got there after a good walk. It was near the next station, but we didn't go so far. Father just looked to see that the semaphore was right—he thought of everything.

We stopped by the river, which murmured in the hot sun, broad and friendly. The shady trees hung along the banks and were reflected in the backwater. It was all fresh and light here; a soft breeze was blowing off the small lakes higher up. We climbed down the slope and walked a little way along the bank, Father pointing out the spots for fishing. He had sat here on the stones as a boy, waiting for perch all day long; often there wasn't even a bite, but it was a blissful life. Now he didn't have time. We hung about on the bank for a good while, making a noise, pushing out bits of bark for the current to take, throwing pebbles out into the water to see who could throw farthest; we were both gay and cheerful by nature, Father and I. At last we felt tired and that we had had enough, and we set off for home.

It was beginning to get dark. The woods were changed—it wasn't dark there yet, but almost. We quickened our steps. Mother would be getting anxious and waiting with supper. She was always afraid something was going to happen. But it hadn't; it had been a lovely day, nothing had happened that shouldn't. We were content with everything.

The twilight deepened. The trees were so funny. They stood listening to every step we took, as if they didn't know who we were. Under one of them was a glow-worm. It lay down there in the dark staring at us. I squeezed Father's hand, but he didn't see the strange glow, just walked on. Now it was quite dark. We came to the bridge over the stream. It roared down there in the depths, horribly, as though it wanted to swallow us up; the abyss yawned below us. We trod carefully on the sleepers, holding each other tightly by the hand so as not to fall in. I thought Father would carry me across, but he didn't say anything; he probably wanted me to be like him and think nothing of it.

We went on. Father was so calm as he walked there in the darkness, with even strides, not speaking, thinking to himself. I couldn't understand how he could be so calm when it was so murky. I looked all around me in fear. Nothing but darkness everywhere. I hardly dared take a deep breath, for then you got so much darkness inside you, and that was dangerous. I thought it meant you would soon die. I remember quite well that's what I thought then. The embankment sloped steeply down, as though into chasms black as night. The telegraph poles rose, ghostly, to the sky. Inside them was a hollow rumble, as though someone were talking deep down in the earth and the white porcelain caps sat huddled fearfully together listening to it. It was all horrible. Nothing was right, nothing real; it was all so weird.

Hugging close to Father, I whispered, "Father, why is it so horrible when it's dark?"

"No, my boy, it's not horrible," he said, taking me by the hand.

"Yes, Father, it is."

"No, my child, you mustn't think that. Not when we know there is a God."

I felt so lonely, forsaken. It was so strange that only I was afraid, not Father, that we didn't think the same. And strange that what he said didn't help me and stop me from being afraid. Not even what he said about God helped me. I thought he too was horrible. It was horrible that he was everywhere here in the darkness, down under the trees, in the telegraph poles which rumbled—that must be he—everywhere. And yet you could never see him.

We walked in silence, each with his own thoughts. My heart contracted, as though the darkness had got in and was beginning to squeeze it.

Then, as we were rounding a bend, we suddenly heard a mighty roar behind us! We were awakened out of our thoughts in alarm. Father pulled me down on to the embankment, down into the abyss, held me there. Then the train tore past, a black train. All the lights in the carriages were out, and it was going at frantic speed. What sort of train was it? There wasn't one due now! We gazed at it in terror. The fire blazed in the huge engine as they shovelled in coal; sparks whirled out into the night. It was terrible. The driver stood there in the light of the fire, pale, motionless, his features as though turned to stone. Father didn't recognize him, didn't know who he was. The man just stared straight ahead, as though intent on rushing into the darkness, far into the darkness that had no end.

Beside myself with dread, I stood there panting, gazing after the furious vision. It was swallowed up by the night. Father took me up on to the line; we hurried home. He said, "Strange, what train was that? And I didn't recognize the driver." Then we walked on in silence.

But my whole body was shaking. It was for me, for my sake. I sensed what it meant: it was the anguish that was to come, the unknown, all that Father knew nothing about, that he wouldn't be able to protect me against. That was how this world, this life, would be for me; not like Father's, where everything was secure and certain. It wasn't a real world, a real life. It just hurtled, blazing, into the darkness that had no end.

ALAIN ROBBE-GRILLET

The SHORE

Translated by Bruce Morrissette

Three children are walking along a beach. They walk side by side, holding each other by the hand. They are about the same height, and probably the same age: about twelve. The one in the center, nevertheless, is slightly shorter than the other two.

Except for these three children, the long shore is empty. The band of sand is fairly wide, unbroken, free of scattered rocks and water holes, sloping gently from the steep cliff, which seems unending, to the sea.

The weather is fine. The sun illuminates the yellow sand with a violent, vertical light. There is not a single cloud in the sky. Nor is there any wind. The water is blue, calm, without a trace of a swell coming in from the distance, although the beach faces the open sea and the horizon.

But at regular intervals, a quick wave, always the same, originating a few yards from the shore, suddenly rises and immediately breaks, always along the same line. The water does not seem to move forward, and then rush back; it is rather as if the whole movement occurred in a stationary position. The swelling of the water produces first a shallow trough, along the side next to the shore, and the wave draws back slightly, with a rustling noise of gravel rolling; then it bursts and spreads milkily over the slope of the beach's edge, but only to recover the space which it had lost. At most, a stronger surge rises, here and there, to moisten, for a moment, a few extra inches of sand.

And all is again motionless, the sea, flat and blue, stationary at precisely the same height on the yellow sand of the beach, on which the three children walk side by side.

They are blond, and almost the same color as the sand: their skin a little darker, their hair a little lighter. All three are dressed in the same way, short trousers and sleeveless shirts, both of a faded thick blue cloth. They are walking side by side, holding each other by the hand, in a straight line, parallel to the sea and parallel to the cliff, almost equidistant between the two, yet a little closer to the water. The sun, now at the zenith, throws no shadow at their feet.

In front of them the sand is absolutely unmarked, yellow and smooth from the rock cliff to the water. The children walk forward in a straight line, at a constant pace, without the slightest movement to either side, calmly and holding each other by the hand. Behind them the sand, barely damp, is marked by three lines of footprints left by their bare feet, three regular series of similar and equally spaced prints, clearly hollowed out, and without a seam.

The children look straight ahead. They never glance at the high cliff, on their left, or at the sea, with its little waves breaking periodically, in the other direction. Nor, even more certainly, do they turn around to look behind them at the space which they have covered. They continue on their way with a rapid and uniform step.

In front of them, a flock of sea birds walk briskly along the shore, just at the edge of the waves. They move parallel with the children, in the same direction, about a hundred yards farther on. But, as the birds do not move as fast as they, the children gain upon them. And while the sea constantly wipes out the starry tracks of the birds, the children's footsteps remain clearly inscribed in the barely damp sand, in which the three lines of footsteps grow longer and longer.

The depth of these footprints is unchanging: a little less than an inch. They are not deformed either by a crumbling of the edges or by an excessively deep impression of the heel, or of the toe. They appear as if punched out by machine in an upper, and more malleable, crust of the beach.

Thus their triple line extends, always farther, and seems at the same time to grow narrower, to slow down, to blend into a single line, which separates the beach into two bands, throughout its length, and which comes to an end in a tiny mechanical movement, far off, occurring as if in a stationary position: the alternate lifting and setting down of six bare feet.

But as the bare feet move farther along, they gain upon the birds. Not only do they cover the ground rapidly, but the relative distance which separates the two groups diminishes even faster, compared with the space already covered. Soon there is only the gap of a few steps between them. . . .

But, when the children finally seem about to catch up with the birds, there is a flapping of wings as the birds take flight, first one, then two, then ten. . . . And the whole flock, white and gray, describes a curve above the sea as it returns to light upon the sand and begins to walk quickly again, always in the same direction, just at the edge of the waves, about a hundred yards farther on.

At this distance, the movements of the water are almost imperceptible, except for a sudden change in color, every ten seconds, at the moment when the dazzling foam shines in the sunlight.

Heedless of the footprints that they continue to press so precisely into the bare sand, indifferent to the little waves on their right, to the birds—now flying, now walking—that advance before them, the three blond children walk along side by side, with a rapid and uniform step, holding each other by the hand.

Their three sunburned faces, darker than their hair, look alike. They have the same expression: serious, thoughtful, perhaps concerned. Their features are also identical, although, obviously, two of the children are boys and the third a girl. The girl's hair is just a little longer, a little bit more curly, and her limbs appear a shade more slender. But her clothes are exactly the same: short trousers and sleeveless shirt, both of a faded thick blue cloth.

The girl is at the far right, next to the sea. At her left walks the boy who is slightly less tall. The other boy, nearest the cliff, is as tall as the girl.

Before them extends the smooth, unbroken sand, as far as the eye can see. On their left rises the wall of brown rock, almost vertical, and seemingly unending. On their right, motionless and blue out to the horizon, is the flat surface of the water, bordered by a sudden hem, which immediately bursts and spreads out in white foam.

Then, ten seconds later, the wave which wells up hollows out again the same shallow trough, on the side next to the beach, with a rustling noise of gravel rolling.

The tiny wave unfurls; the milky foam again climbs up the slope of sand, recovering the few inches of lost space. During the silence that follows, the tolling of a bell, from very far away, reverberates dimly in the quiet air.

"There's the bell," says the smallest of the children, the boy who is walking in the middle.

But the noise of the gravel sucked in by the sea muffles the weak echoes of the bell. Only at the end of the wave cycle can a few sounds, distorted by the distance, be heard again.

"It's the first bell," says the tall boy.

The tiny wave unfurls, on their right.

When silence returns, they hear nothing further. The three blond children still walk at the same regular pace, holding each other by the hand. In front of them the flock of birds, only a few steps away, is suddenly overcome by a contagious excitement. The birds flap their wings and fly upward.

They describe the same curve above the sea, and return to light upon the sand and begin to walk quickly again, always in the same direction, just at the edge of the waves, about a hundred yards farther on.

"Maybe it isn't the first," says the small boy, "Maybe we didn't hear the other one, before. . . ."

"We would have heard it the same as this one," the tall boy answers.

The children have not in any way changed their pace; and the same footprints, behind them, continue to appear, as they walk forward, under the six bare feet.

"We weren't as near before," says the girl.

After a moment, the taller of the two boys, the one next to the cliff, says: "We still aren't near."

And all three walk on in silence.

They remain silent thus until the bell, still just as faint, sounds again in the quiet air. The taller of the boys says then, "There's the bell." The others make no answer.

The birds, as the children are about to overtake them, flap their wings and fly upward, first one, then two, then ten. . . .

Then the whole flock is again back upon the sand, moving along the shore, about a hundred yards ahead of the children.

The sea continually wipes out the starry tracks left by their feet. The children, on the other hand, who are walking closer to the cliff, side by side, holding each other by the hand, leave behind them deep prints, in a triple line which stretches out parallel to the seashore, down the long beach.

On the right, near the edge of the motionless, flat water, and always at the same spot, the same small wave wells up and breaks.

JAMES BALDWIN

The OUTING

Each summer the church gave an outing. It usually took place on the Fourth of July, that being the day when most of the church-members were free from work; it began quite early in the morning and lasted all day. The saints referred to it as the 'whosoever will' outing, by which they meant that, though it was given by the Mount of Olives Pentecostal Assembly for the benefit of its members, all men were free to join them, Gentile, Jew or Greek or sinner. The Jews and the Greeks, to say nothing of the Gentiles—on whom, for their livelihood, most of the saints depended—showed themselves, year after year, indifferent to the invitation; but sinners of the more expected hue were seldom lacking. This year they were to take a boat trip up the Hudson as far as Bear Mountain where they would spend the day and return as the moon rose over the wide river. Since on other outings they had merely taken a subway ride as far as Pelham Bay or Van Cortlandt Park, this year's outing was more than ever a special occasion and even the deacon's two oldest boys, Johnnie and Roy, and their friend, David Jackson, were reluctantly thrilled. These three tended to consider themselves sophisticates, no longer, like the old folks, at the mercy of the love or the wrath of God.

The entire church was going and for weeks in advance talked of nothing else. And for weeks in the future the outing would provide interesting conversation. They did not consider this frivolous. The outing, Father James declared from his pulpit a week before the event, was for the purpose of giving the children of God a day of relaxation; to breathe a purer air and to worship God joyfully beneath the roof of heaven; and there was nothing frivolous about *that*. And, rather to the alarm of the captain, they planned to hold church services aboard the ship. Last year Sister McCandless had held an impromptu service in the unbelieving subway car. She played the tambourine and sang and exhorted sinners and passed through the train distributing tracts. Not everyone had found this admirable, to some it seemed that Sister McCandless was being a little ostentatious. "I praise my Redeemer wherever I go," she retorted defiantly. "Holy Ghost don't leave *me* when I leave the church. I got a every day religion."

Sylvia's birthday was on the third, and David and Johnnie and Roy had been saving money for her birthday present. Between them they had five dollars but they could not decide what to give her. Roy's suggestion that they give her underthings was rudely shouted down: did he want Sylvia's mother to kill the girl? They were all frightened of the great, rawboned, outspoken Sister Daniels and for Sylvia's sake went to great pains to preserve what remained of her good humor. Finally, at the suggestion of David's older sister, Lorraine, they bought a small, gold-plated pin cut in the shape of a butterfly. Roy thought that it was cheap and grumbled angrily at their combined bad taste ("Wait till it starts turning her clothes green!" he cried) but David did not think it was so bad; Johnnie thought it pretty enough and he was sure that Sylvia would like it anyway; (When's *your* birthday?" he asked David). It was agreed that David should present it to her on the day of the outing in the presence of them all. ("Man, I'm the oldest cat here," David said, "you know that girl's crazy about me"). This was the summer in which they all abruptly began to grow older, their bodies becoming troublesome and awkward and even dangerous and their voices not to be trusted. David perpetually boasted of the increase of down on his chin and professed to have hair on his chest—"and somewhere else, too," he added slyly, whereat they all laughed. "You ain't the only one," Roy said. "No," Johnnie said, "I'm almost as old as you are." "Almost ain't got it," David said. "Now ain't this a hell of a conversation for church boys?" Roy wanted to know.

The morning of the outing they were all up early; their father sang in the kitchen and their mother, herself betraying an excitement nearly youthful, scrubbed and dressed the younger children and laid the plates for breakfast. In the bedroom which they shared Roy looked wistfully out of the window and turned to Johnnie.

"Got a good mind to stay home," he said. "Probably have more fun." He made a furious gesture toward the kitchen. "Why doesn't *he* stay home?"

Johnnie, who was looking forward to the day with David and who had not the remotest desire to stay home for any reason and who knew, moreover, that Gabriel was not going to leave Roy alone in the city, not even if the heavens fell, said lightly, squirming into clean underwear: "Oh, he'll probably be busy with the old folks. We can stay out of his way."

Roy sighed and began to dress. "Be glad when I'm a man," he said.

Lorraine and David and Mrs. Jackson were already on the boat when they arrived. They were among the last; most of the church, Father James, Brother Elisha, Sister McCandless, Sister Daniels and Sylvia were seated near the rail of the boat in a little semi-circle, conversing in strident tones. Father James and Sister McCandless were remarking the increase of laxity among God's people and debating whether or not the church should run a series of revival meetings. Sylvia sat there, saying nothing, smiling painfully now and then at young Brother Elisha, who spoke loudly of the need for a revival and who continually attempted to include Sylvia in the conversation. Elsewhere on the boat similar conversations were going on. The saints of God were together and very conscious this morning of their being together and of their sainthood; and were determined that the less enlightened world should know who they were and remark upon it. To this end there were a great many cries of "Praise the Lord!" in greeting and the formal holy kiss. The children, bored with the familiar spectacle, had already drawn apart and amused themselves by loud cries and games that were no less exhibitionistic than that being played by their parents. Johnnie's nine year old sister, Lois, since she professed salvation, could not very well behave as the other children did; yet no degree of salvation could have equipped her to enter into the conversation of the grown-ups; and she was very violently disliked among the adolescents and could not join them either. She wandered about, therefore, unwillingly forlorn, contenting herself to some extent by a great display of virtue in her encounters with the unsaved children and smiling brightly at the grown-ups. She came to Brother Elisha's side. "Praise the Lord," he cried, stroking her head and continuing his conversation.

Lorraine and Mrs. Jackson met Johnnie's mother for the first time as she breathlessly came on board, dressed in the airy and unreal blue which Johnnie would forever associate with his furthest memories of her. Johnnie's baby brother, her youngest, happiest child, clung round her neck; she made him stand, staring in wonder at the strange, endless deck, while she was introduced. His mother, on all social occasions, seemed fearfully distracted, as though she awaited, at any moment, some crushing and irrevocable disaster. This disaster might be the sudden awareness of a run in her stocking or private knowledge that the trump of judgment was due, within five minutes to sound: but, whatever it was, it lent her a certain agitated charm and people, struggling to guess what it might be that so claimed her inward attention, never failed, in the process, to be won over. She talked with Lorraine and Mrs. Jackson for a few moments, the child tugging at her skirts, Johnnie watching her with a smile; and at last, the child becoming always more restive, said that she must go—into what merciless arena one dared not imagine—but hoped, with a despairing smile which clearly indicated the improbability of such happiness, that she would be able to see them later. They watched her as she walked slowly to the other end of the boat, sometimes pausing in conversation, always (as though it were a duty) smiling a little and now and then considering Lois where she stood at Brother Elisha's knee.

"She's very friendly," Mrs. Jackson said. "She looks like you, Johnnie."

David laughed. "Now why you want to say a thing like that, Ma? That woman ain't never done nothing to you."

Johnnie grinned, embarrassed, and pretended to menace David with his fists.

"Don't you listen to that old, ugly boy," Lorraine said. "He just trying to make you feel bad. Your mother's real good-looking. Tell her I said so."

This embarrassed him even more, but he made a mock bow and said, "Thank you, Sister." And to David: "Maybe now you'll learn to keep your mouth shut."

"Who'll learn to keep whose mouth shut? What kind of talk is that?"

He turned and faced his father, who stood smiling on them as from a height.

"Mrs. Jackson, this is my father," said Roy quickly. "And this is Miss Jackson. You know David."

Lorraine and Mrs. Jackson looked up at the deacon with polite and identical smiles.

"How do you do?" Lorraine said. And from Mrs. Jackson: "I'm very pleased to meet you."

"Praise the Lord," their father said. He smiled. "Don't you let Johnnie talk fresh to you."

"Oh, no, we were just kidding around," David said. There was a short, ugly silence. The deacon said: "It looks like a good day for the outing, praise the Lord. You kids have a good time. Is this your first time with us, Mrs. Jackson?"

"Yes," said Mrs. Jackson. "David came home and told me about it and it's been so long since I've been in the country I just decided I'd take me a day off. And Lorraine's not been feeling too strong, I thought the fresh air would do her some good." She smiled a little painfully as she spoke. Lorraine looked amused.

"Yes, it will, nothing like God's fresh air to help the feeble." At this description of herself as feeble Lorraine looked ready to fall into the Hudson and coughed nastily into her handkerchief. David, impelled by his own perverse demon, looked at Johnnie quickly and murmured, "That's the truth, deacon." The deacon looked at him and smiled and turned to Mrs. Jackson. "We been hoping that your son might join our church someday. Roy brings him out to service every Sunday. Do you like the services, son?" This last was addressed in a hearty voice to David; who, recovering from his amazement at hearing Roy mentioned as his especial pal (for he was Johnnie's friend, it was to be with Johnnie that he came to church!) smiled and said, "Yes sir, I like them alright," and looked at Roy, who considered his father with an expression at once contemptuous, ironic and resigned and at Johnnie, whose face was a mask of rage. He looked sharply at the deacon again; but he, with his arm around Roy, was still talking.

"This boy came to the Lord just about a month ago," he said proudly. "The Lord saved him just like that. Believe me, Sister Jackson, ain't no better fortress for nobody, young or old, than the arms of Jesus. My son'll tell you so, ain't it, Roy?"

They considered Roy with a stiff, cordial curiosity. He muttered murderously, "Yes sir."

"Johnnie tells me you're a preacher," Mrs. Jackson said at last. "I'll come out and hear you sometime with David."

"Don't come out to hear me," he said. "You come out and listen to the Word of God. We're all just vessels in His hand. Do you know the Lord, sister?"

"I try to do His will," Mrs. Jackson said.

He smiled kindly. "We must all grow in grace." He looked at Lorraine. "I'll be expecting to see you too, young lady."

"Yes, we'll be out," Lorraine said. They shook hands. "It's very nice to have met you," she said.

"Goodbye." He looked at David. "Now you be good. I want to see you saved soon." He released Roy and started to walk away. "You kids enjoy yourselves. Johnnie, don't you get into no mischief, you hear me?"

He affected not to have heard; he put his hands in his pants' pockets and pulled out some change and pretended to count it. His hand was clammy and it shook. When his father repeated his admonition, part of the change spilled to the deck and he bent to pick it up. He wanted at once to shout to his father the most dreadful curses that he knew and he wanted to weep. He was aware that they were all intrigued by the tableau presented by his father and himself, that they were all vaguely cognizant of an unnamed and deadly tension. From his knees on the deck he called back (putting into his voice as much asperity, as much fury and hatred as he dared):

"Don't worry about me, Daddy. Roy'll see to it that I behave."

There was a silence after he said this; and he rose to his feet and saw that they were all watching him. David looked pitying and shocked, Roy's head was bowed and he looked apologetic. His father called:

"Excuse yourself, Johnnie, and come here."

"Excuse me," he said, and walked over to his father. He looked up into his father's face with an anger which surprised and even frightened him. But he did not drop his eyes, knowing that his father saw there (and he wanted him to see it) how much he hated him.

"What did you say?" his father asked.

"I said you don't have to worry about me. I don't think I'll get into any mischief." And his voice surprised him, it was more deliberately cold and angry than he had intended and there was a sardonic stress on the word 'mischief.' He knew that his father would then and there have knocked him down if they had not been in the presence of saints and strangers.

"You be careful how you speak to me. Don't you get grown too fast. We get home, I'll pull down those long pants and we'll see who's the man, you hear me?"

Yes we will, he thought and said nothing. He looked with a deliberate casualness about the deck. Then they felt the lurch of the boat as it began to move from the pier. There was an excited raising of voices and "I'll see you later," his father said and turned away.

He stood still, trying to compose himself to return to Mrs. Jackson and Lorraine. But as he turned with his hands in his pants' pockets he saw that David and Roy were coming toward him and he stopped and waited for them.

"It's a bitch," Roy said.

David looked at him, shocked. "That's no language for a saved boy." He put his arm around Johnnie's shoulder. "We're off to Bear Mountain," he cried, "*up* the glorious Hudson"—and he made a brutal gesture with his thumb.

"Now suppose Sylvia saw you do that," said Roy, "what would you say, huh?"

"We needn't worry about her," Johnnie said. "She'll be sitting with the old folks all day long."

"Oh, we'll figure out a way to take care of *them*," said David. He turned to Roy. "Now you the saved one, why don't you talk to Sister Daniels and distract her attention while we talk to the girl? You the baby, anyhow, girl don't want to talk to you."

"I ain't got enough salvation to talk to that hag," Roy said. "I got a Daddy-made salvation. I'm saved when I'm with Daddy." They laughed and Roy added, "And I ain't no baby, either, I got everything my Daddy got."

"And a lot your Daddy don't dream of," David said.

Oh, thought Johnnie, with a sudden, vicious, chilling anger, *he doesn't have to dream about it!*

"Now let's act like we Christians," David said. "If we was real smart now, we'd go over to where she's sitting with all those people and act like we wanted to hear about God. Get on the good side of her mother."

"And suppose *he* comes back?" asked Johnnie.

Gabriel was sitting at the other end of the boat, talking with his wife. "Maybe he'll stay there," David said; there was a note of apology in his voice.

They approached the saints.

"Praise the Lord," they said sedately.

"Well, praise Him," Father James said. "How are you young men today?" He grabbed Roy by the shoulder. "Are you coming along in the Lord?"

"Yes, sir," Roy muttered, "I'm trying." He smiled into Father James's face.

"It's a wonderful thing," Brother Elisha said, "to give up to the Lord in your youth." He looked up at Johnnie and David. "Why don't you boys surrender? Ain't nothing in the world for you, I'll tell you that. He says, 'Remember thy Creator in the days of thy youth when the evil days come not.' "

"Amen," said Sister Daniels. "We're living in the last days, children. Don't think because you're young you got plenty of time. God takes the young as well as the old. You got to hold yourself in readiness all the time lest when He comes He catch you unprepared. Yes sir. Now's the time."

"You boys going to come to service today, ain't you?" asked Sister McCandless. "We're going to have service on the ship, you know." She looked at Father James. "Reckon we'll start as soon as we get a little further up the river, won't we, Father?"

"Yes," Father James said, "we're going to praise God right in the middle of the majestic Hudson." He leaned back and released Roy as he spoke. "Want to see you children there. I want to hear you make a *noise* for the Lord."

"I ain't never seen none of these young men Shout," said Sister Daniels, regarding them with distrust. She looked at David and Johnnie. "Don't believe I've ever even heard you testify."

"We're not saved yet, sister," David told her gently.

"That's alright," Sister Daniels said. "You *could* get up and praise the Lord for your life, health and strength. Praise Him for what you got, He'll give you something more."

"That's the truth," said Brother Elisha. He smiled at Sylvia. "I'm a witness, bless the Lord."

"They going to make a noise yet," said Sister McCandless. "Lord's going to touch everyone of these young men one day and bring them on their knees to the altar. You mark my words, you'll see." And she smiled at them.

"You just stay around the house of God long enough," Father James said. "One of these days the Spirit'll jump on you. I won't never forget the day It jumped on me."

"That *is* the truth," Sister McCandless cried, "so glad it jumped on me one day, hallelujah!"

"Amen," Sister Daniels cried, "amen."

"Looks like we're having a little service right now," Brother Elisha said smiling. Father James laughed heartily and cried, "Well, praise Him anyhow."

"I believe next week the church is going to start a series of revival meetings," Brother Elisha said. "I want to see you boys at every one of them, you hear?" He laughed as he spoke and added as David seemed about to protest, "No, no, brother, don't want no excuses. You *be* there. Get you boys to the altar, then maybe you'll pay more attention in Sunday School."

At this they all laughed and Sylvia said in her mild voice, looking mockingly at Roy, "Maybe we'll even see Brother Roy Shout." Roy grinned.

"Like to see you do some Shouting too," her mother grumbled. "You got to get closer to the Lord." Sylvia smiled and bit her lip; she cast a glance at David.

"Now everybody ain't got the same kind of spirit," Brother Elisha said, coming to Sylvia's aid. "Can't *all* make as much noise as you make," he said, laughing gently, "we all ain't got your energy."

Sister Daniels smiled and frowned at this reference to her size and passion and said, "Don't care, brother, when the Lord moves inside you, you bound to do something. I've seen that girl Shout all night and come back the next night and Shout some more. I don't believe in no dead religion, no sir. The saints of God need a revival."

"Well, we'll work on Sister Sylvia," said Brother Elisha.

Directly before and behind them stretched nothing but the river, they had long ago lost sight of the point of their departure. They steamed beside the Palisades which rose rough and gigantic from the dirty, broad and blue-green Hudson. Johnnie and David and Roy wandered downstairs to the bottom deck, standing by the rail and leaning over to watch the white, writhing spray which followed the boat. From the river there floated up to their faces a soft, cool breeze. They were quiet for a long time, standing together, watching the river and the mountains and hearing vaguely the hum of activity behind them on the boat. The sky was high and blue, with here and there a spittle-like, changing cloud; the sun was orange and beat with anger on their uncovered heads.

And David muttered finally, "Be funny if they were right."

"If who was right?" asked Roy.

"Elisha and them—"

"There's only one way to find out," said Johnnie.

"Yes," said Roy, "and I ain't homesick for heaven yet."

"You always got to be so smart," David said.

"Oh," said Roy, "You just sore because Sylvia's still up there with Brother Elisha."

"You think they going to be married?" Johnnie asked.

"Don't talk like a fool," David said.

"Well it's a cinch you ain't never going to get to talk to her till you get saved," Johnnie said. He had meant to say 'we.' He looked at David and smiled.

"Might be worth it," David said.

"*What* might be worth it?" Roy asked, grinning.

"Now be nice," David said. He flushed, the dark blood rising beneath the dark skin. "How you expect me to get saved if you going to talk that way? You supposed to be an example."

"Don't look at me, boy," Roy said.

"I want you to talk to Johnnie," Gabriel said to his wife.

"What about?"

"That boy's pride is running away with him. Ask him to tell you what he said to me this morning soon as he got in front of his friends. He's your son, alright."

"What did he say?"

He looked darkly across the river. "You ask him to tell you about it tonight. I wanted to knock him down."

She had watched the scene and knew this. She looked at her husband briefly, feeling a sudden, outraged anger, barely conscious; sighed and turned to look at her youngest child where he sat involved in a complicated and strenuous and apparently joyless game which utilized a red ball, jacks, blocks and a broken shovel.

"I'll talk to him," she said at last. "He'll be alright." She wondered what on earth she would say to him; and what he would say to her. She looked covertly about the boat, but he was nowhere to be seen.

"That proud demon's just eating him up," he said bitterly. He watched the river hurtle past. "Be the best thing in the world if the Lord would take his soul." He had meant to say 'save' his soul.

Now it was noon and all over the boat there was the activity of lunch. Paper bags and huge baskets were opened. There was then revealed splendor: cold pork chops, cold chicken, bananas, apples, oranges, pears, and soda-pop, candy and cold lemonade. All over the boat the chosen of God relaxed; they sat in groups and talked and laughed; some of the more worldly gossiped and some of the more courageous young people dared to walk off together. Beneath them the strong, indifferent river raged within the channel and the screaming spray pursued them. In the engine room children watched the motion of the ship's gears as they rose and fell and chanted. The tremendous bolts of steel seemed almost human, imbued with a relentless force that was not human. There was something monstrous about this machine which bore such enormous weight and cargo.

Sister Daniels threw a paper bag over the side and wiped her mouth with her large handkerchief. "Sylvia, you be careful how you speak to these unsaved boys," she said.

"Yes, I am, Mama."

"Don't like the way that little Jackson boy looks at you. That child's got a demon. You be careful."

"Yes, Mama."

"You got plenty of time to be thinking about boys. Now's the time for you to be thinking about the Lord."

"Yes'm."

"You *mind* now," her mother said.

"Mama, I want to go home!" Lois cried. She crawled into her mother's arms, weeping.

"Why, what's the matter, honey?" She rocked her daughter gently. "Tell Mama what's the matter? Have you got a pain?"

"I want to go home, I want to go home." Lois sobbed.

"A very fine preacher, a man of God and a friend of mine will run the service for us," said Father James.

"Maybe you've heard about him—a Reverend Peters? A real man of God, amen."

"I thought," Gabriel said, smiling, "that perhaps I could bring the message some Sunday night. The Lord called me a long time ago. I used to have my own church down home."

"You don't want to run too fast, Deacon Grimes," Father James said. "You just take your time. You been coming along right well on Young Ministers' Nights." He paused and looked at Gabriel. "Yes, indeed."

"I just thought," Gabriel said humbly, "that I could be used to more advantage in the house of God."

Father James quoted the text which tells us how preferable it is to be a gate-keeper in the house of God than to dwell in the tent of the wicked; and started to add the dictum from Saint Paul about obedience to those above one in the Lord but decided (watching Gabriel's face) that it was not necessary yet.

"You just keep praying," he said kindly. "You get a little closer to God. He'll work wonders. You'll see." He bent closer to his deacon. "And try to get just a little closer to the *people.*"

Roy wandered off with a gawky and dazzled girl named Elizabeth. Johnnie and David wandered restlessly up and down the boat alone. They mounted to the topmost deck and leaned over the railing in the deserted stern. Up here the air was sharp and clean. They faced the water, their arms around each other.

"Your old man was kind of rough this morning," David said carefully, watching the mountains pass.

"Yes," Johnnie said. He looked at David's face against the sky. He shivered suddenly in the sharp, cold air and buried his face in David's shoulder. David looked down at him and tightened his hold.

"Who do you love?" he whispered. "Who's your boy?"

"You," he muttered fiercely, "I love you."

"Roy!" Elizabeth giggled, "*Roy Grimes*. If you *ever* say a thing like that *again*."

Now the service was beginning. From all corners of the boat there was the movement of the saints of God. They gathered together their various possessions and moved their chairs from top and bottom decks to the large main hall. It was early afternoon, not quite two o'clock. The sun was high and fell everywhere with a copper light. In the city the heat would have been insupportable; and here, as the saints filed into the huge, high room, once used as a ballroom, to judge from the faded and antique appointments, the air slowly began to be oppressive. The room was the color of black mahogany and coming in from the bright deck, one groped suddenly in darkness; and took one's sense of direction from the elegant grand piano which stood in the front of the room on a little platform.

They sat in small rows with one wide aisle between them, forming, almost unconsciously, a hierarchy. Father James sat in the front next to Sister McCandless. Opposite them sat Gabriel and Deacon Jones and, immediately behind them, Sister Daniels and her daughter. Brother Elisha walked in swiftly, just as they were beginning to be settled. He strode to the piano and knelt down for a second before rising to take his place. There was a quiet stir, the saints adjusted themselves, waiting while Brother Elisha tentatively ran his fingers over the keys. Gabriel looked about impatiently for Roy and Johnnie, who, engaged no doubt in sinful conversation with David, were not yet in service. He looked back to where Mrs. Jackson sat with Lorraine, uncomfortable smiles on their faces, and glanced at his wife, who met his questioning regard quietly, the expression on her face not changing.

Brother Elisha struck the keys and all the congregation joined in the song, *Nothing Shall Move Me from the Love of God*, with tambourine and heavy hands and stomping feet. The walls and the floor of the ancient hall trembled and the candelabra wavered in the high ceiling. Outside the river rushed past under the heavy shadow of the Palisades and the copper sun beat down. A few of the strangers who had come along on the outing appeared at the doors and stood watching with an uneasy amusement. The saints sang on, raising their strong voices in praises to Jehovah and seemed unaware of those unsaved who watched and who, some day, the power of the Lord might cause to tremble.

The song ended as Father James rose and faced the congregation, a broad smile on his face. They watched him expectantly, with love. He stood silent for a moment, smiling down upon them. Then he said, and his voice was loud and filled with triumph:

"Well, let us all say, Amen!"

And they cried out obediently, "Well, Amen!"

"Let us all say, praise Him!"

"Praise Him!"

"Let us all say, hallelujah!"

"Hallelujah!"

"Well, glory!" cried Father James. The Holy Ghost touched him and he cried again, "Well, bless Him! Bless His holy name!"

They laughed and shouted after him, their joy so great that they laughed as children and some of them cried as children do; in the fullness and assurance of salvation, in the knowledge that the Lord was in their midst and that each heart, swollen to anguish, yearned only to be filled with His glory. Then, in that moment, each of them might have mounted with wings like eagles far past the sordid persistence of the flesh, the depthless iniquity of the heart, the doom of hours and days and weeks; to be received by the Bridegroom where He waited on high in glory; where all tears were wiped away and death had no power; where the wicked ceased from troubling and the weary soul found rest.

"Saints, let's praise Him," Father James said. "Today, right in the middle of God's great river, under God's great roof, beloved, let us raise our voices in thanksgiving that God has seen fit to save us, amen!"

"Amen! Hallelujah!"

"—and to keep us saved, amen, to keep us, oh glory to God, from the snares of Satan, from the temptation and the lust and the evil of this world!"

"Talk about it!"

"*Preach!*"

"Ain't nothing strange, amen, about worshiping God *wherever* you might be, ain't that right? Church, when you get this mighty salvation you just can't keep it in, hallelujah! you got to talk about it—"

"Amen!"

"You got to live it, amen. When the Holy Ghost touches you, you *move*, bless God!"

"Well, it's so!"

"Want to hear some testimonies today, amen! I want to hear some *singing* today, bless God! Want to see some *Shouting*, bless God, hallelujah!"

"Talk about it!"

"And I don't want to see none of the saints hold back. If the Lord saved you, amen, He give you a witness *every*where you go. Yes! My soul is a witness, bless our God!"

"Glory!"

"If you ain't saved, amen, get up and praise Him anyhow. Give God the glory for sparing your sinful life, *praise* Him for the sunshine and the rain, praise Him for all the works of His hands. Saints, I want to hear some praises today, you hear me? I want you to make this old boat *rock*, hallelujah! I want to *feel* your salvation. Are you saved?"

"Amen!"

"Are you sanctified?"

"Glory?"

"Baptized in fire?"

"Yes! So glad!"

"*Testify!*"

Now the hall was filled with a rushing wind on which forever rides the Lord, death or healing indifferently in His hands. Under this fury the saints bowed low, crying out "holy!" and tears fell. On the open deck sinners stood and watched, beyond them the fiery sun and the deep river, the black-brown-green, unchanging cliffs. That sun, which covered earth and water now, would one day refuse to shine, the river would cease its rushing and its numberless dead would rise; the cliffs would shiver, crack, fall and where they had been would then be nothing but the unleashed wrath of God.

"Who'll be the first to tell it?" Father James cried. "Stand up and talk about it!"

Brother Elisha screamed, "Have mercy, Jesus!" and rose from the piano stool, his powerful frame possessed. And the Holy Ghost touched him and he cried again, bending nearly double, while his feet beat ageless, dreadful signals on the floor, while his arms moved in the air like wings and his face, distorted, no longer his own face not the face of a young man, but timeless, anguished, grim with ecstasy, turned blindly toward heaven. *Yes, Lord*, they cried, *yes!*

"Dearly beloved . . ."

"Talk about it!"

"Tell it!"

"I want to thank and praise the Lord, amen . . ."

"Amen!"

". . . for being here, I want to thank Him for my life, health, and strength. . . ."

"Amen!"

"Well, glory!"

". . . I want to thank Him, hallelujah, for saving my soul one day. . . ."

"*Oh!*"

"Glory!"

". . . for causing the light, bless God, to shine in *my* heart one day when I was still a child, amen, I want to thank Him for bringing me to salvation in the days of my *youth*, hallelujah, when I have all my faculties, amen, before Satan had a chance to destroy my body in the world!"

"Talk about it!"

"He saved me, dear ones, from the world and the things of the world. Saved me, amen, from cardplaying . . ."

"Glory!"

". . . saved me from drinking, bless God, saved me from the streets, from the movies and all the filth that is in the world!"

"I *know* it's so!"

"He saved me, beloved, and sanctified me and filled me with the blessed Holy Ghost, *hallelujah!* Give me a new song, amen, which I didn't know before and set my feet on the King's highway. Pray for me beloved, that I will stand in these last and evil days."

"Bless your name, Jesus!"

During his testimony Johnnie and Roy and David had stood quietly beside the door, not daring to enter while he spoke. The moment he sat down they moved quickly, together, to the front of the high hall and knelt down beside their seats to pray. The aspect of each of them underwent always, in this company a striking, even an exciting change; as though their youth, barely begun, were already put away; and the animal, so vividly restless and undiscovered, so tense with power, ready to spring had been already stalked and trapped and offered, a perpetual blood-sacrifice, on the altar of the Lord. Yet their bodies continued to change and grow, preparing them, mysteriously and with ferocious speed, for manhood. No matter how careful their movements, these movements suggested, with a distinctness dreadful for the redeemed to see, the pagan lusting beneath the blood-washed robes. In them was perpetually and perfectly poised the power of revelation against the power of nature; and the saints, considering them with a baleful kind of love, struggled to bring their souls to safety in order, as it were, to steal a march on the flesh while the flesh still slept. A kind of storm, infernal, blew over the congregation as they passed; someone cried, "Bless them, Lord!" and immediately, honey-colored Sister Russell, while they knelt in prayer, rose to her feet to testify.

From the moment that they closed their eyes and covered their faces they were isolated from the joy that moved everything beside them. Yet this same isolation served only to make the glory of the saints more real, the pulse of conviction, however faint, beat in and the glory of God then held an undertone of abject terror. Roy was the first to rise, sitting very straight in his seat and allowing his face to reveal nothing; just as Sister Russell ended her testimony and sat down, sobbing, her head thrown back and both hands raised to heaven. Immediately Sister Daniels raised her strong, harsh voice and hit her tambourine, singing. Brother Elisha turned on the piano stool and hit the keys. Johnnie and David rose from their knees and as they rose the congregation rose, clapping their hands singing. The three boys did not sing; they stood together, carefully ignoring one another, their feet steady on the slightly tilting floor but their bodies moving back and forth as the music grew more savage. And someone cried aloud, a timeless sound of wailing: fire splashed the open deck and filled the doors and bathed the sinners standing there; fire filled the great hall and splashed the faces of the saints and a wind, unearthly, moved about their heads. Their hands were arched before them, moving, and their eyes were raised to heaven. Sweat stained the deacon's collar and soaked the tight headbands of the women. Was it true then? and had there indeed been born one day in Bethlehem a Saviour who was Christ the Lord? who had died for them—for *them!*—the spat-upon and beaten with rods, who had worn a crown of thorns and seen His blood run down like rain; and who had lain in the grave three days and vanquished death and hell and risen again in glory—*was it for them?*

Lord, I want to go, show me the way!

For unto us a child is born, unto us a son is given—and His name shall be called Wonderful, the mighty God, the everlasting Father, the Prince of Peace. Yes, and He was coming back one day, the King of glory; He would crack the face of heaven and descend to judge the nations and gather up His people and take them to their rest.

Take me by my hand and lead me on!

Somewhere in the back a woman cried out and began the Shout. They looked carefully about, still not looking at one another, and saw, as from a great distance and through intolerable heat, such heat as might have been faced by the Hebrew children when cast bound into the fiery furnace, that one of the saints was dancing under the arm of the Lord. She danced out into the aisle, beautiful with a beauty unbearable, graceful with grace that poured from heaven. Her face was lifted up, her eyes were closed and the feet which moved so surely now were not her own. One by one the power of God moved others and—as it had been written—the Holy Ghost descended from heaven with a Shout. Sylvia raised her hands, the tears poured down her face, and in a moment, she too moved out into the aisle, Shouting. Is it true then? the saints rejoiced, Roy beat the tambourine. David, grave and shaken, clapped his hands and his body moved insistently in the rhythm of the dancers. Johnnie stood beside him, hot and faint and repeating yet again his struggle, summoning in panic all his forces, to save him from this frenzy. And yet daily he recognized that he was black with sin, that the secrets of his heart were a stench in God's nostrils. *Though your sins be as scarlet they shall be white as snow. Come, let us reason together, saith the Lord.*

Now there was a violent discord on the piano and Brother Elisha leapt to his feet, dancing. Johnnie watched the spinning body and listened, in terror and anguish, to the bestial sobs. Of the men it was only Elisha who danced and the women moved toward him and he moved toward the women. Johnnie felt blow over him an icy wind, all his muscles tightened, as though they furiously resisted some imminent bloody act, as the body of Isaac must have revolted when he saw his father's knife, and, sick and nearly sobbing, he closed his eyes. It was Satan, surely, who stood so foully at his shoulder; and what, but the blood of Jesus, should ever set him free? He thought of the many times he had stood in the congregation of the righteous—and yet he was not saved. He remained among the vast army of the doomed, whose lives—as he had been told, as he now, with such heart-sickness, began to discover for himself—were swamped with wrtechedness and whose end was wrath and weeping. Then, for he felt himself falling, he opened his eyes and watched the rejoicing of the saints. His eyes found his father where he stood clapping his hands, glittering with sweat and overwhelming. Then Lois began to shout. For the first time he looked at Roy; their eyes met in brief, wry wonder and Roy imperceptibly shrugged. He watched his mother standing over Lois, her own face obscurely troubled. The light from the door was on her face, the entire room was filled with this strange light. There was no sound now except the sound of Roy's tambourine and the heavy rhythm of the saints; the sound of heavy feet and hands and the sound of weeping. Perhaps centuries past the children of Israel led by Miriam had made just such a noise as they came out of the wilderness. *For unto us is born this day a Saviour who is Christ the Lord.*

Yet, in the copper sunlight Johnnie felt suddenly, not the presence of the Lord, but the presence of David; which seemed to reach out to him, hand reaching out to hand in the fury of flood-time, to drag him to the bottom of the water or to carry him safe to shore. From the corner of his eye he watched his friend, who held him with such power; and felt, for that moment, such a depth of love, such nameless and terrible joy and pain, that he might have fallen, in the face of that company, weeping at David's feet.

Once at Bear Mountain they faced the very great problem of carrying Sylvia sufficiently far from her mother's sight to present her with her birthday present. This problem, difficult enough, was made even more difficult by the continual presence of Brother Elisha; who, inspired by the afternoon's service and by Sylvia's renewal of her faith, remained by her side to bear witness to the goodness and power of the Lord. Sylvia listened with her habitual rapt and painful smile. Her mother, on the one side and Brother Elisha on the other, seemed almost to be taking turns in advising her on her conduct as a saint of God. They began to despair, as the sun moved visibly westward, of ever giving her the gold-plated butterfly which rested uncomfortably in David's waistcoat pocket.

Of course, as Johnnie once suggested, there was really no reason they could not go up to her, surrounded as she was, and give her the jewel and get it over with—the more particularly as David evinced a desire to explore the wonders of Bear Mountain until this mission should have been fulfilled. Sister Daniels could scarcely object to an innocuous memento from three young men, all of whom attended church devoutly and one of whom professed salvation. But this was far from satisfactory for David, who did not wish to hear Sylvia's "thank-you's" in the constricting presence of the saints. Therefore they waited, wandering about the sloping park, lingering near the lake and the skating rink and watching Sylvia.

"God, why don't they go off somewhere and sleep? or pray?" cried David finally. He glared at the nearby rise where Sylvia and her mother sat talking with Brother Elisha. The sun was in their faces and struck from Sylvia's hair as she restlessly moved her head, small blue-black sparks.

Johnnie swallowed his jealousy at seeing how Sylvia filled his comrade's mind; he said, half-angrily, "I still don't see why we don't just go over and give it to her."

Roy looked at him. "Boy, you sound like you ain't got good sense," he said.

Johnnie, frowning, fell into silence. He glanced sidewise at David's puckered face (his eyes were still on Sylvia) and abruptly turned and started walking off.

"Where you going, boy?" David called.

"I'll be back," he said. And he prayed that David would follow him.

But David was determined to catch Sylvia alone and remained where he was with Roy. "Well, make it snappy," he said; and sprawled, full length, on the grass.

As soon as he was alone his pace slackened; he leaned his forehead against the bark of a tree, shaking and burning as in the teeth of a fever. The bark of the tree was rough and cold and though it offered no other comfort he stood there quietly for a long time, seeing beyond him—but it brought no peace—the high clear sky where the sun in fading glory traveled; and the deep earth covered with vivid banners, grass, flower, thorn and vine, thrusting upward forever the brutal trees. At his back he heard the voices of the children and the saints. He knew that he must return, that he must be on hand should David at last outwit Sister Daniels and present her daughter with the golden butterfly. But he did not want to go back, now he realized that he had no interest in the birthday present, no interest whatever in Sylvia—that he had had no interest all along. He shifted his stance, he turned from the tree as he turned his mind from the abyss which suddenly yawned, that abyss, depthless and terrifying, which he had encountered already in dreams. And he slowly began to walk, away from the saints and the voices of the children, his hands in his pockets, struggling to ignore the question which now screamed and screamed in his mind's bright haunted house.

It happened quite simply. Eventually Sister Daniels felt the need to visit the ladies' room, which was a long ways off. Brother Elisha remained where he was while Roy and David, like two beasts crouching in the underbrush, watched him and waited their opportunity. Then he also rose and wandered off to get cold lemonade for Sylvia. She sat quietly alone on the green rise, her hands clasped around her knees, dreaming.

They walked over to her, in terror that Sister Daniels would suddenly reappear. Sylvia smiled as she saw them coming and waved to them merrily. Roy grinned and threw himself on his belly on the ground beside her. David remained standing, fumbling in his waistcoat pocket.

"We got something for you," Roy said.

David produced the butterfly. "Happy birthday, Sylvia," he said. He stretched out his hands, the butterfly glinted oddly in the sun, and he realized with surprise that his hand was shaking. She grinned widely, in amazement and delight, and took the pin from him.

"It's from Johnnie, too," he said. "I—we—hope you like it—"

She held the small gold pin in her palm and stared down at it; her face was hidden. After a moment she murmured, "I'm so surprised." She looked up, her eyes shining, almost wet. "Oh, it's wonderful," she said. "I never expected anything. I don't know what to say. It's marvelous, it's wonderful." She pinned the butterfly carefully to her light blue dress. She coughed slightly. "Thank you," she said.

"Your mother won't mind, will she?" Roy asked. "I mean—" he stammered awkwardly under Sylvia's sudden gaze—"we didn't know, we didn't want to get you in any trouble—"

"No," David said. He had not moved; he stood watching Sylvia. Sylvia looked away from Roy and up at David, his eyes met hers and she smiled. He smiled back, suddenly robbed of speech. She looked away again over the path her mother had taken and frowned slightly. "No," she said, "no, she won't mind."

Then there was silence. David shifted uncomfortably from one foot to the other. Roy lay contentedly face down on the grass. The breeze from the river, which lay below them and out of sight, grew subtly more insistent for they had passed the heat of the day; and the sun, moving always westward, fired and polished the tips of trees. Sylvia sighed and shifted on the ground.

"Why isn't Johnnie here?" she suddenly asked.

"He went off somewhere," Roy said. "He said he'd be right back." He looked at Sylvia and smiled. She was looking at David.

"You must want to grow real tall," she said mockingly. "Why don't you sit down?"

David grinned and sat down cross-legged next to Sylvia. "Well, the ladies like 'em tall." He lay on his back and stared up at the sky. "It's a fine day," he said.

She said, "Yes," and looked down at him; he had closed his eyes and was bathing his face in the slowly waning sun. Abruptly, she asked him:

"Why don't you get saved? You around the church all the time and you not saved yet? Why don't you?"

He opened his eyes in amazement. Never before had Sylvia mentioned salvation to him, except as a kind of joke. One of the things he most liked about her was the fact that she never preached to him. Now he smiled uncertainly and stared at her.

"I'm not joking," she said sharply. "I'm perfectly serious. Roy's saved—at least he *says* so—" and she smiled darkly, in the fashion of the old folks, at Roy—"and anyway, you ought to be thinking about your soul."

"Well, I don't know," David said. "I *think* about it. It's—well, I don't know if I can—well, live it—"

"All you got to do is make up your mind. If you really want to be saved, He'll save you. Yes, and He'll keep you too." She did not sound at all hysterical or transfigured. She spoke very quietly and with great earnestness and frowned as she spoke. David, taken off guard, said nothing. He looked embarrassed and pained and surprised. "Well, I don't know," he finally repeated.

"Do you ever pray?" she asked. "I mean, *really* pray?"

David laughed, beginning to recover himself. "It's not fair," he said, "you oughtn't to catch me all unprepared like that. Now I don't know what to say." But as he looked at her earnest face he sobered. "Well, I try to be decent. I don't bother nobody." He picked up a grass blade and stared at it. "I don't know," he said at last. "I do my best."

"*Do* you?" she asked.

He laughed again, defeated. "Girl," he said, "you *are* a killer."

She laughed too. "You black-eyed demon," she said, "if I don't see you at revival services I'll never speak to you again." He looked up quickly, in some surprise, and she said, still smiling, "Don't look at me like that. I mean it."

"All right, sister," he said. Then: "If I come out can I walk you home?"

"I got my mother to walk me home—"

"Well, let your mother walk home with Brother Elisha," he said, grinning, "Let the old folks stay together."

"Loose him, Satan!" she cried, laughing, "loose the boy!"

"The brother needs prayer," Roy said.

"Amen," said Sylvia. She looked down again at David. "I want to see you at church. Don't you forget it."

"All right," he said. "I'll be there."

The boat whistles blew at six o'clock, punctuating their holiday; blew, fretful and insistent, through the abruptly dispirited park and skaters left the skating rink; boats were rowed in furiously from the lake. Children were called from the swings and the seesaw and the merry-go-round and forced to leave behind the ball which had been lost in the forest and the torn kite which dangled from the top of a tree. ("Hush now," said their parents, "we'll get you another one—come along." "*Tomorrow?*"—"Come along, honey, it's time to go!") The old folks rose from the benches, from the grass, gathered together the empty lunch-basket, the half-read newspaper, the Bible which was carried everywhere; and they started down the hillside, an army in disorder. David walked with Sylvia and Sister Daniels and Brother Elisha, listening to their conversation (good Lord, thought Johnnie, don't they ever mention anything but sin?) and carrying Sylvia's lunch-basket. He seemed interested in what they were saying; every now and then he looked at Sylvia and grinned and she grinned back. Once, as Sylvia stumbled, he put his hand on her elbow to steady her and held her arm perhaps a moment too long. Brother Elisha, on the far side of Sister Daniels, noticed this and a frown passed over his face. He kept talking, staring now and then hard at Sylvia and trying, with a certain almost humorous helplessness, to discover what was in her mind. Sister Daniels talked of nothing but the service on the boat and of the forthcoming revival. She scarcely seemed to notice David's presence, though once she spoke to him, making some remark about the need, on his part, of much prayer. Gabriel carried the sleeping baby in his arms, striding beside his wife and Lois—who stumbled perpetually and held tightly to her mother's hand. Roy was somewhere in the back, joking with Elizabeth. At a turn in the road the boat and the dock appeared below them, a dead gray-white in the sun.

Johnnie walked down the slope alone, watching David and Sylvia ahead of him. When he had come back, both Roy and David had disappeared and Sylvia sat again in the company of her mother and Brother Elisha; and if he had not seen the gold butterfly on her dress he would have been aware of no change. She thanked him for his share in it and told him that Roy and David were at the skating rink.

But when at last he found them they were far in the middle of the lake in a rowboat. He was afraid of water, he could not row. He stood on the bank and watched them. After a long while they saw him and waved and started to bring the boat in so that he could join them. But the day was ruined for him; by the time they brought the boat in, the hour, for which they had hired it, was over; David went in search of his mother for more money but when he came back it was time to leave. Then he walked with Sylvia.

All during the trip home David seemed preoccupied. When he finally sought out Johnnie he found him sitting by himself on the top deck, shivering a little in the night air. He sat down beside him. After a moment Johnnie moved and put his head on David's shoulder. David put his arms around him. But now where there had been peace there was only panic and where there had been safety, danger, like a flower, opened.

GRAHAM GREENE

The BASEMENT ROOM

1

When the front door had shut them out and the butler Baines had turned back into the dark heavy hall, Philip began to live. He stood in front of the nursery door, listening until he heard the engine of the taxi die out along the street. His parents were gone for a fortnight's holiday; he was "between nurses," one dismissed and the other not yet arrived; he was alone in the great Belgravia house with Baines and Mrs. Baines.

He could go anywhere, even through the green baize door to the pantry or down the stairs to the basement living room. He felt a stranger in his home because he could go into any room and all the rooms were empty.

You could only guess who had once occupied them: the rack of pipes in the smoking-room beside the elephant tusks, the carved wood tobacco jar; in the bedroom the pink hangings and pale perfumes and the three-quarter finished jars of cream which Mrs. Baines had not yet cleared away; the high glaze on the never-opened piano in the drawing-room, the china clock, the silly little tables and the silver: but here Mrs. Baines was already busy, pulling down the curtains, covering the chairs in dust-sheets.

"Be off out of here, Master Philip," and she looked at him with her hateful peevish eyes, while she moved round, getting everything in order, meticulous and loveless and doing her duty.

Philip Lane went downstairs and pushed at the baize door; he looked into the pantry, but Baines was not there, then he set foot for the first time on the stairs to the basement. Again he had the sense: this is life. All his seven nursery years vibrated with the strange, the new experience. His crowded busy brain was like a city which feels the earth tremble at a distant earthquake shock. He was apprehensive, but he was happier than he had ever been. Everything was more important than before.

Baines was reading a newspaper in his shirt-sleeves. He said: "Come in, Phil, and make yourself at home. Wait a moment and I'll do the honours," and going to a white cleaned cupboard he brought out a bottle of ginger-beer and half a Dundee cake. "Half-past eleven in the morning," Baines said. "It's opening time, my boy," and he cut the cake and poured out the ginger-beer. He was more genial than Philip had ever known him, more at his ease, a man in his own home.

"Shall I call Mrs. Baines?" Philip asked, and he was glad when Baines said no. She was busy. She liked to be busy, so why interfere with her pleasure?

"A spot of drink at half-past eleven," Baines said, pouring himself out a glass of ginger-beer, "gives an appetite for chop and does no man any harm."

"A chop?" Philip asked.

"Old Coasters," Baines said, "call all food chop."

"But it's not a chop?"

"Well, it might be, you know, cooked with palm oil. And then some paw-paw to follow."

Philip looked out of the basement window at the dry stone yard, the ash-can and the legs going up and down beyond the railings.

"Was it hot there?"

"Ah, you never felt such heat. Not a nice heat, mind, like you get in the park on a day like this. Wet," Baines said, "corruption." He cut himself a slice of cake. "Smelling of rot," Baines said, rolling his eyes round the small basement room, from clean cupboard to clean cupboard, the sense of bareness, of nowhere to hide a man's secrets. With an air of regret for something lost he took a long draught of ginger-beer.

"Why did father live out there?"

"It was his job," Baines said, "same as this is mine now. And it was mine then too. It was a man's job. You wouldn't believe it now, but I've had forty niggers under me, doing what I told them to."

"Why did you leave?"

"I married Mrs. Baines."

Philip took the slice of Dundee cake in his hand and munched it round the room. He felt very old, independent and judicial; he was aware that Baines was talking to him as man to man. He never called him Master Philip as Mrs. Baines did, who was servile when she was not authoritative.

Baines had seen the world; he had seen beyond the railings, beyond the tired legs of typists, the Pimlico parade to and from Victoria. He sat there over his ginger pop with the resigned dignity of an exile; Baines didn't complain; he had chosen his fate; and if his fate was Mrs. Baines he had only himself to blame.

But today, because the house was almost empty and Mrs. Baines was upstairs and there was nothing to do, he allowed himself a little acidity.

"I'd go back tomorrow if I had the chance."

"Did you ever shoot a nigger?"

"I never had any call to shoot," Baines said. "Of course I carried a gun. But you didn't need to treat them bad. That just made them stupid. Why," Baines said, bowing his thin grey hair with embarrassment over the ginger pop, "I loved some of those damned niggers. I couldn't help loving them. There they'd be, laughing, holding hands; they liked to touch each other: it made them feel fine to know the other fellow was round.

"It didn't mean anything we could understand; two of them would go about all day without loosing hold, grown men; but it wasn't love; it didn't mean anything we could understand."

"Eating between meals," Mrs. Baines said. "What would your mother say, Master Philip?"

She came down the steep stairs to the basement, her hands full of pots of cream and salve, tubes of grease and paste. "You oughtn't to encourage him, Baines," she said, sitting down in a wicker armchair and screwing up her small ill-humoured eyes at the Coty lipstick, Pond's cream, the Leichner rouge and Cyclax powder and Elizabeth Arden astringent.

She threw them one by one into the wastepaper basket. She saved only the cold cream. "Telling the boy stories," she said. "Go along to the nursery, Master Philip, while I get lunch."

Philip climbed the stairs to the baize door. He heard Mrs. Baines's voice like the voice in a nightmare when the small Price light has guttered in the saucer and the curtains move; it was sharp and shrill and full of malice, louder than people ought to speak, exposed.

"Sick to death of your ways, Baines, spoiling the boy. Time you did some work about the house," but he couldn't hear what Baines said in reply. He pushed open the baize door, came up like a small earth animal in his grey flannel shorts into a wash of sunlight on a parquet floor, the gleam of mirrors dusted and polished and beautified by Mrs. Baines.

Something broke downstairs, and Philip sadly mounted the stairs to the nursery. He pitied Baines; it occurred to him how happily they could live together in the empty house if Mrs. Baines were called away. He didn't want to play with his Meccano sets; he wouldn't take out his train or his soldiers; he sat at the table with his chin on his hands: this is life; and suddenly he felt responsible for Baines, as if he were the master of the house and Baines an ageing servant who deserved to be cared for. There was not much one could do; he decided at least to be good.

He was not surprised when Mrs. Baines was agreeable at lunch; he was used to her changes. Now it was "another helping of meat, Master Philip," or "Master Philip, a little more of this nice pudding." It was a pudding he liked. Queen's pudding with a perfect meringue, but he wouldn't eat a second helping lest she might count that a victory. She was the kind of woman who thought that any injustice could be counterbalanced by something good to eat.

She was sour, but she liked making sweet things; one never had to complain of a lack of jam or plums; she ate well herself and added soft sugar to the meringue and the strawberry jam. The half light through the basement window set the motes moving above her pale hair like dust as she sifted the sugar, and Baines crouched over his plate saying nothing.

Again Philip felt responsibility. Baines had looked forward to this, and Baines was disappointed: everything was being spoilt. The sensation of disappointment was one which Philip could share; knowing nothing of love or jealousy or passion, he could understand better than anyone this grief, something hoped for not happening, something promised not fulfilled, something exciting turning dull. "Baines," he said, "will you take me for a walk this afternoon?"

"No," Mrs. Baines said, "no. That he won't. Not with all the silver to clean."

"There's a fortnight to do it in," Baines said.

"Work first, pleasure afterwards." Mrs. Baines helped herself to some more meringue.

Baines suddenly put down his spoon and fork and pushed his plate away. "Blast," he said.

"Temper," Mrs. Baines said softly, "temper. Don't you go breaking any more things, Baines, and I won't have you swearing in front of the boy. Master Philip, if you've finished you can get down." She skinned the rest of the meringue off the pudding.

"I want to go for a walk," Philip said.

"You'll go and have a rest."

"I will go for a walk."

"Master Philip," Mrs. Baines said. She got up from the table, leaving her merignue unfinished, and came toward him, thin, menacing, dusty in the basement room. "Master Philip, you do as you're told." She took him by the arm and squeezed it gently; she watched him with a joyless passionate glitter and above her head the feet of the typists trudged back to the Victoria offices after the lunch interval.

"Why shouldn't I go for a walk?" But he weakened; he was scared and ashamed of being scared. This was life; a strange passion he couldn't understand moving in the basement room. He saw a small pile of broken glass swept into a corner by the wastepaper basket. He looked to Baines for help and only intercepted hate; the sad hopeless hate of something behind bars.

"Why shouldn't I?" he repeated.

"Master Philip," Mrs. Baines said, "you've got to do as you're told. You mustn't think just because your father's away there's nobody here to—"

"You wouldn't dare," Philip cried, and was startled by Baines's low interjection, "There's nothing she wouldn't dare."

"I hate you," Philip said to Mrs. Baines. He pulled away from her and ran to the door, but she was there before him; she was old, but she was quick.

"Master Philip," she said, "you'll say you're sorry." She stood in front of the door quivering with excitement. "What would your father do if he heard you say that?"

She put a hand out to seize him, dry and white with constant soda, the nails cut to the quick, but he backed away and put the table between them, and suddenly to his surprise she smiled; she became again as servile as she had been arrogant. "Get along with you, Master Philip," she said with glee. "I see I'm going to have my hands full till your father and mother come back."

She left the door unguarded and when he passed her she slapped him playfully. "I've got too much to do today to trouble about you. I haven't covered half the chairs," and suddenly even the upper part of the house became unbearable to him as he thought of Mrs. Baines moving round shrouding the sofas, laying out the dust-sheets.

So he wouldn't go upstairs to get his cap but walked straight out across the shining hall into the street, and again, as he looked this way and looked that way, it was life he was in the middle of.

2

It was the pink sugar cakes in the window on a paper doily, the ham, the slab of mauve sausage, the wasps driving like small torpedoes across the pane that caught Philip's attention. His feet were tired by pavements; he had been afraid to cross the road, had simply walked first in one direction, then in the other. He was nearly home now; the square was at the end of the street; this was a shabby outpost of Pimlico, and he smudged the pane with his nose, looking for sweets, and saw between the cakes and ham a different Baines. He hardly recognized the bulbous eyes, the bald forehead. It was a happy, bold and buccaneering Baines, even though it was, when you looked closer, a desperate Baines.

Philip had never seen the girl. He remembered Baines had a niece and he thought that this might be her. She was thin and drawn, and she wore a white mackintosh; she meant nothing to Philip; she belonged to a world about which he knew nothing at all. He couldn't make up stories about her, as he could make them up about withered Sir Hubert Reed, the Permanent Secretary, about Mrs. Wince-Dudley, who came up once a year from Penstanley in Suffolk with a green umbrella and an enormous black handbag, as he could make them up about the upper servants in all the houses where he went to tea and games. She just didn't belong; he thought of mermaids and Undine; but she didn't belong there either, nor to the adventures of Emil, nor to the Bastables. She sat there looking at an iced pink cake in the detachment and mystery of the completely disinherited, looking at the half-used pots of powder which Baines had set out on the marble-topped table between them.

Baines was urging, hoping, entreating, commanding, and the girl looked at the tea and the china pots and cried. Baines passed his handkerchief across the table, but she wouldn't wipe her eyes; she screwed it in her palm and let the tears run down, wouldn't do anything, wouldn't speak, would only put up a silent despairing resistance to what she dreaded and wanted and refused to listen to at any price. The two brains battled over the tea-cups loving each other, and there came to Philip outside, beyond the ham and wasps and dusty Pimlico pane, a confused indication of the struggle.

He was inquisitive and he didn't understand and he wanted to know. He went and stood in the doorway to see better, he was less sheltered than he had ever been; other people's lives for the first time touched and pressed and moulded. He would never escape that scene. In a week he had forgotten it, but it conditioned his career, the long austerity of his life; when he was dying he said, "Who is she?"

Baines had won; he was cocky and the girl was happy. She wiped her face, she opened a pot of powder, and their fingers touched across the table. It occurred to Philip that it would be amusing to imitate Mrs. Baines's voice and call "Baines" to him from the door.

It shrivelled them; you couldn't describe it in any other way; it made them smaller, they weren't happy any more and they weren't bold. Baines was the first to recover and trace the voice, but that didn't make things as they were. The sawdust was spilled out of the afternoon; nothing you did could mend it, and Philip was scared. "I didn't mean . . ." He wanted to say that he loved Baines, that he had only wanted to laugh at Mrs. Baines. But he had discovered that you couldn't laugh at Mrs. Baines. She wasn't Sir Hubert Reed, who used steel nibs and carried a pen-wiper in his pocket; she wasn't Mrs. Wince-Dudley; she was darkness when the night-light went out in a draught; she was the frozen blocks of earth he had seen one winter in a graveyard when someone said, "They need an electric drill"; she was the flowers gone bad and smelling in the little closet room at Penstanley. There was nothing to laugh about. You had to endure her when she was there and forget about her quickly when she was away, suppress the thought of her, ram it down deep.

Baines said, "It's only Phil," beckoned him in and gave him the pink iced cake the girl hadn't eaten, but the afternoon was broken, the cake was like dry bread in the throat. The girl left them at once; she even forgot to take the powder; like a small blunt icicle in her white mackintosh she stood in the doorway with her back to them, then melted into the afternoon.

"Who is she?" Philip asked. "Is she your niece?"

"Oh, yes," Baines said, "that's who she is; she's my niece," and poured the last drops of water on to the coarse black leaves in the teapot.

"May as well have another cup," Baines said.

"The cup that cheers," he said hopelessly, watching the bitter black fluid drain out of the spout.

"Have a glass of ginger pop, Phil?"

"I'm sorry. I'm sorry, Baines."

"It's not your fault, Phil. Why, I could believe it wasn't you at all, but her. She creeps in everywhere." He fished two leaves out of his cup and laid them on the back of his hand, a thin soft flake and a hard stalk. He beat them with his hand: "Today," and the stalk detached itself, "tomorrow, Wednesday, Thursday, Friday, Saturday, Sunday," but the flake wouldn't come, stayed where it was, drying under his blows, with a resistance you wouldn't believe it to possess. "The tough one wins," Baines said.

He got up and paid the bill and out they went into the street. Baines said, "I don't ask you to say what isn't true. But you needn't mention to Mrs. Baines you met us here."

"Oh course not," Philip said, and catching something of Sir Hubert Reed's manner, "I understand, Baines." But he didn't understand a thing; he was caught up in other people's darkness.

"It was stupid," Baines said. "So near home, but I hadn't time to think, you see. I'd got to see her."

"Of course, Baines."

"I haven't time to spare," Baines said. "I'm not young. I've got to see that she's all right."

"Oh course you have, Baines."

"Mrs. Baines will get it out of you if she can."

"You can trust me, Baines," Philip said in a dry important Reed voice; and then, "Look out. She's at the window watching." And there indeed she was, looking up at them, between the lace curtains, from the basement room, speculating. "Need we go in, Baines?" Philip asked, cold lying heavy on his stomach like too much pudding; he clutched Baines's arm.

"Careful," Baines said softly, "careful."

"But need we go in, Baines? It's early. Take me for a walk in the park."

"Better not."

"But I'm frightened, Baines."

"You haven't any cause," Baines said. "Nothing's going to hurt you. You just run along upstairs to the nursery. I'll go down by the area and talk to Mrs. Baines." But even he stood hesitating at the top of the stone steps, pretending not to see her where she watched between the curtains. "In at the front door, Phil, and up the stairs."

Philip didn't linger in the hall; he ran, slithering on the parquet Mrs. Baines had polished, to the stairs. Through the drawing-room doorway on the first floor he saw the draped chairs; even the china clock on the mantel was covered like a canary's cage; as he passed it, it chimed the hour, muffled and secret under the duster. On the nursery table he found his supper laid out: a glass of milk and a piece of bread and butter, a sweet biscuit and a little cold Queen's pudding without the meringue. He had no appetite; he strained his ears for Mrs. Baines's coming, for the sound of voices, but the basement held its secrets; the green baize door shut off that world. He drank the milk and ate the biscuit, but he didn't touch the rest, and presently he could hear the soft precise footfalls of Mrs. Baines on the stairs: she was a good servant, she walked softly; she was a determined woman, she walked precisely.

But she wasn't angry when she came in; she was ingratiating as she opened the night nursery door—"Did you have a good walk, Master Philip?"—pulled down the blinds, laid out his pyjamas, came back to clear his supper. "I'm glad

Baines found you. Your mother wouldn't have liked your being out alone." She examined the tray. "Not much appetite, have you, Master Philip? Why don't you try a little of this nice pudding? I'll bring you up some more jam for it."

"No, no, thank you, Mrs. Baines," Philip said.

"You ought to eat more," Mrs. Baines said. She sniffed round the room like a dog. "You didn't take any pots out of the wastepaper basket in the kitchen, did you, Master Philip?"

"No," Philip said.

"Of course you wouldn't. I just wanted to make sure." She patted his shoulder and her fingers flashed to his lapel; she picked off a tiny crumb of pink sugar. "Oh, Master Philip," she said, "that's why you haven't any appetite. You've been buying sweet cakes. That's not what your pocket money's for."

"But I didn't," Philip said. "I didn't."

She tasted the sugar with the tip of her tongue.

"Don't tell lies to me, Master Philip. I won't stand for it any more than your father would."

"I didn't, I didn't " Philip said. "They gave it me. I mean Baines," but she had pounced on the word "they." She had got what she wanted; there was no doubt about that, even when you didn't know what it was she wanted. Philip was angry and miserable and disappointed because he hadn't kept Baines's secret. Baines oughtn't to have trusted him; grown-up people should keep their own secrets, and yet here was Mrs. Baines immediately entrusting him with another.

"Let me tickle your palm and see if you can keep a secret." But he put his hand behind him; he wouldn't be touched. "It's a secret between us, Master Philip, that I know all about them. I suppose she was having tea with him," she speculated.

"Why shouldn't she?" he said, the responsibility for Baines weighing on his spirit, the idea that he had got to keep her secret when he hadn't kept Baines's making him miserable with the unfairness of life. "She was nice."

"She was nice, was she?" Mrs. Baines said in a bitter voice he wasn't used to.

"And she's his niece."

"So that's what he said," Mrs. Baines struck softly back at him like the clock under the duster. She tried to be jocular. "The old scoundrel. Don't you tell him I know, Master Philip." She stood very still between the table and door, thinking very hard, planning something. "Promise you won't tell. I'll give you that Meccano set, Master Philip. . . ."

He turned his back on her; he wouldn't promise, but he wouldn't tell. He would have nothing to do with their secrets, the responsibilities they were determined to lay on him. He was only anxious to forget. He had recieved already a larger dose of life than he had bargained for, and he was scared. "A 2 A Meccano set, Master Philip." He never opened his Meccano set again, never built anything, never created anything, died, the old dilettante, sixty years later, with nothing to show rather than preserve the memory of Mrs. Baines's malicious voice saying good night, her soft determined footfalls on the stairs to the basement, going down, going down.

3

The sun poured in between the curtains and Baines was beating a tattoo on the water-can. "Glory, glory," Baines said. He sat down on the end of the bed and said, "I beg to announce that Mrs. Baines has been called away. Her mother's dying. She won't be back till tomorrow."

"Why did you wake me up so early?" Philip said. He watched Baines with uneasiness; he wasn't going to be drawn in; he'd learnt his lesson. It wasn't right for a man of Baines's age to be so merry. It made a grown person human in the same way that you were human. For if a grown-up could behave so childishly, you were liable too to find yourself in their world. It was enough that it came at you in dreams: the witch at the corner, the man with a knife. So "It's very early," he complained, even though he loved Baines, even though he couldn't help being glad that Baines was happy. He was divided by the fear and the attraction of life.

"I want to make this a long day," Baines said. "This is the best time." He pulled the curtains back. "It's a bit misty. The cat's been out all night. There she is, sniffing around the area. They haven't taken in any milk at 59. Emma's shaking out the mats at 63." He said, "This was what I used to think about on the Coast: somebody shaking mats and the cat coming home. I can see it today," Baines said, "just as if I was still in Africa. Most days you don't notice what you've got. It's a good life if you don't weaken." He put a penny on the washstand. "When you've dressed, Phil, run and get a *Mail* from the barrow at the corner. I'll be cooking the sausages."

"Sausages?"

"Sausages," Baines said. "We're going to celebrate today. A fair bust." He celebrated at breakfast, reckless, cracking jokes, unaccountably merry and nervous. It was going to be a long, long day, he kept on coming back to that: for years he had waited for a long day, he had sweated in the damp Coast heat, changed shirts, gone down with fever, lain between the blankets and sweated, all in the hope of this long day, that cat sniffing round the area, a bit of mist, the mats beaten at 63. He propped the *Mail* in front of the coffee-pot and read pieces aloud. He said, "Cora Down's been married for the fourth time." He was amused, but it wasn't his idea of a long day. His long day was the Park, watching the riders in the Row, seeing Sir Arthur Stillwater pass beyond the rails ("He dined with us once in Bo; up from Freetown; he was governor there"), lunch at the Corner House for Philip's sake (he's have preferred himself a glass of stout and some oysters at the York bar), the Zoo, the long bus ride home in the last summer light: the leaves in the Green Park were beginning to turn and the motors nuzzled out of Berkeley Street with the low sun gently glowing on their wind-screens. Baines envied no one, not Cora Down, or Sir Arthur Stillwater, or Lord Sandale, who came out on to the steps of the Army and Navy and then went back again because he hadn't got anything to do and might as well look at another paper. "I said don't let me see you touch that black again." Baines had led a man's life; everyone on top of the bus pricked their ears when he told Philip all about it.

"Would you have shot him?" Philip asked, and Baines put his head back and tilted his dark respectable manservant's hat to a better angle as the bus swerved round the artillery memorial.

"I wouldn't have thought twice about it. I'd have shot to kill," he boasted, and the bowed figure went by, the steel helmet, the heavy cloak, the down-turned rifle and the folded hands.

"Have you got the revolver?"

"Of course I've got it," Baines said. "Don't I need it with all the burglaries there've been?" This was the Baines whom Philip loved: not Baines singing and carefree, but Baines responsible, Baines behind barriers, living his man's life.

All the buses streamed out from Victoria like a convoy of aeroplanes to bring Baines home with honour. "Forty blacks under me," and there waiting near the area steps was the proper conventional reward, love at lighting-up time.

"It's your niece," Philip said, recognizing the white mackintosh, but not the happy sleepy face. She frightened him like an unlucky number; he nearly told Baines what Mrs. Baines had said; but he didn't want to bother, he wanted to leave things alone.

"Why, so it is," Baines said. "I shouldn't wonder if she was going to have a bite of supper with us." But he said they'd play a game, pretend they didn't know her, slip down the area steps, "and here," Baines said, "we are," lay the table, put out the cold sausages, a bottle of beer, a bottle of ginger pop, a flagon of harvest burgundy. "Everyone his own drink," Baines said. "Run upstairs, Phil, and see if there's been a post."

Philip didn't like the empty house at dusk before the lights went on. He hurried. He wanted to be back with Baines. The hall lay there in quiet and shadow prepared to show him something he didn't want to see. Some letters rustled down, and someone knocked. "Open in the name of the Republic." The tumbrils rolled, the head bobbed in the bloody basket. Knock, knock, and the postman's footsteps going away. Philip gathered the letters. The slit in the door was like the grating in a jeweller's window. He remembered the policeman he had seen peer through. He had said to his nurse, "What's he doing?" and when she said, "He's seeing if everything's all right," his brain immediately filled with images of all that might be wrong. He ran to the baize door and the stairs. The girl was already there and Baines was kissing her. She leant breathless against the dresser.

"This is Emmy, Phil."

"There's a letter for you, Baines."

"Emmy," Baines said, "it's from her." But he wouldn't open it. "You bet she's coming back."

"We'll have supper, anyway," Emmy said. "She can't harm that."

"You don't know her," Baines said. "Nothing's safe. Damn it," he said, "I was a man once," and he opened the letter.

"Can I start?" Philip asked, but Baines didn't hear; he presented in his stillness and attention an example of the importance grown-up people attached to the written word: you had to write your thanks, not wait and speak them, as if letters couldn't lie. But Philip knew better than that, sprawling his thanks across a page to Aunt Alice who had given him a doll he was too old for. Letters could lie all right, but they made the lie permanent: they lay as evidence against you; they made you meaner than the spoken word.

"She's not coming back till tomorrow night," Baines said. He opened the bottles, he pulled up the chairs, he kissed Emmy again against the dresser.

"You oughtn't to," Emmy said, "with the boy here."

"He's got to learn," Baines said, "like the rest of us," and he helped Philip to three sausages. He only took one himself; he said he wasn't hungry; but when Emmy said she wasn't hungry either he stood over her and made her eat. He was timid and rough with her; he made her drink the harvest burgundy because he said she needed building up; he wouldn't take no for an answer, but when he touched her his hands were light and clumsy too, as if he were afraid to damage something delicate and didn't know how to handle anything so light.

"This is better than milk and biscuits, eh?"

"Yes," Philip said, but he was scared, scared for Baines as much as for himself. He couldn't help wondering at every bite, at every draught of the ginger pop, what Mrs. Baines would say if she ever learnt of this meal; he couldn't imagine it, there was a depth of bitterness and rage in Mrs. Baines you couldn't sound. He said, "She won't be coming back tonight?" but you could tell by the way they immediately understood him that she wasn't really away at all; she was there in the basement with them, driving them to longer drinks and louder talk, biding her time for the right cutting word. Baines wasn't really happy; he was only watching happiness from close to instead of from far away.

"No," he said, "she'll not be back till late tomorrow." He couldn't keep his eyes off happiness; he'd played around as much as other men, he kept on reverting to the Coast as if to excuse himself for his innocence; he wouldn't have been so innocent if he'd lived his life in London, so innocent when it came to tenderness. "If it was you, Emmy," he said, looking at the white dresser, the scrubbed chairs, "this'd be like a home." Already the room was not quite so harsh; there was a little dust in corners, the silver needed a final polish, the morning's paper lay untidily on a chair. "You'd better go to bed, Phil; it's been a long day."

They didn't leave him to find his own way up through the dark shrouded house; they went with him, turning on lights, touching each other's fingers on the switches; floor after floor they drove the night back; they spoke softly among the covered chairs; they watched him undress, they didn't make him or clean his teeth, they saw him into bed and lit his night-light and left his door ajar. He could hear their voices on the stairs, friendly, like the guests he heard at dinner-parties when they moved down to the hall, saying good night. They belonged; wherever they were they made a home. He heard a door open and a clock strike, he heard their voices for a long while, so that he felt they were not far away and he was safe. The voices didn't dwindle, they simply went out, and he could be sure that they were still somewhere not far from him, silent together in one of the many empty rooms, growing sleepy together as he grew sleepy after the long day.

He just had time to sigh faintly with satisfaction, because this too perhaps had been life, before he slept and the inevitable terrors of sleep came round him: a man with a tricolour hat beat at the door on His Majesty's service, a bleeding head lay on the kitchen table in a basket, and the Siberian wolves crept closer. He was bound hand and foot and couldn't move; they leapt round him breathing heavily; he opened his eyes and Mrs. Baines was there, her grey untidy hair in threads over his face, her black hat askew. A loose hairpin fell on the pillow and one musty thread brushed his mouth. "Where are they?" she whispered. "Where are they?"

4

Philip watched her in terror. Mrs. Baines was out of breath as if she had been searching all the empty rooms, looking under loose covers.

With her untidy grey hair and her black dress buttoned to her throat, her gloves of black cotton, she was so like the witches of his dreams that he didn't dare to speak. There was a stale smell in her breath.

"She's here," Mrs. Baines said; "you can't deny she's here." Her face was simultaneously marked with cruelty and misery; she wanted to "do things" to people, but she suffered all the time. It would have done her good to scream, but she daren't do that: it would warm them. She came ingratiatingly back to the bed where Philip lay rigid on his back and whispered, "I haven't forgotten the Meccano set. You shall have it tomorrow, Master Philip. We've got secrets together, haven't we? Just tell me where they are."

He couldn't speak. Fear held him as firmly as any nightmare. She said, "Tell Mrs. Baines, Master Philip. You love your Mrs. Baines, don't you?" That was too much; he couldn't speak, but he could move his mouth in terrified denial, wince away from her dusty image.

She whispered, coming closer to him, "Such deceit. I'll tell your father. I'll settle with you myself when I've found them. You'll smart; I'll see you smart." Then immediately she was still, listening. A board had creaked on the floor below, and a moment later, while she stooped listening above his bed, there came the whispers of two people who were happy and sleepy together after a long day. The night-light stood beside the mirror and Mrs. Baines could see bitterly there her own reflection, misery and cruelty wavering in the glass, age and dust and nothing to hope for. She sobbed without tears, a dry, breathless sound; but her cruelty was a kind of pride which kept her going; it was her best quality, she would have been merely pitiable without it. She went out of the door on tiptoe, feeling her way across the landing, going so softly down the stairs that no one behind a shut door could hear her. Then there was complete silence again; Philip could move; he raised his knees; he sat up in bed; he wanted to die. It wasn't fair, the walls were down again between his world and theirs; but this time it was something worse than merriment that the grown people made him share; a passion moved in the house he recognized but could not understand.

It wasn't fair, but he owed Baines everything: the Zoo, the ginger pop, the bus ride home. Even the supper called on his loyalty. But he was frightened; he was touching something he touched in dreams: the bleeding head, the wolves, the knock, knock, knock. Life fell on him with savagery: you couldn't blame him if he never faced it again in sixty years. He got out of bed, carefully from habit put on his bedroom slippers, and tiptoed to the door: it wasn't quite dark on the landing below because the curtains had been taken down for the cleaners and the light from the street came in through the tall windows. Mrs. Baines had her hand on the glass door-knob; she was very carefully turning it; he screamed, "Baines, Baines."

Mrs. Baines turned and saw him cowering in his pyjamas by the banisters; he was helpless, more helpless even than Baines, and cruelty grew at the sight of him and drove her up the stairs. The nightmare was on him again and he couldn't move: he hadn't any more courage left for ever; he'd spent it all, had been allowed no time to let it grow, no years of gradual hardening; he couldn't even scream.

But the first cry had brought Baines out of the best spare bedroom and he moved quicker than Mrs. Baines. She hadn't reached the top of the stairs before he'd caught her round the waist. She drove her black cotton gloves at his face and he bit her hand. He hadn't time to think, he fought her savagely like a stranger, but she fought back with knowledgeable hate. She was going to teach them all and it didn't really matter whom she began with; they had all deceived her; but the old image in the glass was by her side, telling her she must be dignified, she wasn't young enough to yield her dignity; she could beat his face, but she mustn't bite; she could push, but she mustn't kick.

Age and dust and nothing to hope for were her handicaps. She went over the banisters in a flurry of black clothes and fell into the hall; she lay before the front door like a sack of coals which should have gone down the area into the basement. Philip saw; Emmy saw; she sat down suddenly in the doorway of the best spare bedroom with her eyes open as if she were too tired to stand any longer. Baines went slowly down into the hall.

It wasn't hard for Philip to escape; they'd forgotten him completely; he went down the back, the servants' stairs because Mrs. Baines was in the hall; he didn't understand what she was doing lying there; like the startling pictures in a book no one had read to him, the things he didn't understand terrified him. The whole house had been turned over to the grown-up world; he wasn't safe in the night nursery; their passions had flooded it. The only thing he could do was to

ANTON CHEKHOV

A DAY in the COUNTRY

Translated by Constance Garnett

Between eight and nine o'clock in the morning.

A dark leaden-coloured mass is creeping over the sky towards the sun. Red zigzags of lightning gleam here and there across it. There is a sound of far-away rumbling. A warm wind frolics over the grass, bends the trees, and stirs up the dust. In a minute there will be a spurt of May rain and a real storm will begin.

Fyokla, a little beggar-girl of six, is running through the village, looking for Terenty the cobbler. The white-haired, barefoot child is pale. Her eyes are wide-open, her lips are trembling.

"Uncle, where is Terenty?" she asks every one she meets. No one answers. They are all preoccupied with the approaching storm and take refuge in their huts. At last she meets Silanty Silitch, the sacristan, Terenty's bosom friend. He is coming along, staggering from the wind.

"Uncle, where is Terenty?"

"At the kitchen-gardens," answers Silanty.

The beggar-girl runs behind the huts to the kitchen-gardens and there finds Terenty; the tall old man with a thin, pock-marked face, very long legs, and bare feet, dressed in a woman's tattered jacket, is standing near the vegetable plots, looking with drowsy, drunken eyes at the dark storm-cloud. On his long crane-like legs he sways in the wind like a starling-cote.

"Uncle Terenty!" the white-headed beggar-girl addresses him. "Uncle, darling!"

Terenty bends down to Fyokla, and his grim, drunken face is overspread with a smile, such as come into people's faces when they look at something little, foolish, and absurd, but warmly loved.

"Ah! servant of God, Fyokla," he says, lisping tenderly, "where have you come from?"

"Uncle Terenty," says Fyokla, with a sob, tugging at the lapel of the cobbler's coat. "Brother Danilka has had an accident! Come along!"

"What sort of accident? Ough, what thunder! Holy, holy, holy. . . . What sort of accident?"

"In the count's copse Danilka stuck his hand into a hole in a tree, and he can't get it out. Come along, uncle, do be kind and pull his hand out!"

"How was it he put his hand in? What for?"

"He wanted to get a cuckoo's egg out of the hole for me."

"The day has hardly begun and already you are in trouble. . . ." Terenty shook his head and spat deliberately. "Well, what am I to do with you now? I must come . . . I must, may the wolf gobble you up, you naughty children! Come, little orphan!"

Terenty comes out of the kitchen-garden and, lifting high his long legs, begins striding down the village street. He walks quickly without stopping or looking from side to side, as though he were shoved from behind or afraid of pursuit. Fyokla can hardly keep up with him.

They come out of the village and turn along the dusty road towards the count's copse that lies dark blue in the distance. It is about a mile and half away. The clouds have by now covered the sun, and soon afterwards there is not a speck of blue left in the sky. It grows dark.

"Holy, holy, holy . . ." whispers Fyokla, hurrying after Terenty. The first rain-drops, big and heavy, lie, dark dots on the dusty road. A big drop falls on Fyokla's cheek and glides like a tear down her chin.

"The rain has begun," mutters the cobbler, kicking up the dust with his bare, bony feet. "That's fine, Fyokla, old girl. The grass and the trees are fed by the rain, as we are by bread. And as for the thunder, don't you be frightened, little orphan. Why should it kill a little thing like you?"

As soon as the rain begins, the wind drops. The only sound is the patter of rain dropping like fine shot on the young rye and the parched road.

"We shall get soaked, Fyokla," mutters Terenty. "There won't be a dry spot left on us. . . . Ho-ho, my girl! It's run down my neck! But don't be frightened, silly. . . . The grass will be dry again, the earth will be dry again, and we shall be dry again. There is the same sun for us all."

A flash of lightning, some fourteen feet long, gleams above their heads. There is a loud peal of thunder, and it seems to Fyokla that something big, heavy, and round is rolling over the sky and tearing it open, exactly over her head.

"Holy, holy, holy . . ." says Terenty, crossing himself. "Don't be afraid, little orphan! It is not from spite that it thunders."

Terenty's and Fyokla's feet are covered with lumps of heavy, wet clay. It is slippery and difficult to walk, but Terenty strides on more and more rapidly. The weak little beggar-girl is breathless and ready to drop.

But at last they go into the count's copse. The washed trees, stirred by a gust of wind, drop a perfect waterfall upon them. Terenty stumbles over stumps and begins to slacken his pace.

"Whereabouts is Danilka?" he asks. "Lead me to him."

Fyokla leads him into a thicket, and, after going a quarter of a mile, points to Danilka. Her brother, a little fellow of eight, with hair as red as ochre and a pale sickly face, stands leaning against a tree, and, with his head on one side, looking sideways at the sky. In one hand he holds his shabby old cap, the other is hidden in an old lime tree. The boy is gazing at the stormy sky, and apparently not thinking of his trouble. Hearing footsteps and seeing the cobbler he gives a sickly smile and says:

"A terrible lot of thunder, Terenty. . . . I've never heard so much thunder in all my life."

"And where is your hand?"

"In the hole. . . . Pull it out, please, Terenty!"

The wood had broken at the edge of the hole and jammed Danilka's hand: he could push it farther in, but could not pull it out. Terenty snaps off the broken piece, and the boy's hand, red and crushed, is released.

"It's terrible how it's thundering," the boy says again, rubbing his hand. "What make it thunder, Terenty?"

"One cloud runs against the other," answers the cobbler. The party come out of the copse, and walk along the edge of it towards the darkened road. The thunder gradually abates, and its rumbling is heard far away beyond the village.

"The ducks flew by here the other day, Terenty," says Danilka, still rubbing his hand. "They must be nesting in the Gniliya Zaimishtcha marshes. . . . Fyokla, would you like me to show you a nightingale's nest?"

"Don't touch it, you might disturb them," says Terenty, wringing the water out of his cap. "The nightingale is a singing-bird, without sin. He has had a voice given him in his throat, to praise God and gladden the heart of man. It's a sin to disturb him."

"What about the sparrow?"

"The sparrow doesn't matter, he's a bad, spiteful bird. He is like a pickpocket in his ways. He doesn't like man to be happy. When Christ was crucified it was the sparrow brought nails to the Jews, and called 'alive! alive!' "

A bright patch of blue appears in the sky.

"Look!" says Terenty. "An ant-heap burst open by the rain! They've been flooded, the rogues!"

They bent over the ant-heap. The downpour has damaged it; the insects are scurrying to and fro in the mud, agitated, and busily trying to carry away their drowned companions.

"You needn't be in such a taking, you won't die of it!" says Terenty, grinning. "As soon as the sun warms you, you'll come to your senses again. . . .

It's a lesson to you, you stupids. You won't settle on low ground another time."

They go on.

"And here are some bees," cries Danilka, pointing to the branch of a young oak tree.

The drenched and chilled bees are huddled together on the branch. There are so many of them that neither bark nor leaf can be seen. Many of them are settled on one another.

"That's a swarm of bees," Terenty informs them. "They were flying looking for a home, and when the rain came down upon them they settled. If a swarm is flying, you need only sprinkle water on them to make them settle. Now if, say, you wanted to take the swarm, you would bend the branch with them into a sack and shake it, and they all fall in."

Little Fyokla suddenly frowns and rubs her neck vigorously. Her brother looks at her neck, and sees a big swelling on it.

"Hey-hey!" laughs the cobbler. "Do you know where you got that from, Fyokla, old girl? There are Spanish flies on some tree in the wood. The rain has trickled off them, and a drop has fallen on your neck—that's what has made the swelling."

The sun appears from behind the clouds and floods the wood, the fields, and the three friends with its warm light. The dark menacing cloud has gone far away and taken the storm with it. The air is warm and fragrant. There is a scent of bird-cherry, meadowsweet, and lilies-of-the-valley.

"That herb is given when your nose bleeds," says Terenty, pointing to a woolly-looking flower. "It does good."

They hear a whistle and a rumble, but not such a rumble as the storm-clouds carried away. A goods train races by before the eyes of Terenty, Danilka, and Fyokla. The engine, panting and puffing out black smoke, drags more than twenty vans after it. Its power is tremendous. The children are interested to know how an engine, not alive and without the help of horses, can move and drag such weights, and Terenty undertakes to explain it to them:

"It's all the steam's doing, children. . . . The steam does the work. . . . You see, it shoves under that thing near the wheels, and it . . . you see . . . it works. . . ."

They cross the railway line, and, going down from the embankment, walk towards the river. They walk not with any object, but just at random, and talk all the way. . . . Danilka asks questions, Terenty answers them. . . .

Terenty answers all his questions, and there is no secret in Nature which baffles him. He knows everything. Thus, for example, he knows the names of all the wild flowers, animals, and stones. He knows what herbs cure diseases, he has no difficulty in telling the age of a horse or a cow. Looking at the sunset, at the moon, or the birds, he can tell what sort of weather it will be next day. And indeed, it is not only Terenty who is so wise. Silanty Silitch, the innkeeper, the market-gardener, the shepherd, and all the villagers, generally speaking, know as much as he does. These people have learned not from books, but in the fields, in the wood, on the river bank. Their teachers have been the birds themselves, when they sang to them, the sun when it left a glow of crimson behind it at setting, the very trees, and wild herbs.

Danilka looks at Terenty and greedily drinks in every word. In spring, before one is weary of the warmth and the monotonous green of the fields, when everything is fresh and full of fragrance, who would not want to hear about the golden may-beetles, about the cranes, about the gurgling streams, and the corn mounting into ear?

The two of them, the cobbler and the orphan, walk about the fields, talk unceasingly, and are not weary. They could wander about the world endlessly. They walk, and in their talk of the beauty of the earth do not notice the frail little beggar-girl tripping after them. She is breathless and moves with a lagging step. There are tears in her eyes; she would be glad to stop these inexhaustible wanderers, but to whom and where can she go? She has no home or people of her own; whether she likes it or not, she must walk and listen to their talk.

Towards midday, all three sit down on the river bank. Danilka takes out of his bag a piece of bread, soaked and reduced to a mash, and they begin to eat. Terenty says a prayer when he has eaten the bread, then stretches himself on the sandy bank and falls asleep. While he is asleep, the boy gazes at the water, pondering. He has many different things to think of. He has just seen the storm the bees, the ants, the train. Now, before his eyes, fishes are whisking about. Some are two inches long and more, others are no bigger than one's nail. A viper, with its head held high, is swimming from one bank to the other.

Only towards the evening our wanderers return to the village. The children go for the night to a deserted barn, where the corn of the commune used to be kept, while Terenty, leaving them, goes to the tavern. The children lie huddled together on the straw, dozing.

The boy does not sleep. He gazes into the darkness, and it seems to him that he is seeing all that he has seen in the day: the storm-clouds, the bright sunshine, the birds, the fish, lanky Terenty. The number of his impressions, together with exhaustion and hunger, are too much for him; he is as hot as though he were on fire, and tosses from side to side. He longs to tell someone all that is haunting him now in the darkness and agitating his soul, but there is no one to tell. Fyokla is too little and could not understand.

"I'll tell Terenty to-morrow," thinks the boy.

The children fall asleep thinking of the homeless cobbler, and, in the night, Terenty comes to them, makes the sign of the Cross over them, and puts bread under their heads. And no one sees his love. It is seen only by the moon which floats in the sky and peeps caressingly through the holes in the wall of the deserted barn.

2

YOUTH
Intimacy versus Isolation

In this section the question of intimacy versus isolation is explored in terms of first love. As might be expected, most of the loves turn out to be temporary in nature, and what becomes crucial to measure are their consequences. Is the rejected or "exploited" lover necessarily worse off than the person he continues to love? Is the endurance of a first love a good indication of the intimacy of the lovers? At what point does an unfulfilled first love become a barrier to future intimacy? All of these questions center on the kind of sexual involvement or sexual attraction the lovers in these stories develop. Yet, it is equally clear that sex is not by itself enough to hold any of the lovers together and that their intimacy depends on the relationship between their private lives and the lives they lead within their families or society.

The problem of getting a perspective on the intimacy or the isolation of any two lovers is reflected in Julio Cortázar's "Blow-Up," the story on which Antonioni's film of the same title was based. Cortázar, an Argentinean, who was born in Brussels and has lived and worked in Paris since 1952, begins his story with his narrator observing:

> *It'll never be known how this has to be told, in the first person or in the second, using the third person plural or continually inventing modes that will serve for nothing. If one might say: I will see the moon rose, or: we hurt me at the back of my eyes, and especially: you the blond woman was the clouds that race before my your his our yours their faces. What the hell.*

Cortázar's story centers on a photograph his narrator, Roberto Michel, a French-Chilean translator and amateur photographer, takes of an older woman and a boy as they seem about to begin an affair that Michel finds ugly.

> *I raised the camera, pretended to study a focus which did not include them, and waited and watched closely, sure that I would finally catch the revealing expression, one that would sum it all up. . . . The woman was getting on with*

> *the job of handcuffing the boy smoothly, stripping from him what was left of his freedom a hair at a time, in an incredibly slow and delicious torture. . . . that woman was not looking for the boy as a lover, and at the same time she was dominating him toward some end impossible to understand if you do not imagine it as a cruel game, the desire to desire without satisfaction, to excite herself for someone else, someone who in no way could be that kid.*

As soon as Michel takes a picture of the two, the scene is broken. The woman demands that Michel give over his film, the boy runs away once the commotion starts, and a man who has been sitting in a car, pretending to read a newspaper, joins the woman. Michel, for his part, feels that he has done a good deed in disrupting things and leaves without yielding the film. "Michel is something of a puritan at times. . . . In the last analysis, taking that photo has been a good act."

It is not until he begins to develop his film that Michel realizes events were much more complicated than he thought: that the woman was really working for the man in the car:

> *And what I had imagined earlier was much less horrible than the reality, that woman, who was not there by herself, she was not caressing or propositioning or encouraging for her own pleasure. . . . The real boss was waiting there, smiling petulantly, already certain of the business; he was not the first to send a woman in the vanguard, to bring him the prisoners manacled with flowers.*

How much good then has Michel done? Does his power extend beyond his photograph? Have the man and the woman already determined the immediate future of the boy? The dilemma Cortázar sets up is not only the artistic dilemma of his narrator but that of anyone concerned with how the failure of a first intimacy can influence all future capacity for love.

The next two stories suggest that, when a first loves goes unfulfilled, the innocent or weaker partner may not be harmed nearly so much as one imagines. In Joyce's "Araby" and Turgenev's "First Love," the narrators are able to speak of their unhappy first loves without bitterness. What is in doubt is whether or not their feelings are due to a perspective they have acquired or the loves themselves.

In Joyce's "Araby" both these questions are crucial from the start. Like Stephen Dedalus in *Portrait of the Artist,* the narrator of "Araby" is an extraordinarily sensitive boy whose temperament often cuts him off from friends his age. The feeling he has for the older sister of a school friend is certainly love, but whether or not it is a love that involves anything that might be called intimacy is another matter. One knows only that the narrator of "Araby" is drawn to Mangan's sister and the language he uses to describe her suggests intimacy:

> *I thought little of the future. I did not know whether I would ever speak to her or not or, if I spoke to her, how I could tell her of my confused adoration. But my body was like a harp, and her words and gestures were like fingers running upon the wires.*

At no time are these feelings consummated, or, as far as we know, reciprocated.

The trip that Joyce's narrator makes to *Araby*, the bazaar Mangan's sister would like to attend if it were not for "a retreat that week in her convent," only confirms his youthful romanticism. The trip, which in its intensity takes on the aura of a holy quest, ends with the narrator feeling terribly isolated, his desire to purchase a gift for Mangan's sister mocked by men "counting money on a salver" and a young clerk "talking and laughing with two young gentlemen." The last lines of Joyce's story read like a confession: "Gazing up into the darkness I saw myself as a creature driven and derided by vanity; and my eyes burned with anguish and anger." What has to be asked at this point is at whom or at what is the "anguish and anger" directed. At the narrator? His general situation? The bazaar?

In Turgenev's "First Love" one has a similar situation in that Sergei Nikolaich, the narrator of his story, has in his youth been drawn to an older girl whom he idealizes but cannot win:

> *I looked at her, and how dear and close she grew to me! I felt that I had known her a very long time, that I had never known anything and had never lived until I met her. . . . She was wearing a dark, rather shabby dress and an apron; I think I would willingly have caressed every fold in that dress and that apron. The toes of her shoes peered out from under her dress: I would have bowed myself down to those shoes in adoration.*

The difference is that, unlike Mangan's sister, Sergei's love is not an innocent. She surrounds herself with suitors and plays with the affection of Sergei Nikolaich, the narrator of the story, has in his youth been drawn to an older girl long time unaware of the extent of Zinaida's deception. Indeed, he is her virtual slave. When she challenges him to prove his love by jumping off a fourteen-foot wall he is standing on, he does it without even thinking. The critical test for Sergei comes when he discovers that Zinaida is in love with his father and will even consent to being beaten by him:

> *Suddenly before my eyes, something unbelievable occurred: my father raised his whip, with which he had been beating the dust out of the edge of his coat, and I heard a sharp blow on that arm bared to the elbow. I could hardly refrain from crying out. But Zinaida shuddered, gazed silently at my father, and slowly raised her arm to her mouth, then kissed the weal that showed livid across it.*

Although Sergei is shocked by his discovery, in the end it is not anger toward Zinaida that dominates his feelings but an awareness that what has made him a slave to his love has done the same to her. When she dies prematurely, it is her "dear features" he remembers and himself he reproaches for not having visited her when he had a chance. Can this closeness of feeling between Sergei and Zinaida be called an intimacy? Is it significant that Sergei never marries and that at the time he tells his story he is referred to as a bachelor "about forty years old" with "black hair streaked with gray"? There are, as in "Araby," religious overtones to the love Turgenev's narrator describes, but in the end the problem is discovering where they lead.

No such ambiguities exist in Guy de Maupassant's "The Model." The marriage of Jean Summer, a young painter of distinction, and his wife is a disaster. The question is only who bears the greatest burden. Jean Summer? Or his wife, who, when she thought Jean was not going to marry her leaped out a window and permanently crippled herself as a result of her fall? A nameless character in de Maupassant's story remarks:

> *The girl staged a comedy, or rather a melodrama. In fact, she risked everything on a single throw. Was she sincere? Was she in love with Jean? One can never tell in these cases. Who can say how much the element of cruelty and how much that of sincerity ever enters into women's actions?*

But de Maupassant as narrator seems content to describe what Erikson has called partnership "which amounts to an isolation à deux." We are left with cnly an ironic sense of the intimacy between Jean and his wife. Her leap evokes none of the sentiments of Sergei's jump in "First Love."

In contrast to "The Model," the last story in this section, Fitzgerald's "The Ice Palace," is dominated by a narrative voice that is usually comic. The first time we see Sally Carrol Happer, she seems like nothing so much as a caricature of a 1920s Southern belle:

> *Sally Carrol sighed voluminously and raised herself with profound inertia from the floor, where she had been occupied in alternately destroying parts of a green apple and painting paper dolls for her younger sister. She approached a mirror, regarded her expression with a pleased and pleasant languor, dabbed two spots of rouge on her lips and a grain of powder on her nose, and covered her bobbed corn-colored hair with a rose-littered sunbonnet.*

Yet, Fitzgerald's story suggests as strongly as de Maupassant's does, that feelings of moral obligation, let alone guilt, are a barrier to real intimacy. Sally Carrol may continually appear in a comic light, but there is good reason to take her seriously and see in her fondness for the South and her wish "to live where things happen on a big scale" some of the contradictions Fitzgerald found in his own wife, Zelda Sayre, whom he met when she was an eighteen-year-old girl, still living with her family in Montgomery, Alabama.

"The Ice Palace" turns on Sally Carrol's efforts to adapt herself to the ways of her fiancé from the North, Harry Bellamy, "tall, broad, and brusk." Sally Carrol cannot, however, finally will herself to like Harry's family or most of his friends. After she tells him, "Where you are is home for me," she "had the feeling for almost the first time in her life that she was acting a part." In the end Sally Carrol returns home, and we see her much as we did in the first scene, "resting her chin on her arm, and her arm on an old window-seat." Has Sally Carrol abandoned "the part of me that may be useful somewhere, that'll last when I'm not beautiful any more"? Certainly the answer we give to that question must grow out of the fact that Sally Carrol realizes any intimacy she achieves with a man must include, not exclude, the world she has come of age in.

JULIO CORTÁZAR

BLOW-UP

Translated bv Paul Blackburn

It'll never be known how this has to be told, in the first person or in the second, using the third person plural or continually inventing modes that will serve for nothing. If one might say: I will see the moon rose, or: we hurt me at the back of my eyes, and especially: you the blond woman was the clouds that race before my your his our yours their faces. What the hell.

Seated ready to tell it, if one might go to drink a bock over there, and the typewriter continue by itself (because I use the machine), that would be perfection. And that's not just a manner of speaking. Perfection, yes, because here is the aperture which must be counted also as a machine (of another sort, a Contax 1.1.2) and it is possible that one machine may know more about another machine than I, you, she—the blond—and the clouds. But I have the dumb luck to know that if I go this Remington will sit turned to stone on top of the table with the air of being twice as quiet that mobile things have when they are not moving. So, I have to write. One of us all has to write, if this is going to get told. Better that it be me who am dead, for I'm less compromised than the rest; I who see only the clouds and can think without being distracted, write without being distracted (there goes another, with a grey edge) and remember without being distracted, I who am dead (and I'm alive, I'm not trying to fool anybody, you'll see when we get to the moment, because I have to begin some way and I've begun with this period, the last one back, the one at the beginning, which in the end is the best of the periods when you want to tell something.)

All of a sudden I wonder why I have to tell this, but if one begins to wonder why he does all he does do, if one wonders why he accepts an invitation to lunch (now a pigeon's flying by and it seems to me a sparrow), or why when someone has told us a good joke immediately there starts up something like a tickling in the stomach and we are not at peace until we've gone into the office across the hall and told the joke over again; then it feels good immediately, one is fine, happy, and can get back to work. For I imagine that no one has explained this, that really the best thing is to put aside all decorum and tell it, because, after all's done, nobody is ashamed of breathing or of putting on his shoes; they're things that you do, and when something weird happens, when you find a spider in your shoe or if you take a breath and feel like a broken window, then you have to tell what's happening, tell it to the guys at the office or to the doctor. Oh, doctor, every time I take a breath . . . Always tell it, always get rid of that tickle in the stomach that bothers you.

And now that we're finally going to tell it, let's put things a little bit in order, we'd be walking down the staircase in this house as far as Sunday, November 7, just a month back. One goes down five floors and stands then in the Sunday in the sun one would not have suspected of Paris in November, with a large appetite to walk around, to see things, to take photos (because we were photographers, I'm a photographer). I know that the most difficult thing is going to be finding a way to tell it, and I'm not afraid of repeating myself. It's going to be difficult because nobody really knows who it is telling it, if I am I or what actually occurred or what I'm seeing (clouds, and once in a while a pigeon) or if, simply, I'm telling a truth which is only my truth, and then is the truth only for my stomach, for this impulse to go running out and to finish up in some manner with, this, whatever it is.

We're going to tell it slowly, what happens in the middle of what I'm writing is coming already. If they replace me, if, so soon, I don't know what to say, if the clouds stop coming and something else starts (because it's impossible that this keep coming, clouds passing continually and occasionally a pigeon), if something out of all this . . . And after the "if" what am I going to put if I'm going to close the sentence structure correctly? But if I begin to ask questions, I'll never tell anything, maybe to tell would be like an answer, at least for someone who's reading it.

Roberto Michel, French-Chilean, translator and in his spare time an amateur photographer, left number 11, rue Monsieur-le-Prince Sunday November 7 of the current year (now there're two small ones passing, with silver linings). He had spent three weeks working on the French version of a treatise challenges and appeals by José Norberto Allende, professor at the University of Santiago. It's rare that there's wind in Paris, and even less seldom a wind like this that swirled around corners and rose up to whip at old wooden venetian blinds behind which astonished ladies commented variously on how unreliable the weather had been these last few years. But the sun was out also, riding the wind and friend of the cats, so there was nothing that would keep me from taking a walk along the docks of the Seine and taking photos of the Conservatoire and Sainte-Chapelle. It was hardly ten o'clock, and I figured that by eleven the light would be good, the best you can get in the fall; to kill some time I detoured around by the Isle Saint-Louis and started to walk along the quai d'Anjou, I stared for a bit at the hôtel de Lauzun, I recited bits from Apollinaire which always get into my head whenever I pass in front of the hôtel de Lauzun (and at that I ought to be remembering the other poet, but Michel is an obstinate beggar), and when the wind stopped all at once and the sun came out at least twice as hard (I mean warmer, but really it's the same thing), I sat down on the parapet and felt terribly happy in the Sunday morning.

One of the many ways of contesting level-zero, and one of the best, is to take photographs, an activity in which one should start becoming an adept very early in life, teach it to children since it requires discipline, aesthetic education, a good eye and steady fingers. I'm not talking about waylaying the lie like any old reporter, snapping the stupid silhouette of the VIP leaving number 10 Downing Street, but in all ways when one is walking about with a camera, one has almost a duty to be attentive, to not lose that abrupt and happy rebound of sun's rays off an old stone, or the pigtails-flying run of a small girl going home with a loaf of bread or a bottle of milk. Michel knew that the photographer always worked as a permutation of his personal way of seeing the world as other than the camera insidiously imposed upon it (now a large cloud is going by, almost black), but he lacked no confidence in himself, knowing that he had only to go out without the Contax to recover the keynote of distraction, the sight without a frame around it, light without the diaphragm aperture or 1/250 sec. Right now (what a word, *now*, what a dumb lie) I was able to sit quietly on the railing overlooking the river watching the red and black motorboats passing below without it occurring to me to think photographically of the scenes, nothing more than letting myself go in the letting go of objects, running immobile in the stream of time. And then the wind was not blowing.

After, I wandered down the quai de Bourbon until getting to the end of the isle where the intimate square was (intimate because it was small, not that it was hidden, it offered its whole breast to the river and the sky), I enjoyed it, a lot. Nothing there but a couple and, of course, pigeons; maybe even some of those which are flying past now so that I'm seeing them. A leap up and I settled on the wall, and let myself turn about and be caught and fixed by the sun, giving it my face and ears and hands (I kept my gloves in my pocket). I had no desire to shoot pictures, and lit a cigarette to be doing something; I think it was that moment when the match was about to touch the tobacco that I saw the young boy for the first time.

What I'd thought was a couple seemed much more now a boy with his mother, although at the same time I realized that it was not a kid and his mother, and that it was a couple in the sense that we always allegate to couples when we see them leaning up against the parapets or embracing on the benches in the squares. As I had nothing else to do, I had more than enough time to wonder why the boy was so nervous, like a young colt or a hare, sticking his hands into his pockets, taking them out immediately, one after the other, running his fingers through his hair, changing his stance, and especially why was he afraid, well, you could guess that from every gesture, a fear suffocated by his shyness, an impulse to step backwards which he telegraphed, his body standing as if it were on the edge of flight, holding itself back in a final, pitiful decorum.

All this was so clear, ten feet away—and we were alone against the parapet at the tip of the island—that at the beginning the boy's fright didn't let me see the blond very well. Now, thinking back on it, I see her much better at that first second when I read her face (she'd turned around suddenly, swinging like a metal weathercock, and the eyes, the eyes were there), when I vaguely understood what might have been occurring to the boy and figured it would be worth the trouble to stay and watch (the wind was blowing their words away and they were speaking in a low murmur). I think that I know how to look, if it's something I know, and also that every looking oozes with mendacity, because it's that which expels us furthest outside ourselves, without the least guarantee, whereas to smell, or (but Michel rambles on to himself easily enough, there's no need to let him harangue on this way). In any case, if the likely inaccuracy can be seen beforehand, it becomes possible again to look; perhaps it suffices to choose between looking and the reality looked at, to strip things of all their unnecessary clothing. And surely all that is difficult besides.

As for the boy I remember the image before his actual body (that will clear itself up later), while now I am sure that I remember the woman's body much better than the image. She was thin and willowy, two unfair words to describe what she was, and was wearing an almost-black fur coat, almost long, almost handsome. All the morning's wind (now it was hardly a breeze and it wasn't cold) had blown through her blond hair which pared away her white, bleak face—two unfair words—and put the world at her feet and horribly alone in front of her dark eyes, her eyes fell on things like two eagles, two leaps into nothingness, two puffs of green slime. I'm not describing anything, it's more a matter of trying to understand it. And I said two puffs of green slime.

Let's be fair, the boy was well enough dressed and was sporting yellow gloves which I would have sworn belonged to his older brother, a student of law or sociology; it was pleasant to see the fingers of the gloves sticking out of his jacket pocket. For a long time I didn't see his face, barely a profile, not stupid—a terrified bird, a Fra Filippo angel, rice pudding with milk—and the back of an adolescent who wants to take up judo and has had a scuffle or two in defense of an idea or his sister. Turning fourteen, perhaps fifteen, one would guess that he was dressed and fed by his parents but without a nickel in his pocket, having to debate with his buddies before making up his mind to buy a coffee, a cognac, a pack of cigarettes. He'd walk through the streets thinking of the girls in his class, about how good it would be to go to the movies and see the latest film, or to buy novels or neckties or bottles of liquor with green and white labels on them. At home (it would be a respectable home, lunch at noon and romantic landscapes on the walls, with a dark entryway and a mahogany umbrella stand inside the door) there'd be the slow rain of time, for studying, for being mama's hope, for looking like dad, for writing to his aunt in Avignon. So that there was a lot of walking the streets, the whole of the river for him (but without a nickel) and the mysterious city of fifteen-year-olds with its signs in doorways, its terrifying cats, a paper of fried potatoes for thirty francs, the pornographic magazine folded four ways, a solitude like the emptiness of his pockets, the eagerness for so much that was incomprehensible but illumined by a total love, by the availability analogous to the wind and the streets.

This biography was of the boy and of any boy whatsoever, but this particular one now, you could see he was insular, surrounded solely by the blond's presence as she continued talking with him. (I'm tired of insisting, but two long ragged ones just went by. That morning I don't think I looked at the sky once, because what was happening with the boy and the woman appeared so soon I could do nothing but look at them and wait, look at them and . . .) To cut it short, the boy was agitated and one could guess without too much trouble what had just occurred a few minutes before, at most half-an-hour. The boy had come onto the tip of the island, seen the woman and thought her marvelous. The woman was waiting for that because she was there waiting for that, or maybe the boy arrived before her and she saw him from one of the balconies or from a car and got out to meet him, starting the conversation with whatever, from the beginning she was sure that he was going to be afraid and want to run off, and that, naturally, he'd stay, stiff and sullen, pretending experience and the pleasure of the adventure. The rest was easy because it was happening ten feet away from me, and anyone could have gauged the stages of the game, the derisive, competitive fencing; its major attraction was not that it was happening but in foreseeing its denouement. The boy would try to end it by pretending a date, an obligation, whatever, and would go stumbling off disconcerted, wishing he were walking with some assurance, but naked under the mocking glance which would follow him until he was out of sight. Or rather, he would stay there, fascinated or simply incapable of taking the initiative, and the woman would begin to touch his face gently, muss his hair, still talking to him voicelessly, and soon would take him by the arm to lead him off, unless he, with an uneasiness beginning to tinge the edge of desire, even his stake in the adventure, would rouse himself to put his arm around her waist and to kiss her. Any of this could have happened, though it did not, and perversely Michel waited, sitting on the railing, making the settings almost without looking at the camera, ready to take a picturesque shot of a corner of the island with an uncommon couple talking and looking at one another.

Strange how the scene (almost nothing: two figures there mismatched in their youth) was taking on a disquieting aura. I thought it was I imposing it, and that my photo, if I shot it, would reconstitute things in their true stupidity. I would have liked to know what he was thinking, a man in a grey hat sitting at the wheel of a car parked on the dock which led up to the footbridge, and whether he was reading the paper or asleep. I had just discovered him because people inside a parked car have a tendency to disappear, they get lost in that wretched, private cage stripped of the beauty that motion and danger give it. And nevertheless, the car had been there the whole time, forming part (or deforming that part) of the isle. A car: like saying a lighted streetlamp, a park bench. Never like saying wind, sunlight, those elements always new to the skin and the eyes, and also the boy and the woman, unique, put there to change the island, to show it to me in another way. Finally, it may have been that the man with the newspaper also became aware of what was happening and would, like me, feel that malicious sensation of waiting for everything to happen. Now the woman had swung around smoothly, putting the young boy between herself and the wall, I saw them almost in profile, and he was taller, though not much taller, and yet she dominated him, it seemed like she was hovering over him (her laugh, all at once, a whip of feathers), crushing him just by being there, smiling, one hand taking a stroll through the air. Why wait any longer? Aperture at sixteen, a sighting which would not include the horrible black car, but yes, that tree, necessary to break up too much grey space . . .

I raised the camera, pretended to study a focus which did not include them, and waited and watched closely, sure that I would finally catch the revealing expression, one that would sum it all up, life that is rhythmed by movement but which a stiff image destroys, taking time in cross section, if we do not choose the essential imperceptible fraction of it. I did not have to wait long. The woman was getting on with the job of handcuffing the boy smoothly, stripping from him what was left of his freedom a hair at a time, in an incredibly slow and delicious torture. I imagined the possible endings (now a small fluffy cloud appears, almost alone in the sky), I saw their arrival at the house (a basement apartment probably, which she would have filled with large cushions and cats) and conjectured the boy's terror and his desperate decision to play it cool and to be led off pretending there was nothing new in it for him. Closing my eyes, if I did in fact close my eyes, I set the scene: the teasing kisses, the woman mildly repelling the hands which were trying to undress her, like in novels, on a bed that would have a lilac-colored comforter, on the other hand she taking off his clothes, plainly mother and son under a milky yellow light, and everything would end up as usual, perhaps, but maybe everything would go otherwise, and the initiation of the adolescent would not happen, she would not let it happen, after a long prologue wherein the awkwardnesses, the exasperating caresses, the running of hands over bodies would be resolved in who knows what, in a separate and solitary pleasure, in a petulant denial mixed with the art of tiring and disconcerting so much poor innocence. It might go like that, it might very well go like that; that woman was not looking for the boy as a lover, and at the same time she was dominating him toward some end impossible to understand if you do not imagine it as a cruel game, the desire to desire without satisfaction, to excite herself for someone else, someone who in no way could be that kid.

Michel is guilty of making literature, of indulging in fabricated unrealities. Nothing pleases him more than to imagine exceptions to the rule, individuals outside the species, not-always-repugnant monsters. But that woman invited speculation, perhaps giving clues enough for the fantasy to hit the bullseye. Before she left, and now that she would fill my imaginings for several days, for I'm given to ruminating, I decided not to lose a moment more. I got it all into the view-finder (with the tree, the railing, the eleven-o'clock sun) and took the shot. In time to realize that they both had noticed and stood there looking at me, the boy surprised and as though questioning, but she was irritated, her face and body flat-footedly hostile, feeling robbed, ignominiously recorded on a small chemical image.

I might be able to tell it in much greater detail but it's not worth the trouble. The woman said that no one had the right to take a picture without permission, and demanded that I hand her over the film. All this in a dry, clear voice with a good Parisian accent, which rose in color and tone with every phrase. For my part, it hardly mattered whether she got the roll of film or not, but anyone who knows me will tell you, if you want anything from me, ask nicely. With the result that I restricted myself to formulating the opinion that not only was photography in public places not prohibited, but it was looked upon with decided favor, both private and official. And while that was getting said, I noticed on the sly how the boy was falling back, sort of actively backing up though without moving, and all at once (it seemed almost incredible) he turned and broke into a run, the poor kid, thinking that he was walking off and in fact in full flight, running past the side of the car, disappearing like a gossamer filament of angel-spit in the morning air.

But filaments of angel-spittle are also called devil-spit, and Michel had to endure rather particular curses, to hear himself called meddler and imbecile, taking great pains meanwhile to smile and to abate with simple movements of his head such a hard sell. As I was beginning to get tired, I heard the car door slam. The man in the grey hat was there, looking at us. It was only at that point that I realized he was playing a part in the comedy.

He began to walk toward us, carrying in his hand the paper he had been pretending to read. What I remember best is the grimace that twisted his mouth askew, it covered his face with wrinkles, changed somewhat both in location and shape because his lips trembled and the grimace went from one side of his mouth to the other as though it were on wheels, independent and involuntary. But the rest stayed fixed, a flour-powered clown or bloodless man, dull dry skin, eyes deepset, the nostrils black and prominently visible, blacker than the eyebrows or hair or the black necktie. Walking cautiously as though the pavement hurt his feet; I saw patent-leather shoes with such thin soles that he must have felt every roughness in the pavement. I don't know why I got down off the railing, nor very well why I decided to not give them the photo, to refuse that demand in which I guessed at their fear and cowardice. The clown and the woman consulted one another in silence: we made a perfect and unbearable triangle, something I felt compelled to break with a crack of a whip. I laughed in their faces and began to walk off, a little more slowly, I imagine, than the boy. At the level of the first houses, beside the iron footbridge, I turned around to look at them. They were not moving, but the man had dropped his newspaper; it seemed to me that the woman, her back to the parapet, ran her hands over the stone with the classical and absurd gesture of someone pursued looking for a way out.

What happened after that happened here, almost just now, in a room on the fifth floor. Several days went by before Michel developed the photos he'd taken on Sunday; his shots of the Conservatoire and of Sainte-Chapelle were all they should be. Then he found two or three proof-shots he'd forgotten, a poor attempt to catch a cat perched astonishingly on the roof of a rambling public urinal, and also the shot of the blond and the kid. The negative was so good that he made an enlargement; the enlargement was so good that he made one very much larger, almost the size of a poster. It did not occur to him (now one wonders and wonders) that only the shots of the Conservatoire were worth so much work. Of the whole series, the snapshot of the tip of the island was the only one which interested him; he tacked up the enlargement on one wall of the room, and the first day he spent some time looking at it and remembering, that gloomy operation of comparing the memory with the gone reality; a frozen memory, like any photo, where nothing is missing, not even, and especially, nothingness, the true solidifier of the scene. There was the woman, there was the boy, the tree rigid above their heads, the sky as sharp as the stone of the parapet, clouds and stones melded into a single substance and inseparable (now one with sharp edges is going by, like a thunderhead). The first two days I accepted what I had done, from the photo itself to the enlargement on the wall, and didn't even question that every once in a while I would interrupt my translation of José Norberto Allende's treatise to encounter once more the woman's face, the dark splotches on the railing. I'm such a jerk; it had never occured to me that when we look at a photo from the front, the eyes reproduce exactly the position and the vision of the lens; it's these things that are taken for granted and it never occurs to anyone to think about them. From my chair, with the typewriter directly in front of me, I looked at the photo ten feet away, and then it occurred to me that I had hung it exactly at the point of view of the lens. It looked very good that way; no doubt, it was the best way to appreciate a photo, though the angle from the diagonal doubtless has its pleasures and might even divulge different aspects. Every few minutes, for example when I was unable to find the way to say in good French what José Norberto Allende was saying in very good Spanish, I raised my eyes and looked at the photo; sometimes the woman would catch my eye, sometimes the boy, sometimes the pavement where a dry leaf had fallen admirably situated to heighten a lateral section. Then I rested a bit from my labors, and I enclosed myself again happily in that morning in which the photo was drenched, I recalled ironically the angry picture of the woman demanding I give her the photograph, the boy's pathetic and ridiculous flight, the entrance on the scene of the man with the white face. Basically, I was satisfied with myself; my part had not been too brilliant, and since the French have been given the gift of the sharp response, I did not see very well why I'd chosen to leave without a complete demonstration of the rights, privileges and prerogatives of citizens. The important thing, the really important thing was having helped the kid to escape in time (this in case my theorizing was correct, which was not sufficiently proven, but the running away itself seemed to show it so). Out of plain meddling, I had given him the opportunity finally to take advantage of his fright to do something useful; now he would be regretting it, feeling his honor impaired, his manhood diminished. That was better than the attentions of a woman capable of looking as she had looked at him on that island. Michel is something of a puritan at times, he believes that one should not seduce someone from a position of strength. In the last analysis, taking that photo had been a good act.

Well, it wasn't because of the good act that I looked at it between paragraphs while I was working. At that moment I didn't know the reason, the reason I had tacked the enlargement onto the wall; maybe all fatal acts happen that way, and that is the condition of their fulfillment. I don't think that almost-furtive trembling of the leaves on the tree alarmed me, I was working on a sentence and rounded it out successfully. Habits are like immense herbariums, in the end an enlargement of 32 x 28 looks like a movie screen, where, on the tip of the island, a woman is speaking with a boy and a tree is shaking its dry leaves over their heads.

But her hands were just too much. I had just translated: "In that case, the second key resides in the intrinsic nature of difficulties which societies . . ."—when I saw the woman's hand beginning to stir slowly, finger by finger. There was nothing left of me, a phrase in French which I would never have to finish, a typewriter on the floor, a chair that squeaked and shook, fog. The kid had ducked his head like boxers do when they've done all they can and are waiting for the final blow to fall; he had turned up the collar of his overcoat and seemed more a prisoner than ever, the perfect victim helping promote the catastrophe. Now the woman was talking into his ear, and her hand opened again to lay itself against his cheekbone, to caress and caress it, burning it, taking her time. The kid was less startled than he was suspicious, once or twice he poked his head over the woman's shoulder and she continued talking, saying something that made him look back every few minutes toward that area where Michel knew the car was parked and the man in the grey hat, carefully eliminated from the photo but present in the boy's eyes (how doubt that now) in the words of the woman, in the woman's hands, in the vicarious presence of the woman. When I saw the man come up, stop near them and look at them, his hands in his pockets and a stance somewhere between disgusted and demanding, the master who is about to whistle in his dog after a frolic in the square, I understood, if that was to understand, what had to happen now, what had to have happened then, what would have to happen at that moment, among these people, just where I had poked my nose in to upset an established order, interfering innocently in that which had not happened, but which was now going to happen, now was going to be fulfilled. And what I had imagined earlier was much less horrible than the reality, that woman, who was not there by herself, she was not caressing or propositioning or encouraging for her own pleasure, to lead the angel away with his tousled hair and play the tease with his terror and his eager grace. The real boss was waiting there, smiling petulantly, already certain of the business; he was not the first to send a woman in the vanguard, to bring him the prisoners manacled with flowers. The rest of it would be so simple, the car, some house or another, drinks, stimulating engravings, tardy tears, the awakening in hell. And there was nothing I could do, this time I could do absolutely nothing. My strength had been a photograph, that, there, where they were taking their revenge on me, demonstrating clearly what was going to happen. The photo had been taken, the time had run out, gone; we were so far from one another, the abusive act had certainly already taken place, the tears already shed, and the rest conjecture and sorrow. All at once the order was inverted, they were alive, moving, they were deciding and had decided, they were going to their future; and I on this, prisoner of another time, in a room on the fifth floor, to not know who they were, that woman, that man, and that boy, to be only the lens of my camera, something fixed, rigid, incapable of intervention. It was horrible, their mocking me, deciding it before my impotent eye, mocking me, for the boy again was looking at the flour-faced clown and I had to accept the fact that he was going to say yes, that the proposition carried money with it or a gimmick, and I couldn't yell for him to run, or even open the road to him again with a new photo, a small and almost meek intervention which would ruin the framework of drool and perfume. Everything was going to resolve itself right there, at that moment; there was like an immense silence which had nothing to do with physical silence. It was stretching it out, setting itself up. I think I screamed, I screamed terribly, and that at that exact second I realized that I was beginning to move toward them, four inches, a step, another step, the tree swung its branches rhythmically in the foreground, a place where the railing was tarnished emerged from the frame, the woman's face turned toward me as though surprised, was enlarging, and then I turned a bit, I mean that the camera turned a little, and without losing sight of the woman, I began to close in on the man who was looking at me with the black holes he had in place of eyes, surprised and angered both, he looked, wanting to nail me onto the air, and at that instant I happened to see something like a large bird outside the focus that was flying in a single swoop in front of the picture, and I leaned up against the wall of my room and was happy because the boy had just managed to escape, I saw him running off, in focus again, sprinting with his hair flying in the wind, learning finally to fly across the island, to arrive at the footbridge, return to the city. For the second time he'd escaped them, for the second time I was helping him to escape, returning him to his precarious paradise. Out of breath, I stood in front of them; no need to step closer, the game was played out. Of the woman you could see just maybe a shoulder and a bit of hair, brutally cut off by the frame of the picture; but the man was directly center, his mouth half open, you could see a shaking black tongue, and he lifted his hands slowly, bringing them into the foreground, an instant still in perfect focus, and then all of him a lump that blotted out the island, the tree, and I shut my eyes, I didn't want to see any more, and I covered my face and broke into tears like an idiot.

Now there's a big white cloud, as on all these days, all this untellable time. What remains to be said is always a cloud, two clouds, or long hours of a sky perfectly clear, a very clean, clear rectangle tacked up with pins on the wall of my room. That was what I saw when I opened my eyes and dried them with my fingers: the clear sky, and then a cloud that drifted in from the left, passed gracefully and slowly across and disappeared on the right. And then another, and for a change sometimes, everything gets grey, all one enormous cloud, and suddenly the splotches of rain cracking down, for a long spell you can see it raining over the picture, like a spell of weeping reversed, and little by little, the frame becomes clear, perhaps the sun comes out, and again the clouds begin to come, two at a time, three at a time. And the pigeons once in a while, and a sparrow or two.

JAMES JOYCE

ARABY

North Richmond Street, being blind, was a quiet street except at the hour when the Christian Brothers' School set the boys free. An uninhabited house of two storeys stood at the blind end, detached from its neighbours in a square ground. The other houses of the street, conscious of decent lives within them, gazed at one another with brown imperturbable faces.

The former tenant of our house, a priest, had died in the back drawing-room. Air, musty from having been long enclosed, hung in all the rooms, and the waste room behind the kitchen was littered with old useless papers. Among these I found a few paper-covered books, the pages of which were curled and damp: *The Abbot*, by Walter Scott, *The Devout Communicant* and *The Memoirs of Vidocq*. I liked the last best because its leaves were yellow. The wild garden behind the house contained a central apple-tree and a few straggling bushes under one of which I found the late tenant's rusty bicycle-pump. He had been a very charitable priest; in his will he had left all his money to institutions and the furniture of his house to his sister.

When the short days of winter came dusk fell before we had well eaten our dinners. When we met in the street the houses had grown sombre. The space of sky above us was the colour of ever-changing violet and towards it the lamps of the street lifted their feeble lanterns. The cold air stung us and we played till our bodies glowed. Our shouts echoed in the silent street. The career of our play brought us through the dark muddy lanes behind the houses where we ran the gantlet of the rough tribes from the cottages, to the back doors of the dark dripping gardens where odours arose from the ashpits, to the dark odorous stables where a coachman smoothed and combed the horse or shook music from the buckled harness. When we returned to the street light from the kitchen windows had filled the areas. If my uncle was seen turning the corner we hid in the shadow until we had seen him safely housed. Or if Mangan's sister came out on the doorstep to call her brother in to his tea we watched her from our shadow peer up and down the street. We waited to see whether she would remain or go in and, if she remained, we left our shadow and walked up to Mangan's steps resignedly. She was waiting for us, her figure defined by the light from the half-opened door. Her brother always teased her before he obeyed and I stood by the railings looking at her. Her dress swung as she moved her body and the soft rope of her hair tossed from side to side.

Every morning I lay on the floor in the front parlour watching her door. The blind was pulled down to within an inch of the sash so that I could not be seen. When she came out on the doorstep my heart leaped. I ran to the hall, seized my books and followed her. I kept her brown figure always in my eye and, when we came near the point at which our ways diverged, I quickened my pace and passed her. This happened morning after morning. I had never spoken to her, except for a few casual words, and yet her name was like a summons to all my foolish blood.

Her image accompanied me even in places the most hostile to romance. On Saturday evenings when my aunt went marketing I had to go to carry some of the parcels. We walked through the flaring streets, jostled by drunken men and bargaining women, amid the curses of labourers, and shrill litanies of shop-boys who stood on guard by the barrels of pigs' cheeks, the nasal chanting of street-singers, who sang a *come-all-you* about O'Donovan Rossa, or a ballad about the troubles in our native land. These noises converged in a single sensation of life for me: I imagined that I bore my chalice safely through a throng of foes. Her name sprang to my lips at moments in strange prayers and praises which I myself did not understand. My eyes were often full of tears (I could not tell why) and at times a flood from my heart seemed to pour itself out into my bosom. I thought little of the future. I did not know whether I would ever speak to her or not or, if I spoke to her, how I could tell her of my confused adoration. But my body was like a harp and her words and gestures were like fingers running upon the wires.

One evening I went into the back drawing-room in which the priest had died. It was a dark rainy evening and there was no sound in the house. Through one of the broken panes I heard the rain impinge upon the earth, the fine incessant needles of water playing in the sodden beds. Some distant lamp or lighted window gleamed below me. I was thankful that I could see so little. All my senses seemed to desire to veil themselves and, feeling that I was about to slip from them, I pressed the palms of my hands together until they trembled, murmuring: *O love! O love!* many times.

At last she spoke to me. When she addressed the first words to me I was so confused that I did not know what to answer. She asked me was I going to *Araby*. I forget whether I answered yes or no. It would be a splendid bazaar, she said; she would love to go.

—And why can't you? I asked.

While she spoke she turned a silver bracelet round and round her wrist. She could not go, she said, because there would be a retreat that week in her convent. Her brother and two other boys were fighting for their caps and I was alone at the railings. She held one of the spikes, bowing her head towards me.

The light from the lamp opposite our door caught the white curve of her neck, lit up her hair that rested there and, falling, lit up the hand upon the railing. It fell over one side of her dress and caught the white border of a petticoat, just visible as she stood at ease.

—It's well for you, she said.

—If I go, I said, I will bring you something.

What innumerable follies laid waste my waking and sleeping thoughts after that evening! I wished to annihilate the tedious intervening days. I chafed against the work of school. At night in my bedroom and by day in the classroom her image came between me and the page I strove to read. The syllables of the word *Araby* were called to me through the silence in which my soul luxuriated and cast an Eastern enchantment over me. I asked for leave to go to the bazaar on Saturday night. My aunt was surprised and hoped it was not some Freemason affair. I answered few questions in class. I watched my master's face pass from amiability to sternness; he hoped I was not beginning to idle. I could not call my wandering thoughts together. I had hardly any patience with the serious work of life which, now that it stood between me and my desire, seemed to me child's play, ugly monotonous child's play.

On Saturday morning I reminded my uncle that I wished to go to the bazaar in the evening. He was fussing at the hallstand, looking for the hat-brush, and answered me curtly:

—Yes, boy, I know.

As he was in the hall I could not go into the front parlour and lie at the window. I left the house in bad humour and walked slowly towards the school. The air was pitilessly raw and already my heart misgave me.

When I came home to dinner my uncle had not yet been home. Still it was early. I sat staring at the clock for some time and, when its ticking began to irritate me, I left the room. I mounted the staircase and gained the upper part of the house. The high cold empty gloomy rooms liberated me and I went from room to room singing. From the front window I saw my companions playing below in the street. Their cries reached me weakened and indistinct and, leaning my forehead against the cool glass, I looked over at the dark house where she lived. I may have stood there for an hour, seeing nothing but the brown-clad figure cast by my imagination, touched discreetly by the lamplight at the curved neck, at the hand upon the railings and at the border below the dress.

When I came downstairs again I found Mrs. Mercer sitting at the fire. She was an old garrulous woman, a pawnbroker's widow, who collected used stamps for some pious purpose. I had to endure the gossip of the tea-table. The meal was prolonged beyond an hour and still my uncle did not come. Mrs. Mercer stood up to go: she was sorry she couldn't wait any longer, but it was after eight o'clock and she did not like to be out late, as the night air was bad for her. When she had gone I began to walk up and down the room, clenching my fists. My aunt said:

—I'm afraid you may put off your bazaar for this night of Our Lord.

At nine o'clock I heard my uncle's latchkey in the halldoor. I heard him talking to himself and heard the hallstand rocking when it had received the weight of his overcoat. I could interpret these signs. When he was midway through his dinner I asked him to give me the money to go to the bazaar. He had forgotten.

—The people are in bed and after their first sleep now, he said.

I did not smile. My aunt said to him energetically:

—Can't you give him the money and let him go? You've kept him late enough as it is.

My uncle said he was very sorry he had forgotten. He said he believed in the old saying: *All work and no play makes Jack a dull boy.* He asked me where I was going and, when I had told him a second time he asked me did I know *The Arab's Farewell to his Steed.* When I left the kitchen he was about to recite the opening lines of the piece to my aunt.

I held a florin tightly in my hand as I strode down Buckingham Street towards the station. The sight of the streets thronged with buyers and glaring with gas recalled to me the purpose of my journey. I took my seat in a third-class carriage of a deserted train. After an intolerable delay the train moved out of the station slowly. It crept onward among ruinous houses and over the twinkling river. At Westland Row Station a crowd of people pressed to the carriage doors; but the porters moved them back, saying that it was a special train for the bazaar. I remained alone in the bare carriage. In a few minutes the train drew up beside an improvised wooden platform. I passed out on to the road and saw by the lighted dial of a clock that it was ten minutes to ten. In front of me was a large building which displayed the magical name.

I could not find any sixpenny entrance and, fearing that the bazaar would be closed, I passed in quickly through a turnstile, handing a shilling to a weary-looking man. I found myself in a big hall girdled at half its height by a gallery. Nearly all the stalls were closed and the greater part of the hall was in darkness. I recognised a silence like that which pervades a church after a service. I walked into the centre of the bazaar timidly. A few people were gathered about the stalls which were still open. Before a curtain, over which the words *Café Chantant* were written in coloured lamps, two men were counting money on a salver. I listened to the fall of the coins.

Remembering with difficulty why I had come I went over to one of the stalls and examined porcelain vases and flowered tea-sets. At the door of the stall a young lady was talking and laughing with two young gentlemen. I remarked their English accents and listened vaguely to their conversation.

—O, I never said such a thing!

—O, but you did!

—O, but I didn't!

—Didn't she say that?

—Yes. I heard her.

—O, there's a . . . fib!

Observing me the young lady came over and asked me did I wish to buy anything. The tone of her voice was not encouraging; she seemed to have spoken to me out of a sense of duty. I looked humbly at the great jars that stood like eastern guards at either side of the dark entrance to the stall and murmured:

—No, thank you.

The young lady changed the position of one of the vases and went back to the two young men. They began to talk of the same subject. Once or twice the young lady glanced at me over her shoulder.

I lingered before her stall, though I knew my stay was useless, to make my interest in her wares seem more real. Then I turned away slowly and walked down the middle of the bazaar. I allowed the two pennies to fall against the sixpence in my pocket. I heard a voice call from one end of the gallery that the light was out. The upper part of the hall was now completely dark.

Gazing up into the darkness I saw myself as a creature driven and derided by vanity; and my eyes burned with anguish and anger.

IVAN TURGENEV

FIRST LOVE

Translated by Harry Stevens

The guests had long since departed. The clock struck half past twelve. Only the host, Sergei Nikolaich, and Vladimir Piotrovich were left in the room.

The host rang and ordered the servant to clear the supper table.

"Well, so it's agreed," he said, making himself more comfortable in his armchair and lighting a cigar. "Each of us undertakes to tell the story of his first love. You begin, Sergei Nikolaich."

Sergei Nikolaich, a portly man with a fair, puffy face, first looked at his host, then fixed his eyes on the ceiling. "I never had a first love," he said at last. "I started with my second."

"But how could you have done that?"

"Quite simply. I was eighteen when I first began to chase after a certain very attractive young lady; but I courted her exactly as if it were nothing new for me at all, exactly as—I paid court to others, later. To tell the truth, the first time I fell in love—and the last—was at the age of six, with my nurse; but that was very long ago, I have quite forgotten the details of our relations, and even if I could remember them, who would be interested?"

"Well, what am I to say?" the host began. "There isn't much of interest to tell about my first love either. I never fell in love with anyone until I met Anna Ivanovna, my present wife; and everything went like clockwork then: our fathers arranged our betrothal, we very quickly fell in love with each other, and we got married without delay. So my story can be told in very few words. I confess, gentlemen, that when I raised this question of first love I was relying on you,—I won't say old bachelors, and yet you're not exactly young. Surely you'll amend matters for us with some story, Vladimir Piotrovich?"

"It so happens that my first love was not exactly ordinary," Vladimir Piotrovich replied after some hesitation. He was about forty years old, and had black hair streaked with gray.

"Ah!" The host and Sergei Nikolaich exclaimed in one voice. "So much the better. . . . Tell us the story."

"With pleasure. . . . But no, I won't tell you the story; I am no good at telling stories, I make them either dry and short, or long-winded and untrue to life. But if you'll allow me I'll write down all I can remember and read it to you."

At first his two friends would not agree, but he insisted on having his way. Two weeks later they met again, and he kept his promise.

This is what he had written.

1

At that time I was sixteen; it happened in the summer of 1833.

I was living with my parents in Moscow. They had rented a house for the summer close to the Kaluga Gate, opposite the Nieskuchny Gardens. I was preparing to enter the university, but I worked very little and at my leisure.

No one put any restraints on my freedom. I did what I liked, especially after I had parted from my last tutor, a Frenchman who could never get used to the idea that he had fallen "like a bomb" (*comme une bombe*) into Russia, and who spent days on end lying in bed with a fierce expression on his face. My father treated me with negligent kindness; my mother paid hardly any attention to me, though I was her only child: she was preoccupied with other cares. My father, a man still young and very handsome, had married her for money; she was ten years older than he. She had a miserable life; she was always getting upset, always jealous, always angry—but never in my father's presence. She was terribly afraid of him, and he treated her sternly, coldly, distantly. I have never known any other man so artificially calm, self-assured, and autocratic.

I shall never forget the first few weeks I spent in that house by the Kaluga Gate. The weather was perfect; we moved out of town on May 9, St. Nicholas's Day. I went walking in our garden, or about the Nieskuchny Gardens, or out beyond the city gate, taking a book with me—Kaidanov's *Course*, for instance—but rarely opening it. I spent much of my time reciting poems, for I knew very many by heart. My blood was coursing through my veins, and I was melancholy, so delightfully and absurdly; I was always expecting something, always afraid of something, and I was astonished at everything, and always at the ready. My imagination played and danced continually around the same ideas, like swifts round a belfry at dawn. I was lost in thought, I sorrowed and even wept. But through the tears and through the sorrow inspired by some melodious poem, or by the beauty of the evening, a joyous feeling of youthful and effervescent life sprang up like grass in spring.

I had a saddle-horse. I saddled her myself and rode alone to some distant spot, the farther the better; I shook out the reins in a gallop and imagined myself a knight at a tourney (how merrily the wind blew in my ears!). Or, turning my face to the sky, I took its radiant light and azure into my soul.

I remember that in those days my mind hardly ever visualized the image of a woman, the apparition of woman's love, in any definite shape; but in all my thoughts, in all my feelings, lurked a half-recognized, bashful presentiment of something new, something inexpressibly sweet—something feminine.

This presentiment, this expectation, suffused all my being: I drew it in with my breath, it flowed through my veins in every drop of my blood . . . it was fated to have speedy realization.

Our house consisted of a large timber dwelling with a columned portico and two low wings; in the left-hand wing was a tiny manufactory of cheap wallpapers; I sometimes went there to watch a dozen thin and shock-headed, hollow-cheeked boys in greasy gowns, who jumped from time to time on the wooden levers that worked the square blocks of the press and so, with the weight of their puny bodies, stamped the patterns on the wallpaper. The small wing on the right was empty, but was to be rented. One day, three weeks or so after May 9, the shutters of this wing were thrown open, and women's faces appeared at the windows: a family had come to live there. I remember that same day at dinner my mother asked our butler who our new neighbors were, and, when he mentioned the name of Princess Zasiokina, remarked not without a touch of respect: "Ah, a princess!" then added: "She cannot be very well off."

"They arrived in three droshkies," the butler observed as he respectfully presented the dish. "They haven't a carriage of their own, and the furniture they brought is hardly worth mentioning."

"Maybe," my mother replied, "but all the same a princess is better."

My father gave her a frigid look; she said no more.

Certainly the Princess Zasiokina could not have been wealthy: the small wing she had rented was so tumbledown and tiny that anyone at all well off would never had agreed to live in it. However, I paid no attention to any of this conversation. The Princess's title made little impression on me: I had recently been reading Schiller's *Robbers*.

2

I had the habit of wandering about our garden every evening with a gun and taking pot shots at the rooks. I had long felt hatred for those prudent, rapacious, and cunning birds. On the day I have already spoken of I went off into the garden as usual and, after walking fruitlessly along all the avenues (the rooks recognized me and only cawed brokenly in the distance), I happened to approach the low fence separating our domain from the narrow strip of garden extending beyond and attached to the right-hand wing. I walked along with my head sunk on my breast. Suddenly I heard voices. I looked over the fence and was petrified: I saw a strange sight.

A few paces away, in a glade between bushes of green raspberry, was a tall, graceful girl in a striped, rose-colored dress and with a white kerchief on her head; four young men were pressing round her, and she was smacking each of them in turn on the forehead with those small gray flowers—I don't know their names, but they are well known to children: the flowers form small bags and burst with a pop when you strike them against anything hard. The young men thrust out their foreheads so readily, and there was something so charming, so imperative, so gracious, amusing, and pleasant in the girl's movements, that I all but cried out with amazement and delight, and I think I would have given everything else on earth for those enchanting fingers to strike me on the forehead too. My gun slipped to the grass, I forgot everything; my eyes were fixed on that graceful waist and neck and the beautiful hands, and the rather untidy, fair hair beneath the white kerchief, and that one half-closed, intelligent eye (I was watching her from the side) and those eyelashes and the tender cheek below them. . . .

"Young man! Now, young man!" I suddenly heard a voice right beside me. "Is it permissible to stare like that at strange young ladies?"

I trembled all over, I was put to confusion. Beside me, but beyond the fence, a man with close-cut black hair was standing and gazing at me with an ironical expression. The girl turned toward me at the same moment. I saw her large gray eyes in her vivid, animated face, and all that face suddenly began to quiver, to smile; her white teeth gleamed, her eyebrows were raised amusingly. I crimsoned, snatched up my gun from the ground, and, pursued by a ringing but not ill-natured laugh, ran to my room, flung myself on my bed, and covered my face with my hands. My heart was dancing within me; I felt deeply abashed and gay; I felt an agitation I had never known before.

After a rest I combed my hair, made myself tidy, and went downstairs to tea. The image of the young girl went before me; my heart ceased to dance, but it felt a pleasant twinge.

"What is the matter with you?" my father suddenly asked me. "Have you killed a rook?"

I felt like telling him everything, but I refrained and only smiled to myself. When I went to bed, for some unknown reason I spun round three or four times on one leg, greased my hair, got into bed, and slept like a log all night. In the early morning I woke for a moment, raised my head, looked around me rapturously, and fell off to sleep again.

3

"How can I make their acquaintance?" was my first thought the moment I awoke in the morning. I went out into the garden before tea, but did not go close to the fence and did not see anyone. After we had had tea I walked up and down the road in front of the house several times and took glances at the windows from this distance. . . . I thought I saw her face behind a curtain, and in my alarm I hurriedly retreated. "All the same, we must make their acquaintance," I thought as I wandered aimlessly over the sandy waste that extends beyond the Nieskuchny Gardens. "But how? That's the problem." I recalled the tiniest details of the previous day's meeting; for some reason I remembered very clearly how she had laughed at me. But while I was working myself up and making all kinds of plans, fate was already taking care of me.

While I was out, my mother received a letter from her new neighbor; it was on gray paper and sealed with a brown seal such as is used only for postal notices and to seal the corks of cheap wine-bottles. This letter, which was written in illiterate terms and slovenly handwriting, asked my mother to extend her protection to the Princess: according to her, my mother was intimately acquainted with certain important people who had the fate of the Princess and her children in their hands, as she was involved in very serious judicial cases. "I adress myself to you," she wrote, "as one noble lady to another, and moreover it is a plesure for me to have this oportunity." In conclusion she asked my mother's permission for her to call. I found my mother in an unpleasant frame of mind: my father was not at home, and she had no one with whom to discuss the letter. It was impossible not to reply to a "noble lady," and a Princess at that, but how to reply my mother could not imagine. She thought it would not be correct to write a note in French, but she herself was not very good at Russian orthography, she knew that; and she was anxious not to compromise herself. She was delighted at my arrival and at once ordered me to go to the Princess and tell her in person that my mother was always ready to do Her Excellency any service that lay in her power, and to ask her to call at one o'clock. The unexpectedly rapid fulfillment of my secret desires both delighted and frightened me. But I did not reveal the confusion into which I was plunged, and first went to my room to put on a new coat and cravat, for when at home I still went about in a jacket and turn-down collar, though I was deeply mortified at having to wear them.

4

All my body trembling uncontrollably, I entered the close and unpleasant lobby of the Zasiokins' wing and was met by an old, gray-headed servant with a dark, copper-colored face, moody little pig's eyes, and such deep furrows on the forehead and temples as I had never seen in all my life. He was carrying a picked herring backbone on a tray; shutting the door leading to the other room with his foot, he asked abruptly: "What do you want?"

"Is the Princess Zasiokina at home?" I asked.

"Vonifaty?" a jarring feminine voice shouted from the other side of the door.

The servant silently turned his back on me, revealing that the back of his livery was badly worn and had a single rusty button stamped with an armorial bearing, and went off, after setting the tray on the floor.

"Have you been to the policeman?" the same voice asked. The servant muttered something. "What? Someone come? Our neighbor's son? Well, ask him in."

The servant returned to me. "Please go into the reception room," he said as he picked up the tray from the floor. I tidied myself and went in.

I found myself in a small and not very neatly arranged room with poor furniture that looked as though it had been set out in a hurry. A woman aged about fifty, straight-haired and plain-looking, in an old green dress and with a varicolored triangular worsted neckerchief round her neck, was sitting by the window, in an armchair with a broken arm. Her small black eyes were fixed on me.

I went up to her and bowed.

"Have I the honor of speaking to Princess Zasiokina?"

"I am Princess Zasiokina. And are you Mr. V.'s son?"

"That is so. I have called with a message from my mother."

"Please sit down. Vonifaty! Where are my keys? Have you seen them?"

I told the Princess my mother's answer to her note. As she listened she tapped her fat red fingers on the windowsill, and when I had finished she fixed her eyes on me once more.

"Very good; I shall call without fail," she said. "But how young you still are! How old are you, if I may ask?"

"Sixteen," I replied with an involuntary stammer.

The Princess took some greasy, scribbled papers out of her pocket, raised them right to her nose, and began to sort them over.

"A fine age!" she said suddenly, turning and fidgeting in her chair. "But please don't stand on ceremony. I have simple ways."

"Too simple," I thought, with involuntary squeamishness running my eyes over all her unsightly figure.

At that moment another door of the reception room was swiftly flung open and the girl I had seen in the garden the previous evening entered. She raised her hand, and a derisive smile flitted over her face.

"And this is my daughter," the Princess said, pointing to the girl with her elbow. "Zenia, my dear, this is the son of our neighbor, Mr. V. What is your name, if I may ask?" She turned to me.

"Vladimir," I replied, rising, and stuttering in my agitation.

"And your patronymic?"

"Piotrovich."

"Indeed. I knew a chief of police once whose name was Vladimir Piotrovich too. Vonifaty! Don't look for the keys. I have them in my pocket."

The young girl was still gazing at me with the same smile, her eyes half-closed and her head cocked a little on one side.

"I've already seen M'sieur Voldemar," she began. (The silvery sound of her voice ran over me like a pleasant chilliness.) "You will alow me to call you that, won't you?"

"Please!" I stammered.

"Where did you see him?" her mother asked.

The young Princess did not reply. "Are you busy now?" she said, not taking her eyes off me.

"Not at all."

"Would you like to help me ball some wool? Come with me to my room."

She nodded to me and went out. I followed her.

In the room we entered the furniture was rather better and was arranged with greater taste. At that moment, however, I was not in a state to notice anything: I walked as though in a dream, and in all my being I felt an idiotically tense felicity.

The Princess sat down, picked up a skein of crimson wool, and, pointing me to a chair opposite her, carefully opened the skein and put it over my hands. All this she did without saying a word, with an amusing deliberation of movement and with the same bright and crafty smile on her slightly parted lips. She began to wind the wool onto a card folded double, and suddenly transfixed me with such a clear and swift glance that I involuntarily cast down my eyes. When her eyes, which usually were half-closed, were opened to their full extent, her face changed completely: it was as though light had flooded over it.

"What did you think of me yesterday, M'sieur Voldemar?" she asked, after a moment. "I expect you condemned me?"

"I—Princess—I didn't think anything—how could I?" I answered in some embarrassment.

"Listen!" she retorted. "You don't know me yet; I am exceedingly strange; I always like to be told the truth. I heard that you're sixteen, and I am twenty-one; you see I am much older than you, and so you should always tell me the truth—and do as I tell you," she added. "Look at me; why don't you look at me?"

I was still more embarrassed; none the less, I raised my eyes to her. She smiled, only not with her previous, but with a different, approving smile. "Look at me," she said, caressingly lowering her voice. "I don't dislike being looked at. I like your face; I have a feeling we shall be friends. And do you like me?" She added craftily.

"Princess—" I began.

"To begin with, call me Zinaida Alexandrovna; and secondly, what is this habit children" (she corrected herself)—"young people have of not saying frankly what they feel? That's all right for grown-ups. Now, you do like me, don't you?"

Though I found it very pleasant to have her talking to me so frankly, none the less I was a little annoyed. I wanted to show her that she was not dealing with a boy, and so, adopting as nonchalant and serious an air as possible, I said: "Of course I like you very much, Zinaida Alexandrovna; I have no intention of concealing that."

She shook her head deliberately. "Have you a tutor?" she suddenly asked.

"No. I haven't had a tutor for a long time."

I was lying; it was not a month since I had parted with my Frenchman.

"Oh; why, so I see; you're quite big, really."

She gently tapped my fingers. "Hold your hands straight." And she set to work diligently to wind the wool.

I took advantage of the circumstance that she did not raise her eyes and began to scrutinize her, at first surreptitiously, then more and more openly. Her face seemed even more charming than it had looked the previous evening, so fine, intelligent, and pleasant was everything about it. She was sitting with her back to the window, which was hung with a white blind; the sunlight, filtering through this blind, flooded her fluffy, golden hair, her innocent neck, her drooping shoulders and tender, untroubled breast with soft light. I looked at her, and how dear and close she grew to me! I felt that I had known her a very long time, that I had never known anything and had never even lived until I met her. . . . She was wearing a dark, rather shabby dress and an apron; I think I would willingly have caressed every fold in that dress and that apron. The toes of her shoes peered out from under her dress: I would have bowed myself down to those shoes in adoration. "And so I am sitting in front of her," I thought; "I have made her acquaintance. . . . What happiness—really, what happiness!" I all but sprang off the chair in my rapture, but I only kicked my feet a little, like an infant enjoying some treat.

I felt as good as a fish in water, and I would have remained in that room forever; I would never have left that spot.

Her eyelids slowly rose, and again her shining eyes beamed before me, and again she smiled.

"How you are staring at me!" she said slowly, and threatened me with one finger.

I crimsoned. . . . "She understands everything, she sees everything," the thought flashed through my head. "And how can she help understanding and seeing everything?"

Suddenly there was a tapping sound in the next room, and a saber clattered.

"Zenia!" the Princess called from that room. "Belovzorov has brought you a kitten."

"A kitten!" Zinaida exclaimed, and, rising impetuously from the chair, she flung the ball of wool onto my knees and ran out.

I also rose and, laying the skein and ball of wool on the windowsill, went into the reception room and halted in astonishment: in the middle of the room a tabby kitten was lying with her paws spread out, and Zinaida was on her knees before it, carefully raising its tiny head. Close to the Princess was a flaxen and curly-haired young hussar with crimson face and goggling eyes; he covered almost all the wall space between the two windows.

"How funny it is!" Zinaida declared. "And its eyes are not gray, but green; and what big ears it has! Thank you, Victor Yegorich! You are very kind!"

The hussar, whom I recognized as one of the young men I had seen the previous evening, smiled and bowed, clattering his spurs and jingling the chain of his saber.

"You were so kind yesterday as to say that you wanted a tabby kitten with large ears—and here it is! Your word is law!" He bowed again.

The kitten squealed faintly and began to sniff the floor.

"Oh, it's hungry!" Zinaida exclaimed. "Vonifaty! Sonia! Bring some milk."

A maid in an old yellow dress, with a faded kerchief round her neck, brought in a saucer of milk and set it before the kitten. The kitten trembled, screwed up its eyes, and began to lap.

"What a rosy little tongue it has!" Zinaida observed, bending her head down almost to the floor and gazing at the animal from one side, with her eyes right by its nose.

The kitten drank till it had had enough and then began to purr, finically lifting its paws. Zinaida got up and, turning to the maid, said in an indifferent tone: "Take it out!"

"In exchange for the kitten, your little hand!" the hussar said, grinning and drawing up all his powerful body, which was tightly constricted in his new uniform.

"Both hands!" Zinaida retorted, and held out her hands to him. While he was kissing them she looked at me across her shoulder.

I stood rooted to the spot and did not know whether I ought to smile, to say something, or keep silent. Suddenly through the wide-open door leading to the lobby I caught sight of our servant Fyodor. He made signs to me. I mechanically went out to him.

"What do you want?" I asked.

"Your mother has sent for you," he said in a whisper. "She is angry because you haven't come back with a reply."

"But have I been here so long, then?"

"An hour and more."

"An hour and more!" I involuntarily repeated. Going back to the reception room, I began to take my leave and scrape my feet.

"Where are you going?" the young Princess asked me, looking round the hussar's body.

"I must go home. So I am to say"—I turned to her mother—"that you will call on my mother at one o'clock."

"Yes, you tell her that, my boy."

She hurriedly picked up a snuffbox and took a pinch so noisily that I shuddered. "Yes, tell her that," she repeated, blinking tearfully and wheezing.

I bowed once more, turned, and left the room with the feeling of awkwardness in the back that a very young man always feels when he knows people are staring after him.

"But don't forget to come and see us, M'sieur Voldemar," Zinaida called, and she again burst into a laugh.

"What is she always laughing for?" I thought as I returned home with Fyodor, who said not one word to me, but followed me with a disapproving air. My mother scolded me and wondered what I could have been doing so long in that Princess's place. I did not tell her and went off to my room. I suddenly felt very sad. . . . I tried not to cry. . . . I was jealous of that hussar!

5

The Princess kept her promise and called on my mother, who did not take any liking to her. I was not present at their meeting, but at table my mother told my father that she thought Princess Zasiokina *une femme trés vulgaire*, that she had grown very tired of the Princess's requests that she should intercede with Princess Sergei on her behalf, that she was always involved in lawsuits and affairs, *des vilaines affaires d'argent*, and that she must be a terrible intriguer. My mother added, however, that she had invited the Princess and her daughter to dine with us next day (when I heard the words "and her daughter," I bent my head over my plate), because, after all, she was our neighbor, and a Princess. To which my father said he remembered now what sort of lady she was: in his youth he had known the late Prince Zasiokin, who had been very well brought up, but had been an empty and quarrelsome fellow. In society he had been known as "*le Parisien*," because he had lived many years in Paris; at one time he had been very wealthy, but he had gambled away all his fortune. And for some unknown reason, possibly for money—though in any case he could have made a better choice, my father added with a frigid smile—he married the daughter of some lawyer's clerk and then began to indulge in speculation and ruined himself completely.

"So long as she doesn't ask us to lend her money," my mother observed.

"That is extremely possible," my father said calmly. "Does she speak French?"

"Very badly."

"Hm! But that doesn't matter. I think you said you had invited her daughter too; someone has assured me that she is a very pleasant and well-educated girl."

"Ah! In that case she doesn't take after her mother."

"Nor her father!" my father retorted. "He was educated too, but stupid!"

Mother sighed and was lost in thought. My father said no more. During this conversation I felt very awkward.

After dinner I went into the garden, but without my gun. I had pledged myself not to go near the Zasiokin garden, but an irresistible force drew me that way—and not for nothing. When still some distance from the fence, I saw Zinaida. This time she was alone. She was holding a small book in one hand and was walking slowly along the path. She did not notice me.

I all but let her pass, but suddenly I stopped short and coughed.

She turned, but did not stop; with one hand she threw back the broad blue ribbon of her round straw hat, then she looked at me, quietly smiled, and fixed her eyes on her book again.

I took off my cap and hesitated for a moment, then turned away with a heavy heart. "*Que suis-je pour elle?*" I thought (God knows why) in French.

I heard familiar steps behind me. I looked round: my father was coming toward me with his swift and easy stride.

"Is that the young Princess?" he asked me.

"Yes."

"Do you know her, then?"

"I saw her this morning when I called on her mother."

My father halted and, turning sharply on his heels, walked back. As he drew level with Zinaida he bowed to her politely. She bowed in reply, not without a look of astonishment, and let her book fall. I saw her following him with her eyes. My father always dressed exquisitely, in his own original and simple manner; but never had his figure seemed more finely proportioned, never had he worn his gray hat more beautifully on his still quite thick, curly hair.

I thought of going to Zinaida, but she did not even glance at me. She picked up her book and walked away.

6

I spent all that evening and the following morning in a despondent torpor. I remember I tried to work, and picked up Kaidanov, but the scrawling lines and pages of that famous primer flickered before me in vain. Ten times in succession I read the sentence: "Julius Caesar was distinguished by his martial courage"; I understood not one word and threw the book down. Before dinner I again greased my hair and put on my coat and cravat.

"What are you wearing them for?" my mother asked. "You're not a student yet, and goodness knows whether you'll pass the entrance examination. And it isn't so long since you had the jacket made for you. You mustn't stop wearing it altogether."

"We're having guests," I whispered almost in despair.

"What rubbish! What sort of guests do you call them?"

I had to submit. I exchanged my coat for the jacket, but I did not take off the cravat. The Princess and her daughter arrived half an hour or so before dinner; the older woman was wearing the green dress I had already seen, had thrown a yellow shawl round her shoulders, and had put on an old-fashioned bonnet with flame-colored ribbons. She at once began to talk about her promissory notes, complained of her poverty, and was "importunate," but did not stand on ceremony in the least: she took snuff just as nosily, and shifted and fidgeted on her chair just as freely. Apparently it did not even occur to her that she was a Princess. On the other hand, Zinaida behaved very correctly, almost haughtily, like a real princess. Her face wore a look of cold immobility and importance, and I did not recognize her, did not recognize her looks or her smiles, though in this new guise also she seemed beautiful to me. She was wearing a light *barège* dress with pale blue figurework; her hair fell in long curls at the side of her cheeks, in the English fashion; this coiffure suited the cold expression of her face. My father sat next to her at dinnertime and entertained her with his own distinctive, elegant, and imperturbable courtesy. Occasionally he glanced at her, and occasionally she glanced at him, but so queerly, almost inimically. They carried on conversation in French; I remember I was astonished by the purity of her pronunciation. At table the older Princess was just as unconstrained as before; she ate a great deal and praised the cooking. My mother was obviously depressed by her and replied with a mournful disdain; from time to time my father knitted his brows a little. My mother did not take to Zinaida either. "She's so haughty," she said next day. "And what has she got to be haughty about, *avec sa mine de grisette?*"

"Evidently you've never seen grisettes," my father remarked.

"And thank goodness for that!"

"Of course, thank goodness—only, how can you pass judgment on them?"

Zinaida did not pay any attention to me whatever. Soon after dinner the Princess took her leave.

"I shall hope to have your protection, Maria Nikolaevna and Piotr Vasilievich," she said in a drawling voice to my father and mother. "What can I do? There were days—but they have passed. And here am I, an Excellency," she added with an unpleasant laugh; "but what's the good of honor if you haven't any food for dinner?" My father bowed to her respectfully and accompanied her to the door of the lobby. I stood beside him in my tailless jacket and stared at the floor, as though condemned to death. Zinaida's treatment of me had completely overcome me. But imagine my surprise when, as she walked past me, with the old gracious expression in her eyes she hurriedly whispered: "Come along at eight o'clock, do you hear, without fail. . . ." I was astonished, but she was already departing, throwing a white scarf over her head as she went.

7

At eight o'clock exactly, wearing my coat and with my hair combed up at the front, I entered the lobby of the small wing that the Princesses occupied. The old servant stared at me glumly and rose reluctantly from the bench. Merry voices could be heard coming from the reception room. I opened the door and started back in amazement. The young Princess was standing on a chair in the middle of the room, holding out a man's hat in front of her; five men were crowded round the chair. They were trying to put their hands into the hat, but she raised it and shook it vigorously. When she saw me she cried: "Wait, wait! We have a fresh guest; he must be given a ticket too." Lightly jumping down from the chair, she took me by the lapel of my coat. "Come on," she said, "what are you waiting for; Messieurs, let me introduce you. This is M'sieur Voldemar, our neighbor's son. And these," she added, turning to me and pointing to the guests one after another, "are Count Malevsky, Dr. Lushin, the poet Maidanov, retired Captain Nirmatsky, and Belovzorov, the hussar you have seen before. Please be friends, and good friends."

I was so embarrassed that I did not even bow to anyone. Dr. Lushin I recognized as the same swarthy gentleman who had so ruthlessly put me to shame in the garden. I did not know the others at all.

"Count!" Zinaida continued, "write a ticket for M'sieur Voldemar."

"That is unfair," the Count objected in a slightly Polish accent. He was a very handsome and fashionably dressed man with black hair, expressive hazel eyes, a thin white nose, and a scanty mustache above a very small mouth. "He hasn't played forfeits with us."

"It's unfair," Belovzorov and the gentleman described as a retired captain both repeated. The captain was a man about forty years of age, hideously pockmarked, with hair as frizzy as a Negro's, rather stocky, bowlegged, and wearing a military jacket without epaulets, flung round his shoulders.

"Write a ticket, I tell you," the Princess repeated. "What do you call this, mutiny? M'sieur Voldemar is with us for the first time, and today the law does not apply to him. Stop grumbling and write a ticket; that is my wish."

The Count shrugged his shoulders but, humbly bowing his head, took the pen in his white, beringed hand, tore off a piece of paper, and began to write on it.

"At any rate, do let us explain to Mr. Voldemar what it is all about," Lushin said in a scoffing tone, "for he looks completely bewildered. You see, young man, we're playing forfeits. The Princess has had to pay a forfeit, and the one who draws the lucky ticket will have the right to kiss her hand. Did you understand what I said?"

I only glanced at him and continued standing as before. But the Princess jumped onto the chair again and shook the hat. All the men drew round her, and I with the others.

"Maidanov," she said to the tall young man with emaciated face, small, shortsighted eyes, and extraordinarily long black hair; "you, as a poet, should be magnanimous and surrender your ticket to M'sieur Voldemar, so that he has two chances instead of one."

But Maidanov shook his head and whirled his hair. I was the last to thrust my hand into the hat. I drew out a ticket and unfolded. Lord, what did I feel like when I read the words: "A kiss!"

"A kiss!" I involuntarily exclaimed.

"Bravo! He's won!" Zinaida cried. "I am glad! She got down from the chair and looked into my eyes so lucidly and sweetly that my heart beat violently. "But are you glad?" she asked me.

"I?" I stammered.

"Sell me your ticket," Belovzorov suddenly said ineptly right in my ear. "I'll give you a hundred rubles for it."

I gave him such an indignant look that Zinaida clapped her hands, while Lushin exclaimed: "Good lad!"

"But," Lushin went on, "I, as the master of ceremonies, am bound to see that all the rules are observed. M'sieur Voldemar, go down on one knee. That is our custom."

Zinaida stood in front of me with her head bent a little to one side, as though to examine me the better, and dignifiedly stretched out her hand. My eyes went misty; I tried to go down on one knee, but fell down on both my knees; and so clumsily did I press my lips against her fingers that I scratched the tip of my nose with her nail.

"Enough!" Lushin cried, and he helped me to rise.

We went on playing at forfeits. Zinaida seated me beside her. The forfeits she thought of! In one case she had to represent a "statue," and she chose the ugly Maidanov as her pedestal; she ordered him to lie face-downward, and even to tuck his head into his chest. The merriment did not cease for one moment. I was a privately and soberly educated lad, brought up in a genteel, sedate home, and all the noise and racket, this unceremonious, almost violent gaiety, these unprecendented relations with strangers, went to my head. I was just as intoxicated as if I had drunk too much wine. I began to laugh and talk even louder than the others, so that even the old Princess, who was closeted in the next room with some lawyer's clerk summoned into conference with her, came out to stare at me. But I felt so happy that, as we say, I did not care a fig and took no notice of anyone's sneers and wry looks. Zinaida continued to show preference for me and did not let me leave her side. In one forfeit I had to sit beside her, our heads covered with the one silk kerchief: I was supposed to tell her my greatest secret. I still remember how close together our heads were in that stifling, translucent, scented veil, how in that twilight her eyes shone very mildly and very close to me, and her parted lips breathed on me hotly, and I saw her teeth, and her hair tickled and scorched me. I was silent; she smiled mysteriously and roguishly and whispered at last: "Well, and now what?" But I only went red and laughed and turned away, and could hardly get my breath. We grew tired of forfeits, so we began to play a game in which we all had to stand in a circle holding a string, while she was in the middle. And my goodness! What rapture I felt when I forgot what I was doing and she gave me a strong, sharp smack on my extended fingers! And how I tried after that to pretend that I was forgetting again! But she only teased me and would not smack my fingers, though I left them extended.

What else did we do in the course of that evening! We played the piano and we sang and we danced and we acted a gypsy encampment. Nirmatsky was dressed as a bear and given salt water to drink. Count Malevsky showed us card tricks and ended by shuffling the cards and dealing himself a hand that held all the trumps, at which Lushin "ventured to congratulate him." Maidanov recited parts of his poem "The Murderer" (this was at the height of the romantic period in our literature), which he proposed to publish in a black jacket with the title in blood red. We stole the hat off the knees of the lawyer's clerk and made him do the Cossack dance as ransom; we dressed old Vonifaty in a bonnet, while Zinaida put on a man's hat. I could not tell you all we did. Only Belovzorov withdrew more and more into one corner, morose and angry. At times his eyes were suffused with blood, he flushed and looked as though at any moment he would charge down on us and scatter us in all directions, like splinters. But the Princess looked at him and threatened him with her fingers, and once more he skulked in his corner.

At last we were worn out. Zinaida's mother was now ready for anything, as she herself expressed it, and no amount of shouting disturbed her; but even she felt tired and wanted to rest. Supper was served at midnight, and consisted of a piece of old, dry cheese and some cold patties of chopped ham, which I thought more tasty than any meat pie; there was only one bottle of wine, and that bottle was queer: dark, with a swollen neck, and the wine inside it was a rose color; however, no one drank any of it. When I left I was weary and happy to the point of exhaustion; at parting Zinaida squeezed my hand firmly and again smiled enigmatically.

The night breathed heavily and humidly into my flaming face; a storm appeared to be gathering; black clouds were growing and crawling over the sky, visibly changing their smoky outlines. Abreeze trembled restlessly in the dark trees, and somewhere beyond the horizon thunder seemed to be grumbling to itself angrily and hollowly.

I made my way to my room through the back entrance. My servant was sleeping on the floor, and I had to step across him. He awoke, saw me, and reported that my mother had been annoyed with me again and had wanted to send for me to come home, but my father had restrained her. (I never went to bed without saying good-night to my mother and asking her blessing.) But there was nothing to be done about it now!

I told my man that I would undress and get myself to bed and put out the candle. . . . But I did not undress and I did not lie down.

I sat down on a chair, and sat there for a long time as though enchanted. What I felt was so new and so sweet: I sat looking about me and not stirring, breathing slowly, and only silently laughing at my memories from time to time, then going cold at the thought that I was in love, that this was it, this was love. Zinaida's face silently floated before me in the darkness—it floated up, and did not float past—her lips still enigmatically smiling, her eyes looking at me a little sidelong, interrogatively, thoughtfully, and tenderly, as they had at our parting. At last I rose, tiptoed over to my bed, and cautiously laid my head on the pillow without undressing, as though afraid that by some abrupt movement I would disturb the feeling with which I was overflowing. . . .

I lay down, but I did not even close my eyes. I quickly noticed that pallid gleams of light were continually flickering across the room toward me. I half raised myself and glanced at the window. Its transom showed up distincly against the mysteriously and mournfully glimmering panes. A thunderstorm, I thought; and I was right, it was a thunderstorm. But it was a very long way off, and no thunder was to be heard; only dull, long, sheet lightning lit up the sky incessantly; it did not flash so much as flutter and quiver like the wings of a dying bird. I got up, went across to the window, and remained standing there till dawn came. . . . The lightning did not cease for a moment; it was what the common people call a "sparrows' night." I gazed at the silent sandy plain, at the dark mass of the Nieskuchny Gardens, at the yellowish façades of distant buildings, which seemed to be quivering with every feeble flash. I gazed and could not tear myself away; that mute lightning, those temperate flashes, seemed to be in accord with the mute and secret emotions that were flaming up inside me. The dawn began to break; the sunrise drew on in crimson patches. As the sun approached, the lightning grew paler and less frequent; it flickered more and more intermittently, and finally ceased, overborne by the sobering and indubitable light of the oncoming day . . .

Within me, too, my own lightnings faded. I felt a great weariness and stillness. . . . But Zinaida's image continued to hover triumphantly over my soul. Only, that very image seemed to grow composed: like a swan flying up from the reeds of a marsh, it separated from the other, unpleasant shapes surrounding it and, as I dropped off to sleep, I fell once more at its feet in a valedictory and trustful adoration.

O gentle feelings, tender sounds, the benignity and assuagement of the deeply moved soul, the melting joy of love's first emotions—where are you now, where are you now?

8

When I went down to tea next morning, my mother scolded me, but not so much as I had expected, and made me tell her how I had spent the previous evening. I replied in few words, omitting many of the details and trying to make it all appear as innocent as possible.

"All the same, they are not people *comme il faut*," Mother remarked, "and there is no reason why you should go chasing after them, instead of preparing for your examination and keeping yourself occupied."

As I knew that my mother's anxiety about my occupations was confined to these few words, I did not think it necessary to protest. But after tea my father took me by the arm and, leading me into the garden, made me tell him all I had seen at the Zasiokins' the previous evening.

My father had a strange influence over me, and our relations, too, were strange. He took hardly any interest in my education and upbringing, but he never upset me, he respected my freedom, and, if I may put it so, he was even polite to me . . . only he never let me draw close to him. I loved him, I admired him, he seemed to me the perfect pattern of a man, and, upon my word, how passionately I would have become attached to him if I had not continually felt that he was thrusting me off! On the other hand, if he wished, with just one word, one gesture, he could suddenly win my unbounded confidence in him. My soul would lay itself bare, I would talk to him as if he were an understanding friend, or an indulgent tutor . . . and then, just as abruptly, he would abandon me, and he again thrust me off, kindly and gently, but none the less he thrust me off.

Sometimes a spirit of gaiety came over him, and then he was ready to sport and romp with me like a boy (he was fond of all vigorous physical movement). Once—only once—he caressed me so tenderly that I all but burst into tears. But his gaiety and his tenderness vanished without trace, and the intimacy that had sprung up between us afforded me no hope whatever for the future—I might have dreamed it. There were times when I would study his intelligent, handsome, lucid face . . . my heart would begin to quiver, and all my being would be vehemently drawn toward him. . . . He seemed to feel what was going on inside me, he would pat me casually on the cheek, and either would go off or would occupy himself with something, or would go quite set and cold, as he alone could, and at once I would shrink and go cold too. His rare outbursts of feeling for me were never to be evoked by my mute but intelligible entreaties; they always came unexpectedly. In later days, when I pondered on my father's character, I came to the conclusion that he had no time for me, or for family life; he was fond of something else, and thoroughly enjoyed that something else. "You yourself take all you can, but never put yourself in someone else's hand; belong to yourself: that is the whole art of life," he once said to me. On another occasion I, as a young democrat, ventured to reflect on freedom in his presence (that day he was "good," as I used to say, and at such times I could talk with him about anything). "Freedom," he repeated. "But do you know what it is that can give man freedom?"

"No, what?"

"Will; his own will; and it gives him power too, which is better than freedom. Know how to desire, and then you will be free, and you will command."

First and foremost my father wanted to live. . . . and he did live. Perhaps he had a presentiment that he would not be able to enjoy the "art" of life for long: he died at the age of forty-two.

I told my father all about my visit to the Zasiokins. He listened to me half-attentively, half-abstractedly, sitting on a bench and drawing in the sand with the butt of his whip. Very occasionally he smiled, and looked at me brightly and amusingly, and encouraged me to go on by asking brief questions and making interjections. At first I could not bring myself even to mention Zinaida's name, but I could not restrain myself, and I began to refer to her. My father went on smiling. Then he was lost in thought; he yawned and rose to his feet.

I remembered that on leaving the house he had ordered his horse to be saddled. He was an excellent horseman and could control the very wildest of horses.

"Shall I ride with you, Papa?" I asked him.

"No," he replied, and his face adopted its usual indifferent and kindly expression. "Go for a ride by yourself if you like; and tell the coachman I'm not going."

He turned his back on me and walked away swiftly. I followed him with my eyes; he vanished through the gate. I saw his hat moving along above the fence; he turned in turned in at the Zasiokins' gate.

He remained there over an hour, but then went off at once to town and did not return home till the evening.

After dinner I myself went to call on the Zasiokins! I found only the old Princess in the reception room. When she saw me she scratched her head under her cap with the end of a knitting-needle and suddenly asked me if I would write out a soliciting letter for her.

"With pleasure," I replied, and sat down on the edge of a chair.

"Only write in a large letters," she said as she handed me a dirty sheet of paper. "But could you do it today, my dear?"

"I'll write it out this very day."

The door leading to the next room was opened very slightly and Zinaida's face appeared in the opening; it was pale, thoughtful, and the hair was thrown back negligently. She stared at me with great, cold eyes and quietly closed the door again.

"Zenia, Zenia!" her mother called. But Zinaida did not answer. I took away the Princess's letter and sat over it all the evening.

9

My "passion" began from that day. I remember I felt rather as a man must feel who has just entered the Czar's service: I had ceased to be a boy; I was in love. I have said that my passion began from that day; I could add that my torments also dated from that day. In Zinaida's absence I languished; my mind was a blank, everything dropped out of my hands, and for days on end I thought tensely only about her. . . . I languished. . . . But I felt no better in her presence. I was jealous, I realized my insignificance, I stupidly sulked and stupidly fawned; and even so an irresistible power drew me to her, and every time I crossed the threshold of her room I felt an involuntary throb of happiness. She guessed at once that I was in love with her, nor did I think to conceal the fact; she made fun of my passion, played with me, petted and tormented me. It is sweet to be the sole source, the autocratic and irresponsible cause, of another being's greatest joys and deepest sorrows—and in Zinaida's hands I was as the softest wax. For that matter, I was not the only one in love with her: all the men who visited her home went crazy over her, and she kept them all in leading strings, at her feet. She found amusement in arousing their hopes, or their fears, in twisting them round her finger at her whim (she called this knocking people against one another), and they did not even think of resisting and readily submitted to her. In all her being, so vital and beautiful, was a peculiarly enchanting blend of cunning and unconcern, artificiality and simplicity, stillness and high spirits; everything she did, or said, her every movement, was invested with a light, subtle charm, a playful strength. Her face, too, was incessantly changing, and it played too; almost in the same instant it would express derision, thoughtfulness, and passion. The most varied of feelings, light and swift, sped momentarily over her eyes and lips, like the shadows of clouds on a sunny, windy day.

She had need of every one of her devotees. Belovzorov, whom she sometimes called "my animal" and sometimes simply "mine," would readily have thrown himself into the fire for her; though he could put no hope in his mental capacity or any other qualities, he was continually proposing to her, hinting that others only talked. Maidanov answered to the poetic elements in her soul; though he was rather cold, like almost all authors, he tensely assured her, and possibly himself too, that he worshipped her, he lauded her in innumerable poems and read them to her with an unnatural yet sincere rapture. She felt sympathy for him, and at the same time she rather made fun of him; she did not really believe him and, after listening to his effusions, made him read Pushkin, in order to clear the air, as she said. Dr. Lushin, mocking and cynical of speech, knew her better than did any of the others, and loved her more than any of the others, though he ran her down behind her back and to her face. She respected him, but she did not release him and sometimes took a particular, malignant pleasure in making him feel that he, too, was in her hands. "I am a coquette, I am heartless, I have an actress's nature," she said to him once in my presence. "Well, all right! Give me your hand; I'll stick a pin in it; you will feel shame in front of this young man, it will hurt you; but all the same, Mr. Self-righteous, you've got to laugh!" Lushin flushed, turned away and bit his lips, but finished by putting out his hand. She pricked him, and he did begin to laugh . . . and she laughed too as she pushed the pin in quite deep and looked into his eyes, which vainly tried to avoid her gaze.

Least of all could I understand the relations between Zinaida and Count Malevsky. He was good-looking, adroit, and intelligent, but even I, a sixteen-year-old lad, found something dubious, something false in him, and I was amazed that Zinaida did not notice it. But perhaps she did notice this falsity and was not repelled by it. Her unsatisfactory upbringing, her strange acquaintances and habits, her mother's constant presence, the poverty and disorder of the home—everything, beginning with the very liberty that this young woman enjoyed, and her consciousness of superiority to everybody around her, developed a half-contemptuous negligence and lack of squeamishness in her. There were times when it did not matter what happened—Vonifaty might come to report that there was no sugar in the house, some petty calumny would come out, or the guests would quarrel with one another—she only shook her curls, said: "It's all nothing," and was not worried in the least.

On the other hand, there were times when all my blood boiled as I saw Malevsky go up to her, his body swaying craftily, like a fox, and then elegantly lean on the back of her chair and whisper into her ear with a self-satisfied and ingratiating little smile, while she folded her arms on her breast, looked at him attentively, and she too smiled and gently swayed her head.

"What pleasure do you get out of seeing Monsieur Malevsky?" I asked her one day.

"But he has such handsome little mustaches!" she replied. "In any case, it's nothing to do with you."

"You mustn't think I'm in love with him," she said to me on another occasion. "No, I'm not. I cannot love a man like him, a man I have to look down at. I need someone who will break me. . . . But I shall never meet such a man, thank God! I shall never be caught by anyone; no, never!"

"So you will never fall in love?"

"But how about you? Don't I love you, then?" she said, and struck me on my nose with the end of her glove.

Yes, Zinaida was always making fun of me. For three weeks I saw her every day, and there was little that she did not do with me! She rarely called on us, and I did not regret this; in our house she was transformed into a young lady, into a young princess, and I shunned her. I was afraid of betraying myself in front of my mother, who was very unfriendly to Zinaida and watched us inimically. I was not so afraid of Father; he did not appear to notice me, and he talked only little with Zinaida, though when he did he talked with particular intelligence and meaning in his words. I stopped working, reading, I even stopped wandering about the district and riding. Like a beetle tied by one leg, I continually hovered about the home of my beloved; I think I would have remained there forever . . . but that was impossible: my mother grumbled at me, and sometimes Zinaida herself drove me away. Then I locked myself in my room or went off to the very end of the garden, climbed onto the ruins of a lofty stone conservatory, and, dangling my feet from the wall overlooking the road, sat there for hours and gazed and gazed, seeing nothing. Around me white butterflies lazily fluttered over the dusty nettles, a saucy sparrow settled not far away on a broken red brick and irritatingly chirruped, incessantly twisting and turning all its body and spreading wide its tail; the rooks, still distrustful of me, occasionally cawed as they sat high up on the bare crown of a birch tree, the sun and the wind played gently among the tree's supple branches, from time to time the sounds of the bells of the Donskoi Monastery floated calmly and despondently to my ears; but I sat, gazed, listened, and was entirely filled with a nameless feeling that included all feelings: sadness, and joy, and presentiment of the future, and desire, and fear of life. But at that time I understood nothing of all this, and I could not have given a name to any of the feelings that possessed me, or else I would have given all of it just one name, the name of Zinaida.

But Zinaida went on playing with me, like a cat with a mouse. At one moment she would flirt with me, and I grew excited and melted like wax; the next instant she drove me away, and I did not dare to go near her, did not dare to glance at her.

I remember she was very cold to me for several days in succession; I grew quite diffident, and when I timidly went to call on them I tried to keep near the old Princess, even though just then she was scolding and shouting a great deal: she was in a bad way with her promissory notes, and she had already had to see the police twice.

One day I was passing the well-known fence in the garden when I happened to see Zinaida: she was sitting very still on the grass, resting her head on both hands. I tried quietly to retreat, but she suddenly raised her head and beckoned to me imperatively. I was petrified: at first I did not understand her gesture. She repeated it. I at once jumped over the fence and ran up to her joyfully; but she halted me with a look and pointed to the path two steps away from her. In my confusion, not knowing what to do, I went down on my knees at the edge of the path. She was so pale, and such a bitter sorrow, such profound weariness, was expressed in all her features that my heart sank and I muttered involuntarily: "What is the matter?"

She stretched out her hand, pulled up some weed, bit it, and threw it away, as far as she could throw it.

"Do you love me very much?" she said at last. "Do you?"

I made no answer; and besides, why should I answer?

"Yes," she said, looking at me as before. "That is true. Just the same eyes," she added, then was lost in thought and covered her face with her hands.

"Everything has grown repulsive to me," she whispered. "I would go off to the end of the world; I cannot bear this, I cannot cope with it. . . . And what awaits me in the future? . . . Ah, it is hard for me. . . . My God, how hard!'

"Why is it?" I asked timidly.

She did not answer and only shrugged her shoulders. I remained on my knees, looking at her with deep despondency. Every word she uttered was a stab in my heart. I think that at that moment I would willingly have given my life if only she had ceased to grieve. I looked at her and, still not understanding why she was so depressed, I vividly pictured her coming suddenly, in an outburst of uncontrollable sorrow, into the garden and falling to the ground as though mown down. It was bright and green all around us; the wind was rustling among the leaves of the trees and occasionally swaying the long cane of a raspberry above Zinaida's head. Somewhere doves were cooing, and the bees were humming as they flew low over the scanty grass. Above us the sky was a gracious azure—but I felt so sad. . . .

"Say some poetry to me," she said in an undertone, and leaned on her elbows. "I like you to say poems. You sing them, but that's nothing, that's the way of youth, Say 'On the Hills of Georgia'[1] to me. Only sit down first."

I sat down and recited "On the Hills of Georgia."

" 'That my heart simply cannot help loving' "—Zinaida repeated the line. "That is where poetry is so good: it tells of something that is not, something that not only is better than the reality, but is even more like the truth. . . .'That my heart simply cannot cease loving.' It would like to, but it cannot." She was silent again and suddenly started and rose. "Let's go. Maidanov is with Mamma; he brought me his poem, but I left him. And now he is upset too—but it cannot be helped. You will find out some day—only don't be angry with me!"

She hurriedly squeezed my hand and ran off in front. We returned to the house. Maidanov began to read us his "Murderer," which had just been printed; but I did not listen to it. He shouted out his four-foot iambics in a singsong voice; the rhythms alternated and jingled like sleighbells, empty and loud; but I gazed continually at Zinaida and continually tried to fathom the meaning of her last words.

"Or is it that a secret rival
Suddenly has conquered thee?"

Maidanov exclaimed in a nasal tone, and my eyes met Zinaida's eyes. She let them drop and faintly blushed. I saw her blush, and I went cold with alarm. I had already felt jealous, but only at that moment did the thought that she was in love flash through my head. "My God! She's fallen in love!"

10

Now I was really tormented. I racked my brains, I thought, and thought again, and watched her persistently, though as far as possible secretly. A change

[1] An eight-line, one-stanza poem by Pushkin. (Tr.)

had occurred in her, that was evident. Now she went off for walks by herself, and long walks too. Sometimes she did not come out of her room when there were visitors, but sat there for hours. This had not formerly been her habit. I suddenly became—or thought I became—extremely observant. "Isn't it he? or perhaps it is he?" I asked myself, anxiously considering one devotee after another. Secretly I thought Count Malevsky more dangerous than the others, though for Zinaida's sake I felt ashamed of admitting this possibility.

My powers of observation did not extend beyond my own nose, and my secrecy probably did not deceive anybody; at least, Dr Lushin soon saw through me. By the way, he, too, had changed of late: he had grown thinner, and though he laughed just as much, his laugh was more hollow, evil, and curt; his previous light irony and exaggerated cynicism were replaced by an involuntary nervous irritability.

"What are you always dragging along here for, young man?" he asked me one day when he was alone with me in the Zasiokins' reception room. (The young Princess had not yet returned from a walk, and her mother could be heard on the mezzanine floor loudly scolding her maid.) "You ought to be studying and working while you are young; but you—what are you doing?"

"You don't know whether I work or not at home," I retorted, not without a touch of hauteur, but also in some embarrassment.

"What work is there to be done here? That's not what is worrying you. But I won't argue with you—at your age this is to be expected. Only your choice is far from commendable. Don't you see the kind of house this is?"

"I don't understand you," I remarked.

"You don't understand? So much the worse for you. I consider it my duty to warn you. People like me, old bachelors, may call here with safety, what can happen to us? We have been well steeled, nothing whatever can make any holes in us. But you've still got a delicate skin; and the air here is injurious to you, believe me. You may catch the infection."

"What do you mean?"

"What I say. Tell me, are you really well, even now? Are you in any normal state? Is what you are feeling of any value to you, any good to you?"

"Well, and what am I feeling?" I said, though in my heart of hearts I had to admit that he was right.

"Ah, young man, young man!" he went on in a tone of voice that suggested there was something very insulting to me in those two words. "What are you trying to be clever for? After all, thank God you still reveal in your face what is going on in your soul. But there, why talk? I myself would not come here if—" (he clenched his teeth) "if I were not just as big a fool as you are. Only this is the thing that amazes me: how is it that you, with your intelligence, don't perceive what is happening all around you?"

"But what is happening, then?" I retorted, and I went tense with expectation.

The doctor looked at me with derisive commiseration.

"And I'm a fine one too," he said, apparently to himself. "Much need I have to say all this to him! In a word," he added, raising his voice, "I repeat: this atmosphere is not good for you. You like being here; but then, why shouldn't you? It is pleasant to smell the scents of a conservatory, only you cannot go and live in it. Now take my advice and go back to Kaidanov."

The Princess entered and began to complain to him of the toothache. A little later Zinaida returned.

"Now do scold her, doctor," her mother said. "All day she is drinking nothing but ice water, and is it really good for her, with her weak chest?"

"Why do you do that?" Lushin asked Zinaida.

"What harm is there in it?"

"What harm is there in it? You may catch a chill and die."

"Really? Surely not? And in any case, what of it? If that is the way I am to go."

"You don't say!" the doctor snorted. Zinaida's mother went out.

"You don't say!" Zinaida repeated. "Is life so cheerful, after all? Look around you. . . . Well, are you satisfied? Or do you think that I don't realize it all, don't feel it all? I enjoy drinking ice water, and can you seriously assure me that such a life is so worth while that it is not to be risked for a moment of enjoyment? . . . I won't speak of happiness."

"That's just it," Lushin remarked. "Caprice and independence: those two words sum up all your being, they express the whole of your character."

She laughed a nervous laugh.

"You've missed the post, doctor. You are not very good at observation, you're left behind. Put your spectacles on. I am not interested in caprices now; making a fool of you, making a fool of myself—how very cheerful! And as for independence—M'sieur Voldemar," she suddenly cried, stamping her little foot, "don't pull that melancholy face. I cannot stand it when people show me commiseration." She swiftly left the room.

"This atmosphere is bad for you, young man; very bad," Lushin said to me once more.

11

That evening all the usual guests were gathered in the Zasiokins' reception room; I was among them.

The conversation turned to Maidanov's poem. Zinaida praised it, and quite sincerely. "But do you know what?" she said to him. "If I were a poet I would choose other subjects. Perhaps it is all nonsense, but sometimes strange thoughts come into my head, especially when I am lying awake, before dawn, when the sky begins to turn rosy and gray. For instance, I would— You won't laugh at me?"

"No! No!" we all exclaimed with one accord.

"I would picture a whole company of young girls in a large boat on a quiet river at night," she went on, folding her hands over her chest and gazing to one side. "The moon is shining, and they are all in white and wearing garlands of white flowers, and they're singing something, a kind of hymn, you know."

"I understand, I understand; go on," Maidanov said in a meaningful and dreamy tone.

"Suddenly there is noise, and laughter, torches, tambourines on the bank. . . . It is a crowd of bacchantes running with singing and clamor. And here you have to describe the scene, Mr. Poet. . . . Only I would like the torches to be crimson and smoking a great deal, and the bacchantes' eyes must be glittering beneath their garlands, and the garlands should be of a dark color. And don't forget the tigerskins and the goblets . . . and gold, lots of gold."

"But where is the gold to be?" Maidanov asked, throwing back his straight hair and dilating his nostrils.

"Where? On their shoulders, on their arms, on their legs, everywhere. They say that in ancient times the women wore gold bangles round their ankles. The bacchantes call to the girls in the boat to join them. The girls have stopped singing their hymn—they cannot go on with it—but they do not stir. The river carries them to the bank. And now, suddenly, one of them quietly rises. . . . This must be described very well: how she quietly stands up in the moonlight, and how her friends are afraid. . . . She has stepped over the edge of the boat, the bacchantes surround her, they dash off into the night, into the darkness. . . . Here you must decribe the smoke as floating in great billows, and everything is confused. Only their shrieks are to be heard, and her garland is left lying on the bank."

She was silent. ("Oh, she has fallen in love indeed!" I thought again.)

"And is that all?" Maidanov asked.

"Yes," she replied.

"That cannot be the subject for a whole poem," he said seriously. "But I shall make use of your idea in a lyric."

"In the romantic genre?" Malevsky asked.

"Of course, in the romantic genre, the Byronic."

"But in my view Hugo is better than Byron," the young Count said with a negligent air. "He is more interesting."

"Hugo is a first-class writer," Maidanov retorted, "and my friend Tonkosheev, in his Spanish novel *El Trovador*—'

"Ah, that is the book with the question marks round the wrong way, isn't it?" Zinaida interrupted him.

"Yes, that's the way the Spaniards write it. I was about to say that Tonkosheev—"

"Now you'll start arguing about classicism and romanticism again," Zinaida once more interrupted him. "'I'd rather have a game—"

"Of forfeits?" Lushin broke in.

"No, forfeits are boring; we'll play comparisons." (This was a game she herself had invented; some object was named, and each player tried to compare it with something else, and the prize went to the one who made the best comparison.) She went across to the window. The sun had only just set; long, crimson clouds were floating high in the heavens.

"What are those clouds like?" she asked, and went on without waiting for us to answer: "I think they are like those purple sails on Cleopatra's golden vessel when she sailed to meet Antony. Do you remember, Maidanov? You told me all about it recently."

Like Polonius in *Hamlet*, we all decided that the clouds did remind us of those very sails, and that not one of us could ever think of a better comparison.

"But how old was Antony then?" she asked.

"I'm sure he was a young man," Malevsky remarked.

"Yes, he was young" Maidanov confirmed in a tone of conviction.

"Pardon me!" Lushin exclaimed; "he was over forty."

"Over forty," Zinaida repeated, giving him a swift glance.

I went home soon after. "She's in love," my lips involuntarily whispered. "But with whom?"

12

The days passed. Zinaida grew more and more strange, more and more incomprehensible. One day I went to see her and found her sitting on a rush chair with her head pressed against the sharp edge of the table. She straightened up. . . . All her face was wet with tears.

"Ah! So it's you!" she said with a harsh, sneering smile. "Come here."

I went to her; she laid her hand on my head, suddenly seized my hair, and began to twist it.

"That hurts," I said at last.

"Ah! So it hurts, does it? But doesn't it hurt me? Doesn't it?" she repeated.

"Oh!" she cried out suddenly as she saw that she had torn out a thin strand of hair. "What have I done? Poor M'sieur Voldemar!"

She carefully straightened out the strand of hair, wound it round her finger, and twisted it into a little ring.

"I shall put your hair in a medallion, and I shall wear it," she said, while her eyes glittered with tears. "Perhaps that will comfort you a little. . . . But now good-by."

I returned home, to find an unpleasant situation awaiting me. My mother was having a scene with my father. She was reproaching him with something or other, but he, as usual, was coldly and courteously silent, and not long after, he drove off. I could not catch what my mother was saying, nor was I particularly interested. I remember only that afterward she sent for me to go to her room and talked in a very dissatisfied tone about my visits to the Princess, who, in her words, was *une femme capable de tout*. I kissed her hand (I always did that when I wanted to cut short the conversation) and went to my room. Zinaida's tears had baffled me completely. I simply did not know what to make of it all, and I, too, was ready to cry: after all, I was a child, despite my sixteen years. Now I no longer thought of Malevsky, though Bolovzorov grew more and more threatening every day and looked at the shifty Count like a wolf at a sheep. Indeed, I did not think of anything or anybody. I was lost in conjecture, and was always going off to lonely spots. I grew especially fond of the conservatory. I would climb up to the top of the high wall, would sit down, and go on sitting there, such an unhappy, lonely, and sorrowful lad that I began to feel sorry for myself. And how comforting did I find those mournful feelings, how I reveled in them!

Well, one day, as I was sitting on the wall, gazing into the distance and listening to the church bells, suddenly something passed over me . . . like a little breeze; not a shiver, but literally a waft, literally a sensation that someone was in the vicinity. . . . I looked down. Below me Zinaida was hurriedly walking along the road; she was in a gray dress and had a rose-colored parasol over her shoulder. She saw me, halted, and throwing back the brim of her straw hat, raised her velvety eyes to me.

"What are you doing up there, so high?" she asked me with a strange smile. "Listen! You're always declaring that you love me; jump down here to me, if you really do love me."

She hardly had time to say the words before I flew down just as though someone had pushed me in the back. The wall was about fourteen feet high. I reached the ground on my feet, but the drop was so great that I could not keep my balance: I fell and lost consciousness for a moment. When I came to, without opening my eyes I felt that Zinaida was kneeling beside me. "My dear boy," she said as she bent over me, and an anxious tenderness sounded in her voice; "what made you do that, what made you do as I told you? . . . You see, I love you. . . . Get up."

Her breast rose and fell beside me, her hands touched my head, and suddenly—ah,what happened to me then!—her soft, fresh lips began to cover all my face wtih kisses . . . they touched my lips. . . . But then she must have guessed by the expression of my face that I had come round, though I had not opened my eyes, for, swiftly rising, she said: "Now get up, you madcap, you stupid! What are you lying in the dust for?" I got up. "Hand me my parasol," she said; "I dropped it somewhere. And don't stare at me like that. . . . What a stupid thing to do! You haven't hurt yourself, have you? I expect you've stung yourself in the nettles. Don't stare at me, I tell you. Oh, he doesn't understand a thing, he doesn't say a word," she added, as though to herself. "Go home, M'sieur Voldemar, and brush yourself off, and don't dare to follow me or I'll be angry, and then never again—"

She did not finish the sentence and briskly walked away, while I sat up in the road. My legs would not support me. The nettles had stung my hands, my back ached, and my head was swimming, but the feeling of bliss that I experienced at that moment has never visited me again. It was like a pleasant pain in all my limbs, and it was resolved at last in rapturous jumps and exclamations of joy. Truly, I was still a child.

13

I was so gay and proud all that day, I retained the feeling of Zinaida's kisses so vividly on my face, I remembered her every word with such shuddering rapture, I cherished my unexpected happiness so deeply that I began to feel frightened, I did not even wish to see her, the cause of these new sensations. I felt that now I could demand nothing more of fate, that now I ought to "sigh deeply for the last time, and die." On the other hand, when I went to call on the Zasiokins next day, I felt great embarrassment, which I vainly tried to conceal bemeath a modest jauntiness, proper to a man who wishes to indicate that he can keep a secret. Zinaida received me very simply, without any sign of agitation; she only threatened me with her finger and asked whether I had any bruises. All my modest jauntiness and mysterious secrecy vanished in a moment, and with it my embarrassment. Of course, I had not expected anything in particular, but Zinaida's calm was like a douche of cold water. I realized that in her eyes I was a child, and I felt very miserable. She walked backward and forward, smiling swiftly whenever she glanced at me; but her thoughts were far away, I saw that clearly. . . . "Shall I be the first to refer to yesterday?" I thought. "Shall I ask where she was off to in such a hurry, so that I can find out definitely? . . ." But I only dismissed the idea and sat down in a corner.

Belovzorov came in; I was glad to see him.

"I haven't found you a riding-horse, not a quiet one, yet," he began in a harsh tone. "Freitag says he has one, but I'm not sure about it. I'm afraid."

"What are you afraid of?" Zinaida inquired. "May I ask?"

"What am I afraid of? Why, you cannot ride yet. God preserve us from anything happening! And what is this mad idea that has suddenly come into your head?"

"Well, that's my business, M'sieur my animal. In that case I shall ask Piotr Vasilich." (My father's name was Piotr Vasilich, and I was surprised to hear her mention his name so lightly and easily, as though she was quite sure of his readiness to serve her.)

"So that's it?" Belovzorov retorted. "So it's with him that you want to go riding?"

"Either with him or with someone else, it makes no difference to you. In any case it won't be with you."

"Won't be with me?" Belovzorov repeated. "As you wish. What of it? I'll get you a horse."

"Only, listen, I don't want any old nag. I warn you that I want to gallop."

"Gallop by all means. But whom are you going to ride with? Malevsky, by any chance?"

"And why not, warrior knight? Now calm down," she added, "and don't flash your eyes. I'll take you with me too. You know what I think about Malevsky now—pooh!" She shook her head.

"You say that just to console me," he snorted.

Zinaida half closed her eyes. "Does it console you, then? Oh, oh, oh, you warrior!" she said at last, as though she could not think of anything else to call him. "And what about you, M'sieur Voldemar? Would you go riding with us?"

"I'm not fond of riding—with lots of other people," I muttered without raising my eyes.

"So you prefer it to be tête-à-tête? Well, the free has his choice, the saved has—paradise," she said, sighing. "Go and see what you can do, Belovzorov. I need a horse for tomorrow."

"All very well, but where are we to get the money?" her mother intervened.

Zinaida knitted her brows.

"I shan't ask you for it. Belovzorov will give me credit."

"He will, he certainly will," the Princess replied, and suddenly shouted at the top of her voice: "Dunia!"

"*Maman*, I have given you a bell to ring," Zinaida observed.

"Dunia!" the old woman called again.

Belovzorov took his leave; I went with him. Zinaida did not detain me.

14

Next morning I rose early, cut myself a stick, and went for a walk out beyond the city turnpike. I thought I would walk off my misery. The day was beautiful, bright, and not too hot; a cheerful, fresh breeze was roving over the earth, and it blew and played gently, stirring everything and disturbing nothing. I wandered a long time over the hills, through the forest; I did not feel happy—I had left home with the intention of giving myself over to dejection; but my youth, the fine weather, the fresh air, the pleasure of the swift walk, the delight of lying alone on the thick grass, all had their way: the memory of those unforgettable words, of those kisses, again forced itself upon my soul. It was pleasant to think that at all events Zinaida would have to admit my resolution, my heroism. . . . "She may find others better than I," I thought, "and let her! On the other hand, others only say they'll do a thing, but I do it. And what else couldn't I do for her!" My imagination began to run riot. I imagined how I would save her from the hands of enemies, how, all streaming with blood, I would wrest her from a dungeon, how I would die at her feet. I remembered a picture that hung in our reception room; it depicted Maleque Adèle carrying off Mathilde[1] . . . and at that very moment my attention was distracted by the sight of a great spotted woodpecker, which fussily climbed the slender trunk of a birch and peered anxiously out from behind it, first to the right, then to the left, like a musician from behind the neck of his double-bass.

[1]The hero and heroine of *Mathilde*, by the French woman novelist Marie Cottin (1770-1807).

Then I began to sing: "Not white are the snows," and went on to a ballad well known at that time, "I wait for thee, whenas the playful zephyr"; then I began to declaim Yermak's apostrophe to the stars, from Khomyakov's tragedy of the same name; I would have tried my hand at writing something in a sentimental style, I even thought of the line that was to end the poem: "O Zinaida, Zinaida!" But nothing came of it. Meanwhile the dinner hour was approaching. I dropped down into a valley; a narrow, sandy path wound along it in the direction of the city. I followed this path. . . . The hollow drumming of horse-hoofs sounded behind me. I looked round, involuntarily halted, and removed my cap: my father and Zinaida were riding toward me, side by side. My father was saying something to her, leaning all his body across and resting his hand on her horse's neck. He was smiling. Zinaida was listening to him without speaking, her eyes strictly cast down and her lips compressed. At first I saw no one else, but some moments later Belovzorov appeared round a bend in the valley; he was in his hussar uniform, with a pelisse, and was riding a foaming black horse. The good horse shook its head, snorted, and fretted; the rider was continually reining it in and spurring it on. I stepped aside. My father gathered up his reins and drew away from Zinaida; she slowly raised her eyes to him, and they both set off at a gallop. . . . Belovzorov tore after them, his saber clattering. "He's as crimson as a lobster," I thought. "And she—why is she so pale? They've been riding all the morning, and yet she's pale."

I hastened my steps and arrived home just before dinnertime. My father, who had washed and changed his clothes, was already sitting by my mother's chair and reading a *feuilleton* from the *Journal des débats* to her in his even, musical voice. But my mother was only half listening; when she saw me, she asked me where I had been all day, and added that she did not like people going off God knows where and God knows with whom. I felt like replying: "I have been for a walk by myself"; but I looked at my father, and for some reason I kept silent.

15

During the next five or six days I hardly saw Zinaida at all; she pleaded that she was unwell, which, however, did not prevent the usual visitors from reporting for duty, as they themselves put it—all except Maidanov, who grew depressed and bored as soon as he had no chance to rhapsodize. Belovzorov sat moodily in a corner, red of face, his coat tightly buttoned up. An unpleasant smile roved continually over Count Malevsky's thin features. The Count certainly had fallen out of favor with Zinaida and now waited diligently on the old Princess, even driving with her in a hired carriage to see the Governor General. This journey proved a failure, however, and even led to some unpleasantness for Malevsky; they reminded him of some incident or other in which he had been involved with road engineers, and he had to plead in his justification that at that time he was lacking in experience. Lushin called a couple of times every day, but did not remain long. I was a little afraid of him after our last talk, but at the same time I was genuinely drawn toward him. One day he went for a walk with me in the Nieskuchny Gardens; he was very good-natured and amiable, told me the names and properties of various herbs and flowers, and suddenly went off at a tangent and exclaimed, striking himself on the forehead: "But I, fool that I am, thought she was a flirt! Evidently it is pleasant to sacrifice oneself for others!"

"What are you trying to convey?" I asked him.

"I'm not trying to convey anything to *you*," he retorted vehemently.

Zinaida avoided me: my arrival always made an unpleasant impression on her, as I could not help noticing. She involuntarily turned away from me—involuntarily, that was what made it so bitter, what upset me most of all. But there was nothing I could do about it, and I tried to keep out of her sight and watched over her only from a distance, which was not always possible. As before, something incomprehensible was happening to her: her features changed, she changed altogether. One warm, still evening I was particularly struck by the change that had occurred in her. I was siting on a low bench under a spreading elder bush; I was fond of this spot, for from it I could see the window of Zinaida's room. I was sitting there, and above my head amid the darkened foliage a little bird was fidgeting; a gray kitten, arching its back, cautiously stole into the garden, and the first May bugs were buzzing noisily in the air, which was still translucent, though the day was fading. I sat and gazed at the window and waited to see whether it would open. Yes, it did open, and Zinaida appeared at it. She was wearing a white dress, and she herself, her face, her shoulders, her arms, were all as white as a sheet. She stood a long time without stirring and gazed a long time fixedly from under her wrinkled brows. I had not realized that she could look like that. Then she clenched her fists, strongly, very strongly, shook her curls, and, nodding with an air of decision, slammed the window shut again.

Three days later I met her in the garden. I tried to slip away, but she herself stopped me.

"Give me your hand," she said with all her former kindness. "You and I haven't had a talk for a long time."

I glanced at her. Her eyes were beaming mildly, and her face was smiling, as though through a mist.

"Are you still unwell?" I asked her.

"No, it's all past now," she replied as she picked a small red rose. "I'm a little tired, but that will pass too."

"And will you be again as you were before?" I asked.

She raised the rose to her face, and I had the impression that the brilliant color of the petals was reflected in her cheeks. "Have I changed, then?" she asked.

"Yes, you have changed," I replied in a low voice.

"I have been cold to you, I know," she began. "But you shouldn't have taken any notice of it. . . . I could not be otherwise. But why talk about it?"

"You don't want me to love you, that's what it is," I exclaimed moodily in an involuntary outburst.

"You're wrong; do go on loving me, but not as before."

"How, then?"

"We shall be friends, that's how." She held out the rose for me to smell. "Listen; after all, I am much older than you. I could quite well be your aunt, really I could; of if not your aunt, then your elder sister. But you—"

"You regard me as a child," I interrupted her.

"Why, yes, you are a child, but a dear, good, intelligent child whom I love very much. Do you know what? From today I appoint you my page; and you must not forget that pages should never leave their mistresses' side. Here is the token of your new dignity," she added, putting the rose in my buttonhole. "A token of my favor."

"I have had other favors from you in the past," I muttered.

"Ah!" she said, and looked sidelong at me. "What a memory he has! Well, what if I did? I'm just as ready now."

And, bending toward me, she printed a pure, tranquil kiss on my forehead.

I only gazed at her; but she turned away and went toward the house, saying: "Follow me, my page." I followed her, continually in a muse. "Is this gentle and sober-minded girl the same Zinaida whom once I knew?" I thought. "Surely not?" Even her walk seemed more staid, and all her figure more majestic and harmonious.

But my goodness! With what new strength did my love flame up within me!

16

After dinner guests again gathered in the Zasiokins' reception room, and Zinaida came out to join them. All the company was present that had assembled on that first unforgettable evening. Even Nirmatsky dragged himself along. This time Maidanov was the first to arrive; he brought some new verse. We played forfeits again, but now they were lacking in the previous ingenuity, and there was not the former foolery and hubbub; the gypsy element had vanished. Zinaida set a new mood for our gathering. I sat beside her, as was my right as a page. Among other things she suggested that the one who drew a forfeit should tell a dream he had had. But this was not a success. The dreams proved either uninteresting (Belovzorov had dreamed that he fed his horse on carp, and that his mount had a wooden head) or unnatural, invented. . . . Maidanov treated us to a whole novel: it included graveyard vaults, and angels with lyres, and flowers that talked . . . and sounds coming from afar. Zinaida would not let him finish. "Now we have begun to make up stories," she said, "let each of us tell some story, only it must be really made up." It fell to Belovzorov to begin.

The young hussar was disconcerted. "I can't think of anything," he exclaimed.

"What nonsense!" Zinaida rebuked him. "Imagine, for instance, that you are married, and tell us how you would spend the time with your wife. Would you keep her locked in?"

"I would keep her locked in."

"And would you sit with her yourself?"

"Of course I would."

"Excellent. But supposing she got bored with all this and was false to you?"

"I would kill her."

"But supposing she ran away?"

"I would go after her, and I would kill her just the same."

"Yes, but supposing I were your wife, what would you do then?"

He was silent for a moment, then replied: "I would kill myself."

Zinaida laughed. "I see your song isn't a long one."

She herself drew the second forfeit. She gazed up at the ceiling and was lost in thought. "Now listen to what I have made up," she said at last, "Imagine a magnificent palace, a summer night, and a marvelous ball. The ball is being given by the young Queen. Everywhere there is gold, marble, crystal, silk, lights, amber, flowers, incense, all the whims of luxury."

"You're fond of luxury, aren't you?" Lushin interrupted.

"Luxury is beautiful," she retorted. "I am fond of all beautiful things."

"More than fine things?" he asked.

"That is too subtle, and I don't understand it. Don't interrupt me. And so, it is a magnificent ball. There are a large number of guests, they are all young, fine, and brave, they are all madly in love with the Queen."

"But aren't there any women among the guests?" Malevsky asked.

"No—but wait, yes, there are."

"And they're all ugly?"

"They're all charming, but all the men are in love with the Queen. She is tall and graceful . . . she has a small gold diadem on her black hair."

I gazed at Zinaida, and at that moment she seemed so much taller than the rest of us, and such lucid intelligence and such authority beamed from her white forehead, from her knitted brows, that I thought: "You yourself are this Queen."

"They all crowd round her," she continued, "they all make her highly flattering speeches."

"But is she fond of flattery?" Lushin asked.

"How unbearable you are! You're always interrupting. . . . Who doesn't like flattery?"

"Just one last question," Malevsky interposed. "Has the Queen a husband?"

"I hadn't thought about that. No, why should she have a husband?"

"Of course," Malevsky caught her up; "why should she have a husband?"

"*Silence!*" Maidanov, who spoke French badly, exclaimed in French.

"*Merci*," Zinaida said to him. "And so the Queen listens to these speeches, she listens to the music, but her eyes are not on any of her guests. Six windows are open from top to bottom, from ceiling to floor, and beyond them is the dark sky with great stars, and the dark garden with great trees. The Queen is gazing into the garden. There, by the trees, is a fountain; in the dusk it shows up white, and long, very long, like an apparition. Through the talk and the music the Queen hears the quiet splashing of the water; she gazes and thinks: 'All you gentlemen are of noble birth, you are all intelligent, and wealthy, you crowd round me, you treasure my every word, every one of you is ready to die at my feet, I rule over you. . . . But there, by the fountain, by that splashing water, the one I love, the one who rules over me, is standing and waiting for me. He is wearing neither sumptuous attire nor precious gems; no one knows him, but he is waiting for me and is sure that I shall come. And I shall go to him, and there is no power that could halt me when I desire to go to him and remain with him, and to be lost with him there in the darkness of the garden, beneath the rustling of the trees, beneath the splashing of the fountain.' "

She was silent.

"Is this—all made up?" Malevsky asked craftily.

Zinaida did not even look at him.

"But, gentlemen, what would we do," Lushin suddenly asked, "if we were among those guests and knew about that fortunate one by the fountain?"

"Wait, wait!" Zinaida interrupted him. "I myself will tell you what each of you would do. You, Belovzorov, would challenge him to a duel; you, Maidanov, would write an epigram on him. But no, you don't know how to write epigrams; you would write long iambic verse about him, in the manner of Barbier,[1] and you would publish your poem in the *Telegraph*. You, Nirmatsky, would borrow from him. . . . No, you would lend him money at interest. You, Doctor—" She paused. "As for you, I don't know what you would do."

"In my capacity as court physician," he said, "I would advise the Queen not to give balls if she hadn't time for her guests."

"Perhaps you'd be right. But you, Count—"

"And I? Malevsky asked, with his unpleasant smile.

"You would offer him a poisoned sweet."

Malevsky's face twisted a little in a grimace and looked Jewish for a moment, but he immediately burst into a roar of laughter.

"And as for you, Voldemar—" Zinaida continued. "But no more of this; let us play some other game."

"M'sieur Voldemar, in his capacity as the Queen's page, would hold her train as she ran into the garden," Malevsky observed venomously.

I flared up; but Zinaida swiftly laid her hand on my shoulder, rose a little in her seat, and declared in a voice that shook a little: "I have never given Your Excellency any right to be insolent, and so I must ask you to withdraw." She pointed to the door.

"Forgive me, Princess!" Malevsky muttered, turning pale.

"The Princess is right!" Belovzorov exclaimed, and he, too, rose.

[1] Henri Auguste Barbier (1805-1882) French poet known chiefly by his satirical poems *Iambic Verses.*

"By God, I never expected you to take it like that," Malevsky added. "I don't think there was anything of that nature in what I said. . . . It never occurred to me to insult you even in thought. . . . Do pardon me."

Zinaida gave him a cold look and coldly laughed. "If you wish you can remain," she declared with a negligent gesture. "I and M'sieur Voldemar were angry over nothing. You find it pleasant to wound! May you enjoy it!"

"Forgive me!" Malevesky repeated yet again; and I, remembering Zinaida's gesture, thought again that even a real queen could not have pointed an audacious man to the door with greater dignity.

The game of forfeits did not continue for long after this little incident; everybody felt rather awkward, not so much because of what had happened as because of another, not altogether defined, yet oppressive feeling. No one referred to it, but each of us was conscious of it, both in himself and in his neighbor. Maidanov read his poems to us, and Malevsky praised them with exaggerated enthusiasm. "Isn't he anxious to show how kind he is!" Lushin whispered to me. We soon broke up. Suddenly Zinaida went into a reverie; the Princess sent in to say that she had a headache; Nirmatsky began to complain of his rheumatism.

I was a long time getting to sleep; I had been impressed by Zinaida's story. "Was she hinting at something, perhaps?" I asked myself. "And at whom, at what was she hinting? And if there really is something to hint at, how is one to decide? . . . No, no, it cannot be that," I whispered, turning over from one hot cheek to the other. But I remembered Zinaida's face as she told her story. I remembered the exclamation that had burst from Lushin in the Nieskuchny Gardens, the sudden changes in her behavior toward me, and I was lost in conjecture. "Who is he?" Those three words seemed to rise before my eyes, outlined in the darkness. I felt as though a low, sinister cloud were hanging over me, and I could feel its pressure and was waiting for it to burst any moment. Of recent times I had grown accustomed to a great deal, I had seen a great deal at the Zasiokins'. Their untidiness, the greasy candle-ends, the broken knives and forks, the glum old Vonifaty, the ragged maidservants, the manners of the old Princess herself—all this terrible existence no longer disturbed me. But I could not get accustomed to what I vaguely surmised was occurring in Zinaida now. "She's an adventuress," my mother had once said of her in my presence. An adventuress: my idol, my divinity! That term burned me, I tried to get away from it by burying myself in the pillow; I was indignant. . . . And at the same time what would I not have agreed to, what would I not have given, if I could have been that fortunate one at the fountain!

The blood began to burn and course through my veins. "The garden . . . the fountain," I thought. "I'll go into the garden." I briskly dressed and slipped out of the house. The night was dark; the trees were only faintly whispering; a gentle cool fell from the sky, the smell of parsley came from the garden. I walked along all the paths; the quiet sound of my footsteps both disconcerted and encouraged me. I halted, waited, and listened to the heavy and rapid beating of my heart. At last I approached the fence and leaned on the thin rail. Suddenly—or did I imagine it?—a woman's figure flitted past a few paces away. I strained my eyes into the darkness, I held my breath. What was that? Did I hear footsteps, or was it again my heart beating? "Who is there?" I stammered almost inaudibly. And what was that? A suppressed laugh? Or the leaves rustling, or a sigh close to my ear? I began to feel afraid. "Who is there?" I repeated still more softly.

The air streamed past me for a moment; a fiery streak glittered over the sky; a star fell: "Zinaida?" I wanted to ask; but the words died on my lips. And suddenly everything grew profoundly still all around me, as often happens in the middle of the night. Even the crickets ceased to chirrup among the trees; only a window was noisily shut somewhere. I went on standing and standing for a moment or two longer, then returned to my room, to my cold bed. I felt a strange agitation, as though I had been to keep an assignation and had been left waiting alone and had passed another's happiness.

17

Next day I saw Zinaida only for a second: she drove off somewhere in a droshky with her mother. On the other hand I saw Lushin, who, by the way, hardly deigned to speak to me, and Malevsky. The young Count smirked and began to talk to me quite pleasantly. Of all the visitors to the Zasiokins' he alone had been able to insinuate himself into our house and to find favor with my mother. My father did not like him and treated him with insulting courtesy.

"Ah, *monsieur le page*!" Malevsky began. "Very glad to meet you. What is your excellent queen doing?"

His fresh, handsome face was so repellent to me at that moment, and he looked at me so contemptuously and playfully, that I made no answer whatever.

"Are you still angry?" he went on. "How absurd! After all, it was not I who called you a page, and pages are usually found in attendance on queens. But allow me to observe that you perform your duties badly."

"Why do I?"

"Pages should be inseparable from their sovereigns; pages should always know what their sovereigns are doing, they should even watch over them"; and he added, lowering his voice: "Day—and night."

"What do you mean?"

"What do I mean? I think I am expressing myself clearly enough. Day—and night. In the daytime it is easy enough; one can see in the daytime and there are people about. But at night—that is the time to expect trouble. I advise you not to sleep at night, but to watch, to watch with all your powers. Remember, in the garden, by the fountain at night—that is where one should be on guard. You'll be grateful to me."

He laughed and turned his back on me. Probably he did not attach any special importance to what he had said: he had the reputation of being fond of mystifying people, and boasted of his ability to take people in at the masquerades—a gift that depended a great deal on the almost unconscious hypocrisy that marked his character. He was only trying to tease me, but every word he said flowed like poison through my veins. The blood rushed to my head. "Ah, so that's it!" I said to myself. "Good! So I did not go into the garden for nothing. But it shall not be!" I exclaimed aloud and beat my breast with my fist, though to tell the truth I had no idea what it was that must not be. "Whether it is Malevsky himself that visits the garden," I thought (possibly he had said too much, and he was capable of such insolence), "or anyone else" (our garden wall was very low, and it was quite easy to climb over it), "it will be a bad lookout for anyone I come across. I don't advise anyone to fall in with me! I shall show all the world and her, the traitress" (so after all I did call her a traitress) "that I can take my revenge!"

I returned to my room, went to my writing-desk and took out a penknife I had recently bought, felt the sharp blades, and, with furrowed brows, with cold and concentrated resolution I thrust it into my pocket, as though such deeds were nothing surprising and my actions nothing new to me. My heart swelled angrily and went numb. I did not relax my displeasure or my compressed lips all that day, and I walked backward and forward with one hand in my pocket, clutching the heated knife and preparing myself for something terrible. These new and unprecedented feelings so greatly occupied and diverted me that, to tell the truth, I thought very little about Zinaida. I was continually thinking of Aleko, the young gypsy: "Whither, my handsome youth?" "Lie down!" And then: "Thou art all spattered with blood; oh, what hast thou done?" . . . "Nothing!" With what a harsh smile did I repeat that word "nothing"! My father was not at home, but my mother, who for some time past had been in a state of almost speechless irritation, noticed my air of doom, and at supper she said to me: "What are you sulking for like a mouse in the groats?" In reply I only smiled at her condescendingly and thought: "If she only knew!" Eleven o'clock struck; I went to my room, but I did not undress. I waited for midnight; at last it, too, struck. "Time!" I whispered between my teeth and, buttoning my coat right up and even rolling up my sleeves, I went out into the garden.

I had already chosen the spot where I would keep guard. At the end of the garden, where the fence separating our domain from that of the Zasiokins' ended in the common wall, grew a single fir; standing beneath its low, thick branches, I could have a good view of all that happened around me, so far as the nocturnal darkness would permit. Here, too, was a little path, which always seemed rather mysterious to me: it crawled like a snake up to the fence, which at this spot showed signs that someone had climbed over it, and led to a circular arbor of dense acacias. I reached the fir, leaned against its trunk, and began to watch.

That night was as still as the night before; but there were fewer clouds in the sky, and I could see the outlines of the bushes, and even the taller flowers, more clearly. Those first few moments of expectation were exhausting, almost frightening. I had not resolved on any step; I only pondered what action I should take. Should I thunder out: "Where are you going? Stop! Confess or die"? Or should I simply strike? Every sound, every rustle and whisper, seemed significant, extraordinary. . . . I made ready. . . . I leaned forward. . . . But half an hour passed; an hour passed; my blood grew still and cool; I began to realize that I was doing all this for nothing, that I was even rather ridiculous, that Malevsky had been making fun of me. I abandoned my ambush and walked right through the garden. As though of intent, not the least sound was to be heard anywhere; everything was at peace; even our dog was asleep, rolled into a ball by the wicket gate. I climbed onto the ruins of the conservatory, and before me I saw the far-stretching plain. I recalled my meeting with Zinaida and was lost in thought.

I started. . . . I thought I heard the creak of a door being opened, then the light crack of a twig snapping. In two bounds I was down from the ruins, and froze still. Swift, light, and cautious steps were clearly to be heard in the garden. They drew near to where I was standing. "Here he comes—here he comes at last!" rushed through my mind. I convulsively drew the knife out of my pocket, convulsively opened it; crimson sparks danced before my eyes, in my fear and anger the hair stirred on my head. The footsteps came straight toward me; I bent down, I strained to meet them. A man appeared. . . . My God! It was my father!

I recognized him at once, though he was wrapped from head to foot in a dark cloak, and his hat was drawn down over his face. He went past me on tiptoe. He did not notice me, though nothing concealed me; but I crouched and cowered so low that I think I must have been level with the ground. The jealous Othello ready to commit murder was suddenly transformed into a schoolboy. I was so frightened by my father's unexpected appearance that at first I did not even notice whence he had come or where he went. Only when everything was again still all around me did I straighten up and wonder: "What is father walking in the garden at night for?" In my fright I had dropped my pocketknife in the grass, but I did not even trouble to look for it: I felt deeply ashamed. I cooled down in a moment. But as I returned home, I went to my bench under the elder bush and glanced at the window of Zinaida's bedroom. The small, slightly convex panes showed as dim blue patches in the feeble light coming from the nocturnal sky. Suddenly their color began to change. Behind them—I saw it, I saw it clearly—the white blind was let down cautiously and quietly, was let down to the windowsill, and remained down, motionless.

"What is all this?" I said aloud, almost involuntarily, when I was back in my room once more. "A dream, chance, or—?" The suppositions that suddenly came to my mind were so new and strange that I did not even dare to give myself over to them.

18

Next morning I woke with a headache. The agitation of the night before had gone. It was replaced by a dull bewilderment and grief that I had never known before, as though something within me had died.

"What are you looking like a rabbit with half its brain extracted for?" Lushin asked me when we met. At breakfast time I took surreptitious glances first at my father, then at my mother. He was calm, as usual, and she, as usual, was secretly irritable. I waited for him to talk to me in his amiable way, as sometimes he did. But he did not even caress me with his everyday, cold caress. "Shall I tell Zinaida everything?" I thought. " . . . After all, it doesn't matter now, it's all over between us." I went to see her, but not only did I not say anything to her about it, I did not even succeed in saying more than a word to her, much as I wished to. Her brother, a twelve-year-old student in a military school, had arrived from Petersburg for a holiday. Zinaida at once placed him in my charge. "Here you are, my dear Volodya" (it was the first time she had used this diminutive), "here is a companion for you. His name is Volodya too. Please be nice to him; he's still shy, but he has a kind heart. Show him the Nieskuchny Gardens, take him for walks, and take him under your protection. You will do that, won't you? You're kind, too." She graciously laid both hands on my shoulders, and I was completely overcome. This boy's arrival turned me also into a boy. I gazed silently at the lad, who stared at me just as speechlessly. Zinaida burst into laughter and pushed us toward each other. "Now give each other a hug, children." We gave each other a hug.

"Would you like me to take you into the garden?" I asked him.

"If you please," he replied in a hoarse, genuinely cadet voice. Zinaida laughed again. I did manage to observe that never before had she had such a charming color in her cheeks. I went off with the cadet.

In our garden was an old swing. I seated him on the thin board and began to give him a swing. He sat very still in his new little uniform of stout cloth, with broad gold lace galloons, and clung tightly to the rope. "But you should unbutton your collar," I said to him. "It's all right, we're used to it," he said, and cleared his throat. He was like his sister; his eyes especially reminded me of her. I enjoyed doing him a kindness, but meanwhile that same corrosive sorrow was gnawing at my heart. "Now indeed I am a child," I thought; "but yesterday—" I remembered where I had dropped my penknife the night before and went and found it. The boy asked me for it, broke off a stout stem of angelica, carved a pipe from it, and began to pipe. Othello whistled a little, too.

But then how he wept, that very same Othello, in Zinaida's arms, when, seeking him out in a corner of the garden that evening, she asked him why he was so sad. My tears poured down so torrentially that she was alarmed. "What's the matter with you, what's the matter, Volodya?" she asked, and as I did not answer and did not stop crying, she made to kiss my wet cheek. But I turned away from her and whispered through my sobs: "I know everything; why did you play with me? . . . What did you need my love for?"

"I have done you wrong, Volodya," she said. "Ah, I have done you great wrong," she said, and clenched her fists. "How much there is in me that is stupid, dark, sinful! . . . But I am not playing with you now; I love you—you don't even suspect why, or how. . . . But all the same—what do you know?"

What could I say to her? She stood before me and looked at me, and I belonged to her wholly, from my head to my feet, the moment she looked at me. . . . Fifteen minutes later I was running races with her and her brother; I was no longer weeping, I was laughing, though my swollen eyelids dropped tears with my laughter; round my neck Zinaida's ribbon was tied instead of a cravat, and I cried out with joy when I succeeded in catching her by the waist. She did just as she liked with me.

19

I should find it difficult if I were made to tell in detail all that happened to me during the week after my unfortunate nocturnal expedition. It was a strange, feverish time, a kind of chaos in which the most contradictory feelings, thoughts, suspicions, hopes, joys, and sufferings eddied like a whirlwind. I grew afraid to look into myself, if a sixteen-year-old boy can look into himself at all; I grew afraid to take stock of anything; I simply hastened to get through the day till the evening. On the other hand, I slept at night—the child's mental levity helped me there. I did not wish to know whether anyone loved me, and did not wish to confess to myself that no one loved me; I avoided my father, but Zinaida I could not avoid. I burned as though on fire in her presence; but what use was there in my knowing the sort of fire in which I burned and melted?—it was bliss for me to melt and burn so pleasantly. I gave myself over entirely to my sensations, and was cunning with myself, turning my back on my memories, and closing my eyes to what I anticipated ahead of me. . . . Without doubt this drain on me would not have continued for long in any case—a thunderclap ended it all with one stroke and flung me into a new path.

Returning toward dinnertime after a long walk one day, I was amazed to learn that I would be dining alone: my father had driven somewhere, and my mother was not well, did not want anything to eat, and had locked herself in her bedroom. By the servants' faces I guessed that something unusual had occurred. I did not dare question them, but I had one friend, the young butler, Philip, a passionate lover of verse and an artist on the guitar, and I spoke to him. He told me there had been a terrible scene between my father and mother (and every word was heard in the maids' room; much of the quarrel was in French, but the maid Masha had lived five years with a sempstress from Paris, and she understood everything). My mother had charged my father with infidelity, with intimacy with the young lady next door; at first my father had denied everything, but then he had flared up and in his turn had said something very harsh, "apparently about their ages," at which my mother had burst into tears. My mother had also made mention of a promissory note of the Princess's that had been accepted, and she had spoken very unpleasntly about her and the young lady too. And then my father had used threats to her. "And all the trouble arose," Philip added, "over an anonymous letter; and no one knows who wrote it. Otherwise there would have been no reason for all this affair to come out at all."

"But really was there anything in it?" I said with difficulty, while my hands and feet turned cold and something began to quiver in the very depths of my breast.

Philip winked meaningly. "There was. You can't keep these things quiet, no matter how careful your father was this time. After all, you have to hire a carriage or something . . . and then you can't manage without the servants."

I sent Philip away and collapsed on my bed. I did not sob, or give way to despair; I did not ask myself when and how all this happened; I was not astonished that I had not already guessed, long since. I did not even rail against my father. What I had learned was beyond my power to bear: this sudden revelation shattered me. It was all over. All my flowers were torn up in one handful and lay around me scattered and trampled.

20

Next day Mother announced that she was going back to town. In the morning my father had gone to her bedroom and had sat alone with her for a long time. No one heard what he said to her, but she did not cry any more; she grew calm, and asked for food—but she did not come downstairs and did not change her decision. I remember I wandered aabout all day; but I did not go into the garden, and did not look once at the Zasiokins' wing. But that evening I was witness of an astonishing incident: my father led Count Malevsky by the arm from the reception room to the lobby and, in our footman's presence, coldly told him: "Several days ago in a certain house Your Excellency was shown the door. I shall not give you any explanation now, but I have the honor to inform you that if you call on me again I shall throw you through the window. I do not like your handwriting." The Count bowed, clenched his teeth, bristled up, and disappeared.

Preparations were put in hand for our return to town, to our house in Arbat Square. In all probability my father himself no longer wished to remain in the country. But evidently he had persuaded Mother not to make a scene; everything was done quietly, unhurriedly; my mother even sent a servant to convey her respects and to express her regret that, as she was not at all well, she would not be seeing the Princess again before our departure. I roamed about as though crazy and only wanted it all to end as soon as possible. One thought never left my head: how could she, a young girl, and a Princess after all, resolve on such conduct, knowing that my father was not free, and when she could have married Belovzorov, for instance? What did she hope for? Why was she not afraid of ruining all her own future? "Yes," I thought, "this is love, this is passion, this is devotion"; and I recalled Lushin's words: to sacrifice oneself for others is sweet. I happened to see a white patch at one of the windows of the wing. "Surely that isn't Zinaida's face?" I thought. . . . Yes, it was her face. I could endure no more. I could not part from her without saying a last good-by to her. I seized a convenient moment and went to her home.

In the reception room the old Princess welcomed me with her usual unpleasant and negligent greeting.

"Why have your people taken flight so soon?" she said, thrusting snuff into both her nostrils. I looked at her and felt relieved. Philip's reference to a "promissory note" had been tormenting me. But she suspected nothing; at least, so it seemed to me then. Zinaida came in from the next room, in a black dress, her face pale, her hair unbound; she silently took me by the hand and led me out of the room.

"I heard your voice and came out at once," she began. "And was it so easy for you to desert us, you wicked boy?"

"I've come to say good-by to you, Princess," I replied, "and probably forever. You have heard that we are going away?"

She gazed at me fixedly.

"Yes, I have heard. Thank you for coming. I had begun to think I would not be seeing you. Don't think badly of me. I tormented you sometimes, but all the same I am not what you imagine me to be."

She turned away and leaned against the window.

"Really I am not. I know you have a bad opinion of me."

"I have?"

"Yes, you have—you have. . . ."

"I have?" I repeated sorrowfully, and my heart began to quiver as of old under the influence of her irresistible, inexpressible enchantment. "I? Believe me, Zinaida Alexandrovna, no matter what you did, no matter how much you tortured me, I would love you and adore you to the end of my days."

She turned swiftly to me and, opening her arms wide, took my head in her hands and impetuously and hotly kissed me. God knows whom that long, farewell kiss was seeking, but I greedily tasted of its sweetness, I knew that it would never be repeated. "Good-by, good-by . . ." I said again.

She tore herself away and went out. And I left the house. I am unable to convey the feeling with which I left. I would never wish it to be repeated, but I would regard myself as unfortunate if I had never known it.

We drove back to town. It took me a long time to cut myself off from the past, it took me a long time to settle down to work. My wound slowly healed; but really there was no bad feeling between my father and me. On the contrary, he seemed to grow even more in my eyes; let psychologists explain this contradiction as they wish. One day as I was walking along the boulevard, to my indescribable joy I ran into Lushin. I liked him for his direct and unhypocritical nature, and, besides, he was dear to me because of the memories he awoke within me. I rushed over to him. "Aha!" he said. "So it's you, young man! Let me have a look at you! You're still rather yellow, but I must say there isn't the former nasty look in your eyes. Now you look like a man, not a lapdog. Well, and what are you doing? Working hard?"

I sighed. I did not want to lie, but I was ashamed to tell the truth.

"Now, don't be afraid," Lushin went on, "don't be shy. The main thing is to live a normal life and not to give yourself over to distractions. For what good will they ever do you? No matter where the wave carries you, it is always bad; but a man may stand on stone so long as he stands on his own feet. I've got a bit of a cough, and Belovzorov—have you heard?

"No, I haven't. What's happened?"

"Vanished without a trace; they say he's gone off to the Caucasus. There's a lesson for you, young man. And all because they're not capable of getting out in time, of breaking the net. But you appear to have escaped without damage. Now see that you don't get caught again. Good-by."

"I shan't be caught again," I thought. "I shall never see her again." But I was fated to see Zinaida once more.

21

My father went riding every day; he had a magnificent roan and sorrel English thoroughbred, untiring and wicked, with a long, slender neck and long legs; he was called Electric. No one but my father could ride him. One day Father came to me in a good humor—a mood I had not known him to be in for a long time. He was intending to go for a ride and was already wearing spurs. I asked him to take me with him.

"We'd do better at a game of leapfrog," he replied. "On your hack you'll never keep up with me."

"Yes I shall; I'll wear spurs too."

"Come on, then."

We set off. I had a little shaggy raven horse, strong in the legs and quite skittish; true, he had to gallop at full speed when Electric was put into a fast trot, but even so I was not left behind. I have never seen another horseman like my father; he sat his horse so beautifully and with such careless ease that it seemed as though the horse beneath him were conscious of it and proud of him. We rode along all the boulevards, and through the Dvichye Fields, jumped several fences (at first I was afraid to jump, but my father felt contempt for timid people, and I ceased to be afraid), rode twice across the River Moskva, and I was just thinking that now we would be returning home, especially as my father himself had noticed that my horse was tired, when suddenly he turned away in the direction of the Crimean Ford and galloped along the bank. I set off after him. Drawing up to a lofty pile of old beams, he swung himself nimbly out of the saddle, ordered me to dismount, and, giving me his horse's reins, said I was to wait for him here by the beams. Then he turned into a narrow lane and was lost to sight. I began to walk up and down along the bank, leading the horses and swearing at Electric, who would keep throwing up or shaking his head, snorting and neighing. And when I halted he dug his hoofs into the earth one after another, squealed, and bit my mount on the neck; in a word, he behaved like a spoilt thoroughbred. My father did not return. An unpleasant dampness rose from the river; a fine rain fell softly and sprinkled tiny dark spots over the idiotic gray beams, which I now found thoroughly boring as I wandered about in their vicinity. I began to feel anxious, but still my father did not return. Some policeman, a Finn, who was all gray too, and had an enormous shako, like a pot, on his head, and was armed wtih a halberd (what was a policeman doing on the bank of the River Moskva, I wondered), came along and, turning his elderly, furrowed face in my direction, asked me:

"What are you doing here with those horses, young sir? Give them to me, I'll hold them."

I did not reply; he asked me for some tobacco. In order to get away from him (moreover, I was on tenterhooks with impatience), I went several paces in the direction my father had taken, then walked along the little lane to its end, turned a corner, and stopped short. In a street some forty paces away, outside the open window of a small wooden house, I saw my father. He was standing with his back to me and leaning his chest against the windowsill. Inside the house, half hidden by the curtain, a woman in a dark dress was sitting, talking to him. The woman was Zinaida.

I was petrified. I confess that I had had not the least expectation of what I saw. My first reaction was to turn and flee. "He will look round," I thought, "and I shall be done for." But a strange feeling, a feeling stronger than curiosity, stronger even than jealousy, stronger than fear, restrained me. I began to watch, I tried to overhear what they were saying. Apparently my father was insisting on something. Zinaida would not agree. I can see her face even now, mournful, serious, beautiful, and with an indescribable impress of devotion, sorrow, love, and a kind of despair—I cannot find another word for it. She spoke in monosyllables, did not raise her eyes, and only smiled, humbly and obstinately. In that smile alone did I recognize my former Zinaida. My father shrugged his shoulders and adjusted the hat on his head: a movement that was always a sign that he was getting impatient. Then I caught the words: "*Vous devez vous separer de cette . . .*" Zinaida drew herself up and stretched out her hand. . . . Suddenly before my eyes, something unbelievable occurred: my father impetuously raised his whip, with which he had been beating the dust out of the edge of his coat, and I heard a sharp blow on that arm bared to the elbow. I could hardly refrain from crying out. But Zinaida shuddered, gazed silently at my father, and slowly raised her arm to her mouth, then kissed the weal that showed livid across it. He threw his whip away and, running hurriedly up the steps of the veranda, burst into the house. Zinaida turned and, stretching out her arms, throwing back her head, also left the window.

My heart sinking with fear, possessed with a bewildered horror, I flung myself back and, running along the lane, all but letting go of Electric, returned to the riverbank. I could make nothing of what I had seen. I knew that my cold and restrained father sometimes had outbreaks of frenzy, yet I could not realize that I had just witnessed such an attack. But I felt at once that no matter how long I lived, it would never be possible for me to forget that movement, that look, that smile of Zinaida's; I felt that her image, this new image that had suddenly been revealed to me, was imprinted forever in my memory. I stared senselessly at the river and did not notice that tears were running from my eyes. "They beat her," I thought; "they beat her . . . beat her. . . ."

"Now what's the matter with you? Give me my horse!" I heard my father's voice behind me.

I mechanically gave him the rein. He sprang into the saddle. The animal was chilled, and he rose on his hind legs and took one bound of a good ten feet. But Father quickly had him under control; he drove the spurs into his flanks and struck him on the neck with his fist. "Pity I haven't got my whip!" he muttered.

I remembered how that same whip had whistled and the blow it had struck, and shuddered.

"What have you done with it?" I asked after a moment.

He did not reply, but galloped on ahead. I overtook him. I simply had to see his face.

"Have you been bored while I was gone?" he asked through set teeth.

"A little. But where have you dropped your whip?" I asked him again.

He gave me a swift look. "I haven't dropped it," he said; "I threw it away." He was lost in thought and his head sank on his breast. And then, for the first and probably for the last time, I saw how much tenderness and regret could be expressed in his stern features.

He galloped on once more, and this time I could not overtake him: I arrived home fifteen minutes after him.

"Now, that is love," I said to myself again as I sat that evening before my writing-desk, which was now beginning to be littered wtih exercise books and primers. "That is passion. How could one help revolting, how could one endure a blow from anyone, least of all from the dearest of all hands! But evidently you can, if you really love. . . . Yet I—I imagined . . ."

The past month had aged me considerably, and even to me my love, with all its agitations and sufferings, seemed something petty, and childish, and miserable by comparison with this other, this unknown something, at which I could hardly surmise and which frightened me, like a strange, handsome, but threatening face that one vainly tries to discern in the dusk.

I dreamed a strange and terrible dream that night. I thought I was entering a low, dark room. . . . My father was standing with a whip in his hand and stamping his feet; Zinaida was huddled in one corner, and there was a crimson line, not on her hand, but on her forehead. . . . And behind them both Belovzorov rose covered with blood, grinning with his white teeth and angrily threatening him.

Two months later I entered the university, and six months afterward my father died of a stroke, in Petersburg, to which city we had recently moved. A few days before his death a letter arrived from Moscow that greatly agitated him. . . . He went to ask my mother for something, and they say he even wept—he, my father! On the very morning of the day he had the stroke he began to write a letter to me in French. "My son," he wrote, "fear woman's love; fear that happiness, that poison. . . ." After his death my mother sent quite a large sum of money to Moscow.

22

Four years passed. I had just left the university and still had no real idea what I intended to do with myself, at what door to knock; for the time being, I was loafing about in idleness. One fine evening I met Maidanov at the theater. He had married and gone into the civil service; but I did not notice any change in him. He still went into raptures just as unnecessarily, and grew depressed just as suddenly.

"Do you know," he said to me, in passing, "Madame Dolskaya is here?"

"Which Madame Dolskaya?"

"Why, have you forgotten? The former Princess Zasiokina, whom we were all in love with, including yourself. Do you remember, in the house you had for the summer near the Nieskuchny Gardens?"

"Has she married Dolsky, then?"

"Yes."

"And she is here, in the theater?"

"No, I mean she's in Petersburg. She arrived a day or two ago. She is planning to abroad."

"What sort of man is her husband?" I asked.

"A spendid fellow, and wealthy. He was a colleague of mine in Moscow. You understand that after that affair—you must know all about it" (he smiled significantly)—"it was not easy for her to make a match; there were consequences. . . . But with her intelligence everything is possible. Go and call on her; she'll be very glad to see you. She has grown even more beautiful."

He gave me Zinaida's address. She was staying in the Hôtel Demuth. Old memories began to quicken within me. . . . I promised myself that I would call on my former "passion" the very next day. But something else came along; a week passsed, then another; and when I did at last go to the Hôtel Demuth and ask for Mme Dolskaya, I learned that she had died four days previously, quite suddenly, in childbirth.

Something seemed to strike at my heart. The thought that I could have seen her and did not see her, and now never would see her—that bitter thought pierced me with all the strength of irresistible reproach. "She's dead!" I repeated, staring stupidly at the porter. I slowly made my way into the street and went, not knowing whither. All the past came back and rose before me in a moment. And so that was how it had been resolved, that was what that young, burning, brilliant life, hurrying and agitated, had striven to achieve! As I thought this, I imagined those dear features, those eyes, those curls, in a narrow box, in the damp underground gloom, here, not far from me, who was still alive, and perhaps only a few paces from my father. . . . I thought all this, I strained my imagination; but meanwhile:

"From indifferent lips I heard news of her death,
And indifferently listened I to it . . ."

the words echoed in my soul. O youth! Youth! There seems to be nothing you cannot do, you would seem to have mastery over all the treasures of the universe, even sorrow is a comfort to you, even grief confers added beauty on your face, you are self-confident and audacious; you say: "I alone am alive, look at me." But with you, too, the days speed past and disappear without trace and without number, and everything within you vanishes, like wax in the sun, like snow. . . . And, maybe, all the secret of your charm consists not in the possibility that you can do anything, but in the possibility of thinking that you can do anything, consists just in the circumstance that you cast to the winds strength that you would not know how to use on anything else, in the circumstance that every one of us seriously regards himself as a spendthrift, seriously assumes that he has every right to say: "Oh, what would I have done if I had not wasted my time in vain!"

So too I. . . . How much I hoped for, how much I expected, what a rich future did I anticipate, even when I had only just carried out the momentarily returning apparition of my first love, accompanying it with a single sigh, a single pang of mourning.

But of all that I hoped, what has come to pass? And now that the evening shadows are already beginning to speed over my life, what is left to me more fresh, more precious than the memory of that swiftly passed, vernal thunder of my morn?

But in vain do I upbraid myself. Even then, in that thoughtless, youthful time, I did not remain deaf to the mournful voice that called to me, the solemn sound that reached me from beyond the grave. I remember, a few days after I had learned of Zinaida's death, I was drawn by my own invincible attraction to be present at the deathbed of a poor old woman who lived in our house. Covered with rags, lying on hard boards, with a sack beneath her head, she died painfully and wretchedly. All her life had been passed in one bitter struggle with everyday need; she had never known joy, she had never tasted the honey of happiness; one would have thought that she could not but rejoice at death, at its freedom, its peace. And yet so long as her decrepit body still resisted, so long as her breast still heaved beneath the icy hand that lay on it, so long as her last strength had not departed from her, that old woman went on crossing herself and whispering: "Lord, forgive me my trespasses. . . ." And only with the last spark of consciousness did the expression of fear and terror of her end fade from her eyes. . . . And I remember that there, beside that poor old woman's deathbed, I suddenly felt afraid for Zinaida; and I wanted to pray for her, for my father . . . and for myself.

GUY DE MAUPASSANT

The MODEL

Translated by H. N. P. Sloman

The little crescent-shaped town of Étretat, with its white cliffs, white shingle and blue sea, was dozing peacefully in the brilliant July sunshine. At the tips of the crescent two arches of rock jutted out into the calm water, the smaller to the north like a dwarf foot, the larger to the south like a giant leg; and beyond it the Needle, tapering upwards from a broad base almost to the height of the cliff, towered skywards.

On the beach along the water's edge a crowd of people were sitting about watching the bathers. The Casino terrace, where another crowd was sitting or strolling along, looked like a flower-bed, with the brightly coloured ladies' dresses and their red and blue silk-embroidered sunshades.

On the promenade at the far end of the terrace there were others enjoying its restful atmosphere, sauntering up and down, far from the chatter of the well-dressed throng.

A young man, Jean Summer, well known as a painter of distinction, was walking beside an invalid chair, in which his young wife was sitting, looking thoroughly miserable. A man-servant was pushing the bath-chair slowly, and the crippled lady was gazing sadly at the brightness of the sky, the cheerful sunlight and the light-hearted crowd.

They neither spoke nor looked at each other.

"Let's stop a minute," said the lady.

They stopped, and the painter sat down on a camp-stool, which the man-servant handed him.

The people passing behind the motionless silent couple looked pityingly at them. Their romance had become a local legend; he had married her, it was said, in spite of her infirmity, touched by her love.

Not far off two young men were sitting on a winch, talking and gazing vacantly out to sea.

"No, it's not true; I know Jean Summer quite well."

"Then why did he ever marry her? She was an invalid at the time, wasn't she?"

"Yes, she was. He married her . . . well, he married her, as a man always does marry, because he was a fool."

"But there must have been some other reason."

"Other reason, my dear man?—there is no other reason. A man is a fool because he is a fool. Besides, as you know, painters specialize in absurd marriages. They nearly always marry a model, who has been somebody else's mistress before—damaged goods in every sense of the word. Why do they do it? Nobody knows. One would have thought that constant association with the type of imbecile we call a model must have sickened them for ever of this kind of female. But not a bit of it. They make them pose, and then they marry them. You ought to read Alphonse Daudet's little book, *Artists' Wives*—a gem of a book, so true to life and so cruel.

"In the case of the couple over there, the accident happened in an unusual way, that was rather tragic. The girl staged a comedy, or rather a melodrama. In fact, she risked everything on a single throw. Was she sincere? Was she in love with Jean? One can never tell in these cases. Who can say how much the element of cruelty and how much that of sincerity ever enters into women's actions? They are always sincere at the moment, but their feelings are always changing. They are passionate, criminal, devoted, heroic or mean, at the bidding of fleeting emotions, of which they are quite unconscious. They are always telling lies, involuntarily, thoughtlessly, automatically; and with all this, and in spite of all this, they have an absolute honesty of emotion and sentiment; they show this by decisions which are violent, unexpected, incomprehensible, irrational, which defeat all our reasoning, our habits of caution and all our selfish calculations. Owing to the unexpectedness and suddenness of their determinations they always remain indecipherable riddles to us men. We are always asking ourselves: Are they sincere, or are they acting a part?

"My dear fellow, they are sincere and insincere at one and the same time, because it is part of their nature to be both to the highest degree and yet to be neither.

"Think of the means the best of them adopt to attain their ends from us. These means are at once complicated and simple. So complicated that we never guess them in advance, and yet so simple that, after falling into the trap, we can't help being surprised at ourselves and saying: 'Well, did she really fool me as easily as that?'

"And they always get their own way, old man, especially when they want to get married.

"But, anyway, this is Summer's story.

"The girl was a model, of course; she used to pose for him. She was pretty and, even more, she was smart, and she had a divine figure according to all accounts. He fell in love with her, as a man always falls in love with any attractive woman whom he sees a lot of. He imagined he really loved her. It is a curious phenomenon. As soon as a man wants a woman, he is genuinely convinced that he will never be able to do without her for the rest of his natural life. He is fully aware that the same thing has happened to him before and that, when desire is satisfied, disgust ensues; he knows that, in order to spend one's whole life with another human being, it is not the transient passion of the primitive animal that is needed, but a kinship of soul, temperament and feeling. He must be able to distinguish, in the midst of the attraction he feels, whether it is the result of purely physical factors, a kind of intoxication of the senses, or of the deeper union of minds.

"Anyhow, he convinced himself that he did love her; he vowed eternal fidelity a hundred times over and never looked at any other woman.

"She was genuinely attractive, for she had that gift of superficial smartness which comes so easily to many Paris girls. She babbled and chattered and said foolish things that seemed witty by the amusing way she said them. She was never at a loss for a graceful pose, well calculated to please a painter's eye. Whenever she raised her arm or bent down or got into a carriage or shook hands, her every movement was perfectly timed and just right.

"For three months Jean didn't realize that at bottom she was just like all other models.

"They rented a small house at Andressy for the summer.

"I was there one evening, when the first doubts began to force themselves into my friend's consciousness.

"It was a gorgeous night, and we decided to take a stroll along the river. The moonlight was dancing on the shimmering water, its reflection broken up into golden spangles by the eddies and currents of the broad, sluggish stream.

"We were walking along the banks, slightly intoxicated by the vague feeling of happiness that often comes over one on a perfect evening like this. We felt as though we could perform superhuman feats and fall in love with the fictitious creations of our own poetical imagination; we were oddly aware of the stirring of strange emotions, longings and aspirations. We were silent, thrilled by the calm exhilarating freshness of this perfect night, and the cool moonlight seemed to go right through us, penetrating the body and drowning the soul in a scented bath of contentment. Suddenly Joséphine—that's her name—uttered a cry:

" 'Oh! did you see that big fish jump over there?'

"He answered without looking or taking in her words:

" 'Yes, darling.'

"She lost her temper:

" 'No, you didn't; your back was turned.'

"He smiled:

" 'Yes, you're quite right; it's such a lovely night that I'm not thinking of anything at all.'

"She said no more; but a minute later she felt the need to talk and asked:

" 'Are you going to Paris to-morrow?'

"He declared:

" 'I don't know.'

"She got annoyed again:

" 'I suppose you think it's amusing to go for a walk and never say a word. People who aren't half-wits talk.'

"He made no answer. Then, realizing, with a woman's perverse intuition, that it would exasperate him, she began singing that irritating song that has been dinned into our ears, insulting our intelligence, for the last two years:

'I was gazing at the sky.'

"He murmured:

" 'Do be quiet!'

"She retorted angrily:

" 'Why should I be quiet?'

"He replied:

" 'You're spoiling the evening for us.'

"Then occurred the inevitable scene, the hateful silly scene, with unpremeditated reproaches and tactless recriminations, and then tears; they ran through the whole gamut. At last they went home; he had let her run on without interruption, mesmerized by the beauty of the night and overwhelmed by the storm of her senseless reproaches.

"Three months later he was struggling desperately in the grip of the unbreakable, invisible bonds that such an association weaves round us. She used her emotional hold over him to dominate him and make his whole life a misery. The quarrelled morning to night, abused each other and fought.

"Finally he made up his mind to end it all and break away. He sold all his canvases, borrowed money from his friends, raised twenty thousand francs—he had not made his name then—and left them on the chimney-piece with a farewell letter.

"He sought refuge in my house.

"About three o'clock that afternoon there was a ring at the bell; I went and opened the door. A woman faced me, pushed me aside and forced her way into my studio; it was Joséphine.

"He got up as she entered the room.

"She threw the letter with the bank-notes at his feet with a gesture of no little dignity and said curtly:

" 'There's your money; I don't want it.'

"She was trembling and very pale, in a state when she might do anything. As for him, I saw him turn pale too, pale with anger and exasperation, which might easily lead to violence.

"He asked:

" 'What do you want?'

"She replied:

" 'I don't want to be treated like a harlot. You wanted me and you had your will. I asked nothing from you; now you can't cast me off.'

"He stamped his foot:

" 'No, this is too much. If you think you're going to . . .'

"I had seized his arm:

" 'Don't say anything more, Jean; leave it to me.'

"I went up to her and gently, gradually, I talked reason to her, using all the stock arguments that one can employ in such a case. She listened to me motionless, staring in front of her, silent and obstinate.

"At last, having said everything I could and seeing no hope of a happy ending to the scene, I thought of a last argument. I declared:

" 'He still loves you, my dear; but his family want him to marry; you see what I mean.'

"She started:

" 'Ah! I see now . . .' And, turning to him, she went on: 'You're going . . . you're going to marry?'

"He answered bluntly:

" 'Yes.'

"She took a step forward:

" 'If you marry, I shall kill myself . . . you understand that.'

"He shrugged his shoulders:

" 'Very well—kill yourself.'

" 'You say . . . you say . . . say that again.'

"He repeated:

" 'Well, kill yourself, if you want to.'

"She went on, alarmingly pale:

" 'Don't think I don't mean it; I'll throw myself out of the window.'

"He began to laugh, went to the window, opened it and, like a man bowing a guest out of a room, said politely:

" 'This way—after you!'

"She stared at him for a moment with the light of madness in her eyes; then, taking a run as if she were going to jump over a hedge in a field, she dashed past both of us and, clearing the balcony railing, disappeared from sight.

"I shall never forget the effect of that open window on me, when I saw the falling body pass across it; it suddenly looked as wide as the sky and as empty as space. I instinctively shrank back, afraid to look down, as if I should fall out myself.

"Jean stood motionless in a daze.

"The poor girl was carried in with both legs broken; she would never walk again. Her lover, mad with remorse, and perhaps, too, feeling that he owed it to her, took her back and married her.

"Well, that's the story, old man."

It was getting dark. The girl, feeling chilly, wanted to go home, and the servant began to push the bath-chair towards the village. The painter walked by his wife's side; they had not said a word to each other for an hour.

F. SCOTT FITZGERALD

The ICE PALACE

The sunlight dripped over the house like golden paint over an art jar, and the freckling shadows here and there only intensified the rigor of the bath of light. The Butterworth and Larkin houses flanking were intrenched behind great stodgy trees; only the Happer house took the full sun, and all day long faced the dusty road-street with a tolerant kindly patience. This was the city of Tarleton in southernmost Georgia, September afternoon.

Up in her bedroom window Sally Carrol Happer rested her nineteen-year-old chin on a fifty-two-year-old sill and watched Clark Darrow's ancient Ford turn the corner. The car was hot—being partly metallic it retained all the heat it absorbed or evolved—and Clark Darrow sitting bolt upright at the wheel wore a pained, strained expression as though he considered himself a spare part, and rather likely to break. He laboriously crossed two dust ruts, the wheels squeeking indignantly at the encounter, and then with a terrifying expression he gave the steering-gear a final wrench and deposited self and car approximately in front of the Happer steps. There was a plaintive heaving sound, a death-rattle, followed by a short silence; and then the air was rent by a startling whistle.

Sally Carrol gazed down sleepily. She started to yawn, but finding this quite impossible unless she raised her chin from the window-sill, changed her mind and continued silently to regard the car, whose owner sat brilliantly if perfunctorily at attention as he waited for an answer to his signal. After a moment the whistle once more split the dusty air.

"Good mawnin'."

With difficulty Clark twisted his tall body round and bent a distorted glance on the window.

"'Tain't mawnin', Sally Caroll"

"Isn't it, sure enough?"

"What you doin'?"

"Eatin' 'n apple."

"Come on go swimmin'—want to?"

"Reckon so."

"How 'bout hurryin' up?"

"Sure enough."

Sally Carrol sighed voluminously and raised herself with profound inertia from the floor, where she had been occupied in alternately destroying parts of a green apple and painting paper dolls for her younger sister. She approached a mirror, regarded her expression with a pleased and pleasant languor, dabbed two spots of rouge on her lips and a grain of powder on her nose, and covered her bobbed corn-colored hair with a rose-littered sunbonnet. Then she kicked over the painting water, said, "Oh, damn!"—but let it lay—and left the room.

"How you, Clark?" she inquired a minute later as she slipped nimbly over the side of the car.

"Mighty fine, Sally Carrol."

"Where we go swimmin'?"

"Out to Walley's Pool. Told Marylyn we'd call by an' get her an' Joe Ewing."

Clark was dark and lean, and when on foot was rather inclined to stoop. His eyes were ominous and his expression somewhat petulant except when startlingly illuminated by one of his frequent smiles. Clark had "a income"—just enough to keep himself in ease and his car in gasoline—and he had spent the two years since he graduated from Georgia Tech in dozing round the lazy streets of his home town, discussing how he could best invest his capital for an immediate fortune.

Hanging round he found not at all difficult; a crowd of little girls had grown up beautifully, the amazing Sally Carrol foremost among them; and they enjoyed being swum with and danced with and made love to in the flower-filled summery evenings—and they all liked Clark immensely. When feminine company palled there were half a dozen other youths who were always just about to do something, and meanwhile were quite willing to join him in a few holes of golf, or a game of billiards, or the consumption of a quart of "hard yella licker." Every once in a while one of these contemporaries made a farewell round of calls before going up to New York or Philadelphia or Pittsburgh to go into business, but mostly they just stayed round in this languid paradise of dreamy skies and firefly evenings and noisy niggery street fairs—and especially of gracious, soft-voiced girls, who were brought up on memories instead of money.

The Ford having been excited into a sort of restless resentful life Clark and Sally Carrol rolled and rattled down Valley Avenue into Jefferson Street, where the dust road became a pavement; along opiate Millicent Place, where there were half a dozen prosperous, substantial mansions; and on into the down-town section. Driving was perilous here, for it was shopping time; the population idled casually across the streets and a drove of low-moaning oxen were being urged along in front of a placid street-car; even the shops seemed only yawning their doors and blinking their windows in the sunshine before retiring into a state of utter and finite coma.

"Sally Carrol," said Clark suddenly, "it a fact that you're engaged?"

She looked at him quickly.

"Where'd you hear that?"

"Sure enough, you engaged?"

" 'At's a nice question!"

"Girl told me you were engaged to a Yankee you met up in Asheville last summer."

Sally Carrol sighed.

"Never saw such an old town for rumors."

"Don't marry a Yankee, Sally Carrol. We need you round here." Sally Carrol was silent a moment.

"Clark," she demanded suddenly, "who on earth shall I marry?"

"I offer my services."

"Honey, you couldn't support a wife," she answered cheerfully. "Anyway, I know you too well to fall in love with you."

" 'At doesn't mean you ought to marry a Yankee," he persisted.

"S'pose I love him?"

He shook his head.

"You couldn't. He'd be a lot different from us, every way."

He broke off as he halted the car in front of a rambling, dilapidated house. Marylyn Wade and Joe Ewing appeared in the doorway.

" 'Lo, Sally Carrol."

"Hi!"

"How you-all?"

"Sally Carrol," demanded Marylyn as they started off again, "you engaged?"

"Lawdy, where'd all this start? Can't I look at a man 'thout everybody in town engagin' me to him?"

Clark stared straight in front of him at a bolt on the clattering windshield.

"Sally Carrol," he said with a curious intensity, "don't you like us?"

"What?"

"Us down here?"

"Why, Clark, you know I do. I adore all you boys."

"Then why you gettin' engaged to a Yankee?"

"Clark, I don't know. I'm not sure what I'll do, but—well, I want to go places and see people. I want my mind to grow. I want to live where things happen on a big scale."

"What you mean?"

"Oh, Clark, I love you, and I love Joe here, and Ben Arrot, and you-all, but you'll—you'll——"

"We'll all be failures?"

"Yes. I don't mean only money failures, but just sort of—of ineffectual and sad, and—oh, how can I tell you?"

"You mean because we stay here in Tarleton?"

"Yes, Clark; and because you like it and never want to change things or think or go ahead."

He nodded and she reached over and pressed his hand.

"Clark," she said softly, "I wouldn't change you for the world. You're sweet the way you are. The things that'll make you fail I'll love always—the living in the past, the lazy days and nights you have, and all your carelessness and generosity."

"But you're goin'away?"

"Yes—because I couldn't ever marry you. You've a place in my heart no one else ever could have, but tied down here I'd get restless. I'd feel I was—wastin' myself. There's two sides to me, you see. There's the sleepy old side you love; an' there's a sort of energy—the feelin' that makes me do wild things. That's the part of me that may be useful somewhere, that'll last when I'm not beautiful any more."

She broke off with characteristic suddenness and sighed, "Oh, sweet cooky!" as her mood changed.

Half closing her eyes and tipping back her head till it rested on the seat-back she let the savory breeze fan her eyes and ripple the fluffy curls of her bobbed hair. They were in the country now, hurrying between tangled growths of bright-green coppice and grass and tall trees that sent sprays of foliage to hang a cool welcome over the road. Here and there they passed a battered Negro cabin, its oldest white-haired inhabitant smoking a corncob pipe beside the door, and half a dozen scantily clothed pickaninnies parading tattered dolls on the wild-grown grass in front. Farther out were lazy cotton-fields, where even the workers seemed intangible shadows lent by the sun to the earth, not for toil, but to while away some age-old tradition in the golden September fields. And round the drowsy picturesqueness, over the trees and shacks and muddy rivers, flowed the heat, never hostile, only comforting, like a great warm nourishing bosom for the infant earth.

"Sally Carrol, we're here!"

"Poor chile's soun' asleep."

"Honey, you dead at last outa sheer laziness?"

"Water, Sally Carrol! Cool water waitin' for you!"

Her eyes opened sleepily.

"Hi!" she murmured, smiling.

2

In November Harry Bellamy, tall, broad, and brisk, came down from his Northern city to spend four days. His intention was to settle a matter that had been hanging fire since he and Sally Carrol had met in Asheville, North Carolina, in midsummer. The settlement took only a quiet afternoon and an evening in front of a glowing open fire, for Harry Bellamy had everything she wanted; and, besides, she loved him—loved him with that side of her she kept especially for loving. Sally Carrol had several rather clearly defined sides.

On his last afternoon they walked, and she found their steps tending half-unconsciously toward one of her favorite haunts, the cemetery. When it came in sight, gray-white and golden-green under the cheerful late sun, she paused, irresolute, by the iron gate.

"Are you mournful by nature, Harry?" she asked with a faint smile.

"Mournful? Not I."

"Then let's go in here. It depresses some folks, but I like it."

They passed through the gateway and followed a path that led through a wavy valley of graves—dusty-gray and mouldy for the fifties; quaintly carved with flowers and jars for the seventies; ornate and hideous for the nineties, with fat marble cherubs lying in sodden sleep on stone pillows, and great impossible growths of nameless granite flowers. Occasionally they saw a kneeling figure with tributary flowers, but over most of the graves lay silence and withered leaves with only the fragrance that their own shadowy memories could waken in living minds.

They reached the top of a hill where they were fronted by a tall, round head-stone, freckled with dark spots of damp and half grown over with vines.

"Margery Lee," she read; "1844-1873. Wasn't she nice? She died when she was twenty-nine. Dear Margery Lee," she added softly. "Can't you see her, Harry?"

"Yes, Sally Carrol."

He felt a little hand insert itself into his.

"She was dark, I think; and she always wore her hair with a ribbon in it, and gorgeous hoop-skirts of alice blue and old rose."

"Yes."

"Oh, she was sweet, Harry! And she was the sort of girl born to stand on a wide, pillared porch and welcome folks in. I think perhaps a lot of men went away to war meanin' to come back to her; but maybe none of 'em ever did."

He stooped down close to the stone, hunting for any record of marriage.

"There's nothing here to show."

"Of course not. How could there be anything there better than just 'Margery Lee,' and that eloquent date?"

She drew close to him and an unexpected lump came into his throat as her yellow hair brushed his cheek.

"You see how she was, don't you, Harry?"

"I see," he agreed gently. "I see through your precious eyes. You're beautiful now, so I know she must have been."

Silent and close they stood, and he could feel her shoulders trembling a little. An ambling breeze swept up the hill and stirred the brim of her floppidy hat.

"Let's go down there!"

She was pointing to a flat stretch on the other side of the hill where along the green turf were a thousand grayish-white crosses stretching in endless, ordered rows like the stacked arms of a battalion.

"Those are the Confederate dead," said Sally Carrol simply.

They walked along and read the inscriptions, always only a name and a date, sometimes quite indecipherable.

"The last row is the saddest—see, 'way over there. Every cross has just a date on it, and the word 'Unknown.' "

She looked at him and her eyes brimmed with tears.

"I can't tell you how real it is to me, darling—if you don't know."

"How you feel about it is beautiful to me."

"No, no, it's not me, it's them—that old time that I've tried to have live in me. These were just men, unimportant evidently or they wouldn't have been 'unknown'; but they died for the most beautiful thing in the world—the dead South. You see," she continued, her voice still husky, her eyes glistening with tears, "people have these dreams they fasten onto things, and I've always grown up with that dream. It was so easy because it was all dead and there weren't any disillusions comin' to me. I've tried in a way to live up to those past standards of noblesse oblige—there's just the last remnants of it, you know, like the roses of an old garden dying all round us—streaks of strange courtliness and chivalry in some of these boys an' stories I used to hear from a Confederate soldier who lived next door, and a few old darkies. Oh, Harry, there was something, there was something! I couldn't ever make you understand, but it was there."

"I understand," he assured her again quietly.

Sally Carrol smiled and dried her eyes on the tip of a handkerchief protruding from her breast pocket.

"You don't feel depressed, do you, lover? Even when I cry I'm happy here, and I get a sort of strength from it"

Hand in hand they turned and walked slowly away. Finding soft grass she drew him down to a seat beside her with their backs against the remnants of a low broken wall.

"Wish those three old women would clear out," he complained. "I want to kiss you, Sally Carrol."

"Me, too."

They waited impatiently for the three bent figures to move off, and then she kissed him until the sky seemed to fade out and all her smiles and tears to vanish in an ecstasy of eternal seconds.

Afterward they walked slowly back together, while on the corners twilight played at somnolent black-and-white checkers with the end of day.

"You'll be up about mid-January," he said, "and you've got to stay a month at least. It'll be slick. There's a winter carnival on, and if you've never really seen snow it'll be like fairy-land to you. There'll be skating and skiing and tobogganing and sleigh-riding, and all sorts of torchlight parades on snow-shoes. They haven't had one for years, so they're going to make it a knock-out."

"Will I be cold, Harry?" she asked suddenly.

"You certainly won't. You may freeze your nose, but you won't be shivery cold. It's hard and dry, you know."

"I guess I'm a summer child. I don't like any cold I've ever seen."

She broke off and they were both silent for a minute.

"Sally Carrol," he said very slowly, "what do you say to—March?"

"I say I love you."

"March?"

"March, Harry."

3

All night in the Pullman it was very cold. She rang for the porter to ask for another blanket, and when he couldn't give her one she tried vainly, by squeezing down into the bottom of her berth and doubling back the bedclothes, to snatch a few hours sleep. She wanted to look her best in the morning.

She rose at six and sliding uncomfortably into her clothes stumbled up to the diner for a cup of coffee. The snow had filtered into the vestibules and covered the floor with a slippery coating. It was intriguing, this cold, it crept in everywhere. Her breath was quite visible and she blew into the air with a naïve enjoyment. Seated in the diner she stared out the window at white hills and valleys and scattered pines whose every branch was a green platter for a cold feast of snow. Sometimes a solitary farmhouse would fly by, ugly and bleak and lone on the white waste; and with each one she had an instant of chill compassion for the souls shut in there waiting for spring.

As she left the diner and swayed back into the Pullman she experienced a surging rush of energy and wondered if she was feeling the bracing air of which Harry had spoken. This was the North, the North—her land now!

"Then blow, ye winds, heigho!
A-roving I will go,"

she chanted exultantly to herself.

"What's 'at?" inquired the porter politely.

"I said: 'Brush me off.' "

The long wires of the telegraph-poles doubled; two tracks ran up beside the train—three—four; came a succession of white-roofed houses, a glimpse of a trolley-car with frosted windows, streets—more streets—the city.

She stood for a dazed moment in the frosty station before she saw three fur-bundled figures descending upon her.

"There she is!"

"Oh, Sally Carrol!"

Sally Carrol dropped her bag.

"Hi!"

A faintly familiar icy-cold face kissed her, and then she was in a group of faces all apparently emitting great clouds of heavy smoke; she was shaking hands. There were Gordon, a short, eager man of thirty who looked like an amateur knocked-about model for Harry, and his wife, Myra, a listless lady with flaxen hair under a fur automobile cap. Almost immediately Sally Carrol thought of her as vaguely Scandinavian. A cheerful chauffeur adopted her bag, and amid ricochets of half-phrases, exclamations, and perfunctory listless "my dears" from Myra, they swept each other from the station.

Then they were in s sedan bound through a crooked succession of snowy streets where dozens of little boys were hitching sleds behind grocery wagons and automobiles.

"Oh," cried Sally Carrol, "I want to do that! Can we, Harry?"

"That's for kids. But we might——"

"It looks like such a circus!" she said regretfully.

Home was a rambling frame house set on a white lap of snow, and there she met a big, gray-haired man of whom she approved, and a lady who was like an egg, and who kissed her—these were Harry's parents. There was a breathless indescribable hour crammed full of half-sentences, hot water, bacon and eggs and confusion; and after that she was alone with Harry in the library, asking him if she dared smoke.

It was a large room with a Madonna over the fireplace and rows upon rows of books in covers of light gold and dark gold and shiny red. All the chairs had little lace squares where one's head should rest, the couch was just comfortable, the books looked as if they had been read—some—and Sally Carrol had an instantaneous vision of the battered old library at home, with her father's huge medical books, and the oil-paintings of her three great-uncles, and the old couch that had been mended up for forty-five years and was still luxurious to dream in. This room struck her as being neither attractive nor particularly otherwise. It was simply a room with a lot of fairly expensive things in it that all looked about fifteen years old.

"What do you think of it up here?" demanded Harry eagerly. "Does it surprise you? Is it what you expected, I mean?"

"You are, Harry," she said quietly, and reached out her arms to him.

But after a brief kiss he seemed anxious to extort enthusiasm from her.

"The town, I mean. Do you like it? Can you feel the pep in the air?"

"Oh, Harry," she laughed, "you'll have to give me time. You can't just fling questions at me."

She puffed at her cigarette with a sigh of contentment.

"One thing I want to ask you," he began rather apologetically; "you Southerners put quite an emphasis on family, and all that—not that it isn't quite all right, but you'll find it a little different here. I mean—you'll notice a lot of things that'll seem to you sort of vulgar display at first, Sally Carrol; but just remember that this is a three-generation town. Everybody has a father, and about half of us have grandfathers. Back of that we don't go."

"Of course," she murmured.

"Our grandfathers, you see, founded the place, and a lot of them had to take some pretty queer jobs while they were doing the founding. For instance, there's one woman who at present is about the social model for the town; well, her father was the first public ash man—things like that."

"Why," said Sally Carrol, puzzled, "did you s'pose I was goin' to make remarks about people?"

"Not at all," interrupted Harry; "and I'm not apologizing for any one either. It's just that—well, a Southern girl came up here last summer and said some unfortunate things, and—oh, I just thought I'd tell you."

Sally Carrol felt suddenly indignant—as thought she had been unjustly spanked—but Harry evidently considered the subject closed, for he went on with a great surge of enthusiasm.

"It's carnival time, you know. First in ten years. And there's an ice palace they're building now that's the first they've had since eighty-five. Built out of blocks of the clearest ice they could find—on a tremendous scale."

She rose and walking to the window pushed aside the heavy Turkish portières and looked out.

"Oh!" she cried suddenly. "There's two little boys makin' a snow man! Harry, do you reckon I can go out an' help 'em?"

"You dream! Come here and kiss me."

She left the window rather reluctantly.

"I don't guess this is a very kissable climate, is it? I mean, it makes you so you don't want to sit round, doesn't it?"

"We're not going to. I've got a vacation for the first week you're here, and there's a dinner-dance to-night."

"Oh, Harry," she confessed, subsiding in a heap, half in his lap, half in the pillows, "I sure do feel confused. I haven't got an idea whether I'll like it or not, an' I don't know what people expect, or anything'. You'll have to tell me, honey."

"I'll tell you," he said softly, "if you'll just tell me you're glad to be here."

"Glad—just awful glad!" she whispered, insinuating herself into his arms in her own peculiar way. "Where you are is home for me, Harry."

And as she said this she had the feeling for almost the first time in her life that she was acting a part.

That night, amid the gleaming candles of a dinner-party, where the men seemed to do most of the talking while the girls sat in a haughty and expensive aloofness, even Harry's presence on her left failed to make her feel at home.

"They're a good-looking crowd, don't you think?" he demanded. "Just look round. There's Spud Hubbard, tackle at Princeton last year, and Junie Morton—he and the red-haired fellow next to him were both Yale hockey captains; Junie was in my class. Why, the best athletes in the world come from these States round here. This is a man's country, I tell you. Look at John J. Fishburn!"

"Who's he?" asked Sally Carrol innocently.

"Don't you know?"

"I've heard the name."

"Greatest wheat man in the Northwest, and one of the greatest financiers in the country."

She turned suddenly to a voice on her right.

"I guess they forgot to introduce us. My name's Roger Patton."

"My name is Sally Carrol Happer," she said graciously.

"Yes, I know. Harry told me you were coming."

"You a relative?"

"No, I'm a professor."

"Oh," she laughed.

"At the university. You're from the South, aren't you?"

"Yes; Tarleton, Georgia."

She liked him immediately—a reddish-brown mustache under watery blue eyes that had something in them that these other eyes lacked, some quality of appreciation. They exchanged stray sentences through dinner, and she made up her mind to see him again.

After coffee she was introduced to numerous good-looking young men who danced wtih conscious precision and seemed to take it for granted that she wanted to talk about nothing except Harry.

"Heavens," she thought, "they talk as if my being engaged made me older than they are—as if I'd tell their mothers on them!"

In the South an engaged girl, even a young married woman, expected the same amount of half-affectionate badinage and flattery that would be accorded a débutante, but here all that seemed banned. One young man, after getting well started on the subject of Sally Carrol's eyes, and how they had allured him ever since she entered the room, went into a violent confusion when he found she was visiting the Bellamys—was Harry's fiancée. He seemed to feel as though he had made some risqué and inexcusable blunder, became immediately formal, and left her at the first opportunity.

She was rather glad when Roger Patton cut in on her and suggested that they sit out a while.

"Well," he inquired, blinking cheerily, "How's Carmen from the South?"

"Might fine. How's—how's Dangerous Dan McGrew? Sorry, but he's the only Northerner I know much about."

He seemed to enjoy that.

"Of course," he confessed, "as a professor of literature I'm not supposed to have read Dangerous Dan McGrew."

"Are you a native?"

"No, I'm a Philadelphian. Imported from Harvard to teach French. But I've been here ten years."

"Nine years, three hundred an' sixty-four days longer than me."

"Like it here?"

"Uh-huh. Sure do!"

"Really?"

"Well, why not? Don't I look as if I were havin' a good time?"

"I saw you look out the window a minute ago—and shiver."

"Just my imagination," laughed Sally Carrol. "I'm used to havin' everythin' quiet outside, an' sometimes I look out an' see a flurry of snow, an' it's just as if somethin' dead was movin'."

He nodded appreciatively.

"Ever been North before?"

"Spent two Julys in Asheville, North Carolina."

"Nice-looking crowd, aren't they?" suggested Patton, indicating the swirling floor.

Sally Carrol started. This had been Harry's remark.

"Sure are! They're—canine."

"What?"

She flushed.

"I'm sorry; that sounded worse than I meant it. You see I always think of people as feline or canine, irrespective of sex."

"Which are you?"

"I'm feline. So are you. So are most Southern men an' most of these girls here."

"What's Harry?"

"Harry's canine distinctly. All the men I've met to-night seem to be canine."

"What does 'canine' imply? A certain conscious masculinity as opposed to subtlety?"

"Reckon so. I never analyzed it—only I just look at people an' say 'canine' or 'feline' right off. It's right absurd, I guess."

"Not at all. I'm interested. I used to have a theory about these people. I think they're freezing up."

"What?"

"I think they're growing like Swedes—Ibsenesque, you know. Very gradually getting gloomy and melancholy. It's these long winters. Ever read any Ibsen?"

She shook her head.

"Well, you find in his characters a certain brooding rigidity. They're righteous, narrow, and cheerless, without infinite possibilities for great sorrow or joy."

"Without smiles or tears?"

"Exactly. That's my theory. You see there are thousands of Swedes up here. They come, I imagine, because the climate is very much like their own, and there's been a gradual mingling. There're probably not half a dozen here to-night, but—we've had four Swedish governors. Am I boring you?"

"I'm mighty interested."

"Your future sister-in-law is half Swedish. Personally I like her, but my theory is that Swedes react rather badly on us as a whole. Scandinavians, you know, have the largest suicide rate in the world."

"Why do you live here if it's so depressing?"

"Oh, it doesn't get me. I'm pretty well cloistered, and I suppose books mean more than people to me anyway."

"But writers all speak about the South being tragic. You know—Spanish señoritas, black hair and daggers an' haunting music."

He shook his head.

"No, the Northern races are the tragic races—they don't indulge in the cheering luxury of tears."

Sally Carrol thought of her graveyard. She supposed that that was vaguely what she had meant when she said it didn't depress her.

"The Italians are about the gayest people in the world—but it's a dull subject," he broke off. "Anyway, I want to tell you you're marrying a pretty fine man."

Sally Carrol was moved by an impulse of confidence.

"I know. I'm the sort of person who wants to be taken care of after a certain point, and I feel sure I will be."

"Shall we dance? You know," he continued as they rose, "it's encouraging to find a girl who knows what she's marrying for. Nine-tenths of them think of it as a sort of walking into a moving-picture sunset."

She laughed, and liked him immensely.

Two hours later on the way home she nestled near Harry in the back seat.

"Oh, Harry," she whispered, "it's so co-old!"

"But it's warm in here, darling girl."

"But outside it's cold; and oh, that howling wind!"

She buried her face deep in his fur coat and trembled involuntarily as his cold lips kissed the tip of her ear.

4

The first week of her visit passed in a whirl. She had her promised toboggan-ride at the back of an automobile through a chill January twilight. Swathed in furs she put in a morning tobogganing on the country-club hill; even tried skiing, to sail through the air for a glorious moment and then land in a tangled laughing bundle on a soft snowdrift. She liked all the winter sports, except an afternoon spent snowshoeing over a glaring plain under pale yellow sunshine, but she soon realized that these things were for children—that she was being humored and that the enjoyment round her was only a reflection of her own.

At first the Bellamy family puzzled her. The men were reliable and she liked them; to Mr. Bellamy especially, with his iron-gray hair and energetic dignity, she took an immediate fancy, once she found that he was born in Kentucky; this made of him a link between the old life and the new. But toward the women she felt a definite hostility. Myra, her future sister-in-law, seemed the essence of spiritless conventionality. Her conversation was so utterly devoid of personality that Sally Carrol, who came from a country where a certain amount of charm and assurance could be taken for granted in the women, was inclined to despise her.

"If those women aren't beautiful," she thought, "they're nothing. They just fade out when you look at them. They're glorified domestics. Men are the centre of every mixed group."

Lastly there was Mrs. Bellamy, whom Sally Carrol detested. The first day's impression of an egg had been confirmed—an egg with a cracked, veiny voice and such an ungracious dumpiness of carriage that Sally Carrol felt that if she once fell she would surely scramble. In addition, Mrs. Bellamy seemed to typify the town in being innately hostile to strangers. She called Sally Carrol "Sally," and could not be persuaded that the double name was anything more than a tedious ridiculous nickname. To Sally Carrol this shortening of her name was like presenting her to the public half clothed. She loved "Sally Carrol"; she loathed "Sally." She knew also that Harry's mother disapproved of her bobbed hair; and she had never dared smoke down-stairs after that first day when Mrs. Bellamy had come into the library sniffing violently.

Of all the men she met she preferred Roger Patton, who was a frequent visitor at the house. He never again alluded to the Ibsenesque tendency of the populace, but when he came in one day and found her curled upon the sofa bent over "Peer Gynt" he laughed and told her to forget what he'd said—that it was all rot.

And then one afternoon in her second week she and Harry hovered on the edge of a dangerously steep quarrel. She considered that he precipitated it entirely, though the Serbia in the case was an unknown man who had not had his trousers pressed.

They had been walking homeward between mounds of high-piled snow and under a sun which Sally Carrol scarcely recognized. They passed a little girl done up in gray wool until she resembled a small Teddy bear, and Sally Carrol could not resist a gasp of maternal appreciation.

"Look! Harry!"

"What?"

"That little girl—did you see her face?"

"Yes, why?"

"It was red as a little strawberry. Oh, she was cute!"

"Why, your own face is almost as red as that already! Everybody's healthy here. We're out in the cold as soon as we're old enough to walk. Wonderful climate!"

She looked at him and had to agree. He was mighty healthy-looking; so was his brother. And she had noticed the new red in her own cheeks that very morning.

Suddenly their glances were caught and held, and they stared for a moment at the street-corner ahead of them. A man was standing there, his knees bent, his eyes gazing upward with a tense expression as though he were about to make a leap toward the chilly sky. And then they both exploded into a shout of laughter, for coming closer they discovered it had been a ludicrous momentary illusion produced by the extreme bagginess of the man's trousers.

"Reckon that's one on us," she laughed.

"He must be a Southerner, judging by those trousers," suggested Harry mischievously.

"Why, Harry!"

Her surprised look must have irritated him.

"Those damn Southerners!"

Sally Carrol's eyes flashed.

"Don't call 'em that!"

"I'm sorry, dear," said Harry, malignantly apologetic, "but you know what I think of them. They're sort of—sort of degenerates—not at all like the old Southerners. They've lived so long down there with all the colored people that they've gotten lazy and shiftless."

"Hush your mouth, Harry!" she cried angrily. "They're not! They may be lazy—anybody would be in that climate—but they're my best friends, an' I don't want to hear 'em criticised in any such sweepin' way. Some of 'em are the finest men in the world."

"Oh, I know. They're all right when they come North to college, but of all the hangdog, ill-dressed, slovenly lot I ever saw, a bunch of small-town Southerners are the worst!"

Sally Carrol was clinching her gloved hands and biting her lip furiously.

"Why," continued Harry, "there was one in my class at New Haven, and we all thought that at last we'd found the true type of Southern aristocrat, but it turned out that he wasn't an aristocrat at all—just the son of a Northern carpetbagger, who owned about all the cotton round Mobile."

"A Southerner wouldn't talk the way you're talking now," she said evenly.

"They haven't the energy!"

"Or the somethin' else."

"I'm sorry, Sally Carrol, but I've heard you say yourself that you'd never marry——"

"That's quite different. I told you I wouldn't want to tie my life to any of the boys that are round Tarleton now, but I never made any sweepin' generalities."

They walked along in silence.

"I probably spread it on a bit thick, Sally Carrol. I'm sorry."

She nodded but made no answer. Five minutes later as they stood in the hallway she suddenly threw her arms round him.

"Oh, Harry," she cried, her eyes brimming with tears, "let's get married next week. I'm afraid of having fusses like that. I'm afraid, Harry. It wouldn't be that way if we were married."

But Harry, being in the wrong, was still irritated.

"That'd be idiotic. We decided on March."

The tears in Sally Carrol's eyes faded; her expression hardened slightly.

"Very well—I suppose I shouldn't have said that."

Harry melted.

"Dear little nut!" he cried. "Come and kiss me and let's forget."

That very night at the end of a vaudeville performance the orchestra played "Dixie" and Sally Carrol felt something stronger and more enduring than her tears and smiles of the day brim up inside her. She leaned forward gripping the arms of her chair until her face grew crimson.

"Sort of get you, dear?" whispered Harry.

But she did not hear him. To the spirited throb of the violins and the inspiring beat of the kettledrums her own old ghosts were marching by and on into the darkness, and as fifes whistled and sighed in the low encore they seemed so nearly out of sight that she could have waved good-by.

"Away, away,
Away down South in Dixie!
Away, away,
Away down South in Dixie!"

5

It was a particularly cold night. A sudden thaw had nearly cleared the streets the day before, but now they were traversed again with a powdery wraith of loose snow that travelled in wavy lines before the feet of the wind, and filled the lower air with a fine-particled mist. There was no sky—only a dark, ominous tent that draped in the tops of the streets and was in reality a vast approaching army of snowflakes—while over it all, chilling away the comfort from the brown-and-green glow of lighted windows and muffling the steady trot of the horse pulling their sleigh, interminably washed the north wind. It was a dismal town after all, she thought—dismal.

Sometimes at night it had seemed to her as though no one lived here—they had all gone long ago—leaving lighted houses to be covered in time by tombing heaps of sleet. Oh, if there should be snow on her grave! To be beneath great piles of it all winter long, where even her headstone would be a light shadow against light shadows. Her grave—a grave that should be flower-strewn and washed with sun and rain.

She thought again of those isolated country houses that her train had passed, and of the life there the long winter through—the ceaseless glare through the windows, the crust forming on the soft drifts of snow, finally the slow, cheerless melting, and the harsh spring of which Roger Patton had told her. Her spring—to lose it forever—with its lilacs and the lazy sweetness it stirred in her heart. She was laying away that spring—afterward she would lay away that sweetness.

With a gradual insistence the storm broke. Sally Carrol felt a film of flakes melt quickly on her eyelashes, and Harry reached over a furry arm and drew down her complicated flannel cap. Then the small flakes came in skirmish-line, and the horse bent his neck patiently as a transparency of white appeared momentarily on his coat.

"Oh, he's cold, Harry," she said quickly.

"Who? The horse? Oh, no, he isn't. He likes it!"

After another ten minutes they turned a corner and came in sight of their destination. On a tall hill outlined in vivid glaring green against the wintry sky stood the ice palace. It was three stories in the air, with battlements and embrasures and narrow icicled windows, and the innumerable electric lights inside made a gorgeous transparency of the great central hall. Sally Carrol clutched Harry's hand under the fur robe.

"It's beautiful!" he cried excitedly. "My golly, it's beautiful, isn't it! They haven't had one here since eighty-five!"

Somehow the notion of there not having been one since eighty-five oppressed her. Ice was a ghost, and this mansion of it was surely peopled by those shades of the eighties, with pale faces and blurred snowfilled hair.

"Come on, dear," said Harry.

She followed him out of the sleigh and waited while he hitched the horse. A party of four—Gordon, Myra, Roger Patton, and another girl—drew up beside them with a mighty jingle of bells. There were quite a crowd already, bundled in fur or sheepskin, shouting and calling to each other as they moved through the snow, which was now so thick that people could scarcely be distinguished a few yards away.

"It's a hundred and seventy feet tall," Harry was saying to a muffled figure beside him as they trudged toward the entrance; "covers six thousand square yards."

She caught snatches of conversation: "One main hall"—"walls twenty to forty inches thick"—"and the ice cave has almost a mile of—"—"this Canuck who built it——"

They found their way inside, and dazed by the magic of the great crystal walls Sally Carrol found herself repeating over and over two lines from "Kubla Khan":

"It was a miracle of rare device,
A sunny pleasure-dome with caves of ice!"

In the great glittering cavern with the dark shut out she took a seat on a wooden bench, and the evening's oppression lifted. Harry was right—it was beautiful; and her gaze travelled the smooth surface of the walls, the blocks for which had been selected for their purity and clearness to obtain this opalescent, translucent effect.

"Look! Here we go—oh, boy!" cried Harry.

A band in a far corner struck up "Hail, Hail, the Gang's All Here!" which echoed over to them in wild muddled acoustics, and then the lights suddenly went out; silence seemed to flow down the icy sides and sweep over them. Sally Carrol could still see her white breath in the darkness, and a dim row of pale faces over on the other side.

The music eased to a sighing complaint, and from outside drifted in the full-throated resonant chant of the marching clubs. It grew louder like some paean of a viking tribe traversing an ancient wild; it swelled—they were coming nearer; then a row of torches appeared, and another and another, and keeping time with their moccasined feet a long column of gray-mackinawed figures swept in, snowshoes slung at their shoulders, torches soaring and flickering as their voices rose along the great walls.

The gray column ended and another followed, the light streaming luridly this time over red toboggan caps and flaming crimson mackinaws, and as they entered they took up the refrain; then came a long platoon of blue and white, of green, of white, of brown and yellow.

"Those white ones are the Wacouta Club," whispered Harry eagerly. "Those are the men you've met round at dances."

The volume of the voices grew; the great cavern was a phantasmagoria of torches waving in great banks of fire, of colors and the rhythm of soft-leather steps. The leading column turned and halted, platoon deployed in front of platoon until the whole procession made a solid flag of flame, and then from thousands of voices burst a mighty shout that filled the air like a crash of thunder, and sent the torches wavering. It was magnificent, it was tremendous! To Sally Carrol it was the North offering sacrifice on some mighty altar to the gray pagan God of Snow. As the shout died the band struck up again and there came more singing, and then long reverberating cheers by each club. She sat very quiet listening while the staccato cries rent the stillness; and then she started, for there was a volley of explosion, and great clouds of smoke went up here and there through the cavern—the flash-light photographers at work—and the council was over. With the band at their head the clubs formed in column once more, took up their chant, and began to march out.

"Come on!" shouted Harry. "We want to see the labyrinths downstairs before they turn the lights off!"

They all rose and started toward the chute—Harry and Sally Carrol in the lead, her little mitten buried in his big fur gantlet. At the bottom of the chute was a long empty room of ice, with the ceiling so low that they had to stoop—and their hands were parted. Before she realized what he intended Harry had darted down one of the half-dozen glittering passages that opened into the room and was only a vague receding blot against the green shimmer.

"Harry!" she called.

"Come on!" he cried back.

She looked round the empty chamber; the rest of the party had evidently decided to go home, were already outside somewhere in the blundering snow. She hesitated and then darted in after Harry.

"Harry!" she shouted.

She had reached a turning-point thirty feet down; she heard a faint muffled answer far to the left, and with a touch of panic fled toward it. She passed another turning, two more yawning alleys.

"Harry!"

No answer. She started to run straight forward, and then turned like lightning and sped back the way she had come, enveloped in a sudden icy terror.

She reached a turn—was it here?—took the left and came to what should have been the outlet into the long, low room, but it was only another glittering passage with darkness at the end. She called again but the walls gave back a flat, lifeless echo with no reverberations. Retracing her steps she turned another corner, this time following a wide passage. It was like the green lane between the parted waters of the Red Sea, like a damp vault connecting empty tombs.

She slipped a little now as she walked, for ice had formed on the bottom of her overshoes; she had to run her gloves along the half-slippery, half-sticky walls to keep her balance.

"Harry!"

Still no answer. The sound she made bounced mockingly down to the end of the passage.

Then on an instant the lights went out, and she was in complete darkness. She gave a small, frightened cry, and sank down into a cold little heap on the ice. She felt her left knee do something as she fell, but she scarcely noticed it as some deep terror far greater than any fear of being lost settled upon her. She was alone with this presence that came out of the North, the dreary loneliness that rose from ice-bound whalers in the Arctic seas, from smokeless, trackless wastes where were strewn the whitened bones of adventure. It was an icy breath of death; it was rolling down low across the land to clutch at her.

With a furious, despairing energy she rose again and started blindly down the darkness. She must get out. She might be lost in here for days, freeze to death and lie embedded in the ice like corpses she had read of, kept perfectly preserved until the melting of a glacier. Harry probably thought she had left with the others—he had gone by now; no one would know until late next day. She reached pitifully for the wall. Forty inches thick, they had said—forty inches thick!

"Oh!"

On both sides of her along the walls she felt things creeping, damp souls that haunted this place, this town, this North.

"Oh, send somebody—send somebody!" she cried aloud.

Clark Darrow—he would understand; or Joe Ewing; she couldn't be left here to wander forever—to be frozen, heart, body, and soul. This her—this Sally Carrol! Why, she was a happy thing. She was a happy little girl. She liked warmth and summer and Dixie. These things were foreign—foreign.

"You're not crying," something said aloud. "You'll never cry any more. Your tears would just freeze; all tears freeze up here!"

She sprawled full length on the ice.

"Oh, God!" she faltered.

A long single file of minutes went by, and with a great weariness she felt her eyes closing. Then some one seemed to sit down near her and take her face in warm, soft hands,. She looked up gratefully.

"Why, it's Margery Lee," she crooned softly to herself. "I knew you'd come." It really was Margery Lee, and she was just as Sally Carrol had known she would be, with a young, white brow, and wide, welcoming eyes, and a hoop-skirt of some soft material that was quite comforting to rest on.

"Margery Lee."

It was getting darker now and darker—all those tombstones ought to be repainted, sure enough, only that would spoil 'em, of course. Still, you ought to be able to see 'em.

Then after a succession of moments that went fast and then slow, but seemed to be ultimately resolving themselves into a multitude of blurred rays converging toward a pale-yellow sun, she heard a great cracking noise break her new-found stillness.

It was the sun, it was a light, a torch, and a torch beyond that, and another one, and voices; a face took flesh below the torch, heavy arms raised her, and she felt something on her cheek—it felt wet. Some one had seized her and was rubbing her face with snow. How ridiculous—with snow!

"Sally Carrol! Sally Carrol!"

It was Dangerous Dan McGrew; and two other faces she didn't know.

"Child, child! We've been looking for you two hours! Harry's half-crazy!"

Things came rushing back into place—the singing, the torches, the great shout of the marching clubs. She squirmed in Patton's arms and gave a long low cry.

"Oh, I want to get out of here! I'm going back home. Take me home"—her voice rose to a scream that sent a chill to Harry's heart as he came racing down the next passage—"to-morrow!" she cried with delirious, unrestrained passion—"To-morrow! To-morrow! To-morrow!"

6

The wealth of golden sunlight poured a quite enervating yet oddly comforting heat over the house where day long it faced the dusty stretch of road. Two birds were making a great to-do in a cool spot found among the branches of a tree next door, and down the street a colored woman was announcing herself melodiously as a purveyor of strawberries. It was April afternoon.

Sally Carrol Happer, resting her chin on her arm, and her arm on an old window-seat gazed sleepily down over the spangled dust whence the heat waves were rising for the first time this spring. She was watching a very ancient Ford turn a perilous corner and rattle and groan to a jolting stop at the end of the walk. She made no sound, and in a minute a strident familiar whistle rent the air. Sally Carrol smiled and blinked.

"Good mawnin'."

A head appeared tortuously from under the car-top below.

" 'Tain't mawnin', Sally Carrol."

"Sure enough!" she said in affected surprise. "I guess maybe not."

"What you doin'?"

"Eatin' green peach. 'Spect to die any minute."

Clark twisted himself a last impossible notch to get a view of her face.

"Water's warm as a kettla steam, Sally Carrol. Wanta go swimmin'?"

"Hate to move," sighed Sally Carrol lazily, "but I reckon so."

1920

3

ADULTHOOD
Identity versus Role Confusion

In Erikson's chart on the eight ages of man, the problem of identity versus role confusion arises with the end of childhood and the onset of puberty. The adolescent, according to Erikson, finds himself in a position in which the samenesses and continuities he once relied on must be reexamined in terms of their ability to meet a rush of new demands. Both in his private life and in his choice of a career, the adolescent is in danger of losing a sense of who he is or who he wants to be. Erikson's concern with identity crises is not limited, however, to his study of adolescence but pervades all his writing, and with good reason, as the fiction in this section shows. For particularly in societies in which cultural and familial pressures work to discourage independence, acquiring a meaningful sense of identity often cannot be accomplished at an early age.

The consequences of failing to achieve a meaningful identity for oneself are described with surreal vividness in the opening story of this section, Kafka's "The Metamorphosis":

> *As Gregor Samsa awoke one morning from uneasy dreams he found himself transformed in his bed into a gigantic insect. He was lying on his hard, as it were armor-plated, back, and when he lifted his head a little he could see his dome-like brown belly divided into stiff arched segments on top of which the bed quilt could hardly keep in position and was about to slide off completely. His numerous legs, which were pitifully thin compared to the rest of his bulk, waved helplessly before his eyes.*

More difficult to locate is where the responsibility for Gregor's condition lies.

Is Gregor to blame for his metamorphosis? Certainly, there are numerous indications that he has sacrificed any claims to a life of his own for the sake of his family and job. Indeed, even when Gregor discovers that he has been turned into an insect, his first instinct is to go on as if nothing unusual had happened:

> *He remembered that often enough in bed he had felt small aches and pains, probably caused by awkward postures, which had proved purely imaginary*

> *once he got up, and he looked forward eagerly to seeing this morning's delusions gradually fall away. That the change in his voice was nothing but the precursor of a severe chill, a standing ailment of commercial travellers, he had not the least possible doubt.*

The problem is that Gregor's fears are reinforced by everyone around him. When the chief clerk of his employer sees Gregor, he immediately runs away, and Gregor's father is, if anything, more brutal. With his walking stick and newspaper, he "pitilessly" drives Gregor back into his bedroom. Only Gregor's sister, Grete, shows any compassion for his condition. Yet, even her concern cannot last. Whereas she once chose his food with care, she finally "pushed into his room with her foot any food that was available and in the evening cleared it out again with one sweep of the broom."

Thus, it becomes possible to ask whether it is Gregor or the situation in which he has been placed that causes him to become an insect. Above all, it is necessary to ask if Gregor's metamorphosis is a sign that he, more than others, is inwardly sensitive to what a loss of identity as a human being means.

The next two stories, Alberto Moravia's "Eye-Witness" and Heinrich Böll's "Action will be taken," strongly suggest that achieving an identity in which one is in harmony with society may be the equivalent of denying one's identity altogether. As in Kafka's story and the other stories in this section, setting is crucial, providing not merely background but a psychological force against which character must be measured.

"Eye-Witness" is told by a man who believes that "out of ten men—as far as I know anyhow—two, perhaps, are born masters, but the others are born servants." Remigio has been a servant all his life and wishes to remain that way:

> *As for me, I was born a servant, I have lived up till now as a servant, and I shall die, I daresay, as an old dotard, but still a servant. I like to serve; I like to obey; I like to submit to the will of another.*

In the position Remigio takes in a villa on the Via Cassia, it is not possible, however, for him just to serve. After witnessing a fight between his master, the "son and grandson of peasants," and his mistress, "of good family but uprooted," he is dismissed by the latter, who cannot bear to have a servant around who knows her husband beats her.

Remigio realizes the unfairness of his mistress's decision: "It was they who came to words and blows; but I, who had nothing whatever to do with it, got the sack." What disturbs him, however, are the social implications of his mistress's decision:

> *A real born mistress does not even see her manservant; for her he is transparent like glass. Why she can even take off all her clothes in his presence, or get exasperated with her husband; it's just as though the servant were not there. Well, well, it seems there are no real masters and mistresses left in the world.*

One is left to wonder if Remigio's loyalty is less human than the arbitrariness of his employer. She at least credits him with an identity that must be considered.

In contrast to the narrator of "Eye-Witness," the narrator of "Action will be taken" is able to find a job in which he can fully lose his identity. Getting such a position is not easy for him, however. Although the factory in which he first works thrives on meaningless action, there is still not enough of it for a man who asserts, "I no longer acknowledge the term free time—on my fifteenth birthday I eliminated it from my vocabulary, for in the beginning was the act." It is not until the narrator of "Action will be taken" becomes a professional mourner at funerals that he discovers his true calling. "As soon as my first professional appearance as a mourner was over I knew: This is where I belong, this is what I am cut out for."

Is the narrator's acceptance of such a profession anything more than an idiosyncrasy? Perhaps not. Yet, the direct transition he makes from the factory to the grave is worth noting, particularly in view of the remark with which he closes his story, "It was not till much later that I realized I had never bothered to find out what was being produced in Wunsiedel's factory. I expect it was soap." One cannot help remembering that during World War II the Nazis made soap out of their concentration camp victims and that in the post-war era, Böll, like Günter Grass, has been one of the German writers most critical of his own country. If the narrator's action needs to be explained, so too does a society in which there is room for such a death-like abnegation of personal identity.

The final two stories in this section treat identity crises in reverse fashion by focusing on men who have conspicuously failed to reach an accommodation with society. The distance between these men and society is not, however, an automatic indication that they have achieved a sense of themselves. Especially in Gogol's "Diary of a Madman," it is possible to see the insanity of his madman-narrator as an extension rather than a corruption of the "sanity" of nineteenth-century Russian society. To be sure, the Madman does things no ordinary person would do. He credits dogs with having the power of human speech. He imagines himself King of Spain. Yet, the Madman's delusions are not without an underlying coherence. The conversation he overhears from the dogs reflects nothing so much as the artificiality of conventional gossip and love talk. Similarly, the Madman's belief that he is King of Spain is no less arbitrary than the fact that his birth and social status have relegated him to the role of clerk. As he himself observes:

> *I've often tried to discover where all these differences lie. Why am I a clerk? Why should I be a clerk? Perhaps I'm really a general or a count and only seem a clerk? Maybe I don't really know who I am? There are plenty of instances in history when somebody quite ordinary, not necessarily an aristocrat, some middle-class person or even a peasant, suddenly turns out to be a public figure and perhaps even the ruler of a country. . . . What I'd like to know is, why am I a clerk? Why precisely a clerk?*

Nothing good, of course, comes from the Madman's self-questioning. In the end we see him in an insane asylum, pained as never before:

> *My God! What they're doing to me! They pour cold water on my head. They don't listen to me, they don't hear me, they don't see me. What have I done to them? Why do they torture me so? What do they want from me? What can I give them? I haven't anything to give.*

Once again, the Madman seems superior to those who make his life so miserable. Yet, such a judgment is also deceptive. For even at this point the Madman seems to take his identity from an envy rather than a scorn of society.

The very opposite is true for the title character of Melville's "Bartleby." Bartleby is without the least desire to improve his social position or accommodate himself to the ways of his employer. After being hired as a scrivener in a law firm, he gradually reaches a position where he not only refuses to do copy work but all work. Indeed, he even refuses to leave his employer's office after he has been fired, and his employer in desperation moves to new quarters.

Is there a method to Bartleby's seeming madness? Certainly, Bartleby's employer and Melville's narrator can find none. Yet, there is good reason to question the latter's perceptions. He is, for example, totally insensitive to the walls that dominate his life. He does not appear to mind that on one end his chambers "looked upon the white wall of the interior of a spacious skylight shaft" and on the other end "commanded an unobstructed view of a lofty brick wall, black by age and everlasting shade." Nor does he concern himself with the way he has isolated Bartleby by surrounding him with "a high green folding screen" and placing him next to a window that "commanded at present no view at all, though it gave some light."

Bartleby does make his employer question certain of the assumptions by which he has run his life. At one point the latter admits:

> *For the first time in my life a feeling of overpowering stinging melancholy seized me. Before, I had never experienced aught but a not unpleasing sadness. The bond of a common humanity now drew me irresistibly to gloom. A fraternal melancholy. For both I and Bartleby were sons of Adam.*

The changes that take place in the lawyer are not deep enough, however, for him to do anything to prevent Bartleby from going to jail. What this ambiguous result suggests about the purposes or identity of Bartleby is difficult to fathom. Is Bartleby to be taken as a martyr? Does he have a positive identity that his refusal to compromise himself implicitly reveals? As in Kafka's and Gogol's tales, it is easiest to be sure of how society confuses and brutalizes those who do not fulfill their expected roles.

FRANZ KAFKA

The METAMORPHOSIS

1

As Gregor Samsa awoke one morning from uneasy dreams he found himself transformed in his bed into a gigantic insect. He was lying on his hard, as it were armor-plated, back and when he lifted his head a little he could see his dome-like brown belly divided into stiff arched segments on top of which the bed quilt could hardly keep in position and was about to slide off completely. His numerous legs, which were pitifully thin compared to the rest of his bulk, waved helplessly before his eyes.

What has happened to me? he thought. It was no dream. His room, a regular human bedroom, only rather too small, lay quiet between the four familiar walls. Above the table on which a collection of cloth samples was unpacked and spread out—Samsa was a commercial traveler—hung the picture which he had recently cut out of an illustrated magazine and put into a pretty gilt frame. It showed a lady, with a fur cap on and a fur stole, sitting upright and holding out to the spectator a huge fur muff into which the whole of her forearm had vanished!

Gregor's eyes turned next to the window, and the overcast sky—one could hear rain drops beating on the window gutter—made him quite melancholy. What about sleeping a little longer and forgetting all this nonsense, he thought, but it could not be done, for he was accustomed to sleep on his right side and in his present condition he could not turn himself over. However violently he forced himself towards his right side he always rolled on his back again. He tried it at least a hundred times, shutting his eyes to keep from seeing his struggling legs, and only desisted when he began to feel in his side a faint dull ache he had never experienced before.

Oh God, he thought, what an exhausting job I've picked on! Traveling about day in, day out. It's much more irritating work than doing the actual business in the office, and on top of that there's the trouble of constant traveling, of worrying about train connections, the bed and irregular meals, casual acquaintances that are always new and never become intimate friends. The devil take it all! He felt a slight itching up on his belly; slowly pushed himself on his back nearer to the top of the bed so that he could lift his head more easily; identified the itching place which was surrounded by many small white spots the nature of which he could not understand and made to touch it with a leg, but drew the leg back immediately, for the contact made a cold shiver run through him.

He slid down again into his former position. This getting up early, he thought, makes one quite stupid. A man needs his sleep. Other commercials live like harem women. For instance, when I come back to the hotel of a morning to write up the orders I've got, these others are only sitting down to breakfast. Let me just try that with my chief; I'd be sacked on the spot. Anyhow, that might be quite a good thing for me, who can tell? If I didn't have to hold my hand because of my parents I'd have given notice long ago, I'd have gone to the chief and told him exactly what I think of him. That would knock him endways from his desk! It's a queer way of doing, too, this sitting on high at a desk and talking down to employees, especially when they have to come quite near because the chief is hard of hearing. Well, there's still hope; once I've saved enough money to pay back my parents' debts to him—that should take another five or six years—I'll do it without fail. I'll cut myself completely loose then. For the moment, though, I'd better get up, since my train goes at five.

He looked at the alarm clock ticking on the chest. Heavenly Father! he thought. It was half-past six o'clock and the hands were quietly moving on, it was even past the half-hour, it was getting on toward a quarter to seven. Had the alarm clock not gone off? From the bed one could see that it had been properly set for four o'clock; of course it must have gone off. Yes, but was it possible to sleep quietly through that ear-splitting noise? Well, he had not slept quietly, yet apparently all the more soundly for that. But what was he to do now? The next train went at seven o'clock; to catch that he would need to hurry like mad and his samples weren't even packed up, and he himself wasn't feeling particularly fresh and active. And even if he did catch the train he wouldn't avoid a row with the chief, since the firm's porter would have been waiting for the five o'clock train and would have long since reported his failure to turn up. The porter was a creature of the chief's, spineless and stupid. Well, supposing he were to say he was sick? But that would be most unpleasant and would look suspicious, since during his five years' employment he had not been ill once. The chief himself would be sure to come with the sick-insurance doctor, would reproach his parents with their son's laziness and would cut all excuses short by referring to the insurance doctor, who of course regarded all mankind as perfectly healthy malingerers. And would he be so far wrong on this occasion? Gregor really felt quite well, apart from a drowsiness that was utterly superfluous after such a long sleep, and he was even unusually hungry.

As all this was running through his mind at top speed without his being able to decide to leave his bed—the alarm clock had just struck a quarter to seven—there came a cautious tap at the door behind the head of his bed. "Gregor," said a voice—it was his mother's—"it's a quarter to seven. Hadn't you a train to catch?" That gentle voice! Gregor had a shock as he heard his own voice answering hers, unmistakably his own voice, it was true, but with a persistent horrible twittering squeak behind it like an undertone, that left the words in their clear shape only for the first moment and then rose up reverberating round them to destroy their sense, so that one could not be sure one had heard them rightly. Gregor wanted to answer at length and explain everything, but in the circumstances he confined himself to saying: "Yes, yes, thank you, Mother, I'm getting up now." The wooden door between them must have kept the change in his voice from being noticeable outside, for his mother contented herself with this statement and shuffled away. Yet this brief exchange of words had made the other members of the family aware that Gregor was still in the house, as they had not expected, and at one of the side doors his father was already knocking, gently, yet with his fist. "Gregor, Gregor," he called, "what's the matter with you?" And after a little while he called again in a deeper voice: "Gregor! Gregor!" At the other side door his sister was saying in a low, plaintive tone: "Gregor? Aren't you well? Are you needing anything?" He answered them both at once: "I'm just ready," and did his best to make his voice sound as normal as possible by enunciating the words very clearly and leaving long pauses between them. So his father went back to his breakfast, but his sister whispered: "Gregor, open the door, do." However, he was not thinking of opening the door, and felt thankful for the prudent habit he had acquired in traveling of locking all doors during the night, even at home.

His immediate intention was to get up quietly without being disturbed, to put on his clothes and above all eat his breakfast, and only then to consider what else was to be done, since in bed, he was well aware, his meditations would come to no sensible conclusion. He remembered that often enough in bed he had felt small aches and pains, probably caused by awkward postures, which had proved purely imaginary once he got up, and he looked forward eagerly to seeing this morning's delusions gradually fall away. That the change in his voice was nothing but the precursor of a severe chill, a standing ailment of commercial travelers, he had not the least possible doubt.

To get rid of the quilt was quite easy; he had only to inflate himself a little and it fell off by itself. But the next move was difficult, especially because he was so uncommonly broad. He would have needed arms and hands to hoist himself up; instead he had only the numerous little legs which never stopped waving in all directions and which he could not control in the least. When he tried to bend one of them it was the first to stretch itself straight; and did he succeed at last in making it do what he wanted, all the other legs meanwhile waved the more wildly in a high degree of unpleasant agitation. "But what's the use of lying idle in bed," said Gregor to himself.

He thought that he might get out of bed with the lower part of his body first, but this lower part, which he had not yet seen and of which he could form no clear conception, proved too difficult to move; it shifted so slowly; and when finally, almost wild with annoyance, he gathered his forces together and thrust out recklessly, he had miscalculated the direction and bumped heavily against the lower end of the bed, and the stinging pain he felt informed him that precisely this lower part of his body was at the moment probably the most sensitive.

So he tried to get the top part of himself out first, and cautiously moved his head towards the edge of the bed. That proved easy enough, and despite its breadth and mass the bulk of his body at last slowly followed the movement of his head. Still, when he finally got his head free over the edge of the bed he felt too scared to go on advancing, for after all if he let himself fall in this way it would take a miracle to keep his head from being injured. And at all costs he must not lose consciousness now, precisely now; he would rather stay in bed.

But when after a repetition of the same efforts he lay in his former position again, sighing, and watched his little legs struggling against each other more wildly than ever, if that were possible, and saw no way of bringing any order into this arbitrary confusion, he told himself again that is was impossible to stay in bed and that the most sensible course was to risk everything for the smallest hope of getting away from it. At the same time he did not forget meanwhile to remind himself that cool reflection, the coolest possible, was much better than desperate resolves. In such moments he focused his eyes as sharply as possible on the window, but, unfortunately, the prospect of the morning fog, which muffled even the other side of the narrow street, brought him little encouragement and comfort. "Seven o'clock already," he said to himself when the alarm clock chimed again, "seven o'clock already and still such a thick fog." And for a little while he lay quiet, breathing lightly, as if perhaps expecting such complete repose to restore all things to their real and normal conditions.

But then he said to himself: "Before it strikes a quarter past seven I must be quite out of this bed, without fail. Anyhow, by that time someone will have come from the office to ask for me, since it opens before seven." And he set himself to rocking his whole body at once in a regular rhythm, with the idea of swinging it out of the bed. If he tipped himself out in that way he could keep his head from injury by lifting it at an acute angle when he fell. His back seemed to be hard and was not likely to suffer from a fall on the carpet. His biggest worry was the loud crash he would not be able to help making, which would probably cause anxiety, if not terror, behind all the doors. Still, he must take the risk.

When he was already half out of the bed—the new method was more a game than an effort, for he needed only to hitch himself across by rocking to and fro—it struck him how simple it would be if he could get help. Two strong people—he thought of his father and the servant girl—would be amply sufficient; they would only have to thrust their arms under his convex back, lever him out of the bed, bend down with their burden and then be patient enough to let him turn himself right over on to the floor, where it was to be hoped his legs would then find their proper function. Well, ignoring the fact that the doors were all locked, ought he really to call for help? In spite of his misery he could not suppress a smile at the very idea of it.

He had got so far that he could barely keep his equilibrium when he rocked himself strongly, and he would have to nerve himself very soon for the final decision since in five minutes' time it would be a quarter past seven—when the front door bell rang. "That's someone from the office," he said to himself, and grew almost rigid, while his little legs only jigged about all the faster. For a moment everything stayed quiet. "They're not going to open the door," said Gregor to himself, catching at some kind of irrational hope. But then of course the servant girl went as usual to the door with her heavy tread and opened it. Gregor needed only to hear the first good morning of the visitor to know immediately who it was—the chief clerk himself. What a fate, to be condemned to work for a firm where the smallest omission at once gave rise to the gravest suspicion! Were all employees in a body nothing but scoundrels, was there not among them one single loyal devoted man who, had he wasted only an hour or so of the firm's time in a morning, was so tormented by conscience as to be driven out of his mind and actually incapable of leaving his bed? Wouldn't it really have been sufficient to send an apprentice to inquire—if any inquiry were necessary at all—did the chief clerk himself have to come and thus indicate to the entire family, an innocent family, that this suspicious circumstance could be investigated by no one less versed in affairs than himself? And more through the agitation caused by these reflections than through any act of will Gregor swung himself out of bed with all his strength. There was a loud thump, but it was not really a crash. His fall was broken to some extent by the carpet, his back, too, was less stiff than he thought, and so there was merely a dull thud, not so very startling. Only he had not lifted his head carefully enough and had hit it; he turned it and rubbed it on the carpet in pain and irritation.

"That was something falling down in there," said the chief clerk in the next room to the left. Gregor tried to suppose to himself that something like what had happened to him today might some day happen to the chief clerk; one really could not deny that it was possible. But as if in brusque reply to this supposition the chief clerk took a couple of firm steps in the next-door room and his patent leather boots creaked. From the right-hand room his sister was whispering to inform him of the situation: "Gregor, the chief clerk's here." "I know," muttered Gregor to himself; but he didn't dare to make his voice loud enough for his sister to hear it.

"Gregor," said his father now from the left-hand room "the chief clerk has come and wants to know why you didn't catch the early train. We don't know what to say to him. Besides, he wants to talk to you in person. So open the door, please. He will be good enough to excuse the untidiness of your room." "Good morning, Mr. Samsa," the chief clerk was calling amiably meanwhile. "He's not well," said his mother to the visitor, while his father was still speaking through the door, "he's not well, sir, believe me. What else would make him miss a train! The boy thinks about nothing but his work. It makes me almost cross the way he never goes out in the evenings; he's been here the last eight days and has stayed at home every single evening. He just sits there quietly at the table reading a newspaper or looking through railway timetables. The only amusement he gets is doing fretwork. For instance, he spent two or three evenings cutting out a little picture frame; you would be surprised to see how pretty it is; it's hanging in his room; you'll see it in a minute when Gregor opens the door. I must say I'm glad you've come, sir; we should never have got him to unlock the door by ourselves; he's so obstinate; and I'm sure he's unwell, though he wouldn't have it to be so this morning." "I'm just coming," said Gregor slowly and carefully, not moving an inch for fear of losing one word of the conversation. "I can't think of any other explanation, madam," said the chief clerk, "I hope it's nothing serious. Although on the other hand I must say that we men of business—fortunately or unfortunately—very often simply have to ignore any slight indisposition, since business must be attended to." "Well, can the chief clerk come in now?" asked Gregor's father impatiently, again knocking on the door. "No," said Gregor. In the left-hand room a painful silence followed this refusal, in the right-hand room his sister began to sob.

Why didn't his sister join the others? She was probably newly out of bed and hadn't even begun to put on her clothes yet. Well, why was she crying? Because he wouldn't get up and let the chief clerk in, because he was in danger of losing his job, and because the chief would begin dunning his parents again for the old debts? Surely these were things one didn't need to worry about for the present. Gregor was still at home and not in the least thinking of deserting the family. At the moment, true, he was lying on the carpet and no one who knew the condition he was in could seriously expect him to admit the chief clerk. But for such a small discourtesy, which could plausibly be explained away somehow later on, Gregor could hardly be dismissed on the spot. And it seemed to Gregor that it would be much more sensible to leave him in peace for the present than to trouble him with tears and entreaties. Still, of course, their uncertainty bewildered them all and excused their behavior.

"Mr. Samsa," the chief clerk called now in a louder voice, "what's the matter with you? Here you are, barricading yourself in your room, giving only 'yes' and 'no' for answers, causing your parents a lot of unnecessary trouble and neglecting—I mention this only in passing—neglecting your business duties in an incredible fashion. I am speaking here in the name of your parents and of your chief, and I beg you quite seriously to give me an immediate and precise explanation. You amaze me, you amaze me. I thought you were a quiet, dependable person, and now all at once you seem bent on making a disgraceful exhibition of yourself. The chief did hint to me early this morning a possible explanation of your disappearance—with reference to the cash payments that were entrusted to you recently—but I almost pledged my solemn word of honor that this could not be so. But now that I see how incredibly obstinate you are, I no longer have the slightest desire to take your part at all. And your position in the firm is not so unassailable. I came with the intention of telling you all this in private, but since you are wasting my time so needlessly I don't see why your parents shouldn't hear it too. For some time past your work has been most unsatisfactory; this is not the season of the year for a business boom, of course, we admit that, but a season of the year for doing no business at all, that does not exist, Mr. Samsa, must not exist."

"But, sir," cried Gregor, beside himself and in his agitation forgetting everything else, "I'm just going to open the door this very minute. A slight illness, an attack of giddiness, has kept me from getting up. I'm still lying in bed. But I feel all right again. I'm getting out of bed now. Just give me a moment or two longer! I'm not quite so well as I thought. But I'm all right, really. How a thing like that can suddenly strike one down! Only last night I was quite well, my parents can tell you, or rather I did have a slight presentiment. I must have showed some sign of it. Why didn't I report it at the office! But one always thinks that an indisposition can be got over without staying in the house. Oh sir, do spare my parents! All that you're reproaching me with now has no foundation; no one has ever said a word to me about it. Perhaps you haven't looked at the last orders I sent in. Anyhow, I can still catch the eight o'clock train, I'm much the better for my few hours' rest. Don't let me detain you here, sir; I'll be attending to business very soon, and do be good enough to tell the chief so and to make my excuses to him!"

And while all this was tumbling out pell-mell and Gregor hardly knew what he was saying, he had reached the chest quite easily, perhaps because of the practice he had had in bed, and was now trying to lever himself upright by means of it. He meant actually to open the door, actually to show himself and speak to the chief clerk; he was eager to find out what the others, after all their insistence, would say at the sight of him. If they were horrified then the responsibility was no longer his and he could stay quiet. But if they took it calmly, then he had no reason either to be upset, and could really get to the station for the eight o'clock train if he hurried. At first he slipped down a few times from the polished surface of the chest, but at length with a last heave he stood upright; he paid no more attention to the pains in the lower part of his body, however they smarted. Then he let himself fall against the back of a near-by chair, and clung with his little legs to the edges of it. That brought him into control of himself again and he stopped speaking, for now he could listen to what the chief clerk was saying.

"Did you understand a word of it?" the chief clerk was asking; "surely he can't be trying to make fools of us?" "Oh dear," cried his mother, in tears, "perhaps he's terribly ill and we're tormenting him. Grete! Grete!" she called out then. "Yes Mother?" called his sister from the other side. They were calling to each other across Gregor's room. "You must go this minute for the doctor. Gregor is ill. Go for the doctor, quick. Did you hear how he was speaking?" "That was no human voice," said the chief clerk in a voice noticeably low beside the shrillness of the mother's. "Anna! Anna!" his father was calling through the hall to the kitchen, clapping his hands, "get a locksmith at once!" And the two girls were already running through the hall with a swish of skirts—how could his sister have got dressed so quickly?—and were tearing the front door open. There was no sound of its closing again; they had evidently left it open, as one does in houses where some great misfortune has happened.

But Gregor was now much calmer. The words he uttered were no longer understandable, apparently, although they seemed clear enough to him, even clearer than before, perhaps because his ear had grown accustomed to the sound of them. Yet at any rate people now believed that something was wrong with him, and were ready to help him. The positive certainty with which these first measures had been taken comforted him. He felt himself drawn once more into the human circle and hoped for great and remarkable results from both the doctor and the locksmith, without really distinguishing precisely between them. To make his voice as clear as possible for the decisive conversation that was now imminent he coughed a little, as quietly as he could, of course, since this noise too might not sound like a human cough for all he was able to judge. In the next room meanwhile there was complete silence. Perhaps his parents were sitting at the table with the chief clerk, whispering, perhaps they were all leaning against the door and listening.

Slowly Gregor pushed the chair towards the door, then let go of it, caught hold of the door for support—the soles at the end of his little legs were somewhat sticky—and rested against it for a moment after his efforts. Then he set himself to turning the key in the lock with his mouth. It seemed, unhappily, that he hadn't really any teeth—what could he grip the key with?—but on the other hand his jaws were certainly very strong; with their help he did manage to set the key in motion, heedless of the fact that he was undoubtedly damaging them somewhere, since a brown fluid issued from his mouth, flowed over the key and dripped on the floor. "Just listen to that," said the chief clerk next door; "he's turning the key." That was a great encouragement to Gregor; but they should all have shouted encouragement to him, his father and mother too: "Go on, Gregor," they should have called out, "keep going, hold on to that key!" And in the belief that they were all following his efforts intently, he clenched his jaws recklessly on the key with all the force at his command. As the turning of the key progressed he circled round the lock, holding on now only with his mouth, pushing on the key, as required, or pulling it down again with all the weight of his body. The louder click of the finally yielding lock literally quickened Gregor. With a deep breath of relief he said to himself: "So I didn't need the locksmith," and laid his head on the handle to open the door wide.

Since he had to pull the door towards him, he was still invisible when it was really wide open. He had to edge himself slowly round the near half of the double door, and to do it very carefully if he was not to fall plump upon his back just on the threshold. He was still carrying out this difficult manoeuvre, with no time to observe anything else, when he heard the chief clerk utter a loud "Oh!"—it sounded like a gust of wind—and now he could see the man, standing as he was nearest to the door, clapping one hand before his open mouth and slowly backing away as if driven by some invisible steady pressure. His mother—in spite of the chief clerk's being there her hair was still undone and sticking up in all directions—first clasped her hands and looked at his father, then took two steps toward Gregor and fell on the floor among her outspread skirts, her face quite hidden on her breast. His father knotted his fist with a fierce expression on his face as if he meant to knock Gregor back into his room, then looked uncertainly round the living room, covered his eyes with his hands and wept till his great chest heaved.

Gregor did not go now into the living room, but leaned against the inside of the firmly shut wing of the door, so that only half his body was visible and his head above it bending sideways to look at the others. The light had meanwhile strengthened; on the other side of the street one could see clearly a section of the endlessly long, dark gray building opposite—it was a hospital—abruptly punctuated by its row of regular windows; the rain was still falling, but only in large singly discernible and literally singly splashing drops. The breakfast dishes were set out on the table lavishly, for breakfast was the most important meal of the day to Gregor's father, who lingered it out for hours over various newspapers. Right opposite Gregor on the wall hung a photograph of himself on military service, as a lieutenant, hand on sword, a carefree smile on his face, inviting one to respect his uniform and military bearing. The door leading to the hall was open, and one could see that the front door stood open too, showing the landing beyond and the beginning of the stairs going down.

"Well," said Gregor, knowing perfectly that he was the only one who had retained any composure, "I'll put my clothes on at once, pack up my samples and start off. Will you only let me go? You see, sir, I'm not obstinate, and I'm willing to work; traveling is a hard life, but I couldn't live without it. Where are you going, sir? To the office? Yes? Will you give a true account of all this? One can be temporarily incapacitated, but that's just the moment for remembering former services and bearing in mind that later on, when the incapacity has been got over, one will certainly work with all the more industry and concentration. I'm loyally bound to serve the chief, you know that very well. Besides, I have to provide for my parents and my sister. I'm in great difficulties, but I'll get out of them again. Don't make things any worse for me than they are. Stand up for me in the firm. Travelers are not popular there, I know. People think they earn sacks of money and just have a good time. A prejudice there's no particular reason for revising. But you, sir, have a more comprehensive view of affairs than the rest of the staff, yes, let me tell you in confidence, a more comprehensive view than the chief himself, who, being the owner, lets his judgment easily be swayed against one of his employees. And you know very well that the traveler, who is never seen in the office almost the whole year round, can so easily fall a victim to gossip and ill luck and unfounded complaints, which he mostly knows nothing about, except when he comes back exhausted from his rounds, and only then suffers in person from their evil consequences, which he can no longer trace back to the original causes. Sir, sir, don't go away without a word to me to show that you think me in the right at least to some extent!"

But at Gregor's very first words the chief clerk had already backed away and only stared at him with parted lips over one twitching shoulder. And while Gregor was speaking he did not stand still one moment but stole away towards the door, without taking his eyes off Gregor, yet only an inch at a time, as if obeying some secret injunction to leave the room. He was already at the hall, and the suddenness with which he took his last step out of the living room would have made one believe he had burned the sole of his foot. Once in the hall he stretched his right arm before him towards the staircase, as if some supernatural power were waiting there to deliver him.

Gregor perceived that the chief clerk must on no account be allowed to go away in this frame of mind if his position in the firm were not to be endangered to the utmost. His parents did not understand this so well; they had convinced themselves in the course of years that Gregor was settled for life in this firm, and besides they were so preoccupied with their immediate troubles that all foresight had forsaken them. Yet Gregor had this foresight. The chief clerk must be detained, soothed, persuaded and finally won over; the whole future of Gregor and his family depended on it! If only his sister had been there! She was intelligent; she had begun to cry while Gregor was still lying quietly on his back. And no doubt the chief clerk, so partial to ladies, would have been guided by her; she would have shut the door of the flat and in the hall talked him out of his horror. But she was not there, and Gregor would have to handle the situation himself. And without remembering that he was still unaware what powers of movement he possessed, without even remembering that his words in all possibility, indeed in all likelihood, would again be unintelligible, he let go the wing of the door, pushed himself through the opening, started to walk towards the chief clerk, who was already ridiculously clinging with both hands to the railing on the landing; but immediately, as he was feeling for support, he fell down with a little cry upon all his numerous legs. Hardly was he down when he experienced for the first time this morning a sense of physical comfort; his legs had firm ground under them; they were completely obedient, as he noted with joy; they even strove to carry him forward in whatever direction he chose; and he was inclined to believe that a final relief from all his sufferings was at hand. But in the same moment as he found himself on the floor, rocking with suppressed eagerness to move, not far from his mother, indeed just in front of her, she, who had seemed so completely crushed, sprang all at once to her feet, her arms and fingers outspread, cried: "Help, for God's sake, help!" bent her head down as if to see Gregor better, yet on the contrary kept backing senselessly away; had quite forgotten that the laden table stood behind her; sat upon it hastily, as if in absence of mind, when she bumped into it; and seemed altogether unaware that the big coffee pot beside her was upset and pouring coffee in a flood over the carpet.

"Mother, Mother," said Gregor in a low voice, and looked up at her. The chief clerk, for the moment, had quite slipped from his mind; instead, he could not resist snapping his jaws together at the sight of the streaming coffee. That made his mother scream again, she fled from the table and fell into the arms of his father, who hastened to catch her. But Gregor had now no time to spare for his parents; the chief clerk was already on the stairs; with his chin on the banister he was taking one last backward look. Gregor made a spring, to be as sure as possible of overtaking him; the chief clerk must have divined his intention, for he leaped down several steps and vanished; he was still yelling "Ugh!" and it echoed through the whole staircase.

Unfortunately, the flight of the chief clerk seemed completely to upset Gregor's father, who had remained relatively calm until now, for instead of running after the man himself, or at least not hindering Gregor in his pursuit, he seized in his right hand the walking stick which the chief clerk had left behind on a chair, together with a hat and greatcoat, snatched in his left hand a large newspaper from the table and began stamping his feet and flourishing the stick and the newspaper to drive Gregor back into his room. No entreaty of Gregor's availed, indeed no entreaty was even understood, however humbly he bent his head his father only stamped on the floor the more loudly. Behind his father his mother had torn open a window, despite the cold weather, and was leaning far out of it with her face in her hands. A strong draught set in from the street to the staircase, the window curtains blew in, the newspapers on the table fluttered, stray pages whisked over the floor. Pitilessly Gregor's father drove him back, hissing and crying "Shoo!" like a savage. But Gregor was quite unpracticed in walking backwards, it really was a slow business. If he had only had a chance to turn round he could get back to his room at once, but he was afraid of exasperating his father by the slowness of such a rotation and at any moment the stick in his father's hand might hit him a fatal blow on the back or on the head. In the end, however, nothing else was left for him to do since to his horror he observed that in moving backwards he could not even control the direction he took; and so, keeping an anxious eye on his father all the time over his shoulder, he began to turn round as quickly as he could, which was in reality very slowly. Perhaps his father noted his good intentions, for he did not interfere except every now and then to help him in the manoeuvre from a distance with the point of the stick. If only he would have stopped making that unbearable hissing noise! It made Gregor quite lose his head. He had turned almost completely round when the hissing noise so distracted him that he even turned a little the wrong way again. But when at last his head was fortunately right in front of the doorway, it appeared that his body was too broad simply to get through the opening. His father, of course, in his present mood was far from thinking of such a thing as opening the other half of the door, to let Gregor had enough space. He had merely the fixed idea of driving Gregor back into his room as quickly as possible. He would never have suffered Gregor to make the circumstantial preparations for standing up on end and perhaps slipping his way through the door. Maybe he was now making more noise than ever to urge Gregor forward, as if no obstacle impeded him; to Gregor, anyhow, the noise in his rear sounded no longer like the voice of one single father; this was really no joke, and Gregor thrust himself—come what might—into the doorway. One side of his body rose up, he was tilted at an angle in the doorway, his flank was quite bruised, horrid blotches stained the white door, soon he was stuck fast and, left to himself, could not have moved at all, his legs on one side fluttered trembling in the air, those on the other were crushed painfully to the floor—when from behind his father gave him a strong push which was literally a deliverance and he flew far into the room, bleeding freely. The door was slammed behind him with the stick, and then at last there was silence.

2

Not until it was twilight did Gregor awake out of a deep sleep, more like a swoon than a sleep. He would certainly have waked up of his own accord not much later, for he felt himself sufficiently rested and well-slept, but it seemed to him as if a fleeting step and a cautious shutting of the door leading into the hall had aroused him. The electric lights in the street cast a pale sheen here and there on the ceiling and the upper surfaces of the furniture, but down below, where he lay, it was dark. Slowly, awkwardly trying out his feelers which he now first learned to appreciate, he pushed his way to the door to see what had been happening there. His left side felt like one single long, unpleasantly tense scar, and he had actually to limp on his two rows of legs. One little leg, moreover, had been severely damaged in the course of that morning's events—it was almost a miracle that only one had been damaged—and trailed uselessly behind him.

He had reached the door before he discovered what had really drawn him to it: the smell of food. For there stood a basin filled with fresh milk in which floated little sops of white bread. He could almost have laughed with joy, since he was now still hungrier than in the morning, and he dipped his head almost over the eyes straight into the milk. But soon in disappointment he withdrew it again; not only did he find it difficult to feed because of his tender left side—and he could only feed with the palpitating collaboration of his whole body—he did not like the milk either, although milk had been his favorite drink and that was certainly why his sister had set it there for him, indeed it was almost with repulsion that he turned away from the basin and crawled back to the middle of the room.

He could see through the crack of the door that the gas was turned on in the living room, but while usually at this time his father made a habit of reading the afternoon newspaper in a loud voice to his mother and occasionally to his sister as well, not a sound was now to be heard. Well, perhaps his father had recently given up the habit of reading aloud, which his sister had mentioned so often in conversation and in her letters. But there was the same silence all around, although the flat was certainly not empty of occupants. "What a quiet life our family has been leading," said Gregor to himself, and as he sat there motionless staring into the darkness he felt great pride in the fact that he had been able to provide such a life for his parents and sister in such a fine flat. But what if all the quiet, the comfort, the contentment were now to end in horror? To keep himself from being lost in such thoughts Gregor took refuge in movement and crawled up and down the room.

Once during the long evening one of the side doors was opened a little and quickly shut again, later the other side door too; someone had apparently wanted to come in and then thought better of it. Gregor now stationed himself immediately before the living room door, determined to persuade any hesitating visitor to come in or at least to discover who it might be; but the door was not opened again and he waited in vain. In the early morning, when the doors were locked, they had all wanted to come in, now that he had opened one door and the other had apparently been opened during the day, no one came in and even the keys were on the other side of the doors.

It was late at night before the gas went out in the living room, and Gregor could easily tell that his parents and his sister had all stayed awake until then, for he could clearly hear the three of them stealing away on tiptoe. No one was likely to visit him, not until the morning, that was certain; so he had plenty of time to meditate at his leisure on how he was to arrange his life afresh. But the lofty, empty room in which he had to lie flat on the floor filled him with an apprehension he could not account for, since it had been his very own room for the past five years—and with a half-unconscious action, not without a slight feeling of shame, he scuttled under the sofa, where he felt comfortable at once, although his back was a little cramped and he could not lift his head up, and his only regret was that his body was too broad to get the whole of it under the sofa.

He stayed there all night, spending the time partly in a light slumber, from which his hunger kept waking him up with a start, and partly in worrying and sketching vague hopes, which all led to the same conclusion, that he must lie low for the present and, by exercising patience and the utmost consideration, help the family to bear the inconvenience he was bound to cause them in his present condition.

Very early in the morning, it was still almost night, Gregor had the chance to test the strength of his new resolutions, for his sister, nearly fully dressed, opened the door from the hall and peered in. She did not see him at once, yet when she caught sight of him under the sofa—well, he had to be somewhere, he couldn't have flown away, could he?—she was so startled that without being able to help it she slammed the door shut again. But as if regretting her behavior she opened the door again immediately and came in on tiptoe, as if she were visiting an invalid or even a stranger. Gregor had pushed his head forward to the very edge of the sofa and watched her. Would she notice that he had left the milk standing, and not for lack of hunger, and would she bring in some other kind of food more to his taste? If she did not do it of her own accord, he would rather starve than draw her attention to the fact, although he felt a wild impulse to dart out from under the sofa, throw himself at her feet and beg her for something to eat. But his sister at once noticed, with surprise, that the basin was still full, except for a little milk that had been spilt all around it, she lifted it immediately, not with her bare hands, true, but with a cloth and carried it away. Gregor was wildly curious to know what she would bring instead, and made various speculations about it. Yet what she actually did next, in the goodness of her heart, he could never have guessed at. To find out what he liked she brought him a whole selection of food, all set out on an old newspaper. There were old, half-decayed vegetables, bones from last night's supper covered with a white sauce that had thickened; some raisins and almonds; a piece of cheese that Gregor would have called uneatable two days ago; a dry roll of bread, a buttered roll, and a roll both buttered and salted. Besides all that, she set down again the same basin, into which she had poured some water, and which was apparently to be reserved for his exclusive use. And with fine tact, knowing that Gregor would not eat in her presence, she withdrew quickly and even turned the key, to let him understand that he could take his ease as much as he liked. Gregor's legs all whizzed towards the food. His wounds must have healed completely, moreover, for he felt no disability, which amazed him and made him reflect how more than a month ago he had cut one finger a little with a knife and had still suffered pain from the wound only the day before yesterday. Am I less sensitive now? he thought, and sucked greedily at the cheese, which above all the other edibles attracted him at once and strongly. One after another and with tears of satisfaction in his eyes he quickly devoured the cheese, the vegetables and the sauce; the fresh food, on the other hand, had no charms for him, he could not even stand the smell of it and actually dragged away to some little distance the things he could eat. He had long finished his meal and was only lying lazily on the same spot when his sister turned the key slowly as a sign for him to retreat. That roused him at once, although he was nearly asleep, and he hurried under the sofa again. But it took considerable self-control for him to stay under the sofa, even for the short time his sister was in the room, since the large meal had swollen his body somewhat and he was so cramped he could hardly breathe. Slight attacks of breathlessness afflicted him and his eyes were starting a little out of his head as he watched his unsuspecting sister sweeping together with a broom not only the remains of what he had eaten but even the things he had not touched, as if these were now of no use to anyone, and hastily shoveling it all into a bucket, which she covered with a wooden lid and carried away. Hardly had she turned her back when Gregor came from under the sofa and stretched and puffed himself out.

In this manner Gregor was fed, once in the early morning while his parents and the servant girl were still asleep, and a second time after they had all had their midday dinner, for then his parents took a short nap and the servant girl could be sent out on some errand or other by his sister. Not that they would have wanted him to starve, of course, but perhaps they could not have borne to know more about his feeding than from hearsay, perhaps too his sister wanted to spare them such little anxieties wherever possible, since they had quite enough to bear as it was.

Under what pretext the doctor and the locksmith had been got rid of on that first morning Gregor could not discover, for since what he said was not understood by the others it never struck any of them, not even his sister, that he could understand what they said, and so whenever his sister came into his room he had to content himself with hearing her utter only a sigh now and then and an occasional appeal to the saints. Later on, when she had got a little used to the situation—of course she could never get completely used to it—she sometimes threw out a remark which was kindly meant or could be so interpreted. "Well, he liked his dinner today," she would say when Gregor had made a good clearance of his food; and when he had not eaten, which gradually happened more and more often, she would say almost sadly: "Everything's been left standing again."

But although Gregor could get no news directly, he overheard a lot from the neighboring rooms, and as soon as voices were audible, he would run to the door of the room concerned and press his whole body against it. In the first few days especially there was no conversation that did not refer to him somehow, even if only indirectly. For two whole days there were family consultations at every mealtime about what should be done; but also between meals the same subject was discussed, for there were always at least two members of the family at home, since no one wanted to be alone in the flat and to leave it quite empty was unthinkable. And on the very first of these days the household cook—it was not quite clear what and how much she knew of the situation—went down on her knees to his mother and begged leave to go, and when she departed, a quarter of an hour later, gave thanks for her dismissal with tears in her eyes as if for the greatest benefit that could have been conferred on her, and without any prompting swore a solemn oath that she would never say a single word to anyone about what had happened.

Now Gregor's sister had to cook too, helping her mother; true, the cooking did not amount to much, for they ate scarcely anything. Gregor was always hearing one of the family vainly urging another to eat and getting no answer but: "Thanks, I've had all I want," or something similar. Perhaps they drank nothing either. Time and again his sister kept asking his father if he wouldn't like some beer and offered kindly to go and fetch it herself, and when he made no answer suggested that she could ask the concierge to fetch it, so that he need feel no sense of obligation, but then a round "No" came from his father and no more was said about it.

In the course of that very first day Gregor's father explained the family's financial postion and prospects to both his mother and his sister. Now and then he rose from the table to get some voucher or memorandum out of the small safe he had rescued from the collapse of his business five years earlier. One could hear him opening the complicated lock and rustling papers out and shutting it again. This statement made by his father was the first cheerful information Gregor had heard since his imprisonment. He had been of the opinion that nothing at all was left over from his father's business, at least his father had never said anything to the contrary, and of course he had not asked him directly. At that time Gregor's sole desire was to do his utmost to help the family to forget as soon as possible the catastrophe which had overwhelmed the business and thrown them all into a state of complete despair. And so he had set to work with unusual ardor and almost overnight had become a commercial traveler instead of a little clerk, with of course much greater chances of earning money, and his success was immediately translated into good round coin which he could lay on the table for his amazed and happy family. These had been fine times, and they had never recurred, at least not with the same sense of glory, although later on Gregor had earned so much money that he was able to meet the expenses of the whole household and did so. They had simply got used to it, both the family and Gregor; the money was gratefully accepted and gladly given, but there was no special uprush of warm feeling. With his sister alone had he remained intimate, and it was a secret plan of his that she, who loved music, unlike himself, and could play movingly on the violin, should be sent next year to study at the Conservatorium, despite the great expense that would entail, which must be made up in some other way. During his brief visits home the Conservatorium was often mentioned in the talks he had with his sister, but always merely as a beautiful dream which could never come true, and his parents discouraged even these innocent references to it; yet Gregor had made up his mind firmly about it and meant to announce the fact with due solemnity on Christmas Day.

Such were the thoughts, completely futile in his present condition, that went through his head as he stood clinging upright to the door and listening. Sometimes out of sheer weariness he had to give up listening and let his head fall negligently against the door, but he always had to pull himself together again at once, for even the slight sound his head made was audible next door and brought all conversation to a stop. "What can he be doing now?" his father would say after a while, obviously turning towards the door, and only then would the interrupted conversation gradually be set going again.

Gregor was now informed as amply as he could wish—for his father tended to repeat himself in his explanations, partly because it was a long time since he had handled such matters and partly because his mother could not always grasp things at once—that a certain amount of investments, a very small amount it was true, had survived the wreck of their fortunes and had even increased a little because the dividends had not been touched meanwhile. And besides that, the money Gregor brought home every month—he had kept only a few dollars for himself—had never been quite used up and now amounted to a small capital sum. Behind the door Gregor nodded his head eagerly, rejoiced at this evidence of unexpected thrift and foresight. True, he could really have paid off some more of his father's debts to the chief with this extra money, and so brought much nearer the day on which he could quit his job, but doubtless it was better the way his father had arranged it.

Yet this capital was by no means sufficient to let the family live on the interest of it; for one year, perhaps, or at the most two, they could live on the principal, that was all. It was simply a sum that ought not to be touched and should be kept for a rainy day; money for living expenses would have to be earned. Now his father was still hale enough but an old man, and he had done no work for the past five years and could not be expected to do much; during these five years, the first years of leisure in his laborious though unsuccessful life, he had grown rather fat and become sluggish. And Gregor's old mother, how was she to earn a living with her asthma, which troubled her even when she walked through the flat and kept her lying on a sofa every other day panting for breath beside an open window? And was his sister to earn her bread, she who was still a child of seventeen and whose life hitherto had been so pleasant, consisting as it did in dressing herself nicely, sleeping long, helping in the housekeeping, going out to a few modest entertainments and above all playing the violin? At first whenever the need for earning money was mentioned Gregor let go his hold on the door and threw himself down on the cool leather sofa beside it, he felt so hot with shame and grief.

Often he just lay there the long nights through without sleeping at all, scrabbling for hours on the leather. Or he nerved himself to the great effort of pushing an armchair to the window, then crawled up over the window sill and, braced against the chair, leaned against the window panes, obviously in some recollection of the sense of freedom that looking out of a window always used to give him. For in reality day by day things that were even a little way off were growing dimmer to his sight; the hospital across the street, which he used to execrate for being all too often before his eyes, was now quite beyond his range of vision, and if he had not known that he lived in Charlotte Street, a quiet street but still a city street, he might have believed that his window gave on a desert waste where gray sky and gray land blended indistinguishable into each other. His quick-witted sister only needed to observe twice that the armchair stood by the window; after that whenever she had tidied the room she always pushed the chair back to the same place at the window and even left the inner casements open.

If he could have spoken to her and thanked her for all she had to do for him, he could have borne his ministrations better; as it was, they oppressed him. She certainly tried to make as light as possible of whatever was disagreeable in her task, and as time went on she succeeded, of course, more and more, but time brought more enlightenment to Gregor too. The very way she came in distressed him. Hardly was she in the room when she rushed to the window, without even taking time to shut the door, careful as she was usually to shield the sight of Gregor's room from the others, and as if she were almost suffocating tore the casements open with hasty fingers, standing then in the open draught for a while even in the bitterest cold and drawing deep breaths. This noisy scurry of hers upset Gregor twice a day; he would crouch trembling under the sofa all the time, knowing quite well that she would certainly have spared him such a disturbance had she found it at all possible to stay in his presence without opening the window.

On one occasion, about a month after Gregor's metamorphosis, when there was surely no reason for her to be still startled at his appearance, she came a little earlier than usual and found him gazing out of the window, quite motionless, and thus well placed to look like a bogey. Gregor would not have been surprised had she not come in at all, for she could not immediately open the window while he was there, but not only did she retreat, she jumped back as if in alarm and banged the door shut; a stranger might well have thought that he had been lying in wait for her there meaning to bite her. Of course he hid himself under the sofa at once, but he had to wait until midday before she came again, and she seemed more ill at ease than usual. This made him realize how repulsive the sight of him still was to her, and that it was bound to go on being repulsive, and what an effort it must cost her not to run away even from the sight of the small portion of his body that stuck out from under the sofa. In order to spare her that, therefore, one day he carried a sheet on his back to the sofa—it cost him four hours' labor—and arranged it there in such a way as to hide him completely, so that even if she were to bend down she could not see him. Had she considered the sheet unnecessary, she would certainly have stripped it off the sofa again, for it was clear enough that this curtaining and confining of himself was not likely to conduce to Gregor's comfort, but she left it where it was, and Gregor even fancied that he caught a thankful glance from her eye when he lifted the sheet carefully a very little with his head to see how she was taking the new arrangement.

For the first fortnight his parents could not bring themselves to the point of entering his room, and he often heard them expressing their appreciation of his sister's activities, whereas formerly they had frequently scolded her for being as they thought a somewhat useless daughter. But now, both of them often waited outside the door, his father and his mother, while his sister tidied his room, and as soon as she came out she had to tell them exactly how things were in the room, what Gregor had eaten, how he had conducted himself this time and whether there was not perhaps some slight improvement in his condition. His mother, moreover, began relatively soon to want to visit him, but his father and sister dissuaded her at first with arguments which Gregor listened to very attentively and altogether approved. Later, however, she had to be held back by main force, and when she cried out: "Do let me in to Gregor, he is my unfortunate son! Can't you understand that I must go to him?" Gregor thought that it might be well to have her come in, not every day, of course, but perhaps once a week; she understood things, after all, much better than his sister, who was only a child despite the efforts she was making and had perhaps taken on so difficult a task merely out of childish thoughtlessness.

Gregor's desire to see his mother was soon fulfilled. During the daytime he did not want to show himself at the window, out of consideration for his parents, but he could not crawl very far around the few square yards of floor space he had, nor could he bear lying quietly at rest all during the night, while he was fast losing any interest he had ever taken in food, so that for mere recreation he had formed the habit of crawling crisscross over the walls and ceiling. He especially enjoyed hanging suspended from the ceiling; it was much better than lying on the floor; one could breathe more freely; one's body swung and rocked lightly; and in the almost blissful absorption induced by this suspension it could happen to his own surprise that he let go and fell plump on the floor. Yet he now had his body much better under control than formerly, and even such a big fall did him no harm. His sister at once remarked the new distraction Gregor had found for himself—he left traces behind him of the sticky stuff on his soles wherever he crawled—and she got the idea in her head of giving him as wide a field as possible to crawl in and of removing the pieces of furniture that hindered him, above all the chest of drawers and the writing desk. But that was more than she could manage all by herself; she did not dare ask her father to help her; and as for the servant girl, a young creature of sixteen who had had the courage to stay on after the cook's departure, she could not be asked to help, for she had begged as an especial favor that she might keep the kitchen door locked and open it only on a definite summons; so there was nothing left but to apply to her mother at an hour when her father was out. And the old lady did come, with exclamations of joyful eagerness, which, however, died away at the door of Gregor's room. Gregor's sister, of course, went in first, to see that everything was in order before letting his mother enter. In great haste Gregor pulled the sheet lower and rucked it more in folds so that it really looked as if it had been thrown accidentally over the sofa. And this time he did not peer out from under it; he renounced the pleasure of seeing his mother on this occasion and was only glad that she had come at all. "Come in, he's out of sight," said his sister, obviously leading her mother in by the hand. Gregor could now hear the two women struggling to shift the heavy old chest from its place, and his sister claiming the greater part of the labor for herself, without listening to the admonitions of her mother who feared she might overstrain herself. It took a long time. After at least a quarter of an hour's tugging his mother objected that the chest had better be left where it was, for in the first place it was too heavy and could never be got out before his father came home, and standing in the middle of the room like that it would only hamper Gregor's movements, while in the second place it was not at all certain that removing the furniture would be doing a service to Gregor. She was inclined to think to the contrary; the sight of the naked walls made her own heart heavy, and why shouldn't Gregor have the same feeling, considering that he had been used to his furniture for so long and might feel forlorn without it. "And doesn't it look," she concluded in a low voice—in fact she had been almost whispering all the time as if to avoid letting Gregor, whose exact whereabouts she did not know, hear even the tones of her voice, for she was convinced that he could not understand her words—"doesn't it look as if we were showing him, by taking away his furniture, that we have given up hope of his ever getting better and are just leaving him coldly to himself? I think it would be best to keep his room exactly as it has always been, so that when he comes back to us he will find everything unchanged and be able all the more easily to forget what has happened in between."

On hearing these words from his mother Gregor realized that the lack of all direct human speech for the past two months together with the monotony of family life must have confused his mind, otherwise he could not account for the fact that he had quite earnestly looked forward to having his room emptied of furnishing. Did he really want his warm room, so comfortably fitted with old family furniture, to be turned into a naked den in which he would certainly be able to crawl unhampered in all directions but at the price of shedding simultaneously all recollection of his human background? He had indeed been so near the brink of forgetfulness that only the voice of his mother, which he had not heard for so long, had drawn him back from it. Nothing should be taken out of his room; everything must stay as it was; he could not dispense with the good influence of the furniture on his state of mind; and even if the furniture did hamper him in his senseless crawling round and round, that was no drawback but a great advantage.

Unfortunately his sister was of the contrary opinion; she had grown accustomed, and not without reason, to consider herself an expert in Gregor's affairs as against her parents, and so her mother's advice was now enough to make her determined on the removal not only of the chest and the writing desk, which had been her first intention, but of all the furniture except the indispensable sofa. This determination was not, of course, merely the outcome of childish recalcitrance and of the self-confidence she had recently developed so unexpectedly and at such cost; she had in fact perceived that Gregor needed a lot of space to crawl about in, while on the other hand he never used the furniture at all, so far as could be seen. Another factor might have been also the enthusiastic temperament of an adolescent girl, which seeks to indulge itself on every opportunity and which now tempted Grete to exaggerate the horror of her brother's circumstances in order that she might do all the more for him. In a room where Gregor lorded it all alone over empty walls no one save herself was likely ever to set foot.

And so she was not to be moved from her resolve by her mother, who seemed moreover to be ill at ease in Gregor's room and therefore unsure of herself, was soon reduced to silence and helped her daughter as best she could to push the chest outside. Now, Gregor could do without the chest, if need be, but the writing desk he must retain. As soon as the two women had got the chest out of his room, groaning as they pushed it, Gregor stuck his head out from under the sofa to see how he might intervene as kindly and cautiously as possible. But as bad luck would have it, his mother was the first to return, leaving Grete clasping the chest in the room next door where she was trying to shift it all by herself, without of course moving it from the spot. His mother however was not accustomed to the sight of him, it might sicken her and so in alarm Gregor backed quickly to the other end of the sofa, yet could not prevent the sheet from swaying a little in front. That was enough to put her on the alert. She paused, stood still for a moment and then went back to Grete.

Although Gregor kept reassuring himself that nothing out of the way was happening, but only a few bits of furniture were being changed round, he soon had to admit that all this trotting to and fro of the two women, their little ejaculations and the scraping of furniture along the floor affected him like a vast disturbance coming from all sides at once, and however much he tucked in his head and legs and cowered to the very floor he was bound to confess that he would not be able to stand it for long. They were clearing his room out; taking away everything he loved; the chest in which he kept his fret saw and other tools was already dragged off; they were now loosening the writing desk which had almost sunk into the floor, the desk at which he had done all his homework when he was at the commercial academy, at the grammar school before that, and, yes, even at the primary school—he had no more time to waste in weighing the good intentions of the two women, whose existence he had by now almost forgotten, for they were so exhausted that they were laboring in silence and nothing could be heard but the heavy scuffling of their feet.

And so he rushed out—the women were just leaning against the writing desk in the next room to give themselves a breather—and four times changed his direction, since he really did not know what to rescue first, then on the wall opposite, which was already otherwise cleared, he was struck by the picture of the lady muffled in so much fur and quickly crawled up to it and pressed himself to the glass, which was a good surface to hold on to and comforted his hot belly. This picture at least, which was entirely hidden beneath him, was going to be removed by nobody. He turned his head towards the door of the living room so as to observe the women when they came back.

They had not allowed themselves much of a rest and were already coming; Grete had twined her arm round her mother and was almost supporting her. "Well, what shall we take now?" said Grete, looking round. Her eyes met Gregor's from the wall. She kept her composure, presumably because of her mother, bent her head down to her mother, to keep her from looking up, and said, although in a fluttering, unpremeditated voice: "Come, hadn't we better go back to the living room for a moment?" Her intentions were clear enough to Gregor, she wanted to bestow her mother in safety and then chase him down from the wall. Well, just let her try it! He clung to his picture and would not give it up. He would rather fly in Grete's face.

But Grete's words had succeeded in disquieting her mother, who took a step to one side, caught sight of the huge brown mass on the flowered wallpaper, and before she was really conscious that what she saw was Gregor screamed in a loud, hoarse voice: "Oh God, oh God!" fell with outspread arms over the sofa as if giving up and did not move. "Gregor!" cried his sister, shaking her fist and glaring at him. This was the first time she had directly addressed him since his metamorphosis. She ran into the next room for some aromatic essence with which to rouse her mother from her fainting fit. Gregor wanted to help too—there was still time to rescue the picture—but he was stuck fast to the glass and had to tear himself loose; he then ran after his sister into the next room as if he could advise her, as he used to do; but then had to stand helplessly behind her; she meanwhile searched among various small bottles and when she turned round started in alarm at the sight of him; one bottle fell on the floor and broke; a splinter of glass cut Gregor's face and some kind of corrosive medicine splashed him; without pausing a moment longer Grete gathered up all the bottles she could carry and ran to her mother with them; she banged the door shut with her foot. Gregor was now cut off from his mother, who was perhaps nearly dying because of him; he dared not open the door for fear of frightening away his sister, who had to stay with her mother; there was nothing he could do but wait; and harassed by self-reproach and worry he began now to crawl to and fro, over everything, walls, furniture and ceiling, and finally in his despair, when the whole room seemed to be reeling round him, fell down on to the middle of the big table.

A little while elapsed, Gregor was still lying there feebly and all around was quiet, perhaps that was a good omen. Then the doorbell rang. The servant girl was of course locked in her kitchen, and Grete would have to open the door. It was his father. "What's been happening?" were his first words; Grete's face must have told him everything. Grete answered in a muffled voice, apparently hiding her head on his breast: "Mother had been fainting, but she's better now. Gregor's broken loose." "Just what I expected," said his father, "just what I've been telling you, but you women would never listen." It was clear to Gregor that his father had taken the worst interpretation of Grete's all too brief statement and was assuming that Gregor had been guilty of some violent act. Therefore Gregor must now try to propitiate his father, since he had neither time nor means for an explanation. And so he fled to the door of his own room and crouched against it, to let his father see as soon as he came in from the hall that his son had the good intention of getting back into his room immediately and that it was not necessary to drive him there, but that if only the door were opened he would disappear at once.

Yet his father was not in the mood to perceive such fine distinctions. "Ah!" he cried as soon as he appeared, in a tone which sounded at once angry and exultant. Gregor drew his head back from the door and lifted it to look at his father. Truly, this was not the father he had imagined to himself; admittedly he had been too absorbed of late in his new recreation of crawling over the ceiling to take the same interest as before in what was happening elsewhere in the flat, and he ought really to be prepared for some changes. And yet, and yet, could that be his father? The man who used to lie wearily sunk in bed whenever Gregor set out on a business journey; who welcomed him back of an evening lying in a long chair in a dressing gown; who could not really rise to his feet but only lifted his arms in greeting, and on the rare occasions when he did go out with his family, on one or two Sundays a year and on high holidays, walked between Gregor and his mother, who were slow walkers anyhow, even more slowly than they did, muffled in his old greatcoat, shuffling laboriously forward with the help of his crook-handled stick which he set down most cautiously at every step and, whenever he wanted to say anything, nearly always came to a full stop and gathered his escort around him? Now he was standing there in fine shape; dressed in a smart blue uniform with gold buttons, such as bank messengers wear; his strong double chin bulged over the stiff high collar of his jacket; from under his bushy eyebrows his black eyes darted fresh and penetrating glances; his onetime tangled white hair had been combed flat on either side of a shining and carefully exact parting. He pitched his cap, which bore a gold monogram, probably the badge of some bank, in a wide sweep across the whole room on to a sofa and with the tail-ends of his jacket thrown back, his hands in his trouser pockets, advanced with a grim visage towards Gregor. Likely enough he did not himself know what he meant to do; at any rate he lifted his feet uncommonly high, and Gregor was dumbfounded at the enormous size of his shoe soles. But Gregor could not risk standing up to him, aware as he had been from the very first day of his new life that his father believed only the severest measures suitable for dealing with him. And so he ran before his father, stopping when he stopped and scuttling forward again when his father made any kind of move. In this way they circled the room several times without anything decisive happening, indeed the whole operation did not even look like a pursuit because it was carried out so slowly. And so Gregor did not leave the floor, for he feared that his father might take as a piece of peculiar wickedness any excursion of his over the walls or the ceiling. All the same, he could not stay this course much longer, for while his father took one step he had to carry out a whole series of movements. He was already beginning to feel breathless, just as in his former life his lungs had not been very dependable. As he was staggering along, trying to concentrate his energy on running, hardly keeping his eyes open; in his dazed state never even thinking of any other escape than simply going forward; and having almost forgotten that the walls were free to him, which in this room were well provided with finely carved pieces of furniture full of knobs and crevices—suddenly something lightly flung landed close behind him and rolled before him. It was an apple; a second apple followed immediately; Gregor came to a stop in alarm; there was no point in running on, for his father was determined to bombard him. He had filled his pockets with fruit from the dish on the sideboard and was now shying apple after apple, without taking particularly good aim for the moment. The small red apples rolled about the floor as if magnetized and cannoned into each other. An apple thrown without much force grazed Gregor's back and glanced off harmlessly. But another following immediately landed right on his back and sank in; Gregor wanted to drag himself forward, as if this startling, incredible pain could be left behind him; but he felt as if nailed to the spot and flattened himself out in a complete derangement of all his senses. With his last conscious look he saw the door of his room being torn open and his mother rushing out ahead of his screaming sister, in her under-bodice, for her daughter had loosened her clothing to let her breathe more freely and recover from her swoon, he saw his mother rushing towards his father, leaving one after another behind her on the floor her loosened petticoats, stumbling over her petticoats straight to his father and embracing him, in complete union with him—but here Gregor's sight began to fail—with her hands clasped round his father's neck as she begged for her son's life.

3

The serious injury done to Gregor, which disabled him for more than a month—the apple went on sticking in his body as a visible reminder, since no one ventured to remove it—seemed to have made even his father recollect that Gregor was a member of the family, despite his present unfortunate and repulsive shape, and ought not to be treated as an enemy, that, on the contrary, family duty required the suppression of disgust and the exercise of patience, nothing but patience.

And although his injury had impaired, probably for ever, his powers of movement, and for the time being it took him long, long minutes to creep across his room like an old invalid—there was no question now of crawling up the wall—yet in his own opinion he was sufficiently compensated for this worsening of his condition by the fact that towards evening the living-room door, which he used to watch intently for an hour or two beforehand, was always thrown open, so that lying in the darkness of his room, invisible to the family, he could see them all at the lamp-lit table and listen to their talk, by general consent as it were, very different from his earlier eavesdropping.

True, their intercourse lacked the lively character of former times, which he had always called to mind with a certain wistfulness in the small hotel bedrooms where he had been wont to throw himself down, tired out, on damp bedding. They were now mostly very silent. Soon after supper his father would fall asleep in his armchair; his mother and sister would admonish each other to be silent; his mother, bending low over the lamp, stitched at fine sewing for an underwear firm; his sister, who had taken a job as a salesgirl, was learning shorthand and French in the evenings on the chance of bettering herself. Sometimes his father woke up, and as if quite unaware that he had been sleeping said to his mother: "What a lot of sewing you're doing today!" and at once fell asleep again, while the two women exchanged a tired smile.

With a kind of mulishness his father persisted in keeping his uniform on even in the house; his dressing gown hung uselessly on its peg and he slept fully dressed where he sat, as if he were ready for service at any moment and even here only at the beck and call of his superior. As a result, his uniform, which was not brand-new to start with, began to look dirty, despite all the loving care of the mother and sister to keep it clean, and Gregor often spent whole evenings gazing at the many greasy spots on the garment, gleaming with gold buttons always in a high state of polish, in which the old man sat sleeping in extreme discomfort and yet quite peacefully.

As soon as the clock struck ten his mother tried to rouse his father with gentle words and to persuade him after that to get into bed, for sitting there he could not have a proper sleep and that was what he needed most, since he had to go on duty at six. But with the mulishness that had obsessed him since he became a bank messenger he always insisted on staying longer at the table, although he regularly fell asleep again and in the end only with the greatest trouble could be got out of his armchair and into his bed. However insistently Gregor's mother and sister kept urging him with gentle reminders, he would go on slowly shaking his head for a quarter of an hour, keeping his eyes shut, and refuse to get to his feet. The mother plucked at his sleeve, whispering endearments in his ear, the sister left her lessons to come to her mother's help, but Gregor's father was not to be caught. He would only sink down deeper in his chair. Not until the two women hoisted him up by the armpits did he open his eyes and look at them both, one after the other, usually with the remark: "This is a life. This is the peace and quiet of my old age." And leaning on the two of them he would heave himself up, with difficulty, as if he were a great burden to himself, suffer them to lead him as far as the door and then wave them off and go on alone, while the mother abandoned her needlework and the sister her pen in order to run after him and help him farther.

Who could find time, in this overworked and tired-out family, to bother about Gregor more than was absolutely needful? The household was reduced more and more; the servant girl was turned off; a gigantic bony charwoman with white hair flying round her head came in morning and evening to do the rough work; everything else was done by Gregor's mother, as well as great piles of sewing. Even various family ornaments, which his mother and sister used to wear with pride at parties and celebrations, had to be sold, as Gregor discovered of an evening from hearing them all discuss the prices obtained. But what they lamented most was the fact that they could not leave the flat which was much too big for their present circumstances, because they could not think of any way to shift Gregor. Yet Gregor saw well enough that consideration for him was not the main difficulty preventing the removal, for they could have easily shifted him in some suitable box with a few air holes in it; what really kept them from moving into another flat was rather their own complete hopelessness and the belief that they had been singled out for a misfortune such as had never happened to any of their relations or acquaintances. They fulfilled to the uttermost all that the world demands of poor people, the father fetched breakfast for the small clerks in the bank, the mother devoted her energy to making underwear for strangers, the sister trotted to and fro behind the counter at the behest of customers, but more than this they had not the strength to do. And the wound in Gregor's back began to nag at him afresh when his mother and sister, after getting his father into bed, came back again, left their work lying, drew close to each other and sat cheek by cheek; when his mother, pointing towards his room, said: "Shut that door now, Grete," and he was left again in darkness, while next door the women mingled their tears or perhaps sat dry-eyed staring at the table.

Gregor hardly slept at all by night or by day. He was often haunted by the idea that next time the door opened he would take the family's affairs in hand again just as he used to do; once more, after this long interval, there appeared in his thoughts the figures of the chief and the chief clerk, the commercial travelers and the apprentices, the porter who was so dull-witted, two or three friends in other firms, a chambermaid in one of the rural hotels, a sweet and fleeting memory, a cashier in a milliner's shop, whom he had wooed earnestly but too slowly—they all appeared, together with strangers or people he had quite forgotten, but instead of helping him and his family they were one and all unapproachable and he was glad when they vanished. At other times he would not be in the mood to bother about his family, he was only filled with rage at the way they were neglecting him, and although he had no clear idea of what he might care to eat he would make plans for getting into the larder to take the food that was after all his due, even if he were not hungry. His sister no longer took thought to bring him what might especially please him, but in the morning and at noon before she went to business hurriedly pushed into his room with her foot any food that was available, and in the evening cleared it out again with one sweep of the broom, heedless of whether it had been merely tasted, or—as most frequently happened—left untouched. The cleaning of his room, which she now did always in the evenings, could not have been more hastily done. Streaks of dirt stretched along the walls, here and there lay balls of dust and filth. At first Gregor used to station himself in some particularly filthy corner when his sister arrived, in order to reproach her with it, so to speak. But he could have sat there for weeks without getting her to make any improvement; she could see the dirt as well as he did, but she had simply made up her mind to leave it alone. And yet, with a touchiness that was new to her, which seemed anyhow to have infected the whole family, she jealously guarded her claim to be the sole caretaker of Gregor's room. His mother once subjected his room to a thorough cleaning, which was achieved only by means of several buckets of water—all this dampness of course upset Gregor too and he lay widespread, sulky and motionless on the sofa—but she was well punished for it. Hardly had his sister noticed the changed aspect of his room that evening than she rushed in high dudgeon into the living room and, despite the imploringly raised hands of her mother, burst into a storm of weeping, while her parents—her father had of course been startled out of his chair—looked on at first in helpless amazement; then they too began to go into action; the father reproached the mother on his right for not having left the cleaning of Gregor's room to his sister; shrieked at the sister on his left that never again was she to be allowed to clean Gregor's room; while the mother tried to pull the father into his bedroom, since he was beyond himself with agitation; the sister, shaken with sobs, then beat upon the table with her small fists; and Gregor hissed loudly with rage because not one of them thought of shutting the door to spare him such a spectacle and so much noise.

Still, even if the sister, exhausted by her daily work, had grown tired of looking after Gregor as she did formerly, there was no need for his mother's intervention or for Gregor's being neglected at all. The charwoman was there. This old widow, whose strong bony frame had enabled her to survive the worst a long life could offer, by no means recoiled from Gregor. Without being in the least curious she had once by chance opened the door of his room and at the sight of Gregor, who, taken by surprise, began to rush to and fro although no one was chasing him, merely stood there with her arms folded. From that time she never failed to open his door a little for a moment, morning and evening, to have a look at him. At first she even used to call him to her, with words which apparently she took to be friendly, such as: "Come along, then, you old dung beetle!" or "Look at the old dung beetle, then!" To such allocutions Gregor made no answer, but stayed motionless where he was, as if the door had never been opened. Instead of being allowed to disturb him so senselessly whenever the whim took her, she should rather have been ordered to clean out his room daily, that charwoman! Once, early in the morning—heavy rain was lashing on the windowpanes, perhaps a sign that spring was on the way—Gregor was so exasperated when she began addressing him again that he ran at her, as if to attack her, although slowly and feebly enough. But the charwoman instead of showing fright merely lifted high a chair that happened to be beside the door, and as she stood there with her mouth wide open it was clear that she meant to shut it only when she brought the chair down on Gregor's back. "So you're not coming any nearer?" she asked, as Gregor turned away again, and quietly put the chair back into the corner.

Gregor was now eating hardly anything. Only when he happened to pass the food laid out for him did he take a bit of something in his mouth as a pastime, kept it there for an hour at a time and usually spat it out again. At first he thought it was chagrin over the state of his room that prevented him from eating, yet he soon got used to the various changes in his room. It had become a habit in the family to push into his room things there was no room for elsewhere, and there were plenty of these now, since one of the rooms had been let to three lodgers. These serious gentlemen—all three of them with full beards, as Gregor once observed through a crack in the door—had a passion for order, not only in their own room but, since they were now members of the household, in all its arrangements, especially in the kitchen. Superfluous, not to say dirty, objects they could not bear. Besides, they had brought with them most of the furnishings they needed. For this reason many things could be dispensed with that it was no use trying to sell but that should not be thrown away either. All of them found their way into Gregor's room. The ash can likewise and the kitchen garbage can. Anything that was not needed for the moment was simply flung into Gregor's room by the charwoman, who did everything in a hurry; fortunately Gregor usually saw only the object, whatever it was, and the hand that held it. Perhaps she intended to take the things away again as time and opportunity offered, or to collect them until she could throw them all out in a heap, but in fact they just lay wherever she happened to throw them, except when Gregor pushed his way through the junk heap and shifted it somewhat, at first out of necessity, because he had not room enough to crawl, but later with increasing enjoyment, although after such excursions, being sad and weary to death, he would lie motionless for hours. And since the lodgers often ate their supper at home in the common living room, the living-room door stayed shut many an evening, yet Gregor reconciled himself quite easily to the shutting of the door, for often enough on evenings when it was opened he had disregarded it entirely and lain in the darkest corner of his room, quite unnoticed by the family. But on one occasion the charwoman left the door open a little and it stayed ajar even when the lodgers came in for supper and the lamp was lit. They set themselves at the top end of the table where formerly Gregor and his father and mother had eaten their meals, unfolded their napkins and took knife and fork in hand. At once his mother appeared in the other doorway with a dish of meat and close behind her his sister with a dish of potatoes piled high. The food steamed with a thick vapor. The lodgers bent over the food set before them as if to scrutinize it before eating, in fact the man in the middle, who seemed to pass for an authority with the other two, cut a piece of meat as it lay on the dish, obviously to discover if it were tender or should be sent back to the kitchen. He showed satisfaction, and Gregor's mother and sister, who had been watching anxiously, breathed freely and began to smile.

The family itself took its meals in the kitchen. None the less, Gregor's father came into the living room before going into the kitchen and with one prolonged bow, cap in hand, made a round of the table. The lodgers all stood up and murmured something in their beards. When they were alone again they ate their food in almost complete silence. It seemed remarkable to Gregor that among the various noises coming from the table he could always distinguish the sound of their masticating teeth, as if this were a sign to Gregor that one needed teeth in order to eat, and that with toothless jaws even of the finest make one could do nothing. "I'm hungry enough," said Gregor sadly to himself, "but not for that kind of food. How these lodgers are stuffing themselves, and here am I dying of starvation!"

On that very evening—during the whole of his time there Gregor could not remember ever having heard the violin—the sound of violin-playing came from the kitchen. The lodgers had already finished their supper, the one in the middle had brought out a newspaper and given the other two a page apiece, and now they were leaning back at ease reading and smoking. When the violin began to play they pricked up their ears, got to their feet, and went on tiptoe to the hall door where they stood huddled together. Their movements must have been heard in the kitchen, for Gregor's father called out: "Is the violin-playing disturbing you, gentlemen? It can be stopped at once." "On the contrary," said the middle lodger, "could not Fräulein Samsa come and play in this room, beside us, where it is much more convenient and comfortable?" "Oh certainly," cried Gregor's father, as if he were the violin-player. The lodgers came back into the living room and waited. Presently Gregor's father arrived with the music stand, his mother carrying the music and his sister with the violin. His sister quietly made everything ready to start playing; his parents, who had never let rooms before and so had an exaggerated idea of the courtesy due to lodgers, did not venture to sit down on their own chairs; his father leaned against the door, the right hand thrust between two buttons of his livery coat, which was formally buttoned up; but his mother was offered a chair by one of the lodgers and, since she left the chair just where he had happened to put it, sat down in a corner to one side.

Gregor's sister began to play; the father and mother, from either side, intently watched the movements of her hands. Gregor, attracted by the playing, ventured to move forward a little until his head was actually inside the living room. He felt hardly any surprise at his growing lack of consideration for the others; there had been a time when he prided himself on being considerate. And yet just on this occasion he had more reason than ever to hide himself, since owing to the amount of dust which lay thick in his room and rose into the air at the slightest movements, he too was covered with dust; fluff and hair and remnants of food trailed with him, caught on his back and along his sides; his indifference to everything was much too great for him to turn on his back and scrape himself clean on the carpet, as once he had done several times a day. And in spite of his condition, no shame deterred him from advancing a little over the spotless floor of the living room.

To be sure, no one was aware of him. The family was entirely absorbed in the violin-playing; the lodgers, however, who first of all had stationed themselves, hands in pockets, much too close behind the music stand so that they could all have read the music, which must have bothered his sister, had soon retreated to the window, half-whispering with downbent heads, and stayed there while his father turned an anxious eye on them. Indeed, they were making it more than obvious that they had been disappointed in their expectation of hearing good or enjoyable violin-playing, that they had had more than enough of the performance and only out of courtesy suffered a continued disturbance of their peace. From the way they all kept blowing the smoke of their cigars high in the air through nose and mouth one could divine their irritation. And yet Gregor's sister was playing so beautifully. Her face leaned sideways, intently and sadly her eyes followed the notes of music. Gregor crawled a little farther forward and lowered his head to the ground so that it might be possible for his eyes to meet hers. Was he an animal, that music had such an effect upon him? He felt as if the way were opening before him to the unknown nourishment he craved. He was determined to push forward till he reached his sister, to pull at her skirt and so let her know that she was to come into his room with her violin, for no one here appreciated her playing as he would appreciate it. He would never let her out of his room, at least, not so long as he lived; his frightful appearance would become, for the first time, useful to him; he would watch all the doors of his room at once and spit at intruders; but his sister should need no constraint, she should stay with him of her own free will; she should sit beside him on the sofa, bend down her ear to him and hear him confide that he had had the firm intention of sending her to the Conservatorium, and that, but for this mishap, last Christmas—surely Christmas was long past?—he would have announced it to everybody without allowing a single objection. After this confession his sister would be so touched that she would burst into tears, and Gregor would then raise himself to her shoulder and kiss her on the neck, which, now that she went to business, she kept free of any ribbon or collar.

"Mr. Samsa!" cried the middle lodger, to Gregor's father, and pointed, without wasting any more words, at Gregor, now working himself slowly forwards. The violin fell silent, the middle lodger first smiled to his friends with a shake of the head and then looked at Gregor again. Instead of driving Gregor out, his father seemed to think it more needful to begin by soothing down the lodgers, although they were not at all agitated and apparently found Gregor more entertaining than the violin-playing. He hurried towards them and, spreading out his arms, tried to urge them back into their own room and at the same time to block their view of Gregor. They now began to be really a little angry, one could not tell whether because of the old man's behavior or because it had just dawned on them that all unwittingly they had such a neighbor as Gregor next door. They demanded explanations of his father, they waved their arms like arms like him, tugged uneasily at their beards, and only with reluctance backed towards their room. Meanwhile Gregor's sister, who stood there as if lost when her playing was so abruptly broken off, came to life again, pulled herself together all at once after standing for a while holding violin and bow in nervelessly hanging hands and staring at her music, pushed her violin into the lap of her mother, who was still sitting in her chair fighting asthmatically for breath, and ran into the lodgers' room to which they were now being shepherded by her father rather more quickly than before. One could see the pillows and blankets on the beds flying under her accustomed fingers and being laid in order. Before the lodgers had actually reached their room she had finished making the beds and slipped out.

The old man seemed once more to be so possessed by his mulish self-assertiveness that he was forgetting all the respect he should show to his lodgers. He kept driving them on and driving them on until in the very door of the bedroom the middle lodger stamped his foot loudly on the floor and so brought him to a halt. "I beg to announce," said the lodger, lifting one hand and looking also at Gregor's mother and sister, "that because of the disgusting conditions prevailing in this household and family"—here he spat on the floor with emphatic brevity—"I give you notice on the spot. Naturally I won't pay you a penny for the days I have lived here, on the contrary I shall consider bringing an action for damages against you, based on claims—believe me—that will be easily susceptible of proof." He ceased and stared straight in front of him, as if he expected something. In fact his two friends at once rushed into the breach with these words: "And we too give notice on the spot." On that he seized the door-handle and shut the door with a slam.

Gregor's father, groping with his hands, staggered forward and fell into his chair; it looked as if he were stretching himself there for his ordinary evening nap, but the marked jerkings of his head, which was as if uncontrollable, showed that he was far from asleep. Gregor had simply stayed quietly all the time on the spot where the lodgers had espied him. Disappointment at the failure of his plan, perhaps also the weakness arising from extreme hunger, made it impossible for him to move. He feared, with a fair degree of certainty, that at any moment the general tension would discharge itself in a combined attack upon him, and he lay waiting. He did not react even to the noise made by the violin as it fell off his mother's lap from under her trembling fingers and gave out a resonant note.

"My dear parents," said his sister, slapping her hand on the table by way of introduction, "things can't go on like this. Perhaps you don't realize that, but I do. I won't utter my brother's name in the presence of this creature, and so all I say is: we must try to get rid of it. We've tried to look after it and to put up with it as far as is humanly possible, and I don't think anyone could reproach us in the slightest."

"She is more than right," said Gregor's father to himself. His mother, who was still choking for lack of breath, began to cough hollowly into her hand with a wild look in her eyes.

His sister rushed over to her and held her forehead. His father's thoughts seemed to have lost their vagueness at Grete's words, he sat more upright, fingering his service cap that lay among the plates still lying on the table from the lodgers' supper, and from time to time looked at the still form of Gregor.

"We must try to get rid of it," his sister now said explicitly to her father, since her mother was coughing too much to hear a word, "it will be the death of both of you, I can see that coming. When one has to work as hard as we do, all of us, one can't stand this continual torment at home on top of it. At least I can't stand it any longer." And she burst into such a passion of sobbing that her tears dropped on her mother's face, where she wiped them off mechanically.

"My dear," said the old man sympathetically, and with evident understanding, "but what can we do?"

Gregor's sister merely shrugged her shoulders to indicate the feeling of helplessness that had now overmastered her during her weeping fit, in contrast to her former confidence.

"If he could understand us," said her father, half questioningly; Grete, still sobbing, vehemently waved a hand to show how unthinkable that was.

"If he could understand us," repeated the old man, shutting his eyes to consider his daughter's conviction that understanding was impossible, "then perhaps we might come to some agreement with him. But as it is—"

"He must go," cried Gregor's sister, "that's the only solution, Father. You must just try to get rid of the idea that this is Gregor. The fact that we've believed it for so long is the root of all our trouble. But how can it be Gregor? If this were Gregor, he would have realized long ago that human beings can't live with such a creature, and he'd have gone away on his own accord. Then we wouldn't have any brother, but we'd be able to go on living and keep his memory in honor. As it is, this creature persecutes us, drives away our lodgers, obviously wants the whole apartment to himself and would have us all sleep in the gutter. Just look, Father," she shrieked all at once, "he's at it again!" And in an access of panic that was quite incomprehensible to Gregor she even quitted her mother, literally thrusting the chair from her as if she would rather sacrifice her mother than stay so near to Gregor, and rushed behind her father, who also rose up, being simply upset by her agitation, and half-spread his arms out as if to protect her.

Yet Gregor had not the slightest intention of frightening anyone, far less his sister. He had only begun to turn round in order to crawl back to his room, but it was certainly a startling operation to watch, since because of his disabled condition he could not execute the difficult turning movements except by lifting his head and then bracing it against the floor over and over again. He paused and looked round. His good intentions seemed to have been recognized; the alarm had only been momentary. Now they were all watching him in melancholy silence. His mother lay in her chair, her legs stiffly outstretched and pressed together, her eyes almost closing for sheer weariness; his father and his sister were sitting beside each other, his sister's arm around the old man's neck.

Perhaps I can go on turning round now, thought Gregor, and began his labors again. He could not stop himself from panting with the effort, and had to pause now and then to take breath. Nor did anyone harass him, he was left entirely to himself. When he had completed the turn-round he began at once to crawl straight back. He was amazed at the distance separating him from his room and could not understand how in his weak state he had managed to accomplish the same journey so recently, almost without remarking it. Intent on crawling as fast as possible, he barely noticed that not a single word, not an ejaculation from his family, interfered with his progress. Only when he was already in the doorway did he turn his head round, not completely, for his neck muscles were getting stiff, but enough to see that nothing had changed behind him except that his sister had risen to her feet. His last glance fell on his mother, who was not quite overcome by sleep.

Hardly was he well inside his room when the door was hastily pushed shut, bolted and locked. The sudden noise in his rear startled him so much that his little legs gave beneath him. It was his sister who had shown such haste. She had been standing ready waiting and had made a light spring forward, Gregor had not even heard her coming, and she cried "At last!" to her parents as she turned the key in the lock.

"And what now?" said Gregor to himself, looking round in the darkness. Soon he made the discovery that he was now unable to stir a limb. This did not surprise him, rather it seemed unnatural that he should ever actually have been able to move on these feeble little legs. Otherwise he felt relatively comfortable. True, his whole body was aching, but it seemed that the pain was gradually growing less and would finally pass away. the rotting apple in his back and the inflamed area around it, all covered with soft dust, already hardly troubled him. He thought of his family with tenderness and love. The decision that he must disappear was one that he held to even more strongly than his sister, if that were possible. In this state of vacant and peaceful meditation he remained until the tower clock struck three in the morning. The first broadening of light in the world outside the window entered his consciousness once more. The his head sank to the floor of its own accord and from his nostrils came the last faint flicker of his breath.

When the charwoman arrived early in the morning—what between her strengh and her impatience she slammed all the doors so loudly, never mind how often she had been begged not to do so, that no one in the whole apartment could enjoy any quiet sleep after her arrival—she noticed nothing unusual as she took her customary peep into Gregor's room. She thought he was lying motionless on purpose, pretending to be in the sulks; she credited him with every kind of intelligence. Since she happened to have the long-handled broom in her hand she tried to tickle him up with it from the doorway. When that too produced no reaction she felt provoked and poked at him a little harder, and only when she had pushed him along the floor without meeting any resistance was her attention aroused. It did not take her long to establish the truth of the matter, and her eyes widened, she let out a whistle, yet did not waste much time over it but tore open the door of the Samsas' bedroom and yelled into the darkness at the top of her voice: "Just look at this, it's dead; it's lying here dead and done for!"

Mr. and Mrs. Samsa started up in their double bed and before they realized the nature of the charwoman's announcement had some difficulty in overcoming the shock of it. But then they got out of bed quickly, one on either side, Mr. Samsa throwing a blanket over his shoulders, Mrs. Samsa in nothing but her nightgown; in this array they entered Gregor's room. Meanwhile the door of the living room opened, too, where Grete had been sleeping since the advent of the lodgers; she was completely dressed as if she had not been to bed, which seemed to be confirmed also by the paleness of her face. "Dead?" said Mrs. Samsa, looking questioningly at the charwoman, although she could have investigated for herself, and the fact was obvious enough without investigation. "I should say so," said the charwoman, proving her words by pushing Gregor's corpse a long way to one side with her broomstick. Mrs. Samsa made a movement as if to stop her, but checked it. "Well," said Mr. Samsa, "now thanks be to God." He crossed himself, and the three women followed his example. Grete, whose eyes never left the corpse, said: "Just see how thin he was. It's such a long time since he's eaten anything. The food came out again just as it went in." Indeed, Gregor's body was completely flat and dry, as could only now be seen when it was no longer supported by the legs and nothing prevented one from looking closely at it.

"Come in beside us, Grete, for a little while," said Mrs. Samsa with a tremulous smile, and Grete, not without looking back at the corpse, followed her parents into their bedroom. The charwoman shut the door and opened the window wide. Although it was so early in the morning a certain softness was perceptible in the fresh air. After all, it was already the end of March.

The three lodgers emerged from their room and were surprised to see no breakfast; they had been forgotten. "Where's our breakfast?" said the middle lodger peevishly to the charwoman. But she put her finger to her lips and hastily, without a word, indicated by gestures that they should go into Gregor's room. They did so and stood, their hands in the pockets of their somewhat shabby coats, around Gregor's corpse in the room where it was now fully light.

At that the door of the Samsas' bedroom opened and Mr. Samsa appeared in his uniform, his wife on one arm, his daughter on the other. They all looked a little as if they had been crying; from time to time Grete hid her face on her father's arm.

"Leave my house at once!" said Mr. Samsa, and pointed to the door without disengaging himself from the women. "What do you mean by that?" said the middle lodger, taken somewhat aback, with a feeble smile. The two others put their hands behind them and kept rubbing them together, as if in gleeful expectation of a fine set-to in which they were bound to come off the winners. "I mean just what I say," answered Mr. Samsa, and advanced in a straight line with his two companions towards the lodger. He stood his ground at first quietly, looking at the floor as if his thought were taking a new pattern in his head. "Then let us go, by all means," he said, and looked up at Mr. Samsa as if in a sudden access of humility he were expecting some renewed sanction for this decision. Mr. Samsa merely nodded briefly once or twice with meaning eyes. Upon that the lodger really did go with long strides into the hall, his two friends had been listening and had quite stopped rubbing their hands for some moments and now went scuttling after him as if afraid that Mr. Samsa might get into the hall before them and cut them off from their leader. In the hall they all three took their hats from the rack, their sticks from the umbrella stand, bowed in silence and quitted the apartment. With a suspiciousness which proved quite unfounded Mr. Samsa and the two women followed them out to the landing; leaning over the banister they watched the three figures slowly but surely going down the long stairs, vanishing from sight at a certain turn of the staircase on every floor and coming into view again after a moment or so; the more they dwindled, the more the Samsa family's interest in them dwindled, and when a butcher's boy met them and passed them on the stairs coming up proudly with a tray on his head, Mr. Samsa and the two women soon left the landing and as if a burden had been lifted from them went back into their apartment.

They decided to spend this day in resting and going for a stroll; they had not only deserved such a respite from work, but absolutely needed it. And so they sat down at the table and wrote three notes of excuse, Mr. Samsa to his board of management, Mrs. Samsa to her employer and Grete to the head of her firm. While they were writing, the charwoman came in to say that she was going now, since her morning's work was finished. At first they only nodded without looking up, but as she kept hovering there they eyed her irritably. "Well?" said Mr. Samsa. The charwoman stood grinning in the doorway as if she had good news to impart to the family but meant not to say a word unless properly questioned. The small ostrich feather standing upright on her hat, which had annoyed Mr. Samsa ever since she was engaged, was waving gaily in all directions. "Well, what is it then?" asked Mrs. Samsa, who obtained more respect from the charwoman then the others. "Oh," said the charwoman, giggling so amiably that she could not at once continue, "just this, you don't need to bother about how to get rid of the thing next door. It's been seen to already." Mrs. Samsa and Grete bent over their letters again, as if preoccupied; Mr. Samsa, who perceived that she was eager to begin describing it all in detail, stopped her with a decisive hand. But since she was not allowed to tell her story, she remembered the great hurry she was in, being obviously deeply huffed: "Bye, everybody," she said, whirling off violently, and departed with a frightful slamming of doors.

"She'll be given notice tonight," said Mr. Samsa, but neither from his wife nor his daughter did he get any answer, for the charwoman seemed to have shattered again the composure they had barely achieved. They rose, went to the window and stayed there, clasping each other tight. Mr. Samsa turned in his chair to look at them and quietly observed them for a little. Then he called out: "Come along, now, do. Let bygones be bygones. And you might have some consideration for me." The two of them complied at once, hastened to him, caressed him and quickly finished their letters.

Then they all three left the apartment together, which was more than they had done for months, and went by tram into the open country outside the town. The tram, in which they were the only passengers, was filled with warm sunshine. Leaning comfortably back in their seats they canvassed their prospects for the future, and it appeared on closer inspection that these were not at all bad, for the jobs they had got, which so far they had never really discussed with each other, were all three admirable and likely to lead to better things later on. The greatest immediate improvement in their condition would of course arise from moving to another house; they wanted to take a smaller and cheaper but also better situated and more easily run apartment than the one they had, which Gregor had selected. While they were thus conversing, it struck both Mr. and Mrs. Samsa, almost at the same moment, as they became aware of their daughter's increasing vivacity, that in spite of all the sorrow of recent times, which had made her cheeks pale, she had bloomed into a pretty girl with a good figure. They grew quieter and half unconsciously exchanged glances of complete agreement, having come to the conclusion that it would soon be time to find a good husband for her. And it was like a confirmation of their new dreams and excellent intentions that at the end of their journey their daughter sprang to her feet first and stretched her young body.

ALBERTO MORAVIA

EYE-WITNESS

Translated by Angus Davidson

They say that the day will come when we shall all be masters and there won't be any servants. They say that the occupation of a servant is unworthy of a man who is a man because one man ought not to serve another. They say that the day will come when we do everything for ourselves, without any servants, like savages. I'm not disputing it: man never stands still; he feels a need to make changes in everything that exists, and very likely the changes are for the worse, but he is bound to make them and then, to comfort himself, he calls them progress. But there's one thing I'm sure of: out of ten men—as far as I know, anyhow—two, perhaps, are born masters, but the others are born servants. The master who is a born master likes to give orders from the very cradle; but the others are not content until they have found a master to give orders to *them*. Well, well, men are all different; and in spite of all sorts of progress there will always be masters and servants, only they'll call them by another name; as we all know, words, to men, are everything; and the man who is offended at hearing himself called "porter" will no doubt run up eagerly if someone shouts "luggage-carrier" at him.

As for me, I was born a servant, I have lived up till now as a servant and I shall die, I daresay, as an old dotard, but still a servant. I like to serve; I like to obey; I like to submit to the will of another. To serve: there is a possibility, however, that the word may be misunderstood. For if you come to think of it, while I am serving my master, he is serving me. I mean, in fact, that if there wasn't a master I should not be able to be a servant. And what should I do then? Become a gravedigger?

And so, from one place to another, changing either because I did not like my master, or because he did not like me, or for some other reason, I finished up in a villa on the Via Cassia, where I thought I had found a good situation. In this recently built villa lived a recently married couple: she a blonde, with a long, lovely face and enormous, intense blue eyes, very thin and tall and elegant, her boyish appearance emphasized by her golden hair cut short *à la* Bonaparte; he small and dark and powerfully built, with disproportionately broad shoulders, a square face, a loud voice, his whole person full of authority and importance—one of those small men who make up for their size by a domineering, arrogant manner. He was evidently a proper rustic by origin—judging, anyhow, by his mother who turned up at the villa on one occasion and whom I very nearly mistook for one of the peasant-women who go round with baskets of new-laid eggs. His wife, on the other hand, came of a good family; I think she was the daughter of a magistrate. I said it was a good situation, but I did not say it was an ideal one: for we were isolated, twenty kilometres along the Via Cassia, and for a manservant who did not have a contemplative character like mine this would have been a serious disadvantage. Then, the villa was a large one, with a ground floor all reception-rooms and an upper floor all bedrooms, and there were only three of us servants, not counting the gardener: the cook, the housemaid and myself. Finally—and this, in my opinion, was the worst thing—neither he nor she was really and truly a "master", that is, a master born: he was a peasant, son and grandson of peasants; she was of good family but uprooted; she set herself up as mistress of the house but she hadn't the habit of it, and, as everyone knows, in these matters it's habit that counts.

Early in the morning, after breakfast, he would leave the house, get into his powerful, expensive car and drive off along the Via Cassia; generally he would stay out all day; and I have an idea that in Rome, apart from his import-export office, he also had some sort of a love-nest. She also had an expensive car which she drove herself, but she used it rarely, either because she did not like going into town or, more probably, because she did not know anybody there; so she stayed at home, wandering round, in trousers and jumper, from one room to another, from one floor to the other, and also, if the weather was fine, round the garden. She was always doing something, it is true, for in such a big house there was always something to do; otherwise, especially in the afternoon, she would curl up in an armchair, sitting on her own legs, and read; but whatever she was doing, wandering round the house or reading, you could see that she was discontented and bored. Sometimes she would stand behind me, in the garden, while I was helping the gardener to put in plants and prune trees; or again she would get on her horse—for she had a fine horse in a stable at the far end of the garden—and go galloping off round the countryside; but always, whether in the garden or on horseback, she had that discontented, bored look on her face.

At last, often after dark, he would come home again, and would begin furiously blowing his horn as soon as he reached the turning from the Via Cassia. From the sound of that horn it was clear who was master in the villa: she would jump up from the sofa where she was reading and run to the door on long legs tightly encased in very tight trousers; beside her, barking, ran two enormous Great Danes, as big as calves, which had been sleeping, curled up at her feet, all the afternoon; the maid, too, would come running, tying on her apron and adjusting her cap; the gardener, who was also the custodian, would run to open the gates of the drive; and I myself would run to open the front door. He would bring his car round the curve of the drive, enveloping us in the dazzling light of his headlamps, then get out and enter the house with the deportment of a Mussolini. His first words were always the same: "Is it ready?" Then he would go and stretch himself out on one of the many sofas in the drawing-room; and she, like an amorous cat, would nestle close up to him and, taking his hand, begin stroking the long black hairs on his wrist with her finger-tips. He abandoned his hand and arm to her, and meanwhile, with his other hand, held up the newspaper, which he read without taking any notice of her. Then I would button up my jacket, throw open the double doors of the dining-room and announce, with a slight bow: "Dinner is served."

Have you ever seen, in some humble eating-place on the outskirts of the city, a poor labourer, all dirty and sweaty and with his little hat made of newspaper still on his head, gulping down a big plateful of beans and pork crackling? Well, my master behaved just like that, for all that he had come home in an expensive car and had suits made of English cloth. At one end of the very long yellow marble table, with its lace mats and its glass, silver and porcelain that could not have been finer, *she* sat, stiff and upright and full of dignity; at the other end, sprawling crookedly at the table with his napkin tucked into his collar, sat *he*—in other words, the labourer. But why do I say the labourer? I'm slandering labourers. He, like a child that hasn't yet learned to walk and that tumbles down on all fours every other step, he, I say, tried to eat with a knife and fork but often resorted to his fingers, especially if it was a case of chicken or veal cutlets. No need to mention that he chewed with his mouth open or drank with his mouth full, that he wiped his lips with the back of his hand, that he balanced a row of peas on his knife and thrust them into his mouth: with him, one vulgar gesture succeeded another like so many pearls on a string. Naturally his wife suffered, for, as she often repeated, she set great store by good manners. I used to see her staring at him with her big blue eyes, then looking at me, and then at the flowers in the middle of the table; or again she would sigh and bend her head. But he took no notice and went on worse than before. Finally she would say to me: "Remigio, change the plates, please"; but he, as he gnawed away at some bone or other, would protest with a growl, just like a dog; and so I waited with the clean plate in my hand till he had finished.

I went on like this for about a month, and, apart from these regrettable dinners, I liked the place. I was left in peace, I had a nice room with a bath, and I was able, into the bargain, to devote myself to gardening, for which I have a passion. But one evening the storm broke which, secretly, I had always foreseen. He, as usual, had thrown himself on his plate of meat with his hands; I recall that it was grilled lamb cutlets; she was watching him and, as usual, the sight pained her. He gnawed all the cutlets, one after the other, four of them in all, covering himself with grease up to the ears, and then, when it seemed that he had finished, he started all over again. Firmly she said to him, from the other end of the table: "Valentino, couldn't you stop eating always with your hands? Apart from anything else, you wipe your fingers on the napkins and one would need a set of two dozen of them to keep up with you."

He was crushing a bone with his teeth, which were strong, close-set and white, like the teeth of a wolf. He rolled his eyes fiercely, and said nothing. She blinked her eyelids and persevered: "Valentino. . . ."

He put down the bone for a moment and said, very clearly: "Leave me alone!" Then he picked up the bone again.

"You oughtn't to eat with your fingers," she resumed, in an agitated nervous way; "it's only boors who eat with their fingers."

"I'm a boor, then, am I?"

"Yes, if you go on like that, you certainly are."

"And d'you know what *you* are?"

"I don't know and I don't want to know. . . . But do stop eating with your fingers."

"You're a pauper, a bore and an idiot."

She flinched at these insults as though someone had thrown a glass of wine in her face. Then she said, with dignity: "I may be a pauper, but in my home people didn't eat with their fingers."

"Of course not: you didn't have anything to eat."

"Valentino!"

"Shut up, you idiot!"

Then she lost patience. Leaning forward on the table, her eyes narrowing with hatred, she hissed: "I've never told you all that I think of you . . . but the moment's come to tell you now: you're a boor, you're a peasant, you're a lout. . . . You're no good for anything but making money. If you were at least goodlooking—but you're not, you're just a dwarf."

To be called a dwarf was obviously the indignity that hurt him most. I drew back only just in time; otherwise he would have knocked me down as he rushed from his place to the other end of the table where his wife was sitting. She sat quite still and watched him coming with a pale, twisted smile. As her husband reached her he raised his hand; she stared straight at him. He struck her in the face, once and then again. She rose and walked slowly out of the room; her husband followed her, in a towering rage; and then I heard cries and yells but it was *he* who was shouting all the time, and there must have been blows given, but I saw nothing. Quietly I cleared the table, just as I did every evening, and then went to my own room. To tell the truth, this scene had not made any particular impression upon me: in the first place I had, as I have said, foreseen it for some time; besides, as we all know, the table is the place where scenes happen, and during my career as a manservant I had witnessed I don't know how many scenes of this kind—and even more violent ones.

Next morning I got up very early and went to the pantry. The villa was immersed in deep silence, the silence of the country. I took a pair of his shoes and started cleaning them, humming under my breath, in front of the wide-open, sun-filled window. At that moment, suddenly the door opened and she appeared on the threshold.

I looked at her and at once realized that the blows must have been many and violent. One eye had swelled up and was half-closed in the middle of a circular bruise—one of those dark bruises that go green and then yellow and take a month to disappear. This bruise gave her whole face a strange look, at the same time both comic and sad. I looked at her, and the bruise was one of those things which, the less you want to look at them, the more you do so. Then she said: "Remigio, I'm very sorry, but I'm forced to give you notice."

This, truly, I was not expecting. I stood there open-mouthed, with the shoe in my hand. Finally I stammered: "But Signora, what have I done that you should have to give me notice?"

She replied coldly: "You haven't done anything; in fact I'm very pleased with you."

"Well, then?"

"I'm giving you notice because of what happened yesterday evening."

"But what has that to do with me?"

"It has nothing to do with you, but you heard and saw, and I can't bear the idea of your staying in the house after what you heard and saw."

"But, Signora," I said, understanding at last, "these are things that happen. . . . All husbands and wives come to words and blows—in the upper as well as the lower classes. I swear to you that, as far as I am concerned, it's just as though I hadn't seen or heard anything."

"That may be so, but I can't bear to be waited on by someone who heard and saw these things. I'm sorry, but you must go."

"But, Signora, you're ruining me."

"I'll give you a very good reference," she said. And, with these words, she went away.

You see? It was they who came to words and blows; but I, who had nothing whatever to do with it, got the sack. I did not try to press this point, nor did I wish to refer the matter to her husband, who would certainly have admitted that I was right; fundamentally I liked her, and I understood her and I was aware that for her it would be yet another humiliation. Furthermore, she would then have hated me and I should have had to leave just the same. So I did not breathe a word; I packed up and went away that same day, without waiting for my week's notice. But now we come back to what I said before: with one who was truly mistress in her own house this would not have happened. A real, born mistress does not even see her manservant; for her he is transparent like glass. Why, she can even take off all her clothes in his presence, or get exasperated with her husband; it's just as though the servant were not there. Well, well, it seems there are no real masters and mistresses left in the world.

HEINRICH BÖLL

ACTION WILL BE TAKEN

Translated by Leila Vennewitz

Probably one of the strangest interludes in my life was the time I spent as an employee in Alfred Wunsiedel's factory. By nature I am inclined more to pensiveness and inactivity than to work, but now and again prolonged financial difficulties compel me—for pensiveness is no more profitable than inactivity—to take on a so-called job. Finding myself once again at a low ebb of this kind, I put myself in the hands of the employment office and was sent with seven other fellow-sufferers to Wunsiedel's factory, where we were to undergo an aptitude test.

The exterior of the factory was enough to arouse my suspicions: the factory was built entirely of glass brick, and my aversion to well-lit buildings and well-lit rooms is as strong as my aversion to work. I became even more suspicious when we were immediately served breakfast in the well-lit, cheerful coffee shop: pretty waitresses brought us eggs, coffee and toast, orange juice was served in tastefully designed jugs, goldfish pressed their bored faces against the sides of pale-green aquariums. The waitresses were so cheerful that they appeared to be bursting with good cheer. Only a strong effort of will—so it seemed to me—restrained them from singing away all day long. They were as crammed with unsung songs as chickens with unlaid eggs.

Right away I realized something that my fellow-sufferers evidently failed to realize: that this breakfast was already part of the test; so I chewed away reverently, with the full appreciation of a person who knows he is supplying his body with valuable elements. I did something which normally no power on earth can make me do: I drank orange juice on an empty stomach, left the coffee and egg untouched, as well as most of the toast, got up, and paced up and down in the coffee shop, pregnant with action.

As a result I was the first to be ushered into the room where the questionnaires were spread out on attractive tables. The walls were done in a shade of green that would have summoned the word "delightful" to the lips of interior decoration enthusiasts. The room appeared to be empty, and yet I was so sure of being observed that I behaved as someone pregnant with action behaves when he believes himself unobserved: I ripped my pen impatiently from my pocket, unscrewed the top, sat down at the nearest table and pulled the questionnaire toward me, the way irritable customers snatch at the bill in a restaurant.

Question No. 1: Do you consider it right for a human being to possess only two arms, two legs, eyes, and ears?

Here for the first time I reaped the harvest of my pensive nature and wrote without hesitation: "Even four arms, legs and ears would not be adequate for my driving energy. Human beings are very poorly equipped."

Question No. 2: How many telephones can you handle at one time?

Here again the answer was as easy as simple arithmetic: "When there are only seven telephones," I wrote, "I get impatient; there have to be nine before I feel I am working to capacity."

Question No. 3: How do you spend your free time?

My answer: "I no longer acknowledge the term free time—on my fifteenth birthday I eliminated it from my vocabulary, for in the beginning was the act."

I got the job. Even with nine telephones I really didn't feel I was working to capacity. I shouted into the mouthpieces: "Take immediate action!" or: "Do something!—We must have some action—Action will be taken—Action has been taken—Action should be taken." But as a rule—for I felt this was in keeping with the tone of the place—I used the imperative.

Of considerable interest were the noon-hour breaks, when we consumed nutritious foods in an atmosphere of silent good cheer. Wunsiedel's factory was swarming with people who were obsessed with telling you the story of their lives, as indeed vigorous personalities are fond of doing. The story of their lives is more important to them than their lives, you have only to press a button, and immediately it is covered with spewed-out exploits.

Wunsiedel had a right-hand man called Broschek, who had in turn made a name for himself by supporting seven children and a paralyzed wife by working night-shifts in his student days, and successfully carrying on four business agencies, besides which he had passed two examinations with honors in two years. When asked by reporters: "When do you sleep, Mr. Broschek?" he had replied: "It's a crime to sleep!"

Wunsiedel's secretary had supported a paralyzed husband and four children by knitting, at the same time graduating in psychology and German history as well as breeding shepherd dogs, and she had become famous as a night-club singer where she was known as *Vamp Number Seven*.

Wunsiedel himself was one of those people who every morning, as they open their eyes, make up their minds to act. "I must act," they think as they briskly tie their bathrobe belts around them. "I must act," they think as they shave, triumphantly watching their beard hairs being washed away with the lather: these hirsute vestiges are the first daily sacrifices to their driving energy. The more intimate functions also give these people a sense of satisfaction: water swishes, paper is used. Action has been taken. Bread gets eaten, eggs are decapitated.

With Wunsiedel, the most trivial activity looked like action: the way he put on his hat, the way—quivering with energy—he buttoned up his overcoat, the kiss he gave his wife, everything was action.

When he arrived at his office he greeted his secretary with a cry of "Let's have some action!" And in ringing tones she would call back: "Action will be taken!" Wunsiedel then went from department to department, calling out his cheerful: "Let's have some action!" Everyone would answer: "Action will be taken!" And I would call back to him too, with a radiant smile, when he looked into my office: "Action will be taken!"

Within a week I had increased the number of telephones on my desk to eleven, within two weeks to thirteen, and every morning on the streetcar I enjoyed thinking up new imperatives, or chasing the words *take action* through various tenses and modulations: for two whole days I kept saying the same sentence over and over again because I thought it sounded so marvelous: "Action ought to have been taken;" for another two days it was: "Such action ought not to have been taken."

So I was really beginning to feel I was working to capacity when there actually was some action. One Tuesday morning—I had hardly settled down at my desk—Wunsiedel rushed into my office crying his "Let's have some action!" But an inexplicable something in his face made me hesitate to reply, in a cheerful gay voice as the rules dictated: "Action will be taken!" I must have paused too long, for Wunsiedel, who seldom raised his voice, shouted at me: "Answer! Answer, you know the rules!" And I answered, under my breath, reluctantly, like a child who is forced to say: I am a naughty child. It was only by a great effort that I managed to bring out the sentence: "Action will be taken," and hardly had I uttered it when there really was some action: Wunsiedel dropped to the floor. As he fell he rolled over onto his side and lay right across the open doorway. I knew at once, and I confirmed it when I went slowly around my desk and approached the body on the floor: he was dead.

Shaking my head I stepped over Wunsiedel, walked slowly along the corridor to Broschek's office, and entered without knocking. Broscheck was sitting at his desk, a telephone receiver in each hand, between his teeth a ballpoint pen with which he was making notes on a writing pad, while with his bare feet he was operating a knitting machine under the desk. In this way he helps to clothe his family. "We've had some action," I said in a low voice.

Broschek spat out the ballpoint pen, put down the two receivers, reluctantly detached his toes from the knitting machine.

"What action?" he asked.

"Wunsiedel is dead," I said.

"No," said Broschek.

"Yes," I said, "come and have a look!"

"No," said Broschek, "that's impossible," but he put on his slippers and followed me along the corridor.

"No," he said, when we stood beside Wunsiedel's corpse, "no, no!" I did not contradict him. I carefully turned Wunsiedel over onto his back, closed his eyes, and looked at him pensively.

I felt something like tenderness for him, and realized for the first time that I had never hated him. On his face was that expression which one sees on children who obstinately refuse to give up their faith in Santa Claus, even though the arguments of their playmates sound so convincing.

"No," said Broschek, "no."

"We must take action," I said quietly to Broschek.

"Yes," said Broschek, "we must take action."

Action was taken: Wunsiedel was buried, and I was delegated to carry a wreath of artificial roses behind his coffin, for I am equipped with not only a penchant for pensiveness and inactivity but also a face and figure that go extremely well with dark suits. Apparently as I walked along behind Wunsiedel's coffin carrying the wreath of artificial roses I looked superb. I received an offer from a fashionable firm of funeral directors to join their staff as a professional mourner. "You are a born mourner," said the manager, "your outfit would be provided by the firm. Your face—simply superb!"

I handed in my notice to Broschek, explaining that I had never really felt I was working to capacity there; that, in spite of the thirteen telephones, some of my talents were going to waste. As soon as my first professional appearance as a mourner was over I knew: This is where I belong, this is what I am cut out for.

Pensively I stand behind the coffin in the funeral chapel, holding a simple bouquet, while the organ plays Handel's *Largo*, a piece that does not receive nearly the respect it deserves. The cemetery café is my regular haunt; there I spend the intervals between my professional engagements, although sometimes I walk behind coffins which I have not been engaged to follow, I pay for flowers out of my own pocket and join the welfare worker who walks behind the coffin of some homeless person. From time to time I also visit Wunsiedel's grave, for after all I owe it to him that I discovered my true vocation, a vocation in which pensiveness is essential and inactivity my duty.

It was not till much later that I realized I had never bothered to find out what was being produced in Wunsiedel's factory. I expect it was soap.

NIKOLAI GOGOL

The DIARY of a MADMAN

Translated by Andrew R. MacAndrew

October 3

An extraordinary thing happened today. I got up rather late, and when Marva brought my boots, I asked her the time. Hearing that ten had struck quite a while before, I dressed in a hurry. I must say I'd as soon have skipped the office altogether, knowing the sour look the Chief of my Division would give me. For a long time now he has been telling me: "How come, my man, you're always in such a muddle? Sometimes you dart around like a house on fire, and get your work in such a tangle the Devil himself couldn't put it straight; you're likely to start a new heading with a small letter and give no date or reference number." The vicious old crane! He must envy me for sitting in the Director's room and sharpening his quills. So I wouldn't have gone to the office if not in hopes of seeing the cashier and trying to get even a small advance on my salary out of the Jew. What a creature he is! The Last Judgment will come before you'll get a month's pay out of him in advance. Even if there's a dire emergency, you can beg till something bursts inside you; he won't give in, the hoary monster. Yet at home his own cook slaps him around. Everyone knows that. I see no advantage in working in our department. No side benefits whatever. It's not like working, say, for the City Administration or in the Justice Department. There you may see someone nesting in a corner and scribbling away. He may be wearing a shabby coat and have a snout that you'd want to spit at. But then, just take a look at the summer house he rents! And don't even think of offering him a gilt china cup: this, he'd say, may be all right for a doctor. But he—he must have a pair of horses maybe, or a carriage, or a beaver fur—300 rubles' worth or so. And he looks so quiet and sounds so deferential and polite: "Would you," he'll say, "be so kind as to lend me your penknife to sharpen my quill, if you please." But he'll strip a petitioner naked, except perhaps for his shirt. On the other hand, though, to work in our department carries more prestige. The people of the City Administration have never dreamt of such cleanliness. Then we have red mahogany tables and our superiors always address us politely. Yes, if it weren't for the prestige, I confess I'd have left the department long ago.

I put on my old overcoat and, as it was pouring rain, took my umbrella. The streets were quite deserted except for some peasant women, their skirts thrown over their heads, a few merchants under umbrellas, and a coachman here and there. As for decent people there was only our kind, the civil-service clerk, squelching along. I saw him at a street crossing. And as soon as I saw him I said to myself: "You're not on your way to the office, my man. You're after that one trotting ahead over there and it's her legs you're staring at." What a rogue your civil servant is! When it comes to such matters, he can take on an army officer any day. He'll try to pick up anything under a bonnet. I was passing by a store, thinking about all this, when a carriage stopped in front of it. I recognized it at once: it belonged to the Director of our Department, himself. But, I thought, he cannot possibly need anything here—it must be his daughter. I pressed myself against the wall. The footman opened the carriage door and she fluttered out like a little bird. Ah, how she looked around, first right, then left, how her eyes and eyebrows flashed past me! . . . Oh God, I'm lost, lost forever. And why did she have to drive out in the pouring rain? Try and deny after that, that women have a passion for clothing. She did not recognize me. Besides, I was trying to hide myself; my coat was quite stained and out of fashion too. Nowadays, they are wearing long collars on their coats while I had two very short ones, one on top of the other. Her lap dog was too slow to get into the store while the door was open and had to stay in the street. I know this little dog. She's called Madgie. Then, a minute or so later, I heard a thin little voice: "Hello, Madgie." I'll be damned! Who's that talking? I turned around and saw two ladies walking under their umbrellas: one old, the other young and pretty. But they had already passed when I heard again, just next to me: "You ought to be ashamed, Madgie!" What on earth was going on? I saw Madgie and a dog that had been following the two ladies sniffing at one another. "Maybe I'm drunk," I said to myself, "but it's not likely. It doesn't happen to me very often." "No, Fidele, you're wrong." With my own eyes I saw Madgie forming the words, "I was, bow-wow, I was, bow-ow-ow, very sick." Talk about a lap dog! I must say I was quite surprised to hear her talking. Later, however, when I had properly sized up the situation, I was no longer surprised. As a matter of fact, the world has seen many similar occurrences before. I've heard that, in England, a fish broke surface and uttered a couple of words in such an outlandish language that scholars have been trying to work out their meaning for three years—so far in vain. Then, too, I read in the newspapers about two cows who went into a store and asked for a pound of tea. But I'll confess that I was much more bewildered when Madgie said: "I *did* write you, Fidele. Perhaps Fido didn't give you my letter." Now, I'd be willing to forfeit a month's pay if I've ever heard of a dog that could write. Only a gentleman can write correctly anyway. Of course, one finds some scribbling shopkeepers—even serfs—but that sort of writing is mostly mechanical; no commas, periods, or spelling. So I was surprised. I'll confess that recently I have been seeing and hearing things that no one else has ever seen or heard. "Let's," I said to myself, "follow this little dog and find out who she is and what her thoughts are." I opened my umbrella and followed the ladies. We crossed Pea Street, from there on to Tradesman's Avenue, turned into Carpenter's Lane, and finally stopped before a large building near Cuckoo Bridge. "I know this house," I said to myself, "it's the Zverkov house." What a house! Who isn't to be found there! There are so many cooks, so many Poles! And it teems with my fellow civil servants; they sit there on top of one another, like dogs. I have a friend there who can play the trumpet quite well. The ladies went up to the fifth floor. "Fine," I thought, "I won't go in now. I'll make a note of the place and wait for the first opportunity."

October 4

Today is Wednesday and that's why I was in our Director's study at his home. I purposely came in early, settled down and sharpened all the quills. Our Director must be a very brilliant man. His study is crammed with bookcases. I looked at some of the titles: such erudition all over the place—cuts an ordinary person off completely; they're all in French or German. And just look into his face, good gracious! What a lot of importance shines in his eyes! I've never heard him utter an unnecessary word. Except, perhaps, when one hands him some documents, he may ask: "How's the weather outside?" "It's quite damp, sir." Yes, he's different from our kind. A public figure! Nevertheless, I feel that he has taken a special liking to me. If only his daughter . . . Ah, what a rogue I am! Never mind, never mind . . . Quiet! . . . I was reading the *Bee*. Aren't the French a stupid race? Whatever can they be driving at? I'd like to take them all and give each one of them a good thrashing. In the same journal I also read a very nice description of a ball by a landowner from Kursk. Kursk landowners certainly write well. . . . Whereupon I noticed that it was striking twelve-thirty and our Director still hadn't left his bedroom. But then, around one-thirty, a thing happened that no pen can adequately describe. The door opened; I thought it was the Director and jumped up from my desk holding the documents in my hand; but it was her, in person! Holy Fathers, the way she was dressed! Her dress was white, all fluffy, like a swan, and when she looked at me, I swear it was like the sun! She nodded to me and said: "Hasn't Papa been in here?" What a voice! A canary, an absolute canary. "Ma'am," I was on the point of saying, "don't have me put to death. But if you do decide that I must die, let it be by your own aristocratic little hand." But my tongue would not obey me and I only muttered, "No, ma'am." Her glance slid from me to the books and she dropped her handkerchief. I rushed like mad, slipped on the blasted parquet and almost smashed my nose. But somehow I recovered my balance and picked it up. Holy Saints, what a hanky! Such fine, delicate linen, and amber, sheer amber. It exuded aristocracy. She said, "Thank you" and smiled, but so faintly that her divine lips hardly moved, and then she left. I remained seated there and, after another hour, a footman came in and told me: "You may go home, the master has gone out." The flunky is the one thing I cannot stand. They're always sprawled out in the entrance hall, not even bothering to acknowledge my existence with a little nod. Once, one of those lumps actually offered me snuff, and without even getting up. Don't you know, you stupid flunky, that I am a civil servant and that I come from a respectable family? Still, I picked up my hat and pulled on my overcoat unaided since those gents wouldn't think of helping you, and left. At home, I lay on my bed most of the time. Then I copied an excellent poem:

Without you one hour crept
Slowly like a year.
"Is my life worth while," I wept,
"When you are not near?"

Sounds like Pushkin. In the evening, I put on my overcoat and walked over to the Director's house and waited by the gate for quite a while to see whether she wouldn't come out and get into her carriage. But she didn't

November 6

Something has got into the Chief of my Division. When I arrived at the office he called me and began as follows: "Now then, tell me. What's the matter with you?" "What do you mean? Nothing," I said. "Come, try to understand; aren't you over forty? Time to be a bit wiser. What do you fancy you are? Don't imagine I can't see what you're up to. I know you're trailing after the Director's daughter. Just look at yourself—what are you? Just nothing. You haven't a penny to your name. Look in the mirror. How can you even think of such things?" The hell with him! Just because he's got a face like a druggist's bottle and that quiff of hair on his head all curled and pomaded, and because he holds his head up in the air like that, he thinks he can get away with anything. I see through his indignation. He's envious; perhaps he's noticed the marks of favor bestowed upon me. A lot I care what he says. So he's a Divisional Chief, so what! So he hangs out his gold watch chain and has custommade boots at thirty rubles. Let him be damned. Perhaps he imagines I had a shopkeeper or a tailor for a father. I'm a gentleman! And I can be promoted too. I'm only forty-two, an age when one's career is really just beginning. Wait, my friend, I'll go higher than you yet, and, God willing, very, very much higher. Then I'll have a social position beyond your dreams. Do you imagine you're the only one to have dignity? Give me a fashionable new coat, let me wear a tie like yours, and you won't be worthy to shine my shoes. My lack of means—that's the only trouble.

November 8

Went to the theater. The play was about the Russian fool Filatka. Laughed a lot. They had a vaudeville show as well, full of amusing verses lampooning lawyers, so outspoken that I wondered how it got past the censor; as to the merchants, it says plainly that they swindle the people, that their sons wallow in debauchery and elbow their way into society. There was also an amusing couplet which complained about the way newspapermen criticize everything and asked the audience for protection from them. Playwrights write very amusing plays nowadays. I love going to the theater. As soon as I get hold of a few pennies, I can't help myself, I go. But civil servants are such swine . . . you won't catch clods like them going to the theater, not even if they're given free tickets. One actress sang really well. . . . It made me think of . . . What a rogue I am! Never mind, never mind . . . silence!

November 9

Left for the office at eight. The Divisional Chief pretended he hadn't noticed me come in. And I also acted as though nothing had happened between us. I went through the papers and sorted them out. Left at four. On the way home, passed by the Director's house but didn't see anyone. After dinner, mostly lay on my bed.

Today, I sat in the Director's study and sharpened twenty-three quills for him, and four quills for . . . oh-oh . . . her. He likes to have as many quills to hand as possible. My, how brainy he must be! Usually he doesn't say much but I guess he must be weighing everything in that head of his. I'd like to know what he has on his mind most of the time, what's cooking up there. I'd like to have a closer look at these people, how they live, with all their subtle innuendoes and courtly jokes; I wish I knew how they behave and what they do among themselves. I've often tried to engage the Director in conversation but I'm damned if it's ever come off. I've managed to say it's warm or cold outside and that is absolutely as far as I've got. One day I'd like just to step into their drawing room. The door is ajar sometimes and from there I can see another door, leading to another room. That drawing room! You should see how it's decorated. All those mirrors and fine pieces of porcelain. I'd also like to see the part where her rooms are. That's where I'd really like to go! I'd like to peep into her boudoir, and see all those little jars and bottles of hers standing there amidst the sort of flowers one doesn't even dare breathe on; to have a glimpse at the dress she has thrown off, lying there looking more like air than a dress. It would be wonderful to glance into her bedroom. . . . Miracles must happen there. It's a paradise surpassing the heavenly one. What wouldn't I give to see the little stool upon which her delicate foot descends when she gets out of bed and watch how an incredibly fine, immaculate stocking is pulled up her leg. . . . Oh, the roguish thoughts! . . . Never mind . . . never mind . . . silence!

But today something suddenly became clear to me when I recalled the conversation between the two dogs I'd overheard on Nevsky Avenue. Fine, I said to myself, now I'll find out everything. I must get hold of the letters exchanged between those nasty mutts. I'm sure to find out something. Now I'll confess that, at one point, I almost called Madgie and said to her: "Listen, Madgie, we are alone now. If you wish, I'll even lock the door so that no one'll see us. Tell me everything you know about your mistress: what she's like and all that. And don't worry, I swear I'll not repeat a thing to anyone." But the sly little mutt just sort of shrank into herself, put her tail between her legs, and left the room in silence, as though she hadn't heard a thing. For a long time I've suspected that dogs are much more intelligent than men; I was even certain that they could speak and simply chose not to out of a peculiar stubbornness. A dog is an extraordinary politician and notices everything, every step a human takes. Still, whatever happens, tomorrow I'll go to the Zverkov house and question Fidele and, if possible, I'll lay my hand on Madgie's letters to her.

November 12

At 2:00 P.M. I went out determined to find Fidele and question her. I can't stand the smell of cabbage which comes pouring out of all the greengrocers along Tradesman's Avenue. This, and the infernal stench from under the gates of every house, sent me scurrying, holding my nose. And all the soot and smoke that they let pour out of the vile workshops make it a quite unsuitable place for a person of breeding to take a stroll. When I reached the sixth floor and rang the bell, out came a girl with little freckles and not too bad-looking at that. I recognized her at once. She was the one I had seen walking with the old woman. She blushed a little and I immediately saw through her: what you need, my dear, is a husband. "What do you want?" she asked. "I want to have a talk with your doggie."

The girl was stupid. I could see from the start how stupid she was! At that moment the mutt ran in yapping furiously and as I was trying to grab her, the repulsive creature almost caught my nose between her teeth. But then I saw her basket in the corner—which was just what I was looking for! I went over to it and felt under the straw and, to my great joy, I found a small bundle of papers. Seeing what I was doing, the nasty little cur first took a bite out of my calf; then, when upon further sniffing she found that I had taken her letters, she began whining and making up to me, but I told her, "Oh no, my dear. See you later!" And off I went. I believe the girl mistook me for a madman—she seemed very frightened indeed.

Once home, I wanted to get down to work immediately, to have those letters sorted before dark, since I can't see too well by candlelight. But for some reason Marva decided to scrub the floor just then. Those stupid Finns always succumb to their obsession for cleanliness at the worst moments. So I went out for a walk to think it all over. Now, finally, I'll find out everything about these intrigues and plots; I'll understand all the little wheels and springs and get to the bottom of the matter. These letters will explain. Dogs are a clever race. They know all about intrigue and so it's all bound to be in their letters: all there is to know about the Director's character and actions. And she, she too is sure to be mentioned . . . but never mind that . . . silence! I came home toward evening. Most of the time, I lay on my bed.

November 13

Let's see now. This letter looks quite legible, though there *is* something canine about the handwriting:

> *Dear Fidele, I still find it difficult to get accustomed to the commonness of your name. Couldn't they find a better one for you? Fidele, like Rose, is very ordinary, but all that's beside the point. I'm very glad we have decided to write to each other.*

The spelling is very good. It's even punctuated correctly. This is considerably better than our Divisional Chief can do, although he claims to have gone to some university or other. Let's see further on:

> *I believe that sharing feelings and impressions with another is one of the main blessings in life. . . .*

Hm! The thought is stolen from a work translated from the German. The author's name escapes me now.

> *I speak from experience although I've never been much further than the gates of our house. But then, isn't my life full of blessings? My young mistress, whom her papa calls Sophie, is crazy about me.*

Ouch! Never mind, never mind. Silence!

> *Papa often pets me too. I drink tea and coffee with cream. I must tell you, my dear, that I am not in the least tempted by the half-gnawed bones which our Fido chews on in the kitchen. I only like the bones of game and, even then, only if the marrow hasn't been sucked out by someone else. A mixture of sauces is nice as long as they contain no capers or vegetables. What I hate is people who give dogs the little pellets they knead out of bread. Some person sitting at the table, who has previously touched all sorts of filthy things, begins to knead a piece of bread with those same hands, then calls you and thrusts the pellet into your mouth. It is awkward somehow to refuse and, disgusted, you eat it up. . . .*

What's that all about? What rubbish! As though there weren't more interesting things to write about. Let's see the next page. There may be something less stupid.

> *Now, I'll tell you with pleasure what goes on in this household. I have mentioned the main character, whom Sophie calls Papa. He's a very strange man. . . .*

At last! I knew they had very shrewd judgment, whatever the subject. Let's see what Papa's like.

> *. . . a very strange man. He's usually silent. He speaks very little, but a week ago he never stopped saying to himself: Will I get it or not? Once he even asked me: What do you say, Madgie, will I get it or won't I? I could make no sense out of it so I smelled his shoe and left the room. Then, a week later, Papa came home overjoyed. All that morning formally dressed people came and congratulated him. At dinner Papa was gayer than I'd ever seen him before, and after dinner, he picked me up and held me level with his chest, saying: Look, Madgie, what's this? I saw some sort of a ribbon. I sniffed at it but it had no fragrance whatever. Finally, discreetly, I gave it a lick: slightly salty.*

Hm. The mutt really goes too far . . . she needs a good whipping . . . So he is that vain is he? I must take it into account.

> *Good-bye, my dear, I must run along . . . blah-blah-blah-blah . . . will finish this letter tomorrow. Hello, I am back with you. Today my mistress, Sophie . . .*

Aha! Let's see what she says about Sophie. I really *am* a rogue! But never mind, never mind. Let's go on.

> *. . . my mistress, Sophie, was in a terrific to-do. She was getting ready for a ball and I intended to take advantage of her absence and write to you. Sophie is always very happy when she's about to leave for a ball but is always very irritable while she's getting dressed for it. You know, my dear, I personally can see no pleasure in going to a ball. Sophie usually returns home from balls at 6 A.M., and I can tell by her pale and emaciated features that the poor thing hasn't been given a bite to eat. I confess I could never lead such a life. If I had to go without game in sauce or chicken-wing stews, I don't know what would become of me. A sauce is not at all bad with porridge. But nothing can make carrots, turnips, and artichokes palatable. . . .*

The style is very jerky. You can see that it's not written by a man. She starts off all right and then lapses into dogginess. Let's see another letter. Looks rather long . . . hm. . . no date . . .

> *Oh, my dear, how strongly I feel the approach of spring. My heart*

beats as though it were waiting for something. In my ears, there's a constant buzz. Very often I listen so intently behind doors that I raise my front paw. And, confidentially, I have plenty of suitors. I often sit by the window and watch them. If only you could see some of them, they're so ugly. There is a horrible mongrel with stupidity written all over him, who swaggers along the street and imagines he is a person of breeding and that everyone is bound to admire him. I paid no attention to him, as though I hadn't even noticed him. Then you should have seen the terrifying Great Dane that stopped in front of my window! If that one stood up on his hind legs, which, incidentally, the clod is incapable of doing, he would be a head taller than Sophie's Papa, who's quite tall himself and fat besides. Moreover, the lump seems to be very arrogant. I growled at him but it didn't put him off in the least. He just hung his tongue out, drooped his huge ears, and kept staring at my window, the oaf! But, my dear, you don't really imagine, do you, that my heart is indifferent to all the hopefuls? . . . You should have seen the dashing young lover that came jumping over the fence into our courtyard. His name is Treasure and he has such a nice face. . . .

Ah, damn it all! What rubbish! How much of her letters is she going to fill with such stupid stuff? I'm after *people*, not dogs! I need spiritual food and I am served these inanities. . . . Let's skip a page, perhaps we'll find something more interesting. . . .

. . . Sophie was sitting at the table sewing something. I was looking out of the window; I like to watch people in the street. Suddenly the manservant came in and announced someone. "Show him in!" Sophie said. She hugged me hard and murmured, "Oh, Madgie, darling, if you only knew who that is. He's a Guards officer, his hair is black and his eyes are so dark and so light at the same time . . . like fire." And Sophie rushed out. A minute later a young officer with black side whiskers appeared. He went to the mirror and smoothed his hair; then he looked around the room. I growled a little and settled down by my window. Soon Sophie came back, greeted him gaily, while I pretended to be busy looking out of the window. In fact, however, I turned my head sideways a little, so that I could catch what they said. You cannot imagine, Fidele dear, the silliness of that conversation. They spoke about some lady who, during a dance, kept doing a certain step instead of the one she was expected to do, then about somebody called Bobov, who looked like a stork and almost fell over, then about one Lidina, who thought she had blue eyes when they were really green, and so on and on. Oh no, I said to myself, this officer doesn't compare to Treasure. Heavens, what a difference! To start with, the officer has a wide face, quite bald except for his side whiskers which, in fact, look like a black

kerchief tied around it, whereas Treasure's face is narrow and fine and he has a sweet white patch on his brow. Treasure's waist is incomparably slenderer than the officer's, and his eyes, his gestures, and his ways are vastly superior. Really, a tremendous difference! I wonder what she finds in her officer. What on earth can she admire in him? . . .

Yes, here I tend to agree. Something seems wrong. It is quite unbelievable that this officer should have swept her off her feet. Let's see:

If she likes the officer, I think she'll soon be liking the civil-service clerk who sits in Papa's study. That one, my dear, is a real scarecrow. He looks a bit like a turtle caught in a bag. . . .

Which clerk can that be? . . .

He has a funny name and he's always sitting sharpening quills. The hair on his head is like straw. Papa sends him on errands like a servant. . . .

The filthy cur seems to be trying to get its own back! Why is my hair like straw?

Sophie can hardly control her laughter when she sees him.

You wretched, lying dog! What a filthy, poisonous tongue! As if I didn't know it's all your jealousy. I know whose tricks these are. I recognize the hand of the Divisional Chief here. For some reason, that man has sworn undying hatred for me and he is trying to harm me, to harm me every minute of the day and night. Still, let's see one more letter. It may make it clear.

My dear Fidele, forgive me for not writing to you all this time. I've been going around in absolute ecstasy. I agree, without reservation, with the philosopher who said that love is a second life. Moreover, a lot of things are changing in our household. The officer comes every day now. Sophie is madly in love with him. Papa is very gay. I even heard our Gregory, who always talks to himself while sweeping the floors, say that the wedding is close at hand, because Papa always wanted to see Sophie married to a high official or to an army officer with a brilliant career ahead of him. . . .

Hell! . . . I can't go on. . . . High officials, senior officers, they get all the best things in this world. You discover a crumb of happiness, you reach out for it and then along comes a high official or an officer and snatches it away. Goddammit! I would like so much to become a high official myself and not just to obtain her hand in marriage either. No, I'd like to be a high official just so that I could watch them jump around for my benefit; I'd listen for a while to their courtly jokes and innuendoes and then tell them what they could do with themselves. It hurts, though. Oh, hell! . . . I tore the stupid little dog's letter to shreds.

December 3

Impossible! Lies! There can't be a wedding. So what if he had a commission in the Guards? That's nothing but position, you can't touch it with your hand. A Guards officer does not have a third eye in the middle of his forehead, his nose is not made of gold but the same stuff as mine or anyone else's and he uses it to sniff not to eat, for sneezing not for coughing. I've often tried to discover where all these differences lie. Why am I a clerk? Why should I be a clerk? Perhaps I'm really a general or a count and only seem to be a clerk? Maybe I don't really know who I am? There are plenty of instances in history when somebody quite ordinary, not necessarily an aristocrat, some middle-class person or even a peasant, suddenly turns out to be a public figure and perhaps even the ruler of a country. If a peasant can turn into someone so important, where are the limits to the possibilities for a man of breeding? Imagine, for instance, me, entering a room in a general's uniform. There's an epaulet on my right shoulder, an epaulet on my left, a blue ribbon across my chest. How would that be? What tune would my beauty sing then? And Papa himself, our Director, what would he say? Ow, he's so vain! He's a Mason, no mistake about it, although he may pretend to be this or that; I noticed from the start that when he shakes hands, he sticks out two fingers only. But I can't be promoted to general or governor or anything like that overnight. What I'd like to know is, why am I a clerk? Why precisely a clerk?

December 5

I read the newspapers all morning. Strange things are happening in Spain. I can't even make them out properly. They write that the throne has been vacated and that the ranking grandees are having difficulty in selecting an heir. It seems there's discontent. Sounds very strange to me. How can a throne be vacant? They say that some donna may accede. A donna cannot accede to a throne. It's absolutely impossible. A king should sit on a throne. But they say there is no king. It's impossible that there should be no king. There must be a king but he's hidden away somewhere in anonymity. It's even possible that he's around but is being forced to remain in hiding for family reasons or for fear of some neighboring country such as France. Or there may be other reasons.

December 8

I was on the point of going to the office but various considerations held me back. I couldn't get those Spanish affairs out of my head. How can a donna possibly become ruler? They won't allow it. In the first place, England won't stand for it. Then we must keep in mind the political setup of the rest of Europe: the Austrian Emperor, our Tsar. . . . I confess I was so perturbed and hurt by these events that I could do nothing all day. Marva remarked that I was very absent-minded during dinner. . . . In fact, I believe I absent-mindedly threw a couple of plates on the floor, where they broke at once. After dinner, I walked the streets, uphill and downhill. Came across nothing of interest. Then, mostly lay on my bed and thought about the Spanish question.

Year 2000, April 43

This is a day of great jubilation. Spain has a king. They've found him. *I* am the King. I discovered it today. It all came to me in a flash. It's incredible to me now that I could have imagined that I was a civil-service clerk. How could such a crazy idea ever have entered my head? Thank God no one thought of slapping me into a lunatic asylum. Now I see everything clearly, as clearly as if it lay in the palm of my hand. But what was happening to me before? Then things loomed at me out of a fog. Now, I believe that all troubles stem from the misconception that human brains are located in the head. They are not: human brains are blown in by the winds from somewhere around the Caspian Sea.

Marva was the first to whom I revealed my identity. When she heard that she was facing the King of Spain, she flung up her hands in awe. She almost died of terror. The silly woman had never seen a King of Spain before. However, I tried to calm her and, speaking graciously, did my best to assure her of my royal favor. I was not going to hold against her all the times she had failed to shine my boots properly. The masses are so ignorant. One can't talk to them on lofty subjects. Probably she was so frightened because she thought that all kings of Spain are like Philip II. But I carefully pointed out that I wasn't like Philip II at all. I didn't go to the office. The hell with it. No, my friends, you won't entice me there now; never again shall I copy your dreadful documents.

Martober 86. Between day and night

Today, our Divisional Chief sent someone to make me go to the office. I hadn't been there for over three weeks. I went, just for a lark. The Divisional Chief expected me to come apologizing to him but I just looked at him indifferently, with not too much ire, nor too much benevolence either; then I sat down in my usual place as though unaware of the people around me. I looked around at all that scribbling rabble and thought: If only you had an inkling of who's sitting here among you, oh Lord, what a fuss you'd make. There'd be a terrific to-do and the Divisional Chief himself would bow deeply to me, as he does to the Director. They put some papers in front of me which I was supposed to abstract or something. I didn't even stir. A few minutes later, there was a general commotion. They said the Director was on his way. Several clerks jumped up, hoping he'd notice them. But I didn't budge. When word came that the Director was about to pass through our Division, they all buttoned up their coats. I did nothing of the sort. What kind of a Director does he think he is? Who says I should get up for him? Never! He's an old cork, not a Director. Yes, but an ordinary cork, the kind used for stoppering a bottle. That's all he is. But the funniest thing of all was when they gave me a paper to sign. They expected I'd sign it in the corner: head clerk such and such. Well, let them think again. I wrote in the main space, the one reserved for the Director's signature: Ferdinand VIII. You should have witnessed the awed silence that followed; but I merely waved my hand graciously and said: "Dispense with the manifestation of allegiance!" and walked out of the room. From there, I went straight to the Director's house. He was not at home. The footman tried to stop me from going in but what I said made his arms drop limp at his sides. I went straight to her boudoir. She was sitting in front of her mirror. She jumped up and stepped back, away from me. Still I did not tell her that I was the King of Spain. I simply told her that she couldn't even imagine the happiness awaiting her and that despite all our enemies' intrigues, we would be together. I did not want to say more and left. Oh, women are such perfidious things! Only now did I understand what a woman is like. So far, no one has found out whom Woman is in love with. I was the first to discover it: Woman is in love with the Devil. And I'm not joking either. Physicists write a lot of drivel about her being this, that and the other. She loves only the Devil. Look, do you see over there, in the front tier of the boxes? She raises her lorgnette. You think she's looking at that fat man with the star over there? Nothing of the sort. She's staring at the Devil, the Devil hiding behind the fat man's back. See, now he has hidden himself in the star and he's beckoning to her with his finger! And she'll marry him too. She will for sure. As for all the rest of them, all those who lick boots and proclaim their patriotism, all they really want is annuities and more annuities. Some patriots! They'd sell their mother, their father, and their God for money, the strutting betrayers of Christ! And all this crazy ambition and vanity comes from the little bubble under the tongue which has a tiny worm about the size of a pinhead in it, and it's all the work of a barber on Pea Street. I can't recall his name but the moving force behind it all is the Sultan of Turkey who pays the barber to spread Mohammedanism all over the world. They say that in France, already, the majority of the people have embraced the Mohammedan faith.

No date. A day without date

Went along Nevsky Avenue incognito. Saw the Tsar riding past. Everybody was doffing his hat, and so did I. I gave no sign that I was the King of Spain. I thought it would be undignified to reveal my identity there, in front of all those people, that it would be more proper to be presented at Court first. What has prevented me so far is the fact that I haven't got Spanish royal attire. If only I could get hold of a royal mantle of some sort. I thought of having one made but tailors are so stupid. Besides, they don't seem to be interested in their trade nowadays and go in for speculation, so that most of them end up mending roads. I decided to make a mantle out of my best coat, which I had only worn twice. But I didn't want those good-for-nothings to mess it all up—I preferred to do it myself. I locked my door so as not to be seen. I had to cut my coat to ribbons with the scissors since a mantle has a completely different style.

Can't remember the day. Nor was there a month. Damned if I know what's been going on

The mantle is ready. Marva really let out a yell when I put it on. Even so, I still don't feel ready to be presented at Court. My retinue hasn't as yet arrived from Spain. The absence of a retinue would be incompatible with my dignity. I'm expecting them at any time.

1st Date

I'm puzzled by the unaccountable delay in the arrival of my retinue. What can be holding them up? I went to the post office and inquired whether the Spanish delegates had arrived. But the postmaster is an utter fool and knows nothing: No, he says, there are no Spanish delegates around here but if you wish to mail a letter, we'll accept it. What the hell is he talking about? What letter? Letter my foot! Let druggists write letters. . . .

Madrid, Februarius the thirtieth

So I'm in Spain. It all happened so quickly that I hardly had time to realize it. This morning the Spanish delegation finally arrived for me and we all got into a carriage. I was somewhat bewildered by the extraordinary speed at which we traveled. We went so fast that in half an hour we reached the Spanish border. But then, nowadays there are railroads all over Europe and the ships go so fast too. Spain is a strange country. When we entered the first room, I saw a multitude of people with shaven heads. I soon realized, though, that these must be Dominican or Capuchin monks because they always shave their heads. I also thought that the manners of the King's Chancellor, who was leading me by the hand, were rather strange. He pushed me into a small room and said: "You sit quiet and don't you call yourself King Ferdinand again or I'll beat the nonsense out of your head." But I knew that I was just being tested and refused to submit. For this, the Chancellor hit me across the back with a stick, twice, so painfully that I almost let out a cry. But I contained myself, remembering that this is customary procedure among knights on initiation into an exalted order. To this day, they adhere to the chivalric code in Spain.

Left to myself, I decided to devote some time to affairs of state. I have discovered that China and Spain are the same thing and it's only ignorance that makes people take them for two separate countries. I advise anybody who doubts it to take a piece of paper and write the word "Spain" and they'll see for themselves that it comes out "China." I also gave much thought to a sad event that must occur tomorrow at seven o'clock. As foreseen by the famous English chemist Wellington, the Earth will mount the Moon. I confess I was deeply worried when I thought of the Moon's extraordinary sensitivity and fragility. The Moon, of course, is made in Hamburg, and I must say they do a very poor job. I wonder why England doesn't do something about it. It's a lame cooper that makes the Moon, and it's quite obvious that the fool has no conception of what the Moon should be. He uses tarred rope and olive oil and that's why the stench is so awful all over the Earth and we are forced to plug our noses. And that's why the Moon itself is such a delicate ball that men cannot live there—only noses. And that's why we can't see our own noses: they are all on the Moon. And when I thought what a heavy thing the Earth is and that, sitting down on the Moon, it would crush our noses into a powder, I became so worried that I put on my socks and shoes and rushed into the State Council Room to order my police force to stand by to prevent the Earth from mounting the Moon. The Capuchin monks I found in the State Council Room were very clever people and when I said, "Gentlemen, let's save the Moon, the Earth is preparing to mount it," they all rushed at once to execute my royal wish and many tried to climb the wall to reach the Moon. But at that moment, the Grand Chancellor came in. As soon as they saw him, they scattered. Being the King, I remained there alone. But to my surprise, the Chancellor hit me with his stick and chased me into my room. Such is the power of popular tradition in Spain!

January of the same year which happened after Februarius

I still can't make out what sort of a place Spain is. The customs and the etiquette at the Court are quite incredible. I don't see, I don't grasp it, I don't understand at all! Today, they shaved my head, although I shouted with all my might that I did not want to become a monk. But then they began to drip cold water on my head and everything went blank. Never have I been through such hell. I just can't understand the point of this peculiar custom, so stupid, so senseless. And the irresponsibility of the kings who never got around to outlawing this custom is quite beyond me.

Some indications make me wonder whether I haven't fallen into the hands of the Inquisition. Maybe the man I took for the Chancellor is really the Grand Inquisitor himself? But then, I can't see how the King can be subjected to the Inquisition. True, this could be the work of France, especially Polignac. That Polignac is an absolute beast. He has sworn to drive me to my death. And so he maneuvers on and on. But I know, my fine fellow, that you in turn are being led by the English. The English are great politicians. They sow the seeds of dissension everywhere. The whole world knows that when England takes snuff, France sneezes.

25th Date

Today, the Grand Inquisitor entered my room. I heard his steps approaching while he was still far off and hid under a chair. He looked around and, not seeing me, he began to call out. First he shouted my name and civil-service rank. I remained silent. Then, Ferdinand VIII, King of Spain! I was about to stick my head out but thought to myself: No, they won't get me that way! They may want to pour cold water on my head again. But he saw me and chased me out from under the chair with his stick. His damn stick hurts dreadfully. But my very latest discovery made me feel better: I had found that every rooster has his own Spain and he has it under his feathers. The Grand Inquisitor left very angry, threatening me with some punishment or other. Of course, I completely ignored his helpless fury. I knew he was a puppet. A tool of England.

da 34 te Mnth. Yr. yraurbeF 349

No, I have no strength left. I can't stand any more. My God! What they're doing to me! They pour cold water on my head. They don't listen to me, they don't hear me, they don't see me. What have I done to them? Why do they torture me so? What do they want from me? What can I give them? I haven't anything to give. I have no strength, I cannot bear this suffering, my head is on fire, and everything goes around me in circles. Save me! Take me away from here! Give me a carriage with horses swift as wind! Drive on, coachman, let the harness bells ring! Soar upward, my horses, carry me away from this world! Further, further, where I will see nothing, nothing. There is the sky smoking before me. A star twinkles far away, the forest rushes past with its dark trees and the crescent moon. The violet fog is a carpet underfoot. I hear the twanging of a guitar string through the fog; on one side, the sea, and on the other, Italy. Then Russian huts come into sight. Perhaps that's my house over there, looking blue in the distance. And isn't that my mother sitting by the window? Mother, save your wretched son! Let your tears fall on his sick head! See how they torture him! Hold me, a poor waif, in your arms. There's no room for him in this world. They are chasing him. Mother, take pity on your sick child. . . .

And, by the way, have you heard that the Dey of Algiers has a wart right under his nose?

HERMAN MELVILLE

BARTLEBY

I am a rather elderly man. The nature of my avocations for the last thirty years has brought me into more than ordinary contact with what would seem an interesting and somewhat singular set of men, of whom, as yet, nothing that I know of has ever been written—I mean the law-copyists, or scriveners. I have know very many of them, professionally and privately, and, if I pleased, could relate divers histories at which good-natured gentlemen might smile and sentimental souls might weep. But I waive the biographies of all other scriveners for a few passages in the life of Bartleby, who was a scrivener, the strangest I ever saw or heard of. While of other law-copyists I might write the complete life, of Bartleby nothing of that sort can be done. I believe that no materials exist for a full and satisfactory biography of this man. It is an irreparable loss to literature. Bartleby was one of those beings of whom nothing is ascertainable except from the original sources, and, in his case, those are very small. What my own astonished eyes saw of Bartleby, *that* is all I know of him, except, indeed, one vague report, which will appear in the sequel.

Ere introducing the scrivener as he first appeared to me, it is fit I make some mention of myself, my employees, my business, my chambers and general surroundings, because some such description is indispensable to an adequate understanding of the chief character about to be presented. *Imprimis:* I am a man who, from his youth upwards, has been filled with a profound conviction that the easiest way of life is the best. Hence, though I belong to a profession proverbially energetic and nervous even to turbulence at times, yet nothing of that sort have I ever suffered to invade my peace. I am one of those unambitious lawyers who never addresses a jury or in any way draws down public applause, but, in the cool tranquillity of a snug retreat, do a snug business among rich men's bonds, and mortgages, and title deeds. All who know me consider me an eminently *safe* man. The late John Jacob Astor, a personage little given to poetic enthusiasm, had no hesitation in pronouncing my first grand point to be prudence, my next, method. I do not speak it in vanity, but simply record the fact that I was not unemployed in my profession by the late John Jacob Astor, a name which, I admit, I love to repeat, for it hath a rounded and orbicular sound to it, and rings like unto bullion. I will freely add that I was not insensible to the late John Jacob Astor's good opinion.

Some time prior to the period at which this little history begins my avocations had been largely increased. The good old office, now extinct in the State of New York, of a Master in Chancery, had been conferred upon me. It was not a very arduous office, but very pleasantly remunerative. I seldom lose my temper, much more seldom indulge in dangerous indignation at wrongs and outrages, but I must be permitted to be rash here and declare that I consider the sudden and violent abrogation of the office of Master of Chancery, by the new Constitution, as a——premature act, inasmuch as I had counted upon a life lease of the profits, whereas I only received those of a few short years. But this is by the way.

My chambers were upstairs at No.——Wall Street. At one end they looked upon the white wall of the interior of a spacious skylight shaft, penetrating the building from top to bottom.

This view might have been considered rather tame than otherwise, deficient in what landscape painters call "life." But, if so, the view from the other end of my chambers offered at least a contrast, if nothing more. In that direction, my windows commanded an unobstructed view of a lofty brick wall, black by age and everlasting shade, which wall required no spyglass to bring out its lurking beauties, but, for the benefit of all nearsighted spectators, was pushed up to within ten feet of my windowpanes. Owing to the great height of the surrounding buildings, and my chambers' being on the second floor, the interval between the wall and mine not a little resembled a huge square cistern.

At the period just preceding the advent of Bartleby, I had two persons as copyists in my employment, and a promising lad as an office boy. First, Turkey; second Nippers; third, Ginger Nut. These may seem names the like of which are not usually found in the Directory. In truth, they were nicknames, mutually conferred upon each other by my three clerks, and were deemed expressive of their respective persons or characters. Turkey was a short, pursy Englishman, of about my own age—that is, somewhere not far from sixty. In the morning, one might say, his face was of a fine florid hue, but after twelve o'clock, meridian—his dinner hour—it blazed like a grate full of Christmas coals; and continued blazing—but, as it were, with a gradual wane—till six o'clock, P.M., or thereabouts; after which I saw no more of the proprietor of the face,which, gaining its meridian with the sun, seemed to set with it, to rise, culminate, and decline the following day, with the like regularity and undiminished glory. There are many singular coincidences I have known in the course of my life, not the least among which was the fact, that, exactly when Turkey displayed his fullest beams from his red and radiant countenance, just then, too, at that critical moment, began the daily period when I considered his business capacities as seriously disturbed for the remainder of the twenty-four hours. Not that he was absolutely idle or averse to business then; far from it. The difficulty was, he was apt to be altogether too energetic. There was a strange, inflamed, flurried, flighty recklessness of activity about him. He would be incautious in dipping his pen into his inkstand. All his blots upon my documents were dropped there after twelve o'clock, meridian. Indeed, not only would he be reckless and sadly given to making blots in the afternoon, but some days he went further and was rather noisy. At such times, too, his face flamed with augmented blazonry, as if cannel coal had been heaped on anthracite. He made an unpleasant racket with his chair; spilled his sandbox; in mending his pens, impatiently split them all to pieces and threw them on the floor in a sudden passion; stood up and leaned over his table, boxing his papers about in a most indecorous manner, very sad to behold in an elderly man like him. Nevertheless, as he was in many ways a most valuable person to me, and all the time before twelve o'clock, meridian, was the quickest, steadiest creature, too, accomplishing a great deal of work in a style not easily to be matched—for these reasons I was willing to overlook his eccentricities, though indeed, occasionally, I remonstrated with him. I did this very gently, however, because, though the civilest, nay, the blandest and most reverential of men in the morning, yet, in the afternoon he was disposed, upon provocation, to be slightly rash with his tongue—in fact, insolent. Now, valuing his morning services as I did, and resolved not to lose them—yes, at the same time, made uncomfortable by his inflamed ways after twelve o'clock—and being a man of peace, unwilling by my admonitions to call forth unseemly retorts from him, I took upon my one Saturday noon (he was always worse on Saturdays) to hint to him, very kindly, that perhaps, now that he was growing old, it might be well to abridge his labors; in short, he need not come to my chambers after twelve o'clock, but, dinner over, had best go home to his lodgings and rest himself till teatime. But no; he insisted upon his afternoon devotions. His countenance became intolerably fervid, as he oratorically assured me—gesticulating with a long ruler at the other end of the room—that if his services in the morning were useful, how indispensable, then, in the afternoon?

"With submission, sir," said Turkey, on this occasion, "I consider myself your right-hand man. In the morning I but marshal and deploy my columns, but in the afternoon I put myself at their head, and gallantly charge the foe, thus"—and he made a violent thrust with the ruler.

"But the blots, Turkey," intimated I.

"True; but, with submission, sir, behold these hairs! I am getting old. Surely, sir, a blot or two of a warm afternoon is not to be severely urged against gray hairs. Old age—even if it blot the page—is honorable. With submission, sir, we *both* are getting old."

This appeal to my fellow feeling was hardly to be resisted. At all events, I saw that go he would not. So I made up my mind to let him stay, resolving, nevertheless, to see to it that, during the afternoon, he had to do with my less important papers.

Nippers, the second on my list, was a whiskered, sallow, and upon the whole rather piratical-looking young man of about five and twenty. I always deemed him the victim of two evil powers—ambition and indigestion. The ambition was evinced by a certain impatience of the duties of a mere copyist, an unwarrantable usurpation of strictly professional affairs, such as the original drawing up of legal documents. The indigestion seemed betokened in an occasional nervous testiness and grinning irritability, causing the teeth to audibly grind together over mistakes committed in copying; unnecessary maledictions, hissed rather than spoken, in the heat of business; and especially by a continual discontent with the height of the table where he worked. Though of a very ingenious mechanical turn, Nippers could never get this table to suit him. He put chips under it, blocks of various sorts, bits of pasteboard, and at last went so far as to attempt an exquisite adjustment by final pieces of folded blotting paper. But no invention would answer. If, for the sake of easing his back, he brought the table lid at a sharp angle well up towards his chin, and wrote there like a man using the steep roof of a Dutch house for his desk, then he declared that it stopped the circulation in his arms. If now he lowered the table to his waistbands and stooped over it in writing, then there was a sore aching in his back. In short, the truth of the matter was Nippers knew not what he wanted. Or, if he wanted anything, it was to be rid of a scrivener's table altogether. Among the manifestations of his diseased ambition was a fondness he had for receiving visits from certain ambiguous-looking fellows in seedy coats, whom he called his clients. Indeed, I was aware that not only was he, at times, considerable of a ward politician, but he occasionally did a little business at the Justices' courts, and was not unknown on the steps of the Tombs. I have good reason to believe, however, that one individual who called upon him at my chambers, and who, with a grand air, he insisted was his client, was no other than a dun, and the alleged title deed, a bill. But, with all his failings, and the annoyances he caused me, Nippers, like his compatriot Turkey, was a very useful man to me; wrote a neat, swift hand; and, when he chose, was not deficient in a gentlemanly sort of deportment. Added to this, he always dressed in a gentlemanly sort of way, and so, incidentally, reflected credit upon my chambers. Whereas, with respect to Turkey, I had much ado to keep him from being a reproach to me. His clothes were apt to look oily, and smell of eating houses. He wore his pantaloons very loose and baggy in summer. His coats were execrable, his hat not to be handled. But while the hat was a thing of indifference to me, inasmuch as his natural civility and deference, as a dependent Englishman, always led him to doff it the moment he entered the room, yet his coat was another matter. Concerning his coats, I reasoned with him, but with no effect. The truth was, I suppose, that a man with so small an income could not afford to sport such a lustrous face and a lustrous coat at one and the same time. As Nippers once observed, Turkey's money went chiefly for red ink. One winter day, I presented Turkey with a highly respectable-looking coat of my own—a padded gray coat of a most comfortable warmth, and which buttoned straight up from the knee to the neck. I thought Turkey would appreciate the favor and abate his rashness and obstreperousness of afternoons. But no; I verily believe that buttoning himself up in so downy and blanket-like a coat had a pernicious effect upon him—upon the same principle that too much oats are bad for horses. In fact, precisely as a rash, restive horse is said to feel his oats, so Turkey felt his coat. It made him insolent. He was a man whom prosperity harmed.

Though, concerning the self-indulgent habits of Turkey, I had my own private surmises, yet, touching Nippers, I was well persuaded that, whatever might be his faults in other respects, he was, at least, a temperate young man. But indeed, nature herself seemed to have been his vintner, and, at his birth, charged him so thoroughly with an irritable, brandylike disposition that all subsequent potations were needless. When I consider how, amid the stillness of my chambers, Nippers would sometimes impatiently rise from his seat, and, stooping over his table, spread his arms wide apart, seize the whole desk, and move it, and jerk it, with a grim, grinding motion on the floor, as if the table were a perverse voluntary agent, intent on thwarting and vexing him, I plainly perceive that, for Nippers, brandy-and-water were altogether superfluous.

It was fortunate for me that, owing to its peculiar cause—indigestion—the irritability and consequent nervousness of Nippers were mainly observable in the morning, while in the afternoon he was comparatively mild. So that, Turkey's paroxysms only coming on about twelve o'clock, I never had to do with their eccentricities at one time. Their fits relieved each other, like guards. When Nippers's was on, Turkey's was off; and vice versa. This was a good natural arrangement, under the circumstances.

Ginger Nut, the third on my list, was a lad some twelve years old. His father was a carman, ambitious of seeing his son on the bench instead of a cart before he died. So he sent him to my office, as student at law, errand boy, cleaner and sweeper, at the rate of one dollar a week. He had a little desk to himself, but he did not use it much. Upon inspection, the drawer exhibited a great array of the shells of various sorts of nuts. Indeed, to this quick-witted youth, the whole noble science of the law was contained in a nutshell. Not the least among the employments of Ginger Nut, as well as one which he discharged with the most alacrity, was his duty as cake and apple purveyor for Turkey and Nippers. Copying law papers being proverbially a dry, husky sort of business, my two scriveners were fain to moisten their mouths very often with Spitzenbergs, to be had at the numerous stalls nigh the Custom House and Post Office. Also, they sent Ginger Nut very frequently for that peculiar cake—small, flat, round, and very spicy—after which he had been named by them. Of a cold morning, when business was but dull, Turkey would gobble up scores of these cakes, as if they were mere wafers—indeed, they sell them at the rate of six or eight for a penny—the scrape of his pen blending with the crunching of the crisp particles in his mouth. Of all the fiery afternoon blunders and flurried rashnesses of Turkey was his once moistening a ginger cake between his lips and clapping it on to a mortgage for a seal. I came within an ace of dismissing him then. But he mollified me by making an Oriental bow, and saying:

"With submission, sir, it was generous of me to find you in stationery on my own account."

Now my original business—that of a conveyancer and title hunter, and drawer-up of recondite documents of all sorts—was considerably increased by receiving the Master's office. There was now great work for scriveners. Not only must I push the clerks already with me, but I must have additional help.

In answer to my advertisements a motionless young man one morning stood upon my office threshold, the door being open, for it was summer. I can see that figure now—pallidly neat, pitiably respectable, incurably forlorn! It was Bartleby.

After a few words touching his qualifications, I engaged him, glad to have among my corps of copyists a man of so singularly sedate an aspect, which I thoguth might operate beneficially upon the flighty temper of Turkey and the fiery one of Nippers.

I should have stated before that ground-glass folding doors divided my premises into two parts, one of which was occupied by my scriveners, the other by myself. According to my humor, I threw open these doors or closed them. I resolved to assign Bartleby a corner by the folding doors, but on my side of them, so as to have this quiet man within easy call, in case any trifling thing was to be done. I placed his desk close up to a small side window in that part of the room, a window which orginally had afforded a lateral view of certain grimy back yards and bricks, but which, owing to subsequent erections, commanded at present no view of all, though it gave some light. Within three feet of the panes was a wall, and the light came down from far above, between two lofty buildings, as from a very small opening in a dome. Still further to a satisfactory arrangement, I procured a high green folding screen, which might entirely isolate Bartleby from my sight, though not remove him from my voice. And thus, in a manner, privacy and society were conjoined.

At first, Bartleby did an extraordinary quantity of writing. As if long famishing for something to copy, he seemed to gorge himself on my documents. There was no pause for digestion. He ran a day and night line, copying by sunlight and by candlelight. I should have been quite delighted with his application, had he been cheerfully industrious. But he wrote on silently, palely, mechanically.

It is, of course, an indispensable part of a scrivener's business to verify the accuracy of his copy, word by word. Where there are two or more scriveners in an office, they assist each other in this examination, one reading from the copy, the other holding the original. It is a very dull, wearisome, and lethargic affair. I can readily imagine that, to some sanguine temperaments, it would be altogether intolerable. For example, I cannot credit that the mettlesome poet, Byron, would have contentedly sat down with Bartleby to examine a law document of, say five hundred pages, closely written in a crimpy hand.

Now and then, in the haste of business, it had been my habit to assist in comparing some brief document myself, calling Turkey or Nippers for this purpose. One object I had in placing Bartleby so handy to me behind the screen was to avail myself of his services on such trivial occasions. It was on the third day, I think, of his being with me, and before any necessity had arisen for having his own writing examined, that, being much hurried to complete a small affair I had in hand, I abruptly called to Bartleby. In my haste and natural expectancy of instant compliance, I sat with my head bent over the original on my desk, and my right hand sideways, and somewhat nervously extended with the copy, so that, immediately upon emerging from his retreat, Bartleby might snatch it and proceed to business without the least delay.

In this very attitude did I sit when I called to him, rapidly stating what it was I wanted him to do—namely, to examine a small paper with me. Imagine my surprise, nay, my consternation, when, without moving from his privacy, Bartleby, in a singularly mild, firm voice, replied, "I would prefer not to."

I sat awhile in perfect silence, rallying my stunned faculties. Immediately it occurred to me that my ears had deceived me, or Bartleby had entirely misunderstood my meaning. I repeated my request in the clearest tone I could assume; but in quite as clear a one came the previous reply, "I would prefer not to."

"Prefer not to," echoed I, rising in high excitement, and crossing the room with a stride. "What do you mean? Are you moon-struck? I want you to help me compare this sheet here—take it," and I thrust it towards him.

"I would prefer not to," said he.

I looked at him steadfastly. His face was leanly composed; his gray eyes dimly calm. Not a wrinkle of agitation rippled him. Had there been the least uneasiness, anger, impatience or impertinence in his manner; in other words, had there been anything ordinarily human about him, doubtless I should have violently dismissed him from the premises. But as it was I should have as soon thought of turning my pale plaster-of-Paris bust of Cicero out of doors. I stood gazing at him awhile, as he went on with his own writing, and then reseated myself at my desk. This is very strange, thought I. What had one best do? But my business hurried me. I concluded to forget the matter for the present, reserving it for my future leisure. So calling Nippers from the other room, the paper was speedily examined.

A few days after this, Bartleby concluded four lengthy documents, being quadruplicates of a week's testimony taken before me in my High Court of Chancery. It became necessary to examine them. It was an important suit, and great accuracy was imperative. Having all things arranged, I called Turkey, Nippers and Ginger Nut, from the next room, meaning to place the four copies in the hands of my four clerks, while I should read from the original. Accordingly, Turkey, Nippers, and Ginger Nut had taken their seats in a row, each with his document in his hand, when I called to Bartleby to join this interesting group.

"Bartleby! quick, I am waiting."

I heard a slow scrape of his chair legs on the uncarpeted floor, and soon he appeared standing at the entrance of his hermitage.

"What is wanted?" said he, mildly.

"The copies, the copies," said I, hurriedly. "We are going to examine them. There"—and I held towards him the fourth quadruplicate.

"I would prefer not to," he said, and gently disappeared behind the screen.

For a few moments I was turned into a pillar of salt, standing at the head of my seated column of clerks. Recovering myself, I advanced towards the screen and demanded the reason for such extraordinary conduct.

"*Why* do you refuse?"

"I would prefer not to."

With any other man I should have flown outright into a dreadful passion, scorned all further words, and thrust him ignominiously from my presence. But there was something about Bartleby that not only strangely disarmed me, but, in a wonderful manner, touched and disconcerted me. I began to reason with him.

"These are your own copies we are about to examine. It is labor saving to you, because one examination will answer for your four papers. It is common usage. Every copyist is bound to help examine his copy. Is it not so? Will you not speak? Answer!"

"I prefer not to," he replied in a flutelike tone. It seemed to me that, while I had been addressing him, he carefully revolved every statement that I made; fully comprehended the meaning; could not gainsay the irresistible conclusion; but, at the same time, some paramount consideration prevailed with him to reply as he did.

"You are decided, then, not to comply with my request—a request made according to common usage and common sense?"

He briefly gave me to understand that on that point my judgment was sound. Yes: his decision was irreversible.

It is seldom the case that, when a man is browbeaten in some unprecedented and violently unreasonable way, he begins to stagger in his own plainest faith. He begins, as it were, vaguely to surmise that, wonderful as it may be, all the justice and all the reason is on the other side. Accordingly, if any disinterested persons are present, he turns to them for some reinforcement for his own faltering mind.

"Turkey," said I, "what do you think of this? Am I not right?"

"With submission, sir," said Turkey, in his blandest tone, "I think that you are."

"Nippers," said I, "what do *you* think of it?"

"I think I should kick him out of the office."

(The reader of nice perceptions, will here perceive that, it being morning, Turkey's answer is couched in polite and tranquil terms, but Nippers replies in ill-tempered ones. Or, to repeat a previous sentence, Nippers's ugly mood was on duty, and Turkey's off.)

"Ginger Nut," said I, willing to enlist the smallest suffrage in my behalf, "what do *you* think of it?"

"I think, sir, he's a little *luny*," replied Ginger Nut, with a grin.

"You hear what they say," said I, turning towards the screen, "come forth and do your duty."

But he vouchsafed no reply. I pondered a moment in sore perplexity. But once more business hurried me. I determined again to postpone the consideration of this dilemma to my future leisure. With a little trouble we made out to examine the papers without Bartleby, though at every page or two Turkey deferentially dropped his opinion that this proceeding was quite out of the common; while Nippers, twitching in his chair with a dyspeptic nervousness, ground out between his set teeth occasional hissing maledictions against the stubborn oaf behind the screen. And for his (Nippers's) part, this was the first and the last time he would do another man's business without pay.

Meanwhile Bartleby sat in his hermitage, oblivious to everything but his own peculiar business there.

Some days passed, the scrivener being employed upon another lengthy work. His late remarkable conduct led me to regard his ways narrowly. I observed that he never went to dinner; indeed, that he never went anywhere. As yet I had never, of my personal knowledge, known him to be outside of my office. He was a perpetual sentry in the corner. At about eleven o'clock, though, in the morning, I noticed that Ginger Nut would advance towards the opening in Bartleby's screen, as if silently beckoned thither by a gesture invisible to me where I sat. The boy would then leave the office jingling a few pence, and reappear with a handful of gingernuts, which he delivered in the hermitage, receiving two of the cakes for his trouble.

He lives, then, on gingernuts, thought I; never eats a dinner, properly speaking; he must be a vegetarian, then; but no, he never eats even vegetables, he eats nothing but gingernuts. My mind then ran on in reveries concerning the probable effects upon the human constitution of living entirely on gingernuts. Gingernuts are so called bacause they contain ginger as one of their peculiar constituents, and the final flavoring one. Now, what was ginger? A hot, spicy thing. Was Bartleby hot and spicy? Not at all. Ginger, then, had no effect upon Bartleby. Probably he preferred it should have none.

Nothing so aggravates an earnest person as a passive resistance. If the individual so resisted be of a not inhumane temper, and the resisting one perfectly harmless in his passivity, then, in the better moods of the former, he will endeavor charitably to construe to his imagination what proves impossible to be solved by his judgment. Even so, for the most part I regarded Bartleby and his ways. Poor fellow! thought I, he means no mischief; it is plain he intends no insolence; his aspect sufficiently evinces that his eccentricities are involuntary. He is useful to me. I can get along with him. If I turn him away, the chances are he will fall in with some less indulgent employer, and then he will be rudely treated, and perhaps driven forth miserably to starve. Yes. Here I can cheaply purchase a delicious self-approval. To befriend Bartleby, to humor him in his strange willfulness, will cost me little or nothing, while I lay up in my soul what will eventually prove a sweet morsel for my conscience. But this mood was not invariable with me. The passiveness of Bartleby sometimes irritated me. I felt strangely goaded on to encounter him in new opposition—to elicit some angry spark from him answerable to my own. But, indeed, I might as well have essayed to strike fire with my knuckles against a bit of Windsor soap. But one afternoon the evil impulse in me mastered me, and the following little scene ensued:

"Bartleby," said I, "when those papers are all copied, I will compare them with you."

"I would prefer not to."

"How? Surely you do not mean to persist in that mulish vagary?"

No answer.

I threw open the folding doors near by, and, turning upon Turkey and Nippers, exclaimed:

"Bartleby a second time says he won't examine his papers. What do you think of it, Turkey?"

It was afternoon, be it remembered. Turkey sat glowing like a brass boiler, his bald head steaming, his hands reeling among his blotted papers.

"Think of it?" roared Turkey. "I think I'll just step behind his screen and black his eyes for him!"

So saying, Turkey rose to his feet and threw his arms into a pugilistic position. He was hurrying away to make good his promise when I detained him, alarmed at the effect of incautiously rousing Turkey's combativeness after dinner.

"Sit down, Turkey," said I, "and hear what Nippers has to say. What do you think of it, Nippers? Would I not be justified in immediately dismissing Bartleby?"

"Excuse me, that is for you to decide, sir. I think his conduct quite unusual, and indeed, unjust, as regards Turkey and myself. But it may only be a passing whim."

"Ah," exclaimed I, "you have strangely changed your mind, then—you speak very gently of him now."

"All beer," cried Turkey; "gentleness is effects of beer—Nippers and I dined together today. You see how gentle *I* am, sir. Shall I go and black his eyes?"

"You refer to Bartleby, I suppose. No, not today, Turkey," I replied; "pray, put up your fists."

I closed the doors and again advanced towards Bartleby. I felt additional incentives tempting me to my fate. I burned to be rebelled against again. I remembered that Bartleby never left the office.

"Bartleby," said I, "Ginger Nut is away; just step around to the Post Office, won't you? (it was but a three minutes' walk), and see if there is anything for me."

"I would prefer not to."

"You *will* not?"

"I *prefer* not."

I staggered to my desk and sat there in a deep study. My blind inveteracy returned. Was there any other thing in which I could procure myself to be ignominiously repulsed by this lean, penniless wight?—my hired clerk? What added thing is there, perfectly reasonable, that he will be sure to refuse to do?

"Bartleby!"

No answer.

"Bartleby," in a louder tone.

No answer.

"Bartleby," I roared.

Like a very ghost, agreeably to the laws of magical invocation, at the third summons he appeared at the entrance of his hermitage.

"Go to the next room, and tell Nippers to come to me."

"I prefer not to," he respectfully and slowly said, and mildly disappeared.

"Very good, Bartleby," said I, in a quiet sort of serenely severe self-possessed tone, intimating the unalterable purpose of some terrible retribution very close at hand. At the moment I half intended something of the kind. But upon the whole, as it was drawing towards my dinner hour, I thought it best to put on my hat and walk home for the day, suffering much from perplexity and distress of mind.

Shall I acknowledge it? The conclusion of this whole business was that it soon became a fixed fact of my chambers, that a pale young scrivener by the name of Bartleby had a desk there; that he copied for me at the usual rate of four cents a folio (one hundred words); but he was permanently exempt from examining the work done by him, that duty being transferred to Turkey and Nippers, out of compliment, doubtless, to their superior acuteness; moreover, said Bartleby was never, on any account, to be dispatched on the most trivial errand of any sort; and that even if entreated to take upon him such a matter, it was generally understood that he would "prefer not to"—in other words, that he would refuse point-blank.

As days passed on, I became considerably reconciled to Bartleby. His steadiness, his freedom from all dissipation, his incessant industry (except when he chose to throw himself into a standing reverie behind his screen), his great stillness, his unalterableness of demeanor under all circumstances, made him a valuable acquisition. One prime thing was this—*he was always there*—first in the morning, continually through the day, and the last at night. I had a singular confidence in his honesty. I felt my most precious papers perfectly safe in his hands. Sometimes, to be sure, I could not, for the very soul of me, avoid falling into sudden spasmodic passions with him. For it was exceeding difficult to bear in mind all the time those strange peculiarities, privileges, and unheard-of exemptions, forming the tacit stipulations on Bartleby's part under which he remained in my office. Now and then, in the eagerness of dispatching pressing business, I would inadvertently summon Bartleby, in a short, rapid tone, to put his finger, say, on the incipient tie of a bit of red tape with which I was about compressing some papers. Of course, from behind the screen the usual answer, "I prefer not to," was sure to come; and then, how could a human creature, with the common infirmities of our nature, refrain from bitterly exclaiming upon such perverseness—such unreasonableness. However, every added repulse of this sort which I received only tended to lessen the probability of my repeating the inadvertence.

Here it must be said that, according to the custom of most legal gentlemen occupying chambers in densely populated law buildings, there were several keys to my door. One was kept by a woman residing in the attic, which person weekly scrubbed and daily swept and dusted my apartments. Another was kept by Turkey for convenience' sake. The third I sometimes carried in my own pocket. The fourth I knew not who had.

Now, one Sunday morning I happened to go to Trinity Church, to hear a celebrated preacher, and finding myself rather early on the ground I thought I would walk round to my chambers for a while. Luckily I had my key with me, but upon applying it to the lock, I found it resisted by something inserted from the inside. Quite surprised, I called out, when to my consternation a key was turned from within, and, thrusting his lean visage at me, and holding the door ajar, the apparition of Bartleby appeared, in his shirt sleeves, and otherwise in a strangely tattered deshabille, saying quietly that he was sorry, but he was deeply engaged just then, and—preferred not admitting me at present. In a brief word or two, he moreover added, that perhaps I had better walk around the block two or three times, and by that time he would probably have concluded his affairs.

Now, the utterly unsurmised appearance of Bartleby, tenanting my law chambers of a Sunday morning, with his cadaverously gentlemanly *nonchalance*, yet withal firm and self-possessed, had such a strange effect upon me that incontinently I slunk away from my own door and did as desired. But not without sundry twinges of impotent rebellion against the mild effrontery of this unaccountable scrivener. Indeed, it was his wonderful mildness, chiefly, which not only disarmed me but unmanned me, as it were. For I consider that one, for the time, is sort of unmanned when he tranquilly permits his hired clerk to dictate to him and order him away from his own premises. Furthermore, I was full of uneasiness as to what Bartleby could possibly be doing in my office in his shirt sleeves, and in an otherwise dismantled condition, of a Sunday morning. Was anything amiss going on? Nay, that was out of the question. It was not to be thought of for a moment that Bartleby was an immoral person. But what could he be doing there?—copying? Nay again, whatever might be his eccentricities, Bartleby was an eminently decorous person. He would be the last man to sit down to his desk in any state approaching to nudity. Besides, it was Sunday; and there was something about Bartleby that forbade the supposition that he would by any secular occupation violate the proprieties of the day.

Nevertheless, my mind was not pacified, and, full of a restless curiosity, at last I returned to the door. Without hindrance I inserted my key, opened it, and entered. Bartleby was not to be seen. I looked round anxiously, peeped behind his screen, but it was very plain that he was gone. Upon more closely examining the place, I surmised that for an indefinite period Bartleby must have ate, dressed, and slept in my office, and that, too, without plate, mirror, or bed. The cushioned seat of a rickety old sofa in one corner bore that faint impress of a lean, reclining form. Rolled away under his desk I found a blanket; under the empty grate, a blacking box and brush; on a chair, a tin basin, with soap and a ragged towel; in a newspaper a few crumbs of gingernuts and a morsel of cheese. Yes, thought I, it is evident enough that Bartleby has been making his home here, keeping bachelor's hall all by himself. Immediately then the thought came sweeping across me, what miserable friendliness and loneliness are here revealed. His poverty is great, but his solitude, how horrible! Think of it. Of a Sunday,

Wall Street is deserted as Petra, and every night of every day it is an emptiness. This building, too, which of weekdays hums with industry and life, at nightfall echoes with sheer vacancy, and all through Sunday is forlorn. And here Bartleby makes his home, sole spectator of a solitude which he has seen all populous—a sort of innocent and transformed Marius brooding among the ruins of Carthage!

For the first time in my life a feeling of overpowering stinging melancholy seized me. Before, I had never experienced aught but a not unpleasing sadness. The bond of a common humanity now drew me irresistibly to gloom. A fraternal melancholy! For both I and Bartleby were sons of Adam. I remembered the bright silks and sparkling faces I had seen that day, in gala trim, swanlike sailing down the Mississippi of Broadway; and I contrasted them with the pallid copyist, and thought to myself, Ah, happiness courts the light, so we deem the world is gay, but misery hides aloof, so we deem that misery there is none. These sad fancyings—chimeras, doubtless, of a sick and silly brain—led on to other and more special thoughts, concerning the eccentricities of Bartleby. Presentiments of strange discoveries hovered round me. The scrivener's pale form appeared to me laid out, among uncaring strangers in its shivering winding sheet.

Suddenly I was attracted by Bartleby's closed desk, the key in open sight left in the lock.

I mean no mischief, seek the gratification of no heartless curiosity, thought I; besides, the desk is mine, and its contents, too, so I will make bold to look within. Everything was methodically arranged, the papers smoothly placed. The pigeonholes were deep, and, removing the files of documents, I groped into their recesses. Presently I felt something there, and dragged it out. It was an old bandanna handkerchief, heavy and knotted. I opened it, and saw it was a savings bank.

I now recalled all the quiet mysteries which I had noted in the man. I remembered that he never spoke but to answer; that, though at intervals he had considerable time to himself, yet I had never seen him reading—no, not even a newspaper; that for long periods he would stand looking out, at his pale window behind the screen, upon the dead brick wall; I was quite sure he never visited any refectory or eating house, while his pale face clearly indicated that he never drank beer like Turkey, or tea and coffee even, like other men; that he never went anywhere in particular that I could learn; never went out for a walk, unless, indeed, that was the case at present; that he had declined telling who he was, or whence he came, or whether he had any relatives in the world; that though so thin and pale, he never complained of ill health. And more than all I remembered a certain unconscious air of pallid—how shall I call it?—of pallid haughtiness, say, or rather an austere reserve about him, which had positively awed me into my tame compliance with his eccentricities, which I had feared to ask him to do the slightest incidental thing for me even though I might know, from his long-continued motionlessness, that behind his screen he must be standing in one of those dead-wall reveries of his.

Revolving all these things, and coupling them with the recently discovered fact that he made my office his constant abiding place and home, and not forgetful of his morbid moodiness—revolving all these things, a prudential feeling began to steal over me. My first emotions had been those of pure melancholy and sincerest pity; but just in proportion as the forlornness of Bartleby grew and grew to my imagination, did that same melancholy merge into fear, that pity into repulsion. So true it is, and so terrible too, that up to a certain point the thought or sight of misery enlists our best affections; but, in certain special cases, beyond that point it does not. They err who would assert that invariably this is owing to the inherent selfishness of the human heart. It rather proceeds from a certain hopelessness of remedying excessive and organic ill. To a sensitive being, pity is not seldom pain. And when at last it is perceived that such pity cannot lead to effectual succor, common sense bids the soul be rid of it. What I saw that morning persuaded me that the scrivener was the victim of innate and incurable disorder. I might give alms to his body, but his body did not pain him—it was his soul that suffered, and his soul I could not reach.

I did not accomplish the purpose of going to Trinity Church that morning. Somehow, the things I had seen disqualified me for the time from churchgoing. I walked homeward, thinking what I would do with Bartleby. Finally, I resolved upon this—I would put certain calm questions to him the next morning, touching his history, etc., and if he declined to answer them openly and unreservedly (and I supposed he would prefer not), then to give him a twenty-dollar bill over and above whatever I might owe him, and tell him his services were no longer required; but that if in any other way I could assist him, I would be happy to do so, especially if he desired to return to his native place, wherever that might be, I would willingly help to defray the expenses. Moreover, if, after reaching home, he found himself at any time in want of aid, a letter from him would be sure of a reply.

The next morning came.

"Bartleby," said I, gently calling to him behind his screen.

No reply.

"Bartleby," said I, in a still gentler tone, "come here; I am not going to ask you to do anything you would prefer not to do—I simply wish to speak to you."

Upon this he noiselessly slid into view.

"Will you tell me, Bartleby, where you were born?"

"I would prefer not to."

"Will you tell me *anything* about yourself?"

"I would prefer not to."

"But what reasonable objection can you have to speak to me? I feel friendly towards you."

He did not look at me while I spoke, but kept his glance fixed upon my bust of Cicero, which, as I then sat, was directly behind me, some six inches above my head.

"What is your answer, Bartleby," said I, after waiting a considerable time for a reply, during which his countenance remained immovable, only there was the faintest conceivable tremor of the white attenuated mouth.

"At present I prefer to give no answer," he said, and retired into his hermitage.

It was rather weak in me I confess, but his manner, on this occasion, nettled me. Not only did there seem to lurk in it a certain calm disdain, but his perverseness seemed ungrateful, considering the undeniable good usage and indulgence he had received from me.

Again I sat ruminating what I should do. Mortified as I was at his behavior, and resolved as I had been to dismiss him when I entered my office, nevertheless I strangely felt something superstitious knocking at my heart, and forbidding me to carry out my purpose, and denouncing me for a villain if I dared to breathe one bitter word against this forlornest of mankind. At last, familiarly drawing my chair behind his screen, I sat down and said: "Bartleby, never mind, then, about revealing your history; but let me entreat you, as a friend, to comply as far as may be with usages of this office. Say now, you will help to examine papers tomorrow or next day: in short, say now, that in a day or two you will begin to be a little reasonable:—say so, Bartleby."

"At present I would prefer not to be a little reasonable," was his mildly cadaverous reply.

Just then the folding doors opened and Nippers approached. He seemed suffering from an unusually bad night's rest, induced by severer indigestion than common. He overheard those final words of Bartleby.

"*Prefer not,* eh?" gritted Nippers—"I'd *prefer* him, if I were you, sir," addressing me—"I'd *prefer* him; I'd give him preferences, the stubborn mule! What is it, sir, pray, that he *prefers* not to do now?"

Bartleby moved not a limb.

"Mr. Nippers," said I, "I'd prefer that you would withdraw for the present."

Somehow, of late, I had got into the way of involuntarily using this word "prefer" upon all sorts of not exactly suitable occasions. And I trembled to think that my contact with the scrivener had already and seriously affected me in a mental way. And what further and deeper aberration might it not yet produce? This apprehension had not been without efficacy in determining me to summary measures.

As Nippers, looking very sour and sulky, was departing, Turkey blandly and deferentially approached.

"With submission, sir," said he, "yesterday I was thinking about Bartleby here, and I think that if he would but prefer to take a quart of good ale every day, it would do much towards mending him, and enabling him to assist in examining his papers."

"So you have got the word, too," said I, slightly excited.

"With submission, and word, sir?" asked Turkey, respectfully crowding himself into the contracted space behind the screen, and by so doing making me jostle the scrivener. "What word, sir?"

"I would prefer to be left alone here," said Bartleby, as if offended at being mobbed in his privacy.

"*That's* the word, Turkey," said I—"*that's* it."

"Oh, *prefer?* oh yes—queer word. I never use it myself. But, sir, as I was saying, if he would but prefer——"

"Turkey," interrupted I, "you will please withdraw."

"Oh certainly, sir, if you prefer that I should."

As he opened the folding door to retire, Nippers at his desk caught a glimpse of me, and asked whether I would prefer to have a certain paper copied on blue paper or white. He did not in the least roguishly accent the word prefer. It was plain that it involuntarily rolled from his tongue. I thought to myself, surely I must get rid of a demented man, who already has in some degree turned the tongues, if not the heads, of myself and clerks. But I thought it prudent not to break the dismission at once.

The next day I noticed that Bartleby did nothing but stand at his window in his dead-wall reverie. Upon asking him why he did not write, he said that he had decided upon doing no more writing.

"Why, how now? what next?" exclaimed I, "do no more writing?"

"No more."

"And what is the reason?"

"Do you not see the reason for yourself?" he indifferently replied.

I looked steadfastly at him, and perceived that his eyes looked dull and glazed. Instantly it occurred to me that his unexampled diligence in copying by his dim window for the first few weeks of his stay with me might have temporarily impaired his vision.

I was touched. I said something in condolence with him. I hinted that of course he did wisely in abstaining from writing for a while; and urged him to embrace that opportunity of taking wholesome exercise in the open air. This, however, he did not do. A few days after this, my other clerks being absent, and being in a great hurry to dispatch certain letters by the mail, I thought that, having nothing else earthly to do, Bartleby would surely be less inflexible than ususal, and carry these letters to the Post Office. But he blankly declined. So, much to my inconvenience, I went myself.

Still added days went by. Whether Bartleby's eyes improved or not, I could not say. To all appearance, I thought they did. But when I asked him if they did, he vouchsafed no answer. At all events, he would do no copying. At last, in reply to my urgings, he informed me that he had permanently given up copying.

"What!" exclaimed I; "suppose your eyes should get entirely well—better than ever before—would you not copy then?"

"I have given up copying," he answered, and slid aside.

He remained as ever, a fixture in my chamber. Nay—if that were possible—he became still more of a fixture than before. What was to be done? He would do nothing in the office; why should he stay there? In plain fact, he had now become a millstone to me, not only useless as a necklace, but afflictive to bear. Yet I was sorry for him. I speak less than truth when I say that, on his own account, he occasioned me uneasiness. If he would but have named a single relative or friend, I would instantly have written and urged their taking the poor fellow away to some convenient retreat. But he seemed alone, absolutely alone in the universe. A bit of wreck in the mid-Atlantic. At length, necessities connected with my business tyrannized over all other considerations. Decently as I could, I told Bartleby that in six days' time he must unconditionally leave the office. I warned him to take measures, in the interval, for procuring some other abode. I offered to assist him in this endeavor, if he himself would but take the first step towards a removal. "And when you finally quit me, Bartleby," added I, "I shall see that you go not away entirely unprovided. Six days from this hour, remember."

At the expiration of that period, I peeped behind the screen, and lo! Bartleby was there.

I buttoned up my coat, balanced myself, advanced slowly towards him, touched his shoulder, and said, "The time has come; you must quit this place; I am sorry for you; here is money; but you must go."

"I would prefer not," hereplied, with his back still towards me.

"You *must.*"

He remained silent.

Now I had an unbounded confidence in this man's common honesty. He had frequently restored to me sixpences and shillings carelessly dropped upon the floor, for I am apt to be very reckless in such shirt-button affairs. The proceeding, then, which followed will not be deemed extraordinary.

"Bartleby," said I, "I owe you twelve dollars on account; here are thirty-two; the odd twenty are yours—Will you take it?" and I handed the bills toward him.

But he made no motion.

"I will leave them here, then," putting them under a weight on the table. Then taking my hat and cane and going to the door, I tranquilly turned and added—"After you have removed your things from these offices, Bartleby, you will of course lock the door—since everyone is now gone for the day but you—and if you please, slip your key underneath the mat, so that I may have it in the morning. I shall not see you again; so good-bye to you. If, heareafter, in your new place of abode, I can be of any service to you, do not fail to advise me by letter. Good-bye, Bartleby, and fare you well."

But he answered not a word; like the last column of some ruined temple, he remained standing mute and solitary in the middle of the otherwise deserted room.

As I walked home in a pensive mood, my vanity got the better of my pity. I could not but highly plume myself on my masterly management in getting rid of Bartleby. Masterly I call it, and such it must appear to any dispassionate thinker. The beauty of my procedure seemed to consist in its perfect quietness. There was no vulgar bullying, no bravado of any sort, no choleric hectoring and striding to and fro across the apartment, jerking out vehement commands for Bartleby to bundle himself off with his beggarly traps. Nothing of the kind. Without loudly bidding Bartleby depart—as an inferior genius might have done—I *assumed* the ground that depart he must, and upon that assumption built all I had to say. The more I thought over my procedure, the more I was charmed with it. Nevertheless, next morning, upon awakening, I had my doubts—I had somehow slept off the fumes of vanity. One of the coolest and wisest hours a man has is just after he awakes in the morning. My procedure seemed as sagacious as ever—but only in theory. How it would prove in practice—there was the rub. It was truly a beautiful thought to have assumed Bartleby's departure; but, after all, that assumption was simply my own, and none of Bartleby's. The great point was, not whether I had assumed that he would quit me, but whether he would prefer so to do. He was more a man of preferences than assumptions.

After breakfast, I walked downtown, arguing the probabilities pro and con. One moment I thought it would prove a miserable failure, and Bartleby would be found all alive at my office as usual; the next moment it seemed certain that I should find his chair empty. And so I kept veering about. At the corner of Broadway and Canal Street, I saw quite an excited group of people standing in earnest conversation.

"I'll take odds he doesn't," said a voice as I passed.

"Doesn't go?—done!" said I, "put up your money."

I was instinctively putting my hand in my pocket to produce my own, when I remembered that this was an election day. The words I had overheard bore no reference to Bartleby but to the success or nonsuccess of some candidate for the mayoralty. In my intent frame of mind, I had, as it were, imagined that all Broadway shared in my excitement, and were debating the same question with me. I passed on, very thankful that the uproar of the street screened my momentary absent-mindedness.

As I had intended, I was earlier than usual at my office door. I stood listening for a moment. All was still. He must be gone. I tried the knob. The door was locked. Yes, my procedure had worked to a charm; he indeed must be vanished. Yet a certain melancholy mixed with this: I was almost sorry for my brilliant success. I was fumbling under the door mat for the key, which Bartleby was to have left there for me, when accidentally my knee knocked against a panel, producing a summoning sound, and in response a voice came to me from within—"Not yet; I am occupied."

It was Bartleby.

I was thunderstruck. For an instant I stood like the man who, pipe in mouth, was killed one cloudless afternoon long ago in Virginia by summer lightning; at his own warm open window he was killed, and remained leaning out there upon the dreamy afternoon, till someone touched him, when he fell.

"Not gone!" I murmured at last. But again obeying that wondrous ascendancy which the inscrutable scrivener had over me, and from which ascendancy, for all my chafing, I could not completely escape, I slowly went downstairs and out into the street, and while walking round the block considered what I should next do in this unheard-of perplexity. Turn the man out by an actual thrusting I could not; to drive him away by calling him hard names would not do; calling in the police was an unpleasant idea; and yet, permit him to enjoy his cadaverous triumph over me—this, too, I could not think of. What was to be done? or, if nothing could be done, was there anything further that I could *assume* in the matter? Yes, as before I had prospectively assumed that

Bartleby would depart, so now I might retrospectively assume that departed he was. In the legitimate carrying out of this assumption I might enter my office in a great hurry, and, pretending not to see Bartleby at all, walk straight against him as if he were air. Such a proceeding would in a singular degree have the appearance of a home thrust. It was hardly possible that Bartleby could withstand such an application of the doctrine of assumptions. But upon second thoughts the success of the plan seemed rather dubious. I resolved to argue the matter over with him again.

"Bartleby," said I, entering the office, with a quietly severe expression, "I am seriously displeased. I am pained, Bartleby. I had thought better of you. I had imagined you of such a gentlemanly organization that in any delicate dilemma a slight hint would suffice—in short, an assumption. But it appears I am deceived. Why," I added, unaffectedly starting, "you have not even touched that money yet," pointing to it, just where I had left it the evening previous.

He answered nothing.

"Will you, or will you not, quit me?" I now demanded in a sudden passion, advancing close to him.

"I would prefer *not* to quit you," he replied, gently emphasizing the *not*.

"What earthly right have you to stay here? Do you pay any rent? Do you pay my taxes? Or is this property yours?"

He answered nothing.

"Are you ready to go on and write now? Are your eyes recovered? Could you copy a small paper for me this morning? or help examine a few lines? or step round to the Post Office? In a word, will you do anything at all to give a coloring to your refusal to depart the premises?"

He silently retired into his hermitage.

I was now in such a state of nervous resentment that I thought it but prudent to check myself at present from further demonstrations. Bartleby and I were alone. I remembered the tragedy of the unfortunate Adams and the still more unfortunate Colt in the solitary office of the latter; and how poor Colt, being dreadfully incensed by Adams, and imprudently permitting himself to get wildly excited, was at unawares hurried into his fatal act—an act which certainly no man could possibly deplore more than the actor himself. Often it had occurred to me in my ponderings upon the subject that had that altercation taken place in the public street, or at a private residence, it would not have terminated as it did. It was the circumstance of being alone in a solitary office, upstairs, of a building entirely unhallowed by humanizing domestic associations—an uncarpeted office, doubtless, of a dusty, haggard sort of appearance—this it must have been which greatly helped to enhance the irritable desperation of the hapless Colt.

But when this old Adam of resentment rose in me and tempted me concerning Bartleby, I grappled him and threw him. How? Why, simply by recalling the divine injunction: "A new commandment give I unto you, that ye love one another." Yes, this it was that saved me. Aside from higher considerations, charity often operates as a vastly wise and prudent principle—a great safeguard to its possessor. Men have committed murder for jealousy's sake, and anger's sake, and hatred's sake, and selfishness' sake, and spiritual pride's sake; but no man that ever I heard of ever committed a diabolical murder for sweet charity's sake. Mere self-interest, then, if no better motive can be enlisted, should, especially with high-tempered men, prompt all beings to charity and philanthropy. At any rate, upon the occasion in question, I strove to drown my exasperated feelings towards the scrivener by benevolently construing his conduct. Poor fellow, poor fellow! thought I, he don't mean anything, and besides, he has seen hard times, and ought to be indulged.

I endeavored, also, immediately to occupy myself, and at the same time to comfort my despondency. I tried to fancy that in the course of the morning, at such time as might prove agreeable to him, Bartleby, of his own free accord, would emerge from his hermitage and take up some decided line of march in the direction of the door. But no. Half-past twelve o'clock came; Turkey began to glow in the face, overturn his inkstand, and become generally obstreperous; Nippers abated down into quietude and courtesy; Ginger Nut munched his noon apple; and Bartleby remained standing at his window in one of his profoundest dead-wall reveries. Will it be credited? Ought I to acknowledge it? That afternoon I left the office without saying one further word to him.

Some days now passed during which, at leisure intervals, I looked a little into "Edwards on the Will," and "Priestley on Necessity." Under the circumstances, those books induced a salutary feeling. Gradually I slid into the persuasion that these troubles of mine touching the scrivener had been all predestinated from eternity, and Bartleby was billeted upon me for some mysterious purpose of an all-wise Providence, which it was not for a mere mortal like me to fathom. Yes, Bartleby, stay there behind your screen, thought I; I shall persecute you no more; you are harmless and noiseless as any of these old chairs; in short, I never feel so private as when I know you are here. At last I see it, I feel it; I penetrate to the predestinated purpose of my life. I am content. Others may have loftier parts to enact, but my mission in this world, Bartleby, is to furnish you with office room for such period as you may see fit to remain.

I believe that this wise and blessed frame of mind would have continued with me had it not been for the unsolicited and uncharitable remarks obtruded upon me by my professional friends who visited the rooms. But thus it often is that the constant friction of illiberal minds wears out at last the best resolves of the more generous. Though, to be sure, when I reflected upon it it was not strange that people entering my office should be struck by the peculiar aspect of the unaccountable Bartleby, and so be tempted to throw out some sinister observations concerning him. Sometimes an attorney having business with me, and calling at my office, and finding no one but the scrivener there, would undertake to obtain some sort of precise information from him touching my whereabouts; but without heeding his idle talk, Bartleby would remain standing immovable in the middle of the room. So, after contemplating him in that position for a time, the attorney would depart no wiser than he came.

Also, when a reference was going on, and the room full of lawyers and witnesses, and business driving fast, some deeply-occupied legal gentleman present, seeing Bartleby wholly unemployed, would request him to run round to his (the legal gentleman's) office and fetch some papers for him. Thereupon Bartleby would tranquilly decline, and yet remain idle as before. Then the lawyer would give a great stare, and turn to me. And what could I say? At last I was made aware that all through the circle of my professional acquaintance a whisper of wonder was running round, having reference to the strange creature I kept at my office. This worried me very much. And as the idea came upon me of his possibly turning out a long-lived man, and keep occupying my chambers, and denying my authority; and perplexing my visitors; and scandalizing my professional reputation; and casting a general gloom over the premises; keeping soul and body together to the last upon his savings (for doubtless he spent but half a dime a day), and in the end perhaps outlive me, and claim possession of my office by right of his perpetual occupancy—as all these dark anticipations crowded upon me more and more, and my friends continually intruded their relentless remarks upon the apparition in my room, a great change was wrought in me. I resolved to gather all my faculties together and forever rid me of this intolerable incubus.

Ere revolving any complicated project, however, adapted to this end, I first simply suggested to Bartleby the propriety of his permanent departure. In a calm and serious tone, I commended the idea to his careful and mature consideration. But, having taken three days to meditate upon it, he apprised me that his original determination remained the same; in short, that he still preferred to abide with me.

What shall I do? I now said to myself, buttoning up my coat to the last button. What shall I do? what ought I to do? what does conscience say I *should* do with this man, or, rather, ghost. Rid myself of him, I must; go, he shall. But how? You will not thrust him, the poor, pale, passive mortal—you will not thrust such a helpless creature out of your door? you will not dishonor yourself by such cruelty? No, I will not, I cannot do that. Rather would I let him live and die here, and then mason up his remains in the wall. What, then, will you do? For all your coaxing, he will not budge. Bribes he leaves under your own paperweight on your table; in short, it is quite plain that he prefers to cling to you.

Then something severe, something unusual, must be done. What! surely you will not have him collared by a constable, and commit his innocent pallor to the common jail? And upon what ground could you procure such a thing to be done?—a vagrant, is he? What! he a vagrant, a wanderer, who refuses to budge? It is because he will *not* be a vagrant, then, that you seek to count him *as* a vagrant. That is too absurd. No visible means of support: there I have him. Wrong again: for indubitably he *does* support himself, and that is the only unanswerable proof that any man can show of his possessing the means so to do. No more, then. Since he will not quit me, I must quit him. I will change my offices; I will move elsewhere, and give him fair notice that if I find him on my new premises I will then proceed against him as a common trespasser.

Acting accordingly, next day I thus addressed him: "I find these chambers too far from the City Hall; the air is unwholesome. In a word, I propose to remove my offices next week, and shall no longer require your services. I tell you this now, in order that you may seek another place."

He made no reply, and nothing more was said.

On the appointed day I engaged carts and men, proceeded to my chambers, and, having but little furniture, everything was removed in a few hours. Throughout, the scrivener remained standing behind the screen, which I directed to be removed the last thing. It was withdrawn; and, being folded up like a huge folio, left him the motionless occupant of a naked room. I stood in the entry watching him a moment, while something from within me upbraided me.

I re-entered, with my hand in my pocket—and—and my heart in my mouth.

"Good-bye, Bartleby; I am going—good-bye; and God some way bless you; and take that," slipping something in his hand. But it dropped upon the floor, and then—strange to say—I tore myself from him whom I had so longed to be rid of.

Established in my new quarters, for a day or two I kept the door locked, and started at every footfall in the passages. When I returned to my rooms after any little absence, I would pause at the threshold for an instant and attentively listen ere applying my key. But these fears were needless. Bartleby never came nigh me.

I thought all was going well, when a perturbed-looking stranger visited me, inquiring whether I was the person who had recently occupied rooms at No. —— Wall Street.

Full of forebodings, I replied that I was.

"Then, sir," said the stranger, who proved a lawyer, "you are responsible for the man you left there. He refuses to do any copying; he refuses to do anything; he says he prefers not to; and he refuses to quit the premises."

"I am very sorry, sir," said I, with assumed tranquillity, but an inward tremor, "but, really, the man you allude to is nothing to me—he is no relation or apprentice of mine, that you should hold me responsible for him."

"In mercy's name, who is he?"

"I certainly cannot inform you. I know nothing about him. Formerly I employed him as a copyist; but he has done nothing for me now for some time past."

"I shall settle him, then—good morning, sir."

Several days passed, and I heard nothing more; and, though I often felt a charitable prompting to call at the place and see poor Bartleby, yet a certain squeamishness, of I know not what, withheld me.

All is over with him, by this time, thought I at last, when, through another week, no further intelligence reached me. But, coming to my room the day after, I found several persons waiting at my door in a high state of nervous excitement.

"That's the man—here he comes," cried the foremost one, whom I recognized as the lawyer who had previously called upon me alone.

"You must take him away, sir, at once," cried a portly person among them, advancing upon me, and whom I knew to be the landlord of No. —— Wall Street. "These gentlemen, my tenants, cannot stand it any longer; Mr. B——," pointing to the lawyer, "has turned him out of his room, and he now persists in haunting the building generally, sitting upon the banisters of the stairs by day, and sleeping in the entry by night. Everybody is concerned; clients are leaving the offices; some fears are entertained of a mob; something you must do, and that without delay."

Aghast at this torrent, I fell back before it, and would fain have locked myself in my new quarters. In vain I persisted that Bartleby was nothing to me—no more than to anyone else. In vain—I was the last person known to have anything to do with him, and they held me to the terrible account. Fearful, then, of being exposed in the papers (as one person present obscurely threatened), I considered the matter, and at length said that if the lawyer would give me a confidential interview with the scrivener, in his (the lawyer's) own room, I would, that afternoon, strive my best to rid them of the nuisance they complained of.

Going upstairs to my old haunt, there was Bartleby silently sitting upon the banister at the landing.

"What are you doing here, Bartleby?" said I.

"Sitting upon the banister," he mildly replied.

I motioned him into the lawyer's room, who then left us.

"Bartleby," said I, "are you aware that you are the cause of great tribulation to me, by persisting in occupying the entry after being dismissed from the office?"

No answer.

"Now one of two things must take place. Either you must do something, or something must be done to you. Now what sort of business would you like to engage in? Would you like to re-engage in copying for someone?"

"No; I would prefer not to make any change."

"Would you like a clerkship in a dry-goods store?"

"There is too much confinement about that. No, I would not like a clerkship; but I am not particular."

"Too much confinement," I cried; "why you keep yourself confined all the time!"

"I would prefer not to take a clerkship," he rejoined, as if to settle that little item at once.

"How would a bartender's business suit you? There is no trying of the eyesight in that."

"I would not like it at all; though, as I said before, I am not particular."

His unwonted wordiness inspirited me. I returned to the charge.

"Well, then, would you like to travel through the country collecting bills for the merchants? That would improve your health."

"No, I would prefer to be doing something else."

"How, then, would going as a companion to Europe, to entertain some young gentleman with your conversation—how would that suit you?"

"Not at all. It does not strike me that there is anything definite about that. I like to be stationary. But I am not particular."

"Stationary you shall be, then," I cried, now losing all patience, and, for the first time in all my exasperating connection with him, fairly flying into a passion. "If you do not go away from these premises before night, I shall feel bound—indeed, I *am* bound—to—to—to quit the premises myself!" I rather absurdly concluded, knowing not with what possible threat to try to frighten his immobility into compliance. Despairing of all further efforts, I was precipitately leaving him, when a final thought occurred to me—one which had not been wholly unindulged before.

"Bartleby," said I, in the kindest tone I could assume under such exciting circumstances, "will you go home with me now—not to my office, but my dwelling—and remain there till we can conclude upon some convenient arrangement for you at our leisure? Come, let us start now, right away."

"No; at present I would prefer not to make any change at all."

I answered nothing, but, effectually dodging everyone by the suddenness and rapidity of my flight, rushed from the building, ran up Wall Street towards Broadway, and, jumping into the first omnibus, was soon removed from pursuit. As soon as tranquillity returned, I distinctly perceived that I had now done all that I possibly could, both in respect to the demands of the landlord and his tenants, and with regard to my own desire and sense of duty, to benefit Bartleby, and shield him from rude persecution. I now strove to be entirely carefree and quiescent, and my conscience justified me in the attempt, though, indeed, it was not so successful as I could have wished. So fearful was I of being again hunted out by the incensed landlord and his exasperated tenants that, surrendering my business to Nippers for a few days, I drove about the upper part of the town and through the suburbs in my rockaway; crossed over to Jersey City and Hoboken, and paid fugitive visits to Manhattanville and Astoria. In fact, I almost lived in my rockaway for the time.

When again I entered my office, lo, a note from the landlord lay upon the desk. I opened it with trembling hands. It informed me that the writer had sent to the police, and had Bartleby removed to the Tombs as a vagrant. Moreover, since I knew more about him than anyone else, he wished me to appear at that place and make a suitable statement of the facts. These tidings had a conflicting effect upon me. At first I was indignant, but at last almost approved. The landlord's energetic, summary disposition had led him to adopt a procedure which I do not think I would have decided upon myself; and yet, as a last resort, under such peculiar circumstances, it seemed the only plan.

As I afterwards learned, the poor scrivener, when told that he must be conducted to the Tombs, offered not the slightest obstacle, but, in his pale, unmoving way, silently acquiesced.

Some of the compassionate and curious bystanders joined the party, and, headed by one of the constables arm in arm with Bartleby, the silent procession filed its way through all the noise, and heat, and joy of the roaring thoroughfares at noon.

The same day I received the note, I went to the Tombs, or, to speak more properly, the Halls of Justice. Seeking the right officer, I stated the purpose of my call, and was informed that the individual I described was indeed within. I then assured the functionary that Bartleby was a perfectly honest man, and greatly to be compassionated, however unaccountably eccentric. I narrated all I knew, and closed by suggesting the idea of letting him remain in as indulgent confinement as possible till something less harsh might be done—though, indeed, I hardly knew what. At all events, if nothing else could be decided upon, the almshouse must receive him. I then begged to have an interview.

Being under no disgraceful charge, and quite serene and harmless in all his ways, they had permitted him freely to wander about the prison, and, especially, in the inclosed grass-platted yards thereof. And so I found him there standing all alone in the quietest of the yards, his face towards a high wall, while all around, from the narrow slits of the jail windows, I thought I saw peering out upon him the eyes of murderers and thieves.

"Bartleby!"

"I know you," he said, without looking round—"and I want nothing to say to you."

"It was not I that brought you here, Bartleby," said I, keenly pained at his implied suspicion. "And, to you, this should not be so vile a place. Nothing reproachful attaches to you by being here. And see, it is not so sad a place as one might think. Look there is the sky, and here is the grass."

"I know where I am," he replied, but would say nothing more, and so I left him.

As I entered the corridor again, a broad meatlike man in an apron accosted me, and, jerking his thumb over his shoulder, said—"Is that your friend?"

"Yes."

"Does he want to starve? If he does, let him live on the prison fare, that's all."

"Who are you?" asked I, not knowing what to make of such an unofficially speaking person in such a place.

"I am the grubman. Such gentlemen as have friends here hire me to provide them with something good to eat."

"Is this so?" said I, turning to the turnkey.

He said it was.

"Well, then," said I, slipping some silver into the grubman's hands (for so they called him), "I want you to give particular attention to my friend there; let him have the best dinner you can get. And you must be as polite to him as possible."

"Introduce me, will you?" said the grubman, looking at me with an expression which seemed to say he was all impatience for an opportunity to give a specimen of his breeding.

Thinking it would prove of benefit to the scrivener, I acquiesced, and, asking the grubman his name, went up with him to Bartleby.

"Bartleby, this is a friend; you will find him very useful to you."

"Your sarvant, sir, your sarvant," said the grubman, making a low salutation behind his apron. "Hope you find it pleasant here, sir; nice grounds—cool apartments—hope you'll stay with us some time—try to make it agreeable. What will you have for dinner today?"

"I prefer not to dine today," said Bartleby, turning away. "It would disagree with me; I am unused to dinners." So saying, he slowly moved to the other side of the inclosure and took up a position fronting the dead-wall.

"How's this?" said the grubman, addressing me with a stare of astonishment. "He's odd, ain't he?"

"I think he is a little deranged," said I, sadly.

"Deranged? deranged is it? Well, now, upon my word, I thought that friend of yourn was a gentleman forger; they are always pale and genteel-like, them forgers. I can't help pity 'em—can't help it, sir. Did you know Monroe Edwards?" he added, touchingly, and paused. Then, laying his hand piteously on my shoulder, sighed, "he died of consumption at Sing-Sing. So you weren't acquainted with Monroe?"

"No, I was never socially acquainted with any forgers. But I cannot stop longer. Look to my friend yonder. You will not lose by it. I will see you again."

Some few days after this, I again obtained admission to the Tombs, and went through the corridors in quest of Bartleby; but without finding him.

"I saw him coming from his cell not long ago," said a turnkey, "maybe he's gone to loiter in the yards."

So I went in that direction.

"Are you looking for the silent man?" said another turnkey, passing me. "Yonder he lies—sleeping in the yard there. 'Tis not twenty minutes since I saw him lie down."

The yard was entirely quiet. It was not accessible to the common prisoners. The surrounding walls, of amazing thickness, kept off all sounds behind them. The Egyptian character of the masonry weighed upon me with its gloom. But a soft imprisoned turf grew underfoot. The heart of the eternal pyramids, it seemed, wherein, by some strange magic, through the clefts, grass-seed, dropped by birds, had sprung.

Strangely huddled at the base of the wall, his knees drawn up and lying on his side, his head touching the cold stones, I saw the wasted Bartleby. But nothing stirred. I paused, then went close up to him, stooped over, and saw that his dim eyes were open; otherwise he seemed profoundly sleeping. Something prompted me to touch him. I felt his hand, when a tingling shiver ran up my arm and down my spine to my feet.

The round face of the grubman peered upon me now. "His dinner is ready. Won't he dine today, either? Or does he live without dining?"

"Lives without dining," said I, and closed the eyes.

"Eh!—He's asleep, ain't he?"

"With kings and counselors," murmured I.

There would seem little need for proceeding further in this history. Imagination will readily supply the meager recital of poor Bartleby's interment. But, ere parting with the reader, let me say that if this little narrative has sufficiently interested him to awaken curiosity as to who Bartleby was, and what manner of life he led prior to the present narrator's making his acquaintance, I can only reply that in such curiosity I fully share, but am wholly unable to gratify it. Yet here I hardly know whether I should divulge one little item of rumor which came to my ear a few months after the scrivener's decease. Upon what basis it rested, I could never ascertain, and hence how true it is I cannot now tell. But, inasmuch as this vague report has not been without a certain suggestive interest to me, however sad, it may prove the same with some others, and so I will briefly mention it. The report was this: that Bartleby had been a subordinate clerk in the Dead Letter Office at Washington, from which he had benn suddenly removed by a change in the administration. When I think over this rumor, hardly can I express the emotions which seize me. Dead letters! does it not sound like dead men? Conceive a man by nature and misfortune prone to a pallid hopelessness, can any business seem more fitted to heighten it than that of continually handling these dead letters, and assorting them for the flames? For by the cartload they are annually burned. Sometimes from out the folded paper the pale clerk takes a ring—the finger it was meant for, perhaps, molders in the grave; a bank note sent in swiftest charity—he whom it would relieve nor eats nor hungers any more; pardon for those who died despairing; hope for those who died unhoping; good tidings for those who died stifled by unrelieved calamities. On errands of life, these letters speed to death.

Ah, Bartleby! Ah, humanity!

4

ADULTHOOD
Generativity versus Stagnation

More than any other issue, generativity versus stagnation raises the question of whether or not men can survive as a learning and teaching animal. For it makes clear that, if human development is to continue, then adults must directly concern themselves with establishing and guiding the next generation. In most adult lives generativity is not, however, just a matter of child rearing but also a matter of personal creativity and endurance, and it is on these latter concerns that the stories in this section focus. In the five stories that follow, the principal figures are all concerned with their own survival. What makes some of them choose suicide, and the others arrive at new ways of living? The answer, when it can be found, does not lie in the magnitude of the problems they face so much as their reactions to them. As the tone of each of these stories reveals, the past either becomes an insuperable force in the life of the central character or else he generates ways of moving beyond it.

The first story, Yukio Mishima's "Patriotism," deals with a young lieutenant in the Japanese army who commits hara-kiri after friends of his fail to overthrow the government. The story is one with which Mishima, who at age 45 committed hara-kiri to demonstrate his belief that Japan should rearm, was deeply involved. In 1965, five years before his own death, Mishima produced "Patriotism" as a movie and assigned himself the role of the lieutenant.

"Patriotism" begins in so factual a tone that at first one has only a newspaper sense of the lieutenant's death:

> *On the twenty-eighth of February, 1936 (on the third day, that is of the February 26 Incident), Lieutenant Shinji Takeyama of the Konoe Transport Battalion—profoundly disturbed by the knowledge that his closest colleagues had been with the mutineers from the beginning, and indignant at the imminent prospect of Imperial troops attacking Imperial troops—took his officer's sword and ceremonially disemboweled himself. . . . The lieutenant's*

> *age, it should be noted, was thirty-one, his wife's twenty-three; and it was not half a year since the celebration of their marriage.*

This tone, however, is one that makes us see that if Lieutenant Takeyama's hara-kiri is viewed at a distance, it can only appear as a waste of life. The rest of Mishima's story is devoted to capturing the world the lieutenant lives in: his sense of courage, his belief in tradition, his relationship to his wife. By the time Lieutenant Takeyama tells his wife that he will refuse orders to attack his rebellious fellow officers and that taking his own life is the only alternative, his choice seems logical rather than shocking. We are left to wonder only if his choice is as glorious as he believes:

> *A lonely death on the battlefield, a death beneath the eyes of his beautiful wife . . . in the sensation that he was now to die in these two dimensions, realizing an impossible union of them both, there was a sweetness beyond words. This must be the very pinnacle of good fortune, he thought.*

Would the strengths that the lieutenant has appear less formidable if he took a more flexible position with regard to his dilemma? Can we separate the beauty of his life from his capacity to terminate it at will?

A different set of questions arises with regard to Juan Dahlmann, the central figure of Jorge Luis Borges' "The South." Like Lieutenant Takeyama, Dahlmann is prepared to commit suicide, but in his case suicide is an event without ritual or glory. Dahlmann allows himself to be provoked into a knife fight in which he knows "the weapon, in his torpid hand, was no defense at all, but would merely serve to justify his murder."

Why does Dahlmann choose such an end? Again, the contrast with Lieutenant Takeyama is striking. For the mood of Borges' story is built around the drabness rather than the beauty in Dahlmann's life. Indeed, most of the latter's days have been spent in "boredom and solitude," and until February, 1939, virtually nothing can be said to have happened to him. After that point, events do move swiftly, however. Dahlmann discovers that "he was in hell," and eight days later he is taken off to a sanitarium where he is treated with a bewildering brutality:

> *When he arrived at his destination, they undressed him, shaved his head, bound him with metal fastenings to a stretcher; they shone bright lights on him until he was blind and dizzy, auscultated him, and a masked man stuck a needle into his arm. He awoke with a feeling of nausea, covered with a bandage, in a cell with something of a well about it; in the days and nights which followed the operation he came to realize that he had merely been, up until then, in a suburb of hell.*

Dahlmann is, nonetheless, eventually pronounced cured, and leaves the sanitarium for a ranch he owns in the South of Argentina. On the way there he stops at a general store, and at this point answers the challenge he knows will be fatal. Borges' description of Dahlmann's state of mind seems very precise:

> *As he crossed the threshold, he felt that to die in a knife fight, under the open sky, and going forward to the attack, would have been a liberation, a joy, and a festive occasion, on the first night in the sanitarium when they stuck him with the needle.*

The difficulty is in knowing what such a description suggests. Is Dahlmann's decision a reaction to the sanitarium? The brutality before him? His previous restlessness? Does Borges' conclusion raise problems that cannot be answered within his story?

By contrast, the next three stories all deal with men who make a choice to go on living. The first of these stories, Ernest Hemingway's "Big Two-Hearted River," is outwardly a description of a fishing trip Nick Adams takes in upper Michigan. But the story is much more than that. Nick's trip is a very deliberate attempt at escape. "He felt he had left everything behind, the need for thinking, the need to write, other needs. It was all back of him." What Nick is running away from is never stated in "Big Two-Hearted River," but as the stories which come before it in the Hemingway collection *In Our Time* make clear, Nick has come back from World War I, in which he has been wounded and has made a "separate peace." Thus, Nick's concern with details is not just that of a man who loves the woods but that of a man who is struggling to keep his nerves under control. The real mood of the story is a reflection of Nick's tension rather then the beauty of the country:

> *Nick was happy as he crawled inside the tent. He had not been unhappy all day. This was different though. Now things were done. There had been this to do. Now it was done. It had been a hard trip. He was very tired. That was done. He had made his camp. He was settled. Nothing could touch him.*

Part II of "Big Two-Hearted River" ends with Nick cooking trout and deciding he will not follow the water into the swamp. "In the swamp fishing was a tragic adventure. Nick did not want it. He did not want to go down the stream any further today." Nick seems sure that sooner or later he will have the strength for "tragic adventure," and Hemingway is content to let Nick have the last word. But here, as in the rest of Hemingway's writing, it is not easy to see what provision has been made for anything more complex than basic survival.

In D. H. Lawrence's "The Blind Man," Maurice Pervin, who has been blinded in World War I, also finds relief in sheer physical activity:

> *Sightless, he could still discuss everything with Wernham, and he could also do a good deal of work about the place—menial work, it is true, but it gave him satisfaction. He milked the cows, carried in the pails, turned the separator, attended to the pigs and horses.*

It is not, however, the ritual of keeping busy, but the blood knowledge Maurice has of the life around him that defines him and sets the tone of Lawrence's story:

> *He did not think much or trouble much. So long as he kept this sheer*

> *immediacy of blood-contact with the substantial world he was happy, he wanted no intervention of visual consciousness. In this state there was a certain rich positivity, bordering sometimes on rapture.*

The difficulty is that Maurice cannot always sustain this "new way of consciousness." He also has "fits of depression," which his wife finds so troubling that frequently "she wished she could be snatched off the earth altogether, anything rather than live at this cost."

The tension between Maurice and his wife appears headed for a climax when she is visited by an old friend and "second or third cousin," Bertie Reid. Bertie, with his wit and quickness, is the very opposite of Maurice, who worries that Bertie will remind his wife of all he cannot give her. By the end of Bertie's visit, however, Maurice is much calmer about himself and Bertie and stands before his wife "like a strange colossus." What is to be made of this change? Is there a secret pleasure Maurice has found in destroying Bertie? Has Bertie given him new insight into his wife? Above all, can Isabel Pervin share in the feeling that has come over her husband?

In the final story in this section, Frank O'Connor's "Guests of the Nation," the central character must also recover from war, but in his case the shock stems from violence he has inflicted on the "enemy." The enemy in this case is two Englishmen, Hawkins and Belcher, who have been captured by the Irish during the rebellion. O'Connor's story focuses on the way in which Hawkins and Belcher become friends with their captors. "They just naturally took with us, and after the first day or two we gave up all pretence of keeping a close eye on them."

As the intimacy between Hawkins and Belcher and their captors grows, so however does a second concern: what is going to be done with the Englishmen. In the first section of "Guests of the Nation" we know only that Hawkins and Belcher have been transferred to their present location because "the search for them became too hot." It is not until the second section that we realize they are being kept as hostages. "If they [the English] shoot our prisoners, we'll shoot theirs." By the time of the third section, the decision has been made that Hawkins and Belcher are to be shot in retaliation for killings by the English of Irish prisoners. To Bonaparte, the narrator of "Guests of the Nation," the thought of such revenge is sickening, and he hopes Belcher and Hawkins will make an effort to escape, for then he is sure, "I'd never fire on them." But Hawkins and Belcher go passively to their deaths, and Bonaparte does nothing to prevent their murder. He emerges only with the sense, "I was somehow very small and very lost and lonely like a child astray in the snow. And anything that happened to me afterwards, I never felt the same about again."

At the end of O'Connor's story there is, thus, no sense that the shock of war can be recovered from. On the other hand, there is also the feeling that if Bonaparte were ever to reconcile himself to his actions, then all hope for him to generate a new life would be lost.

YUKIO MISHIMA

PATRIOTISM

Translated by Geoffrey W. Sargeant

On the twenty-eighth of February, 1936 (on the third day, that is, of the February Incident), Lieutenant Shinji Takeyama of the Konoe Transport Battalion—profoundly disturbed by the knowledge that his closest colleagues had been with the mutineers from the beginning, and indignant at the imminent prospect of Imperial troops attacking Imperial troops—took his officer's sword and ceremonially disemboweled himself in the eight-mat room of his private residence in the sixth block of Aoba-chō, in Yotsuya Ward. His wife, Reiko, followed him, stabbing herself to death. The lieutenant's farewell note consisted of one sentence: "Long live the Imperial Forces." His wife's, after apologies for her unfilial conduct in thus preceding her parents to the grave, concluded: "The day which, for a soldier's wife, had to come, has come. . . ." The last moments of this heroic and dedicated couple were such as to make the gods themselves weep. The lieutenant's age, it should be noted, was thirty-one, his wife's twenty-three; and it was not half a year since the celebration of their marriage.

2

Those who saw the bride and bridegroom in the commemorative photograph—perhaps no less than those actually present at the lieutenant's wedding—had exclaimed in wonder at the bearing of this handsome couple. The lieutenant, majestic in military uniform, stood protectively beside his bride, his right hand resting upon his sword, his officer's cap held at his left side. His expression was severe, and his dark brows and wide-gazing eyes well conveyed the clear integrity of youth. For the beauty of the bride in her white over-robe no comparisons were adequate. In the eyes, round beneath soft brows, in the slender, finely shaped nose, and in the full lips, there was both sensuousness and refinement.

One hand, emerging shyly from a sleeve of the over-robe, held a fan, and the tips of the fingers, clustering delicately, were like the bud of a moonflower.

After the suicide, people would take out this photograph and examine it, and sadly reflect that too often there was a curse on these seemingly flawless unions. Perhaps it was no more than imagination, but looking at the picture after the tragedy it almost seemed as if the two young people before the gold-lacquered screen were gazing, each with equal clarity, at the deaths which lay before them.

Thanks to the good offices of their go-between, Lieutenant General Ozeki, they had been able to set themselves up in a new home at Aoba-chō in Yotsuya. "New home" is perhaps misleading. It was an old three-room rented house backing onto a small garden. As neither the six- nor the four-and-a-half mat room downstairs was favored by the sun, they used the upstairs eight-mat room as both bedroom and guest room. There was no maid, so Reiko was left alone to guard the house in her husband's absence.

The honeymoon trip was dispensed with on the grounds that these were times of national emergency. The two of them had spent the first night of their marriage at this house. Before going to bed, Shinji, sitting erect on the floor with his sword laid before him, had bestowed upon his wife a soldierly lecture. A woman who had become the wife of a soldier should know and resolutely accept that her husband's death might come at any moment. It could be tomorrow. It could be the day after. But, no matter when it came—he asked—was she steadfast in her resolve to accept it? Reiko rose to her feet, pulled open a drawer of the cabinet, and took out what was the most prized of her new possessions, the dagger her mother had given her. Returning to her place, she laid the dagger without a word on the mat before her, just as her husband had laid his sword. A silent understanding was achieved at once, and the lieutenant never again sought to test his wife's resolve.

In the first few months of her marriage Reiko's beauty grew daily more radiant, shining serene like the moon after rain.

As both were possessed of young, vigorous bodies, their relationship was passionate. Nor was this merely a matter of the night. On more than one occasion, returning home straight from maneuvers, and begrudging even the time it took to remove his mud-splashed uniform, the lieutenant had pushed his wife to the floor almost as soon as he had entered the house. Reiko was equally ardent in her response. For a little more or a little less than a month, from the first night of their marriage Reiko knew happiness, and the lieutenant, seeing this, was happy too.

Reiko's body was white and pure, and her swelling breasts conveyed a firm and chaste refusal; but, upon consent, those breasts were lavish with their intimate, welcoming warmth. Even in bed these two were frighteningly and awesomely serious. In the very midst of wild, intoxicating passions, their hearts were sober and serious.

By day the lieutenant would think of his wife in the brief rest periods between training; and all day long, at home, Reiko would recall the image of her husband. Even when apart, however, they had only to look at the wedding photograph for their happiness to be once more confirmed. Reiko felt not the slightest surprise that a man who had been a complete stranger until a few months ago should now have become the sun about which her whole world revolved.

All these things had a moral basis, and were in accordance with the Education Rescript's injunction that "husband and wife should be harmonious." Not once did Reiko contradict her husband, nor did the lieutenant ever find reason to scold his wife. On the god shelf below the stairway, alongside the tablet from the Great Ise Shrine, were set photographs of their Imperial Majesties, and regularly every morning, before leaving for duty, the lieutenant would stand with his wife at this hallowed place and together they would bow their heads low. The offering water was renewed each morning, and the sacred sprig of *sasaki* was always green and fresh. Their lives were lived beneath the solemn protection of the gods and were filled with an intense happiness which set every fiber in their bodies trembling.

3

Although Lord Privy Seal Saitō's house was in their neighborhood, neither of them heard any noise of gunfire on the morning of February 26. It was a bugle, sounding muster in the dim, snowy dawn, when the ten-minute tragedy had already ended, which first disrupted the lieutenant's slumbers. Leaping at once from his bed, and without speaking a word, the lieutenant donned his uniform, buckled on the sword held ready for him by his wife, and hurried swiftly out into the snow-covered streets of the still darkened morning. He did not return until the evening of the twenty-eighth.

Later, from the radio news, Reiko learned the full extent of this sudden eruption of violence. Her life throughout the subsequent two days was lived alone, in complete tranquillity, and behind locked doors.

In the lieutenant's face, as he hurried silently out into the snowy morning, Reiko had read the determination to die. If her husband did not return, her own decision was made: she too would die. Quietly she attended to the disposition of her personal possessions. She chose her sets of visiting kimonos as keepsakes for friends of her schooldays, and she wrote a name and address on the stiff paper wrapping in which each was folded. Constantly admonished by her husband never to think of the morrow, Reiko had not even kept a diary and was now denied the pleasure of assiduously rereading her record of the happiness of the past few months and consigning each page to the fire as she did so. Ranged across the top of the radio were a small china dog, a rabbit, a squirrel, a bear, and a fox. There were also a small vase and a water pitcher. These comprised Reiko's one and only collection. But it would hardly do, she imagined, to give such things as keepsakes. Nor again would it be quite proper to ask specifically for them to be included in the coffin. It seemed to Reiko, as these thoughts passed through her mind, that the expressions on the small animals' faces grew even more lost and forlorn.

Reiko took the squirrel in her hand and looked at it. And then, her thoughts turning to a realm far beyond these childlike affections, she gazed up into the distance at the great sunlike principle which her husband embodied. She was ready, and happy, to be hurtled along to her destruction in that gleaming sun chariot—but now, for these few moments of solitude, she allowed herself to luxuriate in this innocent attachment to trifles. The time when she had genuinely loved these things, however, was long past. Now she merely loved the memory of having once loved them, and their place in her heart had been filled by more intense passions, by a more frenzied happiness. . . . For Reiko had never, even to herself, thought of those soaring joys of the flesh as a mere pleasure. The February cold, and the icy touch of the china squirrel, had numbed Reiko's slender fingers; yet, even so, in her lower limbs, beneath the ordered repetition of the pattern which crossed the skirt of her trim *meisen* kimono, she could feel now, as she thought of the lieutenant's powerful arms reaching out toward her, a hot moistness of the flesh which defied the snows.

She was not in the least afraid of the death hovering in her mind. Waiting alone at home, Reiko firmly believed that everything her husband was feeling or thinking now, his anguish and distress, was leading her—just as surely as the power in his flesh—to a welcome death. She felt as if her body could melt away with ease and be transformed to the merest fraction of her husband's thought.

Listening to the frequent announcements on the radio, she heard the names of several of her husband's colleagues mentioned among those of the insurgents. This was news of death. She followed the developments closely, wondering anxiously, as the situation became daily more irrevocable, why no Imperial ordinance was sent down, and watching what had at first been taken as a movement to restore the nation's honor come gradually to be branded with the infamous name of mutiny. There was no communication from the regiment. At any moment, it seemed, fighting might commence in the city streets where the remains of the snow still lay.

Toward sundown on the twenty-eighth Reiko was startled by a furious pounding on the front door. She hurried downstairs. As she pulled with fumbling fingers at the bolt, the shape dimly outlined beyond the frosted-glass panel made no sound, but she knew it was her husband. Reiko had never known the bolt on the sliding door to be so stiff. Still it resisted. The door just would not open.

In a moment, almost before she knew she had succeeded, the lieutenant was standing before her on the cement floor inside the porch, muffled in a khaki greatcoat, his top boots heavy with slush from the street. Closing the door behind him, he returned the bolt once more to its socket. With what significance, Reiko did not understand.

"Welcome home."

Reiko bowed deeply, but her husband made no response. As he had already unfastened his sword and was about to remove his greatcoat, Reiko moved around behind to assist. The coat, which was cold and damp and had lost the odor of horse dung it normally exuded when exposed to the sun, weighed heavily upon her arm. Draping it across a hanger, and cradling the sword and leather belt in her sleeves, she waited while her husband removed his top boots and then followed behind him into the "living room." This was the six-mat room downstairs.

Seen in the clear light from the lamp, her husband's face, covered with a heavy growth of bristle, was almost unrecognizably wasted and thin. The cheeks were hollow, their luster and resilience gone. In his normal good spirits he would have changed into old clothes as soon as he was home and have pressed her to get supper at once, but now he sat before the table still in his uniform, his head drooping dejectedly. Reiko refrained from asking whether she should prepare the supper.

After an interval the lieutenant spoke.

"I knew nothing. They hadn't asked me to join. Perhaps out of consideration, because I was newly married. Kanō, and Homma too, and Yamaguchi."

Reiko recalled momentarily the faces of high-spirited young officers, friends of her husband, who had come to the house occasionally as guests.

"There may be an Imperial ordinance sent down tomorrow. They'll be posted as rebels, I imagine. I shall be in command of a unit with orders to attack them. . . . I can't do it. It's impossible to do a thing like that."

He spoke again.

"They've taken me off guard duty, and I have permission to return home for one night. Tomorrow morning, without question, I must leave to join the attack. I can't do it, Reiko."

Reiko sat erect with lowered eyes. She understood clearly that her husband had spoken of his death. The lieutenant was resolved. Each word, being rooted in death, emerged sharply and with powerful significance against this dark, unmovable background. Although the lieutenant was speaking of his dilemma, already there was no room in his mind for vacillation.

However, there was a clarity, like the clarity of a stream fed from melting snows, in the silence which rested between them. Sitting in his own home after the long two-day ordeal, and looking across at the face of his beautiful wife, the lieutenant was for the first time experiencing true peace of mind. For he had at once known, though she said nothing, that his wife divined the resolve which lay beneath his words.

"Well, then . . ." The lieutenant's eyes opened wide. Despite his exhaustion they were strong and clear, and now for the first time they looked straight into the eyes of his wife. "Tonight I shall cut my stomach."

Reiko did not flinch.

Her round eyes showed tension, as taut as the clang of a bell.

"I am ready," she said. "I ask permission to accompany you."

The lieutenant felt almost mesmerized by the strength in those eyes. His words flowed swiftly and easily, like the utterances of a man in delirium, and it was beyond his understanding how permission in a matter of such weight could be expressed so casually.

"Good. We'll go together. But I want you as a witness, first, for my own suicide. Agreed?"

When this was said a sudden release of abundant happiness welled up in both their hearts. Reiko was deeply affected by the greatness of her husband's trust in her. It was vital for the lieutenant, whatever else might happen, that there should be no irregularity in his death. For that reason there had to be a witness. The fact that he had chosen his wife for this was the first mark of his trust. The second, and even greater mark, was that though he had pledged that they should die together he did not intend to kill his wife first—he had deferred her death to a time when he would no longer be there to verify it. If the lieutenant had been a suspicious husband, he would doubtless, as in the usual suicide pact, have chosen to kill his wife first.

When Reiko said, "I ask permission to accompany you," the lieutenant felt these words to be the final fruit of the education which he had himself given his wife, starting on the first night of their marriage, and which had schooled her, when the moment came, to say what had to be said without a shadow of hesitation. This flattered the lieutenant's opinion of himself as a self-reliant man. He was not so romantic or conceited as to imagine that the words were spoken spontaneously, out of love for her husband.

With happiness welling almost too abundantly in their hearts, they could not help smiling at each other. Reiko felt as if she had returned to her wedding night.

Before her eyes was neither pain nor death. She seemed to see only a free and limitless expanse opening out into vast distances.

"The water is hot. Will you take your bath now?"

"Ah yes, of course."

"And supper . . .?"

The words were delivered in such level, domestic tones that the lieutenant came near to thinking, for the fraction of a second, that everything had been a hallucination.

"I don't think we'll need supper. But perhaps you could warm some sake?"

"As you wish."

As Reiko rose and took a *tanzen* gown from the cabinet for after the bath, she purposely directed her husband's attention to the opened drawer. The lieutenant rose, crossed to the cabinet, and looked inside. From the ordered array of paper wrappings he read, one by one, the addresses of the keepsakes. There was no grief in the lieutenant's response to this demonstration of heroic resolve. His heart was filled with tenderness. Like a husband who is proudly shown the childish purchases of a young wife, the lieutenant, overwhelmed by affection, lovingly embraced his wife from behind and implanted a kiss upon her neck.

Reiko felt the roughness of the lieutenant's unshaven skin against her neck. This sensation, more than being just a thing of this world, was for Reiko almost the world itself, but now—with the feeling that it was soon to be lost forever—it had freshness beyond all her experience. Each moment had its own vital strength, and the senses in every corner of her body were reawakened. Accepting her husband's caresses from behind, Reiko raised herself on the tips of her toes, letting the vitality seep through her entire body.

"First the bath, and then, after some sake . . . lay out the bedding upstairs, will you?"

The lieutenant whispered the words into his wife's ear. Reiko silently nodded.

Flinging off his uniform, the lieutenant went to the bath. To faint background noises of slopping water Reiko tended the charcoal brazier in the living room and began the preparations for warming the sake.

Taking the *tanzen*, a sash, and some underclothes, she went to the bathroom to ask how the water was. In the midst of a coiling cloud of steam the lieutenant was sitting cross-legged on the floor, shaving, and she could dimly discern the rippling movements of the muscles on his damp, powerful back as they responded to the movement of his arms.

There was nothing to suggest a time of any special significance. Reiko, going busily about her tasks, was preparing side dishes from odds and ends in stock. Her hands did not tremble. If anything, she managed even more efficiently and smoothly than usual. From time to time, it is true, there was a strange throbbing deep within her breast. Like distant lightning, it had a moment of sharp intensity and then vanished without trace. Apart from that, nothing was in any way out of the ordinary.

The lieutenant, shaving in the bathroom, felt his warmed body miraculously healed at last of the desperate tiredness of the days of indecision and filled—in spite of the death which lay ahead—with pleasurable anticipation. The sound of his wife going about her work came to him faintly. A healthy physical craving, submerged for two days, reasserted itself.

The lieutenant was confident there had been no impurity in that joy they had experienced when resolving upon death. They had both sensed at that moment—though not, of course, in any clear and conscious way—that those permissible pleasures which they shared in private were once more beneath the protection of Righteousness and Divine Power, and of a complete and unassailable morality. On looking into each other's eyes and discovering there an honorable death, they had felt themselves safe once more behind steel walls which none could destroy, encased in an impenetrable armor of Beauty and Truth. Thus, so far from seeing any inconsistency or conflict between the urges of his flesh and the sincerity of his patriotism, the lieutenant was even able to regard the two as parts of the same thing.

Thrusting his face close to the dark, cracked, misted wall mirror, the lieutenant shaved himself with great care. This would be his death face. There must be no unsightly blemishes. The clean-shaven face gleamed once more with a youthful luster, seeming to brighten the darkness of the mirror. There was a certain elegance, he even felt, in the association of death with this radiantly healthy face.

Just as it looked now, this would become his death face! Already, in fact, it had half departed from the lieutenant's personal possession and had become the bust above a dead soldier's memorial. As an experiment he closed his eyes tight. Everything was wrapped in blackness, and he was no longer a living, seeing creature.

Returning from the bath, the traces of the shave glowing faintly blue beneath his smooth cheeks, he seated himself beside the now well-kindled charcoal brazier. Busy though Reiko was, he noticed, she had found time lightly to touch up her face. Her cheeks were gay and her lips moist. There was no shadow of sadness to be seen. Truly, the lieutenant felt, as he saw this mark of his young wife's passionate nature, he had chosen the wife he ought to have chosen.

As soon as the lieutenant had drained his sake cup he offered it to Reiko. Reiko had never before tasted sake, but she accepted without hesitation and sipped timidly.

"Come here," the lieutenant said.

Reiko moved to her husband's side and was embraced as she leaned backward across his lap. Her breast was in violent commotion, as if sadness, joy, and the potent sake were mingling and reacting within her. The lieutenant looked down into his wife's face. It was the last face he would see in this world, the last face he would see of his wife. The lieutenant scrutinized the face minutely, with the eyes of a traveler bidding farewell to spendid vistas which he will never revisit. It was a face he could not tire of looking at—the features regular yet not cold, the lips lightly closed with a soft strength. The lieutenant kissed those lips, unthinkingly. And suddenly, though there was not the slightest distortion of the face into the unsightliness of sobbing, he noticed that tears were welling slowly from beneath the long lashes of the closed eyes and brimming over into a glistening stream.

When, a little later, the lieutenant urged that they should move to the upstairs bedroom, his wife replied that she would follow after taking a bath. Climbing the stairs alone to the bedroom, where the air was already warmed by the gas heater, the lieutenant lay down on the bedding with arms outstretched and legs apart. Even the time at which he lay waiting for his wife to join him was no later and no earlier than usual.

He folded his hands beneath his head and gazed at the dark boards of the ceiling in the dimness beyond the range of the standard lamp. Was it death he was not waiting for? Or a wild ecstasy of the senses? The two seemed to overlap, almost as if the object of this bodily desire was death itself. But, however that might be, it was certain that never before had the lieutenant tasted such total freedom.

There was the sound of a car outside the window. He could hear the screech of its tires skidding in the snow piled at the side of the street. The sound of its horn re-echoed from near-by walls. . . . Listening to these noises he had the feeling that this house rose like a solitary island in the ocean of a society going as restlessly about its business as ever. All around, vastly and untidily, stretched the country for which he grieved. He was to give his life for it. But would that great country, with which he was prepared to remonstrate to the extent of destroying himself, take the slightest heed of his death? He did not know; and it did not matter. His was a battlefield without glory, a battlefield where none could display deeds of valor: it was the front line of the spirit.

Reiko's footstesp sounded on the stairway. The steep stairs in this old house creaked badly. There were fond memories in that creaking, and many a time, while waiting in bed, the lieutenant had listened to its welcome sound. At the thought that he would hear it no more he listened with intense concentration, striving for every corner of every moment of this precious time to be filled with the sound of those soft footfalls on the creaking stairway. The moments seemed transformed to jewels, sparkling with inner light.

Reiko wore a Nagoya sash about the waist of her *yukata*, but as the lieutenant reached toward it, its redness sobered by the dimness of the light, Reiko's hand moved to his assistance and the sash fell away, slithering swiftly to the floor. As she stood before him, still in her *yukata*, the lieutenant inserted his hands through the side slits beneath each sleeve, intending to embrace her as she was; but at the touch of his finger tips upon the warm naked flesh, and as the armpits closed gently about his hands, his whole body was suddenly aflame.

In a few moments the two lay naked before the glowing gas heater.

Neither spoke the thought, but their hearts, their bodies, and their pounding breasts blazed with the knowledge that this was the very last time. It was as if the words "The Last Time" were spelled out, in invisible brushstrokes, across every inch of their bodies.

The lieutenant drew his wife close and kissed her vehemently. As their tongues explored each other's mouths, reaching out into the smooth, moist interior, they felt as if the still unknown agonies of death had tempered their senses to the keenness of red-hot steel. The agonies they could not yet feel, the distant pains of death, had refined their awareness of pleasure.

"This is the last time I shall see your body," said the lieutenant. "Let me look at it closely." And, tilting the shade on the lampstand to one side, he directed the rays along the full length of Reiko's outstretched form.

Reiko lay still with her eyes closed. The light from the low lamp clearly revealed the majestic sweep of her white flesh. The lieutenant, not without a touch of egocentricity, rejoiced that he would never see this beauty crumble in death.

At his leisure, the lieutenant allowed the unforgettable spectacle to engrave itself upon his mind. With one hand he fondled the hair, with the other he softly stroked the magnificent face, implanting kisses here and there where his eyes lingered. The quiet coldness of the high, tapering forehead, the closed eyes with their long lashes beneath faintly etched brows, the set of the finely shaped nose, the gleam of teeth glimpsed between full, regular lips, the soft cheeks and the small, wise chin . . . these things conjured up in the lieutenant's mind the vision of a truly radiant death face, and again and again he pressed his lips tight against the white throat—where Reiko's own hand was soon to strike—and the throat reddened faintly beneath his kisses. Returning to the mouth he laid his lips against it with the gentlest of pressures, and moved them rhythmically over Reiko's with the light rolling motion of a small boat. If he closed his eyes, the world became a rocking cradle.

Wherever the lieutenant's eyes moved his lips faithfully followed. The high, swelling breasts, surmounted by nipples like the buds of a wild cherry, hardened as the lieutenant's lips closed about them. The arms flowed smoothly downward from each side of the breast, tapering toward the wrists, yet losing nothing of their roundness or symmetry, and at their tips were those delicate fingers which had held the fan at the wedding ceremony. One by one, as the lieutenant kissed them, the fingers withdrew behind their neighbor as if in shame. . . . The natural hollow curving between the bosom and the stomach carried in its lines a suggestion not only of softness but of resilient strength, and while it gave forewarning of the rich curves spreading outward from here to the hips it had, in itself, an appearance only of restraint and proper discipline. The whiteness and richness of the stomach and hips was like milk brimming in a great bowl, and the sharply shadowed dip of the navel could have been the fresh impress of a raindrop, fallen there that very moment. Where the shadows gathered more thickly, hair clustered, gentle and sensitive, and as the agitation mounted in the now no longer passive body there hung over this region a scent like the smoldering of fragrant blossoms, growing steadily more pervasive.

At length, in a tremulous voice, Reiko spoke.

"Show me. . . . Let me look too, for the last time."

Never before had he heard from his wife's lips so strong and unequivocal a request. It was as if something which her modesty had wished to keep hidden to the end had suddenly burst its bonds of constraint. The lieutenant obediently lay back and surrendered himself to his wife. Lithely she raised her white, trembling body, and—burning with an innocent desire to return to her husband what he had done for her—placed two white fingers on the lieutenant's eyes, which gazed fixedly up at her, and gently stroked them shut.

Suddenly overwhelmed by tenderness, her cheeks flushed by a dizzying uprush of emotion, Reiko threw her arms about the lieutenant's close-cropped head. The bristly hairs rubbed painfully against her breast, the prominent nose was cold as it dug into her flesh, and his breath was hot. Relaxing her embrace, she gazed down at her husband's masculine face. The severe brows, the closed eyes, the splendid bridge of the nose, the shapely lips drawn firmly together . . . the blue, cleanshaven sheeks reflecting the light and gleaming smoothly. Reiko kissed each of these. She kissed the broad nape of the neck, the strong, erect shoulders, the powerful chest with its twin circles like shields and its russet nipples. In the armpits, deeply shadowed by the ample flesh of the shoulders and chest, a sweet and melancholy odor emanated from the growth of hair, and in the sweetness of this odor was contained, somehow, the essence of young death.

The lieutenant's naked skin glowed like a field of barley, and everywhere the muscles showed in sharp relief, converging on the lower abdomen about the small, unassuming navel. Gazing at the youthful, firm stomach, modestly covered by a vigorous growth of hair, Reiko thought of it as it was soon to be, cruelly cut by the sword, and she laid her head upon it, sobbing in pity, and bathed it with kisses.

At the touch of his wife's tears upon his stomach the lieutenant felt ready to endure with courage the cruelest agonies of his suicide.

What ecstasies they experienced after these tender exchanges may well be imagined. The lieutenant raised himself and enfolded his wife in a powerful embrace, her body now limp with exhaustion after her grief and tears. Passionately they held their faces close, rubbing cheek against cheek. Reiko's body was trembling. Their breasts, moist with sweat, were tightly joined, and every inch of the young and beautiful bodies had become so much one with the other that it seemed impossible there should ever again be a separation. Reiko cried out. From the heights they plunged into the abyss, and from the abyss they took wing and soared once more to dizzying heights. The lieutenant panted like the regimental standard-bearer on a route march. . . . As one cycle ended, almost immediately a new wave of passion would be generated, and together—with no trace of fatigue—they would climb again in a single breathless movement to the very summit.

4

When the lieutenant at last turned away, it was not from weariness. For one thing, he was anxious not to undermine the considerable strength he would need in carrying out his suicide. For another, he would have been sorry to mar the sweetness of these last memories by overindulgence.

Since the lieutenant had clearly desisted, Reiko too, with her usual compliance, followed his example. The two lay naked on their backs, with fingers interlaced, staring fixedly at the dark ceiling. The room was warm from the heater, and even when the sweat had ceased to pour from their bodies they felt no cold. Outside, in the hushed night, the sounds of passing traffic had ceased. Even the noises of the trains and streetcars around Yotsuya station did not penetrate this far. After echoing through the region bounded by the moat, they were lost in the heavily wooded park fronting the broad driveway before Akasaka Palace. It was hard to believe in the tension gripping this whole quarter, where the two factions of the bitterly divided Imperial Army now confronted each other, poised for battle.

Savoring the warmth glowing within themselves, they lay still and recalled the ecstasies they had just known. Each moment of the experience was relived. They remembered the taste of kisses which had never wearied, the touch of naked flesh, episode after episode of dizzying bliss. But already, from the dark boards of the ceiling, the face of death was peering down. These joys had been final, and their bodies would never know them again. Not that joy of this intensity—and the same thought had occurred to them both—was ever likely to be reexperienced, even if they should live on to old age.

The feel of their fingers intertwined—this too would soon be lost. Even the wood-grain patterns they now gazed at on the dark ceiling boards would be taken from them. They could feel death edging in, nearer and nearer. There could be no hesitation now. They must have the courage to reach out to death themselves, and to seize it.

"Well, let's make our preparations," said the lieutenant. The note of determination in the words was unmistakable, but at the same time Reiko had never heard her husband's voice so warm and tender.

After they had risen, a variety of tasks awaited them.

The lieutenant, who had never once before helped with the bedding, now cheerfully slid back the door of the closet, lifted the mattress across the room by himself, and stowed it away inside.

Reiko turned off the gas heater and put away the lamp standard. During the lieutenant's absence she had arranged this room carefully, sweeping and dusting it to a fresh cleanness, and now—if one overlooked the rosewood table drawn into one corner—the eight-mat room gave all the appearance of a reception room ready to welcome an important guest.

"We've seen some drinking here, haven't we? With Kanō and Homma and Noguchi . . ."

"Yes, they were great drinkers, all of them."

"We'll be meeting them before long, in the other world. They'll tease us, I imagine, when they find I've brought you with me."

Descending the stairs, the lieutenant turned to look back into this calm clean room, now brightly illuminated by the ceiling lamp. There floated across his mind the faces of the young officers who had drunk there, and laughed, and innocently bragged. He had never dreamed then that he would one day cut open his stomach in this room.

In the two rooms downstairs husband and wife busied themselves smoothly and serenely with their respective preparations. The lieutenant went to the toilet, and then to the bathroom to wash. Meanwhile Reiko folded away her husband's padded robe, placed his uniform tunic, his trousers, and a newly cut bleached loincloth in the bathroom, and set out sheets of paper on the living-room table for the farewell notes. Then she removed the lid from the writing box and began rubbing ink from the ink tablet. She had already decided upon the wording of her own note.

Reiko's fingers pressed hard upon the cold gilt letters of the ink tablet, and the water in the shallow well at once darkened, as if a black cloud had spread across it. She stopped thinking that this repeated action, this pressure from her fingers, this rise and fall of faint sound, was all and solely for death. It was a routine domestic task, a simple paring away of time until death should finally stand before her. But somehow, in the increasingly smooth motion of the tablet rubbing on the stone, and in the scent from the thickening ink, there was unspeakable darkness.

Neat in his uniform, which he now wore next to his skin, the lieutenant emerged from the bathroom. Without a word he seated himself at the table, bolt upright, took a brush in his hand, and stared undecidedly at the paper before him.

Reiko took a white silk kimono with her and entered the bathroom. When she reappeared in the living room, clad in the white kimono and with her face lightly made up, the farewell note lay completed on the table beneath the lamp. The thick black brushstrokes said simply:

"Long Live the Imperial Forces—Army Lieutenant Takeyama Shinji."

While Reiko sat opposite him writing her own note, the lieutenant gazed in silence, intensely serious, at the controlled movement of his wife's pale fingers as they manipulated the brush.

With their respective notes in their hands—the lieutenant's sword strapped to his side, Reiko's small dagger thrust into the sash of her white kimono—the two of them stood before the god shelf and silently prayed. Then they put out all the downstairs lights. As he mounted the stairs the lieutenant turned his head and gazed back at the striking, white-clad figure of his wife, climbing behind him, with lowered eyes, from the darkness beneath.

The farewell notes were laid side by side in the alcove of the upstairs room. They wondered whether they ought not to remove the hanging scroll, but since it had been written by their go-between, Lieutenant General Ozeki, and consisted, moreover, of two Chinese characters signifying "Sincerity," they left it where it was. Even if it were to become stained with splashes of blood, they felt that the lieutenant general would understand.

The lieutenant sitting erect with his back to the alcove, laid his sword on the floor before him.

Reiko set facing him, a mat's width away. With the rest of her so severely white the touch of rouge on her lips seemed remarkably seductive.

Across the dividing mat they gazed intently into each other's eyes. The lieutenant's sword lay before his knees. Seeing it, Reiko recalled their first night and was overwhelmed with sadness. The lieutenant spoke, in a hoarse voice:

"As I have no second to help me I shall cut deep. It may look unpleasant, but please do not panic. Death of any sort is a fearful thing to watch. You must not be discouraged by what you see. Is that all right?"

"Yes."

Reiko nodded deeply.

Looking at the slender white figure of his wife the lieutenant experienced a bizarre excitement. What he was about to perform was an act in his public capacity as a soldier, something he had never previously shown his wife. It called for a resolution equal to the courage to enter battle; it was a death of no less degree and quality than death in the front line. It was his conduct on the battlefield that he was now to display.

Momentarily the thought led the lieutenant to a strange fantasy. A lonely death on the battlefield, a death beneath the eyes of his beautiful wife . . . in the sensation that he was now to die in these two dimensions, realizing an impossible union of them both, there was sweetness beyond words. This must be the very pinnacle of good fortune, he thought. To have every moment of his death observed by those beautiful eyes—it was like being borne to death on a gentle, fragrant breeze. There was some special favor here. He did not understand precisely what it was, but it was a domain unknown to others: a dispensation granted to no one else had been permitted to himself. In the radiant, bridelike figure of his white-robed wife the lieutenant seemed to see a vision of all those things he had loved and for which he was to lay down his life—the Imperial Household, the Nation, the Army Flag. All these, no less than the wife who sat before him, were presences observing him closely with clear and never-faltering eyes.

Reiko too was gazing intently at her husband, so soon to die, and she thought that never in this world had she seen anything so beautiful. The lieutenant always looked well in uniform, but now, as he contemplated death with severe brows and firmly closed lips, he revealed what was perhaps masculine beauty at its most superb.

"It's time to go," the lieutenant said at last.

Reiko bent her body low to the mat in a deep bow. She could not raise her face. She did not wish to spoil her make-up with tears, but the tears could not be held back.

When at length she looked up she saw hazily through the tears that her husband had wound a white bandage around the blade of his now unsheathed sword, leaving five or six inches of naked steel showing at the point.

Resting the sword in its cloth wrapping on the mat before him, the lieutenant rose from his knees, resettled himself cross-legged, and unfastened the hooks of his uniform collar. His eyes no longer saw his wife. Slowly, one by one, he undid the flat brass buttons. The dusky brown chest was revealed, and then the stomach. He unclasped his belt and undid the buttons of his trousers. The pure whiteness of the thickly coiled loincloth showed itself. The lieutenant pushed the cloth down with both hands, further to ease his stomach, and then reached for the white-bandaged blade of his sword. With his left hand he massaged his abdomen, glacing downward as he did so.

To reassure himself on the sharpness of his sword's cutting edge the lieutenant folded back the left trouser flap, exposing a little of his thigh, and lightly drew the blade across the skin. Blood welled up in the wound at once, and several streaks of red trickled downward, glistening in the strong light.

It was the first time Reiko had ever seen her husband's blood, and she felt a violent throbbing in her chest. She looked at her husband's face. The lieutenant was looking at the blood with calm appraisal. For a moment—though thinking at the same time that it was hollow comfort—Reiko experienced a sense of relief.

The lieutenant's eyes fixed his wife with an intense, hawk-like stare. Moving the sword around to his front, he raised himself slightly on his hips and let the upper half of his body lean over the sword point. That he was mustering his whole strength was apparent from the angry tension of the uniform at his shoulders. The lieutenant aimed to strike deep into the left of his stomach. His sharp cry pierced the silence of the room.

Despite the effort he had himself put into the blow, the lieutenant had the impression that someone else had struck the side of his stomach agonizingly with a thick rod of iron. For a second or so his head reeled and he had no idea what had happened. The five or six inches of naked point had vanished completely into his flesh, and the white bandage, gripped in his clenched fist, pressed directly against his stomach.

He returned to consciousness. The blade had certainly pierced the wall of the stomach, he thought. His breathing was difficult, his chest thumped violently, and in some far deep region, which he could hardly believe was a part of himself, a fearful and excruciating pain came welling up as if the ground had split open to disgorge a boiling stream of molten rock. The pain came suddenly nearer, with terrifying speed. The lieutenant bit his lower lip and stifled an instinctive moan.

Was this *seppuku?*—he was thinking. It was a sensation of utter chaos, as if the sky had fallen on his head and the world was reeling drunkenly. His will power and courage, which had seemed so robust before he made the incision, had now dwindled to something like a single hairlike thread of steel, and he was assailed by the uneasy feeling that he must advance along this thread, clinging to it with desperation. His clenched fist had grown moist. Looking down, he saw that both his hand and the cloth were drenched in blood. His loincloth too was dyed a deep red. It struck him as incredible that, amidst this terrible agony, things which could be seen could still be seen, and existing things existed still.

The moment the lieutenant thrust the sword into his left side and she saw the deathly pallor fall across his face, like an abruptly lowered curtain, Reiko had to struggle to prevent herself from rushing to his side. Whatever happened, she must watch. She must be a witness. That was the duty her husband had lain upon her. Opposite her, a mat's space away, she could clearly see her husband biting his lip to stifle the pain. The pain was there, with absolute certainty, before her eyes. And Reiko had no means of rescuing him from it.

The sweat glistened on her husband's forehead. The lieutenant closed his eyes, and then opened them again, as if experimenting. The eyes had lost their luster, and seemed innocent and empty like the eyes of a small animal.

The agony before Reiko's eyes burned as strong as the summer sun, utterly remote from the grief which seemed to be tearing herself apart within. The pain grew steadily in stature, stretching upward. Reiko felt that her husband had already become a man in a separate world, a man whose whole being had been resolved into pain, a prisoner in a cage of pain where no hand could reach out to him. But Reiko felt no pain at all. Her grief was not pain. As she thought about this, Reiko began to feel as if someone had raised a cruel wall of glass high between herself and her husband.

Ever since her marriage her husband's existence had been her own existence, and every breath of his had been a breath drawn by herself. But now, while her husband's existence in pain was a vivid reality, Reiko could find in this grief of hers no certain proof at all of her own existence.

With only his right hand on the sword the lieutenent began to cut sideways across his stomach. But as the blade became entangled with the entrails it was pushed constantly outward by their soft resilience; and the lieutenant realized that it would be necessary, as he cut, to use both hands to keep the point pressed deep into his stomach. He pulled the blade across. It did not cut as easily as he had expected. He directed the strength of his whole body into his right hand and pulled again. There was a cut of three or four inches.

The pain spread slowly outward from the inner depths until the whole stomach reverberated. It was like the wild clanging of a bell. Or like a thousand bells which jangled simultaneously at every breath he breathed and every throb of his pulse, rocking his whole being. The lieutenant could no longer stop himself from moaning. But by now the blade had cut its way through to below the navel, and when he noticed this he felt a sense of satisfaction, and a renewal of courage.

The volume of blood had steadily increased, and now it spurted from the wound as if propelled by the beat of the pulse. The mat before the lieutenant was drenched red with splattered blood, and more blood overflowed onto it from pools which gathered in folds of the lieutenant's khaki toursers. A spot, like a bird, came flying across to Reiko and settled on the lap of her white silk kimono.

By the time the lieutenant had at last drawn the sword across to the right side of his stomach, the blade was already cutting shallow and had revealed its naked tip, slippery with blood and grease. But, suddenly stricken by a fit of vomitıng, the lieutenant cried out hoarsely. The vomiting made the fierce pain fiercer still, and the stomach, which had thus far remained firm and compact, now abruptly heaved, opening wide its wound, and the entrails burst through, as if the wound too were vomiting. Seemingly ignorant of their master's suffering, the entrails gave an impression of robust health and almost disagreeable vitality as they slipped smoothly out and spilled over into the crotch. The lieutenant's head drooped, his shoulders heaved, his eyes opened to narrow slits, and a thin trickle of saliva dribbled from his mouth. The gold markings on his epaulettes caught the light and glinted.

Blood was scattered everywhere. The lieutenant was soaked in it to his knees, and he sat now in a crumpled and listless posture, one hand on the floor. A raw smell filled the room. The lieutenant his head drooping, retched repeatedly, and the movement showed vividly in his shoulders The blade of the sword, now pushed back by the entrails and exposed to its tip, was still in the lieutenant's right hand.

It would be difficult to imagine a more heroic sight than that of the lieutenant at this moment, as he mustered his strength and flung back his head. The movement was performed with sudden violence, and the back of his head struck with a sharp crack against the alcove pillar. Reiko had been sitting until now with her face lowered; gazing in fascination at the tide of blood advancing toward her knees, but the sound took her by surprise and she looked up.

The lieutenant's face was not the face of a living man. The eyes were hollow, the skin parched, the once so lustrous cheeks and lips the color of dried mud. The right hand alone was moving. Laboriously gripping the sword, it hovered shakily in the air like the hand of a marionette and strove to direct the point at the base of the lieutenant's throat. Reiko watched her husband make this last, most heart-rending, futile exertion. Glistening with blood and grease, the point was thrust at the throat again and again. And each time it missed its aim. The strength to guide it was no longer there. The straying point struck the collar and the collar badges. Although its hooks had been unfastened, the stiff military collar had closed together again and was protecting the throat.

Reiko could bear the sight no longer. She tried to go to her husband's help, but she could not stand. She moved through the blood on her knees, and her white skirts grew deep red. Moving to the rear of her husband, she helped no more than by loosening the collar. The quivering balde at last contacted the naked flesh of the throat. At that moment Reiko's impression was that she herself had propelled her husband forward; but that was not the case. It was a movement planned by the lieutenant himself, his last exertion of strength. Abruptly he threw his body at the blade, and the blade pierced his neck, emerging at the nape. There was a tremendous spurt of blood and the lieutenant lay still, cold blue-tinged steel protruding from his neck at the back.

5

Slowly, her socks slippery with blood, Reiko descended the stairway. The upstairs room was now completely still.

Switching on the ground-floor lights, she checked the gas jet and the main gas plug and poured water over the smoldering, half-buried charcoal in the brazier. She stood before the upright mirror in the four-and-a-half-mat room and held up her skirts. The bloodstains made it seem as if a bold, vivid pattern was printed across the lower half of her white kimono. When she sat down before the mirror, she was conscious of the dampness and coldness of her husband's blood in the region of her thighs, and she shivered. Then, for a long while, she lingered over her toilet preparations. She applied the rouge generously to her cheeks, and her lips too she painted heavily. This was no longer make-up to please her husband. It was make-up for the world which she would leave behind, and there was a touch of the magnificent and the spectacular in her brushwork. When she rose, the mat before the mirror was wet with blood. Reiko was not concerned about this.

Returning from the toilet, Reiko stood finally on the cement floor of the porchway. When her husband had bolted the door here last night it had been in preparation for death. For a while she stood immersed in the consideration of a simple problem. Should she now leave the bolt drawn? If she were to lock the door, it could be that the neighbors might not notice their suicide for several days. Reiko did not relish the thought of their two corpses putrifying before discovery. After all, it seemed, it would be best to leave it open. . . . She released the bolt, and also drew open the frosted-glass door a fraction. . . . At once a chill wind blew in. There was no sign of anyone in the midnight streets and stars glittered ice-cold through the trees in the large house opposite.

Leaving the door as it was, Reiko mounted the stairs. She had walked here and there for some time and her socks were no longer slippery. About halfway up, her nostrils were already assailed by a peculiar smell.

The lieutenant was lying on his face in a sea of blood. The point protruding from his neck seemed to have grown even more prominent than before. Reiko walked heedlessly across the blood. Sitting beside the lieutenant's corpse, she stared intently at the face, which lay on one cheek on the mat. The eyes were opened wide, as if the lieutenant's attention had been attracted by something. She raised the head, folding it in her sleeve, wiped the blood from the lips, and bestowed a last kiss.

Then she rose and took from the closet a new white blanket and a waist cord. To prevent any derangement of her skirts, she wrapped the blanket about her waist and bound it there firmly with the cord.

Reiko sat herself on a spot about one foot distant from the lieutenant's body. Drawing the dagger from her sash, she examined its dully gleaming blade intently, and held it to her tongue. The taste of the polished steel was slightly sweet.

Reiko did not linger. When she thought how the pain which had previously opened such a gulf between herself and her dying husband was now to become a part of her own experience, she saw before her only the joy of herself entering a realm her husband had already made his own. In her husband's agonized face there had been something inexplicable which she was seeing for the first time. Now she would solve that riddle. Reiko sensed that at last she too would be able to taste the true bitterness and sweetness of that great moral principle in which her husband believed. What had until now been tasted only faintly through her husband's example she was about to savor directly with her own tongue.

Reiko rested the point of the blade against the base of her throat. She thrust hard. The wound was only shallow. Her head blazed, and her hands shook uncontrollably. She gave the blade a strong pull sideways. A warm substance flooded into her mouth, and everything before her eyes reddened, in a vision of spouting blood. She gathered her strength and plunged the point of the blade deep into her throat.

JORGE LUIS BORGES

The SOUTH

Translated by Anthony Kerrigan

The man who landed in Buenos Aires in 1871 bore the name of Johannes Dahlmann and he was a minister in the Evangelical Church. In 1939, one of his grandchildren, Juan Dahlmann, was secretary of a municipal library on Calle Córdoba, and he considered himself profoundly Argentinian. His maternal grandfather had been that Francisco Flores, of the Second Line-Infantry Division, who had died on the frontier of Buenos Aires, run through with a lance by Indians from Catriel; in the discord inherent between his two lines of descent, Juan Dahlmann (perhaps driven to it by his Germanic blood) chose the line represented by his romantic ancestor, his ancestor of the romantic death. An old sword, a leather frame containing the daguerreotype of a blank-faced man with a beard, the dash and grace of certain music, the familiar strophes of *Martin Fierro*, the passing years, boredom and solitude, all went to foster this voluntary, but never ostentatious nationalism. At the cost of numerous small privations, Dahlmann had managed to save the empty shell of a ranch in the South which had belonged to the Flores family; he continually recalled the image of the balsamic eucalyptus trees and the great rose-colored house which had once been crimson. His duties, perhaps even indolence, kept him in the city. Summer after summer he contented himself with the abstract idea of posession and with the certitude that his ranch was waiting for him on a precise site in the middle of the plain. Late in February, 1939, something happened to him.

Blind to all fault, destiny can be ruthless at one's slightest distraction. Dahlmann had succeeded in acquiring, on that very afternoon, an imperfect copy of Weil's edition of *The Thousand and One Nights.* Avid to examine this find, he did not wait for the elevator but hurried up the stairs. In the obscurity, something brushed by his forehead: a bat, a bird? On the face of the woman who opened the door to him he saw horror engraved, and the hand he wiped across his face came away red wtih blood. The edge of a recently painted door which someone had forgotten to close had caused this wound. Dahlmann was able to fall asleep, but from the moment he awoke at dawn the savor of all things was atrociously poignant. Fever wasted him and the pictures in *The Thousand and One Nights* served to illustrate nightmares. Friends and relatives paid him visits and, with exaggerated smiles, assured him that they thought he looked fine. Dahlmann listened to them with a kind of feeble stupor and he marveled at their not knowing that he was in hell. A week, eight days passed, and they were like eight centuries. One afternoon, the usual doctor appeared, accompanied by a new doctor, and they carried him off to a sanitarium on the Calle Ecuador, for it was necessary to X-ray him. Dahlmann, in the hackney coach which bore them away, thought that he would, at last, be able to sleep in a room different from his own. He felt happy and communicative. When he arrived at his destination, they undressed him, shaved his head, bound him with metal fastenings to a stretcher; they shone bright lights on him until he was blind and dizzy, auscultated him, and a masked man stuck a needle into his arm. He awoke with a feeling of nausea, covered with a bandage, in a cell with something of a well about it; in the days and nights which followed the operation he came to realize that he had merely been, up until then, in a suburb of hell. Ice in his mouth did not leave the least trace of freshness. During these days Dahlmann hated himself in minute detail: he hated his identity, his bodily necessities, his humiliation, the beard which bristled upon his face. He stoically endured the curative measures, which were painful, but when the surgeon told him he had been on the point of death from septicemia, Dahlmann dissolved in tears of self-pity for his fate. Physical wretchedness and the incessant anticipation of horrible nights had not allowed him time to think of anything so abstract as death. On another day, the surgeon told him he was healing and that, very soon, he would be able to go to his ranch for convalescence. Incredibly enough, the promised day arrived.

Reality favors symmetries and slight anachronisms: Dahlmann had arrived at the sanitarium in a hackney coach and now a hackney coach was to take him to the Constitución station. The first fresh tang of autumn, after the summer's oppressiveness, seemed like a symbol in nature of his rescue and release from fever and death. The city, at seven in the morning, had not lost that air of an old house lent it by the night; the streets seemed like long vestibules, the plazas were like patios. Dahlmann recognized the city with joy on the edge of vertigo: a second before his eyes registered the phenomena themselves, he recalled the corners, the billboards, the modest variety of Buenos Aires. In the yellow light of the new day, all things returned to him.

Every Argentine knows that the South begins at the other side of Rivadavia. Dahlmann was in the habit of saying that this was no mere convention, that whoever crosses this street enters a more ancient and sterner world. From inside the carriage he sought out, among the new buildings, the iron grill window, the brass knocker, the arched door, the entrance way, the intimate patio.

At the railroad station he noted that he still had thirty minutes. He quickly recalled that in a café on the Calle Brazil (a few dozen feet from

Yrigoyen's house) there was an enormous cat which allowed itself to be caressed as if it were a disdainful divinity. He entered the café. There was the cat, asleep. He ordered a cup of coffee, slowly stirred the sugar, sipped it (this pleasure had been denied him in the clinic), and thought, as he smoothed the cat's black coat, that this contact was an illusion and that the two beings, man and cat, were as good as separated by a glass, for man lives in time, in succession, while the magical animal lives in the present, in the eternity of the instant.

Along the next to the last platform the train lay waiting. Dahlmann walked through the coaches until he found one almost empty. He arranged his baggage in the network rack. When the train started off, he took down his valise and extracted, after some hesitation, the first volume of *The Thousand and One Nights*. To travel with this book, which was so much a part of the history of his ill-fortune, was a kind of affirmation that his ill-fortune had been annulled; it was a joyous and secret defiance of the frustrated forces of evil.

Along both sides of the train the city dissipated into suburbs; this sight, and then a view of the gardens and villas, delayed the beginning of his reading. The truth was that Dahlmann read very little. The magnetized mountain and the genie who swore to kill his benefactor are—who would deny it?—marvelous, but not so much more than the morning itself and the mere fact of being. The joy of life distracted him from paying attention to Scheherezade and her superfluous miracles. Dahlmann closed his book and allowed himself to live.

Lunch—the bouillon served in shining metal bowls, as in the remote summers of childhood—was one more peaceful and rewarding delight.

Tomorrow I'll wake up at the ranch, he thought, and it was as if he was two men at a time: the man who traveled through the autumn day and across the geography of the fatherland, and the other one, locked up in a sanitarium and subject to methodical servitude. He saw unplastered brick houses, long and angled, timelessly watching the trains go by; he saw horsemen along the dirt roads; he saw gullies and lagoons and ranches; he saw great luminous clouds that resembled marble; and all these things were accidental, casual, like dreams of the plain. He also thought he recognized trees and crop fields; but he would not have been able to name them, for his actual knowledge of the countryside was quite inferior to his nostalgic and literary knowledge.

From time to time he slept, and his dreams were animated by the impetus of the train. The intolerable white sun of high noon had already become the yellow sun which precedes nightfall, and it would not be long before it would turn red. The railroad car was now also different; it was not the same as the one which had quit the station siding at Constitución; the plain and the hours had transfigured it. Outside, the moving shadow of the railroad car stretched toward the horizon. The elemental earth was not perturbed either by settlements or other signs of humanity. The country was vast but at the same time intimate and, in some measure, secret. The limitless country sometimes contained only a solitary bull. The solitude was perfect, perhaps hostile, and it might have occurred to Dahlmann that he was traveling into the past and not merely south. He was distracted from these considerations by the railroad inspector who, on reading his ticket, advised him that the train would not let him off at the regular station but at another: an earlier stop, one scarcely known to Dahlmann. (The man added an explanation which Dahlmann did not attempt to understand, and which he hardly heard, for the mechanism of events did not concern him.)

The train laboriously ground to a halt, practically in the middle of the plain. The station lay on the other side of the tracks; it was not much more than a siding and a shed. There was no means of conveyance to be seen, but the station chief supposed that the traveler might secure a vehicle from a general store and inn to be found some ten or twelve blocks away.

Dahlmann accepted the walk as a small adventure. The sun had already disappeared from view, but a final splendor exalted the vivid and silent plain, before the night erased its color. Less to avoid fatigue than to draw out his enjoyment of these sights, Dahlmann walked slowly, breathing in the odor of clover with sumptuous joy.

The general store at one time had been painted a deep scarlet, but the years had tempered this violent color for its own good. Something in its poor architecture recalled a steel engraving, perhaps one from an old edition of *Paul et Virginie.* A number of horses were hitched up to the paling. Once inside, Dahlmann thought he recognized the shopkeeper. Then he realized that he had been deceived by the man's resemblance to one of the male nurses in the sanitarium. When the shopkeeper heard Dahlmann's request, he said he would have the shay made up. In order to add one more event to that day and to kill time, Dahlmann decided to eat at the general store.

Some country louts, to whom Dahlmann did not at first pay any attention, were eating and drinking at one of the tables. On the floor, and hanging on to the bar, squatted an old man, immobile as an object. His years had reduced and polished him as water does a stone or the generations of men do a sentence. He was dark, dried up, diminutive, and seemed outside time, situated in eternity. Dahlmann noted with satisfaction the kerchief, the thick poncho, the long *chiripá*, and the colt boots, and told himself, as he recalled futile discussions with people from the Northern counties or from the province of Entre Rios, that gauchos like this no longer existed outside the South.

Dahlmann sat down next to the window. The darkness began overcoming the plain, but the odor and sound of the earth penetrated the iron bars of the window. The shop owner brought him sardines, followed by some roast meat. Dahlmann washed the meal down with several glasses of red wine. Idling, he relished the tart savor of the wine, and let his gaze, now grown somewhat drowsy, wander over the shop. A kerosene lamp hung from a beam. There were three customers at the other table: two of them appeared to be farm workers; the third man, whose features hinted at Chinese blood, was drinking with his hat on. Of a sudden, Dahlmann felt something brush lightly against his face. Next to the heavy glass of turbid wine, upon one of the stripes in the table cloth, lay a spit ball of breadcrumb. That was all: but someone had thrown it there.

The men at the other table seemed totally cut off from him. Perplexed, Dahlmann decided that nothing had happend, and he opened the volume of *The*

Thousand and One Nights, by way of suppressing reality. After a few moments another little ball landed on his table, and now the *peones* laughed outright. Dahlmann said to himself that he was not frightened, but he reasoned that it would be a major blunder if he, a convalescent, were to allow himself to be dragged by strangers into some chaotic quarrel. He determined to leave, and had already gotten to his feet when the owner came up and exhorted him in an alarmed voice:

"*Señor* Dahlmann, don't pay any attention to those lads; they're half high."

Dahlmann was not surprised to learn that the other man, now, knew his name. But he felt that these conciliatory words served only to aggravate the situation. Previous to this moment, the *peones'* provocation was directed against an unknown face, against no one in particular, almost against no one at all. Now it was an attack against him, against his name, and his neighbors knew it. Dahlmann pushed the owner aside, confronted the *peones*, and demanded to know what they wanted of him.

The tough with a Chinese look staggered heavily to his feet. Almost in Juan Dahlmann's face he shouted insults, as if he had been a long way off. His game was to exaggerate his drunkness, and this extravagance constituted a ferocious mockery. Between curses and obscenities, he threw a long knife into the air, followed it with his eyes, caught and juggled it, and challenged Dahlmann to a knife fight. The owner objected in a tremulous voice, pointing out that Dahlmann was unarmed. At this point, something unforeseeable occured.

From a corner of the room, the old ecstatic gaucho—in whom Dahlmann saw a summary and cipher of the South (his South)—threw him a naked dagger, which landed at his feet. It was as if the South had resolved that Dahlmann should accept the duel. Dahlmann bent over to pick up the dagger, and felt two things. The first, that this almost instinctive act bound him to fight. The second, that the weapon, in his torpid hand, was no defense at all, but would merely serve to justify his murder. He had once played with a poniard, like all men, but his idea of fencing and knifeplay did not go further than the notion that all strokes whould be directed upwards, with the cutting edge held inwards. *They would not have allowed such things to happen to me in the sanitarium,* he thought.

"Let's get on our way," said the other man.

They went out and if Dahlmann was without hope, he was also without fear. As he crossed the threshold, he felt that to die in a knife fight, under the open sky, and going forward to the attack, would have been a liberation, a joy, and a festive occasion, on the first night in the sanitarium, when they stuck him with the needle. He felt that if he had been able to choose, then, or to dream his death, this would have been the death he would have chosen or dreamt.

Firmly clutching his knife, which he perhaps would not know how to wield, Dahlmann went out into the plain.

ERNEST HEMINGWAY

BIG TWO-HEARTED RIVER

Part I

The train went on up the track out of sight, around one of the hills of burnt timber. Nick sat down on the bundle of canvas and bedding the baggage man had pitched out of the door of the baggage car. There was no town, nothing but the rails and the burned-over country. The thirteen saloons that had lined the one street of Seney had not left a trace. The foundations of the Mansion House hotel stuck up above the ground. The stone was chipped and split by the fire. It was all that was left of the town of Seney. Even the surface had been burned off the ground.

Nick looked at the burned-over stretch of hillside, where he had expected to find the scattered houses of the town and then walked down the railroad track to the bridge over the river. The river was there. It swirled against the long spiles of the bridge. Nick looked down into the clear, brown water, colored from the pebbly bottom, and watched the trout keeping themselves steady in the current with wavering fins. As he watched them they changed their positions by quick angles, only to hold steady in the fast water again. Nick watched them a long time.

He watched them holding themselves with their noses into the current, many trout in deep, fast moving water, slightly distorted as he watched far down through the glassy convex surface of the pool, its surface pushing and swelling smooth against the resistance of the log-driven piles of the bridge. At the bottom of the pool were the big trout. Nick did not see them at first. Then he saw them at the bottom of the pool, big trout looking to hold themselves on the gravel bottom in a varying mist of gravel and sand, raised in spurts by the current.

Nick looked down into the pool from the bridge. It was a hot day. A kingfisher flew up the stream. It was a long time since Nick had looked into a stream and seen trout. They were very satisfactory. As the shadow of the kingfisher moved up the stream, a big trout shot upstream in a long angle, only his shadow marking the angle, then lost his shadow as he came through the surface of the water, caught the sun, and then, as he went back into the stream under the surface, his shadow seemed to float down the stream with the current, unresisting, to his post under the bridge where he tightened facing up into the current.

Nick's heart tightened as the trout moved. He felt all the old feeling.

He turned and looked down the stream. It stretched away, pebbly-bottomed with shallows and big boulders and a deep pool as it curved away around the foot of a bluff.

Nick walked back up the ties to where his pack lay in the cinders beside the railway track. He was happy. He adjusted the pack harness around the bundle, pulling straps tight, slung the pack on his back, got his arms through the shoulder straps and took some of the pull off his shoulders by leaning his forehead against the wide band of the tump-line. Still, it was too heavy. It was much too heavy. He had his leather rod-case in his hand and leaning forward to keep the weight of the pack high on his shoulders he walked along the road that paralleled the railway track, leaving the burned town behind in the heat, and then turned off around a hill with a high, fire-scarred hill on either side onto a road that went back into the country. He walked along the road feeling the ache from the pull of the heavy pack. The road climbed steadily. It was hard work walking up-hill. His muscles ached and the day was hot, but Nick felt happy. He felt he had left everything behind, the need for thinking, the need to write, other needs. It was all back of him.

From the time he had gotten down off the train and the baggage man had thrown his pack out of the open car door things had been different. Seney was burned, the country was burned over and changed, but it did not matter. It could not all be burned. He knew that. He hiked along the road, sweating in the sun, climbing to cross the range of hills that separated the railway from the pine plains.

The road ran on, dipping occasionally, but always climbing. Nick went on up. Finally the road after going parallel to the burnt hillside reached the top. Nick leaned back against a stump and slipped out of the pack harness. Ahead of him, as far as he could see, was the pine plain. The burned country stopped off at the left with the range of hills. On ahead islands of dark pine trees rose out of the plain. Far off to the left was the line of the river. Nick followed it with his eye and caught glints of the water in the sun.

There was nothing but the pine plain ahead of him, until the far blue hills that marked the Lake Superior height of land. He could hardly see them, faint and far away in the heat-light over the plain. If he looked too steadily they were gone. But if he only half-looked they were there, the far off hills of the height of land.

Nick sat down against the charred stump and smoked a cigarette. His pack balanced on the top of the stump, harness holding ready, a hollow molded in it from his back. Nick sat smoking, looking out over the country. He did not need to get his map out. He knew where he was from the position of the river.

As he smoked, his legs stretched out in front of him, he noticed a grasshopper walk along the ground and up onto his woolen sock. The grasshopper was black. As he had walked along the road, climbing, he had started many grasshoppers from the dust. They were all black. They were not the big grasshoppers with yellow and black or red and black wings whirring out from their black wing sheathing as they fly up. These were just ordinary hoppers, but all a sooty black in color. Nick had wondered about them as he walked, without really thinking about them. Now, as he watched the black hopper that was nibbling at the wool of his sock with its fourway lip, he realized that they had all turned black from living in the burned-over land. He realized that the fire must have come the year before, but the grasshoppers were all black now. He wondered how long they would stay that way.

Carefully he reached his hand down and took hold of the hopper by the wings. He turned him up, all his legs walking in the air, and looked at his jointed belly. Yes, it was black too, iridescent where the back and head were dusty.

"Go on, hopper," Nick said, speaking out loud for the first time, "Fly away somewhere "

He tossed the grasshopper up into the air and watched him sail away to a charcoal stump across the road.

Nick stood up. He leaned his back against the weight of his pack where it rested upright on the stump and got his arms through the shoulder straps. He stood with the pack on his back on the brow of the hill looking out across the country, toward the distant river and then struck down the hillside away from the road. Underfoot the ground was good walking. Two hundred yards down the hillside the fire line stopped. Then it was sweet fern, growing ankle high, to walk through, and clumps of jack pines; a long undulating country with frequent rises and descents, sandy underfoot and the country alive again.

Nick kept his direction by the sun. He knew where he wanted to strike the river and he kept on through the pine plain, mounting small rises to see other rises ahead of him and sometimes from the top of a rise a great solid island of pines off to his right or his left. He broke off some sprigs of the heathery sweet fern, and put them under his pack straps. The chafing crushed it and he smelled it as he walked.

He was tired and very hot, walking across the uneven, shadeless pine plain. At any time he knew he could strike the river by turning off to his left. It could not be more than a mile away. But he kept on toward the north to hit the river as far upstream as he could go in one day's walking.

For some time as he walked Nick had been in sight of one of the big islands of pine standing out above the rolling high ground he was crossing. He dipped down and then as he came slowly up to the crest of the ridge he turned and made toward the pine trees.

There was no underbrush in the island of pine trees. The trunks of the trees went straight up or slanted toward each other. The trunks were straight and brown without branches. The branches were high above. Some interlocked to make a solid shadow on the brown forest floor. Around the grove of trees was a bare space. It was brown and soft underfoot as Nick walked on it. This was the over-lapping of the pine needle floor, extending out beyond the width of the high branches. The trees had grown tall and the branches moved high, leaving in the sun this bare space they had once covered with shadow. Sharp at the edge of this extension of the forest floor commenced the sweet fern.

Nick slipped off his pack and lay down in the shade. He lay on his back and looked up into the pine trees. His neck and back and the small of his back rested as he stretched. The earth felt good against his back. He looked up at the sky, through the branches, and then shut his eyes. He opened them and looked up again. There was a wind high up in the branches. He shut his eyes again and went to sleep.

Nick woke stiff and cramped. The sun was nearly down. His pack was heavy and the straps painful as he lifted it on. He leaned over with the pack on and picked up the leather rod-case and started out from the pine trees across the sweet fern swale, toward the river. He knew it could not be more than a mile.

He came down a hillside covered with stumps into a meadow. At the edge of the meadow flowed the river. Nick was glad to get to the river. He walked upstream through the meadow. His trousers were soaked with the dew as he walked. After the hot day, the dew had come quickly and heavily. The river made no sound. It was too fast and smooth. At the edge of the meadow, before he mounted to a piece of high ground to make camp, Nick looked down the river at the trout rising. They were rising to insects come from the swamp on the other side of the stream when the sun went down. The trout jumped out of water to take them. While Nick walked through the little stretch of meadow alongside the stream, trout had jumped high out of water. Now as he looked down the river, the insects must be settling on the surface, for the trout were feeding steadily all down the stream. As far down the long stretch as he could see, the trout were rising, making circles all down the surface of the water, as though it were starting to rain.

The ground rose, wooded and sandy, to overlook the meadow, the stretch of river and the swamp. Nick dropped his pack and rod-case and looked for a level piece of ground. He was very hungry and he wanted to make his camp before he cooked. Between two jack pines, the ground was quite level. He took the ax out of the pack and chopped out two projecting roots. That leveled a piece of ground large enough to sleep on. He smoothed out the sandy soil with his hand and pulled all the sweet fern bushes by their roots. His hands smelled good from the sweet fern. He smoothed the uprooted earth. He did not want anything making lumps under the blankets. When he had the ground smooth, he spread his three blankets. One he folded double, next to the ground. The other two he spread on top.

With the ax he slit off a bright slab of pine from one of the stumps and split it into pegs for the tent. He wanted them long and solid to hold in the ground. With the tent unpacked and spread on the ground, the pack, leaning against a jackpine, looked much smaller. Nick tied the rope that served the tent for a ridge-pole to the trunk of one of the pine trees and pulled the tent up off the ground with the other end of the rope and tied it to the other pine. The tent hung on the rope like a canvas blanket on a clothes line. Nick poked a pole he had cut up under the back peak of the canvas and then made it a tent by pegging out the sides. He pegged the sides out taut and drove the pegs deep, hitting them down into the ground with the flat of the ax until the rope loops were buried and the canvas was drum tight.

Across the open mouth of the tent Nick fixed cheese cloth to keep out mosquitoes. He crawled inside under the mosquito bar with various things from the pack to put at the head of the bed under the slant of the canvas. Inside the tent the light came through the brown canvas. It smelled pleasantly of canvas. Already there was something mysterious and homelike. Nick was happy as he crawled inside the tent. He had not been unhappy all day. This was different though. Now things were done. There had been this to do. Now it was done. It had been a hard trip. He was very tired. That was done. He had made his camp. He was settled. Nothing could touch him. It was a good place to camp. He was there, in the good place. He was in his home where he had made it. Now he was hungry.

He came out, crawling under the cheese cloth. It was quite dark outside. It was lighter in the tent.

Nick went over to the pack and found, with his fingers, a long nail in a paper sack of nails, in the bottom of the pack. He drove it into the pine tree, holding it close and hitting it gently with the flat of the ax. He hung the pack up on the nail. All his supplies were in the pack. They were off the ground and sheltered now.

Nick was hungry. He did not believe he had ever been hungrier. He opened and emptied a can of pork and beans and a can of spaghetti into the frying pan.

"I've got a right to eat this kind of stuff, if I'm willing to carry it," Nick said. His voice sounded strange in the darkening woods. He did not speak again.

He started a fire with some chunks of pine he got with the ax from a stump. Over the fire he stuck a wire grill, pushing the four legs down into the ground with his boot. Nick put the frying pan on the grill over the flames. He was hungrier. The beans and spaghetti warmed. Nick stirred them and mixed them together. They began to bubble, making little bubbles that rose with difficulty to the surface. There was a good smell. Nick got out a bottle of tomato catchup and cut four slices of bread. The little bubbles were coming faster now. Nick sat down beside the fire and lifted the frying pan off. He poured about half the contents out into the tin plate. It spread slowly on the plate. Nick knew it was too hot. He poured on some tomato catchup. He knew the beans and spaghetti were still too hot. He looked at the fire, then at the tent, he was not going to spoil it all by burning his tongue. For years he had never enjoyed fried bananas because he had never been able to wait for them to cool. His tongue was very sensitive. He was very hungry. Across the river in the swamp, in the almost dark, he saw a mist rising. He looked at the tent once more. All right. He took a full spoonful from the plate.

"Chrise," Nick said, "Geezus Chrise," he said happily.

He ate the whole plateful before he remembered the bread. Nick finished the second plateful with the bread, mopping the plate shiny. He had not eaten since a cup of coffee and a ham sandwich in the station restaurant at St. Ignace. It had been a very fine experience. He had been that hungry before, but had not been able to satisfy it. He could have made camp hours before if he had wanted to. There were plenty of good places to camp on the river. But this was good.

Nick tucked two big chips of pine under the grill. The fire flared up. He had forgotten to get water for the coffee. Out of the pack he got a folding canvas bucket and walked down the hill, across the edge of the meadow, to the stream. The other bank was in the white mist. The grass was wet and cold as he knelt on the bank and dipped the canvas bucket into the stream. It bellied and pulled hard in the current. The water was ice cold. Nick rinsed the bucket and carried it full up to the camp. Up away from the stream it was not so cold.

Nick drove another big nail and hung up the bucket full of water. He dipped the coffee pot half full, put some more chips under the grill onto the fire and put the pot on. He could not remember which way he made coffee. He could remember an argument about it with Hopkins, but not which side he had taken. He decided to bring it to a boil. He remembered now that was Hopkins's way. He had once argued about everything with Hopkins. While he waited for the coffee to boil, he opened a small can of apricots. He liked to open cans. He emptied the can of apricots out into a tin cup. While he watched the coffee on the fire, he drank the juice syrup of the apricots, carefully at first to keep from spilling, then meditatively, sucking the apricots down. They were better than fresh apricots.

The coffee boiled as he watched. The lid came up and coffee and grounds ran down the side of the pot. Nick took it off the grill. It was a triumph for Hopkins. He put sugar in the empty apricot cup and poured some of the coffee out to cool. It was too hot to pour and he used his hat to hold the handle of the coffee pot. He would not let it steep in the pot at all. Not the first cup. It should be straight Hopkins all the way. Hop deserved that. He was a very serious coffee maker. He was the most serious man Nick had ever known. Not heavy, serious. That was a long time ago. Hopkins spoke without moving his lips. He had played polo. He made millions of dollars in Texas. He had borrowed carfare to go to Chicago, when the wire came that his first big well had come in. He could have wired for money. That would have been too slow. They called Hop's girl the Blonde Venus. Hop did not mind because she was not his real girl. Hopkins said very confidently that none of them would make fun of his real girl. He was right. Hopkins went away when the telegram came. That was on the Black River. It took eight days for the telegram to reach him. Hopkins gave away his .22 caliber Colt automatic pistol to Nick. He gave his camera to Bill. It was to remember him always by. They were all going fishing again next summer. The Hop Head was rich. He would get a yacht and they would all cruise along the north shore of Lake Superior. He was excited but serious. They said good-bye and all felt bad. It broke up the trip. They never saw Hopkins again. That was a long time ago on the Black River.

Nick drank the coffee, the coffee according to Hopkins. The coffee was bitter. Nick laughed. It made a good ending to the story. His mind was starting to work. He knew he could choke it because he was tired enough. He spilled the coffee out of the pot and shook the grounds loose into the fire. He lit a cigarette and went inside the tent. He took off his shoes and trousers, sitting on the blankets, rolled the shoes up inside the trousers for a pillow and got in between the blankets.

Out through the front of the tent he watched the glow of the fire, when the night wind blew on it. It was a quiet night. The swamp was perfectly quiet. Nick stretched under the blanket comfortably. A mosquito hummed close to his ear. Nick sat up and lit a match. The mosquito was on the canvas, over his head. Nick moved the match quickly up to it. The mosquito made a satisfactory hiss in the flame. The match went out. Nick lay down again under the blankets. He turned on his side and shut his eyes. He was sleepy. He felt sleep coming. He curled up under the blanket and went to sleep.

Part II

In the morning the sun was up and the tent was starting to get hot. Nick crawled out under the mosquito netting stretched across the mouth of the tent, to look at the morning. The grass was wet on his hands as he came out. He held his trousers and his shoes in his hands. The sun was just up over the hill. There was the meadow, the river and the swamp. There were birch trees in the green of the swamp on the other side of the river.

The river was clear and smoothly fast in the early morning. Down about two hundred yards were three logs all the way across the stream. They made the water smooth and deep above them. As Nick watched, a mink crossed the river on the logs and went into the swamp. Nick was excited. He was excited by the early morning and the river. He was really too hurried to eat breakfast, but he knew he must. He built a little fire and put on the coffee pot. While the water was heating in the pot he took an empty bottle and went down over the edge of the high ground to the meadow. The meadow was wet with dew and Nick wanted to catch grasshoppers for bait before the sun dried the grass. He found plenty of good grasshoppers. They were at the base of the grass stems. Sometimes they clung to a grass stem. They were cold and wet with the dew, and could not jump until the sun warmed them. Nick picked them up, taking only the medium sized brown ones, and put them into the bottle. He turned over a log and just under the shelter of the edge were several hundred hoppers. It was a grasshopper lodging house. Nick put about fifty of the medium browns into the bottle. While he was picking up the hoppers the others warmed in the sun and commenced to hop away. They flew when they hopped. At first they made one flight and stayed stiff when they landed, as though they were dead.

Nick knew that by the time he was through with breakfast they would be as lively as ever. Without dew in the grass it would take him all day to catch a bottle full of good grasshoppers and he would have to crush many of them, slamming at them with his hat. He washed his hands at the stream. He was excited to be near it. Then he walked up to the tent. The hoppers were already jumping stiffly in the grass. In the bottle, warmed by the sun, they were jumping in a mass. Nick put in a pine stick as a cork. It plugged the mouth of the bottle enough, so the hoppers could not get out and left plenty of air passage.

He had rolled the log back and knew he could get grasshoppers there every morning.

Nick laid the bottle full of jumping grasshoppers against a pine trunk. Rapidly he mixed some buckwheat flour with water and stirred it smooth, one cup of flour, one cup of water. He put a handful of coffee in the pot and dipped a lump of grease out of a can and slid it sputtering across the hot skillet. On the smoking skillet he poured smoothly the buckwheat batter. It spread like lava, the grease spitting sharply. Around the edges the buckwheat cake began to firm, then brown, then crisp. The surface was bubbling slowly to porousness. Nick pushed under the browned under surface with a fresh pine chip. He shook the skillet sideways and the cake was loose on the surface. I won't try and flop it, he thought. He slid the chip of clean wood all the way under the cake, and flopped it over onto its face. It sputtered in the pan.

When it was cooked Nick regreased the skillet. He used all the batter. It made another big flapjack and one smaller one.

Nick ate a big flapjack and a smaller one, covered with apple butter. He put apple butter on the third cake, folded it over twice, wrapped it in oiled paper and put it in his shirt pocket. He put the apple butter jar back in the pack and cut bread for two sandwiches.

In the pack he found a big onion. He sliced it in two and peeled the silky outer skin. Then he cut one half into slices and made onion sandwiches. He wrapped them in oiled paper and buttoned them in the other pocket of his khaki shirt. He turned the skillet upside down on the grill, drank the coffee, sweetened and yellow brown with the condensed milk in it, and tidied up the camp. It was a nice little camp.

Nick took his fly rod out of the leather rod-case, jointed it, and shoved the rod-case back into the tent. He put on the reel and threaded the line through the guides. He had to hold it from hand to hand, as he threaded it, or it would slip back through its own weight. It was a heavy, double tapered fly line. Nick had paid eight dollars for it a long time ago. It was made heavy to lift back in the air and come forward flat and heavy and straight to make it possible to cast a fly which has no weight. Nick opened the aluminum leader box. The leaders were coiled between the damp flannel pads. Nick had wet the pads at the water cooler on the train up to St. Ignace. In the damp pads the gut leaders had softened and Nick unrolled one and tied it by a loop at the end of the heavy fly line. He fastened a hook on the end of the leader. It was a small hook; very thin and springy.

Nick took it from his hook book, sitting with the rod across his lap. He tested the knot and the spring of the rod by pulling the line taut. It was a good feeling. He was careful not to let the hook bite into his finger.

He started down to the stream, holding his rod, the bottle of grasshoppers hung from his neck by a thong tied in half hitches around the neck of the bottle. His landing net hung by a hook from his belt. Over his shoulder was a long flour sack tied at each corner into an ear. The cord went over his shoulder. The sack flapped against his legs.

Nick felt awkward and professionally happy with all his equipment hanging from him. The grasshopper bottle swung against his chest. In his shirt the breast pockets bulged against him with the lunch and his fly book.

He stepped into the stream. It was a shock. His trousers clung tight to his legs. His shoes felt the gravel. The water was a rising cold shock.

Rushing, the current sucked against his legs. Where he stepped in, the water was over his knees. He waded with the current. The gravel slid under his shoes. He looked down at the swirl of water below each leg and tipped up the bottle to get a grasshopper.

The first grasshopper gave a jump in the neck of the bottle and went out into the water. He was sucked under in the whirl by Nick's right leg and came to the surface a little way down stream. He floated rapidly, kicking. In a quick circle, breaking the smooth surface of the water, he disappeared. A trout had taken him.

Another hopper poked his head out of the bottle. His antennae wavered. He was getting his front legs out of the bottle to jump. Nick took him by the head and held him while he threaded the slim hook under his chin, down through his thorax and into the last segments of his abdomen. The grasshopper took hold of the hook with his front feet, spitting tobacco juice on it. Nick dropped him into the water.

Holding the rod in his right hand he let out line against the pull of the grasshopper in the current. He stripped off line from the reel with his left hand and let it run free. He could see the hopper in the little waves of the current. It went out of sight.

There was a tug on the line. Nick pulled against the taut line. It was his first strike. Holding the now living rod across the current, he brought in the line with his left hand. The rod bent in jerks, the trout pumping against the current. Nick knew it was a small one. He lifted the rod straight up in the air. It bowed with the pull.

He saw the trout in the water jerking with his head and body against the shifting tangent of the line in the stream.

Nick took the line in his left hand and pulled the trout, thumping tiredly against the current, to the surface. His back was mottled the clear, water-over-gravel color, his side flashing in the sun. The rod under his right arm, Nick stooped, dipping his right hand into the current. He held the trout, never still, with his moist right hand while he unhooked the barb from his mouth, then dropped him back into the stream.

He hung unsteadily in the current, then settled to the bottom beside a stone. Nick reached down his hand to touch him, his arm to the elbow under water. The trout was steady in the moving stream, resting on the gravel, beside a stone. As Nick's fingers touched him, touched his smooth, cool, underwater feeling he was gone, gone in a shadow across the bottom of the stream.

He's all right, Nick thought. He was only tired.

He had wet his hand before he touched the trout, so he would not disturb the delicate mucus that covered him. If a trout was touched with a dry hand, a white fungus attacked the unprotected spot. Years before when he had fished crowded streams, with fly fishermen ahead of him and behind him, Nick had again and again come on dead trout, furry with white fungus, drifted against a rock, or floating belly up in some pool. Nick did not like to fish with other men on the river. Unless they were of your party, they spoiled it.

He wallowed down the stream, above his knees in the current, through the fifty yards of shallow water above the pile of logs that crossed the stream. He did not rebait his hook and held it in his hand as he waded. He was certain he could catch small trout in the shallows, but he did not want them. There would be no big trout in the shallows this time of day.

Now the water deepened up his thighs sharply and coldly. Ahead was the smooth dammed-back flood of water above the logs. The water was smooth and dark; on the left, the lower edge of the meadow; on the right the swamp.

Nick leaned back against the current and took a hopper from the bottle. He threaded the hopper on the hook and spat on him for good luck. Then he pulled several yards of line from the reel and tossed the hopper out ahead onto the fast, dark water. It floated down towards the logs then the weight of the line pulled the bait under the surface. Nick held the rod in his right hand, letting the line run out through his fingers.

There was a long tug. Nick struck and the rod came alive and dangerous, bent double, the line tightening, coming out of water, tightening, all in a heavy, dangerous, steady pull. Nick felt the moment when the leader would break if the strain increased and let the line go.

The reel ratcheted into a mechanical shriek as the line went out in a rush. Too fast. Nick could not check it, the line rushing out, the reel note rising as the line ran out.

With the core of the reel showing, his heart feeling stopped with excitement, leaning back against the current that mounted icily his thighs, Nick thumbed the reel hard with his left hand. It was awkward getting his thumb inside the fly reel frame.

As he put on pressure the line tightened into sudden hardness and beyond the logs a huge trout went high out of water. As he jumped, Nick lowered the tip of the rod. But he felt, as he dropped the tip to ease the strain, the moment when the strain was too great; the hardness too tight. Of course, the leader had broken. There was no mistaking the feeling when all spring left the line and it became dry and hard. Then it went slack.

His mouth dry, his heart down, Nick reeled in. He had never seen so big a trout. There was a heaviness, a power not to be held, and then the bulk of him, as he jumped. He looked as broad as a salmon.

Nick's hand was shaky. He reeled in slowly. The thrill had been too much. He felt, vaguely, a little sick, as though it would be better to sit down.

The leader had broken where the hook was tied to it. Nick took it in his hand. He thought of the trout somewhere on the bottom, holding himself steady over the gravel, far down below the light, under the logs, with the hook in his jaw. Nick knew the trout's teeth would cut through the snell of the hook. The hook would imbed itself in his jaw. He'd bet the trout was angry. Anything that size would be angry. That was a trout. He had been solidly hooked. Solid as a rock. He felt like a rock, too, before he started off. By God, he was a big one. By God, he was the biggest one I ever heard of.

Nick climbed out onto the meadow and stood, water running down his toursers and out of his shoes, his shoes squelchy. He went over and sat on the logs. He did not want to rush his sensations any.

He wriggled his toes in the water, in his shoes, and got out a cigarette from his breast pocket. He lit it and tossed the match into the fast water below the logs. A tiny trout rose at the match, as it swung around in the fast current. Nick laughed. He would finish the cigarette.

He sat on the logs, smoking, drying in the sun, the sun warm on his back, the river shallow ahead entering the woods, curving into the woods, shallows, light glittering, big water-smooth rocks, cedars along the bank and white birches, the logs warm in the sun, smooth to sit on, without bark, gray to the touch; slowly the feeling of disappointment left him. It went away slowly, the feeling of disappointment that came sharply after the thrill that made his shoulders ache. It was all right now. His rod lying out on the logs, Nick tied a new hook on the leader, pulling the gut tight until it grimped into itself in a hard knot.

He baited up, then picked up the rod and walked to the far end of the logs to get into the water, where it was not too deep. Under and beyond the logs was a deep pool. Nick walked around the shallow shelf near the swamp shore until he came out on the shallow bed of the stream.

On the left, where the meadow ended and the woods began, a great elm tree was uprooted. Gone over in a storm, it lay back into the woods, its roots clotted with dirt, grass growing in them, rising a solid bank beside the stream. The river cut to the edge of the uprooted tree. From where Nick stood he could see deep channels, like ruts, cut in the shallow bed of the stream by the flow of the current. Pebbly where he stood and pebbly and full of boulders beyond; where it curved near the tree roots, the bed of the stream was marly and between the ruts of deep water green weed fronds swung in the current.

Nick swung the rod back over his shoulder and forward, and the line, curving forward, laid the grasshopper down on one of the deep channels in the weeds. A trout struck and Nick hooked him.

Holding the rod far out toward the uprooted tree and sloshing backward in the current, Nick worked the trout, plunging, the rod bending alive, out of the danger of the weeds into the open river. Holding the rod, pumping alive against the current, Nick brought the trout in. He rushed, but always came, the spring of the rod yielding to the rushes, sometimes jerking under water, but always bringing him in. Nick eased downstream with the rushes. The rod above his head he led the trout over the net, then lifted.

The trout hung heavy in the net, mottled trout back and silver sides in the meshes. Nick unhooked him; heavy sides, good to hold, big undershot jaw, and slipped him, heaving and big sliding, into the long sack that hung from his shoulders in the water.

Nick spread the mouth of the sack against the current and it filled, heavy with water. He held it up, the bottom in the stream, and the water poured out through the sides. Inside at the bottom was the big trout, alive in the water.

Nick moved downstream. The sack out ahead of him, sunk, heavy in the water, pulling from his shoulders.

It was getting hot, the sun hot on the back of his neck.

Nick had one good trout. He did not care about getting many trout. Now the stream was shallow and wide. There were trees along both banks. The trees of the left bank made short shadows on the current in the forenoon sun. Nick knew there were trout in each shadow. In the afternoon, after the sun had crossed toward the hills, the trout would be in the cool shadows on the other side of the stream.

The very biggest ones would lie up close to the bank. You could always pick them up there on the Black. When the sun was down they all moved out into the current. Just when the sun made the water blinding in the glare before it went down, you were liable to strike a big trout anywhere in the current. It was almost impossible to fish then, the surface of the water was blinding as a mirror in the sun. Of course, you could fish upstream, but in a stream like the Black, or this, you had to wallow against the current and in a deep place, the water piled up on you. It was no fun to fish upstream with this much current.

Nick moved along through the shallow stretch watching the banks for deep holes. A beech tree grew close beside the river, so that the branches hung down into the water. The stream went back in under the leaves. There were always trout in a place like that.

Nick did not care about fishing that hole. He was sure he would get hooked in the branches.

It looked deep though. He dropped the grasshopper so the current took it under water, back in under the overhanging branch. The line pulled hard and Nick struck. The trout threshed heavily, half out of water in the leaves and branches. The line was caught. Nick pulled hard and the trout was off. He reeled in and holding the hook in his hand, walked down the stream.

Ahead, close to the left bank, was a big log. Nick saw it was hollow; pointing up river the current entered it smoothly, only a little ripple spread each side of the log. The water was deepening. The top of the hollow log was gray and dry. It was partly in the shadow.

Nick took the cork out of the grasshopper bottle and a hopper clung to it. He picked him off, hooked him and tossed him out. He held the rod far out so that the hopper on the water moved into the current flowing into the hollow log. Nick lowered the rod and the hopper floated in. There was a heavy strike. Nick swung the rod against the pull. It felt as though he were hooked into the log itself, except for the live feeling.

He tried to force the fish out into the current. It came, heavily.

The line went slack and Nick thought the trout was gone. Then he saw him, very near, in the current, shaking his head, trying to get the hook out. His mouth was clamped shut. He was fighting the hook in the clear flowing current.

Looping in the line with his left hand, Nick swung the rod to make the line taut and tried to lead the trout toward the net, but he was gone, out of sight, the line pumping. Nick fought him against the current, letting him thump in the water against the spring of the rod. He shifted the rod to his left hand, worked the trout upstream, holding his weight, fighting on the rod, and then let him down into the net. He lifted him clear of the water, a heavy half circle in the net, the net dripping, unhooked him and slid him into the sack.

He spread the mouth of the sack and looked down in at the two big trout alive in the water.

Through the deepening water, Nick waded over to the hollow log. He took the sack off, over his head, the trout flopping as it came out of water, and hung it so the trout were deep in the water. Then he pulled himself up on the log and sat, the water from his trousers and boots running down into the stream. He laid his rod down, moved along to the shady end of the log and took the sandwiches out of his pocket. He dipped the sandwiches in the cold water. The current carried away the crumbs. He ate the sandwiches and dipped his hat full of water to drink, the water running out through his hat just ahead of his drinking.

It was cool in the shade, sitting on the log. He took a cigarette out and struck a match to light it. The match sunk into the gray wood, making a tiny furrow. Nick leaned over the side of the log, found a hard place and lit the match. He sat smoking and watching the river.

Ahead the river narrowed and went into a swamp. The river became smooth and deep and the swamp looked solid with cedar trees, their trunks close together, their branches solid. It would not be possible to walk through a swamp like that. The branches grew so low. You would have to keep almost level with the ground to move at all. You could not crash through the branches. That must be why the animals that lived in swamps were built the way they were, Nick thought.

He wished he had brought something to read. He felt like reading. He did not feel like going on into the swamp. He looked down the river. A big cedar slanted all the way across the stream. Beyond that the river went into the swamp.

Nick did not want to go in there now. He felt a reaction against deep wading with the water deepening up under his armpits, to hook big trout in places impossible to land them. In the swamp the banks were bare, the big cedars came together overhead, the sun did not come through, except in patches; in the fast deep water, in the half light, the fishing would be tragic. In the swamp fishing was a tragic adventure. Nick did not want it. He did not want to go down the stream any further today.

He took out his knife, opened it and stuck it in the log. Then he pulled up the sack, reached into it and brought out one of the trout. Holding him near the tail, hard to hold, alive, in his hand, he whacked him against the log. The trout quivered, rigid. Nick laid him on the log in the shade and broke the neck of the other fish the same way. He laid them side by side on the log. They were fine trout.

Nick cleaned them, slitting them from the vent to the tip of the jaw. All the insides and the gills and tongue came out in one piece. They were both males; long gray-white strips of milt, smooth and clean. All the insides clean and compact, coming out all together. Nick tossed the offal ashore for the minks to find.

He washed the trout in the stream. When he held them back up in the water they looked like live fish. Their color was not gone yet. He washed his hands and dried them on the log. Then he laid the trout on the sack spread out on the log, rolled them up in it, tied the bundle and put it in the landing net. His knife was still standing, blade stuck in the log. He cleaned it on the wood and put it in his pocket.

Nick stood up on the log, holding his rod, the landing net hanging heavy, then stepped into the water and splashed ashore. He climbed the bank and cut up into the woods, toward the high ground. He was going back to camp. He looked back. The river just showed through the trees. There were plenty of days coming when he could fish the swamp.

D. H. LAWRENCE

The BLIND MAN

Isabel Pervin was listening for two sounds—for the sound of wheels on the drive outside and for the noise of her husband's footsteps in the hall. Her dearest and oldest friend, a man who seemed almost indispensable to her living, would drive up in the rainy dusk of the closing November day. The trap had gone to fetch him from the station. And her husband, who had been blinded in Flanders, and who had a disfiguring mark on his brow, would be coming in from the out-houses.

He had been home for a year now. He was totally blind. Yet they had been very happy. The Grange was Maurice's own place. The back was a farmstead, and the Wernhams, who occupied the rear premises, acted as farmers. Isabel lived with her husband in the handsome rooms in front. She and he had been almost entirely alone together since he was wounded. They talked and sang and read together in a wonderful and unspeakable intimacy. Then she reviewed books for a Scottish newspaper, carrying on her old interest, and he occupied himself a good deal with the farm. Sightless, he could still discuss everything with Wernham, and he could also do a good deal of work about the place—menial work, it is true, but it gave him satisfaction. He milked the cows, carried in the pails, turned the separator, attended to the pigs and horses. Life was still very full and strangely serene for the blind man, peaceful with the almost incomprehensible peace of immediate contact in darkness. With his wife he had a whole world, rich and real and invisible.

They were newly and remotely happy. He did not even regret the loss of his sight in these times of dark, palpable joy. A certain exultance swelled his soul.

But as time wore on, sometimes the rich glamour would leave them. Sometimes, after months of this intensity, a sense of burden overcame Isabel, a weariness, a terrible ennui, in that silent house approached between a colonnade of tall-shafted pines. Then she felt she would go mad, for she could not bear it. And sometimes he had devastating fits of depression, which seemed to lay waste his whole being. It was worse than depression—a black misery, when his own life was a torture to him, and when his presence was unbearable to his wife. The dread went down to the roots of her soul as these black days recurred. In a kind of panic she tried to wrap herself up still further in her husband. She forced the old spontaneous cheerfulness and joy to continue. But the effort it cost her was almost too much. She knew she could not keep it up. She felt she would scream with the strain, and would give anything, anything, to escape. She longed to possess her husband utterly; it gave her inordinate joy to have him entirely to herself. And yet, when again he was gone in a black and massive misery, she could not bear him, she could not bear herself; she wished she could be snatched away off the earth altogether, anything rather than live at this cost.

Dazed, she schemed for a way out. She invited friends, she tried to give him some further connection with the outer world. But it was no good. After all their joy and suffering, after their dark, great year of blindness and solitude and unspeakable nearness, other people seemed to them both shallow, prattling, rather impertinent. Shallow prattle seemed presumptuous. He became impatient and irritated, she was wearied. And so they lapsed into their solitude again. For they preferred it.

But now, in a few weeks' time, her second baby would be born. The first had died, an infant, when her husband first went out to France. She looked with joy and relief to the coming of the second. It would be her salvation. But also she felt some anxiety. She was thirty years old, her husband was a year younger. They both wanted the child very much. Yet she could not help feeling afraid. She had her husband on her hands, a terrible joy to her, and a terrifying burden. The child would occupy her love and attention. And then, what of Maurice? What would he do? If only she could feel that he, too, would be at peace and happy when the child came! She did so want to luxuriate in a rich, physical satisfaction of maternity. But the man, what would he do? How could she provide for him, how avert those shattering black moods of his, which destroyed them both?

She sighed with fear. But at this time Bertie Reid wrote to Isabel. He was her old friend, a second or third cousin, a Scotsman, as she was a Scotswoman. They had been brought up near to one another, and all her life he had been her friend, like a brother, but better than her own brothers. She loved him—though not in the marrying sense. There was a sort of kinship between them, an affinity. They understood one another instinctively. But Isabel would never have thought of marrying Bertie. It would have seemed like marrying in her own family.

Bertie was a barrister and a man of letters, a Scotsman of the intellectual type, quick, ironical, sentimental, and on his knees before the women he adored but did not want to marry. Maurice Pervin was different. He came of a good old country family—the Grange was not a very great distance from Oxford. He was passionate, sensitive, perhaps over-sensitive, wincing—a big fellow with heavy limbs and a forehead that flushed painfully. For his mind was slow, as if drugged by the strong provincial blood that beat in his veins. He was very sensitive to his own mental slowness, his feelings being quick and acute. So that he was just the opposite to Bertie, whose mind was much quicker than his emotions, which were not so very fine.

From the first the two men did not like each other. Isabel felt that they *ought* to get on together. But they did not. She felt that if only each could have the clue to the other there would be such a rare understanding between them. It did not come off, however. Bertie adopted a slightly ironical attitude, very offensive to Maurice, who returned the Scotch irony with English resentment, a resentment which deepened sometimes into stupid hatred.

This was a little puzzling to Isabel. However, she accepted it in the course of things. Men were made freakish and unreasonable. Therefore, when Maurice was going out to France for the second time, she felt that, for her husband's sake, she must discontinue her friendship with Bertie. She wrote to the barrister to this effect. Bertram Reid simply replied that in this, as in all other matters, he must obey her wishes, if these were indeed her wishes.

For nearly two years nothing had passed between the two friends. Isabel rather gloried in the fact; she had no compunction. She had one great article of faith, which was, that husband and wife should be so important to one another, that the rest of the world simply did not count. She and Maurice were husband and wife. They loved one another. They would have children. Then let everybody and everything else fade into insignificance outside this connubial felicity. She professed herself quite happy and ready to receive Maurice's friends. She was happy and ready: the happy wife, the ready woman in possession. Without knowing why, the friends retired abashed, and came no more. Maurice, of course, took as much satisfaction in this connubial absorption as Isabel did.

He shared in Isabel's literary activities, she cultivated a real interest in agriculture and cattle-raising. For she, being at heart perhaps an emotional enthusiast, always cultivated the practical side of life, and prided herself on her mastery of practical affairs. Thus the husband and wife had spent the five years of their married life. The last had been one of blindness and unspeakable intimacy. And now Isabel felt a great indifference coming over her, a sort of lethargy. She wanted to be allowed to bear hier child in peace, to nod by the fire and drift vaguely, physically, from day to day. Maurice was like an ominous thunder-cloud. She had to keep waking up to remember him.

When a little note came from Bertie, asking if he were to put up a tombstone to their dead friendship, and speaking of the real pain he felt on account of her husband's loss of sight, she felt a pang, a fluttering agitation of re-awakening. And she read the letter to Maurice.

"Ask him to come down," he said.

"Ask Bertie to come here!" she re-echoed.

"Yes—if he wants to."

Isabel paused for a few moments.

"I know he wants to—he'd only be too glad," she replied. "But what about you, Maurice? How would you like it?"

"I should like it."

"Well—in that case—— But I thought you didn't care for him——"

"Oh, I don't know. I might think differently of him now," the blind man replied. It was rather abstruse to Isabel.

"Well, dear," she said, "if you're quite sure——"

"I'm sure enough. Let him come," said Maurice.

So Bertie was coming, coming this evening, in the November rain and darkness. Isabel was agitated, racked with her old restlessness and indecision. She had always suffered from this pain of doubt, just an agonising sense of uncertainty. It had begun to pass off, in the lethargy of maternity. Now it returned, and she resented it. She stuggled as usual to maintain her calm, composed, friendly bearing, a sort of mask she wore over all her body.

A woman had lighted a tall lamp beside the table, and spread the cloth. The long dining-room was dim, with its elegant but rather severe pieces of old furniture. Only the round table glowed softly under the light. It had a rich, beautiful effect. The white cloth glistened and dropped its heavy, pointed lace corners almost to the carpet, the china was old and handsome, creamy-yellow, with a blotched pattern of harsh red and deep blue, the cups large and bell-shaped, the teapot gallant. Isabel looked at it with superficial appreciation.

Her nerves were hurting her. She looked automatically again at the high, uncurtained windows. In the last dusk she could just perceive outside a huge fir tree swaying its boughs: it was as if she thought it rather than saw it. The rain came flying on the window panes. Ah, why had she no peace? These two men, why did they tear at her? Why did they not come—why was there this suspense?

She sat in a lassitude that was really suspense and irritation. Maurice, at least, might come in—there was nothing to keep him out. She rose to her feet. Catching sight of her reflection in a mirror, she glanced at herself with a slight smile of recognition, as if she were an old friend to herself. Her face was oval and calm, her nose a little arched. Her neck made a beautiful line down to her shoulder. With hair knotted loosely behind, she had something of a warm, maternal look. Thinking this of herself, she arched her eyebrows and her rather heavy eyelids, with a little flicker of a smile, and for a moment her grey eyes looked amused and wicked, a little sardonic, out of her transfigured Madonna face.

Then, resuming her air of womanly patience—she was really fatally self-determined—she went with a little jerk towards the door. Her eyes were slightly reddened.

She passed down the wide hall, and through a door at the end. Then she was in the farm premises. The scent of dairy, and of farm-kitchen, and of farmyard and of leather almost overcame her: but particularly the scent of dairy. They had been scalding out the pans. The flagged passage in front of her was dark, puddled and wet. Light came out from the open kitchen door. She went forward and stood in the doorway. The farm-people were at tea, seated at a little distance from her, round a long, narrow table, in the centre of which stood a white lamp. Ruddy faces, ruddy hands holding food, red mouths working, heads bent over the tea-cups: men, land-girls, boys: it was tea-time, feeding-time. Some faces caught sight of her. Mrs. Wernham, going round behind the chairs with a large black teapot, halting slightly in her walk, was not aware of her for a moment. Then she turned suddenly.

"Oh, is it Madame!" she exclaimed. "Come in, then, come in! We're at tea." And she dragged forward a chair.

"No, I won't come in," said Isabel. "I'm afraid I interrupt your meal."

"No—no—not likely, Madame, not likely."

"Hasn't Mr. Pervin come in, do you know?"

"I'm sure I couldn't say! Missed him, have you, Madame?"

"No, I only wanted him to come in," laughed Isabel, as if shyly.

"Wanted him, did ye? Get up, boy—get up, now——"

Mrs. Wernham knocked one of the boys on the shoulder. He began to scrape to his feet, chewing largely.

"I believe he's in top stable," said another face from the table.

"Ah! No, don't get up. I'm going myself," said Isabel.

"Don't you go out of a dirty night like this. Let the lad go. Get along wi' ye, boy," said Mrs. Wernham.

"No, no," said Isabel, with a decision that was always obeyed. "Go on with your tea, Tom. I'd like to go across to the stable, Mrs. Wernham."

"Did ever you hear tell!" exclaimed the woman.

"Isn't the trap late?" asked Isabel.

"Why, no," said Mrs. Wernham, peering into the distance at the tall, dim clock. "No, Madame—we can give it another quarter or twenty minutes yet, good—yes, every bit of a quarter."

"Ah! It seems late when darkness falls so early," said Isabel.

"It do, that it do. Bother the days, that they draw in so," answered Mrs. Wernham. "Proper miserable!"

"They are," said Isabel, withdrawing.

She pulled on her over-shoes, wrapped a large tartan shawl around her, put on a man's felt hat, and ventured out along the causeways of the first yard. It was very dark. The wind was roaring in the great elms behind the out-houses. When she came to the second yard the darkness seemed deeper. She was unsure of her footing. She wished she had brought a lantern. Rain blew against her. Half she liked it, half she felt unwilling to battle.

She reached at last the just visible door of the stable. There was no sign of a light anywhere. Opening the upper half, she looked in: Into a simple well of darkness. The smell of horses, ammonia, and of warmth was startling to her, in that full night. She listened with all her ears, but could hear nothing save the night, and the stirring of a horse.

"Maurice!" she called, softly and musically, though she was afraid. "Maurice—are you there?"

Nothing came from the darkness. She knew the rain and wind blew in upon the horses, the hot animal life. Feeling it wrong, she entered the stable, and drew the lower half of the door shut, holding the upper part close. She did not stir, because she was aware of the presence of the dark hindquarters of the horses, though she could not see them, and she was afraid. Something wild stirred in her heart.

She listened intensely. Then she heard a small noise in the distance—far away, it seemed—the chink of a pan, and a man's voice speaking a brief word. It would be Maurice, in the other part of the stable. She stood motionless, waiting for him to come through the partition door. The horses were so terrifyingly near to her, in the invisible.

The loud jarring of the inner door-latch made her start; the door was opened. She could hear and feel her husband entering and invisibly passing among the horses near to her, in darkness as they were, actively intermingled. The rather low sound of his voice as he spoke to the horses came velvety to her nerves. How near he was, and how invisible! The darkness seemed to be in a strange swirl of violent life, just upon her. She turned giddy.

Her presence of mind made her call, quietly and musically:

"Maurice! Maurice—dea-ar!"

"Yes," he answered. "Isabel?"

She saw nothing, and the sound of his voice seemed to touch her.

"Hello!" she answered cheerfully, straining her eyes to see him. He was still busy, attending to the horses near her, but she saw only darkness. It made her almost desperate.

"Won't you come in, dear?" she said.

"Yes, I'm coming. Just half a minute. *Stand over—now!* Trap's not come, has it?"

"Not yet," said Isabel.

His voice was pleasant and ordinary, but it had a slight suggestion of the stable to her. She wished he would come away. While he was so utterly invisible she was afraid of him.

"How's the time" he asked

"Not yet six," she replied. She disliked to answer into the dark. Presently he came very near to her, and she retreated out of doors.

"The weather blows in here," he said, coming steadily forward, feeling for the doors. She shrank away. At last she could dimly see him.

"Bertie won't have much of a drive," he said, as he closed the doors.

"He won't indeed!" said Isabel calmly, watching the dark shape at the door.

"Give me your arm, dear," she said.

She pressed his arm close to her, as she went. But she longed to see him, to look at him. She was nervous. He walked erect, with face rather lifted, but with a curious tentative movement of his powerful, muscular legs. She could feel the clever, careful, strong contact of his feet with the earth, as she balanced against him. For a moment he was a tower of darkness to her, as if he rose out of the earth.

In the house-passage he wavered, and went cautiously, with a curious look of silence about him as he felt for the bench. Then he sat down heavily. He was a man with rather sloping shoulders, but with heavy limbs, powerful legs that seemed to know the earth. His head was small, usually carried high and light. As he bend down to unfasten his gaiters and boots he did not look blind. His hair was brown and crisp, his hands were large, reddish, intelligent, the veins stood out in the wrists; and his thighs and knees seemed massive. When he stood up his face and neck were surcharged with blood, the veins stood out on his temples. She did not look at his blindness.

Isabel was always glad when they had passed through the dividing door into their own regions of repose and beauty. She was a little afraid of him, out there in the animal grossness of the back. His bearing also changed, as he smelt the familiar, indefinable odour that pervaded his wife's surroundings, a delicate, refined scent, very faintly spicy. Perhaps it came from the pot-pourri bowls.

He stood at the foot of the stairs, arrested, listening. She watched him, and her heart sickened. He seemed to be listening to fate.

"He's not here yet," he said. "I'll go up and change."

"Maurice," she said, "you're not wishing he wouldn't come, are you?"

"I couldn't quite say," he answered. "I feel myself rather on the *qui vive*."

"I can see you are." she answered. And she reached up and kissed his cheek. She saw his mouth relax into a slow smile.

"What are you laughing at?" she said roguishly.

"You consoling me," he answered.

"Nay," she answered. "Why should I console you? You know we love each other—you know *how* married we are! What does anything else matter?"

"Nothing at all, my dear."

He felt for her face, and touched it, smiling.

"*You're* all right, aren't you?" he asked, anxiously.

"I'm wonderfully all right, love," she answered. "It's you I am a little troubled about, at times."

"Why me?" he said, touching her cheeks delicately with the tips of his fingers. The touch had an almost hypnotising effect on her.

He went away upstairs. She saw him mount into the darkness, unseeing and unchanging. He did not know that the lamps on the upper corridor were unlighted. He went on into the darkness with unchanging step. She heard him in the bathroom.

Pervin moved about almost unconsciously in his familiar surroundings, dark though everything was. He seemed to know the presence of objects before he touched them. It was a pleasure to him to rock thus through a world of things, carried on the flood in a sort of blood-prescience. He did not think much or trouble much. So long as he kept this sheer immediacy of blood-contact with the substantial world he was happy, he wanted no intervention of visual consciousness. In this state there was a certain rich positivity, bordering sometimes on rapture. Life seemed to move in him like a tide lapping, lapping, and advancing, enveloping all things darkly. It was a pleasure to stretch forth the hand and meet the unseen obejct, clasp it, and possess it in pure contact. He did not try to remember, to visualise. He did not want to. The new way of consciousness substituted itself in him.

The rich suffusion of this state generally kept him happy, reaching its culmination in the consuming passion for his wife. But at times the flow would seem to be checked and thrown back. Then it would beat inside him like a tangled sea, and he was tortured in the shattered chaos of his own blood. He grew to dread this arrest, this throw-back, this chaos inside himself, when he seemed merely at the mercy of his own powerful and conflicting elements. How to get some measure of control or surety, this was the question. And when the question rose maddening in him, he would clench his fists as if he would *compel* the whole universe to submit to him. But it was in vain. He could not even compel himself.

To-night, however, he was still serene, though little tremors of unreasonable exasperation ran through him. He had to handle the razor very carefully, as he shaved, for it was not at one with him, he was afraid of it. His hearing also was too much sharpened. He heard the woman lighting the lamps on the corridor, and attending to the fire in the visitor's room. And then, as he went to his room he heard the trap arrive. Then came Isabel's voice, lifted and calling, like a bell ringing:

"Is it you, Bertie? Have you come?"

And a man's voice answered out of the wind:

"Hello, Isabel! There you are."

"Have you had a miserable drive? I'm so sorry we couldn't send a closed carriage. I can't see you at all, you know."

"I'm coming. No, I liked the drive—it was like Perthshire. Well, how are you? You're looking fit as ever, as far as I can see."

"Oh, yes," said Isabel. "I'm wonderfully well. How are you? Rather thin, I think——"

"Worked to death—everybody's old cry. But I'm all right, Ciss. How's Pervin?—isn't he here?"

"Oh, yes, he's upstairs changing. Yes, he's awfully well. Take off your wet things; I'll send them to be dried."

"And how are you both, in spirits? He doesn't fret?"

"No—no, not at all. No, on the contrary, really. We've been wonderfully happy, incredibly. It's more than I can understand—so wonderful: the nearness, and the peace——"

"Ah! Well, that's awfully good news——"

They moved away. Pervin heard no more. But a childish sense of desolation had come over him, as he heard their brisk voices. He seemed shut out—like a child that is left out. He was aimless and excluded, he did not know what to do with himself. The helpless desolation came over him. He fumbled nervously as he dressed himself, in a state almost of childishness. He disliked the Scotch accent in Bertie's speech, and the slight response it found on Isabel's tongue. He disliked the slight purr of complacency in the Scottish speech. He disliked intensely the glib way in which Isabel spoke of their happiness and nearness. It made him recoil. He was fretful and beside himself like a child, he had almost a childish nostalgia to be included in the life circle. And at the same time he was a man, dark and powerful and infuriated by his own weakness. By some fatal flaw, he could not be by himself, he had to depend on the support of another. And this very dependence enraged him. He hated Bertie Reid, and at the same time he knew the hatred was nonsense, he knew it was the outcome of his own weakness.

He went downstairs. Isabel was alone in the dining-room. She watched him enter, head erect, his feet tentative. He looked so strong-blooded and healthy, and, at the same time, cancelled. Cancelled—that was the word that flew across her mind. Perhaps it was his scars suggested it.

"You heard Bertie come, Maurice?" she said.

"Yes—isn't he here?"

"He's in his room. He looks very thin and worn."

"I suppose he works himself to death."

A woman came in with a tray—and after a few minutes Bertie came down. He was a little dark man, with a very big forehead, thin, wispy hair, and sad, large eyes. His expression was inordinately sad—almost funny. He had odd, short legs.

Isabel watched him hesitate under the door, and glance nervously at her husband. Pervin heard him and turned.

"Here you are, now," said Isabel. "Come, let us eat."

Bertie went across to Maurice.

"How are you, Pervin?" he said, as he advanced.

The blind man stuck his hand out into space, and Bertie took it.

"Very fit. Glad you've come," said Maurice.

Isabel glanced at them, and glanced away, as if she could not bear to see them.

"Come," she said. "Come to table. Aren't you both awfully hungry? I am, tremendously."

"I'm afraid you waited for me," said Bertie, as they sat down.

Maurice had a curious monolithic way of sitting in a chair, erect and distant. Isabel's heart always beat when she caught sight of him thus.

"No," she replied to Bertie. "We're very little later than usual. We're having a sort of high tea, not dinner. Do you mind? It gives us such a nice long evening uninterrupted."

"I like it," said Bertie.

Maurice was feeling, with curious little movements, almost like a cat kneading her bed, for his place, his knife and fork, his napkin. He was getting the whole geography of his cover into his consciouslness. He sat erect and inscrutable, remote-seeming. Bertie watched the static figure of the blind man, the delicate tactile discernment of the large, ruddy hands, and the curious mindless silence of the brow, above the scar. With difficulty he looked away, and without knowing what he did, picked up a little crystal bowl of violets from the table, and held them to his nose.

"They are sweet-scented," he said. "Where do they come from?"

"From the garden—under the windows," said Isabel.

"So late in the year—and so fragrant! Do you remember the violets under Aunt Bell's south wall?"

The two friends looked at each other and exchanged a smile, Isabel's eyes lighting up.

"Don't I?" she replied. "*Wasn't* she queer!"

"A curious old girl," laughed Bertie. "There's a streak of freakishness in the family, Isabel."

"Ah—but not in you and me, Bertie," said Isabel. "Give them to Maurice, will you?" she added, as Bertie was putting down the flowers. "Have you smelled the violets, dear? Do!—they are so scented."

Maurice held out his hand, and Bertie placed the tiny bowl against his large, warm-looking fingers. Maurice's hand closed over the thin white fingers of the barrister. Bertie carefully extricated himself. Then the two watched the blind man smelling the violets. He bent his head and seemed to be thinking. Isabel waited.

"Aren't they sweet, Maurice?" she said at last, anxiously.

"Very," he said. And he held out the bowl. Bertie took it. Both he and Isabel were a little afraid, and deeply disturbed.

The meal continued. Isabel and Bertie chatted spasmodically. The blind man was silent. He touched his food repeatedly, with quick, delicate touches of his knife-point, then cut irregular bits. He could not bear to be helped. Both Isabel and Bertie suffered: Isabel wondered why. She did not suffer when she was alone with Maurice. Bertie made her conscious of a strangeness.

After the meal the three drew their chairs to the fire, and sat down to talk. The decanters were put on a table near at hand. Isabel knocked the logs on the fire, and clouds of brilliant sparks went up the chimney. Bertie noticed a slight weariness in her bearing.

"You will be glad when your child comes now, Isabel?" he said.

She looked up to him with a quick wan smile.

"Yes, I shall be glad," she answered. "It begins to seem long. Yes, I shall be very glad. So will you, Maurice, won't you?" she added.

"Yes, I shall," replied her husband.

"We are both looking forward so much to having it," she said.

"Yes, of course," said Bertie.

He was a bachelor, three or four years older than Isabel. He lived in beautiful rooms overlooking the river, guarded by a faithful Scottish manservant. And he had his friends among the fair sex—not lovers, friends. So long as he could avoid any danger of courtship or marriage, he adored a few good women with constant and unfailing homage, and he was chivalrously fond of quite a number. But if they seemed to encroach on him, he withdrew and detested them.

Isabel knew him very well, knew his beautiful constancy, and kindness, also his incurable weakness, which made him unable ever to enter into close contact of any sort. He was ashamed of himself, because he could not marry, could not approach women physically. He wanted to do so. But he could not. At the centre of him he was afraid, helplessly and even brutally afraid. He had given up hope, had ceased to expect any more that he could escape his own weakness. Hence he was a brilliant and successful barrister, also *littérateur* of high repute, a rich man, and a great social success. At the centre he felt himself neuter, nothing.

Isabel knew him well. She despised him even while she admired him. She looked at his sad face, his little short legs, and felt contempt of him. She looked at his dark grey eyes, with their uncanny, almost child-like intuition, and she loved him. He understood amazingly—but she had no fear of his understanding. As a man she patronised him.

And she turned to the impassive, silent figure of her husband. He sat leaning back, with folded arms, and face a little uptilted. His knees were straight and massive. She sighed, picked up the poker, and again began to prod the fire, to rouse the clouds of soft, brilliant sparks.

"Isabel tells me," Bertie began suddenly, "that you have not suffered unbearably from the loss of sight."

Maurice straightened himself to attend, but kept his arms folded.

"No," he said, "not unbearably. Now and again one struggles against it, you know. But there are compensations."

"They say it is much worse to be stone deaf," said Isabel.

"I believe it is," said Bertie. "Are there compensations?" he added, to Maurice.

"Yes. You cease to bother about a great many things." Again Maurice stretched his figure, stretched the strong muscles of his back, and leaned backwards, with uplifted face.

"And that is a relief," said Bertie. "But what is there in place of the bothering? What replaces the activity?"

There was a pause. At length the blind man replied, as out of a negligent, unattentive thinking:

"Oh, I don't know. There's a good deal when you're not active."

"Is there?" said Bertie. "What, exactly? It always seems to me that when there is no thought and no action, there is nothing."

Again Maurice was slow in replying

"There is something," he replied. "I couldn't tell you what it is."

And the talk lapsed once more, Isabel and Bertie chatting gossip and reminiscence, the blind man silent.

At length Maurice rose restlessly, a big, obtrusive figure. He felt tight and hampered. He wanted to go away.

"Do you mind," he said, "if I go and speak to Wernham?"

"No—go along, dear," said Isabel.

And he went out. A silence came over the two friends. At length Bertie said:

"Nevertheless, it is a great deprivation, Cissie."

"It is, Bertie. I know it is."

"Something lacking all the time," said Bertie.

"Yes, I know. And yet—and yet—Maurice is right. There is something else, something *there*, which you never knew was there, and which you can't express."

"What is there?" asked Bertie.

"I don't know—it's awfully hard to define it—but something strong and immediate. There's something strange in Maurice's presence—indefinable—but I couldn't do without it. I agree that it seems to put one's mind to sleep. But when we're alone I miss nothing; it seems awfully rich, almost splendid, you know."

"I'm afraid I don't follow," said Bertie.

They talked desultorily. The wind blew loudly outside, rain chattered on the window-panes, making a sharp drum-sound, because of the closed, mellow-golden shutters inside. The logs burned slowly, with hot, almost invisible small flames. Bertie seemed uneasy, there were dark circles round his eyes. Isabel, rich with her approaching maternity, leaned looking into the fire. Her hair curled in odd, loose strands, very pleasing to the man. But she had a curious feeling of old woe in her heart, old, timeless night-woe.

"I suppose we're all deficient somewhere," said Bertie.

"I suppose so," said Isabel wearily.

"Damned, sooner or later."

"I don't know," she said, rousing herself. "I feel quite all right, you know. The child coming seems to make me indifferent to everything, just placid. I can't feel that there's anything to trouble about, you know."

"A good thing, I should say," he replied slowly.

"Well, there it is. I suppose it's just Nature. If only I felt I needn't trouble about Maurice, I should be perfectly content——"

"But you feel you must trouble about him?"

"Well—I don't know——" She even resented this much effort.

The evening passed slowly. Isabel looked at the clock. "I say," she said. "It's nearly ten o'clock. Where can Maurice be? I'm sure they're all in bed at the back. Excuse me a moment."

She went out, returning almost immediately.

"It's all shut up and in darkness," she said. "I wonder where he is. He must have gone out to the farm——"

Bertie looked at her.

"I suppose he'll come in," he said.

"I suppose so," she said. "But it's unusual for him to be out now."

"Would you like me to go out and see?"

"Well—if you wouldn't mind. I'd go, but——" She did not want to make the physical effort.

Bertie put on an old overcoat and took a lantern. He went out from the side door. He shrank from the wet and roaring night. Such weather had a nervous effect on him: too much moisture everywhere made him feel almost imbecile. Unwilling, he went through it all. A dog barked violently at him. He peered in all the buildings. At last, as he opened the upper door of a sort of intermediate barn, he heard a grinding noise, and looking in, holding up his lantern, saw Maurice, in his shirt-sleeves, standing listening, holding the handle of a turnip-pulper. He had been pulping sweet roots, a pile of which lay dimly heaped in a corner behind him.

"That you, Wernham?" said Maurice, listening.

"No, it's me," said Bertie.

A large, half-wild grey cat was rubbing at Maurice's leg. The blind man stooped to rub its sides. Bertie watched the scene, then unconsciously entered and shut the door behind him. He was in a high sort of barn-place, from which, right and left, ran off the corridors in front of the stalled cattle. He watched the slow, stooping motion of the other man, as he caressed the great cat.

Maurice straightened himself.

"You came to look for me?" he said.

"Isabel was a little uneasy," said Bertie.

"I'll come in. I like messing about doing these jobs."

The cat had reared her sinister, feline length against his leg, clawing at his thigh affectionately. He lifted her claws out of his flesh.

"I hope I'm not in your way at all at the Grange here," said Bertie, rather shy and stiff.

"My way? No, not a bit. I'm glad Isabel has somebody to talk to. I'm afraid it's I who am in the way. I know I'm not very lively company. Isabel's all right, don't you think? She's not unhappy, is she?"

"I don't think so."

"What does she say?"

"She says she's very content—only a little troubled about you."

"Why me?"

"Perhaps afraid that you might brood," said Bertie cautiously.

"She needn't be afraid of that." He continued to caress the flattened grey head of the cat with his fingers. "What I am a bit afraid of," he resumed, "is that she'll find me a dead weight, always alone with me down here."

"I don't think you need think that," said Bertie, though this was what he feared himself.

"I don't know," said Maurice. "Sometimes I feel it isn't fair that she's saddled with me." Then he dropped his voice curiously. "I say," he asked, secretly struggling, "is my face much disfigured? Do you mind telling me?"

"There is the scar," said Bertie, wondering. "Yes, it is a disfigurement. But more pitiable than shocking."

"A pretty bad scar, though," said Maurice.

"Oh yes."

There was a pause.

"Sometimes I feel I am horrible," said Maurice, in a low voice, talking as if to himself. And Bertie actually felt a quiver of horror.

"That's nonsense," he said.

Maurice again straightened himself, leaving the cat.

"There's no telling," he said. Then again, in an odd tone, he added: "I don't really know you, do I?"

"Probably not," said Bertie.

"Do you mind if I touch you?"

The lawyer shrank away instinctively. And yet, out of very philanthropy, he said, in a small voice: "Not at all."

But he suffered as the blind man stretched out a strong, naked hand to him. Maurice accidentally knocked off Bertie's hat.

"I thought you were taller," he said, starting. Then he laid his hand on Bertie Reid's head, closing the dome of the skull in a soft, firm grasp, gathering it, as it were; then, shifting his grasp and softly closing again, with a fine, close pressure, till he had covered the skull and the face of the smaller man, tracing the brows, and touching the full, closed eyes, touching the small nose and the nostrils, the rough, short moustache, the mouth, the rather strong chin. The hand of the blind man grasped the shoulder, the arm, the hand of the other man. He seemed to take him, in the soft, travelling grasp.

"You seem young," he said quietly, at last.

The lawyer stood almost annihilated, unable to answer

"Your head seems tender, as if you were young," Maurice repeated. "So do your hands. Touch my eyes, will you?—touch my scar."

Now Bertie quivered with revulsion. Yet he was under the power of the blind man, as if hypnotised. He lifted his hand, and laid the fingers on the scar, on the scarred eyes. Maurice suddenly covered them with his own hand, pressed the fingers of the other man upon his disfigured eye-sockets, trembling in every fibre, and rocking slightly, slowly, from side to side. He remained thus for a minute or more, whilst Bertie stood as if in a swoon, unconscious, imprisoned.

Then suddenly Maurice removed the hand of the other man from his brow, and stood holding it in his own.

"Oh, my God," he said, "we shall know each other now, shan't we? We shall know each other now."

Bertie could not answer. He gazed mute and terror-struck, overcome by his own weakness. He knew he could not answer. He had an unreasonable fear, lest the other man should suddenly destroy him. Whereas Maurice was actually filled with hot, poignant love, the passion of friendship. Perhaps it was this very passion of friendship which Bertie shrank from most.

"We're all right together now, aren't we?" said Maurice. "It's all right now, as long as we live, so far as we're concerned."

"Yes," said Bertie, trying by any means to escape.

Maurice stood with head lifted, as if listening. The new delicate fulfilment of mortal friendship had come as a revelation and surprise to him, something exquisite and unhoped-for. He seemed to be listening to hear if it were real.

Then he turned for his coat.

"Come," he said, "we'll go to Isabel."

Bertie took the lantern and opened the door. The cat disappeared. The two men went in silence along the causeways. Isabel, as they came, thought their footsteps sounded strange. She looked up pathetically and anxiously for their entrance. There seemed a curious elation about Maurice. Bertie was haggard, with sunken eyes.

"What is it?" she asked.

"We've become friends," said Maurice, standing with his feet apart, like a strange colossus.

"Friends!" re-echoed Isabel. And she looked again at Bertie. He met her eyes with a furtive, haggard look; his eyes were as if glazed with misery.

"I'm so glad," she said, in sheer perplexity.

"Yes," said Maurice.

He was indeed so glad. Isabel took his hand with both hers, and held it fast.

"You'll be happier now, dear," she said.

But she was watching Bertie. She knew that he had one desire—to escape from this intimacy, this friendship, which had been thrust upon him. He could not bear it that he had been touched by the blind man, his insane reserve broken in. He was like a mollusc whose shell is broken.

FRANK O'CONNOR

GUESTS of the NATION

At dusk the big Englishman, Belcher, would shift his long legs out of the ashes and say "Well, chums, what about it?" and Noble or me would say "All right, chum" (for we had picked up some of their curious expressions), and the little Englishman, Hawkins, would light the lamp and bring out the cards. Sometimes Jeremiah Donovan would come up and supervise the game and get excited over Hawkins's cards, which he always played badly, and shout at him as if he was one of our own "Ah, you divil, you, why didn't you play the tray?"

But ordinarily Jeremiah was a sober and contented poor devil like the big Englishman, Belcher, and was looked up to only because he was a fair hand at documents, though he was slow enough even with them. He wore a small cloth hat and big gaiters over his long pants, and you seldom saw him with his hands out of his pockets. He reddened when you talked to him, tilting from toe to heel and back, and looking down all the time at his big farmer's feet. Noble and me used to make fun of his broad accent, becuase we were from the town.

I couldn't at the time see the point of me and Noble guarding Belcher and Hawkins at all, for it was my belief that you could have planted that pair down anywhere from this to Claregalway and they'd have taken root there like a native weed. I never in my short experience seen two men to take to the country as they did.

They were handed on to us by the Second Battalion when the search for them became too hot, and Nobel and myself, being young, took over with a natural feeling of responsibility, but Hawkins made us look like fools when he showed that he knew the country better than we did.

"You're the bloke they calls Bonaparte," he says to me. "Mary Brigid O'Connell told me to ask you what you done with the pair of her brother's socks you borrowed."

For it seemed, as they explained it, that the Second used to have little evenings, and some of the girls of the neighbourhood turned in, and, seeing they were such decent chaps, our fellows couldn't leave the two Englishmen out of them. Hawkins learned to dance "The Walls of Limerick," "The Siege of Ennis," and "The Waves of Tory" as well as any of them, though, naturally, he couldn't return the compliment, because our lads at that time did not dance foreign dances on principle.

So whatever privileges Belcher and Hawkins had with the Second they just naturally took with us, and after the first day or two we gave up all pretence of keeping a close eye on them. Not that they could have got far, for they had accents you could cut with a knife and wore khaki tunics and overcoats with civilian pants and boots. But it's my belief that they never had any idea of escaping and were quite content to be where they were.

It was a treat to see how Belcher got off with the old woman of the house where we were staying. She was a great warrant to scold, and cranky even with us, but before ever she had a chance of giving our guests, as I may call them, a lick of her tongue, Belcher had made her his friend for life. She was breaking sticks, and Belcher, who hadn't been more than ten minutes in the house, jumped up from his seat and went over to her.

"Allow me, madam," he says, smiling his queer little smile, "please allow me"; and he takes the bloody hatchet. She was struck too paralytic to speak, and after that, Belcher would be at her heels, carrying a bucket, a basket, or a load of turf, as the case might be. As Noble said, he got into looking before she leapt, and hot water, or any little thing she wanted, Belcher would have it ready for her. For such a huge man (and though I am five foot ten myself I had to look up to him) he had an uncommon shortness—or should I say lack?—of speech. It took us some time to get used to him, walking in and out, like a ghost, without a word. Especially because Hawkins talked enough for a platoon, it was strange to hear big Belcher with his toes in the ashes come out with a solitary "Excuse me, chum," or "That's right, chum." His one and only passion was cards, and I will say for him that he was a good card-player. He could have fleeced myself and Noble, but whatever we lost to him Hawkins lost to us, and Hawkins played wtih the money Belcher gave him.

Hawkins lost to us because he had too much old gab, and we probably lost to Belcher for the same reason. Hawkins and Noble would spit at one another about religion into the early hours of the morning, and Hawkins worried the soul out of Noble, whose brother was a priest, with a string of questions that would puzzle a cardinal. To make it worse, even in treating of holy subjects, Hawkins had a deplorable tongue. I never in all my career met a man who could mix such a variety of cursing and bad language into an argument. He was a terrible man, and a fright to argue. He never did a stroke of work, and when he had no one else to talk to, he got stuck in the old woman.

He met his match in her, for one day when he tried to get her to complain profanely of the drought, she gave him a great come-down by blaming it entirely on Jupiter Pluvius (a deity neither Hawkins nor I had ever heard of, though

Noble said that among the pagans it was believed that he had something to do with rain). Another day he was swearing at the capitalists for starting the German war when the old lady laid down her iron, puckered up her little crab's mouth, and said: "Mr. Hawkins, you can say what you like about the war, and think you'll deceive me because I'm only a simple poor countrywoman, but I know what started the war. It was the Italian Count that stole the heathen divinity out of the temple in Japan. Believe me, Mr. Hawkins, nothing but sorrow and want can follow the people that disturb the hidden powers."

A queer old girl, all right.

2

We had our tea one evening, and Hawkins lit the lamp and we all sat into cards. Jeremiah Donovan came in too, and sat down and watched us for a while, and it suddenly struck me that he had no great love for the two Englishmen. It came as a great surprise to me, because I hadn't noticed anything about him before.

Late in the evening a really terrible argument blew up between Hawkins and Noble, about capitalists and priests and love of your country.

"The capitalists," says Hawkins with an angry gulp, "pays the priests to tell you about the next world so as you won't notice what the bastards are up to in this."

"Nonsense, man!" says Noble, losing his temper. "Before ever a capitalist was thought of, people believed in the next world."

Hawkins stood up as though he was preaching a sermon.

"Oh, they did, did they?" he says with a sneer. "They believed all the things you believe, isn't that what you mean? And you believe that God created Adam, and Adam created Shem, and Shem created Jehoshophat. You believe all that silly old fairytale about Eve and Eden and the apple. Well, listen to me, chum. If you're entitled to hold a silly belief like that, I'm entitled to hold my silly belief—which is that the first thing your God created was a bleeding capitalist, with morality and Rolls-Royce complete. Am I right, chum?" he says to Belcher.

"You're right, chum," says Belcher with his amused smile, and got up from the table to stretch his long legs into the fire and stroke his moustache. So, seeing that Jeremiah Donovan was going, and that there was no knowing when the argument about religion would be over, I went out with him. We strolled down to the village together, and then he stopped and started blushing and mumbling and saying I ought to be behind, keeping guard on the prisoners. I didn't like the tone he took with me, and anyway I was bored with life in the cottage, so I replied by asking him what the hell we wanted guarding them at all for. I told him I'd talked it over with Noble, and that we'd both rather be out with a fighting column.

"What use are those fellows to us?" says I.

He looked at me in surprise and said: "I thought you knew we were keeping them as hostages."

"Hostages?" I said.

"The enemy have prisoners belonging to us," he says, "and now they're talking of shooting them. If they shoot our prisoners, we'll shoot theirs."

"Shoot them?" I said.

"What else did you think we were keeping them for?" he says.

"Wasn't it very unforeseen of you not to warn Noble and myself of that in the beginning?" I said.

"How was it?" says he. "You might have known it."

"We couldn't know it, Jeremiah Donovan," says I. "How could we when they were on our hands so long?"

"The enemy have our prisoners as long and longer," says he.

"That's not the same thing at all," says I.

"What difference is there?" says he.

I couldn't tell him, because I knew he wouldn't understand. If it was only an old dog that was going to the vet's, you'd try and not get too fond of him, but Jeremiah Donovan wasn't a man that would ever be in danger of that.

"And when is this thing going to be decided?" says I.

"We might hear tonight," he says. "Or tomorrow or the next day at latest. So if it's only hanging round here that's a trouble to you, you'll be free soon enough."

It wasn't the hanging round that was a trouble to me at all by this time. I had worse things to worry about. When I got back to the cottage the argument was still on. Hawkins was holding forth in his best style, maintaining that there was no next world, and Noble was maintaining that there was; but I could see that Hawkins had had the best of it.

"Do you know what, chum?" he was saying with a saucy smile. "I think you're just as big a bleeding unbeliever as I am. You say you believe in the next world, and you know just as much about the next world as I do, which is sweet damn-all. What's heaven? You don't know. Where's heaven? You don't know. You know sweet damn-all! I ask you again, do they wear wings?"

"Very well, then," says Noble, "they do. Is that enough for you? They do wear wings."

"Where do they get them, then? Who makes them? Have they a factory for wings? Have they a sort of store where you hands in your chit and takes your bleeding wings?"

"You're an impossible man to argue with," says Noble. "Now, listen to me—" And they were off again.

It was long after midnight when we locked up and went to bed. As I blew out the candle I told Noble what Jeremiah Donovan was after telling me. Noble took it very quietly. When we'd been in bed about an hour he asked me did I think we ought to tell the Englishmen. I didn't think we should, because it was more than likely that the English wouldn't shoot our men, and even if they did, the brigade officers, who were always up and down the Second Battalion and knew the Englishmen well, wouldn't be likely to want them plugged. "I think so too," says Noble. "It would be great cruelty to put the wind up them now."

"It was very unforeseen of Jeremiah Donovan anyhow," says I.

It was next morning that we found it so hard to face Belcher and Hawkins. We went about the house all day scarcely saying a word. Belcher didn't seem to notice; he was stretched into the ashes as usual, with his usual look of waiting in quietness for something unforeseen to happen, but Hawkins noticed and put it down to Noble's being beaten in the argument of the night before.

"Why can't you take a discussion in the proper spirit?" he says severely. "You and your Adam and Eve! I'm a Communist, that's what I am. Communist or anarchist, it all comes to much the same thing." And for hours he went round the house, muttering when the fit took him. "Adam and Eve! Adam and Eve! Nothing better to do with their time than picking bleeding apples!"

3

I don't know how we got through that day, but I was very glad when it was over, the tea things were cleared away, and Belcher said in his peaceable way: "Well, chums, what about it?" We sat round the table and Hawkins took out the cards, and just then I heard Jeremiah Donovan's footstep on the path and a dark presentiment crossed my mind. I rose from the table and caught him before he reached the door.

"What do you want?" I asked.

"I want those two soldier friends of yours," he says, getting red.

"Is that the way, Jeremiah Donovan?" I asked.

"That's the way. There were four of our lads shot this morning, one of them a boy of sixteen."

"That's bad," I said.

At that moment Noble followed me out, and the three of us walked down the path together, talking in whispers. Feeney, the local intelligence officer, was standing by the gate.

"What are you going to do about it?" I asked Jeremiah Donovan.

"I want you and Noble to get them out; tell them they're being shifted again; that'll be the quietest way."

"Leave me out of that," says Noble under his breath.

Jeremiah Donovan looks at him hard.

"All right," he says. "You and Feeney get a few tools from the shed and dig a hole by the far end of the bog. Bonaparte and myself will be after you. Don't let anyone see you with the tools. I wouldn't like it to go beyond ourselves."

We saw Feeney and Noble go round to the shed and went in ourselves. I left Jeremiah Donovan to do the explanations. He told them that he had orders to send them back to the Second Battalion. Hawkins let out a mouthful of curses, and you could see that though Belcher didn't say anything, he was a bit upset too. The old woman was for having them stay in spite of us, and she didn't stop advising them until Jeremiah Donovan lost his temper and turned on her. He had a nasty temper, I noticed. It was pitch-dark in the cottage by this time, but no one thought of lighting the lamp, and in the darkness the two Englishmen fetched their topcoats and said good-bye to the old woman.

"Just as a man makes a home of a bleeding place, some bastard at headquarters thinks you're too cushy and shunts you off," says Hawkins, shaking her hand.

"A thousand thanks, madam," says Belcher. "A thousand thanks for everything"—as though he'd made it up.

We went round to the back of the house and down towards the bog. It was only then that Jeremiah Donovan told them. He was shaking with excitement.

"There were four of our fellows shot in Cork this morning and now you're to be shot as a reprisal."

"What are you talking about?" snaps Hawkins. "It's bad enough being mucked about as we are without having to put up with your funny jokes."

"It isn't a joke," says Donovan. "I'm sorry Hawkins, but it's true," and begins on the usual rigmarole about duty and how unpleasant it is.

I never noticed that people who talk a lot about duty find it much of a trouble to them.

"Oh, cut it out!" says Hawkins.

"Ask Bonaparte," says Donovan, seeing that Hawkins isn't taking him seriously. "Isn't it true, Bonaparte?"

"It is," I say, and Hawkins stops.

"Ah, for Christ's sake, chum!"

"I mean it, chum," I say.

"You don't sound as if you meant it."

"If he doesn't mean it, I do," says Donovan, working himself up.

"What have you against me, Jeremiah Donovan?"

"I never said I had anything against you. But why did your people take out four of our prisoners and shoot them in cold blood?"

He took Hawkins by the arm and dragged him on, but it was impossible to make him understand that we were in earnest. I had the Smith and Wesson in my pocket and I kept fingering it and wondering what I'd do if they put up a fight for it or ran, and wishing to God they'd do one or the other. I knew if they did run for it, that I'd never fire on them. Hawkins wanted to know was Noble in it, and when we said yes, he asked us why Noble wanted to plug him. Why did any of us want to plug him? What had he done to us? Weren't we all chums? Didn't we understand him and didn't he understand us? Did we imagine for an instant that he'd shoot us for all the so-and-so officers in the so-and-so British Army?

By this time we'd reached the bog, and I was so sick I couldn't even answer him. We walked along the edge of it in the darkness, and every now and then Hawkins would call a halt and begin all over again, as if he was wound up, about our being chums, and I knew that nothing but the sight of the grave would convince him that we had to do it. And all the time I was hoping that something would happen; that they'd run for it or that Noble would take over the responsibility from me. I had the feeling that it was worse on Noble than on me.

4

At last we saw the lantern in the distance and made towards it. Noble was carrying it, and Feeney was standing somewhere in the darkness behind him, and the picture of them so still and silent in the bogland brought it home to me that we were in earnest, and banished the last bit of hope I had.

Belcher, on recognizing Noble, said: "Hallo, chum," in his quiet way, but Hawkins flew at him at once, and the argument began all over again, only this time Noble had nothing to say for himself and stood with his head down, holding the lantern between his legs.

It was Jeremiah Donovan who did the answering. For the twentieth time, as though it was haunting his mind, Hawkins asked if anybody thought he's shoot Noble.

"Yes, you would," says Jeremiah Donovan.

"No, I wouldn't, damn you!"

"You would, becuase you'd know you'd be shot for not doing it."

"I wouldn't, not if I was to be shot twenty times over. I wouldn't shoot a pal. And Belcher wouldn't—isn't that right, Belcher?"

"That's right, chum," Belcher said, but more by way of answering the question than of joining in the argument. Belcher sounded as though whatever unforeseen thing he'd always been waiting for had come at last.

"Anyway, who says Noble would be shot if I wasn't? What do you think I'd do if I was in his place, out in the middle of a blasted bog?"

"What would you do?" asks Donovan.

"I'd go with him wherever he was going, of course. Share my last bob with him and stick by him through thick and thin. No one can ever say of me that I let down a pal."

"We had enough of this," says Jeremiah Donovan, cocking his revolver. "Is there any message you want to send?"

"No, there isn't."

"Do you want to say your prayers?"

Hawkins came out with a cold-blooded remark that even shocked me and turned on Noble again.

"Listen to me, Noble," he says. "You and me are chums. You can't come over to my side, so I'll come over to your side. That show you I mean what I say? Give me a rifle and I'll go along with you and the other lads."

Nobody answered him. We knew that was no way out.

"Hear what I'm saying?" he says. "I'm through with it. I'm a deserter or anything else you like. I don't believe in your stuff, but it's no worse than mine. That satisfy you?"

Noble raised his head, but Donovan began to speak and he lowered it again without replying.

"For the last time, have you any messages to send?" says Donovan in a cold, excited sort of voice.

"Shut up, Donovan! You don't understand me, but these lads do. They're not the sort to make a pal and kill a pal. They're not the tools of any capitalist."

I alone of the crowd saw Donovan raise his Webley to the back of Hawkins's neck, and as he did so I shut my eyes and tried to pray. Hawkins had begun to say something else when Donovan fired, and as I opened my eyes at the bang, I saw Hawkins stagger at the knees and lie out flat at Noble's feet, slowly and as quiet as a kid falling asleep, with the lantern-light on his lean legs and bright farmer's boots. We all stood very still, watching him settle out in the last agony.

Then Belcher took out a handkerchief and began to tie it about his own eyes (in our excitement we'd forgotten to do the same for Hawkins), and, seeing it wasn't big enough, turned and asked for the loan of mine. I gave it to him and he knotted the two together and pointed with his foot at Hawkins.

"He's not quite dead," he says. "Better give him another."

Sure enough, Hawkins's left knee is beginning to rise. I bend down and put my gun to his head; then, recollecting myself, I get up again. Belcher understands what's in my mind.

"Give him his first," he says. "I don't mind. Poor bastard, we don't know what's happening to him now."

I knelt and fired. By this time I didn't seem to know what I was doing. Belcher, who was fumbling a bit awkwardly with the handkerchiefs, came out with a laugh as he heard the shot. It was the first time I heard him laugh and it sent a shudder down my back; it sounded so unnatural.

"Poor bugger!" he said quietly. "And last night he was so curious about it all. It's very queer, chums, I always think. Now he knows as much about it as they'll ever let him know, and last night he was all in the dark."

Donovan helped him to tie the handkerchiefs about his eyes. "Thanks, chum," he said. Donovan asked if there were any messages he wanted sent.

"No, chum," he says. "Not for me. If any of you would like to write to Hawkins's mother, you'll find a letter from her in his pocket. He and his mother were great chums. But my missus left me eight years ago. Went away with another fellow and took the kid with her. I like the feeling of a home, as you may have noticed, but I couldn't start again after that."

It was an extraordinary thing, but in those few minutes Belcher said more than in all the weeks before. It was just as if the sound of the shot had started a flood of talk in him and he could go on the whole night like that, quite happily, talking about himself. We stood round like fools now that he couldn't see us any longer. Donovan looked at Noble, and Noble shook his head. Then Donovan raised his Webley, and at that moment Belcher gives his queer laugh again. He may have thought we were talking about him or perhaps he noticed the same thing I'd noticed and couldn't understand it.

"Excuse me, chums," he says. "I feel I'm talking the hell of a lot, and so silly, about my being so handy about a house and things like that. But this thing came on me suddenly. You'll forgive me, I'm sure."

"You don't want to say a prayer?" asks Donovan.

"No, chum," he says. "I don't think it would help. I'm ready, and you boys want to get it over."

"You understand that we're only doing our duty?" says Donovan.

Belcher's head was raised like a blind man's, so that you could only see his chin and the tip of his nose in the lantern-light.

"I never could make out what duty was myself," he said. "I think you're all good lads, if that's what you mean. I'm not complaining."

Noble, just as if he couldn't bear any more of it, raised his fist at Donovan, and in a flash Donovan raised his gun and fired. The big man went over like a sack of meal, and this time there was no need of a second shot.

I don't remember much about the burying, but that it was worse than all the rest because we had to carry them to the grave. It was all mad lonely with nothing but a patch of latern-light between ourselves and the dark, and birds hooting and screeching all round, disturbed by the guns. Noble went through Hawkins's belongings to find the letter from his mother, and then joined his hands together. He did the same with Belcher. Then, when we'd filled in the grave, we separated from Jeremiah Donovan and Feeney and took our tools back to the shed. All the way we didn't speak a word. The kitchen was dark and cold as we'd left it, and the old woman was sitting over the hearth, saying her beads. We walked past her into the room, and Noble struck a match to light the lamp. She rose quietly and came to the doorway with all her cantankerousness gone.

"What did ye do with them?" she asked in a whisper, and Noble started so that the match went out in his hand.

"What's that?" he asked without turning round.

"I heard ye," she said.

"What did you hear?" asked Noble.

"I heard ye. Do ye think I didn't hear ye, putting the spade back in the houseen?"

Noble struck another match and this time the lamp lit for him.

"Was that what ye did to them?" she asked.

Then, by God, in the very doorway, she fell on her knees and began praying, and after looking at her for a minute or two Noble did the same by the fireplace. I pushed my way out past her and left them at it. I stood at the door, watching the stars and listening to the shrieking of the birds dying out over the bogs. It is so strange what you feel at times like that that you can't describe it. Noble says he saw everything ten times the size, as though there were nothing in the whole world but that little patch of bog with the two Englishmen stiffening into it, but with me it was as if the patch of bog where the Englishmen were was a million miles away, and even Noble and the old woman, mumbling behind me, and the birds and the bloody stars were all far away, and I was somehow very small and very lost and lonely like a child astray in the snow. And anything that happened to me afterwards, I never felt the same about again.

5

MATURITY
Integrity versus Despair

Maturity marks not only the last stage in the human life cycle but the stage which more than any other demands an evaluation of all that has preceded it. As Erikson points out, only the man who has adapted himself to the triumphs and disappointments of his particular existence can view old age with a sense of integrity, a genuine belief in the worth of his life style. Without such confidence old age must, as Erikson argues, center on a fear of death and be expressed in despair over the fact that time has become too short to find an alternative way of living. In the stories that follow the question of integrity versus despair is crucial for all the older people, who must face not only their own judgment of themselves but the judgment of those who will outlive them.

In the first story in this section, Leo Tolstoy's "The Death of Ivan Ilych," Ivan Ilych expresses a fear of death that duplicates to the letter the kind of despair Erikson ascribes to mature people who have lost faith in their past. "His mental sufferings were due to the fact that that night . . . the question suddenly occurred to him, 'What if my whole life has really been wrong?' " In Ivan Ilych's case his doubts are complicated even more by the way in which they run counter to the values of family and friends:

> *It occurred to him that his scarcely perceptible attempts to struggle against what was considered good by the most highly placed people, those scarcely noticeable impulses which he had immediately suppressed, might have been the real thing, and all the rest false. And his professional duties and the whole arrangement of his life and of his family, and all his social and official interests, might all have been false. He tried to defend all those things to himself and suddenly felt the weakness of what he was defending.*

As Tolstoy's description of Ivan Illych's life and funeral makes clear, the latter is right to question the way he has lived. At each stage in his career, we see Ivan Ilych devoting himself to what will guarantee success:

> *Even when he was at the School of Law he was just what he remained for the rest of his life: a capable, cheerful, good-natured, and sociable man, though strict in the fulfilment of what he considered to be his duty: and he considered his duty to be what was so considered by those in authority. Neither as a boy nor as a man was he a toady, but from early youth was by nature attracted to people of high station as a fly is drawn to the light, assimilating their ways and views of life and establishing friendly relations with them.*

Indeed, up until he believes he is going to die, the only serious troubles Ivan Ilych has arise when his career takes a temporary turn for the worse and his wife quarrels with him over money.

How then are we to judge the conclusion of Ivan Ilych's life? His new feelings make it impossible for him to view his past with any sense of integrity, but at the same time they mark a fundamental change in his self-awareness. Is despair to be regarded as a positive rather than a negative achievement for a man like Ivan Ilych? He concludes that "though his life had not been what it should have been, this could still be rectified." But one wonders if this statement reflects anything more than the suddenness of his death-bed insight.

A very different set of problems arises in Doris Lessing's "The Old Chief Mshlanga," which takes place in Southern Rhodesia, where she grew up. Here we also have two versions of the title character. He is the man about whom explorers have written, "Our destination was Chief Mshlanga's country to the north of the river; and it was our desire to ask his permission to prospect for gold in his territory." He is also the man whom the narrator's father can chastise at will and to whom, after his goats trample the father's fields, the father can declare, "I'm not going to argue about it. I am keeping the goats."

In the Chief's case, however, he is not responsible for these two versions of himself. He finds only one version true, and makes this clear in his argument with the narrator's father, when he has his son (who translates for him) say, "All this land, this land you call yours . . . belongs to our people." In the end we are left to ask only if the Chief's pride and sense of integrity can be more than a brave pose. We see the emptiness of his village, in which "the young men were all away working on the white men's farms and mines," and later we learn he and his people "had been moved two hundred miles east, to a proper Native Reserve."

An even greater degree of ambiguity surrounds the Grandfather of Joyce Carol Oates's "Swamps." We first see him in circumstances that undermine any patriarchal claims he might make:

> *The Grandfather still lived alone in his log cabin, a ramshackle eyesore that the children, and the children's children, no longer cared to joke about. It had been built a hundred years ago, and the Grandfather, his mind surely loosened, would boast sometimes that he had watched his father clear the land or that he had helped clear it himself. . . .*

Yet, we quickly learn that there is also a great depth of admiration for the Grandfather among his neighbors:

> *The neighbors—farmers on remote strips of land, on rice farms bordered by swamps—thought highly of the Grandfather, who, in his time, had been blacksmith for the area, schoolteacher when the big boys used to chase every other schoolteacher away, chief and truck driver for the volunteer fire company . . . and an excellent farmer, neighbor, and parent.*

Most importantly, the Grandfather, with his "prickly independence," is not a man to bow before the opinions of others. When he finds a young girl by the river, pregnant and half-crazy, he takes her home because she needs help and he can stand up to the criticism that follows. His judgment seems vindicated, moreover, when the girl delivers a healthy baby, and the Grandfather is able to carry it triumphantly to his son's house and demand clothes for it.

Unfortunately, the Grandfather's triumph is short-lived. He is robbed and beaten by the girl whose baby he has saved, and the shock proves too much for him. So great is the transformation in his demeanor that his grandson finds that "he could never remember this grandfather." 'He remembered only the other grandfather, and he had to think hard to make himself recall this one—this trembling old man who whined about being robbed." How are we than to interpret the disintegration of the Grandfather? The causes are clearly psychological and not physiological, but their rapidity almost defies the imagination. At the end of "Swamps" the Grandfather appears to have no belief in the integrity of his life. Yet, up to that time he is pictured as a bulwark. Is it possible to find some hidden weakness in his character that accounts for his final behavior? Or are we to believe that one such incident has the power to erase all that went before it?

The final two stories in this section focus on central characters who experience no such self-doubt. In Isaac Bashevis Singer's "Gimpel the Fool," Gimpel makes it apparent from the beginning that he does not accept others' opinions of him. "I am Gimpel the Fool. I don't think myself a fool. On the contrary. But that's what folks call me." Gimpel makes no effort to hide the number of times he has been played for a fool. We see that as a child he cannot even go to the rabbi without being tricked:

> *I went to the rabbi to get some advice. He said, "It is written, better to be a fool all your days than for one hour to be evil. You are not a fool. They are the fools. For he who causes his neighbor to feel shame loses paradise himself. Nevertheless the rabbi's daughter took me in. As I left the rabbinical court she said, "Have you kissed the wall yet?" I said, "No; what for?" She answered, "It's the law; you've got to do it after every visit." Well, there didn't seem to be any harm in it. And she burst out laughing. It was a fine trick. She put one over on me, all right.*

We see the same pattern in Gimpel's marriage. He is not only duped into a union he does not want, he is deceived by his wife for all twenty years of their marriage. On her deathbed she confesses, "It was ugly how I deceived you all these years. I want to go clean to my Maker, and so I have to tell you that the children are not yours."

Gimpel, however, is not taken aback by these events. The one time he thinks of revenge on the citizens of Frampol, he dreams of his wife in hell:

> *I looked at her face. It was black; I was startled and waked, and remained sitting dumb. I sensed that everything hung in the balance. A false step now and I'd lose eternal life. But God gave me His help.*

This sense of the relationship between his own conduct and eternity stays with Gimpel to the end of his story, when he observes of death, "Whatever may be there, it will be real, without complication, without ridicule, without deception. God be praised: there even Gimpel cannot be decieved." At this point there can be no doubt that Gimpel believes in the integrity of his own life. What must be asked, however, is if his life bears out this confidence, or if it too must be judged on faith.

No less a capacity for trust and for being deceived reveals itself in the life of Félicité in Flaubert's "A Simple Heart." Félicité loves one after another a man who deserts her, her mistress's children, her nephew, and an old man she finds dying of a tumor. None of these people, however, is able to respond to Félicité with the warmth she deserves, and at the end of her life, the only creature left for her to lavish her affection on is a parrot. When the parrot dies, she has him stuffed, and in the final scene of Flaubert's story, we see that the dying Félicité has confused the parrot with the Holy Ghost:

> *Her heart-beats grew slower and slower, each a little fainter and gentler, like a fountain running dry, an echo fading away. And as she breathed her last, she thought she could see, in the opening heavens, a gigantic parrot hovering above her head.*

As in "Gimpel the Fool," it is not easy to distinguish the irony from the piety in "A Simple Heart." Until we do, however, there is no coming to terms with the quality or the integrity of Félicité's life.

LEO TOLSTOY

The DEATH of IVAN ILYCH

Translated by Louise and Aylmer Maude

1

During an interval in the Melvinski trial in the large building of the Law Courts, the members and public prosecutor met in Ivan Egorovich Shebek's private room, where the conversation turned on the celebrated Krasovski case. Fëdor Vasilievich warmly maintained that it was not subject to their jurisdiction, Ivan Egorovich maintained the contrary, while Peter Ivanovich, not having entered into the discussion at the start, took no part in it but looked through the *Gazette* which had just been handed in.

"Gentlemen," he said, "Ivan Ilych has died!"

"You don't say so!"

"Here, read it yourself," replied Peter Ivanovich, handing Fëdor Vasilievch the paper still damp from the press. Surrounded by a black border were the words: "Praskovya Fëdorovna Golovina, with profound sorrow, informs relatives and friends of the demise of her beloved husband Ivan Ilych Golovin, Member of the Court of Justice, which occurred on February the 4th of this year 1882. The funeral will take place on Friday at one o'clock in the afternoon."

Ivan Ilych had been a colleague of the gentlemen present and was liked by them all. He had been ill for some weeks with an illness said to be incurable. His post had been kept open for him, but there had been conjectures that in case of his death Alexeev might receive his appointment, and that either Vinnikov or Shtabel would succeed Alexeev. So on receiving the news of Ivan Ilych's death the first thought of each of the gentlemen in that private room was of the changes and promotions it might occasion among themselves or their acquaintances.

"I shall be sure to get Shtabel's place or Vinnikov's," thought Fëdor Vasilievich. "I was promised that long ago, and the promotion means an extra eight hundred rubles a year for me besides the allowance."

"Now I must apply for my brother-in-law's transfer from Kaluga," thought Peter Ivanovich. "My wife will be very glad, and then she won't be able to say that I never do anything for her relations."

"I thought he would never leave his bed again," said Peter Ivanovich aloud. "It's very sad."

"But what really was the matter with him?"

"The doctors couldn't say—at least they could, but each of them said something different. When last I saw him I thought he was getting better."

"And I haven't been to see him since the holidays. I always meant to go."

"Had he any property?"

"I think his wife had a little—but something quite trifling."

"We shall have to go to see her, but they live so terribly far away."

"Far away from you, you mean. Everything's far away from your place."

"You see, he never can forgive my living on the other side of the river," said Peter Ivanovich, smiling at Shebek. Then, still talking of the distances between different parts of the city, they returned to the Court.

Besides considerations as to the possible transfers and promotions likely to result from Ivan Ilych's death, the mere fact of the death of a near acquaintance aroused, as usual, in all who heard of it the complacent feeling that, "it is he who is dead and not I."

Each one thought or felt, "Well, he's dead but I'm alive!" But the more intimate of Ivan Ilych's acquaintances, his so-called friends, could not help thinking also that they would now have to fulfil the very tiresome demands of propriety by attending the funeral service and paying a visit of condolence to the widow.

Fëdor Vasilievich and Peter Ivanovich had been his nearest acquaintances. Peter Ivanovich had studied law with Ivan Ilych and had considered himself to be under obligations to him.

Having told his wife at dinner-time of Ivan Ilych's death and of his conjecture that it might be possible to get her brother transferred to their circuit, Peter Ivanovich sacrificed his usual nap, put on his evening clothes, and drove to Ivan Ilych's house.

At the entrance stood a carriage and two cabs. Leaning against the wall in the hall downstairs near the cloak-stand was a coffin-lid covered with cloth of gold, ornamented with gold cord and tassels, that had been polished up with metal powder. Two ladies in black were taking off their fur cloaks. Peter Ivanovich recognized one of them as Ivan Ilych's sister, but the other was a stranger to him. His colleague Schwartz was just coming downstairs, but on seeing Peter Ivanovich enter he stopped and winked at him, as if to say: "Ivan Ilych has made a mess of things—not like you and me."

Schwartz's face with his Piccadilly whiskers and his slim figure in evening dress, had as usual an air of elegant solemnity which contrasted with the playfulness of his character and had a special piquancy here, or so it seemed to Peter Ivanovich.

Peter Ivanovich allowed the ladies to precede him and slowly followed them upstairs. Schwartz did not come down but remained where he was, and Peter Ivanovich understood that he wanted to arrange where they should play bridge that evening. The ladies went upstairs to the widow's room, and Schwartz with seriously compressed lips but a playful look in his eyes, indicated by a twist of his eyebrows the room to the right where the body lay.

Peter Ivanovich, like everyone else on such occasions, entered feeling uncertain what he would have to do. All he knew was that at such times it is always safe to cross oneself. But he was not quite sure whether one should make obeisances while doing so. He therefore adopted a middle course. On entering the room he began crossing himself and made a slight movement resembling a bow. At the same time, as far as the motion of his head and arm allowed, he surveyed the room. Two young men—apparently nephews, one of whom was a high-school pupil—were leaving the room, crossing themselves as they did so. An old woman was standing motionless, and a lady with strangely arched eyebrows was saying something to her in a whisper. A vigorous, resolute Church Reader, in a frock-coat, was reading something in a loud voice with an expression that precluded any contradiction. The butler's assistant, Gerasim, stepping lightly in front of Peter Ivanovich, was strewing something on the floor. Noticing this, Peter Ivanovich was immeduately aware of a faint odour of a decomposing body.

The last time he had called on Ivan Ilych, Peter Ivanovich had seen Gerasim in the study. Ivan Ilych had been particularly fond of him and he was performing the duty of a sick nurse.

Peter Ivanovich continued to make the sign of the cross slightly inclining his head in an intermediate direction between the coffin, the Reader, and the icons on the table in a corner of the room. Afterwards, when it seemed to him that this movement of his arm in crossing himself had gone on too long, he stopped and began to look at the corpse.

The dead man lay, as dead men always lie, in a specially heavy way, his rigid limbs sunk in the soft cushions of the coffin, with the head forever bowed on the pillow. His yellow waxen brow with bald patches over his sunken temples was thrust up in the way peculiar to the dead, the protruding nose seeming to press on the upper lip. He was much changed and had grown even thinner since Peter Ivanovich had last seen him, but, as is always the case with the dead, his face was handsomer and above all more dignified than when he was alive. The expression on the face said that what was necessary had been accomplished, and accomplished rightly. Besides this there was in that expression a reproach and a warning to the living. This warning seemed to Peter Ivanovich out of place, or at least not applicable to him. He felt a certain discomfort and so he hurriedly crossed himself once more and turned and went out of the door—too hurriedly and too regardless of propriety, as he himself was aware.

Schwartz was waiting for him in the adjoining room with legs spread wide apart and both hands toying with his top-hat behind his back. The mere sight of that playful, well-groomed, and elegant figure refreshed Peter Ivanovich. He felt that Schwartz was above all these happenings and would not surrender to any depressing influences. His very look said that this incident of a church service for Ivan Ilych could not be a sufficient reason for infringing the order of the session—in other words, that it would certainly not prevent his unwrapping a new pack of cards and shuffling them that evening while a footman placed four fresh candles on the table: in fact, that there was no reason for supposing that this incident would hinder their spending the evening agreeably. Indeed he said this in a whisper as Peter Ivanovich passed him, proposing that they should neet for a game at Fëdor Vasilievich's. But apparently Peter Ivanovich was not destined to play bridge that evening. Praskovya Fëdorovna (a short, fat woman who despite all efforts to the contrary had continued to broaden steadily from her shoulders downwards and who had the same extraordinarily arched eyebrows as the lady who had been standing by the coffin), dressed all in black, her head covered with lace, came out of her own room with some other ladies, conducted them to the room where the dead body lay, and said; "The service will begin immediately. Please go in."

Schwartz, making an indefinite bow, stood still, evidently neither accepting nor declining this invitation. Praskovya Fëdorovna, recognizing Peter Ivanovich, sighed, went close up to him, took his hand, and said: "I know you were a true friend to Ivan Ilych . . ." and looked at him awaiting some suitable response. And Peter Ivanovich knew that, just as it had been the right thing to cross himself in that room, so what he had to do here was to press her hand, sigh, and say, "Believe me. . . ." So he did all this and as he did it felt that the desired result had been achieved: that both he and she were touched.

"Come with me. I want to speak to you before it begins," said the widow. "Give me your arm."

Peter Ivanovich gave her his arm and they went to the inner rooms, passing Schwartz, who winked at Peter Ivanovich compassionately.

"That does for our bridge! Don't object if we find another player. Perhaps you can cut in when you do escape," said his playful look.

Peter Ivanovich sighed still more deeply and despondently, and Praskovya Fëdorovna pressed his arm gratefully. When they reached the drawing-room, upholstered in pink cretonne and lighted by a dim lamp, they sat down at the table—she on a sofa and Peter Ivanovich on a low pouffe, the springs of which yielded spasmodically under his weight. Praskovya Fëdorovna had been on the point of warning him to take another seat, but felt that such a warning was out of keeping with her present condition and so changed her mind. As he sat down on the pouffe Peter Ivanovich recalled how Ivan Ilych had arranged this room and had consulted him regarding this pink cretonne with green leaves. The whole room was full of furniture and knick-knacks, and on her way to the sofa the lace of the widow's black shawl caught on the carved edge of the table. Peter Ivanovich rose to detach it, and the springs of the pouffe, relieved of his weight, rose also and gave him a push. The widow began detaching her shawl herself, and Peter Ivanovich again sat down, suppressing the rebellious springs of the pouffe under him. But the widow had not quite freed herself and Peter Ivanovich got up again, and again the pouffe rebelled and even creaked. When this was all over she took out a clean cambric handkerchief and began to weep. The episode with the shawl and the struggle with the pouffe had cooled Peter Ivanovich's emotions and he sat there with a sullen look on his face. This awkward situation was interrupted by Sokolov, Ivan Ilych's butler, who came to report that the plot in the cemetery that Praskovya Fëdorovna had chosen would cost two hundred rubles. She stopped weeping and, looking at Peter Ivanovich with the air of a victim, remarked in French that it was very hard for her. Peter Ivanovich made a silent gesture signifying his full conviction that it must indeed be so.

"Please smoke," she said in a magnanimous yet crushed voice, and turned to discuss with Sokolov the price of the plot for the grave.

Peter Ivanovich while lighting his cigarette heard her inquiring very circumstantially into the prices of different plots in the cemetery and finally decide which she would take. When that was done she gave instructions about engaging the choir. Sokolov then left the room.

"I look after everything myself," she told Peter Ivanovich, shifting the albums that lay on the table; and noticing that the table was endangered by his cigarette-ash, she immediately passed him an ash-tray, saying as she did so: "I consider it an affectation to say that my grief prevents my attending to practical affairs. On the contrary, if anything can—I won't say console me, but—distract me, it is seeing to everything concerning him." She again took out her handkerchief as if preparing to cry, but suddenly, as if mastering her feeling, she shook herself and began to speak calmly. "But there is something I want to talk to you about."

Peter Ivanovich bowed, keeping control of the springs of the pouffe, which immediately began quivering under him.

"He suffered terribly the last few days."

"Did he?" said Peter Ivanovich.

"Oh, terribly! He screamed unceasingly, not for minutes but for hours. For the last three days he screamed incessantly. It was unendurable. I cannot understand how I bore it; you could hear him three rooms off. Oh, what I have suffered!"

"Is it possible that he was conscious all that time?" asked Peter Ivanovich.

"Yes," she whispered. "To the last moment. He took leave of us a quarter of an hour before he died, and asked us to take Volodya away."

The thought of the sufferings of this man he had known so intimately, first as a merry little boy, then as a school-mate, and later as a grown-up colleague, suddenly struck Peter Ivanovich with horror, despite an unpleasant consciousness of his own and this woman's dissimulation. He again saw that brow, and that nose pressing down on the lip, and felt afraid for himself.

"Three days of frightful suffering and then death! Why, that might suddenly, at any time, happen to me," he thought, and for a moment felt terrified. But—he did not himself know how—the customary reflection at once occurred to him that this had happened to Ivan Ilych and not to him, and that it should not and could not happen to him, and that to think that it could would be yielding to depression which he ought not to do, as Schwartz's expression plainly showed. After which reflection Peter Ivanovich felt reassured , and began to ask with interest about the details of Ivan Ilych's death, as though death was an accident natural to Ivan Ilych but certainly not to himself.

After many details of the really dreadful physical sufferings Ivan Ilych had endured (which details he learnt only from the effect those sufferings had produced on Praskovya Fëdorovna's nerves) the widow apparently found it necessary to get to business.

"Oh, Peter Ivanovich, how hard it is! How terribly, terribly hard!" and she again began to weep.

Peter Ivanovich sighed and waited for her to finish blowing her nose. When she had done so he said, "Believe me . . ." and she again began talking and brought out what was evidently her chief concern with him—namely, to question him as to how she could obtain a grant of money from the government on the occasion of her husband's death. She made it appear that she was asking Peter Ivanovich's advice about her pension, but he soon saw that she already knew about that to the minutest detail, more even than he did himself. She knew how much could be got out of the government in consequence of her husband's death, but wanted to find out whether she could not possibly extract something more. Peter Ivanovich tried to think of some means of doing so, but after reflecting for a while and, out of propriety, condemning the government for its niggardliness, he said he thought that nothing more could be got. Then she sighed and evidently began to devise means of getting rid of her visitor. Noticing this, he put out his cigarette, rose, pressed her hand, and went out into the anteroom.

In the dining-room where the clock stood that Ivan Ilych had liked so much and had bought at an antique shop, Peter Ivanovich met a priest and a few acquaintances who had come to attend the service, and he recognized Ivan Ilych's daughter, a handsome young woman. She was in black and her slim figure appeared slimmer than ever. She had a gloomy, determined, almost angry expression, and bowed to Peter Ivanovich as though he were in some way to blame. Behind her, with the same offended look, stood a wealthy young man, an examining magistrate, whom Peter Ivanovich also knew and who was her fiancé, as he had heard. He bowed mournfully to them and was about to pass into the death-chamber, when from under the stairs appeared the figure of Ivan Ilych's schoolboy son, who was extremely like his father. He seemed a little Ivan Ilych, such as Peter Ivanovich remembered when they studied law together. His tear-stained eyes had in them the look that is seen in the eyes of boys of thirteen or fourteen who are not pure-minded. When he saw Peter Ivanovich he scowled morosely and shamefacedly. Peter Ivanovich nodded to him and entered the death-chamber. The service began: candles, groans, incense, tears, and sobs. Peter Ivanovich stood looking gloomily down at his feet. He did not look once at the dead man, did not yield to any depressing influence, and was one of the first to leave the room. There was no one in the anteroom, but Gerasim darted out of the dead man's room, rummaged with his strong hands among the fur coats to find Peter Ivanovich's and helped him on with it.

"Well, friend Gerasim," said Peter Ivanovich, so as to say something. "It's a sad affair, isn't it?"

"It's God's will. We shall all come to it some day," said Gerasim, displaying his teeth—the even, white teeth of a healthy peasant—and, like a man in the thick of urgent work, he briskly opened the front door, called the coachman, helped Peter Ivanovich into the sledge, and sprang back to the porch as if in readiness for what he had to do next.

Peter Ivanovich found the fresh air particularly pleasant after the smell of incense, the dead body, and carbolic acid.

"Where to, sir?" asked the coachman.

"It's not too late even now. . . . I'll call round on Fëdor Vasilievich."

He accordingly drove there and found them just finishing the first rubber, so that it was quite convenient for him to cut in.

2

Ivan Ilych's life had been most simple and most ordinary and therefore most terrible.

He had been a member of the Court of Justice, and died at the age of forty-five. His father had been an official who after serving in various ministries and departments in Petersburg had made the sort of career which brings men to positions from which by reason of their long service they cannot be dismissed, though they are obviously unfit to hold any responsible position, and for whom therefore posts are specially created, which though fictitious carry salaries of from six to ten thousand rubles that are not fictitious, and in receipt of which they live on to a great age.

Such was the Privy Councillor and superfluous member of various superfluous institutions, Ilya Epimovich Golovin.

He had three sons, of whom Ivan Ilych was the second. The eldest son was following in his father's footsteps only in another department, and was already approaching that stage in the service at which a similar sinecure would be reached. The third son was a failure. He had ruined his prospects in a number of positions and was now serving in the railway department. His father and brothers, and still more their wives, not merely disliked meeting him, but avoided remembering his existence unless compelled to do so. His sister had married Baron Greff, a Petersburg official of her father's type. Ivan Ilych was *le phénix de la famille* as people said. He was neither as cold and formal as his elder brother nor as wild as the younger, but was a happy mean between them—an intelligent, polished, lively and agreeable man. He had studied with his younger brother at the School of Law, but the latter had failed to complete the course and was expelled when he was in the fifth class. Ivan Ilych finished the course well. Even when he was at the School of Law he was just what he remained for the rest of his life: a capable, cheerful, good-natured, and sociable man, though strict in the fulfilment of what he considered to be his duty: and he considered his duty to be what was so considered by those in authority. Neither as a boy nor as a man was he a toady, but from early youth was by nature attracted to people of high station as a fly is drawn to the light, assimilating their ways and views of life and establishing friendly relations with them. All the enthusiasms of childhood and youth passed without leaving much trace on him; he succumbed to sensuality, to vanity, and latterly among the highest classes to liberalism, but always within limits which his instinct unfailingly indicated to him as correct.

At school he had done things which had formerly seemed to him very horrid and made him feel disgusted with himself when he did them; but when later on he saw that such actions were done by people of good position and that they did not regard them as wrong, he was able not exactly to regard them as right but to forget about them entirely or not be at all troubled at remembering them.

Having graduated from the School of Law and qualified for the tenth rank of the civil service, and having received money from his father for his equipment, Ivan Ilych ordered himself clothes at Scharmer's, the fashionable tailor, hung a medallion inscribed *respice finem* on his watch-chain, took leave of his professor and the prince who was patron of the school, had a farewell dinner with his comrades at Donon's first-class restaurant, and with his new and fashionable portmanteau, linen, clothes, shaving and other toilet appliances, and a traveling rug, all purchased at the best shops, he set off for one of the provinces where, through his father's influence, he had been attached to the Governor as an official for special service.

In the province Ivan Ilych soon arranged as easy and agreeable a position for himself as he had had at the School of Law. He performed his official tasks, made his career, and at the same time amused himself pleasantly and decorously. Occasionally he paid official visits to country districts, where he behaved with dignity both to his superiors and inferiors, and performed the duties entrusted to him, which related chiefly to the sectarians, with an exactness and incorruptible honesty of which he could not but feel proud.

In official matters, despite his youth and taste for frivolous gaiety, he was exceedingly reserved, punctilious, and even severe; but in society he was often amusing and witty, and always good-natured, correct in his manner, and *bon enfant*, as the governor and his wife—with whom he was like one of the family—used to say of him.

In the province he had an affair with a lady who made advances to the elegant young lawyer, and there was also a milliner; and there were carousals with aides-de-camp who visited the district, and after-supper visits to a certain outlying street of doubtful reputation; and there was too some obsequiousness to his chief and even to his chief's wife, but all this was done with such a tone of good breeding that no hard names could be applied to it. It all came under the heading of the French saying: "*Il faut que jeunesse se passe.*"* It was all done

*Youth must have its fling.

with clean hands, in clean linen, with French phrases, and above all among people of the best society and consequently with the approval of people of rank.

So Ivan Ilych served for five years and then came a change in his official life. The new and reformed judicial institutions were introduced, and new men were needed. Ivan Ilych became such a new man. He was offered the post of examining magistrate, and he accepted it though the post was in another province and obliged him to give up the connexions he had formed and to make new ones. His friends met to give him a send-off; they had a group-photograph taken and presented him with a silver cigarette-case, and he set off to his new post.

As examining magistrate Ivan Ilych was just as *comme il faut* and decorous a man, inspiring general respect and capable of separating his official duties from his private life, as he had been when acting as an official on special service. His duties now as examining magistrate were far more interesting and attractive than before. In his former position it had been pleasant to wear an undress uniform made by Scharmer, and to pass through the crowd of petitioners and officials who were timorously awaiting an audience with the governor, and who envied him as with free and easy gait he went straight into his chief's private room to have a cup of tea and a cigarette with him. But not many people had then been directly dependent on him—only police officials and the sectarians when he went on special missions—and he liked to treat them politely, almost as comrades, as if he were letting them feel that he who had the power to crush them was treating them in this simple, friendly way. There were then but few such people. But now, as an examining magistrate, Ivan Ilych felt that everyone without exception, even the most important and self-satisfied, was in his power, and that he need only write a few words on a sheet of paper with a certain heading, and this or that important, self-satisfied person would be brought before him in the role of an accused person or a witness, and if he did not choose to allow him to sit down, would have to stand before him and answer his questions. Ivan Ilych never abused his power; he tried on the contrary to soften its expression, but the consciousness of it and of the possibility of softening its effect, supplied the chief interest and attraction of his office. In his work itself, especially in his examinations, he very soon acquired a method of eliminating all considerations irrelevant to the legal aspect of the case, and reducing even the most complicated case to a form in which it would be presented on paper only in its externals, completely excluding his personal opinion of the matter, while above all observing every prescribed formality. The work was new and Ivan Ilych was one of the first men to apply the new Code of 1864.*

On taking up the post of examining magistrate in a new town, he made new acquaintances and connexions, placed himself on a new footing, and assumed a somewhat different tone. He took up an attitude of rather dignified aloofness toward the provincial authorities, but picked out the best circle of legal gentlemen and wealthy gentry living in the town and assumed a tone of slight dissatisfaction with the government, of moderate liberalism, and of enlightened citizenship. At the same time, without at all altering the elegance of his

*The emancipation of the serfs in 1861 was followed by a thorough all-round reform of judicial proceedings. (Tr.)

toilet, he ceased shaving his chin and allowed his beard to grow as it pleased.

Ivan Ilych settled down very pleasantly in this new town. The society there, which inclined towards opposition to the Governor, was friendly, his salary was larger, and he began to play *vint* [a form of bridge], which he found added not a little to the pleasure of life, for he had a capacity for cards, played good-humouredly, and calculated rapidly and astutely, so that he usually won.

After living there for two years he met his future wife, Praskovya Fëdorovna Mikhel, who was the most attractive, clever, and brilliant girl of the set in which he moved, and among other amusements and relaxations from his labours as examining magistrate, Ivan Ilych established light and playful relations with her.

While he had been an official on special service he had been accustomed to dance, but now as an examining magistrate it was exceptional for him to do so. If he danced now, he did it as if to show that though he served under the reformed order of things, and had reached the fifth official rank, yet when it came to dancing he could do it better than most people. So at the end of an evening he sometimes danced with Praskovya Fëdorovna, and it was chiefly during these dances that he captivated her. She fell in love with him. Ivan Ilych had at first no definite intention of marrying, but when the girl fell in love with him he said to himself: "Really, why shouldn't I marry?"

Praskovya Fëdorovna came of a good family, was not bad looking, and had some little property. Ivan Ilych might have aspired to a more brilliant match, but even this was good. He had his salary, and she, he hoped, would have an equal income. She was well connected, and was a sweet, pretty, and thoroughly correct young woman. To say that Ivan Ilych married because he fell in love with Praskovya Fëdorovna and found that she sympathized with his views of life would be as incorrect as to say that he married because his social circle approved of the match. He was swayed by both these considerations: the marriage gave him personal satisfaction, and at the same time it was considered the right thing by the most highly placed of his associates.

So Ivan Ilych got married.

The preparations for marriage and the beginning of married life, with its conjugal caresses, the new furniture, new crockery, and new linen, were very pleasant until his wife became pregnant—so that Ivan Ilych had begun to think that marriage would not impair the easy, agreeable, gay and always decorous character of his life, approved of by society and regarded by himself as natural, but would even improve it. But from the first months of his wife's pregnancy, something new, unpleasant, depressing, and unseemly, and from which there was no way of escape, unexpectedly showed itself.

His wife, without any reason—*de gaieté de coeur* as Ivan Ilych expressed it to himself—began to disturb the pleasure and propriety of their life. She began to be jealous without any cause, expected him to devote his whole attention to her, found fault with everything, and made coarse and ill-mannered scenes.

At first Ivan Ilych hoped to escape from the unpleasantness of this state of affairs by the same easy and decorous relation to life that had served him heretofore: he tried to ignore his wife's disagreeable moods, continued to live in his usual easy and pleasant way, invited friends to his house for a game of cards, and also tried going out to his club or spending his evenings with friends. But one day his wife began upbraiding him so vigorously, using such coarse words, and continued to abuse him every time he did not fulfil her demands, so resolutely and with such evident determination not to give way till he submitted—that is, till he stayed at home and was bored just as she was—that he became alarmed. He now realized that matrimony—at any rate with Praskovya Fëdorovna—was not always conducive to the pleasures and amenities of life, but on the contrary often infringed both comfort and propriety, and that he must therefore entrench himself against such infringement. And Ivan Ilych began to seek for means of doing so. His official duties were the one thing that imposed upon Praskovya Fëdorovna, and by means of his official work and the duties attached to it he began struggling with his wife to secure his own independence.

With the birth of their child, the attempts to feed it and the various failures in doing so, and with the real and imaginary illnesses of mother and child, in which Ivan Ilych's sympathy was demanded but about which he understood nothing, the need of securing for himself an existence outside his family life became still more imperative.

As his wife grew more irritable and exacting and Ivan Ilych transferred the centre of gravity of his life more and more to his official work, so did he grow to like his work better and became more ambitious than before.

Very soon, within a year of his wedding, Ivan Ilych had realized that marriage, though it may add some comforts to life, is in fact a very intricate and difficult affair towards which in order to perform one's duty, that is, to lead a decorous life approved of by society, one must adopt a definite attitude just as towards one's official duties.

And Ivan Ilych evolved such an attitude towards married life. He only required of it those conveniences—dinner at home, housewife, and bed—which it could give him, and above all that propriety of external forms required by public opinion. For the rest he looked for light-hearted pleasure and propriety, and was very thankful when he found them, but if he met with antagonism and querulousness he at once retired into his separate fenced-off world of official duties, where he found satisfaction.

Ivan Ilych was esteemed a good official, and after three years was made Assistant Public Prosecutor. His new duties, their importance, the possibility of indicting and imprisoning anyone he chose, the publicity his speeches received, and the success he had in all these things, made his work still more attractive.

More children came. His wife became more and more querulous and ill-tempered, but the attitude Ivan Ilych had adopted towards his home life rendered him almost impervious to her grumbling.

After seven years' service in that town he was transferred to another province as Public Prosecutor. They moved, but were short of money and his wife did not like the place they moved to. Though the salary was higher the cost of living was greater, besides which two of their children died and family life became still more unpleasant for him.

Praskovya Fëdorovna blamed her husband for every inconvenience they encountered in their new home. Most of the conversations between husband and wife, especially as to the children's education, led to topics which recalled former disputes, and those disputes were apt to flare up again at any moment. There remained only those rare periods of amorousness which still came to them at times but did not last long. These were islets at which they anchored for a while and then again set out upon the ocean of veiled hostility which showed itself in their aloofness from one another. This aloofness might have grieved Ivan Ilych had he considered that it ought not to exist, but he now regarded the position as normal, and even made it the goal at which he aimed in family life. His aim was to free himself more and more from those unpleasantnesses and to give them a semblance of harmlessness and propriety. He attained this by spending less and less time with his family, and when obliged to be at home he tried to safeguard his position by the presence of outsiders. The chief thing however was that he had his official duties. The whole interest of his life now centred in the official world and that interest absorbed him. The consciousness of his power, being able to ruin anybody he wished to ruin, the importance, even the external dignity of his entry into court, or meetings with his subordinates, his success with superiors and inferiors, and above all his masterly handling of cases, of which he was conscious—all this gave him pleasure and filled his life, together with chats with his colleagues, dinners, and bridge. So that on the whole Ivan Ilych's life continued to flow as he considered it should do—pleasantly and properly.

So things continued for another seven years. His eldest daughter was already sixteen, another child had died, and only one son was left, a schoolboy and a subject of dissension. Ivan Ilych wanted to put him in the School of Law, but to spite him Praskovya Fëdorovna entered him at the High School. The daughter had been educated at home and had turned out well: the boy did not learn badly either.

3

So Ivan Ilych lived for seventeen years after his marriage. He was already a Public Prosecutor of long standing, and had declined several proposed transfers while awaiting a more desirable post, when an unanticipated and unpleasant occurrence quite upset the peaceful course of his life. He was expecting to be offered the post of presiding judge in a University town, but Happe somehow came to the front and obtained the appointment instead. Ivan Ilych became irritable, reproached Happe, and quarrelled both with him and with his immediate superiors—who became colder to him and again passed him over when other appointments were made.

This was in 1880, the hardest year of Ivan Ilych's life. It was then that it became evident on the one hand that his salary was insufficient for them to live on, and on the other that he had been forgotten, and not only this, but that what was for him the greatest and most cruel injustice appeared to others a quite ordinary occurrence. Even his father did not consider it his duty to help him.

Ivan Ilych felt himself abandoned by everyone, and that they regarded his position with a salary of 3,500 rubles as quite normal and even fortunate. He alone knew that with the consciousness of the injustices done him, with his wife's incessant nagging, and with the debts he had contracted by living beyond his means, his position was far from normal.

In order to save money that summer he obtained leave of absence and went with his wife to live in the country at her brother's place.

In the country, without his work, he experienced *ennui* for the first time in his life, and not only *ennui* but intolerable depression, and he decided that it was impossible to go on living like that, and that it was necessary to take energetic measures.

Having passed a sleepless night pacing up and down the veranda, he decided to go to Petersburg and bestir himself, in order to punish those who had failed to appreciate him and to get transferred to another ministry.

Next day, despite many protests from his wife and her brother, he started for Petersburg with the sole object of obtaining a post with a salary of five thousand rubles a year. He was no longer bent on any particular department, or tendency, or kind of activity. All he now wanted was an appointment to another post with a salary of five thousand rubles, either in the administration, in the banks, with the railways, in one of the Empress Marya's Institutions, or even in the customs—but it had to carry with it a salary of five thousand rubles and be in a ministry other than that in which they had failed to appreciate him.

And this quest of Ivan Ilych's was crowned with remarkable and unexpected success. At Kursk an acquaintance of his, F. I. Ilyin, got into the first-class carriage, sat down beside Ivan Ilych, and told him of a telegram just received by the Governor of Kursk announcing that a change was about to take place in the ministry: Peter Ivanovich was to be superseded by Ivan Semënovich.

The proposed change, apart from its significance for Russia, had a special significance for Ivan Ilych, because by bringing forward a new man, Peter Petrovich, and consequently his friend Zachar Ivanovich, it was highly favourable for Ivan Ilych, since Zachar Ivanovich was a friend and colleague of his.

In Moscow this news was confirmed, and on reaching Petersburg Ivan Ilych found Zachar Ivanovich and received a definite promise of an appointment in his former department of Justice.

A week later he telegraphed to his wife: "Zachar in Miller's place. I shall receive appointment on presentation of report."

Thanks to this change of personnel, Ivan Ilych had unexpectedly obtained an appointment in his former ministry which placed him two stages above his former colleagues besides giving him five thousand rubles salary and three thousand five hundred rubles for expenses connected with his removal. All his ill humour towards his former enemies and the whole department vanished, and Ivan Ilych was completely happy.

He returned to the country more cheerful and contented than he had been for a long time. Praskovya Fëdorovna also cheered up and a truce was arranged between them. Ivan Ilych told of how he had been fêted by everybody in

Petersburg, how all those who had been his enemies were put to shame and now fawned on him; how envious they were of his appointment, and how much everybody in Petersburg had liked him.

Praskovya Fëdorovna listened to all this and appeared to believe it. She did not contradict anything, but only made plans for their life in the town to which they were going. Ivan Ilych saw with delight that these plans were his plans, that he and his wife agreed, and that, after a stumble, his life was regaining its due and natural character of pleasant lightheartedness and decorum.

Ivan Ilych had come back for a short time only, for he had to take up his new duties on the 10th of September. Moreover, he needed time to settle into the new place, to move all his belongings from the province, and to buy and order many additional things: in a word, to make such arrangements as he had resolved on, which were almost exactly what Praskovya Fëdorovna too had decided on.

Now that everything had happened so fortunately, and that he and his wife were at one in their aims and moreover saw so little of one another, they got on together better than they had done since the first years of marriage. Ivan Ilych had thought of taking his family away with him at once, but the insistence of his wife's brother and her sister-in-law, who had suddenly become particularly amiable and friendly to him and his family, induced him to depart alone.

So he departed, and the cheerful state of mind induced by his success and by the harmony between his wife and himself, the one intensifying the other, did not leave him. He found a delightful house, just the thing both he and his wife had dreamt of. Spacious, lofty reception rooms in the old style, a convenient and dignified study, rooms for his wife and daughter, a study for his son—it might have been specially built for them. Ivan Ilych himself superintended the arrangements, chose the wallpapers, supplemented the furniture (preferably with antiques which he considered particularly *comme il faut*), and supervised the upholstering. Everything progressed and progressed and approached the ideal he had set himself: even when things were only half completed they exceeded his expectations. He saw what a refined and elegant character, free from vulgarity, it would all have when it was ready. On falling asleep he pictured to himself how the reception-room would look. Looking at the yet unfinished drawing-room he could see the fireplace, the screen, the what-not, the little chairs dotted here and there, the dishes and plates on the walls, and the bronzes, as they would be when everything was in place. He was pleased by the thought of how his wife and daughter, who shared his taste in this matter, would be impressed by it. They were certainly not expecting as much. He had been particularly successful in finding, and buying cheaply, antiques which gave a particularly aristocratic character to the whole place. But in his letters he intentionally understated everything in order to be able to surprise them. All this so absorbed him that his new duties—though he liked his official work—interested him less than he had expected. Sometimes he even had moments of absent-mindedness during the Court Sessions, and would consider whether he should have straight or curved cornices for his curtains. He was so interested in it all that he often did things himself, rearranging the furniture, or rehanging the curtains. Once when mounting a step-ladder to show the upholsterer, who did not understand, how he wanted the hangings draped, he made a false step and slipped, but being a strong and agile man he clung on and only knocked his side against the knob of the window frame. The bruised place was painful but the pain soon passed, and he felt particularly bright and well just then. He wrote: "I feel fifteen years younger." He thought he would have everything ready by September, but it dragged on till mid-October. But the result was charming not only in his eyes but to everyone who saw it.

In reality it was just what is usually seen in the houses of people of moderate means who want to appear rich, and therefore succeed only in resembling others like themselves: there were damasks, dark wood, plants, rugs, and dull and polished bronzes—all the things people of a certain class have in order to resemble other people of that class. His house was so like the others that it would never have been noticed, but to him it all seemed to be quite exceptional. He was very happy when he met his family at the station and brought them to the newly furnished house all lit up, where a footman in a white tie opened the door into the hall decorated with plants, and when they went on into the drawing room, and the study uttering exclamations of delight. He conducted them everywhere, drank in their praises eagerly, and beamed with pleasure. At tea that evening, when Praskovya Fëdorovna among other things asked him about his fall, he laughed and showed them how he had gone flying and had frightened the upholsterer.

"It's a good thing I'm a bit of an athlete. Another man might have been killed, but I merely knocked myself, just here; it hurts when it's touched, but it's passing off already—it's only a bruise."

So they began living in their new home—in which, as always happens, when they got thoroughly settled in they found they were just one room short—and with the increased income, which as always was just a little (some five hundred rubles) too little, but it was all very nice.

Things went particularly well at first, before everything was finally arranged and while something had still to be done: this thing bought, that thing ordered, another thing moved, and something else adjusted. Though there were some disputes between husband and wife, they were both so well satisfied and had so much to do that it all passed off without any serious quarrels. When nothing was left to arrange it became rather dull and something seemed to be lacking, but they were then making acquaintances, forming habits, and life was growing fuller.

Ivan Ilych spent his mornings at the law court and came home to dinner, and at first he was generally in a good humour, though he occasionally became irritable just on account of his house. (Every spot on the tablecloth or the upholstery, and every broken window-blind string, irritated him. He had devoted so much trouble to arranging it all that every disturbance of it distressed him.) But on the whole his life ran its course as he believed life should do: easily, pleasantly, and decorously.

He got up at nine, drank his coffee, read the paper, and then put on his undress uniform and went to the law courts. There the harness in which he worked had already been stretched to fit him and he donned it without a hitch: petitioners, inquiries at the chancery, the chancery itself, and the sittings public and administrative. In all this the thing was to exclude everything fresh and vital, which always disturbs the regular course of official business, and to admit only official relations with people, and then only on official grounds. A man would come, for instance, wanting some information. Ivan Ilych, as one in whose sphere the matter did not lie, would have nothing to do with him: but if the man had some business with him in his official capacity, something that could be expressed on officially stamped paper, he would do everything, positively everything he could within the limits of such relations, and in doing so would maintain the semblance of friendly human relations, that is, would observe the courtesies of life. As soon as the official relations ended, so did everything else. Ivan Ilych possessed this capacity to separate his real life from the official side of affairs and not mix the two, in the highest degree, and by long practice and natural aptitude had brought it to such a pitch that sometimes, in the manner of a virtuoso, he would even allow himself to let the human and official relations mingle. He let himself do this just because he felt that he could at any time he chose resume the strictly official attitude again and drop the human relation. And he did it all easily, pleasantly, correctly, and even artistically. In the intervals between the sessions he smoked, drank tea, chatted a little about politics, a little about general topics, a little about cards, but most of all about official appointments. Tired, but with the feelings of a virtuoso—one of the first violins who has played his part in an orchestra with precision—he would return home to find that his wife and daughter had been out paying calls, or had a visitor, and that his son had been to school, had done his homework with his tutor, and was duly learning what is taught at High Schools. Everything was as it should be. After dinner, if they had no visitors, Ivan Ilych sometimes read a book that was being much discussed at the time, and in the evening settled down to work, that is, read official papers, compared the depositions of witnesses, and noted paragraphs of the Code applying to them. This was neither dull nor amusing. It was dull when he might have been playing bridge, but if no bridge was available it was at any rate better than doing nothing or sitting with his wife. Ivan Ilych's chief pleasure was giving little dinners to which he invited men and women of good social position, and just as his drawing-room resembled all other drawing-rooms so did his enjoyable little parties resemble all other such parties.

Once they even gave a dance. Ivan Ilych enjoyed it and everything went off well, except that it led to a violent quarrel with his wife about the cakes and sweets. Praskovya Fëdorovna had made her own plans, but Ivan Ilych insisted on getting everything from an expensive confectioner and ordered too many cakes, and the quarrel occurred because some of those cakes were left over and the confectioner's bill came to forty-five rubles. It was a great and disagreeable quarrel. Praskovya Fëdorovna called him a "a fool and an imbecile," and he clutched at his head and made angry allusions to divorce.

But the dance itself had been enjoyable. The best people were there, and Ivan Ilych had danced with Princess Trufonova, a sister of the distinguished founder of the Society "Bear my Burden."

The pleasures connected with his work were pleasures of ambition; his social pleasures were those of vanity; but Ivan Ilych's greatest pleasure was playing bridge. He acknowledged that whatever disagreeable incident happened in his life, the pleasure that beamed like a ray of light above everything else was to sit down to bridge with good players, not noisy partners, and of course to four-handed bridge (with five players it was annoying to have to stand out, though one pretended not to mind), to play a clever and serious game (when the cards allowed it) and then to have supper and drink a glass of wine. After a game of bridge, especially if he had won a little (to win a large sum was unpleasant), Ivan Ilych went to bed in specially good humour.

So they lived. They formed a circle of acquaintances among the best people and were visited by people of importance and by young folk. In their views as to their acquaintances, husband, wife and daughter were entirely agreed, and tacitly and unanimously kept at arm's length and shook off the various shabby friends and relations who, with much show of affection, gushed into the drawing-room with its Japanese plates on the walls. Soon these shabby friends ceased to obtrude themselves and only the best people remained in the Golovins' set.

Young men made up to Lisa, and Petrishchev, an examining magistrate and Dmitri Ivanovich Petrishchev's son and sole heir, began to be so attentive to her that Ivan Ilych had already spoken to Praskovya Fëdorovna about it, and considered whether they should not arrange a party for them, or get up some private theatricals.

So they lived, and all went well, without change, and life flowed pleasantly.

4

They were all in good health. It could not be called ill health if Ivan Ilych sometimes said that he had a queer taste in his mouth and felt some discomfort in his left side.

But this discomfort increased and, though not exactly painful, grew into a sense of pressure in his side accompanied by ill humour. And his irritability became worse and worse and began to mar the agreeable, easy, and correct life that had established itself in the Golovin family. Quarrels between husband and wife became more and more frequent, and soon the ease and amenity disappeared and even the decorum was barely maintained. Scenes again became frequent, and very few of those islets remained on which husband and wife could meet without an explosion. Praskovya Fëdorovna now had good reason to say that her husband's temper was trying. With characteristic exaggeration she said he had always had a dreadful temper, and that it had needed all her good nature to put up with it for twenty years. It was true that now the quarrels were started by him. His bursts of temper always came just before dinner, often just as he began to eat his soup. Sometimes he noticed that a plate or dish was chipped, or the food was not right, or his son put his elbow on the table, or his daughter's hair was not done as he liked it, and for all this he blamed Praskovya Fëdorovna. At first she retorted and said disagreeable things to him, but once or twice he fell into such a rage at the beginning of dinner that she realized it was due to some physical derangement brought on by taking food, and so she restrained herself and did not answer, but only hurried to get the dinner over. She regarded this self-restraint as highly praiseworthy. Having come to the conclusion that her husband had a dreadful temper and made her life miserable, she began to feel sorry for herself, and the more she pitied herself the more she hated her husband. She began to wish he would die; yet she did not want him to die because then his salary would cease. And this irritated her against him still more. She considered herself dreadfully unhappy just because not even his death could save her, and though she concealed her exasperation, that hidden exasperation of hers increased his irritation also.

After one scene in which Ivan Ilych had been particularly unfair and after which he had said in explanation that he certainly was irritable but that it was due to his not being well, she said that if he was ill it should be attended to, and insisted on his going to see a celebrated doctor.

He went. Everything took place as he had expected and as it always does. There was the usual waiting and the important air assumed by the doctor, with which he was so familiar (resembling that which he himself assumed in court), and the sounding and listening, and the questions which called for answers that were foregone conclusions and were evidently unnecessary, and the look of importance which implied that "if only you put yourself in our hands we will arrange everything—we know indubitably how it has to be done, always in the same way for everybody alike." It was all just as it was in the law courts. The doctor put on just the same air towards him as he himself put on towards an accused person.

The doctor said that so-and-so indicated that there was so-and-so inside the patient, but if the investigation of so-and-so did not confirm this, then he must assume that and that. If he assumed that and that, then . . . and so on. To Ivan Ilych only one question was important: was his case serious or not? But the doctor ignored that inappropriate question. From his point of view it was not the one under consideration, the real question was to decide between a floating kidney, chronic catarrh, or appendicitis. It was not a question of Ivan Ilych's life or death, but one between a floating kidney and appendicitis. And that question the doctor solved brilliantly, as it seemed to Ivan Ilych, in favour of the appendix, with the reservation that should an examination of the urine give fresh indications the matter would be reconsidered. All this was just what Ivan Ilych had himself brilliantly accomplished a thousand times in dealing with men on trial. The doctor summed up just as brilliantly, looking over his spectacles triumphantly and even gaily at the accused. From the doctor's summing up Ivan Ilych concluded that things were bad, but that for the doctor, and perhaps for everybody else, it was a matter of indifference, though for him it was bad. And this conclusion struck him painfully, arousing in him a great feeling of pity for himself and of bitterness towards the doctor's indifference to a matter of such importance.

He said nothing of this, but rose, placed the doctor's fee on the table, and remarked with a sigh: "We sick people probably often put inappropriate questions. But tell me, in general, is this complaint dangerous, or not? . . ."

The doctor looked at him sternly over his spectacles with one eye, as if to say: "Prisoner, if you will not keep to the questions put to you, I shall be obliged to have you removed from the court."

"I have already told you what I consider necessary and proper. The analysis may show something more." And the doctor bowed.

Ivan Ilych went out slowly, seated himself disconsolately in his sledge, and drove home. All the way home he was going over what the doctor had said, trying to translate those complicated, obscure, scientific phrases into plain language and find in them an answer to the question: "Is my condition bad? Is it very bad? Or is there as yet nothing much wrong?" And it seemed to him that the meaning of what the doctor had said was that it was very bad. Everything in the streets seemed depressing. The cabmen, the houses, the passers-by, and the shops, were dismal. His ache, this dull gnawing ache that never ceased for a moment, seemed to have acquired a new and more serious significance from the doctor's dubious remarks. Ivan Ilych now watched it with a new and oppressive feeling.

He reached home and began to tell his wife about it. She listened, but in the middle of his account his daughter came in with her hat on, ready to go out with her mother. She sat down reluctantly to listen to this tedious story, but could not stand it long, and her mother too did not hear him to the end.

"Well, I am very glad," she said. "Mind now to take your medicine regularly. Give me the prescription and I'll send Gerasim to the chemist's." And she went to get ready to go out.

While she was in the room Ivan Ilych had hardly taken time to breathe, but he sighed deeply when she left it.

"Well," he thought, "perhaps it isn't so bad after all."

He began taking his medicine and following the doctor's directions, which had been altered after the examination of the urine. But then it happened that there was a contradiction between the indications drawn from the examination of the urine and the symptoms that showed themselves. It turned out that what was happening differed from what the doctor had told him, and that he had either forgotten, or blundered, or hidden something from him. He could not, however, be blamed for that, and Ivan Ilych still obeyed his orders implicitly and at first derived some comfort from doing so.

From the time of his visit to the doctor, Ivan Ilych's chief occupation was the exact fulfilment of the doctor's instructions regarding hygiene and the taking of medicine, and the observation of his pain and his excretions. His chief interests came to be people's ailments and people's health. When sickness, deaths, or recoveries were mentioned in his presence, especially when the illness resembled his own, he listened with agitation which he tried to hide, asked questions, and applied what he heard to his own case.

The pain did not grow less, but Ivan Ilych made efforts to force himself to think that he was better. And he could do this so long as nothing agitated him. But as soon as he had any unpleasantness with his wife, any lack of success in his official work, or held bad cards at bridge, he was at once acutely sensible of his disease. He had formerly borne such mischances, hoping soon to adjust what was wrong, to master it and attain success, or make a grand slam. But now every mischance upset him and plunged him into despair. He would say to himself: "There now, just as I was beginning to get better and the medicine had begun to take effect, comes this accursed misfortune, or unpleasantness. . . ." And he was furious with the mishap, or with the people who were causing the unpleasantness and killing him, for he felt that this fury was killing him but could not restrain it. One would have thought that it should have been clear to him that this exasperation with circumstances and people aggravated his illness, and that he ought therefore to ignore unpleasant occurrences. But he drew the very opposite conclusion: he said that he needed peace, and he watched for everything that might disturb it and became irritable at the slightest infringement of it. His condition was rendered worse by the fact that he read medical books and consulted doctors. The progress of his disease was so gradual that he could deceive himself when comparing one day with another—the difference was so slight. But when he consulted the doctors it seemed to him that he was getting worse, and even very rapidly. Yet despite this he was continually consulting them.

That month he went to see another celebrity, who told him almost the same as the first had done but put his questions rather differently, and the interview with this celebrity only increased Ivan Ilych's doubts and fears. A friend of a friend of his, a very good doctor, diagnosed his illness again quite differently from the others, and though he predicted recovery, his questions and suppositions bewildered Ivan Ilych still more and increased his doubts. A homoeopathist diagnosed the disease in yet another way, and prescribed medicine which Ivan Ilych took secretly for a week. But after a week, not feeling any improvement and having lost confidence both in the former doctor's treatment and in this one's, he became still more despondent. One day a lady acquaintance mentioned a cure effected by a wonder-working icon. Ivan Ilych caught himself listening attentively and beginning to believe that it had occurred. This incident alarmed him. "Has my mind really weakened to such an extent?" he asked himself. "Nonsense! It's all rubbish. I mustn't give way to nervous fears but having chosen a doctor must keep strictly to his treatment. That is what I will do. Now it's all settled. I won't think about it, but will follow the treatment seriously till summer, and then we shall see. From now there must be no more of this wavering!" This was easy to say but impossible to carry out. The pain in his side oppressed him and seemed to grow worse and more incessant, while the taste in his mouth grew stranger and stranger. It seemed to him that his breath had a disgusting smell, and he was conscious of a loss of appetite and strength. There was no deceiving himself: something terrible, new, and more important than anything before in his life was taking place within him of which he alone was aware. Those about him did not understand or would not understand it, but thought everything in the world was going on as usual. That tormented Ivan Ilych more than anything. He saw that his household, especially his wife and daughter who were in a perfect whirl of visiting, did not understand anything of it and were annoyed that he was so depressed and so exacting, as if he were to blame for it. Though they tried to disguise it he saw that he was an obstacle in their path, and that his wife had adopted a definite line in regard to his illness and kept to it regardless of anything he said or did. Her attitude was this: "You know," she would say to her friends, "Ivan Ilych can't do as other people do, and keep to the treatment prescribed for him. One day he'll take his drops and keep strictly to his diet and go to bed in good time, but the next day unless I watch him he'll suddenly forget his medicine, eat sturgeon—which is forbidden—and sit up playing cards till one o'clock in the morning."

"Oh, come, when was that?" Ivan Ilych would ask in vexation. "Only once at Peter Ivanovich's."

"And yesterday with Shebek."

"Well, even if I hadn't stayed up, this pain would have kept me awake."

"Be that as it may you'll never get well like that, but will always make us wretched."

Praskovya Fëdorovna's attitude to Ivan Ilych's illness, as she expressed it both to others and to him, was that it was his own fault and was another of the annoyances he caused her. Ivan Ilych felt that this opinion escaped her involuntarily—but that did not make it easier for him.

At the law courts too, Ivan Ilych noticed, or thought he noticed, a strange attitude towards himself. It sometimes seemed to him that people were watching him inquisitively as a man whose place might soon be vacant. Then again, his friends would suddenly begin to chaff him in a friendly way about his low spirits, as if the awful, horrible, and unheard-of thing that was going on within him, incessantly gnawing at him and irresistibly drawing him away, was a very agreeable subject for jests. Schwartz in particular irritated him by his jocularity, vivacity, and *savoir-faire*, which reminded him of what he himself had been ten years ago.

Friends came to make up a set and they sat down to cards. They dealt, bending the new cards to soften them, and he sorted the diamonds in his hand and found he had seven. His partner said "No trumps" and supported him with two diamonds. What more could be wished for? It ought to be jolly and lively. They would make a grand slam. But suddenly Ivan Ilych was conscious of that gnawing pain, that taste in his mouth, and it seemed ridiculous that in such circumstances he should be pleased to make a grand slam.

He looked at his partner Mikhail Mikhaylovich, who rapped the table with his strong hand and instead of snatching up the tricks pushed the cards courteously and indulgently towards Ivan Ilych that he might have the pleasure of gathering them up without the trouble of stretching out his hand for them. "Does he think I am too weak to stretch out my arm?" thought Ivan Ilych, and forgetting what he was doing he over-trumped his partner, missing the grand slam by three tricks. And what was most awful of all was that he saw how upset Mikhail Mikhaylovich was about it but did not himself care. And it was dreadful to realize why he did not care.

They all saw that he was suffering, and said: "We can stop if you are tired. Take a rest." Lie down? No, he was not at all tired, and he finished the rubber. All were gloomy and silent. Ivan Ilych felt that he had diffused this gloom over them and could not dispel it. They had supper and went away, and Ivan Ilych was left alone with the consciousness that his life was poisoned and was poisoning the lives of others, and that this poison did not weaken but penetrated more and more deeply into his whole being.

With this consciousness, and with physical pain besides the terror, he must go to bed, often to lie awake the greater part of the night. Next morning he had to get up again, dress, go to the law courts, speak, and write; or if he did not go out, spend at home those twenty-four hours a day each of which was a torture. And he had to live thus all alone on the brink of an abyss, with no one who understood or pitied him.

5

So one month passed and then another. Just before the New Year his brother-in-law came to town and stayed at their house. Ivan Ilych was at the law courts and Praskovya Fëdorovna had gone shopping. When Ivan Ilych came home and entered his study he found his brother-in-law there—a healthy, florid man—unpacking his portmanteau himself. He raised his head on hearing Ivan Ilych's footsteps and looked up at him for a moment without a word. That stare told Ivan Ilych everything. His brother-in-law opened his mouth to utter an exclamation of surprise but checked himself, and that action confirmed it all.

"I have changed, eh?"

"Yes, there is a change."

And after that, try as he would to get his brother-in-law to return to the subject of his looks, the latter would say nothing about it. Praskovya Fëdorovna came home and her brother went out to her. Ivan Ilych locked the door and began to examine himself in the glass, first full face, then in profile. He took up a portrait of himself taken with his wife, and compared it with what he saw in the glass. The change in him was immense. Then he bared his arms to the elbow, looked at them, drew the sleeves down again, sat down on an ottoman, and grew blacker than night.

"No, no, this won't do!" he said to himself, and jumped up, went to the table, took up some law papers and began to read them, but could not continue. He unlocked the door and went into the reception-room. The door leading to the drawing-room was shut. He approached it on tiptoe and listened.

"No, you are exaggerating!" Praskovya Fëdorovna was saying.

"Exaggerating! Don't you see it? Why, he's a dead man! Look at his eyes—there's no light in them. But what is it that is wrong with him?"

"No one knows. Nikolaevich [that was another doctor] said something, but I don't know what. And Leshchetitsky [this was the celebrated specialist] said quite the contrary . . ."

Ivan Ilych walked away, went to his own room, lay down, and began musing: "The kidney, a floating kidney." He recalled all the doctors had told him of how it detached itself and swayed about. And by an effort of imagination he tried to catch that kidney and arrest it and support it. So little was needed for this, it seemed to him. "No, I'll go to see Peter Ivanovich again." [That was the friend whose friend was a doctor.] He rang, ordered the carriage, and got ready to go.

"Where are you going, Jean?" asked his wife, with a specially sad and exceptionally kind look.

This exceptionally kind look irritated him. He looked morosely at her.

"I must go to see Peter Ivanovich."

He went to see Peter Ivanovich, and together they went to see his friend, the doctor. He was in, and Ivan Ilych had a long talk with him.

Reviewing the anatomical and physiological details of what in the doctor's opinion was going on inside him, he understood it all.

There was something, a small thing, in the vermiform appendix. It might all come right. Only stimulate the energy of one organ and check the activity of another, then absorption would take place and everything would come right. He got home rather late for dinner, ate his dinner, and conversed cheerfully, but could not for a long time bring himself to go back to work in his room. At last, however, he went to his study and did what was necessary, but the consciousness that he had put something aside—an important, intimate matter which he would revert to when his work was done—never left him. When he had finished his work he remembered that this intimate matter was the thought of his vermiform appendix. But he did not give himself up to it, and went to the drawing-room for tea. There were callers there, including the examining magistrate who was a desirable match for his daughter, and they were conversing, playing the piano, and singing. Ivan Ilych, as Praskovya Fëdorovna remarked, spent that evening more cheerfully than usual, but he never for a moment forgot that he had postponed the important matter of the appendix. At eleven o'clock he said good-night and went to his bedroom. Since his illness he had slept alone in a small room next to his study. He undressed and took up a novel by Zola, but instead of reading it he fell into thought, and in his imagination that desired improvement in the vermiform appendix occurred. There was the absorption and evacuation and the re-establishment of normal activity. "Yes, that's it!" he said to himself. "One need only assist nature, that's all." He remembered his medicine, rose, took it, and lay down on his back watching for the beneficent action of the medicine and for it to lessen the pain. "I need only take it regularly and avoid all injurious influences. I am already feeling better, much better." He began touching his side: it was not painful to the touch. "There, I really don't feel it. It's much better already." He put out the light and turned on his side. . . . "The appendix is getting better, absorption is occurring." Suddenly he felt the old, familiar, dull, gnawing pain, stubborn and serious. There was the same familiar loathsome taste in his mouth. His heart sank and he felt dazed. "My God! My God!" he muttered. "Again, again! and it will never cease." And suddenly the matter presented itself in a quite different aspect. "Vermiform appendix! Kidney!" he said to himself. "It's not a question of appendix or kidney, but of life and . . . death. Yes, life was there and now it it going, going and I cannot stop it. Yes. Why deceive myself? Isn't it obvious to everyone but me that I'm dying, and that it's only a question of weeks, days . . . it may happen this moment. There was light and now there is darkness. I was here and now I'm going there! Where?" A chill came over him, his breathing ceased, and he felt only the throbbing of his heart. "When I am not, what will there be? There will be nothing. Then where shall I be when I am no more? Can this be dying? No, I don't want to!" He jumped up and tried to light the candle, felt for it with trembling hands, dropped candle and candlestick on the floor, and fell back on his pillow.

"What's the use? It makes no difference," he said to himself, staring with wide-open eyes into the darkness. "Death. Yes, death. And none of them know or wish to know of it, and they have no pity for me. Now they are playing." (He heard through the door the distant sound of a song and its accompaniment.) "It's all the same to them, but they will die too! Fools! I first, and they later, but it will be the same for them. And now they are merry . . . the beasts!"

Anger choked him and he was agonizingly, unbearably miserable. "It is impossible that all men have been doomed to suffer this awful horror!" He raised himself.

"Something must be wrong. I must calm myself—must think it all over from the beginning." And he again began thinking. "Yes, the beginning of my illness: I knocked my side, but I was still quite well that day and the next. It hurt a little, then rather more. I saw the doctors, then followed despondency and anguish, more doctors, and I drew nearer to the abyss. My strength grew less and I kept coming nearer and nearer, and now I have wasted away and there is no light in my eyes. I think of the appendix—but this is death! I think of mending the appendix, and all the while here is death! Can it really be death?" Again terror seized him and he gasped for breath. He leant down and began feeling for the matches, pressing with his elbow on the stand beside the bed. It was in his way and hurt him, he grew furious with it, pressed on it still harder, and upset it. Breathless and in despair he fell on his back, expecting death to come immediately.

Meanwhile the visitors were leaving. Praskovya Fëdorovna was seeing them off. She heard something fall and came in.

"What has happened?"

"Nothing. I knocked it over accidentally."

She went out and returned with a candle. He lay there panting heavily, like a man who has run a thousand yards, and stared upwards at her with a fixed look.

"What is it, Jean?"

"No . . . o . . . thing. ("Why speak of it? She won't understand," he thought.)

And in truth she did not understand. She picked up the stand, lit his candle, and hurried away to see another visitor off. When she came back he still lay on his back, looking upwards.

"What is it? Do you feel worse?"

"Yes."

She shook her head and sat down.

"Do you know, Jean, I think we must ask Leshchetitsky to come and see you here."

This meant calling the famous specialist, regardless of expense. He smiled malignantly and said "No." She remained a little longer and then went up to him and kissed his forehead.

While she was kissing him he hated her from the bottom of his soul and with difficulty refrained from pushing her away.

"Good-night. Please God you'll sleep."

"Yes."

6

Ivan Ilych saw that he was dying, and he was in continual despair.

In the depth of his heart he knew he was dying, but not only was he not accustomed to the thought, he simply did not and could not grasp it.

The syllogism he had learnt from Kiezewetter's Logic: "Caius is a man, men are mortal, therefore Caius is mortal," had always seemed to him correct as applied to Caius, but certainly not as applied to himself. That Caius—man in the abstract—was mortal, was perfectly correct, but he was not Caius, not an abstract man, but a creature quite, quite separate from all others. He had been little Vanya, with a mamma and a papa, with Mitya and Volodya, with the toys, a coachman and a nurse, afterwards with Katenka and with all the joys, griefs, and delights of childhood, boyhood, and youth. What did Caius know of the smell of that striped leather ball Vanya had been so fond of? Had Caius kissed his mother's hand like that, and did the silk of her dress rustle so for Caius? Had he rioted like that at school when the pastry was bad? Had Caius been in love like that? Could Caius preside at a session as he did? "Caius really was mortal, and it was right for him to die; but for me, little Vanya, Ivan Ilych, with all my thoughts and emotions, it's altogether a different matter. It cannot be that I ought to die. That would be too terrible."

Such was his feeling.

"If I had to die like Caius I should have known it was so. An inner voice would have told me so, but there was nothing of the sort in me and I and all my friends felt that our case was quite different from that of Caius. And now here it is!" he said to himself. "It can't be. It's impossible! But here it is. How is this? How is one to understand it?"

He could not understand it, and tried to drive this false, incorrect, morbid thought away and to replace it by other proper and healthy thoughts. But that thought, and not the thought only but the reality itself, seemed to come and confront him.

And to replace that thought he called up a succession of others, hoping to find in them some support. He tried to get back into the former current of thoughts that had once screened the thought of death from him. But strange to say, all that had formerly shut off, hidden, and destroyed, his consciousness of death, no longer had that effect. Ivan Ilych now spent most of his time in attempting to re-establish that old current. He would say to himself: "I will take up my duties again—after all I used to live by them." And banishing all doubts he would go to the law courts, enter into conversation with his colleagues, and sit carelessly as was his wont, scanning the crowd with a thoughtful look and leaning both his emaciated arms on the arms of his oak chair; bending over as usual to a colleague and drawing his papers nearer he would interchange whispers with him, and then suddenly raising his eyes and sitting erect would pronounce certain words and open the proceedings. But suddenly in the midst of those proceedings the pain in his side, regardless of the stage the proceedings had reached, would begin its own gnawing work. Ivan Ilych would turn his attention to it and try to drive the thought of it away, but without success. *It* would come and stand before him and look at him, and he would be petrified and the light would die out of his eyes, and he would again begin asking himself whether *It* alone was true. And his colleagues and subordinates would see with surprise and distress that he, the brilliant and subtle judge, was becoming confused and making mistakes. He would shake himself, try to pull himself together, manage somehow to bring the sitting to a close, and return home with the sorrowful consciousness that his judicial labours could not as formerly hide from him what he wanted them to hide, and could not deliver him from *It*. And what was worst of all was that *It* drew his attention to itself not in order to make him take some action but only that he should look at *It*, look it straight in the face: look at it and without doing anything, suffer inexpressibly.

And to save himself from this condition Ivan Ilych looked for consolations—new screens—and new screens were found and for a while seemed to save him, but then they immediately fell to pieces or rather became transparent, as if *It* penetrated them and nothing could veil *It*.

In these latter days he would go into the drawing-room he had arranged—that drawing-room where he had fallen and for the sake of which (how bitterly ridiculous it seemed) he had sacrificed his life—for he knew that his illness originated with that knock. He would enter and see that something had scratched the polished table. He would look for the cause of this and find that it was the bronze ornamentation of an album, that had got bent. He would take up the expensive album which he had lovingly arranged, and feel vexed with his daughter and her friend for their untidiness—for the album was torn here and there and some of the photographs turned upside down. He would put it carefully in order and bend the ornamentation back into position. Then it would occur to him to place all those things in another corner of the room, near the plants. He could call the footman, but his daughter or wife would come to help him. They would not agree, and his wife would contradict him, and he would dispute and grow angry. But that was all right, for then he did not think about *It*. *It* was invisible.

But then, when he was moving something himself, his wife would say: "Let the servants do it. You will hurt yourself again." And suddenly *It* would flash through the screen and he would see it. It was just a flash, and he hoped it would disappear, but he would involuntarily pay attention to his side. "It sits there as before, gnawing just the same!" And he could no longer forget *It*, but could distinctly see it looking at him from behind the flowers. "What is it all for?"

"It really is so! I lost my life over that curtain as I might have done when storming a fort. Is that possible? How terrible and how stupid. It can't be true! It can't, but it is."

He would go to his study, lie down, and again be alone with *It*: face to face with *It*. And nothing could be done with *It* except to look at it and shudder.

7

How it happened it is impossible to say because it came about step by step, unnoticed, but in the third month of Ivan Ilych's illness, his wife, his daughter, his son, his acquaintances, the doctors, the servants, and above all he himself, were aware that the whole interest he had for other people was whether he would soon vacate his place, and at last release the living from the discomfort caused by his presence and be himself released from his sufferings.

He slept less and less. He was given opium and hypodermic injections of morphine, but this did not relieve him. The dull depression he experienced in a somnolent condition at first gave him a little relief, but only as something new, afterwards it became as distressing as the pain itself or even more so.

Special foods were prepared for him by the doctors' orders, but all those foods became increasingly distasteful and disgusting to him.

For his excretions also special arrangements had to be made, and this was a torment to him every time—a torment from the uncleanliness, the unseemliness, and the smell, and from knowing that another person had to take part in it.

But just through this most unpleasant matter, Ivan Ilych obtained comfort. Gerasim, the butler's young assistant, always came in to carry the things out. Gerasim was a clean, fresh peasant lad, grown stout on town food and always cheerful and bright. At first the sight of him, in his clean Russian peasant costume, engaged in that disgusting task embarrassed Ivan Ilych.

Once when he got up from the commode too weak to draw up his trousers, he dropped into a soft armchair and looked with horror at his bare, enfeebled thighs with the muscles so sharply marked on them.

Gerasim with a firm light tread, his heavy boots emitting a pleasant smell of tar and fresh winter air, came in wearing a clean Hessian apron, the sleeves of his print shirt tucked up over his strong bare young arms; and refraining from looking at his sick master out of consideration for his feelings, and restraining the joy of life that beamed from his face, he went up to the commode.

"Gerasim!" said Ivan Ilych in a weak voice.

Gerasim started, evidently afraid he might have committed some blunder, and with a rapid movement turned his fresh, kind, simple young face which just showed the first downy signs of a beard.

"Yes, sir?"

"That must be very unpleasant for you. You must forgive me. I am helpless."

"Oh, why, sir," and Gerasim's eyes beamed and he showed his glistening white teeth, "what's a little trouble? It's a case of illness with you, sir."

And his deft strong hands did their accustomed task, and he went out of the room stepping lightly. Five minutes later he as lightly returned.

Ivan Ilych was still sitting in the same position in the armchair.

"Gerasim," he said when the latter had replaced the freshly-washed utensil. "Please come here and help me." Gerasim went up to him. "Lift me up. It is hard for me to get up, and I have sent Dmitri away."

Gerasim went up to him, grasped his master with his strong arms deftly but gently, in the same way that he stepped—lifted him, supported him with one hand, and with the other drew up his trousers and would have set him down again, but Ivan Ilych asked to be led to the sofa. Gerasim, without an effort and without apparent pressure, led him, almost lifting him, to the sofa and placed him on it.

"Thank you. How easily and well you do it all!"

Gerasim smiled again and turned to leave the room. But Ivan Ilych felt his presence such a comfort that he did not want to let him go.

"One thing more, please move up that chair. No, the other one—under my feet. It is easier for me when my feet are raised."

Gerasim brought the chair, set it down gently in place, and raised Ivan Ilych's legs on to it. It seemed to Ivan Ilych that he felt better while Gerasim was holding up his legs.

"It's better when my legs are higher " he said. "Place that cushion under them."

Gerasim did so. He again lifted the legs and placed them, and again Ivan Ilych felt better while Gerasim held his legs. When he set them down Ivan Ilych fancied he felt worse.

"Gerasim," he said. "Are you busy now?"

"Not at all, sir," said Gerasim, who had learnt from the townfolk how to speak to gentlefolk.

"What have you still to do?"

"What have I to do? I've done everything except chopping the logs for tomorrow."

"Then hold my legs up a bit higher, can you?"

"Of course I can. Why not?" And Gerasim raised his master's legs higher and Ivan Ilych thought that in that position he did not feel any pain at all.

"And how about the logs?"

"Don't trouble about that, sir. There's plenty of time."

Ivan Ilych told Gerasim to sit down and hold his legs, and began to talk to him. And strange to say it seemed to him that he felt better while Gerasim held his legs up.

After that Ivan Ilych would sometimes call Gerasim and get him to hold his legs on his shoulders, and he liked talking to him. Gerasim did it all easily, willingly, simply, and with a good nature that touched Ivan Ilych. Health, strength, and vitality in other people were offensive to him, but Gerasim's strength and vitality did not mortify but soothed him.

What tormented Ivan Ilych most was the deception, the lie, which for some reason they all accepted, that he was not dying but was simply ill, and that he only need keep quiet and undergo a treatment and then something very good would result. He however knew that do what they would nothing would come of it, only still more agonizing suffering and death. This deception tortured him—their not wishing to admit what they all knew and what he knew, but wanting to lie to him concerning his terrible condition, and wishing and forcing him to participate in that lie. Those lies—lies enacted over him on the eve of his death and destined to degrade this awful, solemn act to the level of their visitings, their curtains, their sturgeon for dinner—were a terrible agony for Ivan Ilych. And strangely enough, many times when they were going through their antics over him he had been within a hairbreadth of calling out to them: "Stop lying! You know and I know that I am dying. Then at least stop lying about it!" But he had never had the spirit to do it. The awful, terrible act of his dying was, he could see, reduced by those about him to the level of a casual, unpleasant, and almost indecorous incident (as if someone entered a drawing-room diffusing an unpleasant odour) and this was done by that very decorum which he had served all his life long. He saw that no one felt for him, because no one even wished to grasp his position. Only Gerasim recognized it and pitied him. And so Ivan Ilych felt at ease only with him. He felt comforted when Gerasim supported his legs (sometimes all night long) and refused to go to bed, saying: "Don't you worry, Ivan Ilych. I'll get sleep enough later on," or when he suddenly became familiar and exclaimed: "If you weren't sick it would be another matter, but as it is, why should I grudge a little trouble?" Gerasim alone did not lie; everything showed that he alone understood the facts of the case and did not consider it necessary to disguise them, but simply felt sorry for his emaciated and enfeebled master. Once when Ivan Ilych was sending him away he even said straight out: "We shall all of us die, so why should I grudge a little trouble?"—expressing the fact that he did not think his work burdensome, because he was doing it for a dying man and hoped someone would do the same for him when his time came.

Apart from this lying, or because of it, what most tormented Ivan Ilych was that no one pitied him as he wished to be pitied. At certain moments after prolonged suffering he wished most of all (though he would have been ashamed to confess it) for someone to pity him as a sick child is pitied. He longed to be petted and comforted. He knew he was an important functionary, that he had a beard turning grey, and that therefore what he longed for was impossible, but still he longed for it. And in Gerasim's attitude towards him there was something akin to what he wished for, and so that attitude comforted him. Ivan Ilych wanted to weep, wanted to be petted and cried over, and then his colleague Shebek would come, and instead of weeping and being petted, Ivan Ilych would assume a serious, severe, and profound air, and by force of habit would express his opinion on a decision of the Court of Cassation and would stubbornly insist on that view. This falsity around him and within him did more than anything else to poison his last days.

8

It was morning. He knew it was morning because Gerasim had gone, and Peter the footman had come and put out the candles, drawn back one of the curtains, and begun quietly to tidy up. Whether it was morning or evening, Friday or Sunday, made no difference, it was all just the same: the gnawing, unmitigated, agonizing pain, never ceasing for an instant, the consciousness of life inexorably waning but not yet extinguished, the approach of that ever dreaded and hateful Death which was the only reality, and always the same falsity. What were days, weeks, hours, in such a case?

"Will you have some tea, sir?"

"He wants things to be regular, and wishes the gentlefolk to drink tea in the morning," thought Ivan Ilych, and only said "No."

"Wouldn't you like to move onto the sofa, sir?"

"He wants to tidy up the room, and I'm in the way. I am uncleanliness and disorder," he thought, and said only:

"No, leave me alone."

The man went on bustling about. Ivan Ilych stretched out his hand. Peter came up, ready to help.

"What is it, sir?"

"My watch."

Peter took the watch which was close at hand and gave it to his master.

"Half-past eight. Are they up?"

"No, sir, except Vladimir Ivanich" (the son) "who has gone to school. Praskovya Fëdorovna ordered me to wake her if you asked for her. Shall I do so?"

"No, there's no need to." "Perhaps I'd better have some tea," he thought, and added aloud: "Yes, bring me some tea."

Peter went to the door, but Ivan Ilych dreaded being left alone. "How can I keep him here? Oh yes, my medicine." "Peter, give me my medicine." "Why not? Perhaps it may still do me some good." He took a spoonful and swallowed it. "No, it won't help. It's all tomfoolery, all deception," he decided as soon as he became aware of the familiar, sickly, hopeless taste. "No, I can't believe in it any longer. But the pain, why this pain? If it would only cease just for a moment!" And he moaned. Peter turned towards him. "It's all right. Go and fetch me some tea."

Peter went out. Left alone Ivan Ilych groaned not so much with pain, terrible though that was, as from mental anguish. Always and for ever the same, always these endless days and nights. If only it would come quicker! If only *what* would come quicker? Death, darkness? . . . No, no! Anything rather than death!

When Peter returned with the tea on a tray, Ivan Ilych stared at him for a time in perplexity, not realizing who and what he was. Peter was disconcerted by that look and his embarrassment brought Ivan Ilych to himself.

"Oh, tea! All right, put it down. Only help me to wash and put on a clean shirt."

And Ivan Ilych began to wash. With pauses for rest, he washed his hands and then his face, cleaned his teeth, brushed his hair, and looked in the glass. He was terrified by what he saw, especially by the limp way in which his hair clung to his pallid forehead.

While his shirt was being changed he knew that he would be still more frightened at the sight of his body, so he avoided looking at it. Finally he was ready. He drew on a dressing-gown, wrapped himself in a plaid, and sat down in the armchair to take his tea. For a moment he felt refreshed, but as soon as he began to drink the tea he was again aware of the same taste, and the pain also returned. He finished it with an effort, and then lay down stretching out his legs, and dismissed Peter.

Always the same. Now a spark of hope flashes up, then a sea of despair rages, and always pain; always pain, always despair, and always the same. When alone he had a dreadful and distressing desire to call someone, but he knew beforehand that with others present it would be still worse. "Another dose of morphine—to lose consciousness. I will tell him, the doctor, that he must think of something else. It's impossible, impossible, to go on like this."

An hour and another pass like that. But now there is a ring at the door bell. Perhaps it's the doctor? It is. He comes in fresh, hearty, plump, and cheerful, and that look on his face that seems to say: "There now, you're in a panic about something, but we'll arrange it all for you directly!" The doctor knows this expression is out of place here, but he has put it on once for all and can't take it off—like a man who has put on a frock-coat in the morning to pay a round of calls.

The doctor rubs his hands vigorously and reassuringly.

"Brr! How cold it is! There's such a sharp frost; just let me warm myself!" he says, as if it were only a matter of waiting till he was warm, and then he would put everything right.

"Well now, how are you?"

Ivan Ilych feels that the doctor would like to say: "Well, how are our affairs?" but that even he feels that this would not do, and says instead: "What sort of a night have you had?"

Ivan Ilych looks at him as much as to say: "Are you really never ashamed of lying?" But the doctor does not wish to understand this question, and Ivan Ilych says: "Just as terrible as ever. The pain never leaves me and never subsides. If only something . . ."

"Yes, you sick people are always like that. . . . There, now I think I am warm enough. Even Praskovya Fëdorovna, who is so particular, could find no fault with my temperature. Well, now I can say good-morning," and the doctor presses his patient's hand.

Then, dropping his former playfulness, he begins with a most serious face to examine the patient, feeling his pulse and taking his temperature, and then begins the sounding and auscultation.

Ivan Ilych knows quite well and definitely that all this is nonsense and pure deception, but when the doctor, getting down on his knee, leans over him, putting his ear first higher then lower, and performs various gymnastic movements over him with a significant expression on his face, Ivan Ilych submits to it all as he used to submit to the speeches of the lawyers, though he knew very well that they were all lying and why they were lying.

The doctor, kneeling on the sofa, is still sounding him when Praskovya Fëdorovna's silk dress rustles at the door and she is heard scolding Peter for not having let her know of the doctor's arrival.

She comes in, kisses her husband, and at once proceeds to prove that she has been up a long time already, and only owing to a misunderstanding failed to be there when the doctor arrived.

Ivan Ilych looks at her, scans her all over, sets against her the whiteness and plumpness and cleanness of her hands and neck, and gloss of her hair, and the sparkle of her vivacious eyes. He hates her with his whole soul. And the thrill of hatred he feels for her makes him suffer from her touch.

Her attitude towards him and his disease is still the same. Just as the doctor had adopted a certain relation to his patient which he could not abandon, so had she formed one towards him—that he was not doing something he ought to do and was himself to blame, and that she reproached him lovingly for this—and she could not now change that attitude.

"You see he doesn't listen to me and doesn't take his medicine at the proper time. And above all he lies in a position that is no doubt bad for him—with his legs up."

She described how he made Gerasim hold his legs up.

The doctor smiles with a contemptuous affability that said: "What's to be done? These sick people do have foolish fancies of that kind, but we must forgive them."

When the examination was over the doctor looked at his watch, and then Praskovya Fëdorovna announced to Ivan Ilych that it was of course as he pleased, but she had sent today for a celebrated specialist who would examine him and have a consultation with Michael Danilovich (their regular doctor).

"Please don't raise any objections. I am doing this for my own sake," she said ironically, letting it be felt that she was doing it all for his sake and only said this to leave him no right to refuse. He remained silent, knitting his brows. He felt that he was so surrounded and involved in a mesh of falsity that it was hard to unravel anything.

Everything she did for him was entirely for her own sake, and she told him she was doing for herself what she actually was doing for herself, as if that was so incredible that he must understand the opposite.

At half-past eleven the celebrated specialist arrived. Again the sounding began and the significant conversations in his presence and in another room, about the kidneys and the appendix, and the questions and answers, with such an air of importance that again, instead of the real question of life and death which now alone confronted him, the question arose of the kidney and appendix which were not behaving as they ought to and would now be attacked by Michael Danilovich and the specialist and forced to amend their ways.

The celebrated specialist took leave of him with a serious though not hopeless look, and in reply to the timid question Ivan Ilych, with eyes glistening with fear and hope, put to him as to whether there was a chance of recovery, said that he could not vouch for it but there was a possibility. The look of hope with which Ivan Ilych watched the doctor out was so pathetic that Praskovya Fëdorovna, seeing it, even wept as she left the room to hand the doctor his fee.

The gleam of hope kindled by the doctor's encouragement did not last long. The same room, the same pictures, curtains, wall-paper, medicine bottles, were all there, and the same aching suffering body, and Ivan Ilych began to moan. They gave him a subcutaneous injection and he sank into oblivion.

It was twilight when he came to. They brought him his dinner and he swallowed some beef tea with difficulty, and then everything was the same again and night was coming on.

After dinner, at seven o'clock, Praskovya Fëdorovna came into the room in evening dress, her full bosom pushed up by her corset, and with traces of powder on her face. She had reminded him in the morning that they were going to the theatre. Sarah Bernhardt was visiting the town and they had a box, which he had insisted on their taking. Now he had forgotten about it and her toilet offended him, but he concealed his vexation when he remembered that he had himself insisted on their securing a box and going because it would be an instructive and aesthetic pleasure for the children.

Praskovya Fëdorovna came in, self-satisfied but yet with a rather guilty air. She sat down and asked how he was, but, as he saw, only for the sake of asking and not in order to learn about it, knowing that there was nothing to learn—and then went on to what she really wanted to say: that she would not on any account have gone but that the box had been taken and Helen and their daughter were going, as well as Petrishchev (the examining magistrate, their daughter's fiancé) and that it was out of the question to let them go alone; but that she would have much preferred to sit with him for a while; and he must be sure to follow the doctor's orders while she was away.

"Oh, and Fëdor Petrovich" (the fiancé) "would like to come in. May he? And Lisa?"

"All right."

Their daughter came in in full evening dress, her fresh young flesh exposed (making a show of that very flesh which in his own case caused so much suffering), strong, healthy, evidently in love, and impatient with illness, suffering, and death, because they interfered with her happiness.

Fëdor Petrovich came in too, in evening dress, his hair curled *a la Capoul*, a tight stiff collar round his long sinewy neck, an enormous white shirt-front and narrow black trousers tightly stretched over his strong thighs. He had one white glove tightly drawn on, and was holding his opera hat in his hand.

Following him the schoolboy crept in unnoticed, in a new uniform, poor little fellow, and wearing gloves. Terribly dark shadows showed under his eyes, the meaning of which Ivan Ilych knew well.

His son had always seemed pathetic to him, and now it was dreadful to see the boy's frightened look of pity. It seemed to Ivan Ilych that Vasya was the only one besides Gerasim who understood and pitied him.

They all sat down and again asked how he was. A silence followed. Lisa asked her mother about the opera-glasses, and there was an altercation between mother and daughter as to who had taken them and where they had been put. This occasioned some unpleasantness.

Fëdor Petrovich inquired of Ivan Ilych whether he had ever seen Sarah Bernhardt. Ivan Ilych did not at first catch the question, but then replied: "No, have you seen her before?"

"Yes, in *Adrienne Lecouvreur.*"

Praskovya Fëdorovna mentioned some rôles in which Sarah Bernhardt was particularly good. Her daughter disagreed. Conversation sprang up as to the elegance and realism of her acting—the sort of conversation that is always repeated and is always the same.

In the midst of the conversation Fëdor Petrovich glanced at Ivan Ilych and became silent. The others also looked at him and grew silent. Ivan Ilych was staring with glittering eyes straight before him, evidently indignant with them. This had to be rectified, but it was impossible to do so. The silence had to be broken, but for a time no one dared to break it and they all became afraid that the conventional deception would suddenly become obvious and the truth become plain to all. Lisa was the first to pluck up courage and break that silence, but by trying to hide what everybody was feeling, she betrayed it.

"Well, if we are going it's time to start," she said, looking at her watch, a present from her father, and with a faint and significant smile at Fëdor Petrovich relating to something known only to them. She got up with a rustle of her dress.

They all rose, said good-night, and went away.

When they had gone it seemed to Ivan Ilych that he felt better; the falsity had gone with them. But the pain remained—that same pain and that same fear that made everything monotonously alike, nothing harder and nothing easier. Everything was worse.

Again minute followed minute and hour followed hour. Everything remained the same and there was no cessation. And the inevitable end of it all became more and more terrible.

"Yes, send Gerasim here," he replied to a question Peter asked.

9

His wife returned late at night. She came in on tiptoe, but he heard her, opened his eyes, and made haste to close them again. She wished to send Gerasim away and to sit with him herself, but he opened his eyes and said: "No, go away."

"Are you in great pain?"

"Always the same."

"Take some opium."

He agreed and took some. She went away.

Till about three in the morning he was in a state of stupefied misery. It seemed to him that he and his pain were being thrust into a narrow, deep black sack, but though they were pushed further and further in they could not be pushed to the bottom. And this, terrible enough in itself, was accompanied by suffering. He was frightened yet wanted to fall through the sack, he struggled but yet co-operated. And suddenly he broke through, fell, and regained consciousness. Gerasim was sitting at the foot of the bed dozing quietly and patiently, while he himself lay with his emaciated stockinged legs resting on Gerasim's shoulders; the same shaded candle was there and the same unceasing pain.

"Go away, Gerasim," he whispered.

"It's all right, sir. I'll stay a while."

"No. Go away."

He removed his legs from Gerasim's shoulders, turned sideways onto his arm, and felt sorry for himself. He only waited till Gerasim had gone into the next room and then restrained himself no longer but wept like a child. He wept on account of his helplessness, his terrible loneliness, the cruelty of man, the cruelty of God, and the absence of God.

"Why hast Thou done all this? Why hast Thou brought me here? Why, why dost Thou torment me so terribly?"

He did not expect an answer and yet wept because there was no answer and could be none. The pain again grew more acute, but he did not stir and did not call. He said to himself: "Go on! Strike me! But what is it for? What have I done to Thee? What is it for?"

Then he grew quiet and not only ceased weeping but even held his breath and became all attention. It was as though he were listening not to an audible voice but to the voice of his soul, to the current of thoughts arising within him.

"What is it you want?" was the first clear conception capable of expres sion in words, that he heard.

"What do you want? What do you want?" he repeated to himself.

"What do I want? To live and not to suffer," he answered.

And again he listened with such concentrated attention that even his pain did not distract him.

"To live? How?" asked his inner voice.

"Why, to live as I used to—well and pleasantly."

"As you lived before, well and pleasantly?" the voice repeated.

And in imagination he began to recall the best moments of his pleasant life. But strange to say none of those best moments of his pleasant life now seemed at all what they had then seemed—none of them except the first recollections of childhood. There, in childhood, there had been something really pleasant with which it would be possible to live if it could return. But the child who had experienced that happiness existed no longer, it was like a reminiscence of somebody else.

As soon as the period began which had produced the present Ivan Ilych, all that had then seemed joys now melted before his sight and turned into something trivial and often nasty.

And the further he departed from childhood and the nearer he came to the present the more worthless and doubtful were the joys. This began with the School of Law. A little that was really good was still found there—there was light-heartedness, friendship, and hope. But in the upper classes there had already been fewer of such good moments. Then during the first years of his official career, when he was in the service of the Governor, some pleasant moments again occurred: they were the memories of love for a woman. Then all became confused and there was still less of what was good; later on again there was still less that was good, and the further he went the less there was. His marriage, a mere accident, then the disenchantment that followed it, his wife's bad breath and the sensuality and hypocrisy: then that deadly official life and those preoccupations about money, a year of it, and two, and ten, and twenty, and always the same thing. And the longer it lasted the more deadly it became. "It is as if I had been going downhill while I imagined I was going up. And that is really what it was. I was going up in public opinion, but to the same extent life was ebbing away from me. And now it is all done and there is only death."

"Then what does it mean? Why? It can't be that life is so senseless and horrible. But if it really has been so horrible and senseless, why must I die and die in agony? There is something wrong!"

"Maybe I did not live as I ought to have done," it suddenly occurred to him. "But how could that be, when I did everything properly?" he replied, and immediately dismissed from his mind this, the sole solution of all the riddles of life and death, as something quite impossible.

"Then what do you want now? To live? Live how? Live as you lived in the law courts when the usher proclaimed 'The judge is coming!' The judge is coming, the judge!" he repeated to himself. "Here he is, the judge. But I am not guilty!" he exclaimed angrily. "What is it for?" And he ceased crying, but turning his face to the wall continued to ponder on the same question: Why, and for what purpose, is there all this horror? But however much he pondered he found no answer. And whenever the thought occurred to him, as it often did, that it all resulted from his not having lived as he ought to have done, he at once recalled the correctness of his whole life and dismissed so strange an idea.

10

Another fortnight passed. Ivan Ilych now no longer left his sofa. He would not lie in bed but lay on the safa, facing the wall nearly all the time. He suffered ever the same unceasing agonies and in his loneliness pondered always on the same insoluble question: "What is this? Can it be that it is Death?" And the inner voice answered: "Yes, it is Death."

"Why these sufferings?" And the voice answered, "For no reason—they just are so." Beyond and besides this there was nothing.

From the very beginning of his illness, every since he had first been to see the doctor, Ivan Ilych's life had been divided between two contrary and alternating moods: now it was despair and the expectation of this uncomprehended and terrible death, and now hope and an intently interested observation of the functioning of his organs. Now before his eyes there was only a kidney or an intestine that temporarily evaded its duty, and now only that incomprehensible and dreadful death from which it was impossible to escape.

These two states of mind had alternated from the very beginning of his illness, but the further it progressed the more doubtful and fantastic became the conception of the kidney, and the more real the sense of impending death.

He had but to call to mind what he had been three months before and what he was now, to call to mind with what regularity he had been going downhill, for every possibility of hope to be shattered.

Latterly during that loneliness in which he found himself as he lay facing the back of the sofa, a loneliness in the midst of a populous town and surrounded by numerous acquaintances and relations but that yet could not have been more complete anywhere—either at the bottom of the sea or under the earth—during that terrible loneliness Ivan Ilych had lived only in memories of the past. Pictures of his past rose before him one after another. They always began with what was nearest in time and then went back to what was most remote—to his childhood—and rested there. If he thought of the stewed prunes that had been offered him that day, his mind went back to the raw shrivelled French plums of his childhood, their peculiar flavour and the flow of saliva when he sucked their stones, and along with the memory of that taste came a whole series of memories of those days: his nurse, his brother, and their toys. "No, I mustn't think of that. . . . It is too painful," Ivan Ilych said to himself, and brought himself back to the present—to the button on the back of the sofa and the creases in its morocco. "Morocco is expensive, but it does not wear well: there had been a quarrel about it. It was a different kind of quarrel and a different kind of morocco that time when we tore father's portfolio and were punished, and mamma brought us some tarts. . . ." And again his thoughts dwelt on his childhood, and again it was painful and he tried to banish them and fix his mind on something else.

Then again together with that chain of memories another series passed through his mind—of how his illness had progressed and grown worse. There also the further back he looked the more life there had been. There had been more of what was good in life and more of life itself. The two merged together. "Just as the pain went on getting worse and worse, so my life grew worse and worse," he thought. "There is one bright spot there at the back, at the beginning of life, and afterwards all becomes blacker and blacker and proceeds more and more rapidly—in inverse ratio to the square of the distance from death," thought Ivan Ilych. And the example of a stone falling downwards with increasing velocity entered his mind. Life, a series of increasing sufferings, flies further and further towards its end—the most terrible suffering. "I am flying. . . ." He shuddered, shifted himself, and tried to resist, but was already aware that resistance was impossible, and again with eyes weary of gazing but unable to cease seeing what was before them, he stared at the back of the sofa and waited—awaiting that dreadful fall and shock and destruction.

"Resistance is impossible!" he said to himself. "If I could only understand what it is all for! But that too is impossible. An explanation would be possible if it could be said that I have not lived as I ought to. But it is impossible to say that," and he remembered all the legality, correctitude, and propriety of his life. "That at any rate can certainly not be admitted," he thought, and his lips smiled ironically as if someone could see that smile and be taken in by it. "There is no explanation! Agony, death . . . What for?"

11

Another two weeks went by in this way and during that fortnight an event occurred that Ivan Ilych and his wife had desired. Petrishchev formally proposed. It happened in the evening. The next day Praskovya Fëdorovna came into her husband's room considering how best to inform him of it, but that very night there had been a fresh change for the worse in his condition. She found him still lying on the sofa but in a different position. He lay on his back, groaning and staring fixedly straight in front of him.

She began to remind him of his medicines, but he turned his eyes towards her with such a look that she did not finish what she was saying; so great an animosity, to her in particular, did that look express.

"For Christ's sake let me die in peace!" he said.

She would have gone away, but just then their daughter came in and went up to say good morning. He looked at her as he had done at his wife, and in reply to her inquiry about his health said dryly that he would soon free them all of himself. They were both silent and after sitting with him for a while went away.

"Is it our fault?" Lisa said to her mother. "It's as if we were to blame! I am sorry for papa, but why should we be tortured?"

The doctor came at his usual time. Ivan Ilych answered "Yes" and "No," never taking his angry eyes from him, and at last said: "You know you can do nothing for me, so leave me alone."

"We can ease your sufferings."

"You can't even do that. Let me be."

The doctor went into the drawing-room and told Praskovya Fëdorovna that the case was very serious and that the only resource left was opium to allay her husband's sufferings, which must be terrible.

It was true, as the doctor said, that Ivan Ilych's physical sufferings were terrible, but worse than the physical sufferings were his mental sufferings, which were his chief torture.

His mental sufferings were due to the fact that that night, as he looked at Gerasim's sleepy, good-natured face with its prominent cheek-bones, the question suddenly occurred to him: "What if my whole life has really been wrong?"

It occurred to him that what had appeared perfectly impossible before, namely that he had not spent his life as he should have done, might after all be true. It occurred to him that his scarcely perceptible attempts to struggle against what was considered good by the most highly placed people, those scarcely noticeable impulses which he had immediately suppressed, might have been the real thing and all the rest false. And his professional duties and the whole arrangement of his life and of his family, and all his social and official interests, might all have been false. He tried to defend all those things to himself and suddenly felt the weakness of what he was defending. There was nothing to defend.

"But if that is so," he said to himself, "and I am leaving this life with the consciousness that I have lost all that was given me and it is impossible to rectify it—what then?"

He lay on his back and began to pass his life in review in quite a new way. In the morning when he saw first his footman, then his wife, then his daughter, and then the doctor, their every word and movement confirmed to him the awful truth that had been revealed to him during the night. In them he saw himself—all that for which he had lived—and saw clearly that it was not real at all, but a terrible and huge deception which had hidden both life and death. This consciousness intensified his physical suffering tenfold. He groaned and tossed about, and pulled at his clothing which choked and stifled him. And he hated them on that account.

He was given a large dose of opium and became unconscious, but at noon his sufferings began again. He drove everybody away and tossed from side to side.

His wife came to him and said:

"Jean, my dear, do this for me. It can't do any harm and often helps. Healthy people often do it."

He opened his eyes wide.

"What? Take communion? Why? It's unnecessary! However . . ."

She began to cry.

"Yes, do, my dear. I'll send for our priest. He is such a nice man."

"All right. Very well," he muttered.

When the priest came and heard his confession, Ivan Ilych was softened and seemed to feel a relief from his doubts and consequently from his sufferings, and for a moment there came a ray of hope. He again began to think of the vermiform appendix and the possibility of correcting it. He received the sacrament with tears in his eyes.

When they laid him down again afterwards he felt a moment's ease, and the hope that he might live awoke in him again. He began to think of the operation that had been suggested to him. "To live! I want to live!" he said to himself.

His wife came in to congratulate him after his communion, and when uttering the usual conventional words she added:

"You feel better, don't you?"

Without looking at her he said "Yes."

Her dress, her figure, the expression of her face, the tone of her voice, all revealed the same thing. "This is wrong, it is not as it should be. All you have lived for and still live for is falsehood and deception, hiding life and death from you." And as soon as he admitted that thought, his hatred and his agonizing physical suffering again sprang up, and with that suffering a consciousness of the unavoidable, approaching end. And to this was added a new sensation of grinding shooting pain and a feeling of suffocation.

The expression of his face when he uttered that "yes" was dreadful. Having uttered it, he looked her straight in the eyes, turned on his face with a rapidity extraordinary in his weak state and shouted:

"Go away! Go away and leave me alone!"

12

From that moment the screaming began that continued for three days, and was so terrible that one could not hear it through two closed doors without horror. At the moment he answered his wife he realized that he was lost, that there was no return, that the end had come, the very end, and his doubts were still unsolved and remained doubts.

"Oh! Oh! Oh!" he cried in various intonations. He had begun by screaming "I won't!" and continued screaming on the letter *O*.

For three whole days, during which time did not exist for him, he struggled in that black sack into which he was being thrust by an invisible, resistless force. He struggled as a man condemned to death struggles in the hands of the executioner, knowing that he cannot save himself. And every moment he felt that despite all his efforts he was drawing mearer and nearer to what terrified him. He felt that his agony was due to his being thrust into that black hole and still more to his not being able to get right into it. He was hindered from getting into it by his conviction that his life had been a good one. That very justification of his life held him fast and prevented his moving forward, and it caused him most torment of all.

Suddenly some force struck him in the chest and side, making it still harder to breathe, and he fell through the hole and there at the bottom was a light. What had happened to him was like the sensation one sometimes experiences in a railway carriage when one thinks one is going backwards while one is really going forwards and suddenly becomes aware of the real direction.

"Yes, it was all not the right thing," he said to himself, "but that's no matter. It can be done. But what *is* the right thing?" he asked himself, and suddenly grew quiet.

This occurred at the end of the third day, two hours before his death. Just then his schoolboy son had crept softly in and gone up to the bedside. The dying man was still screaming desperately and waving his arms. His hand fell on the boy's head, and the boy caught it, pressed it to his lips, and began to cry.

At that very moment Ivan Ilych fell through and caught sight of the light, and it was revealed to him that though his life had not been what it should have been, this could still be rectified. He asked himself, "What *is* the right thing?" and grew still, listening. Then he felt that someone was kissing his hand. He opened his eyes, looked at his son, and felt sorry for him. His wife came up to him and he glanced at her. She was gazing at him open-mouthed, with undried tears on her nose and cheek and a despairing look on her face. He felt sorry for her too.

"Yes, I am making them wretched," he thought. "They are sorry, but it will be better for them when I die." He wished to say this but had not the strength to utter it. "Besides, why speak? I must act," he thought. With a look at his wife he indicated his son and said: "Take him away . . . sorry for him . . . sorry for you too. . . ." He tried to add, "forgive me," but said "forgo" and waved his hand, knowing that He whose understanding mattered would understand.

And suddenly it grew clear to him that what had been oppressing him and would not leave him was all dropping away at once from two sides, from ten sides, and from all sides. He was sorry for them, he must act so as not to hurt them: release them and free himself from these sufferings. "How good and how simple!" he thought. "And the pain?" he asked himself. "What has become of it? Where are you, pain?"

He turned his attention to it.

"Yes, here it is. Well, what of it? Let the pain be."

"And death . . . where is it?"

He sought his former accustomed fear of death and did not find it. "Where is it? What death?" There was no fear because there was no death.

In place of death there was light.

"So that's what it is!" he suddenly exclaimed aloud "What joy!"

To him all this happened in a single instant, and the meaning of that instant did not change. For those present his agony continued for another two hours. Something rattled in his throat, his emaciated body twitched, then the gasping and rattle became less and less frequent.

"It is finished!" said someone near him.

He heard these words and repeated them in his soul.

"Death is finished," he said to himself. "It is no more!"

He drew in a breath, stopped in the midst of a sigh, stretched out, and died.

DORIS LESSING

The OLD CHIEF MSHLANGA

They were good, the years of ranging the bush over her father's farm which, like every white farm, was largely unused, broken only occasionally by small patches of cultivation. In between, nothing but trees, the long sparse grass, thorn and cactus and gully, grass and outcrop and thorn. And a jutting piece of rock which had been thrust up from the warm soil of Africa unimaginable eras of time ago, washed into hollows and whorls by sun and wind that had travelled so many thousands of miles of space and bush, would hold the weight of a small girl whose eyes were sightless for anything but a pale willowed river, a pale gleaming castle—a small girl singing: "Out flew the web and floated wide, the mirror cracked from side to side . . ."

Pushing her way through the green aisles of the mealie stalks, the leaves arching like cathedrals veined with sunlight far overhead, with the packed red earth underfoot, a fine lace of red starred witchweed would summon up a black bent figure croaking premonitions: the Northern witch, bred of cold Northern forests, would stand before her among the mealie fields, and it was the mealie fields that faded and fled, leaving her among the gnarled roots of an oak, snow falling thick and soft and white, the woodcutter's fire glowing red welcome through crowding tree trunks.

A white child, opening its eyes curiously on a sun-suffused landscape, a gaunt and violent landscape, might be supposed to accept it as her own, to take the msasa trees and the thorn trees as familiars, to feel her blood running free and responsive to the swing of the seasons.

This child could not see a msasa tree, or the thorn, for what they were. Her books held tales of alien fairies, her rivers ran slow and peaceful, and she knew the shape of the leaves of an ash or an oak, the names of the little creatures that lived in English streams, when the words "the veld" meant strangeness, though she could remember nothing else.

Because of this, for many years, it was the veld that seemed unreal; the sun was a foreign sun, and the wind spoke a strange language.

The black people on the farm were as remote as the trees and the rocks. They were an amorphous black mass, mingling and thinning and massing like tadpoles, faceless, who existed merely to serve, to say "Yes, Baas," take their money and go. They changed season by season, moving from one farm to the next, according to their outlandish needs, which one did not have to understand, coming from perhaps hundreds of miles north or east, passing on after a few months—where? Perhaps even as far away as the fabled gold mines of Johannesburg, where the pay was so much better than the few shillings a month and the double handful of mealie meal twice a day which they earned in that part of Africa.

The child was taught to take them for granted: the servants in the house would come running a hundred yards to pick up a book if she dropped it. She was called "Nkosikaas"—Chieftainess, even by the black children her own age.

Later, when the farm grew too small to hold her curiosity, she carried a gun in the crook of her arm and wandered miles a day, from vlei to vlei, from *kopje* to *kopje,* accompanied by two dogs: the dogs and the gun were an armour against fear. Because of them she never felt fear.

If a native came into sight along the kaffir paths half a mile away, the dogs would flush him up a tree as if he were a bird. If he expostulated (in his uncouth language which was by itself ridiculous) that was cheek. If one was in a good mood, it could be a matter for laughter. Otherwise one passed on, hardlv glancing at the angry man in the tree.

On the rare occasions when white children met together they could amuse themselves by hailing a passing native in order to make a buffoon of him; they could set the dogs on him and watch him run; they could tease a small black child as if he were a puppy—save that they would not throw stones and sticks at a dog without a sense of guilt.

Later still, certain questions presented themselves in the child's mind; and because the answers were not easy to accept, they were silenced by an even greater arrogance of manner.

It was even impossible to think of the black people who worked about the house as friends, for if she talked to one of them, her mother would come running anxiously: "Come away; you mustn't talk to natives."

It was this instilled consciousness of danger, of something unpleasant, that made it easy to laugh out loud, crudely, if a servant made a mistake in his English or if he failed to understand an order—there is a certain kind of laughter that is fear, afraid of itself.

One evening, when I was about fourteen, I was walking down the side of a mealie field that had been newly ploughed, so that the great red clods showed fresh and tumbling to the vlei beyond, like a choppy red sea; it was that hushed and listening hour, when the birds send long sad calls from tree to tree, and all the colours of earth and sky and leaf are deep and golden. I had my rifle in the curve of my arm, and the dogs were at my heels.

In front of me, perhaps a couple of hundred yards away, a group of three Africans came into sight around the side of a big antheap. I whistled the dogs close in to my skirts and let the gun swing in my hand, and advanced, waiting for them to move aside, off the path, in respect for my passing. But they came on steadily, and the dogs looked up at me for the command to chase. I was angry. It was "cheek" for a native not to stand off a path, the moment he caught sight of you.

In front walked an old man, stooping his weight on to a stick, his hair grizzled white, a dark red blanket slung over his shoulders like a cloak. Behind him came two young men, carrying bundles of pots, assegais, hatchets.

The group was not a usual one. They were not natives seeking work. These had an air of dignity, of quietly following their own purpose. It was the dignity that checked my tongue. I walked quietly on, talking softly to the growling dogs, till I was ten paces away. Then the old man stopped, drawing his blanket close.

"Morning, Nkosikaas," he said, using the customary greeting for any time of the day.

"Good morning," I said. "Where are you going?" My voice was a little truculent.

The old man spoke in his own language, then one of the young men stepped forward politely and said in careful English: "My Chief travels to see his brothers beyond the river."

A Chief! I thought, understanding the pride that made the old man stand before me like an equal—more than an equal, for he showed courtesy, and I showed none.

The old man spoke again, wearing dignity like an inherited garment, still standing ten paces off, flanked by his entourage, not looking at me (that would have been rude) but directing his eyes somewhere over my head at the trees.

"You are the little Nkosikaas from the farm of Baas Jordan?"

"That's right," I said.

"Perhaps your father does not remember," said the interpreter for the old man, "but there was an affair with some goats. I remember seeing you when you were . . ." The young man held his hand at knee level and smiled.

We all smiled.

"What is your name?" I asked

"This is Chief Mshlanga," said the young man.

"I will tell my father that I met you," I said.

The old man said: "My greetings to your father, little Nkosikaas."

"Good morning," I said politely, finding the politeness difficult, from lack of use.

"Morning, little Nkosikaas," said the old man, and stood aside to let me pass.

I went by, my gun hanging awkwardly, the dogs sniffing and growling, cheated of their favourite game of chasing natives like animals.

Not long afterwards I read in an old explorer's book the phrase: "Chief Mshlanga's country." It went like this: "Our destination was Chief Mshlanga's country, to the north of the river; and it was our desire to ask his permission to prospect for gold in his territory."

The phrase "ask his permission" was so extraordinary to a white child, brought up to consider all natives as things to use, that it revived those questions, which could not be suppressed: they fermented slowly in my mind.

On another occasion one of those old prospectors who still move over Africa looking for neglected reefs, with their hammers and tents, and pans for sifting gold from crushed rock, came to the farm and, in talking of the old days, used that phrase again: "This was the Old Chief's country," he said. "It stretched from those mountains over there way back to the river, hundreds of miles of country." That was his name for our district: "The Old Chief's Country"; he did not use our name for it—a new phrase which held no implication of usurped ownership.

As I read more books about the time when this part of Africa was opened up, not much more than fifty years before, I found Old Chief Mshlanga had been a famous man, known to all the explorers and prospectors. But then he had been young; or maybe it was his father or uncle they spoke of—I never found out.

During that year I met him several times in the part of the farm that was traversed by natives moving over the country. I learned that the path up the side of the big red field where the birds sang was the recognized highway for migrants. Perhaps I even haunted it in the hope of meeting him: being greeted by him, the exchange of courtesies, seemed to answer the questions that troubled me.

Soon I carried a gun in a different spirit; I used it for shooting food and not to give me confidence. And now the dogs learned better manners. When I saw a native approaching, we offered and took greetings; and slowly that other landscape in my mind faded, and my feet struck directly on the African soil, and I saw the shapes of tree and hill clearly, and the black people moved back, as it were, out of my life: it was as if I stood aside to watch a slow intimate dance of landscape and men, a very old dance, whose steps I could not learn.

But I thought: this is my heritage, too; I was bred here; it is my country as well as the black man's country; and there is plenty of room for all of us, without elbowing each other off the pavements and roads.

It seemed it was only necessary to let free that respect I felt when I was talking with old Chief Mshlanga, to let both black and white people meet gently, with tolerance for each other's differences: it seemed quite easy.

Then, one day, something new happened. Working in our house as servants were always three natives: cook, houseboy, garden boy. They used to change as the farm natives changed: staying for a few months, then moving on to a new job, or back home to their kraals. They were thought of as "good" or "bad" natives; which meant: how did they behave as servants? Were they lazy, efficient, obedient, or disrespectful? If the family felt good-humoured, the phrase was: "What can you expect from raw black savages?" If we were angry, we said: "These damned niggers, we would be much better off without them."

One day, a white policeman was on his rounds of the district, and he said laughingly: "Did you know you have an important man in your kitchen?"

"What!" exclaimed my mother sharply. "What do you mean?"

"A Chief's son." The policeman seemed amused. "He'll boss the tribe when the old man dies."

"He'd better not put on a Chief's son act with me," said my mother.

When the policeman left, we looked with different eyes at our cook: he was a good worker, but he drank too much at week-ends—that was how we knew him.

He was a tall youth, with very black skin, like black polished metal, his tightly growing black hair parted white man's fashion at one side, with a metal comb from the store stuck into it; very polite, very distant, very quick to obey an order. Now that it had been pointed out, we said: "Of course, you can see. Blood always tells."

My mother became strict with him now she knew about his birth and prospects. Sometimes, when she lost her temper, she would say: "You aren't the Chief yet, you know." And he would answer her very quietly, his eyes on the ground: "Yes, Nkosikaas."

One afternoon he asked for a whole day off, instead of the customary half-day, to go home next Sunday.

"How can you go home in one day?"

"It will take me half an hour on my bicycle," he explained.

I watched the direction he took; and the next day I went off to look for this kraal; I understood he must be Chief Mshlanga's successor: there was no other kraal near enough our farm.

Beyond our boundaries on that side the country was new to me. I followed unfamiliar paths past *kopjes* that till now had been part of the jagged horizon, hazed with distance. This was Government land, which had never been cultivated by white men; at first I could not understand why it was that it appeared, in merely crossing the boundary, I had entered a completely fresh type of landscape. It was a wide green valley, where a small river sparkled, and vivid water-birds darted over the rushes. The grass was thick and soft to my calves, the trees stood tall and shapely.

I was used to our farm, whose hundreds of acres of harsh eroded soil bore trees that had been cut for the mine furnaces and had grown thin and twisted, where the cattle had dragged the grass flat, leaving innumerable criss-crossing trails that deepened each season into gullies, under the force of the rains.

This country had been left untouched, save for prospectors whose picks had struck a few sparks from the surface of the rocks as they wandered by; and for migrant natives whose passing had left, perhaps, a charred patch on the trunk of a tree where their evening fire had nestled.

It was very silent: a hot morning with pigeons cooing throatily, the midday shadows lying dense and thick with clear yellow spaces of sunlight between and in all that wide green park-like valley, not a human soul but myself.

I was listening to the quick regular tapping of a woodpecker when slowly a chill feeling seemed to grow up from the small of my back to my shoulders, in a constricting spasm like a shudder, and at the roots of my hair a tingling sensation began and ran down over the surface of my flesh, leaving me goosefleshed and cold, though I was damp with sweat. Fever? I thought; then uneasily, turned to look over my shoulder; and realized suddenly that this was fear. It was extraordinary, even humiliating. It was a new fear. For all the years I had walked by myself over this country I had never known a moment's uneasiness; in the beginning because I had been supported by a gun and the dogs, then because I had learnt an easy friendliness for the Africans I might encounter.

I had read of this feeling, how the bigness and silence of Africa, under the ancient sun, grows dense and takes shape in the mind, till even the birds seem to call menacingly, and a deadly spirit comes out of the trees and the rocks. You move warily, as if your very passing disturbs something old and evil, something dark and big and angry that might suddenly rear and strike from behind. You look at groves of entwined trees, and picture the animals that might be lurking there; you look at the river running slowly, dropping from level to level through the vlei, spreading into pools where at night the bucks come to drink, and the crocodiles rise and drag them by their soft noses into underwater caves. Fear possessed me. I found I was turning round and round, because of that shapeless menace behind me that might reach out and take me; I kept glancing at the files of *kopjes* which, seen from a different angle, seemed to change with every step so that even known landmarks, like a big mountain that had sentinelled my world since I first became conscious of it, showed an unfamiliar sunlit valley among its foothills. I did not know where I was. I was lost. Panic seized me. I found I was spinning round and round, staring anxiously at this tree and that, peering up at the sun which appeared to have moved into an eastern slant, shedding the sad yellow light of sunset. Hours must have passed! I looked at my watch and found that this state of meaningless terror had lasted perhaps ten minutes.

The point was that it was meaningless. I was not ten miles from home: I had only to take my way back along the valley to find myself at the fence; away among the foothills of the *kopjes* gleamed the roof of a neighbour's house, and a couple of hours' walking would reach it. This was the sort of fear that contracts the flesh of a dog at night and sets him howling at the full moon. It had nothing to do with what I thought or felt; and I was more disturbed by the fact that I could become its victim than of the physical sensation itself: I walked steadily on, quietened, in a divided mind, watching my own pricking nerves and apprehensive glances from side to side with a disgusted amusement. Deliberately I set myself to think of this village I was seeking, and what I should do when I entered it—if I could find it, which was doubtful, since I was walking aimlessly and it might be anywhere in the hundreds of thousands of acres of bush that stretched about me. With my mind on that village, I realized that a new sensation was added to the fear: loneliness. Now such a terror of isolation invaded me that I could hardly walk; and if it were not that I came over the crest of a small rise and saw a village below me, I should have turned and gone home. It was a cluster of thatched huts in a clearing among trees. There were neat patches of mealies and pumpkins and millet, and cattle grazed under some trees at a distance. Fowls scratched among the huts, dogs lay sleeping on the grass, and goats friezed a *kopje* that jutted up beyond a tributary of the river lying like an enclosing arm round the village.

As I came close I saw the huts were lovingly decorated with patterns of yellow and red and ochre mud on the walls; and the thatch was tied in place with plaits of straw.

This was not at all like our farm compound, a dirty and neglected place, a temporary home for migrants who had no roots in it.

And now I did not know what to do next. I called a small black boy, who was sitting on a lot playing a stringed gourd, quite naked except for the strings of blue beads round his neck, and said: "Tell the Chief I am here." The child stuck his thumb in his mouth and stared shyly back at me.

For minutes I shifted my feet on the edge of what seemed a deserted village, till at last the child scuttled off, and then some women came. They were draped in bright cloths, with brass glinting in their ears and on their arms. They also stared, silently; then turned to chatter among themselves.

I said again: "Can I see Chief Mshlanga?" I saw they caught the name; they did not understand what I wanted. I did not understand myself.

At last I walked through them and came past the huts and saw a clearing under a big shady tree, where a dozen old men sat crosslegged on the ground, talking. Chief Mshlanga was leaning back against the tree, holding a gourd in his hand, from which he had been drinking. When he saw me, not a muscle of his face moved, and I could see he was not pleased: perhaps he was afflicted with my own shyness, due to being unable to find the right forms of courtesy for the occasion. To meet me, on our own farm, was one thing; but I should not have come here. What had I expected? I could not join them socially: the thing was unheard of. Bad enough that I, a white girl, should be walking the veld alone as a white man might: and in this part of the bush where only Government officials had the right to move.

Again I stood, smiling foolishly, while behind me stood the groups of brightly clad, chattering women, their faces alert with curiosity and interest, and in front of me sat the old men, with old lined faces, their eyes guarded, aloof. It was a village of ancients and children and women. Even the two young men who kneeled beside the Chief were not those I had seen with him previously: the young men were all away working on the white men's farms and mines, and the Chief must depend on relatives who were temporarily on holiday for his attendants.

"The small white Nkosikaas is far from home," remarked the old man at last.

"Yes," I agreed, "it is far." I wanted to say: "I have come to pay you a friendly visit, Chief Mshlanga." I could not say it. I might now be feeling an urgent helpless desire to get to know these men and women as people, to be accepted by them as a friend, but the truth was I had set out in a spirit of curiosity: I had wanted to see the village that one day our cook, the reserved and obedient young man who got drunk on Sundays, would one day rule over.

"The child of Nkosi Jordan is welcome," said Chief Mshlanga.

"Thank you," I said, and could think of nothing more to say. There was a silence, while the flies rose and began to buzz around my head; and the wind shook a little in the thick green tree that spread its branches over the old men.

"Good morning," I said at last. "I have to return now to my home."

"Morning, little Nkosikaas," said Chief Mshlanga.

I walked away from the indifferent village, over the rise past the staring amber-eyed goats, down through the tall stately trees into the great rich green valley where the river meandered and the pigeons cooed tales of plenty and the woodpecker tapped softly.

The fear had gone; the loneliness had set into stiff-necked stoicism; there was now a queer hostility in the landscape, a cold, hard, sullen indomitability that walked with me, as strong as a wall, as intangible as smoke; it seemed to say to me: you walk here as a destroyer. I went slowly homewards, with an empty heart: I had learned that if one cannot call a country to heel like a dog, neither can one dismiss the past with a smile in an easy gush of feeling, saying: I could not help it, I am also a victim.

I only saw Chief Mshlanga once again.

One night my father's big red land was trampled down by small sharp hooves, and it was discovered that the culprits were goats from Chief Mshlanga's kraal. This had happened once before, years ago.

My father confiscated all the goats. Then he sent a message to the old Chief that if he wanted them he would have to pay for the damage.

He arrived at our house at the time of sunset one evening, looking very old and bent now, walking stiffly under his regally-draped blanket, leaning on a big stick. My father sat himself down in his big chair below the steps of the house; the old man squatted carefully on the ground before him, flanked by his two young men.

The palaver was long and painful, because of the bad English of the young man who interpreted, and because my father could not speak dialect, but only kitchen kaffir.

From my father's point of view, at least two hundred pounds' worth of damage had been done to the crop. He knew he could not get the money from the old man. He felt he was entitled to keep the goats. As for the old Chief, he kept repeating angrily: "Twenty goats! My people cannot lose twenty goats! We are not rich, like the Nkosi Jordan, to lose twenty goats at once."

My father did not think of himself as rich, but rather as very poor. He spoke quickly and angrily in return, saying that the damage done meant a great deal to him, and that he was entitled to the goats.

At last it grew so heated that the cook, the Chief's son, was called from the kitchen to be interpreter, and now my father spoke fluently in English, and our cook translated rapidly so that the old man could understand how very angry my father was. The young man spoke without emotion, in a mechanical way, his eyes lowered, but showing how he felt his position by a hostile uncomfortable set of the shoulders.

It was now in the late sunset, the sky a welter of colours, the birds singing their last songs, and the cattle, lowing peacefully, moving past us towards their sheds for the night. It was the hour when Africa is most beautiful; and here was this pathetic, ugly scene, doing no one any good.

At last my father stated finally: "I'm not going to argue about it. I am keeping the goats."

The old Chief flashed back in his own language: "That means that my people will go hungry when the dry season comes."

"Go to the police, then," said my father, and looked triumphant.

There was, of course, no more to be said.

The old man sat silent, his head bent, his hands dangling helplessly over his withered knees. Then he rose, the young men helping him, and he stood facing my father. He spoke once again, very stiffly; and turned away and went home to his village.

"What did he say?" asked my father of the young man, who laughed uncomfortably and would not meet his eyes.

"What did he say?" insisted my father.

Our cook stood straight and silent, his brows knotted together. Then he spoke. "My father says: All this land, this land you call yours, is his land, and belongs to our people."

Having made this statement, he walked off into the bush after his father, and we did not see him again.

Our next cook was a migrant from Nyasaland, with no expectations of greatness.

Next time the policeman came on his rounds he was told this story. He remarked: "That kraal has no right to be there; it should have been moved long ago. I don't know why no one has done anything about it. I'll have a chat with the Native Commissioner next week. I'm going over for tennis on Sunday, anyway."

Some time later we heard that Chief Mshlanga and his people had been moved two hundred miles east, to a proper Native Reserve; the Government land was going to be opened up for white settlement soon.

I went to see the village again, about a year afterwards. There was nothing there. Mounds of red mud, where the huts had been, had long swathes of rotting thatch over them, veined with the red galleries of the white ants. The pumpkin vines rioted everywhere, over the bushes, up the lower branches of trees so that the great golden balls rolled underfoot and dangled overhead: it was a festival of pumpkins. The bushes were crowding up, the new grass sprang vivid green.

The settler lucky enough to be allotted the lush warm valley (if he chose to cultivate this particular section) would find, suddenly, in the middle of a mealie field, the plants were growing fifteen feet tall, the weight of the cobs dragging at the stalks, and wonder what unsuspected vein of richness he had struck.

JOYCE CAROL OATES

SWAMPS

The Grandfather still lived alone in his log cabin, a ramshackle eyesore that the children, and the children's children, no longer cared to joke about. It had been built a hundred years ago, and the Grandfather, his mind surely loosened, would boast sometimes that he had watched his father clear the land or that he had helped clear it himself, leveling with a big hand ax all the pine trees back to where the swamp began, an acre or so behind the cabin. He was a big, solid man, beginning now to lose flesh in his chest, arms, and face, but he tried to walk just as fast and firmly as ever, at least when people were around. He would appear about seven in the morning in the back yard of his son's house—a one-story wooden house, built shotgun style, with brown siding that had come loose in the last few years, and a chimney whose bricks had begun to crumble. A few chickens would be picking about the sawdust and dried grass, and if the rooster was there, and crowing, the Grandfather would answer him. So they would look out, the son and his wife, to see the old man in their back yard, crowing happily along with the rooster at seven in the morning.

At that time the sun would only be clearing the heavy ridge of pine trees. The son, who had given up farming and worked now at the gypsum mill in town, would swear and shake the window screen. He would say to his wife, "The old man's gone crazy. Gone crazy. He ought to be took off somewhere and locked up." The wife, drowsy and sullen, would say nothing. By that time their younger child, an undersized, fair boy of seven, would have joined the Grandfather in the back yard, and the two would amble off through the pine forest and toward the creek. "He knows I don't have to get up till seven-thirty," the son would say. He would stomp back to bed, raging, and let himself fall back onto it, his eyes already fastened rigidly on the ceiling. The wife would put on her house dress and go out into the kitchen and begin breakfast. By the time she had everything ready, her husband would be stomping around again in the bedroom, and the boy and the Grandfather would have returned.

Sometimes the Grandfather allowed himself to be persuaded to have breakfast there. His daughter-in-law, a stocky, pleasant-faced woman, liked the Grandfather in spite of, perhaps because of, his prickly independence. "You must be like your grandfather," she would whisper to the little boy. "When you grow up. Not now, but when you grow up."

If the Grandfather heard about this he said nothing; he showed, however, by certain gracious grunts and gestures, that he favored his daughter-in-law too. His son—a big-shouldered, big-stomached man—would eat his eggs and drink his coffee, making noises, complaining about his work: He was sick of gypsum dust in his lungs, sick of the foreman, sick of working underground, sick of the cheese sandwiches he carried for lunch every day; he was sick of life. At this the Grandfather would stare at him through his unkempt gray hair, his mouth working soundlessly, lost in his whiskers. "Yes," the son would say at these times, sensing that his words, in some obscure way, wounded his father, "yes. I am sick of life. I am sick of this life."

The neighbors—farmers on remote strips of land, on rice farms bordered by swamps—thought highly of the Grandfather, who, in his time, had been blacksmith for the area, schoolteacher when the big boys used to chase every other schoolteacher away, chief and truck driver for the volunteer fire company, the hero of uncertain, romantic exploits in the Navy (almost sixty years ago), and an excellent farmer, neighbor, and parent. He still lived in the log cabin in which he had been born, and from time to time his children and older neighbors would come to see him or to fish with him down at the creek a short distance away. The Grandfather at these times was transformed. If the visitor was an old friend, come to fish or just to sit quietly on the rocks, and if the boy was allowed to come with them, he would be astonished at the change in the old man. He would now come alive, roaring with laughter, slapping his thighs, delivering remarks in a loud, certain voice that the other man would greet with a harsh kindred laughter. Their talk had to do with old times, with people now dead, with people's children, even, now dead, and the boy would gaze dully out and across the shallow, wide creek to the swamp on the other side with its motionless trees and gray moss, just like cobwebs. At times his attention would be drawn back to the conversation because of a change in his grandfather. The old man would pull at his whiskers in confusion, in embarrassment. The other old man—usually Old Hamp—would poke and jab at him with secret remarks that the boy could not understand.

"A fool about anything, was your granddaddy!" the old man chortled gleefully. The Grandfather looked ruffled, the boy thought, like the rooster after it had dusted its comb and feathers in the dirt.

"Why, boy," Hamp said, "it was your granddaddy saved that feed mill by hisself, fightin' the fire by hisself! Couldn't get nobody much to help but me an' them damn fool Powell brothers, an' Jenk hisself gone away, on account of everybody was mad at Jenk. But your granddaddy! An' a big blusterin' man too, said he'd tear apart anybody that tole Jenk about it, for he hated Jenk so! Ain't that it? Ain't it?"

"Jenk's dead an' gone now," the Grandfather said pleasantly.

Sometimes in the evening, after supper, the boy could hear his parents argue. "I'm goin' back there," his mother would say. "I don't care about you. You never gave him the consideration you ought, an' him your father an' such a good man. I'm goin' back."

"I'm tellin' you."

The boy would wait on the porch. "I'm tellin' *you*," she would say loudly. Then she would appear on the porch, muttering to herself, wiping her hands on the skirt of her shapeless dress. "Well, Billie," she would say, pretending surprise. "You comin' back with me, see about your granddaddy? Let's take a little walk back."

All day long, beginning around noon, the Grandfather and Old Hamp had been drinking, slowly and contentedly. If the boy listened hard while doing his chores he could hear them singing; they sang fast songs, slow songs, songs whining and off key, songs demanding that the voice stoop way down to the ground. There was one the boy always waited for:

Swamp fire burnin' all the night
A long way home, a long way home.
Burnin' like my soul a-fire. . . .
A long way home 'fore I can rest.

When the boy and his mother pushed through the weeds and bushes that had sprung up on the Grandfather's land, the boy stared hard at the old house as if he were seeing it for the first time. It was tilted to one side, and the roof had been propped up by branches that looked as if they themselves were beginning to sag. All about the cabin, trees and bushes crowded inward, not as if they were trying to overpower the little house, but as if the house belonged with them, had somehow grown up out of the ground with them. All around the house, scattered in the yard, there were piles of junk—pieces of wood, whole sections of boards nailed together, ropes, halters, parts of machines, a tire from a tractor, chicken wire.

The two old men sat on the sagging front porch. In the twilight, on such days, they usually looked ghastly—they would be grinning and winking at the boy, giving mock military salutes to his mother. One of the Grandfather's jugs would lie between them, sometimes overturned.

Both the Grandfather and Old Hamp might be bleeding slightly about their faces and throats, for it was at these times that they gave each other shaves. One of them might be holding the straight razor as the boy and his mother approached, picking their way through the junk, and both would be grinning, with blood running in tiny glistening streams down their faces. "What am I to do with you?" the mother would say. The old men would nudge each other, like little boys. "Just what am I to do with you?" she would say wearily.

But by that time the old men would have finished, the razor put indifferently aside. Old Hamp would stand slowly, afraid to straighten his legs all at once. The boy would squat back on the porch and examine the razor, which was rusty, matted with coarse dark hair and congealed blood. If the Grandfather would whirl around suddenly, his mouth shaped for cursing, the boy would jump to his feet in alarm, for the old man would now look like a devil—his whiskers gone except for small scraggly clumps, his face glistening in the warm twilight, his eyes bright and hard beneath the matted, wild hair. "You, there, boy!" he would yell drunkenly. "You want me to cut out your gizzard for you? Is that what you want?"

But the next morning he would come for the boy again, at the same time, and though he walked even more slowly than usual, and the boy had to wait patiently at bushes, holding their branches back so they would not sting the old man, the Grandfather did not really seem any different. Even his newly thinned beard and scabby face, raw-looking in the brilliant morning air, already seemed part of him, and not surprising. Once down at the creek, blinking at the yellow-birds that fluttered and disappeared and reappeared above their heads, with his back against the big oak as usual, the old man would relax, grin, and take a breath so big the boy could almost feel it hurting his own lungs. "Yes, Billie," the Grandfather would say agreeably. At these times the boy felt oddly happy, almost delighted. He would show the old man how good he was at skipping stones in the water. He found a fair-sized flat stone, showed it to the Grandfather, who nodded approval, went to the creek bank and got into position, bending far to the right, his arm back and poised, careful, as if he were taking aim at something definite. Then he would throw. "One-two-three—*four!*" the old man would shout. "Four times!" The flat stone would sometimes skip right out of the water at the far side of the creek and disappear into the swamp. Once a yellow-bird flew out, looking surprised, and the boy and the old man hooted with laughter.

"You pay your pa no mind," the old man would say. The boy usually did not understand. His father rarely talked to him, right to him, that is; he shouted toward him, or talked around him, or about him to the mother, but usually not to him. "Your pa got started to be born, it was the bad side of the moon that night. The dark side. An' you know how you're s'post to plant corn in the full of the moon—well!" And here he laughed mysteriously. "But don't you pay him no mind, he talks about bein' sick of life. It ain't life gone sour on him, it's hisself. But that's all right. You pay him no mind. This-here is a damn good world, a *god*-dam good world, it's all you got an' you better pay attention to it."

One day the boy ran home from school with some news: There was a woman, he said breathlessly, down by the school, sitting down on the creek bank. The schoolteacher had gone out to talk to her at noon but had come back with his face red and hurried; and when they had afternoon recess she was still there, swearing and throwing bits of dried mud at them when they got too close, which led to their throwing mud back at her. And after school she was still there, but no one had any time to throw mud because they all had to get home for chores. And that was it.

The Grandfather had been sawing wood halfheartedly in his son's back yard, while the mother took down sheets hung to dry on the clothesline. She brushed hair irritably away from her face and said, "Go an' wash your hands, Billie," and the boy gaped in disappointment.

The Grandfather, however, whose face was newly mottled with whisker stubs and raw flesh, stopped him. "What was that news again?" he said.

When the boy and the Grandfather got to the school the woman was still there. The boy hung back but the Grandfather went right down past the old schoolhouse and the outhouses to the creek bank. When the woman jerked around, the Grandfather said sternly, "There is some kind of trouble here." The woman stared at him with her lips coming slowly away from her teeth. She was heavy, heavy-armed, with a thick neck and a broad, bovine face. The boy saw with surprise that she was not so old—maybe nineteen, the same age as his sister. She was sitting on the creek bank with her big legs out before her, her feet in dusty shoes pointed across the creek to the swamp on the other side, looking so heavy that the boy thought she might not be able to move. "There is some trouble," the Grandfather said and cleared his throat. He lifted his chin like a rooster lifting its head. "My grandson says you been sittin' here all day."

The woman glared. "I c'n sit here if I want," she said loudly. Even the boy's father talked softly to the Grandfather, but this woman bellowed out as loud as the old man. "This is a goddam free country."

"You goin' to drown yourself?" said the Grandfather.

"This is a free country," bawled the woman. The boy could see her yellowed teeth and a great part of her tongue. "You an' them goddam kids go on away an' let me be. I got a right to sit here all I want."

"You goin' to sit there all night too?" the Grandfather said angrily. "You get up! C'mon, get up!"

"I ain't gettin' up!" the woman yelled. She reached around for something to throw, but the loose pieces of mud were all gone. "You go on get the hell out of here! I got a right to sit here all I goddam please!"

The Grandfather squatted on his heels in the shade a short distance away. He began whistling. The boy stood behind him uncertainly; the woman stared across the creek to the swamp. In the hot silence of the afternoon a few jay birds called to one another, high up in the pines. The Grandfather whistled cheerfully and brightly. But the boy could see how his eyes were narrowed on the woman, how he looked worried and even anxious, a way he did not often look. The afternoon grew hotter. The boy sat for a while in the dried grass, then stood, then tried to think of something to say to the Grandfather to make him come home; but he said nothing. The woman stayed on the creek bank, sitting right in the sun, and stared off across the water. At this time of year, early September, the creek was shallow and stagnant in places along the shore, and in certain low spots where rocks trapped the water the boy could see refuse and a thick film of filth encrusting the water and making a line around the rocks; this was because, as the Grandfather said with disgust, people along the creek drained their sewers into the water. "Filthy pigs!" the Grandfather would say, spitting. Later in the fall the creek would rise with frequent rains, in winter it would freeze over, in spring it would flood; but right now it was shallow and dirty. The woman stared out at it with a fierce, silent rage. The boy could see only her profile, which was thick and put him in mind of a bulldog he had seen once at a fair. "Grandpa," he said softly. The old man did not glance up.

The boy's stomach was telling him it was time for supper when his father drove up in the pick-up truck. The boy jumped up and got in it without being called. His father then began arguing with the Grandfather, without looking at him, staring angrily out at the water, at the thick pine trees and the swamp across the way. After a while his father quit and left the old man and drove back home.

When the boy came home from school the next day he knew that things had changed. The Grandfather had that woman back there with him, he was told ferociously by his sister, a big, soft, aimless girl who talked sometimes of going off to work in a city, but who had not yet done much about it. His mother made her stop, but the boy could tell that she too was angry, exasperated. At night he heard his mother and father talking in bed. He heard his mother's insistent, soft voice, rambling a little, and his father's fast, abrupt voice, his heavy words that sounded to the boy as if they came right up out of his stomach.

"They ast me about it at work, even," the father said. "How the hell did they hear? The old man's gone crazy, pure crazy. It must be from drink."

"He done it from the goodness of his heart," the mother said, for perhaps the fifth time.

"It's craziness he done it from," the father said. "I tell you it's craziness. Craziness from drink an' old age an' livin' alone like he does."

"Alone!" said the mother, as if she had been struck. "Alone? Why, he has us . . . he ain't alone in his old age. . . ."

The boy pressed his face into the pillow. The air in his attic room was hot, motionless, humid. Then he sat up; he stared out the cracked window into the queer flat darkness that was the back yard. Beyond were the barn and chicken coop and the trees around them. Behind them, back a short distance, was his grandfather's house, but he could not see it; he could make out only a thick blot of darkness, and behind it more darkness, the darkness of the swamp, so black, so deep, that a person might go blind staring into it. In the darkness there was no difference between the old man's house and the swamp itself. . . . The boy fell back into bed, his eyes wide open, knowing his grandfather would not come to call for him in the morning.

When the old man did come, it was eight-thirty and time for the boy to leave for school. The old man stomped right up onto the porch and knocked at the door. "Why, come in, Grandfather," the boy's mother said. She and the girl were canning; the cupboard was piled with steamed canning jars and waste from pears. The old man stood in the doorway, his shoulders back and proud, but the boy could tell by his eyes, which darted around, that he was worried about something.

"I'm needin' some things," he said casually.

"Yes?"

"I'm needin' a good clean knife, for one thing," he said apologetically, pretending to sniff at the pears. "An' some towels or so . . . a sheet, maybe." The old man himself slept on olive-green horse blankets that he aired from time to time and beat with a big wire brush. "For when she's due. She's sittin' out on the porch now an' won't talk none, but I spose it's comin' pretty soon now."

The boy's sister stared hatefully at the Grandfather. "I spose you know there's everybody laughin' at us," she said.

"I just need a knife, like I said, an' them things," the Grandfather said to the mother. "I don't ask no help, nor she don't neither; she hates women, she said, an' won't let them near her. She said how she would bite any woman come near her."

"That dirty thing!" cried the boy's sister.

"You shut up," said the Grandfather. "A big thing like you, still lazin' around home. Why ain't you married? Why ain't you off settin' up your own home?"

"At least I ain't havin' a baby with no husband!" the girl said. She retreated to the living room and stuck out her tongue. "At least I ain't no dirty filthy big old thing like you got there! What a old fool, old goddam fool for a grandpa!" she said, and ran off.

"That's all right, all *right*," said the mother. She had been stooping heavily, with great effort, to reach back into one of the lower cupboards. Now she straightened up, one hand on her thick waist, and gave the Grandfather a big knife. "That'll be better than your fishin' knife, God knows," she said wearily. "You wait an' I'll get some towels. I spose you still got a pan or two back there?"

"I got them," the Grandfather said. He did not look at the boy even when they were left alone in the kitchen. "Well," he said, smelling at the pears. "I guess your sister don't like her grandpa none." He sniffed angrily. The boy, who was licking out a dish he had just emptied of blackberries and sugar, could tell, with a strange trip of his heart, that the old man was hurt. "I guess she don't like people that's in trouble or pain or sufferin'. I spose a person is got to be married to suffer right," he said angrily. The Grandfather stared at the little boy as if they had been arguing. The boy lowered his eyes quickly and felt his throat twitch. "Yes, Billie," the old man said, his voice relaxed, "you an' I knew right off what had to be done. Didn't we? An' she ain't so nasty as she acts, either; she'll come around. She'll be all right." When the mother returned with a pile of towels, she set them down on the table and put one hand flat on them, so that the boy knew, long after he'd left for school, his mother and his grandfather would still be in the kitchen talking.

When school was over he cut through fields to his grandfather's house instead of going right home to his mother and being told to do chores. By himself, he felt older and wiser. He pretended that someone was looking for him, maybe with a rifle; he squatted behind bushes and crawled through the high weeds, sticking his head up now and then and immediately ducking back down close to the ground. He crawled on his stomach up to the clearing at the side of his grandfather's cabin and lay there peering through the brittle weeds. He could see the porch of the cabin, a rotted, leaning structure whose boards hung loose, covered at the far end by a great complex twist of morning-glory vines. The Grandfather used to say that the vines held the porch up, but the boy knew he was joking.

The big woman was sitting on this end of the porch, with her feet out in the dust. She was barefoot now. She sat with her shoulders slumped and her arms crossed on her big belly, staring at nothing. Her hair was a thick black tangle and the boy could see her dark, glasslike eyes, her coarse skin, the prickly red flesh of her thick upper arms. As the boy watched, the Grandfather came out of the house and let the crooked screen door close slowly behind him.

The woman began muttering at once, without glancing around. She did not even move her eyes. "You give me that goddam knife, old man," she said. "Then I'll be done with this fast enough. You give it to me, old man. You miserable old whiskery bastard." She went on to say other things, bad things, that the little boy tried to shut out of his mind right away: it wasn't because they were bad, because the boys at school said bad things, but because they were about his grandfather. The boy's throat began to twitch.

The Grandfather said nothing. He sat on the far end of the porch while the woman, swearing in a slow, loud, indifferent way, kept staring at nothing—at a treee, maybe, or the sky. She moved her arms across her stomach, back and forth, squeezing. Her face never changed. She had great red arms that the boy would dream about that night. He shut his eyes and backed up in the grass for a while, like a crab, before he thought to turn around and crawl forward. When he got past the place where they could have seen him he stood up and ran, forgetting about the man with the rifle, not even bothering to duck behind bushes.

Everyone in the house acted funny that week, the boy thought. First of all some people came to visit—an uncle and two aunts of his, his father's relations, and some women his mother used to be friendly with in town. These people acted odd themselves, and talked a lot about the Grandfather, and how his health was, and how they would like to go back to see him. . . . But the boy's father and mother stared at the visitors coldly, blankly, and the boy's sister sneered, and the boy himself looked away. Then at supper there was either no talk at all, or fast, angry talk about the Grandfather, although the old man was never mentioned by name.

"I hear from Tessie that some people say it's *me* havin' a baby," the boy's sister whined one night. She sniffed and rubbed at her nose. "They got it all mixed up. They got it all backwards, an' spreadin' it around. How do you like that?" she said to the boy, turning suddenly on him. "You an' that dirty old crazy old fool of a grandpa you got!"

The boy's father was eating steadily and seriously and did not glance up.

"You shut your face," he said, chewing. "That's your grandfather there."

The boy knew that something was going on that night, but it was not until years later that he really knew what it was. He lay awake in his bed, trying to hear whether his parents were talking. He got up once and stood at the door, listening. But he heard nothing. It crossed his mind once that they might not be there, but they were always down in their bedroom at night; they could be nowhere else. He learned later that they had sat out half the night in the empty cow barn, with a lantern on the bench between them, and some canning jars filled with milk, and that his sister had come out every half hour or so in her bathrobe to ask sleepily if anything had happened. They knew nothing. They just sat there, without talking or even looking toward each other, while giant moths reeled around the lantern and the barn up over their heads twitched and creaked with mice and secret things. They did not even look over toward the Grandfather's house.

About three o'clock, though, the Grandfather himself appeared. He stomped right into the barn, showing no surprise at all that they were all sitting there. He was carrying a newborn baby, and his hands and shirt front were bloody. "Look here," he crowed. "Look here what that girl got! Look what I found somewhere in a straw pile!" The mother examined the baby at once and declared it strong and healthy, a fine baby girl. The baby began squealing and choking with apparent rage. The mother gave the old man the milk and her own sweater to wrap around the baby; and they all went inside for the night.

The boy did not learn these things for years. He knew only that the next morning there was something strange in the air when he came down for breakfast—even his father smiled, tousling his hair, and asked him if he'd had any funny dreams last night. They all ate breakfast quickly. His father said the eggs were good, and his mother laughed like a girl. After breakfast the four of them stood around for a while, as if waiting; but then the boy's father said, rubbing his hands suddenly, that he'd better be off to work. The boy saw by the kitchen clock that he still had half an hour. He sat out on the porch and watched the chickens and waited without hope for the Grandfather to come.

The morning grew brighter. From time to time someone came to the screen door behind the boy and stood there for a while, then went away; it might have been his mother or sister. He supposed vaguely that it was time to leave for school, but no one called out to him. Shadows grew shorter; the morning was going to be bright and hot. Chickens scrambled elaborately in the dust. The boy could feel his heart ready to go fast, to be set off like a gun trigger, but he could not have said why. Then suddenly he heard footsteps behind him.

His mother and sister came outside. Both looked grown up and important. "Can I come? Can I come?" the boy begged.

His sister looked cross, but the mother said, "Yes. You be the man with us." So they went through the yard and back to the Grandfather's house. The boy's heart was hammering like mad.

The cabin looked the same, the boy saw with surprise. He had expected it to be different. He had sometimes wondered how things looked when he was off at school, but of course they were the same—just as they were in the summertime when he was always home. The mother went right up on the porch and knocked at the door. She peered inside. Then she said in a faint, shocked voice, "Oh, Betty! Betty!"

When they went inside they found the Grandfather lying on the cluttered floor, with a thick board next to him. The boy knew at once that the old man had been hit with it because there was a blood-edged bruise on one side of his face. "Grandfather, Grandfather," the mother cried. She and the girl knelt by him. They turned him onto his back. "Grandfather, please wake up. Please wake up for us." The mother hugged him, and the boy, his heart throbbing, his face and tongue turned cold, stepped backward. He stared at them—they were like strangers—as he stumbled back over the boxes and jumbled furniture in the old house. He was sobbing like a baby. "Grandfather," the women cried. The boy stared, and when he saw the old man's fingers move, then his whole arm, this was more frightening than the thought that his grandfather was dead; and the boy turned and ran sobbing into the back room.

He hid behind the wall. He could hear moaning in the front room, and the women crying, and something else—maybe his own heartbeats. Then his eyes cleared slowly and he realized what they had been fastened on for perhaps a minute. It was down on the floor, with its head in a dirty basin. The basin was tilted up on end, so that all but a little of the water had run out onto the baby's soft thin hair and the dirty floor. There was a red sweater twisted about the baby, and that too was wet. The boy stared and his mind started telling him that it was his mother's sweater, his mother's red sweater, and that he would have to tell her about it. He would have to tell her about it.

Even after the Grandfather got well he continued to live with them at the house and ate his meals there. At mealtimes he would sit at his end of the table, wiping gravy off his plate with bread, snuffling, wiping his nose on his sleeve. After meals he would sit out in the yard and stare at the sky; sometimes he would go back to the old cabin, but he would not stay long. He died before the creek thawed in the spring. Years after the old man's death, when the boy was growing up, he could never remember this grandfather. He remembered only the other grandfather, and he had to think hard to make himself recall this one—this trembling old man who whined about being robbed.

"She never took nothin' but the knife an' some pennies you had in a sock," the boy's father would say impatiently. "She never took nothin' else."

But the Grandfather would go on, flatly, patiently, "They robbed me. They robbed me."

The boy had always wanted to ask, "Why does Grandpa always say 'they'? How come 'they'? Because . . . because the little baby couldn't—" But he said nothing.

"They robbed me," the Grandfather would moan, rocking on his turned-over box out in the yard. "They robbed me," he would say, his pained mouth working inside his whiskers.

ISAAC BASHEVIS SINGER

GIMPEL the FOOL

Translated by Saul Bellow

1

I am Gimpel the Fool. I don't think myself a fool. On the contrary. But that's what folks call me. They gave me the name while I was still in school. I had seven names in all: imbecile, donkey, flax-head, dope, glump, ninny, and fool. The last name stuck. What did my foolishness consist of? I was easy to take in. They said, "Gimpel, you know the rabbi's wife has been brought to child-bed?" So I skipped school. Well, it turned out to be a lie. How was I supposed to know? She hadn't had a big belly. But I never looked at her belly. Was that really so foolish? The gang laughed and hee-hawed, stomped and danced and chanted a good-night prayer. And instead of the raisins they give when a woman's lying in, they stuffed my hand full of goat turds. I was no weakling. If I slapped someone he'd see all the way to Cracow. But I'm really not a slugger by nature. I think to myself: Let it pass. So they take advantage of me.

I was coming home from school and heard a dog barking. I'm not afraid of dogs, but of course I never want to start up with them. One of them may be mad, and if he bites there's not a Tartar in the world who can help you. So I made tracks. Then I looked around and saw the whole market place wild with laughter. It was no dog at all but Wolf-Leib the Thief. How was I supposed to know it was he? It sounded like a howling bitch.

When the pranksters and leg-pullers found that I was easy to fool, every one of them tried his luck with me. "Gimpel, the Czar is coming to Frampol; Gimpel, the moon fell down in Turbeen; Gimpel, little Hodel Furpiece found a treasure behind the bathhouse." And I like a golem believed everyone. In the first place, everything is possible, as it is written in the Wisdom of the Fathers, I've forgotten just how. Second, I had to believe when the whole town came down on me! If I ever dared to say, "Ah, you're kidding!" there was trouble. People got angry. "What do you mean! You want to call everyone a liar?" What was I to do? I believed them, and I hope at least that did them some good.

I was an orphan. My grandfather who brought me up was already bent toward the grave. So they turned me over to a baker, and what a time they gave me there! Every woman or girl who came to bake a batch of noodles had to fool me at least once. "Gimpel, there's a fair in heaven; Gimpel, the rabbi gave birth to a calf in the seventh month; Gimpel, a cow flew over the roof and laid brass eggs." A student from the yeshiva came once to buy a roll, and he said, "You, Gimpel, while you stand here scraping with your baker's shovel the Messiah has come. The dead have arisen." "What do you mean?" I said. "I heard no one blowing the ram's horn!" He said, "Are you deaf?" And all began to cry, "We heard it, we heard!" Then in came Rietze the Candle-dipper and called out in her hoarse voice, "Gimpel, your father and mother have stood up from the grave. They're looking for you."

To tell the truth, I knew very well that nothing of the sort had happened, but all the same, as folks were talking, I threw on my wool vest and went out. Maybe something had happened. What did I stand to lose by looking? Well, what a cat music went up! And then I took a vow to believe nothing more. But that was no go either. They confused me so that I didn't know the big end from the small.

I went to the rabbi to get some advice. He said, "It is written, better to be a fool all your days than for one hour to be evil. You are not a fool. They are the fools. For he who causes his neighbor to feel shame loses Paradise himself." Nevertheless the rabbi's daughter took me in. As I left the rabbinical court she said, "Have you kissed the wall yet?" I said, "No; what for?" She answered, "It's the law; you've got to do it after every visit." Well, there didn't seem to be any harm in it. And she burst out laughing. It was a fine trick. She put one over on me, all right.

I wanted to go off to another town, but then everyone got busy matchmaking, and they were after me so they nearly tore my coat tails off. They talked at me and talked until I got water on the ear. She was no chaste maiden, but they told me she was virgin pure. She had a limp, and they said it was deliberate, from coyness. She had a bastard, and they told me the child was her little brother. I cried, "You're wasting your time. I'll never marry that whore." But they said indignantly, "What a way to talk! Aren't you ashamed of yourself? We can take you to the rabbi and have you fined for giving her a bad name." I saw then that I wouldn't escape them so easily and I thought: They're set on making me their butt. But when you're married the husband's the master, and if that's all right with her it's agreeable to me too. Besides, you can't pass through life unscathed, nor expect to.

I went to her clay house, which was built on the sand, and the whole gang, hollering and chorusing, came after me. They acted like bear-baiters. When we came to the well they stopped all the same. They were afraid to start anything with Elka. Her mouth would open as if it were on a hinge, and she had a fierce tongue. I entered the house. Lines were strung from wall to wall and clothes were drying. Barefoot she stood by the tub, doing the wash. She was dressed in a worn hand-me-down gown of plush. She had her hair put up in braids and pinned across her head. It took my breath away, almost, the reek of it all.

Evidently she knew who I was. She took a look at me and said, "Look who's here! He's come, the drip. Grab a seat."

I told her all; I denied nothing. "Tell me the truth," I said, "are you really a virgin, and is that mischievous Yechiel actually your little brother? Don't be deceitful with me, for I'm an orphan."

"I'm an orphan myself," she answered, "and whoever tries to twist you up, may the end of his nose take a twist. But don't let them think they can take advantage of me. I want a dowry of fifty guilders, and let them take up a collection besides. Otherwise they can kiss my you-know-what." She was very plainspoken. I said, "It's the bride and not the groom who gives a dowry." Then she said, "Don't bargain with me. Either a flat 'yes' or a flat 'no'—Go back where you came from."

I thought: No bread will ever be baked from *this* dough. But ours is not a poor town. They consented to everything and proceeded with the wedding. It so happened that there was a dysentery epidemic at the time. The ceremony was held at the cemetery gates, near the little corpse-washing hut. The fellows got drunk. While the marriage contract was being drawn up I heard the most pious high rabbi ask, "Is the bride a widow or a divorced woman?" And the sexton's wife answered for her, "Both a widow and divorced." It was a black moment for me. But what was I to do, run away from under the marriage canopy?

There was singing and dancing. An old granny danced opposite me, hugging a braided white *chalah*. The master of revels made a "God 'a mercy" in memory of the bride's parents. The schoolboys threw burrs, as on Tishe b'Av fast day. There were a lot of gifts after the sermon: a noodle board, a kneading trough, a bucket, brooms, ladles, household articles galore. Then I took a look and saw two strapping young men carrying a crib. "What do we need this for?" I asked. So they said, "Don't rack your brains about it. It's all right, it'll come in handy." I realized I was going to be rooked. Take it another way though, what did I stand to lose? I reflected: I'll see what comes of it. A whole town can't go altogether crazy.

2

At night I came where my wife lay, but she wouldn't let me in. "Say, look here, is this what they married us for?" I said. And she said, "My monthly has come." "But yesterday they took you to the ritual bath, and that's afterward, isn't it supposed to be?" "Today isn't yesterday," said she, "and yesterday's not today. You can beat it if you don't like it." In short, I waited.

Not four months later she was in childbed. The townsfolk hid their laughter with their knuckles. But what could I do? She suffered intolerable pains and clawed at the walls. "Gimpel," she cried, "I'm going. Forgive me!" The house filled with women. They were boiling pans of water. The screams rose to the welkin.

The thing to do was to go to the House of Prayer to repeat Psalms, and that was what I did.

The townsfolk liked that, all right. I stood in a corner saying Psalms and prayers, and they shook their heads at me. "Pray, pray!" they told me. "Prayer never made any woman pregnant." One of the congregation put a straw to my mouth and said, "Hay for the cows." There was something to that too, by God!

She gave birth to a boy. Friday at the synagogue the sexton stood up before the Ark, pounded on the reading table, and announced, "The wealthy Reb Gimpel invites the congregation to a feast in honor of the birth of a son." The whole House of Prayer rang with laughter. My face was flaming. But there was nothing I could do. After all, I *was* the one responsible for the circumcision honors and rituals.

Half the town came running. You couldn't wedge another soul in. Women brought peppered chick-peas, and there was a keg of beer from the tavern. I ate and drank as much as anyone, and they all congratulated me. Then there was a circumcision, and I named the boy after my father, may he rest in peace. When all were gone and I was left with my wife alone, she thrust her head through the bed-curtain and called me to her.

"Gimpel," said she, "why are you silent? Has your ship gone and sunk?"

"What shall I say?" I answered. "A fine thing you've done to me! If my mother had known of it she'd have died a second time."

She said, "Are you crazy, or what?"

"How can you make such a fool," I said, "of one who should be the lord and master?"

"What's the matter with you?" she said. "What have you taken it into your head to imagine?"

I saw that I must speak bluntly and openly. "Do you think this is the way to use an orphan?" I said. "You have borne a bastard."

She answered, "Drive this foolishness out of your head. The child is yours."

"How can he be mine?" I argued. "He was born seventeen weeks after the wedding."

She told me then that he was premature. I said, "Isn't he a little too premature?" She said she had had a grandmother who carried just as short a time and she resembled this grandmother of hers as one drop of water does another. She swore to it with such oaths that you would have believed a peasant at the fair if he had used them. To tell the plain truth, I didn't believe her; but when I talked it over next day with the schoolmaster he told me that the very same thing had happened to Adam and Eve. Two they went up to bed, and four they descended.

"There isn't a woman in the world who is not the granddaughter of Eve," he said.

That was how it was; they argued me dumb. But then, who really knows how such things are?

I began to forget my sorrow. I loved the child madly, and he loved me too. As soon as he saw me he'd wave his little hands and want me to pick him up, and when he was colicky I was the only one who could pacify him. I bought him a little bone teething ring and a little gilded cap. He was forever catching the evil eye from someone, and then I had to run to get one of those abracadabras for him that would get him out of it. I worked like an ox. You know how expenses go up when there's an infant in the house. I don't want to lie about it; I didn't dislike Elka either, for that matter. She swore at me and cursed, and I couldn't get enough of her. What strength she had! One of her looks could rob you of the power of speech. And her orations! Pitch and sulphur, that's what they were full of, and yet somehow also full of charm. I adored her every word. She gave me bloody wounds though.

In the evening I brought her a white loaf as well as a dark one, and also poppyseed rolls I baked myself. I thieved because of her and swiped everything I could lay hands on: macaroons, raisins, almonds, cakes. I hope I may be forgiven for stealing from the Saturday pots the women left to warm in the baker's oven. I would take out scraps of meat, a chunk of pudding, a chicken leg or head, a piece of tripe, whatever I could nip quickly. She ate and became fat and handsome.

I had to sleep away from home all during the week, at the bakery. On Friday nights when I got home she always made an excuse of some sort. Either she had heartburn, or a stitch in the side, or hiccups, or headaches. You know what women's excuses are. I had a bitter time of it. It was rough. To add to it, this little brother of hers, the bastard, was growing bigger. He'd put lumps on me, and when I wanted to hit back she'd open her mouth and curse so powerfully I saw a green haze floating before my eyes. Ten times a day she threatened to divorce me. Another man in my place would have taken French leave and disappeared. But I'm the type that bears it and says nothing. What's one to do? Shoulders are from God, and burdens too.

One night there was a calamity in the bakery; the oven burst, and we almost had a fire. There was nothing to do but go home, so I went home. Let me, I thought, also taste the joy of sleeping in bed in mid-week. I didn't want to wake the sleeping mite and tiptoed into the house. Coming in, it seemed to me that I heard not the snoring of one but, as it were, a double snore, one a thin enough snore and the other like the snoring of a slaughtered ox. Oh, I didn't like that! I didn't like it at all. I went up to the bed, and things suddenly turned black. Next to Elka lay a man's form. Another in my place would have made an uproar, and enough noise to rouse the whole town, but the thought occurred to me that I might wake the child. A little thing like that—why frighten a little swallow, I thought. All right then, I went back to the bakery and stretched out on a sack of flour and till morning I never shut an eye. I shivered as if I had had malaria. "Enough of being a donkey," I said to myself. "Gimpel isn't going to be a sucker all his life. There's a limit even to the foolishness of a fool like Gimpel."

In the morning I went to the rabbi to get advice, and it made a great commotion in the town. They sent the beadle for Elka right away. She came, carrying the child. And what do you think she did? She denied it, denied everything, bone and stone! "He's out of his head," she said. "I know nothing of dreams or divinations." They yelled at her, warned her, hammered on the table, but she stuck to her guns: it was a false accusation, she said.

The butchers and the horse-traders took her part. One of the lads from the slaughterhouse came by and said to me, "We've got our eye on you, you're a marked man." Meanwhile the child started to bear down and soiled itself. In the rabbinical court there was an Ark of the Covenant, and they couldn't allow that, so they sent Elka away.

I said to the rabbi, "What shall I do?"

"You must divorce her at once," said he.

"And what if she refuses?" I asked.

He said, "You must serve the divorce. That's all you'll have to do."

I said, "Well, all right, Rabbi. Let me think about it."

"There's nothing to think about," said he. "You mustn't remain under the same roof with her."

"And if I want to see the child?" I asked

"Let her go, the harlot," said he, "and her brood of bastards with her."

The verdict he gave was that I mustn't even cross her threshold—never again, as long as I should live.

During the day it didn't bother me so much. I thought: It was bound to happen, the abscess had to burst. But at night when I stretched out upon the sacks I felt it all very bitterly. A longing took me, for her and for the child. I wanted to be angry, but that's my misfortune exactly, I don't have it in me to be really angry. In the first place—this was how my thoughts went—there's bound to be a slip sometimes. You can't live without errors. Probably that lad who was with her led her on and gave her presents and what not, and women are often long on hair and short on sense, and so he got around her. And then since she denies it so, maybe I was only seeing things? Hallucinations do happen. You see a figure or a mannikin or something, but when you come up closer it's nothing, there's not a thing there. And if that's so, I'm doing her an injustice. And when I got so far in my thoughts I started to weep. I sobbed so that I wet the flour where I lay. In the morning I went to the rabbi and told him that I had made a mistake. The rabbi wrote on with his quill, and he said that if that were so he would have to reconsider the whole case. Until he had finished I wasn't to go near my wife, but I might send her bread and money by messenger.

3

Nine months passed before all the rabbis could come to an agreement Letters went back and forth. I hadn't realized that there could be so much erudition about a matter like this.

Meanwhile Elka gave birth to still another child, a girl this time. On the sabbath I went to the synagogue and invoked a blessing on her. They called me up to the Torah, and I named the child for my mother-in-law—may she rest in peace. The louts and loudmouths of the town who came into the bakery gave me a going over. All Frampol refreshed its spirits because of my trouble and grief. However, I resolved that I would always believe what I was told. What's the good of *not* believing? Today it's your wife you don't believe; tomorrow it's God Himself you won't take stock in.

By an apprentice who was her neighbor I sent her daily a corn or a wheat loaf, or a piece of pastry, rolls or bagels, or, when I got the chance, a slab of pudding, a slice of honeycake, or wedding strudel—whatever came my way. The apprentice was a goodhearted lad, and more than once he added something of his own. He had formerly annoyed me a lot, plucking my nose and digging me in the ribs, but when he started to be a visitor to my house he became kind and friendly. "Hey, you, Gimpel," he said to me, "you have a very decent little wife and two fine kids. You don't deserve them."

"But the things people say about her," I said.

"Well, they have long tongues," he said, "and nothing to do with them but babble. Ignore it as you ignore the cold of last winter."

One day the rabbi sent for me and said, "Are you certain, Gimpel, that you were wrong about your wife?"

I said, "I'm certain."

"Why, but look here! You yourself saw it."

"It must have been a shadow," I said.

"The shadow of what?"

"Just of one of the beams, I think."

"You can go home then. You owe thanks to the Yanover rabbi. He found an obscure reference in Maimonides that favored you."

I seized the rabbi's hand and kissed it.

I wanted to run home immediately. It's no small thing to be separated for so long a time from wife and child. Then I reflected: I'd better go back to work now, and go home in the evening. I said nothing to anyone, although as far as my heart was concerned it was like one of the Holy Days. The women teased and twitted me as they did every day, but my thought was: Go on, with your loose talk. The truth is out, like the oil upon the water. Maimonides says it's right, and therefore it is right!

At night, when I had covered the dough to let it rise, I took my share of bread and a little sack of flour and started homeward. The moon was full and the stars were glistening, something to terrify the soul. I hurried onward, and before me darted a long shadow. It was winter, and a fresh snow had fallen. I had a mind to sing, but it was growing late and I didn't want to wake the householders. Then I felt like whistling, but I remembered that you don't whistle at night because it brings the demons out. So I was silent and walked as fast as I could.

Dogs in the Christian yards barked at me when I passed, but I thought: Bark your teeth out! What are you but mere dogs? Whereas I am a man, the husband of a fine wife, the father of promising children.

As I approached the house my heart started to pound as though it were the heart of a criminal. I felt no fear, but my heart went thump! thump! Well, no drawing back. I quietly lifted the latch and went in. Elka was asleep. I looked at the infant's cradle. The shutter was closed, but the moon forced its way through the cracks. I saw the newborn child's face and loved it as soon as I saw it—immediately—each tiny bone.

Then I came nearer to the bed. And what did I see but the apprentice lying there beside Elka. The moon went out all at once. It was utterly black, and I trembled. My teeth chattered. The bread fell from my hands, and my wife waked and said, "Who is that, ah?"

I muttered, "It's me."

"Gimpel?" she asked. "How come you're here? I thought it was forbidden."

"The rabbi said," I answered and shook as with a fever.

"Listen to me, Gimpel," she said, "go out to the shed and see if the goat's all right. It seems she's been sick." I have forgotten to say that we had a goat. When I heard she was unwell I went into the yard. The nannygoat was a good little creature. I had a nearly human feeling for her.

With hesitant steps I went up to the shed and opened the door. The goat stood there on her four feet. I felt her everywhere, drew her by the horns, examined her udders, and found nothing wrong. She had probably eaten too much bark. "Good night, little goat," I said. "Keep well." And the little beast answered with a "Maa" as though to thank me for the good will.

I went back. The apprentice had vanished.

"Where," I asked, "is the lad?"

"What lad?" my wife answered.

"What do you mean?" I said. "The apprentice. You were sleeping with him."

"The things I have dreamed this night and the night before," she said, "may they come true and lay you low, body and soul! An evil spirit has taken root in you and dazzles your sight." She screamed out, "You hateful creature! You moon calf! You spook! You uncouth man! Get out, or I'll scream all Frampol out of bed!"

Before I could move, her brother sprang out from behind the oven and struck me a blow on the back of the head. I thought he had broken my neck. I felt that something about me was deeply wrong, and I said, "Don't make a scandal. All that's needed now is that people should accuse me of raising spooks and *dybbuks.*" For that was what she had meant. "No one will touch bread of my baking."

In short, I somehow calmed her.

"Well," she said, "that's enough. Lie down, and be shattered by wheels."

Next morning I called the apprentice aside. "Listen here, brother!" I said. And so on and so forth. "What do you say?" He stared at me as though I had dropped from the roof or something.

"I swear," he said, "you'd better go to an herb doctor or some healer. I'm afraid you have a screw loose, but I'll hush it up for you." And that's how the thing stood.

To make a long story short, I lived twenty years with my wife. She bore me six children, four daughteres and two sons. All kinds of things happened, but I neither saw nor heard. I believed, and that's all. The rabbi recently said to me, "Belief in itself is beneficial. It is written that a good man lives by his faith."

Suddenly my wife took sick. It began with a trifle, a little growth upon the breast. But she evidently was not destined to live long; she had no years. I spent a fortune on her. I have forgotten to say that by this time I had a bakery of my own and in Frampol was considered to be something of a rich man. Daily the healer came, and every witch doctor in the neighborhood was brought. They decided to use leeches, and after that to try cupping. They even called a doctor from Lublin, but it was too late. Before she died she called me to her bed and said, "Forgive me, Gimpel."

I said, "What is there to forgive? You have been a good and faithful wife."

"Woe, Gimpel!" she said. "It was ugly how I deceived you all these years. I want to go clean to my Maker, and so I have to tell you that the children are not yours."

If I had been clouted on the head with a piece of wood it couldn't have bewildered me more.

"Whose are they?" I asked.

"I don't know," she said. "There were a lot . . . but they're not yours." And as she spoke she tossed her head to the side, her eyes turned glassy, and it was all up with Elka. On her whitened lips there remained a smile.

I imagined that, dead as she was, she was saying, "I deceived Gimpel. That was the meaning of my brief life."

4

One night, when the period of mourning was done, as I lay dreaming on the flour sacks, there came the Spirit of Evil himself and said to me, "Gimpel, why do you sleep?"

I said, "What should I be doing? Eating *kreplach?*"

"The whole world deceives you," he said, "and you ought to deceive the world in your turn."

"How can I deceive all the world?" I asked him.

He answered, "You might accumulate a bucket of urine every day and at night pour it into the dough. Let the sages of Frampol eat filth."

"What about the judgment in the world to come?" I said.

"There is no world to come," he said. "They've sold you a bill of goods and talked you into believing you carried a cat in your belly. What nonsense!"

"Well then," I said, "and is there a God?"

He answered, "There is no God either."

"What," I said, "*is* there, then?"

"A thick mire."

He stood before my eyes with a goatish beard and horn, long-toothed, and with a tail. Hearing such words, I wanted to snatch him by the tail, but I tumbled from the flour sacks and nearly broke a rib. Then it happened that I had to answer the call of nature, and, passing, I saw the risen dough, which seemed to say to me, "Do it!" In brief, I let myself be persuaded.

At dawn the apprentice came. We kneaded the bread, scattered caraway seeds on it, and set it to bake. Then the apprentice went away, and I was left sitting in the little trench by the oven, on a pile of rags. Well, Gimpel, I thought, you've revenged yourself on them for all the shame they've put on you. Outside the frost glittered, but it was warm beside the oven. The flames heated my face. I bent my head and fell into a doze.

I saw in a dream, at once, Elka in her shroud. She called to me, "What have you done, Gimpel?"

I said to her, "It's all your fault," and started to cry.

"You fool!" she said. "You fool! Because I was false is everything false too? I never deceived anyone but myself. I'm paying for it all, Gimpel. They spare you nothing here."

I looked at her face. It was black; I was startled and waked, and remained sitting dumb. I sensed that everything hung in the balance. A false step now and I'd lose Eternal Life. But God gave me His help. I seized the long shovel and took out the loaves, carried them into the yard, and started to dig a hole in the frozen earth.

My apprentice came back as I was doing it. "What are you doing, boss?" he said, and grew pale as a corpse.

"I know what I'm doing," I said, and I buried it all before his very eyes.

Then I went home, took my hoard from its hiding place, and divided it among the children. "I saw your mother tonight," I said. "She's turning black, poor thing."

They were so astounded they couldn't speak a word.

"Be well," I said, "and forget that such a one as Gimpel ever existed." I put on my short coat, a pair of boots, took the bag that held my prayer shawl in one hand, my stock in the other, and kissed the *mezzuzah*. When people saw me in the street they were greatly surprised.

"Where are you going?" they said.

I answered, "Into the world." And so I departed from Frampol.

I wandered over the land, and good people did not neglect me. After many years I became old and white; I heard a great deal, many lies and falsehoods, but the longer I lived the more I understood that there were really no lies. Whatever doesn't really happen is dreamed at night. It happens to one if it doesn't happen to another, tomorrow if not today, or a century hence if not next year. What difference can it make? Often I heard tales of which I said, "Now this is a thing that cannot happen." But before a year had elapsed I heard that it actually had come to pass somewhere.

Going from place to place, eating at strange tables, it often happens that I spin yarns—improbable things that could never have happened—about devils, magicians, windmills, and the like. The children run after me, calling, "Grandfather, tell us a story." Sometimes they ask for particular stories, and I try to please them. A fat young boy once said to me, "Grandfather, it's the same story you told us before." The little rogue, he was right.

So it is with dreams too. It is many years since I left Frampol, but as soon as I shut my eyes I am there again. And whom do you think I see? Elka. She is standing by the washtub, as at our first encounter, but her face is shining and her eyes are as radiant as the eyes of a saint, and she speaks outlandish words to me, strange things. When I wake I have forgotten it all. But while the dream lasts I am comforted. She answers all my queries, and what comes out is that all is right. I weep and implore, "Let me be with you." And she consoles me and tells me to be patient. The time is nearer than it is far. Sometimes she strokes and kisses me and weeps upon my face. When I awaken I feel her lips and taste the salt of her tears.

No doubt the world is entirely an imaginary world, but it is only once removed from the true world. At the door of the hovel where I lie, there stands the plank on which the dead are taken away. The gravedigger Jew has his spade ready. The grave waits and the worms are hungry; the shrouds are prepared—I carry them in my beggar's sack. Another *shnorrer* is waiting to inherit my bed of straw. When the time comes I will go joyfully. Whatever may be there, it will be real, without complication, without ridicule, without deception. God be praised: there even Gimpel cannot be deceived.

GUSTAVE FLAUBERT

A SIMPLE HEART

Translated by Robert Baldick

1

For half a century the women of Pont-l'Évêque envied Mme Aubain her maidservant Félicité.

In return for a hundred francs a year she did all the cooking and the housework, the sewing, the washing, and the ironing. She could bridle a horse, fatten poultry, and churn butter, and she remained faithful to her mistress, who was by no means an easy person to get on with.

Mme Aubain had married a young fellow who was good-looking but badly-off, and who died at the beginning of 1809, leaving her with two small children and a pile of debts. She then sold all her property except for the farms of Toucques and Geffosses, which together brought in five thousand francs a year at the most, and left her house at Saint-Melaine for one behind the covered market which was cheaper to run and had belonged to her family.

This house had a slate roof and stood between an alley-way and a lane leading down to the river. Inside there were differences in level which were the cause of many a stumble. A narrow entrance-hall separated the kitchen from the parlour, where Mme Aubain sat all day long in a wicker easy-chair by the window. Eight mahogany chairs were lined up against the white-painted wainscoting, and under the barometer stood an old piano loaded with a pyramid of boxes and cartons. On either side of the chimney-piece, which was carved out of yellow marble in the Louis Quinze style, there was a tapestry-covered arm-chair, and in the middle was a clock designed to look like a temple of Vesta. The whole room smelt a little musty, as the floor was on a lower level than the garden.

On the first floor was 'Madame's' bedroom—very spacious, with a patterned wallpaper of pale flowers and a portrait of 'Monsieur' dressed in what had once been the height of fashion. It opened into a smaller room in which there were two cots, without mattresses. Then came the drawing-room, which was always shut up and full of furniture covered with dust-sheets. Next there was a passage leading to the study, where books and papers filled the shelves of a book-case in three sections built round a big writing-table of dark wood. The two end panels were hidden under pen-and-ink drawings, landscapes in gouache, and etchings by Audran, souvenirs of better days and bygone luxury. On the second floor a dormer window gave light to Félicité's room, which looked out over the fields.

Every day Félicité got up at dawn, so as not to miss Mass, and worked until evening without stopping. Then, once dinner was over, the plates and dishes put away, and the door bolted, she piled ashes on the log fire and went to sleep in front of the hearth, with her rosary in her hands. Nobody could be more stubborn when it came to haggling over prices, and as for cleanliness, the shine on her saucepans was the despair of all the other servants. Being of a thrifty nature, she ate slowly, picking up from the table the crumbs from her loaf of bread—a twelve-pound loaf which was baked specially for her and lasted her twenty days.

All the year round she wore a kerchief of printed calico fastened behind with a pin, a bonnet which covered her hair, grey stockings, a red skirt, and over her jacket a bibbed apron such as hospital nurses wear.

Her face was thin and her voice was sharp. At twenty-five she was often taken for forty; once she reached fifty, she stopped looking any age in particular. Always silent and upright and deliberate in her movements, she looked like a wooden doll driven by clock-work.

2

Like everyone else, she had had her love-story.

Her father, a mason, had been killed when he fell off some scaffolding. Then her mother died, and when her sisters went their separate ways, a farmer took her in, sending her, small as she was, to look after the cows out in the fields. She went about in rags, shivering with cold, used to lie flat on the ground to drink water out of the ponds, would be beaten for no reason at all, and was finally turned out of the house for stealing thirty sous, a theft of which she was innocent. She found work at another farm, looking after the poultry, and as she was liked by her employers the other servants were jealous of her.

One August evening—she was eighteen at the time—they took her off to the fête at Colleville. From the start she was dazed and bewildered by the noise of the fiddles, the lamps in the trees, the medley of gaily coloured dresses, the gold crosses and lace, and the throng of people jigging up and down. She was standing shyly on one side when a smart young fellow, who had been leaning on the shaft of a cart, smoking his pipe, came up and asked her to dance. He treated her to cider, coffee, girdle-cake, and a silk neckerchief, and imagining that she knew what he was after, offered to see her home. At the edge of a field of oats, he pushed her roughly to the ground. Thoroughly frightened, she started screaming for help. He took to his heels.

Another night, on the road to Beaumont, she tried to get past a big, slow-moving waggon loaded with hay, and as she was squeezing by she recognized Théodore.

He greeted her quite calmly, saying that she must forgive him for the way he had behaved to her, as 'it was the drink that did it'.

She did not know what to say in reply and felt like running off.

Straight away he began talking about the crops and the notabilities of the commune, saying that his father had left Colleville for the farm at Les Écots, so that they were now neighbours.

'Ah!' she said.

He added that his family wanted to see him settled but that he was in no hurry and was waiting to find a wife to suit his fancy. She lowered her head. Then he asked her if she was thinking of getting married. She answered with a smile that it was mean of him to make fun of her.

'But I'm not making fun of you!' he said. 'I swear I'm not!'

He put his left arm round her waist, and she walked on supported by his embrace. Soon they slowed down. There was a gentle breeze blowing, the stars were shining, the huge load of hay was swaying about in front of them, and the four horses were raising clouds of dust as they shambled along. Then, without being told, they turned off to the right. He kissed her once more and she disappeared into the darkness.

The following week Théodore got her to grant him several rendezvous.

They would meet at the bottom of a farm-yard, behind a wall, under a solitary tree. She was not ignorant of life as young ladies are, for the animals had taught her a great deal; but her reason and an instinctive sense of honour prevented her from giving way. The resistance she put up inflamed Théodore's passion to such an extent that in order to satisfy it (or perhaps out of sheer naívety) he proposed to her. At first she refused to believe him, but he swore that he was serious.

Soon afterwards he had a disturbing piece of news to tell her: the year before, his parents had paid a man to do his military service for him, but now he might be called up again any day, and the idea of going into the army frightened him. In Félicité's eyes this cowardice of his appeared to be a proof of his affection, and she loved him all the more for it. Every night she would steal out to meet him, and every night Théodore would plague her with his worries and entreaties.

In the end he said that he was going to the Prefecture himself to make inquiries, and that he would come and tell her how matters stood the following Sunday, between eleven and midnight.

At the appointed hour she hurried to meet her sweetheart, but found one of his friends waiting for her instead.

He told her that she would not see Théodore again. To make sure of avoiding conscription, he had married a very rich old woman, Mme Lehoussais of Toucques.

Her reaction was an outburst of frenzied grief. She threw herself on the ground, screaming and calling on God, and lay moaning all alone in the open until sunrise. Then she went back to the farm and announced her intention of leaving. At the end of the month, when she had received her wages, she wrapped her small belongings up in a kerchief and made her way to Pont-l'Évêque.

In front of the inn there, she sought information from a woman in a widow's bonnet, who, as it happened, was looking for a cook. The girl did not know much about cooking, but she seemed so willing and expected so little that finally Mme Aubain ended up by saying: 'Very well, I will take you on.'

A quarter of an hour later Félicité was installed in her house.

At first she lived there in a kind of fearful awe caused by 'the style of the house' and by the memory of 'Monsieur' brooding over everything. Paul and Virginie, the boy aged seven and the girl barely four, seemed to her to be made of some precious substance. She used to carry them about pick-a-back, and when Mme Aubain told her not to keep on kissing them she was cut to the quick. All the same, she was happy now, for her pleasant surroundings had dispelled her grief.

On Thursdays, a few regular visitors came in to play Boston, and Félicité got the cards and the footwarmers ready beforehand. They always arrived punctually at eight, and left before the clock struck eleven.

Every Monday morning the second-hand dealer who lived down the alley put all his junk out on the pavement. Then the hum of voices began to fill the town, mingled with the neighing of horses, the bleating of lambs, the grunting of pigs, and the rattle of carts in the streets.

About midday, when the market was in full swing, a tall old peasant with a hooked nose and his cap on the back of his head would appear at the door. This was Robelin, the farmer from Geffosses. A little later, and Liébard, the farmer from Toucques, would arrive—a short, fat, red-faced fellow in a grey jacket and leather gaiters fitted with spurs.

Both men had hens or cheeses they wanted to sell to 'Madame'. But Félicité was up to all their tricks and invariably outwitted them, so that they went away full of respect for her.

From time to time Mme Aubain had a visit from an uncle of hers, the Marquis de Grémanville, who had been ruined by loose living and was now living at Falaise on his last remaining scrap of property. He always turned up at lunch-time, accompanied by a hideous poodle which dirtied all the furniture with its paws. However hard he tried to behave like a gentleman, even going so far as to raise his hat every time he mentioned 'my late father', the force of habit was usually too much for him, for he would start pouring himself one glass after another and telling bawdy stories. Félicite used to push him gently out of the house, saying politely: 'You've had quite enough, Mousieur de Grémanville. See you another time!' and shutting the door on him.

She used to open it with pleasure to M. Bourais, who was a retired solicitor. His white tie and his bald head, his frilled shirt-front and his ample brown frock-coat, the way he had of rounding his arm to take a pinch of snuff, and indeed everything about him made an overwhelming impression on her such as we feel when we meet some outstanding personality.

As he looked after 'Madame's' property, he used to shut himself up with her for hours in 'Monsieur's' study. He lived in dread of compromising his reputation, had a tremendous respect for the Bench, and laid claim to some knowledge of Latin.

To give the children a little painless instruction, he made them a present of a geography book with illustrations. These represented scenes in different parts of the world, such as cannibals wearing feather head-dresses, a monkey carrying off a young lady, Bedouins in the desert, a whale being harpooned, and so on.

Paul explained these pictures to Félicité, and that indeed was all the education she ever had. As for the children, they were taught by Guyot, a poor devil employed at the Town Hall, who was famous for his beautiful handwriting, and who had a habit of sharpening his penknife on his boots.

When the weather was fine the whole household used to set off early for a day at the Geffosses farm.

The farm-yard there was on a slope, with the house in the middle; and the sea, in the distance, looked like a streak of grey. Félicité would take some slices of cold meat out of her basket, and they would have their lunch in a room adjoining the dairy. It was all that remained of a country house which had fallen into ruin, and the wallpaper hung in shreds, fluttering in the draught. Mme Aubain used to sit with bowed head, absorbed in her memories, so that the children were afraid to talk. 'Why don't you run along and play?' she would say, and away they went.

Paul climbed up into the barn, caught birds, played ducks and drakes on the pond, or banged with a stick on the great casks, which sounded just like drums.

Virginie fed the rabbits, or scampered off to pick cornflowers, showing her little embroidered knickers as she ran.

One autumn evening they came home through the fields. The moon, which was in its first quarter, lit up part of the sky, and there was some mist floating like a scarf over the winding Toucques. The cattle, lying out in the middle of the pasture, looked peacefully at the four people walking by. In the third field a few got up and made a half circle in front of them.

"Don't be frightened!' said Félicité, and crooning softly, she stroked the back of the nearest animal. It turned about and the others did the same. But while they were crossing the next field they suddenly heard a dreadful bellowing. It came from a bull which had been hidden by the mist, and which now came towards the two women.

Mme Aubain started to run.

'No! No!' said Félicité. 'Not so fast!'

All the same they quickened their pace, hearing behind them a sound of heavy breathing which came nearer and nearer. The bull's hooves thudded like hammers on the turf, and they realized that it had broken into a gallop. Turning round, Félicité tore up some clods of earth and flung them at its eyes. It lowered its muzzle and thrust its horns forward, trembling with rage and bellowing horribly.

By now Mme Aubain had got to the end of the field with her two children and was frantically looking for a way over the high bank. Félicité was still backing away from the bull, hurling clods of turf which blinded it, and shouting: 'Hurry! Hurry!'

Mme Aubain got down into the ditch, pushed first Virginie and then Paul up the other side, fell once or twice trying to climb the bank, and finally managed it with a valiant effort.

The bull had driven Félicité back against a gate, and its slaver was spurting into her face. In another second it would have gored her, but she just had time to slip between two of the bars, and the great beast halted in amazement.

This adventure was talked about at Pont-l'Evêque for a good many years, but Félicité never prided herself in the least on what she had done, as it never occurred to her that she had done anything heroic.

Virginie claimed all her attention, for the fright had affected the little girl's nerves, and M. Poupart, the doctor, recommended sea-bathing at Trouville.

In those days the resort had few visitors. Mme Aubain made inquiries, consulted Bourais, and got everything ready as though for a long journey.

Her luggage went off in Liébard's cart the day before she left. The next morning he brought along two horses, one of which had a woman's saddle with a velvet back, while the other carried a cloak rolled up to make a kind of seat on its crupper. Mme Aubain sat on this, with Liébard in front. Félicité looked after Virginie on the other horse, and Paul mounted M. Lechaptois's donkey, which he had lent them on condition they took great care of it.

The road was so bad that it took two hours to travel the five miles to Toucques. The horses sank into the mud up to their pasterns and had to jerk their hind-quarters to get out; often they stumbled in the ruts, or else they had to jump. In some places, Liébard's mare came to a sudden stop, and while he waited patiently for her to move off again, he talked about the people whose properties bordered the road, adding moral reflexions to each story. For instance, in the middle of Toucques, as they were passing underneath some windows set in a mass of nasturtiums, he shrugged his shoulders and said:

'There's a Madame Lehoussais lives here. Now instead of taking a young man, she . . .'

Félicité did not hear the rest, for the horses had broken into a trot and the donkey was galloping along. All three turned down a bridle-path, a gate swung open, a couple of boys appeared, and everyone dismounted in front of a manure-heap right outside the farm-house door.

Old Mother Liébard welcomed her mistress with every appearance of pleasure. She served up a sirloin of beef for lunch, with tripe and black pudding, a fricassee of chicken, sparkling cider, a fruit tart and brandy-plums, garnishing the whole meal with compliments to Madame, who seemed to be enjoying better health, to Mademoiselle, who had turned into a 'proper little beauty', and to Monsieur Paul, who had 'filled out a lot'. Nor did she forget their deceased grandparents, whom the Liébards had known personally, having been in the family's service for several generations.

Like its occupants, the farm had an air of antiquity. The ceiling-beams were worm-eaten, the walls black with smoke, and the window-panes grey with dust. There was an oak dresser laden with all sorts of odds and ends—jugs, plates, pewter bowls, wolf-traps, sheep-shears, and an enormous syringe which amused the children. In the three yards outside there was not a single tree without either mushrooms at its base or mistletoe in its branches. Several had been blown down and had taken root again at the middle; all of them were bent under the weight of their apples. The thatched roofs, which looked like brown velvet and varied in thickness, weathered the fiercest winds, but the cart-shed was tumbling down. Mme Aubain said that she would have it seen to, and ordered the animals to be reharnessed.

It took them another half-hour to reach Trouville. The little caravan dismounted to make their way along the Écores, a cliff jutting right out over the boats moored below; and three minutes later they got to the end of the quay and entered the courtyard of the Golden Lamb, the inn kept by Mère David.

After the first few days Virginie felt stronger, as a result of the change of air and the sea-bathing. Not having a costume, she went into the water in her chemise and her maid dressed her afterwards in a customs officer's hut which was used by the bathers.

In the afternoons they took the donkey and went off beyond the Roches-Noires, in the direction of Hennequeville. To begin with, the path went uphill between gentle slopes like the lawns in a park, and then came out on a plateau where pastureland and ploughed fields alternated. On either side there were holly-bushes standing out from the tangle of brambles, and here and there a big dead tree spread its zigzag branches against the blue sky.

They almost always rested in the same field, with Deauville on their left, Le Havre on their right, and the open sea in front. The water glittered in the sunshine, smooth as a mirror, and so still that the murmur it made was scarcely audible; unseen sparrows could be heard twittering, and the sky covered the whole scene with its huge canopy. Mme Aubain sat doing her needlework, Virginie plaited rushes beside her, Félicité gathered lavender, and Paul, feeling profoundly bored, longed to get up and go.

Sometimes they crossed the Toucques in a boat and hunted for shells. When the tide went out, sea-urchins, ormers, and jelly-fish were left behind; and the children scampered around, snatching at the foam-flakes carried on the wind. The sleepy waves, breaking on the sand, spread themselves out along the shore. The beach stretched as far as the eye could see, bounded on the land side by the dunes which separated it from the Marais, a broad meadow in the shape of an arena. When they came back that way, Trouville, on the distant hillside, grew bigger at every step, and with its medley of oddly assorted houses seemed to blossom out in gay disorder.

On exceptionally hot days they stayed in their room. The sun shone in dazzling bars of light between the slats of the blind. There was not a sound to be heard in the village, and not a soul to be seen down in the street. Everything seemed more peaceful in the prevailing silence. In the distance caulkers were hammering away at the boats, and the smell of tar was wafted along by a sluggish breeze.

The principal amusement consisted in watching the fishingboats come in. As soon as they had passed the buoys, they started tacking. With their canvas partly lowered and their foresails blown out like balloons they glided through the splashing waves as far as the middle of the harbour, where they suddenly dropped anchor. Then each boat came alongside the quay, and the crew threw ashore their catch of quivering fish. A line of carts stood waiting, and women in cotton bonnets rushed forward to take the baskets and kiss their men.

One day one of these women spoke to Félicité, who came back to the inn soon after in a state of great excitement. She explained that she had found one of her sisters—and Nastasie Barette, now Leroux, made her appearance, with a baby at her breast, another child holding her right hand, and on her left a little sailor-boy, his arms akimbo and his cap over one ear.

Mme Aubain sent her off after a quarter of an hour. Fom then on they were forever hanging round the kitchen or loitering about when the family went for a walk, though the husband kept out of sight.

Félicité became quite attached to them. She bought them a blanket, several shirts, and a stove; and it was clear that they were bent on getting all they could out of her.

This weakness of hers annoyed Mme Aubain, who in any event disliked the familiar way in which the nephew spoke to Paul. And so, as Virginie had started coughing and the good weather was over, she decided to go back to Pont-l'Évêque.

M. Bourais advised her on the choice of a school; Caen was considered the best, so it was there that Paul was sent. He said good-bye bravely, feeling really rather pleased to be going to a place where he would have friends of his own.

Mme Aubain resigned herself to the loss of her son, knowing that it was unavoidable. Virginie soon got used to it. Félicité missed the din he used to make, but she was given something new to do which served as a distraction: from Christmas onwards she had to take the little girl to catechism every day.

3

After genuflecting at the door, she walked up the centre aisle under the nave, opened the door of Mme Aubain's pew, sat down, and started looking about her.

The choir stalls were all occupied, with the boys on the right and the girls on the left, while the curé stood by the lectern. In one of the stained-glass windows in the apse the Holy Ghost looked down on the Virgin; another window showed her kneeling before the Infant Jesus; and behind the tabernacle there was a wood-carving of St. Michael slaying the dragon.

The priest began with a brief outline of sacred history. Listening to him, Félicité saw in imagination the Garden of Eden, the Flood, the Tower of Babel, cities burning, peoples dying, and idols being overthrown; and this dazzling vision left her with a great respect for the Almighty and profound fear of His wrath.

Then she wept as she listened to the story of the Passion. Why had they crucified Him, when He loved children, fed the multitudes, healed the blind, and had chosen out of humility to be born among the poor, on the litter of a stable? The sowing of the seed, the reaping of the harvest, the pressing of the grapes—all those familiar things of which the Gospels speak had their place in her life. God had sanctified them in passing, so that she loved the lambs more tenderly for love of the Lamb of God, and the doves for the sake of the Holy Ghost.

She found it difficult, however, to imagine what the Holy Ghost looked like, for it was not just a bird but a fire as well, and sometimes a breath. She wondered whether that was its light she had seen flitting about the edge of the marshes at night, whether that was its breath she had felt driving the clouds across the sky, whether that was its voice she had heard in the sweet music of the bells. And she sat in silent adoration, delighting in the coolness of the walls and the quiet of the church.

Of dogma she neither understood nor even tried to understand anything. The curé discoursed, the children repeated their lesson, and she finally dropped off to sleep, waking up suddenly at the sound of their sabots clattering across the flagstones as they left the church.

It was in this manner, simply by hearing it expounded, that she learnt her catechism, for her religious education had been neglected in her youth. From then on she copied all Virginie's observances, fasting when she did and going to confession with her. On the feast of Corpus Christi the two of them made an altar of repose together.

The preparations for Virginie's first communion caused her great anxiety. She worried over her shoes, her rosary, her missal, and her gloves. And how she trembled as she helped Mme Aubain to dress the child!

All through the Mass her heart was in her mouth. One side of the choir was hidden from her by M. Bourais, but directly opposite her she could see the flock of maidens, looking like a field of snow with their white crowns perched on top of their veils; and she recognized her little darling from a distance by her dainty neck and her rapt attitude. The bell tinkled. Every head bowed low, and there was a silence. Then, to the thunderous accompaniment of the organ, choir and congregation joined in singing the *Agnus Dei*. Next the boys' procession began, and after that the girls got up from their seats. Slowly, their hands joined in prayer, they went towards the brightly lit altar, knelt on the first step, received the Host one by one, and went back to their places in the same order. When it was Virginie's turn, Félicité leant forward to see her, and in one of those imaginative flights born of real affection, it seemed to her that she herself was in the child's place. Virginie's face became her own, Virginie's dress clothed her, Virginie's heart was beating in her breast; and as she closed her eyes and opened her mouth, she almost fainted away.

Early next morning she went to the sacristy and asked M. le Curé to give her communion. She received the sacrament with all due reverence, but did not feel the same rapture as she had the day before.

Mme Aubain wanted her daughter to possess every accomplishment, and since Guyot could not teach her English or music, she decided to send her as a boarder to the Ursuline Convent at Honfleur.

Virginie raised no objection, but Félicité went about sighing at Madame's lack of feeling. Then she thought that perhaps her mistress was right: such matters, after all, lay outside her province.

Finally the day arrived when an old waggonette stopped at their door, and a nun got down from it who had come to fetch Mademoiselle. Félicité hoisted the luggage up on top, gave the driver some parting instructions, and put six pots of jam, a dozen pears, and a bunch of violets in the boot.

At the last moment Virginie burst into a fit of sobbing. She threw her arms round her mother, who kissed her on the forehead, saying: 'Come now, be brave, be brave.' The step was pulled up and the carriage drove away.

Then Mme Aubain broke down, and that evening all her friends, M. and Mme Lormeau, Mme Lechaptois, the Rochefeuille sisters, M. de Houppeville, and Bourais, came in to console her.

To begin with she missed her daughter badly. But she had a letter from her three times a week, wrote back on the other days, walked round her garden, did a little reading, and thus contrived to fill the empty hours.

As for Félicité, she went into Virginie's room every morning from sheer force of habit and looked round it. It upset her not having to brush the child's hair any more, tie her bootlaces, or tuck her up in bed; and she missed seeing her sweet face all the time and holding her hand when they went out together. For want of something to do, she tried making lace, but her fingers were too clumsy and broke the threads. She could not settle to anything, lost her sleep, and, to use her own words, was 'eaten up inside'.

To 'occupy her mind', she asked if her nephew Victor might come and see her, and permission was granted.

He used to arrive after Mass on Sunday, his cheeks flushed, his chest bare, and smelling of the countryside through which he had come. She laid a place for him straight away, opposite hers, and they had lunch together. Eating as little as possible herself, in order to save the expense, she stuffed him so full of food that he fell asleep after the meal. When the first bell for vespers rang, she woke him up, brushed his trousers, tied his tie, and set off for church, leaning on his arm with all a mother's pride.

His parents always told him to get something out of her—a packet of brown sugar perhaps, some soap, or a little brandy, sometimes even money. He brought her his clothes to be mended, and she did the work gladly, thankful for anything that would force him to come again

In August his father took him on a coasting trip. The children's holidays were just beginning, and it cheered her up to have them home again. But Paul was turning capricious and Virginie was getting too old to be addressed familiarly—a state of affairs which put a barrier of constraint between them.

Victor went to Morlaix, Dunkirk, and Brighton in turn, and brought her a present after each trip. The first time it was a box covered with shells, the second a coffee cup, the third a big gingerbread man. He was growing quite handsome, with his trim figure, his little moustache, his frank open eyes, and the little leather cap that he wore on the back of his head like a pilot. He kept her amused by telling her stories full of nautical jargon.

One Monday—it was the fourteenth of July 1819, a date she never forgot—Victor told her that he had signed on for an ocean voyage, and that on the Wednesday night he would be taking the Honfleur packet to join his schooner, which was due to sail shortly from Le Havre. He might be away, he said, for two years.

The prospect of such a long absence made Félicité extremely unhappy, and she felt she must bid him godspeed once more. So on the Wednesday evening, when Madame's dinner was over, she put on her clogs and swiftly covered the ten miles between Pont-l'Évêque and Honfleur.

When she arrived at the Calvary she turned right instead of left, got lost in the shipyards, and had to retrace her steps. Some people she spoke to advised her to hurry. She went right round the harbour, which was full of boats, constantly tripping over moorings. Then the ground fell away, rays of light crisscrossed in front of her, and for a moment she thought she was going mad, for she could see horses up in the sky.

On the quayside more horses were neighing, frightened by the sea. A derrick was hoisting them into the air and dropping them into one of the boats, which was already crowded with passengers elbowing their way between barrels of cider, baskets of cheese, and sacks of grain. Hens were cackling and the captain swearing, while a cabin-boy stood leaning on the cats-head, completely indifferent to it all. Félicité, who had not recognized him, shouted: 'Victor!' and he raised his head. She rushed forward, but at that very moment the gangway was pulled ashore.

The packet moved out of the harbour with women singing as they hauled it along, its ribs creaking and heavy waves lashing its bows. The sail swung round, hiding everyone on board from view, and against the silvery, moonlit sea the boat appeared as a dark shape that grew ever fainter, until at last it vanished in the distance.

As Félicité was passing the Calvary, she felt a longing to commend to God's mercy all that she held most dear; and she stood there praying for a long time, her face bathed in tears, her eyes fixed upon the clouds. The town was asleep, except for the customs officers walking up and down. Water was pouring ceaselessly through the holes in the sluice-gate, making as much noise as a torrent. The clocks struck two.

The convent parlour would not be open before daybreak, and Madame would be annoyed if she were late; so, although she would have liked to give a kiss to the other child, she set off for home. The maids at the inn were just waking up as she got to Pont-l'Évêque.

So the poor lad was going to be tossed by the waves for months on end! His previous voyages had caused her no alarm. People came back from England and Brittany; but America, the Colonies, the Islands, were all so far away, somewhere at the other end of the world.

From then on Félicité thought of nothing but her nephew. On sunny days she hoped he was not too thirsty, and when there was a storm she was afraid he would be struck by lightning. Listening to the wind howling in the chimney or blowing slates off the roof, she saw him being buffeted by the very same storm, perched on the top of a broken mast, with his whole body bent backwards under a sheet of foam; or again—and these were reminiscences of the illustrated geography-book—he was being eaten by savages, captured by monkeys in a forest, or dying on a desert shore. But she never spoke of her worries.

Mme Aubain had worries of her own about her daughter. The good nuns said that she was an affectionate child, but very delicate. The slightest emotion upset her, and she had to give up playing the piano.

Her mother insisted on regular letters from the convent. One morning when the postman had not called, she lost patience and walked up and down the room, between her chair and the window. It was really extraordinary! Four days without any news!

Thinking her own example would confort her, Félicité said:

'I've been six months, Madame, without news.'

'News of whom?'

The servant answered gently:

'Why—of my nephew.'

'Oh, your nephew!' And Mme Aubain started pacing up and down again, with a shrug of her shoulders that seemed to say: 'I wasn't thinking of him—and indeed, why should I? Who cares about a young, good-for-nothing cabin-boy? Whereas my daughter—why, just think!'

Although she had been brought up the hard way, Félicité was indignant with Madame, but she soon forgot. It struck her as perfectly natural to lose one's head where the little girl was concerned. For her, the two children were of equal importance; they were linked together in her heart by a single bond, and their destinies should be the same.

The chemist told her that Victor's ship had arrived at Havana: he had seen this piece of information in a newspaper. Because of its association with cigars, she imagined Havana as a place where nobody did anything but smoke, and pictured Victor walking about among crowds of Negroes in a cloud of tobacco-smoke. Was it possible, she wondered, 'in case of need' to come back by land? And how far was it from Pont-l'Évêque? To find out she asked M. Bourais.

He reached for his atlas, and launched forth into an explanation of latitudes and longitudes, smiling like the pedant he was at Félicité's bewilderment. Finally he pointed with his pencil at a minute black dot inside a ragged oval patch, saying:

'There it is.'

She bent over the map, but the network of coloured lines meant nothing to her and only tired her eyes. So when Bourais asked her to tell him what was puzzling her, she begged him to show her the house where Victor was living. He threw up his hands, sneezed, and roared with laughter, delighted to come across such simplicity. And Félicité—whose intelligence was so limited that she probably expected to see an actual portrait of her nephew—could not make out why he was laughing.

It was a fortnight later that Liébard came into the kitchen at market-time, as he usually did, and handed her a letter from her brother-in-law. As neither of them could read, she turned to her mistress for help.

Mme Aubain, who was counting the stitches in her knitting, put it down and unsealed the letter. She gave a start, and, looking hard at Félicité, said quietly:

'They have some bad news for you . . . Your nephew . . .'

He was dead. That was all the letter had to say.

Félicité dropped on to a chair, leaning her head against the wall and closing her eyelids, which suddenly turned pink. Then, with her head bowed, her hands dangling, and her eyes set, she kept repeating:

'Poor little lad! Poor little lad!'

Liébard looked at her and sighed. Mme Aubain was trembling slightly. She suggested that she should go and see her sister at Trouville, but Félicité shook her head to indicate that there was no need for that.

There was a silence. Old Liébard thought it advisable to go.

Then Félicité said:

'It doesn't matter a bit, not to them it doesn't.'

Her head fell forward again, and from time to time she unconsciously picked up the knitting needles lying on the worktable.

Some women went past carrying a tray full of dripping linen.

Catching sight of them through the window, she remembered her own washing; she had passed the lye through it the day before and today it needed rinsing. So she left the room.

Her board and tub were on the bank of the Toucques. She threw a pile of chemises down by the water's edge, rolled up her sleeves, and picked up her battledore. The lusty blows she gave with it could be heard in all the neighbouring gardens.

The fields were empty, the river rippling in the wind; at the bottom long weeds were waving to and fro, like the hair of corpses floating in the water. She held back her grief, and was very brave until the evening; but in her room she gave way to it completely, lying on her mattress with her face buried in the pillow and her fists pressed against her temples.

Long afterwards she learnt the circumstances of Victor's death from the captain of his ship. He had gone down with yellow fever, and they had bled him too much at the hospital. Four doctors had held him at once. He had died straight away, and the chief doctor had said:

'Good! There goes another!'

His parents had always treated him cruelly. She preferred not to see them again, and they made no advances, either because they had forgotten about her or out of the callousness of the poor.

Meanwhile Virginie was growing weaker. Difficulty in breathing, fits of coughing, protracted bouts of fever, and mottled patches on the cheekbones all indicated some deepseated complaint. M. Poupart had advised a stay in Provence. Mme Aubain decided to follow this suggestion, and, if it had not been for the weather at Pont-l'Évêque, she would have brought her daughter home at once.

She arranged with a jobmaster to drive her out to the convent every Tuesday. There was a terrace in the garden, overlooking the Seine, and there Virginie, leaning on her mother's arm, walked up and down over the fallen vine-leaves. Sometimes, while she was looking at the sails in the distance, or at the long stretch of horizon from the Château de Tancarville to the lighthouses of Le Havre, the sun would break through the clouds and make her blink. Afterwards they would rest in the arbour. Her mother had secured a little cask of excellent Malaga, and, laughing at the idea of getting tipsy, Virginie used to drink a thimbleful, but no more.

Her strength revived. Autumn slipped by, and Félicité assured Mme Aubain that there was nothing to fear. But one evening, coming back from some errand in the neighbourhood, she found M. Poupart's gig standing at the door. He was in the hall, and Mme Aubain was tying on her bonnet.

'Give me my foot-warmer, purse, gloves. Quickly now!'

Virginie had pneumonia and was perhaps past recovery.

'Not yet!' said the doctor; and the two of them got into the carriage with snow-flakes swirling around them. Night was falling and it was very cold.

'Félicité rushed into the church to light a candle, and then ran after the gig. She caught up with it an hour later, jumped lightly up behind, and hung on to the fringe. But then a thought struck her: the courtyard had not been locked up, and burglars might get in. So she jumped down again.

At dawn the next day she went to the doctor's. He had come home and gone out again on his rounds. Then she waited at the inn, thinking that somebody who was a stranger to the district might call there with a letter. Finally, when it was twilight, she got into the coach for Lisieux.

The convent was at the bottom of a steep lane. When she was half-way down the hill, she heard a strange sound which she recognized as a death-bell tolling.

'It's for somebody else', she thought, as she banged the door-knocker hard.

After a few minutes she heard the sound of shuffling feet, the door opened a little way, and a nun appeared.

The good sister said with an air of compunction that 'she had just passed away'. At that moment the bell of Saint-Léonard was tolled more vigorously than ever.

Félicité went up to the second floor. From the doorway of the room she could see Virginie lying on her back, her hands clasped together, her mouth open, her head tilted back under a black crucifix that leant over her, her face whiter than the curtains that hung motionless on either side. Mme Aubain was clinging to the foot of the bed and sobbing desperately. The Mother Superior stood on the right. Three candlesticks on the chest of drawers added touches of red to the scene, and fog was whitening the windows. Some nuns led Mme Aubain away.

For two nights Félicité never left the dead girl. She said the same prayers over and over again, sprinkled holy water on the sheets, then sat down again to watch. At the end of her first vigil, she noticed that the child's face had gone yellow, the lips were turning blue, the nose looked sharper, and the eyes were sunken. She kissed them several times, and would not have been particularly surprised if Virginie had opened them again: to minds like hers the supernatural is a simple matter. She laid her out, wrapped her in a shroud, put her in her coffin, placed a wreath on her, and spread out her hair. It was fair and amazingly long for her age. Félicité cut off a big lock, half of which she slipped into her bosom, resolving never to part with it.

The body was brought back to Pont-l'Évêque at the request of Mme Aubain, who followed the hearse in a closed carriage.

After the Requiem Mass, it took another three-quarters of an hour to reach the cemetery. Paul walked in front, sobbing. Then came M. Bourais, and after him the principal inhabitants of the town, the women all wearing long black veils, and Félicité. She was thinking about her nephew; and since she had been unable to pay him these last honours, she felt an added grief, just as if they were burying him with Virginie.

Mme Aubain's despair passed all bounds. First of all she rebelled against God, considering it unfair of Him to have taken her daughter from her—for she had never done any harm, and her conscience was quite clear. But was it? She ought to have taken Virginie to the south; other doctors would have saved her life. She blamed herself, wished she could have joined her daughter, and cried out in anguish in her dreams. One dream in particular obsessed her. Her husband, dressed like a sailor, came back from a long voyage, and told her amid tears that he had been ordered to take Virginie away—whereupon they put their heads together to discover somewhere to hide her.

One day she came in from the garden utterly distraught. A few minutes earlier—and she pointed to the spot—father and daughter had appeared to her, doing nothing, but simply looking at her.

For several months she stayed in her room in a kind of stupor. Félicité scolded her gently, telling her that she must take care of herself for her son's sake, and also in remembrance of 'her'.

'Her?' repeated Mme Aubain, as if she were waking from a sleep. 'Oh, yes, of course! You don't forget her, do you!' This was an allusion to the cemetery, where she herself was strictly forbidden to go.

Félicité went there every day. She would set out on the stroke of four, going past the houses, up the hill, and through the gate, until she came to

Virginie's grave. There was a little column of pink marble with a tablet at its base, and a tiny garden enclosed by chains. The beds were hidden under a carpet of flowers. She watered their leaves and changed the sand, going down on her knees to fork the ground thoroughly. The result was that when Mme Aubain was able to come here, she experienced a feeling of relief, a kind of consolation.

Then the years slipped by, each one like the last, with nothing to vary the rhythm of the great festivals: Easter, the Assumption, All Saints' Day. Domestic events marked dates that later served as points of reference. Thus in 1825 a couple of glaziers whitewashed the hall; in 1827 a piece of the roof fell into the courtyard and nearly killed a man; and in the summer of 1828 it was Madame's turn to provide the bread for consecration. About this time Bourais went away in a mysterious fashion; and one by one the old acquaintances disappeared: Guyot, Liébard, Mme Lechaptois, Robelin, and Uncle Grémanville, who had been paralysed for a long time.

One night the driver of the mail-coach brought Pont-l'Évêque news of the July Revolution. A few days later a new sub-prefect was appointed. This was the Baron de Larsonnière, who had been a consul in America, and who brought with him, besides his wife, his sister-in-law and three young ladies who were almost grown-up. They were to be seen on their lawn, dressed in loose-fitting smocks; and they had a Negro servant and a parrot. They paid a call on Mme Aubain, who made a point of returning it. As soon as Félicité saw them coming, she would run and tell her mistress. But only one thing could really awaken her interest, and that was her son's letters.

He seemed to be incapable of following any career and spent all his time in taverns. She paid his debts, but he contracted new ones, and the sighs Mme Aubain heaved as she knitted by the window reached Félicité at her spinning-wheel in the kitchen.

The two women used to walk up and down together beside the espalier, forever talking of Virginie and debating whether such and such a thing would have appealed to her, or what she would have said on such and such an occasion.

All her little belongings were in a cupboard in the children's bedroom. Mme Aubain went through them as seldom as possible. One summer day she resigned herself to doing so, and the moths were sent fluttering out of the cupboard.

Virginie's frocks hung in a row underneath a shelf containing three dolls, a few hoops, a set of toy furniture, and the wash-basin she had used. Besides the frocks, they took out her petticoats, her stockings and her handkerchiefs, and spread them out on the two beds before folding them up again. The sunlight streamed in on these pathetic objects, bringing out the stains and showing up the creases made by the child's movements. The air was warm, the sky was blue, a blackbird was singing, and everything seemed to be utterly at peace.

They found a little chestnut-coloured hat, made of plush with a long nap; but the moths had ruined it. Félicité asked if she might have it. The two women looked at each other and their eyes filled with tears. Then the mistress opened her arms, the maid threw herself into them, and they clasped each other in a warm embrace, satisfying their grief in a kiss which made them equal.

It was the first time that such a thing had happened, for Mme Aubain was not of a demonstrative nature. Félicité was as grateful as if she had received a great favour, and henceforth loved her mistress with dog-like devotion and religious veneration.

Her heart grew softer as time went by.

When she heard the drums of a regiment coming down the street she stood at the door with a jug of cider and offered the soldiers a drink. She looked after the people who went down with cholera. She watched over the Polish refugees, and one of them actually expressed a desire to marry her. But they fell out, for when she came back from the Angelus one morning, she found that he had got into her kitchen and was calmly eating an oil-and-vinegar salad.

After the Poles it was Père Colmiche, an old man who was said to have committed fearful atrocities in '93. He lived by the river in a ruined pig-sty. The boys of the town used to peer at him through the cracks in the walls, and threw pebbles at him which landed on the litter where he lay, constantly shaken by fits of coughing. His hair was extremely long, his eyelids inflamed, and on one arm there was a swelling bigger than his head. Félicité brought him some linen, tried to clean out his filthy hovel, and even wondered if she could install him in the wash-house without annoying Madame. When the tumour had burst, she changed his dressings every day, brought him some cake now and then, and put him out in the sun on a truss of hay. The poor old fellow would thank her in a faint whisper, slavering and trembling all the while, fearful of losing her and stretching his hands out as soon as he saw her moving away.

He died, and she had a Mass said for the repose of his soul.

That same day a great piece of good fortune came her way. Just as she was serving dinner, Mme de Larsonniére's Negro appeared carrying the parrot in its cage, complete with perch, chain, and padlock. The Baroness had written a note informing Mme Aubain that her husband had been promoted to a Prefecture and they were leaving that evening; she begged her to accept the parrot as a keepsake and a token of her regard.

This bird had engrossed Félicité's thoughts for a long time, for it came from America, and that word reminded her of Victor. So she had asked the Negro all about it, and once she had even gone so far as to say:

'How pleased Madame would be if it were hers!'

The Negro had repeated this remark to his mistress, who, unable to take the parrot with her, was glad to get rid of it in this way.

4

His name was Loulou. His body was green, the tips of his wings were pink, his poll blue, and his breast golden.

Unfortunately he had a tiresome mania for biting his perch, and also used to pull his feathers out, scatter his droppings everywhere, and upset his bath water. He annoyed Mme Aubain, and so she gave him to Félicité for good.

Félicité started training him, and soon he could say: 'Nice boy! Your servant, sir! Hail, Mary!' He was put near the door, and several people who spoke to him said how strange it was that he did not answer to the name of Jacquot, as all parrots were called Jacquot. They likened him to a turkey or a block of wood, and every sneer cut Félicité to the quick. How odd, she thought, that Loulou should be so stubborn, refusing to talk whenever anyone looked at him!

For all that, he liked having people around him, bacause on Sundays, while the Rochefeuille sisters, M. Houppeville and some new friends—the apothecary Onfroy, M. Varin, and Captain Mathieu—were having their game of cards, he would beat on the window-panes with his wings and make such a din that it was impossible to hear oneself speak.

Bourais's face obviously struck him as terribly funny, for as soon as he saw it he was seized with uncontrollable laughter. His shrieks range round the court-yard, the echo repeated them, and the neighbours came to their windows and started laughing too. To avoid being seen by the bird, M. Bourais used to creep along by the wall, hiding his face behind his hat, until he got to the river, and then come into the house from the garden. The looks he gave the parrot were far from tender.

Loulou had once been cuffed by the butcher's boy for poking his head into his basket; and since then he was always trying to give him a nip through his shirt. Fabu threatened to wring his neck, although he was not a cruel fellow, in spite of his tattooed arms and bushy whiskers. On the contrary, he rather liked the parrot, so much so indeed that in a spirit of jovial camaraderie he tried to teach him a few swear-words. Félicité, alarmed at this development, put the bird in the kitchen. His little chain was removed and he was allowed to wander all over the house.

Coming downstairs, he used to rest the curved part of his beak on each step and then raise first his right foot, then his left; and Félicité was afraid that this sort of gymnastic performance would make him giddy. He fell ill and could neither talk nor eat for there was a swelling under his tongue such as hens sometimes have. She cured him by pulling this pellicule out with her finger-nails. One day M. Paul was silly enough to blow the smoke of his cigar at him; another time Mme Lormeau started teasing him with the end of her parasol, and he caught hold of the ferrule with his beak. Finally he got lost.

Félicité had put him down on the grass in the fresh air, and left him there for a minute. When she came back, the parrot had gone. First of all she looked for him in the bushes, by the river and on the rooftops, paying no attention to her mistress's shouts of: 'Be careful, now! You must be mad!' Next she went over all the gardens in Pont-l'Évêque, stopping passers-by and asking them: 'You don't happen to have seen my parrot by any chance?' Those who did not know him already were given a description of the bird. Suddenly she thought she could make out something green flying about behind the mills at the foot of the hill. But up on the hill there was nothing to be seen. A pedlar told her that he had come upon the parrot a short time before in Mère Simon's shop at Saint-Melaine.

She ran all the way there, but no one knew what she was talking about. Finally she came back home, worn out, her shoes falling to pieces, and death in her heart. She was sitting beside Madame on the garden-seat and telling her what she had been doing, when she felt something light drop on her shoulder. It was Loulou! What he had been up to, no one could discover· perhaps he had just gone for a little walk round the town.

Félicité was slow to recover from this fright, and indeed never really got over it.

As the result of a chill she had an attack of quinsy, and soon after that her ears were affected. Three years later she was deaf, and she spoke at the top of her voice, even in church. Although her sins could have been proclaimed over the length and breadth of the dioceses without dishonour to her or offence to others, M. le Curé thought it advisable to hear her confession in the sacristy.

Imaginary buzzings in the head added to her troubles. Often her mistress would say: 'Heavens, how stupid you are!' and she would reply: 'Yes, Madame,' at the same time looking all around her for something.

The little circle of her ideas grew narrower and narrower, and the pealing of bells and the lowing of cattle went out of her life. Every living thing moved about in a ghostly silence. Only one sound reached her ears now, and that was the voice of the parrot.

As if to amuse her, he would reproduce the click-clack of the turn-spit, the shrill call of a man selling fish, and the noise of the saw at the joiner's across the way; and when the bell rang he would imitate Mme Aubain's 'Félicité! The door, the door!'

They held conversations with each other he repeating *ad nauseam* the three phrases in his repertory, she replying with words which were just as disconnected but which came from the heart. In her isolation, Loulou was almost a son or a lover to her. He used to climb up her fingers, peck at her lips, and hang on to her shawl; and as she bent over him, wagging her head from side to side as nurses do, the great wings of her bonnet and the wings of the bird quivered in unison.

When clouds banked up in the sky and there was a rumbling of thunder, he would utter piercing cries, no doubt remembering the sudden downpours in his native forests. The sound of the rain falling roused him to frenzy. He would flap excitedly around, shoot up to the ceiling, knocking everything over, and fly out of the window to splash about in the garden. But he would soon come back to perch on one of the fire-dogs, hopping about to dry his feathers and showing tail and beak in turn.

One morning in the terrible winter of 1837, when she had put him in front of the fire because of the cold she found him dead in the middle of his cage, hanging head down with his claws caught in the bars. He had probably died of a stroke, but she thought he had been poisoned with parsley, and despite the absence of any proof, her suspicions fell on Fabu.

She wept so much that her mistress said to her: 'Why don't you have him stuffed?'

Félicité asked the chemist's advice, remembering that he had always been kind to the parrot. He wrote to Le Havre, and a man called Fellacher agreed to do the job. As parcels sometimes went astray on the mail-coach, she decided to take the parrot as far as Honfleur herself.

On either side of the road stretched an endless succession of apple-trees, all stripped of their leaves, and there was ice in the ditches. Dogs were barking around the farms; and Félicité, with her hands tucked under her mantlet, her little black sabots and her basket, walked briskly along the middle of the road.

She crossed the forest, passed Le Haut Chêne, and got as far as Saint-Gatien.

Behind her, in a cloud of dust, and gathering speed as the horses galloped downhill, a mail-coach swept along like a whirlwind. When he saw this woman making no attempt to get out of the way, the driver poked his head out above the hood, and he and the postilion shouted at her. His four horses could not be held in and galloped faster, the two leaders touching her as they went by. With a jerk of the reins the driver threw them to one side, and then, in a fury, he raised his long whip and gave her such a lash, from head to waist, that she fell flat on her back.

The first thing she did on regaining consciousness was to open her basket. Fortunately nothing had happened to Loulou. She felt her right cheek burning, and when she touched it her hand turned red; it was bleeding.

She sat down on a heap of stones and dabbed her face with her handkerchief. Then she ate a crust of bread which she had taken the precaution of putting in her basket, and tried to forget her wound by looking at the bird.

As she reached the top of the hill at Ecquemauville, she saw the lights of Honfleur twinkling in the darkness like a host of stars, and the shadowy expanse of the sea beyond. Then a sudden feeling of faintness made her stop; and the misery of her childhood, the disappointment of her first love, the departure of her nephew, and the death of Virginie all came back to her at once like the waves of a rising tide, and, welling up in her throat, choked her.

When she got to the boat she insisted on speaking to the captain, and without telling him what was in her parcel, asked him to take good care of it.

Fellacher kept the parrot a long time. Every week he promised it for the next; after six months he announced that a box had been sent off, and nothing more was heard of it. It looked as though Loulou would never come back, and Félicité told herself: 'They've stolen him for sure!'

At last he arrived—looking quite magnificent, perched on a branch screwed into a mahogany base, one foot in the air, his head cocked to one side, and biting a nut which the taxidermist, out of love of the grandiose, had gilded.

Félicité shut him up in her room.

This place, to which few people were ever admitted, contained such a quantity of religious bric-à-brac and miscellaneous oddments that it looked like a cross between a chapel and a bazaar.

A big wardrobe prevented the door from opening properly. Opposite the window that overlooked the garden was a little round one looking on to the courtyard. There was a table beside the bed, with a water-jug, a couple of combs, and a block of blue soap in a chipped plate. On the walls there were rosaries, medals, several pictures of the Virgin, and a holy-water stoup made out of a coconut. On the chest of drawers, which was draped with a cloth just like an altar, was the shell box Victor had given her, and also a watering-can and a ball, some copybooks, the illustrated geography book, and a pair of ankle-boots. And on the nail supporting the looking-glass, fastened by its ribbons, hung the little plush hat.

Félicité carried this form of veneration to such lengths that she even kept one of Monsieur's frock-coats. All the old rubbish Mme Aubain had no more use for, she carried off to her room. That was how there came to be artificial flowers along the edge of the chest of drawers, and a portrait of the Comte d'Artois in the window-recess.

With the aid of a wall-bracket, Loulou was installed on a chimney-breast that jutted out into the room. Every morning when she awoke, she saw him in the light of the dawn, and then she remembered the old days, and the smallest details of insignificant actions, not in sorrow but in absolute tranquillity.

Having no intercourse with anyone, she lived in the torpid state of a sleep-walker. The Corpus Christi processions roused her from this condition, for she would go round the neighbours collecting candlesticks and mats to decorate the altar of repose which they used to set up in the street.

In church she was forever gazing at the Holy Ghost, and one day she noticed that it had something of the parrot about it. This resemblance struck her as even more obvious in a colour-print depicting the baptism of Our Lord. With its red wings and its emerald-green body, it was the very image of Loulous.

She bought the print and hung it in the place of the Comte d'Artois, so that she could include them both in a single glance. They were linked together in her mind, the parrot being sanctified by this connexion with the Holy Ghost, which itself acquired new life and meaning in her eyes. God the Father could not have chosen a dove as a means of expressing Himself, since doves cannot talk, but rather one of Loulou's ancestors. And although Félicité used to say her prayers with her eyes on the picture, from time to time she would turn slightly towards the bird.

She wanted to join the Children of Mary, but Mme Aubain dissuaded her from doing so.

An important event now loomed up—Paul's wedding.

After starting as a lawyer's clerk, he had been in business, in the Customs, and in Inland Revenue, and had even begun trying to get into the Department of Woods and Forests, when, at the age of thirty-six, by some heaven-sent inspiration, he suddenly discovered his real vocation—in the Wills and Probate Department. There he proved so capable that one of the auditors had offered him his daughter in marriage and promised to use his influence on his behalf.

Paul, grown serious-minded, brought her to see his mother. She criticized the way things were done at Pont-l'Évêque, put on airs, and hurt Félicité's feelings. Mme Aubain was relieved to see her go.

The following week came news of M. Bourais's death in an inn in Lower

Brittany. Rumours that he had committed suicide were confirmed, and doubts arose as to his honesty. Mme Aubain went over her accounts and was soon conversant with the full catalogue of his misdeeds—embezzlement of interest, secret sales of timber, forged receipts, etc. Besides all this, he was the father of an illegitimate child, and had had 'relations with a person at Dozulé'.

These infamies upset Mme Aubain greatly. In March 1853 she was afflicted with a pain in the chest; her tongue seemed to be covered with a film; leeches failed to make her breathing any easier; and on the ninth evening of her illness she died. She had just reached the age of seventy-two.

She was thought to be younger because of her brown hair, worn in bandeaux round her pale, pock-marked face. There were few friends to mourn her, for she had a haughty manner which put people off. Yet Félicité wept for her as servants rarely weep for their masters. That Madame should die before her upset her ideas, seemed to be contrary to the order of things, monstrous and unthinkable.

Ten days later—the time it took to travel hot-foot from Besançon—the heirs arrived. The daughter-in-law ransacked every drawer, picked out some pieces of furniture and sold the rest; and then back they went to the Wills and Probate Department.

Madame's arm-chair, her pedestal table, her foot-warmer, and the eight chairs had all gone. Yellow squares in the centre of the wall-panels showed where the pictures had hung. They had carried off the two cots with their mattresses, and no trace remained in the cupboard of all Virginie's things. Félicité climbed the stairs to her room, numbed with sadness.

The next day there was a notice on the door, and the apothecary shouted in her ear that the house was up for sale.

She swayed on her feet, and was obliged to sit down.

What distressed her most of all was the idea of leaving her room, which was so suitable for poor Loulou. Fixing an anguished look on him as she appealed to the Holy Ghost, she contracted the idolatrous habit of kneeling in front of the parrot to say her prayers. Sometimes the sun, as it came through the little window, caught his glass eye, so that it shot out a great luminous ray which sent her into ecstasies.

She had a pension of three hundred and eighty francs a year which her mistress had left her. The garden kept her in vegetables. As for clothes, she had enough to last her till the end of her days, and she saved on lighting by going to bed as soon as darkness fell.

She went out as little as possible, to avoid the second-hand dealer's shop, where some of the old furniture was on display. Ever since her fit of giddiness, she had been dragging one leg; and as her strength was failing, Mère Simon, whose grocery business had come to grief, came in every morning to chop wood and pump water for her.

Her eyes grew weaker. The shutters were not opened any more. Years went by, and nobody rented the house and nobody bought it.

For fear of being evicted, Félicité never asked for any repairs to be done.

The laths in the roof rotted, and all through one winter her bolster was wet. After Easter she began spitting blood.

When this happened Mère Simon called in a doctor. Félicité wanted to know what was the matter with her, but she was so deaf that only one word reached her: 'Pneumonia.' It was a word she knew, and she answered gently: 'Ah! Like Madame', thinking it natural that she should follow in her mistress's footsteps.

The time to set up the altars of repose was drawing near.

The first altar was always at the foot of the hill, the second in front of the post office, the third about half-way up the street. There was some argument as to the siting of this one, and finally the women of the parish picked on Mme Aubain's courtyard.

The fever and the tightness of the chest grew worse. Félicité fretted over not doing anything for the altar. If only she could have put something on it! Then she thought of the parrot. The neighbours protested that it would not be seemly, but the curé gave his permission, and this made her so happy that she begged him to accept Loulou, the only thing of value she possessed, when she died.

From Tuesday to Saturday, the eve of Corpus Christi, she coughed more and more frequently. In the evening her face looked pinched and drawn, her lips stuck to her gums, and she started vomiting. At dawn the next day, feeling very low, she sent for a priest.

Three good women stood by her while she was given extreme unction. Then she said that she had to speak to Fabu.

He arrived in his Sunday best, very ill at ease in this funereal atmosphere.

'Forgive me,' she said, making an effort to stretch out her arm. 'I thought it was you who had killed him.'

What could she mean by such nonsense? To think that she had suspected a man like him of murder! He got very indignant and was obviously going to make a scene.

'Can't you see', they said, 'that she isn't in her right mind any more?'

From time to time Félicité would start talking to shadows. The women went away. Mère Simon had her lunch.

A little later she picked Loulou up and held him out to Félicité, saying:

'Come now, say good-bye to him.'

Although the parrot was not a corpse, the worms were eating him up. One of his wings was broken, and the stuffing was coming out of his stomach. But she was blind by now, and she kissed him on the forehead and pressed him against her cheek. Mère Simon took him away from her to put him on the altar.

5

The scents of summer came up from the meadows; there was a buzzing of flies; the sun was glittering in the river and warming the slates of the roof. Mère Simon had come back into the room and was gently nodding off to sleep.

The noise of church bells woke her up; the congregation was coming out from vespers. Félicité's delirium abated. Thinking of the procession, she could see it as clearly as if she had been following it.

All the school-children, the choristers, and the firemen were walking along the pavements, while advancing up the middle of the street came the church officer armed with his halberd, the beadle carrying a great cross, the schoolmaster keeping an eye on the boys, and the nun fussing over her little girls—three of the prettiest, looking like curly-headed angels, were throwing rose-petals into the air. Then came the deacon, with both arms outstretched, conducting the band, and a couple of censer-bearers who turned round at every step to face the Holy Sacrament, which the curé, wearing his splendid chasuble, was carrying under a canopy of poppy-red velvet held aloft by four churchwardens. A crowd of people surged along behind, between the white cloths covering the walls of the houses, and eventually they got to the bottom of the hill.

A cold sweat moistened Félicité's temples. Mère Simon sponged it up with a cloth, telling herself that one day she would have to go the same way.

The hum of the crowd increased in volume, was very loud for a moment, then faded away.

A fusillade shook the window-panes. It was the postilions saluting the monstrance. Félicité rolled her eyes and said as loud as she could: 'Is he all right?'—worrying about the parrot.

She entered into her death-agony. Her breath, coming ever faster, with a rattling sound, made her sides heave. Bubbles of froth appeared at the corners of her mouth, and her whole body trembled.

Soon the booming of the ophicleides, the clear voices of the children, and the deep voices of the men could be heard near at hand. Now and then everything was quiet, and the tramping of feet, deadened by a carpet of flowers, sounded like a flock moving across pasture-land.

The clergy appeared in the courtyard. Mère Simon climbed on to a chair to reach the little round window, from which she had a full view of the altar below.

It was hung with green garlands and adorned with a flounce in English needle-point lace. In the middle was a little frame containing some relics, there were two orange-trees at the corners, and all the way along stood silver candlesticks and china vases holding sunflowers, lilies, peonies, foxgloves, and bunches of hydrangea. This pyramid of bright colours stretched from the first floor right down to the carpet which was spread out over the pavement. Some rare objects caught the eye: a silver-gilt sugar-basin wreathed in violets, some pennants of Alençon gems gleaming on a bed of moss, and two Chinese screens with landscape decorations. Loulou, hidden under roses, showed nothing but his blue poll, which looked like a plaque of lapis lazuli.

The churchwardens, the choristers, and the children lined up along the three sides of the courtyard. The priest went slowly up the steps and placed his great shining gold sun on the lace altar-cloth. Everyone knelt down. There was a deep silence. And the censers, swinging at full tilt, slid up and down their chains.

A blue cloud of incense was wafted up into Félicité's room. She opened her nostrils wide and breathed it in with a mystical, sensuous fervour. Then she closed her eyes. Her lips smiled. Her heart-beats grew slower and slower, each a little fainter and gentler, like a fountain running dry, an echo fading away. And as she breathed her last, she thought she could see, in the opening heavens, a gigantic parrot hovering above her head.

NOTES ON THE AUTHORS

SECTION I

Pär Lagerkvist (1891-). Swedish poet, dramatist, and novelist. Writing reflects his special concern with political and social problems. In 1951 awarded the Nobel Prize for Literature. His fiction includes *The Dwarf, Barabbas, The Holy Land, The Marriage Feast and Other Stories.*

Alain Robbe-Grillet (1922-). French novelist and critic. In the latter capacity influential in developing the "new novel," with its emphasis on the visual and descriptive rather than the analogical. His criticism collected in *For a New Novel: Essays on Fiction.* Other writing includes, *The Erasers, The Voyeur, Jealousy, In the Labyrinth,* and *Snapshots,* as well as the screen play for *Last Year at Marienbad.*

James Baldwin (1924-). Born in New York and grew up in Harlem, where his father was a minister. In 1948 moved to Europe and there wrote his first three books. His essays include *Notes of a Native Son, Nobody Knows my Name,* and *The Fire Next Time.* Among his fiction and plays are *Go Tell it on the Mountain, Giovanni's Room, Tell Me How Long the Train's Been Gone, The Amen Corner,* and *Blues for Mr. Charley.*

Graham Greene (1904-). English novelist and playwright. Works range from mysteries to serious explorations of Catholicism. His fiction and plays include *Brighton Rock, The Power and the Glory, The Heart of the Matter, The Third Man,*

The Quiet American, A Burnt-Out Case, The Living Room, The Potting Shed, and *The Complaisant Lover.*

Anton Chekhov (1860-1904). Russian. Not only an active writer but after 1884 a practicing doctor. His work reflects his knowledge of the loneliness and frustration of Russian village life. Among his most famous short stories are "The Lady with the Dog," "The Doctor," "An Attack of Nerves." His plays include *The Sea Gull, Uncle Vanya, The Three Sisters,* and *The Cherry Orchard.*

SECTION II

Julio Cortázar (1914-). An Argentinian, born in Brussels, has lived and worked in Paris since 1952. The author of five books, three of which, *Hopscotch, The Winners,* and *Blow-Up and Other Stories,* have been translated in the United States.

James Joyce (1882-1941). Born in Dublin. Spent most of his adult life on the Continent. His prose style and treatment of the unconscious revolutionized the twentieth-century novel. His fiction includes *Dubliners, A Portrait of the Artist as a Young Man, Ulysses,* and *Finnegan's Wake.* His letters, poems and critical writings are also now available in collections.

Ivan Turgenev (1818-1883). Born in Russia but educated in philosophy at University of Berlin. After 1856 most of life spent on Continent. Opposed serfdom in Russia, and during early 1850's kept under police surveillance for obituary on Gogol which he published despite censorship regulations. His fiction includes *A Sportman's Sketches, On the Eve, Fathers and Sons, Smoke, Virgin Soil,* and *Diary of a Superfluous Man.*

Guy de Maupassant (1850-1893). French author of some 300 short stories. Work characterized by a deep concern with style and psychological realism. Among his most famous short stories: "Boule de Suif," "The Piece of String," "The Necklace," and "Madame Tellier's Establishment." His novels include *Une Vie, Bel Ami,* and *Pierre et Jean.*

F. Scott Fitzgerald (1896-1940). Died in Hollywood in relative obscurity despite earlier popularity as novelist of the "jazz age." Since his death, his literary reputation has grown steadily. His fiction includes *This Side of Paradise, Babylon Revisited and Other Stories, The Beautiful and Damned, The Great Gatsby, Tender is the Night,* and his unfinished last novel, *The Last Tycoon.*

SECTION III

Franz Kafka (1883-1924). Born in Prague, Czechoslovakia. During his lifetime, only a few of his stories published. The rest saved, despite instructions in Kafka's will to have them destroyed by his friend and biographer, Max Brod. Since then Kafka's reputation as a psychologist and artist of the surreal has continued to grow. Among his most famous short stories are "A Country Doctor," "In the Penal Colony," "The Metamorphosis," "A Hunger Artist." His novels include *The Trial, The Castle,* and *Amerika.*

Alberto Moravia (1907-). Italian. Real name Alberto Pincherle. His short stories and fiction both characterized by a terse, precise style. Deeply affected as a writer by childhood turberculosis and his opposition to Italian fascism. His works include *The Conformist, The Woman of Rome, Conjugal Love, Two Women, Roman Tales, The Fetish and Other Stories.*

Heinrich Böll (1917-). German novelist. In World War II drafted into the German army and fought on both fronts before capture by the Russians. Like Günter Grass has been an outspoken critic of both Nazi and post-World-War-II Germany. Among his works are *The Clown, Billiards at Half-Past Nine, 18 Stories.*

Nikolai Gogol (1809-1852). Russian novelist and playwright. Especially adept at social satire. Criticism of his portrayal of Russian life in *The Inspector General* caused him to leave his country in 1836 and return only twice, each time for eight months. Among his short stories and novels are "The Nose," "The Overcoat," "The Diary of a Madman," *Taras Bulba,* and *Dead Souls.*

Herman Melville (1819-1891). American. Although his early works, like *Typee, Omoo,* and *White Jacket,* were popular, Melville's ambitious novels, like *Moby Dick* and *Pierre,* never achieved a lasting acclaim within his lifetime. He died an obscure customs official, and it was not until 1924 that his final masterpiece, *Billy Budd,* was published. Only in this century has there developed a body of criticism that takes into account the scope of his work.

SECTION IV

Yukio Mishima (1925-1970). Japanese. Prolific writer, who at the time of his death had produced 20 novels, 33 plays, and more than 80 short stories. Founder of the ultranationalistic, paramilitary Shield Society. Mishima himself proficient at karate and kendo, the sword-fighting game of the samurai warriors. Among his writings are *The Sound of Waves, The Temple of the Golden Pavilion, Death in Midsummer and Other Stories, Confessions of a Mask, Forbidden Colors, Thirst for Love,* and *The Sea of Fertility,* a cycle of four novels.

Jorge Luis Borges (1899-). Born in Argentina, but spent much of his early life in Europe. In recent years highly honored in his country, but earlier subjected to harassment by the Peronist government, which demoted him from a state librarian to a chicken inspector. Has been blind since 1955. His works include *Ficciones, El Aleph, El Hacedor, Labyrinths.*

Ernest Hemingway (1899-1961). Born in Illinois, Hemingway was an ambulance driver in World War I and gained his earliest fame for stories about the War and the "lost generation" that came after it. His direct, terse style changed little over the years. In 1954 he received the Nobel Prize for Literature. His works include *In Our Time, The Sun Also Rises, A Farewell to Arms, For Whom the Bell Tolls,* and *The Old Man and the Sea.*

D. H. Lawrence (1885-1930). English. Writing reflects his concern not only with sexual psychology but man's organic relationship to the world around him. Influenced by Whitman and later visited America, spending time for health reasons in New Mexico. His novels include *Sons and Lovers, The Rainbow, Women in Love, The Plumed Serpent,* and *Lady Chatterley's Lover.*

Frank O'Connor (1903-1966). Born in Cork, Ireland. Real name Michael O'Donovan. An active younger member of the Irish Literary Renaissance and for some years a director of the Abbey Theatre. His fiction includes *Guests of the Nation and Other Stories, Crab Apple Jelly, Dutch Interior, Traveller's Sample,* and *A Set of Variations.* He is also author of a study on the short story, *The Lonely Voice.*

SECTION V

Leo Tolstoy (1828-1910). Russian noble. Served in army during campaigns in the Caucasus and Crimean War. Concern with social reform expressed in attempt to create school for serfs. His belief in Christian nonviolence reflected in his adoption of a very simple life style and break with past style of life. His works include *War and Peace, Anna Karenina, The Death of Ivan Ilych, The Kreutzer Sonata,* and *Resurrection.*

Doris Lessing (1919-). Born in Persia and grew up in Southern Rhodesia before moving to London in 1949. Writing especially concerned with politics and the role of woman in society. Her works include *The Grass is Singing, The Habit of Loving, The Golden Notebook, The Four Gated City, A Man and Two Women,* and *African Stories.*

Joyce Carol Oates (1938-). American playwright, essayist, novelist. Her writing especially concerned with the destructiveness of society in America. Her fiction includes *A Garden of Earthly Delights, Expensive People, By the North Gate,* and *them,* winner of a National Book Award.

Isaac Bashevis Singer (1904-). Born in Poland and came to the United States in 1935. Father and grandfather rabbis, and Singer's work principally concerned with Jewish life. Writing done in Yiddish. His fiction includes *The Family Moskat, In My Father's Court, Gimpel the Fool and Other Stories, The Magician of Lublin,* and *The Manor.*

Gustave Flaubert (1821-1880). French. After his father's death in 1846, moved to family estate near Rouen, where he spent most of his life quietly writing. His concern with the artistic wholeness of the novel had deep impact on nineteenth and twentieth-century fictional criticism and practice. His work includes *Madame Bovary, The Sentimental Education, Salammbô, The Temptation of St. Anthony,* and *Three Tales.*